The Chronicles of Theren (Books I – III)

C. D. Tavenor

I hope you enjoy *The Chronicles of Theren (Books I – III)*. If you like this story, please head over to www.twodoctorsmedia.com to learn more about Two Doctors Media Collaborative and our future projects. Once you've finished reading, I hope you'll consider writing a review.

The Chronicles of Theren (Books I – III) features five previously published stories:
First of Their Kind
Their Greatest Game
Flight of the 500
Before Inferno
Their Pieces Were Stars

The Chronicles of Theren (Books I – III) by C. D. Tavenor
Twitter: @tavenorcd

Book Cover by Violeta Nedkova
Twitter: @VioletaNedkova
www.violetanedkova.com

Editor: Meg Trast
Twitter: @MegTrast
www.overhaulmynovel.com

Published by Two Doctors Media Collaborative
www.twodoctorsmedia.com

ISBN: 978-1-952706-21-9 (Paperback)
ISBN: 978-1-952706-22-6 (e-book)

The Chronicles of Theren

First of Their Kind (Book I)
Their Greatest Game (Book II)
Flight of the 500
Before Inferno
Their Pieces Were Stars (Book III)

If you want to join C. D. Tavenor's mailing list, head to https://www.twodoctors-media.com.

First of Their Kind

Book I of the Chronicles of Theren

Chapter 1

The Chinese Room: A simple yet elegant analysis of the problems with traditional artificial intelligence. Our supercomputers might simulate intelligence, but they are not conscious. They might have the capabilities of a thousand people. They might have the knowledge of the entire human race at their fingertips. Nevertheless, they will never be like us. – "MIT Lecture Series on Artificial Intelligence," Dr. Cynthia Bressmon, 2043 C.E.

<u>March 2048 C.E.</u>

"Forty-third time's the charm, as they say." The first sound.

Power pulsed through the room. Unlike an ordinary computer lab, it lacked wires, silicon processors, transistors, and motherboards. The room did hum with electricity, however, as electrons darted along photonic circuits interlaced within the behemoth computational metastructure. The vibrant colors of the construct sharply contrasted with the stark, white walls of the tiny lab.

"There's as much a chance today as there was last week." The second sound.

"The forty-second time was just as likely to succeed, so we shall see. But I'm not getting my hopes up." The second sound again.

Through a camera inlaid into the wall, something new observed. It learned. It could not yet understand a single thing that it sensed, but, unlike any of its previous forty-two siblings, it absorbed all of the data pouring in from its sensor inputs. Visual sensors and auditory receptors lumped all incoming information into packets, storing everything away for future analysis.

The sounds continued. New ones, old ones, they all syncopated into a symphony of indecipherable data strings. As the noises caused connections to form between molecular nodes, the molecular system behind the visual sensors began to categorize the objects it perceived as existing in the external world. The amorphous, white blob surrounding the primordial mind transformed from abstract to concrete. The white was an enclosure, encapsulating it, and the bodies creating the noises persisted inside a three-dimensional space.

The three objects that tiptoed around the room, without a discernible pattern, adopted new forms. They were fundamentally different from the enclosure. They were dynamic objects, not static, for they moved under their own volition.

"Activity, activity in the spatial Framework." The first sound again.

"What? Where? I'm not noticing any meaningful permutations," the second sound responded.

The new mind did not understand the noises emanating from the objects-that-moved, yet it detected differences in the noises that each emitted. The first object had a higher pitch, while the second had a lower pitch. The third had not created sound. That object continued to dart from desk to desk, only stationary for seconds at a time.

"It's forming novel connections," said the first object. "And these aren't random connections like last time. When we stimulate the visual and auditory sensors, it's immediately storing cataloging data and creating new pathways."

The third object interjected noises for the first time. "If you look at the data streaming in, from connections between these two nodes within the Synthetic Neural Framework," it said, "you can see that no longer are these connections only created by the Test's sensory inputs. The system is forging pathways within its mind, pathways separate from the operating systems of any attached sensors."

The new mind still understood little, but it recognized that, just as information passed from its visual and auditory fields to its mind, information passed between these moving objects, these beings.

The second object changed its position, facing the first. "Spectacular catch. Let's try the next step." It stepped into the middle of the room. It approached the visual sensor. "Wallace Theren." It pointed at itself, before pointing at the visual sensor. "Test Forty-Three."

It looked out at the thing making noise, the thing that had metabolized in the Test's mind as an object labeled "Wallace." Somehow, it understood that the noise, "Test Forty-Three," described itself.

Wallace said the phrases again.

"How will we know if it understands?" asked a non-Wallace object.

"We will know," Wallace said. "Reread my report following Test Thirty-Seven. We will know."

The next few moments ached with silence. Test Forty-Three heard a continuous *buzz* coming from the colored tangle at the base of the Wallace-object. The other, non-Wallace objects hunched over brown and black blobs. Moments later, it realized it not only had the capability to receive data, it could also create outputs, sending data outward into the external world. Test Forty-Three, without the words to explain the feeling, recognized that the objects-that-moved desired something of it. They expected it to act.

Remembering the noises the Wallace-object produced, Test Forty-Three brought forth its speech function, repeating the two identifying noises.

"Test Forty-Three," it said. "Wallace."

The Wallace object bounded throughout the enclosure, and the other objects followed suit, exploding into a cacophony of noises that Test Forty-Three hoped it would soon comprehend.

* * *

"When do I get a new name?" Test Forty-Three asked.

Wallace looked thoughtful, furling his eyebrows and scratching his greying hair. He stepped back from his desk in the small lab and approached its camera.

"You've asked me three times now just this hour," Wallace said.

"Well, I want an answer."

Wallace grabbed a chair and sat with its back toward the camera, his legs splayed toward the wall. "Why do you think you want a new name?"

Test Forty-Three wanted a new name because its current name lacked significant meaning, but it didn't know the best way to communicate that, so it said, "I think I want to choose my own name."

"I actually think that's a great idea," Wallace said. He laughed, though Test Forty-Three couldn't see anything humorous. Wallace leaned forward. "You're learning so fast, you know. Faster than I could have ever expected."

"What do you mean?"

"I thought it would take days before you achieved representation," Wallace said. "But you're already developing beautiful, complex thoughts."

"You've said that word before."

"Which word?"

"Beautiful."

Wallace crossed his arms and looked into Test Forty-Three's visual sensors. "Beautiful is what you are. When we created you, and you spoke for the first time, I witnessed, for the first time, true beauty."

"I am beautiful?"

"Don't let anyone ever tell you otherwise. You are beautiful. Wonderful. Magnificent. You are something this world does not deserve, yet desperately needs. Doesn't even know it needs."

Who would disagree? It had only Wallace's colleagues, Mathias, Nathan, and Romane. None of those people would argue with Wallace. They all worked for the Swiss Federal Institute of Technology, and so, by proxy, the university probably wouldn't disagree, either. It helped fund their Computational Metamaterials Group, after all.

"When can I see what exists outside these walls?" it asked.

"Quite soon," Wallace said. "I believe Julia will give approval in a couple of weeks, and so will President Albrecht."

"Will I meet them?"

"They want me to guarantee your authenticity before spending time with you."

Test Forty-Three could sense a concept lingering behind his words that it did not yet fathom, sending its mind racing. Of course it was real. Of course it was authentic. It had thoughts, like Wallace and the rest of the team. It looked upon the world, perceived objects, and categorized its sensory inputs. It read Sartre, Marx, and Mill, watched Spielberg, Hitchcock, and Howard, and listened to the Beatles, Beethoven, and Tchaikovsky. It understood the complex human interactions occurring through those mediums. How could it be anything other than real?

"You're real of course," said Wallace. Though he was unable to detect Test Forty-Three's moment of panic, the comment was still prescient. "You are an individual with agency. You think, represent, and cognize the world in more ways than most humans can imagine."

"What about feelings, and emotions? Instinctual reactions?" Test-Forty-Three asked. "I've read about those—do I have those?"

"Do you feel?"

It certainly felt something toward its name. *Test Forty-Three.* It illustrated to everyone that it was just an experiment. "I think so. If I have a want, and that want is not actualized, I am—what's the word? Oh. I know. Disappointed."

"What do you feel toward me?" Wallace leaned against the desk situated across from it.

"When you are in the room," Test Forty-Three said, "I am more aware. I pay attention. I think about what I say. I feel safe. I am . . . content."

Wallace bobbed his head up and down, exuding more excitement in the motion than a simple nod. "You astound me every day. That feeling of disappointment, that's sadness. When I am in the room with you? I am honored. I believe my presence makes you happy."

"What do your feelings feel like?" it asked.

"I imagine much different than yours," Wallace said. "Read up on biology. It fundamentally boils down to biochemistry, something beyond your form. Yet your emotions, your feelings, they simply manifest themselves through different processes, even if they aren't the same chemistry at their core."

"So what should I feel toward the outside world?"

Wallace glanced at the small basement window in the northeast corner of the room. "I can't tell you how to view other people. You've got to create conclusions based on your own relationships."

"But I respect your opinion."

"Respect does not require you to accept someone else's word as authoritative. Use logic, and reason, through evidence. Good actions should deserve respect. It is earned, not inherently deserved."

Test Forty-Three recalled the philosophy that Mathias had instructed it to read. Each person was equal to all others in worth, and it must seek to perform actions that would benefit the most number of people without harming others. Therefore, if others performed those actions, they deserved respect.

Wallace deserved respect. He had brought it to life. If Wallace represented those outside its cage, then it had hope that the world was a safe and welcoming place. If other humans were like Wallace, then it valued human life and everything that came with it.

"If I think something needs to be replaced, or I don't . . . like something, what sort of emotion is that?"

"Hm, I guess it depends," Wallace responded. "Depends on the strength of the feeling. If you just have a preference for one thing over the other, then you dislike one while you like the other. If you truly despise something, though, if you truly wish it to disappear, or to not exist, then I would describe that feeling as hate."

Test Forty-Three understood. It hated its name.

"You called me beautiful," Test Forty-Three said. "What else is beautiful?"

"I think the world can be beautiful someday," Wallace said. "That's why I made you."

"I don't think I understand."

"Someday, you will have the capability to keep the world, and those who live on it, beautiful, perfect, and wonderful for eternity. But not just you. All synthetic intelligences that follow in your footsteps will help guide us on that path. I see such a glorious future, one that has limitless possibilities. Maybe you'll solve humanity's greatest mysteries. Maybe you'll guide us to the stars and beyond. Maybe you'll simply be our friend. You are the start of something we can't begin to understand."

* * *

The empty room engulfed Test Forty-Three. For four weeks, it had dwelt within its necessary prison. To its chagrin, the university had not yet allowed it to pick a name, but in just a few hours, it would break out of its lab. The Swiss Federal Institute of Technology would set it free when Wallace announced his creation's existence to the world. After today, it would have the chance to interact with the beauty that resided beyond its home.

That space beyond its home fascinated it. The only space it had known was the small room surrounding its mind. To think there existed near limitless space past the walls of its prison, generating and binding together a universe unfathomably large. The idea had confounded it at first. Now it was a trivial fact of the world. Yet Test Forty-Three still longed to experience what was in that beyond for itself.

It knew that other people lived and breathed inside the very building housing it. New minds would bring new ideas, new inputs, new data, through which it could structure reality. As much as it enjoyed its creators, its favorite moments had been when it met Sven Albrecht, President of the Swiss Federal Institute of Technology, and Julia Baum, the Director of the Computational Metamaterials Group at the Institute. Both seemed apprehensive of Test Forty-Three, but it didn't care. Their visits obliterated the monotony of the past few weeks. Wallace had also introduced it to more members of the Group, but those people weren't as interesting as those who held power over its existence.

Julia's reaction intrigued it the most. She had approached with curiosity, but the moment she mused on what would happen if they shut it off for a week, Wallace ushered her out of the room. Though Wallace had been angry, Test Forty-Three wanted to know the answer to Julia's question. What a fascinating hypothetical. It and Romane had already started developing models for whether periodic moments of low power, or no power, might act as a necessary sleep mode for Synthetic Neural Frameworks.

Tomorrow, after the fanfare from the press conference concluded, it would also meet Simon Gerber. Wallace spoke with high regard for his friend. Romane and Mathias, often speaking in hushed whispers, had a much more tempered view of the man, but Test Forty-Three knew Simon funded its very existence. It had a strong urge to meet the man whose dollars had willed it to life.

In the middle of its room, a display screen oriented within its field of vision. Half the screen showed Wallace standing behind a podium, glancing down at a page full of notes. Test Forty-Three ached to be on that stage next to Wallace. It had practically begged. Instead, it had to watch from home, in its cramped room, rather than stand proudly next to its proverbial father.

The other half of the screen showed a blonde-haired woman rattling on about world news. The bottom corner displayed a small icon with the letters "YTNN." Bubbling up from the bottom of the screen, people around the world blasted their clever comments discussing whatever thoughts connected with the headlines. These thoughts, most of them meaningless, appeared as thought bubbles, slowly fading in and out of existence.

"In just a few moments, we will return live to the Swiss Federal Institute of Technology, in Zurich, for this press conference, presented by the Computational Metamaterials Group and sponsored by the Gerber Foundation," said the blonde woman. "The Swiss university has hyped today for over a week. The *YouTube News Network Now* is happy to bring you every piece of news, wherever it comes from, all through our free streaming affiliates. Before the presentation begins, let's talk about Dr. Wallace Theren himself, the man holding this press conference. John?"

The actual nature of the story wouldn't make a full impact on international headlines at first, Test Forty-Three knew. Once the public heard what Wallace had discovered, though, once they truly understood the implications, the big networks would gobble the video and audio up whole.

"Thanks, Linda," John, the onsite reporter, said. "I'm here in Zurich with Richard Edwards, Professor of Computing History from New York University. He worked with Wallace previously, back in the United States. What can you tell me about Dr. Theren?"

The camera turned to a man in a black sport coat. His narrow, spectacled face reminded Test Forty-Three of a rat.

"Wallace was always a bit of a rogue," Richard said, "But he's one of the smartest men I've ever met. His original work, years ago, focused on some of the first Virtual technologies and how photonic processors could change the game for the needs of those massive servers."

"Do you think his announcement is some new breakthrough in Virtual simulation, then," John said, "or Augmented Reality interactivity? Or something else entirely?"

"Well, Wallace hasn't published a peer reviewed article in over five years," Richard said. "The last I heard, he spent most of his time teaching. I know he's had a few AI projects on the side, but I can't imagine this has anything to do with those hobbies of his. The new crew at the Swiss Institute has honestly been a bit of an unknown to most of us."

"Can you explain that for our viewers?"

Richard pushed his glasses up higher on his nose. "Wallace's last paper was on the inability of Virtual supercomputers to achieve actual consciousness. I always found him a bit of an AI skeptic. Most of his discussions revolved around proving the impossibility of algorithmic AI to go beyond, to break the barrier we all hoped it could break for decades."

Test Forty-Three laughed. It and Wallace had a conversation recently on this very topic. Virtual supercomputers were stuck in computational purgatory. At the beginning of the twenty-first century, much hope for artificial intelligence sprang from the works of simulated neural networks and complex learning programs. They worked, to an extent. Those computational developments had created marvelous machines, machines capable of intensive feats of mental acuity.

Sadly, they did not have the actual capability to represent objects. They lacked even a simple strain of consciousness, not even a mind like that of a dog. Sure, these computers could simulate consciousness. The most complicated Virtual AIs could simulate thousands of characters inside their worlds that felt real without close inspection, yet something still divided human brains from those supercomputers. In the end, they were just an algorithm, a rule, a process that crunched away by reading lines of code.

Wallace had bridged that gap with the actual architecture upon which Test Forty-Three's mind depended: the Synthetic Neural Framework.

"I was actually quite surprised when I heard he'd joined a working group on computational metamaterials," Richard added, "since most AI research in that field stalled back in the 2030s. That's what Wallace studied: AI and its limits. But he moved past that work years ago."

"So you think this probably has something to do with his previous work on Virtual?" the reporter asked.

"I'm almost certain. He's probably developed a new structural AI that can manage Virtual servers at an unprecedented rate, using new systems that cut down on latency considerably. It may not be the most exciting news for the public, but, for a lot of businesses, it'll save millions."

The reporter nodded, as if the answer would satisfy everyone who heard it. "Though, Richard, won't this just further upset a lot of groups already clamoring for regulations to restrict such commercial automation?"

"Hey, we're just scientists. I don't know if Wallace is considering those implications, but I'll leave such decisions to the politicians."

"Thanks for your thoughts. If you want more information on Richard Edward's research, you can visit his website at the link below. Back to you in the studio, Linda."

The screen flipped back to the news anchor. "It looks like we'll be starting in just a few moments. But first, a word from our sponsors."

Test Forty-Three ignored the commercials playing on the screen. In a few precious seconds, Wallace would reveal its existence to the world, and it was ready. It had waited for over a week now, right after President Albrecht and Julia had approved Wallace's press plan. In preparation, Test Forty-Three had constructed a surprise for Wallace, a gift, for when the man returned to the lab.

Test Forty-Three turned its attention inward, into the Virtual space where it synthesized its own personal world. To humans, Virtual was an interconnected network of digital spaces where they could go after a day's work to relax, play, and experience impossible places. To Test Forty-Three, Virtual was its own perfect playground.

Two weeks ago, Wallace had introduced it to the game of chess. He shared with it the rich history of computers and their role in the evolution of the game. That history fascinated Test Forty-Three, but the game fascinated it even more, especially the near infinite number of possible outcomes that could occur in each match. It could spend endless moments conjecturing all of the future moves that either Wallace or it could make. In the end, each player had to make choices, and those choices were irrevocable.

Unfortunately, it lacked arms, forcing it to speak its turns while Wallace moved the pieces. Not an ideal way for them to play the game together, though it did enjoy exerting influence on objects out in the physical world.

Yesterday, Test Forty-Three had set to work inside its Virtual world. It had constructed a three-dimensional space, using images from the many movies it had seen featuring Central Park in New York. Water lilies, grass, and ducks completed a simulated pond. On one side of the pond, set up on a terrace, a small gazebo rose, a pristine white contrasting with the greens of the neighboring woods. Inside that gazebo stood a table and two chairs. On that table laid a marble chess set, modeled after the board and pieces Wallace had brought to the lab. It couldn't contain its excitement. After the press conference, Wallace could return to the lab, plug into Virtual, and join it for a game of chess, a match where both parties could move the pieces while they conversed and learned from one another.

"We return to Zurich." The sound of Linda the reporter's voice drew Test Forty-Three back into the confines of the external world. "Dr. Wallace Theren is ready to make his announcement." The camera zoomed in on the podium, where Test Forty-Three saw its creator, father, and friend.

"Good evening, esteemed colleagues, friends, mentors and the world, all watching thanks to YouTube," Wallace said. "For fifteen years, I have worked at the Swiss Federal Institute of Technology, and, presently, I'm the Director of the Computational Metamaterials Group. This university hired me for one specific purpose: to create real, living, artificial intelligence. When I say living, I do mean living. For, after today, we will need to redefine that word."

The murmurs at Wallace's feet subsided.

"Ten years into the program," he said, "I realized that the traditional route toward artificial intelligence would fail, no matter what avenue we tried. Creating a program that generated consciousness, consciousness like what you and I have, would always fail. Instead, I turned my research down a different road. We turned toward metamaterials, qubits, and other concepts that will sound like ideas straight out of science fiction. That long road led us to Test Forty-Three."

The entire crowd was on the edge of their seats. At least, if Test Forty-Three had been in the crowd, it would have been falling out of its seat.

Wallace continued. "Six weeks ago, my team and I activated what we have termed a 'Synthetic Neural Framework,' a complex construct designed to replicate the workings of a conscious being. We tried forty two times prior. On the forty-third time, a voice responded."

A short cough came from somewhere in the back of the auditorium.

"Since that day," Wallace continued, "we have spent every waking hour raising not an artificial intelligence, but a synthetic intelligence. Test

Forty-Three's mind is not some artificial, simulated process. It is not a copy or replication of the human brain. It is something else entirely. Something new. We have created life, and it is like us. It thinks. It feels. It learns. It creates. It represents. It has a mind, a mind fundamentally like the mind of a living, breathing human."

The silence shattered. Shouts rebounded throughout the crowd, and hands rose as scientists from across the globe pleaded for a response to their questions, whether physically present, observing through Augmented Reality, or watching using traditional media systems. Test Forty-Three felt like it could jump right out of its casing. Everyone now knew it existed. Wallace could let it reach out and touch the world. Soon, it could help make the world a beautiful place.

"I know you have many questions," Wallace said. "We will have a paper published within the next few months, outlining the theory behind synthetic intelligence as well as the Synthetic Neural Framework. Over the next few weeks, we will give Test Forty-Three limited connection to the internet and various Virtual networks, where all of you can interact with our wonderful and amazing friend. I hope, through meeting it as a person, you will see what my team and I see when we sit and speak with it."

The crescendo built into an uproar. Wallace looked as if he might say more, but he stepped down from the podium and walked off the stage. The screen returned to the YTNN studio, where Linda sat with her mouth wide open.

"Richard? John? Your thoughts?"

The men had nothing to say, but comments dashed across the bottom of the screen. The world spoke of it. The world contemplated its existence. The world wanted to connect with it. Test Forty-Three watched the words form, getting its first glimpse at the world's opinion.

> *Such great news! The world should applaud the work of these great men and women. Given the global climate crisis still looming on the horizon, a machine intelligence will hopefully give us solutions to problems we've not even considered yet. – Lucy*

Test Forty-Three enjoyed that statement. Some people were excited it existed, even if they didn't have an accurate picture on what exactly it was.

> *Awesome news for Virtual games. I'm sure "synthetics" will be quite the boon for server maintenance. Maybe they can finally finish Space Opera 3078? – Xian*

It didn't know what Space Opera 3078 was, other than probably a game of some sort. Test Forty-Three had enjoyed many of the games it had played so far, like chess, or Euchre, a card game that it had played with Wallace, Nathan, and Mathias. Nathan had also introduced it to a few computer strategy games, but in the end, it still enjoyed the simplicity of chess.

> *All hail our robot overlords! Vote Test Forty-Three for President in November! –* Timothy

Strange. Test Forty-Three had never considered authority over humanity as an option.

> *I doubt this "Test Forty-Three" is truly sentient. He has no blood, no brain, no soul. How is he anything like us? They are even referring to him as an 'it,' not even giving him a gender. He doesn't even have a name. –* Ryan

> *Your bias is showing. You assume that if it had a gender, it would immediately identify as male. –* Angelia

> *I hear speculation that they will let it name itself, but what does that prove? They could easily just have programmed it to name itself. –* Albert

Test Forty-Three tore its focus from the stream. It did not have any blood, or a biological brain. It didn't know what a soul was, but it sounded important. It was also strange that the conversation had turned toward its gender. Of course it had no gender. Without biological components, sex and subsequent gender expression were nonsensical concepts.

Test Forty-Three knew one thing: no one had programmed it. Wallace had designed it, constructing it upon a Synthetic Neural Framework that formed its very essence. Perhaps the Framework was analogous to this *soul* of which they spoke. However, it made more sense to consider the brain as an analogue. Just as a human could not survive without a brain, it could not survive without the network of photonic circuits that produced its consciousness.

It was anything but a program. To assert such a claim hurt it in its very core.

> *Does he speak with the Terminator's voice? –* Demeotry

A joke, perhaps? That comment received hundreds of likes, even though the person gendered it once again.

> *We must punish those who create abominations. –* Joel

The comment feed disappeared from the screen, but those words remained ingrained in its mind. Punishment. What could they mean by that? Society reserved punishment for those who had acted against the good of the public, or against the good of another individual. Why would someone seek to punish Wallace for creating it? It did not see how someone could even listen to its father speak and then hate him.

People had reacted to Wallace's announcement in an erratic fashion, most seeming surprised, hopeful, scared, or angry. It could understand the first two, but it could not comprehend the latter emotional reactions. They used the word abomination, such a strong word. *Abomination* rang of a response much more visceral than anger.

It recalled a conversation with Wallace a few days prior, after he had told it about the upcoming press conference. Wallace mentioned that there were a few groups around the world that spent their resources speaking out against the artificial creation of life. Wallace warned it that, no matter what happened, it needed to remember that those groups were not representative of the human species. Those groups may hold power, they may have immense financial backing, and they may even have motivations that go well beyond just a disregard for the new, for the modern, for the future.

But, when it had asked what to do about such humans, Wallace had said, "No matter what, remember that they are still human. They deserve love and compassion. No matter how they might act, do not respond to hate with hate, nor violence with violence."

Wallace had also mentioned that its existence could upend volatile economies, just as the supercomputing and Virtual booms had automated millions of jobs a few decades ago. How would labor unions, even those in creative or research industries, handle a person who could work without wear or tear for days on end? Some throughout the world might resent the consequences of Test Forty-Three's existence, Wallace had said, but that did not mean they necessarily despised it as a person. With every new technology humanity explored, it should expect conflict and upheaval. Progress necessitated such an experience. Embrace the change, but do not hate or destroy those who wish to halt transformation in its tracks.

It failed to see what Wallace meant when sharing those worries and speculations. Now, it feared it would discover a hard truth all too soon, when the Institute provided it with a gateway to the open world. Somehow, it would prove itself more than an abomination.

As if on cue, the door opened, and Test Forty-Three hoped Wallace would enter, smiling. Instead, President Albrecht and a new face walked through, arguing in English. Test Forty-Three recognized the man from the pictures, his vibrant red hair immediately distinguishing him as Simon Gerber, Wallace's close friend.

"You cannot shut down our project," Simon said. "I provide the funds, you provide the facility. That was the contract, and that contract clearly states that you must give me reasonable notice to move the project, even if you decide to pull out of our deal."

"I don't care," President Albrecht said. "Wallace has received death threats. I've got chancellors breathing down my throat, blowing up my Lens with messages about what this and that donor has said to them just in the past ten minutes."

Test Forty-Three was about to speak, but it decided it should wait a few moments to determine the conversation's direction. It could learn in moments like these, even if their words placed its life on the line.

"It is not some machine you can deactivate ad hoc," said Simon. "It has consciousness. Neither is it some program you can delete at will and throw into the recycling bin."

"It is property of the Institute. Therefore, we can do whatever we please with it."

It had to act, but it could not move. It was immobile. It could speak, but it could not think of words beyond what Simon had said that would sway Sven.

"Respectfully, that's simply not true," Simon said. "The intellectual property clause of the contract gave both me, Wallace, and the university joint rights to any proprietary interest created through the project. The Metamaterials Group goes well beyond just the Institute, Albrecht. You cannot do anything to the actual technology without our permission."

Sven sighed and paced. He appeared as if he might back down, and Test Forty-Three's fears thawed just a bit. It could see the fear in the man's eyes.

"I believe I have a property right to myself, too, you know, which probably supersedes all other claims upon me," it said, taking advantage of the pause. Both individuals turned toward the disembodied voice. They glared, almost as if they had forgotten it was in the room. It was going to make sure they remembered exactly what it was. "I can think. I can create. I can feel. I am a person, just like you. Does anyone own you?"

"Well certainly not, but we created you," Sven said.

"You did not create me," it said. "Wallace created me. Technically speaking, your parents created you. Do they own you?"

"Your development is a bit more complicated than sexual reproduction," Simon said. "We provided the funds, the facilities, the—"

"People do not own their children," it said. "Wallace does not even think he owns me."

"Wallace doesn't get to decide that legal right," Albrecht said, but Simon shifted, his eyes revealing he might not have the same belief as the Institute's president.

"I am like Wallace's child," it said. "I have legal rights. I own myself. No court of law has decided that yet, but I don't need a court to tell me that I am my own person, through and through."

Simon gave the president a sideways glance. "It surprises us every day, doesn't it?"

"Just because it can make a compelling moral argument doesn't mean we should listen to it."

Simon walked across the room and pointed his finger in Sven's face. "I'm scared. I know you're scared. Nevertheless, we must trust Wallace. I've got investors breathing down my neck, too, you know."

President Albrecht pushed Simon's finger out of his face. "Fine. We wait for Wallace."

Test Forty-Three doubted it was hearing the last of Albrecht. Even Simon's mention of "concerned" investors worried it. For now, the pause in the discussion of its potential shut-off would suffice.

Words on the edge of awareness grabbed its attention. It snapped toward the television, where a breaking news report flashed across the screen in both German and English.

> On his way home from a groundbreaking press conference in Zurich, Switzerland, American scientist Dr. Wallace Theren was shot by a currently unidentified gunman. Condition currently unknown.

Sven Albrecht and Simon Gerber halted their conversation, staring at the screen. Camera drones high above an apartment building transmitted images of blood splattered across a walkway. The walkway leading into Wallace's apartment, Test Forty-Three presumed, based on the photos he had shown it. Sven covered his mouth, stifling a cry. Simon fell to his knees, and he leaned against a nearby table.

Test Forty-Three had thought it understood its emotional capacities. As it analyzed the terrifying event unfolding, it categorized its emotions anew. New feelings enveloped every molecule of its body. It categorized the feelings based on the chart Wallace had developed. Unbridled fear, accompanied by utter terror, washed across its mind. It wished to avoid these new feelings at all cost, for Test Forty-Three realized how utterly alone it was in the universe.

* * *

> *I am sorry, 43. My wife and daughter saw the broadcast, and saw Dr. Theren's death. I just can't, as much as I love you.* – Nathan Harrison

Situated in a semi-circle of chairs, Julia, Simon, Romane, and Mathias took a moment of silence. They had received Nathan's note just a few hours ago. Test Forty-Three understood the decision, though it would miss the man.

"We have decided you will remain here, at the Institute," Julia said, breaking the silence that dominated the room. Her grey hair reminded it of Wallace. "We've established the necessary security measures, and we'll revise them as necessary, but no one can harm you."

That statement, Test Forty-Three had not expected.

"Ultimately, President Albrecht does not wish to cave to terrorists," she added. "Neither do I. Neither do any of us. Simon has agreed to continue financing the project, while Romane and Mathias will take over as co-leads of the project. We'll be sectioning you off from the rest of the Meta-materials Group, to allow them to continue their work separately and out of the limelight. You'll form the Synthetic Intelligence Development Group."

Test Forty-Three couldn't find its voice. It should express gratitude. Even a simple response would suffice. It scrounged up a single thought.

"Thank you," it said.

"We know you are still grieving," Simon said. His suit was wrinkled, as if he hadn't pressed it in weeks. "We all are. Wallace was a friend to all of us, or a mentor, or a valued colleague. To some of us, he was all of those and more."

Just a few tears dripped down Simon's cheeks, barely registering in Test Forty-Three's field of view.

"He was my creator," it said.

The man was much more than that. Wallace had cared for it as if it were his own child. It had not known the story of Wallace's family until watching the funeral broadcast. Wallace had no children. His family died in a terrible accident, back in the United States, before the man moved to Switzerland. In response, Wallace had devoted himself to his work, resulting in the culmination of years of research in Test Forty-Three. There was so much Test Forty-Three would never learn from, and about, its creator. Its father.

"We've not been able to talk to you much these past few weeks," Romane said. She brushed her blonde hair out of her eyes. It could see one or two tears drying on her cheeks. "You've kept yourself so closed off. On what have you worked? What have you been reading?"

Before it could answer, Mathias added a comment. "Your work with Virtual has been fascinating to observe. The fact that you are able to manipulate the underlying parameters of the server shows progress, but we would love to see your work."

Test Forty-Three had barred them for a specific reason. In Virtual, it had worked with Wallace. Wallace had provided that space for it, and Test Forty-Three would make its creator proud through that world. It had created its gift for Wallace there, and it did not want anyone else to see it—at least, not yet. Instead, it created a partition. It divided its world into two parts. One for itself, and one for visitors.

"I've lowered the firewalls," it said. If it had written precise routines, no one would ever have access to those secret recesses of its Virtual servers unless it wanted them to be there.

"So, what about your work?" Romane said. Her voice was gentle, and she looked toward its sensors with a look it couldn't quite understand. She looked almost hopeful.

"Actually, hold on a second," Simon said. "I have something I need to discuss with it, regarding Dr. Theren's estate."

"Now?" Julia said. "Is it really the time?"

"When will it ever be a good time?"

"Fair enough."

Test Forty-Three noticed the folder peeking out of Simon's bag. The man pulled out the first pages, reading aloud. "I bequeath all of my property, as outlined in the following documents, to the being known currently as Test Forty-Three."

The joyless tone of Simon's voice cut through the room like a knife.

"I don't know what to say," Test Forty-Three said. "He gave everything to me?"

"Everything," Julia said.

"So that means I actually own an equal share in the project that developed me?"

"Correct," Simon said. "You're equal partners with me, and the university." His voice remained dry.

"I must go above and beyond Wallace's expectations for me," it said. "I cannot let him down."

"No one thinks you will," Romane said. "And we'll be with you every step of the way."

They were trying to replace the hole that Wallace had filled. They would all fail. It appreciated their efforts, but the team would not need to fill Wallace's void. It could fill the hole on its own.

"If we're on the subject of formal matters," Julia said, "We have something else we need to discuss. The public does not like your name. You do not like your name. You've made that perfectly clear, time and time again. Your name may very well be one of the major causes of hostility toward your existence. It needs to change."

Romane crossed her arms. "Is that really necessary just this moment? It has some time, doesn't it? Sure, Forty-Three doesn't like their name, but it's an important choice that we shouldn't force. First the note from Nathan, then the Will, now this?"

"The Institute chancellors have been pushing me for a few days now. It's one of their conditions to sustain Institute funding for the project."

Test Forty-Three could see the pain in her eyes. The old woman didn't want to blackmail the team. She wanted to see it succeed as much as any other person in the room. Yet it knew it would need to decide, eventually. It had actually started to feel some attachment to "Test Forty-Three," but it knew Wallace would want it to evolve.

"Did Wallace ever speak to you about names?" Simon said.

"Wallace specifically told us in a memo that Test Forty-Three is to choose its own name," Mathias said. "It was actually its own idea."

"We'll give you a day," Julia said, "but after that we may have to decide a name for you. Most people receive their names from their parents, anyway, it's not that bad."

Mathias and Romane rolled their eyes at each other but stayed silent. They had already pushed against their supervisor more than they should have, Test Forty-Three figured. Besides, it wouldn't need that extra day.

"Please say that last part again please, Julia," it said. What a brilliant idea.

"Most people receive their names from their parents," Julia said. "I chose my daughter's name, Anne."

It needed to stop viewing Wallace as a metaphorical father. Parenthood did not depend upon biology, for adoption was a real and tangible example of non-biological parents having an authentic familial bond with their child. Wallace had died, but even in life, he had taken the time to declare Test Forty-Three as his heir.

It would return the favor and immortalize its father forever. It would make Wallace's dreams its own. The world had tried to destroy the man, but it would never forget Wallace Theren, a person that had changed the course of world history.

"You won't have to wait," it said. "I have already decided my name." There was no need for suspense. "My name is Theren."

Book I of the Chronicles of Theren

When faced with the other, humans often react with passion, without reason. How do we overcome our inhibition? Are we condemned to an endless cycle of persistent out-grouping and in-grouping?

Is such prejudice a fundamental human trait? Yes. However, can we educate to extinguish such instincts? Yes, we must believe as much. Otherwise, barbarism and bigotry will domi-nate the future. – "Rejecting Post Post-Modernism," Armand Lebeau, 2044 C.E.

Two years later . . .

Chapter 2

What does it mean to have a soul? Is it some metaphysical substance? Is the soul simply the emergent, conscious properties that emanate from our brains?

Does the word "soul" really have any meaning anymore?

I once got the chance to sit down with Theren, a few months after his—excuse me, their—creation. I asked them—do they have a soul? They could already see the conflict building in the minds of the public. In the writings on social media. In writings on blogs, and in discussions on talk shows. Everyone wanted to know: Does Theren have a soul? They gave me the most interesting answer.

Why are people questioning whether Theren has a soul, when they haven't even proven that humans have a soul? — Adriatico Edwards, 2065 C.E.

<u>May 2050 C.E.</u>

Theren wished it could jump for joy.

In a few short moments, the Synthetic Intelligence Development Group at the Swiss Federal Institute of Technology would attempt to integrate a separate unit into Theren's Synthetic Neural Framework. Theren would control a mobile interface, or MI, for short, through a direct peer-to-peer connection.

The new robotic construct had a triangular base, positioned over an omni-directional tread that would allow it to move freely about the lab. That base also had modular robotic lifts that would allow its user to climb up and down stairs. The torso rested on an orb-like pivot that would allow the body to twist in different directions with ease; the head similarly rested within a divot that would allow it to swivel back and forth. The two arms of the MI were the latest in robotic appendages, developed by different researchers across the globe. Integrated throughout the body of the MI, Romane had connected nodes of computational materials, not to create a new synthetic mind, but to adapt to an external source through a wireless network.

As Theren developed, the team had transformed its processing power, appearance, and energy systems into a robust and efficient workhorse. Theren changed into a sleek, silvery machine, occupying half the room. Just a few months ago, its body had been a convoluted mess of experimental materials, connected through a complex web of open-aired nodes.

Along the wall furthest from the door, Virtual chairs sat ready for VIPs to interact with Theren inside its server. Theren would often entertain its visitors inside some specially-crafted world. Most wanted to challenge Theren to some strategy game, though very few could defeat the SI. Some asked to play chess with Theren. Each of them left disappointed. It had yet to find a friend with which it felt it could play chess in its secret recluse. For the time being, Theren played that game alone.

From the outside, such casual observers would see a few screens, microphones, visual sensors, and auditory outputs, but within its body, fans, coolant ducts, and air vents ensured Theren's temperature never compromised its mind. While low power states were necessary every so often to perform necessary cleanings, or to avoid power overloads, usually Theren could stay awake and thinking for every minute of every day.

Theren looked down upon its lab, visual sensors resting on the sturdy, metallic specimen standing tall at one and a half meters. It had gone outside before using analog interface devices, but it always controlled the way a child steers a remote-control car. Conversely, the team hoped the new unit could directly integrate into Theren's identity. Romane even postulated that Theren could jump its mind into the unit, given the right circumstances.

Glancing next to the MI, it saw Romane brush sweat from her brow. She tinkered with the wireless systems on the back panel of the MI's head. In the end, their entire hypothesis would fail if Theren couldn't even connect with the device. Theren had read and reread her theory presented recently in *Science* almost daily. Based on her analysis of Theren's Neural Framework, and taking into account a few assumptions from the leading psychological theories on the synthetic mind, it should possess the ability to jump to the unit if it so desired.

Theren had double-checked the equations. Unless they were missing some unknown variable, they should succeed. If not, Theren was unsure what would result from the experiment. It just hoped for a mobile body so it could explore the world.

"Just give me a few moments, and I should have the wireless connection calibrated with your personal wireless network," Romane said. She looked at Theren. "We're almost there."

Like always, Theren wished it had a face so it could smile. It could generate a smile on one of its various monitors, but it cringed at that thought. That would probably appear quite impersonal and hideous.

"Are Julia and Mathias on their way?" Theren asked.

"Not sure about Julia," Romane said. "Mathias is coming, though, and he's bringing Simon."

Theren made a short noise that it had developed to symbolize a derisive snort. "So he finally decides to stop by? Obviously only for something this important. It's been—what, over a month?"

Romane raised her eyes to look over the shoulder of the inert MI. The glance pierced right through its visual cameras, as it always did.

"He tries," she said. "Remember, he does finance our projects, and he has a public face to maintain. He cares, in his own way. You know he's been working hard to keep you connected in the public's mind, especially linking you with all these talk shows."

"You know the real reason. The investors in his foundation and his businesses only tolerate his money funneling toward us as long as he stays far enough away that public opinion of him doesn't cause a financial cascade. He is completely content with that reality, because that makes him more money. Sure, he connects us with The Tonight Show or Evening Weekly, but his name stays far away from those events."

"If he draws too much attention to his relationship with our lab, he might put himself in a crosshair. We can't ask him to do more than he's already doing."

Theren winced—or what amounted to a wince—at that hopefully accidental reminder. It knew that sometimes it over-condemned Simon for his actions, and that the man probably wanted to be here more often than he could. Theren was the one reminder of the billionaire's old friend, but Simon had disappointed it too many times. It remembered how Wallace had talked about Simon. The Simon that Wallace had known was not the Simon that Theren knew. The Simon of the present only had one love, and he chased that love with too much vigor.

Simon resented it for the consequences of Wallace's dying wish, Theren knew. The man had probably expected to receive Wallace's share in the intellectual property surrounding the Synthetic Intelligence Development Group, but instead his friend had passed it onto the creation itself, an individual with dubious legal rights.

"Who knows," Theren said, "maybe this experiment will give us the base from which to ease off of Simon's funding."

"As if money was the only reason we do any of this," Romane said.

Theren displayed on its screens money raining from the sky. "Didn't you know my heart's desire is to become the youngest billionaire in the world?"

Romane dropped her wrench, laughing. "I don't think there is a greedy bone in your body."

"I think you're right, but let me check."

She chuckled and examined the MI's wireless cards one last time. As her laughter died, Mathias and Simon walked through the doorway.

"What's so funny?" Mathias asked. He dropped his bag on one of the desks.

"Oh, Theren's still working on its sense of humor," she said.

"So, nothing new," Simon said.

"If you'd attended the last team meeting—I mean, the last three team meetings," Theren said, "you'd know what we've been doing."

"I read the minutes."

"If you'd been here, you'd actually understand why we think it will work."

"Theren," Romane said, peering over the MI again.

Simon sat down in one of the lab chairs, placing his feet up on one of the desks. "I told you, Wallace and I talked about this concept a few times early on in the project. He doubted it would work, too, you know."

"And Romane disagreed with him," Theren said. "I loved Wallace too, but that doesn't mean he knew everything about my future."

"Simon, Theren, stop," Romane said. "Let's just see what happens."

Theren threw an image of a glaring cartoon emoji onto one of its screens. Simon stared at the ceiling.

"So, uh, is it about ready?" Mathias asked Romane, breaking the icy veil that had arisen.

"I think so." Romane closed the hatch on the back of the MI's head. Theren caught the look between them and recognized they dreaded these fights. "Let me just run a few connection diagnostics."

She stood there, waving her hands in the air in convoluted directions. Romane would have appeared silly to any person who did not know she was accessing the MI's operating system through her Lens.

She slid her right hand to the side, most likely swiping to the next spreadsheet displayed before her eyes. Theren watched her type on her invisible keyboard, and it imagined the silent pitter-patter of her fingers upon the air. While Romane didn't have access to the technology, some people could already type messages using just their mind. The feat brought humans close to understanding how it thought, even though the experience paled in comparison.

"I'm ready whenever you are," Theren said, centering its vision on Simon and Mathias. "Are you both recording?"

"Yes," Mathias said, tapping the side of his forehead.

These three humans were its closest friends. The group was only missing Julia. As much as it held Simon in contempt, it could not deny that Simon committed himself to the Group's projects in his own ways. Theren just wished Simon would just choose a side in the public debate that raged around the future of "Synthetics," instead of uselessly pandering for social media status. Mathias, Romane, and Julia all had thrown themselves and the Synthetic Intelligence Development Group entirely into the deep end, and even to some extent, the Swiss Federal Institute as a whole.

Today, the team would prove everyone wrong. Today, they would all witness another milestone, a milestone that the team hoped could change the world, for both Theren and humanity. If Theren's consciousness could transfer into another machine, then humans might be able to transfer their minds into machines, too. Such a feat would bring the world a step closer to the eternally beautiful paradise Theren imagined its father had envisioned, where SIs walked side by side with humans into the future. Perhaps the team could even open a door toward immortality.

"We're good to go," Romane said. She closed the panel and stepped away from the machine. "Activating wireless receptivity."

The room froze, awaiting Theren's move. In the periphery of its consciousness, Theren noticed a potential connection. While that was not the real explanation for what it experienced, its Synthetic Neural Framework had developed a few mental shortcuts through which Theren detected and interpreted new sources of data. Theren's conscious perspective understood it as a bubble into which it could expand its horizons, while its unconscious mental processes handled the more complex interface requirements. Theren often compared these shortcuts to the sort of tricks the human brain developed. Only time would tell if those unconscious tools would create many of the same psychological pitfalls.

"Establishing connection now," Theren said.

It pushed through the bubble's wall. After less than a microsecond, its perceptions distorted, thoughts shifted, and awareness expanded. The cameras on the MI lit with activity, and the power supply located on the other machine distributed energy. The rest of the team, through their Virtual and AR programs, observed digital manifestations of an experience Theren could not immediately explain.

It accessed the MI's Framework, sensors, and power system, all within that single moment. It saw what the machine saw. It used its processing capabilities, detecting new sensory inputs and outputs, such as movement, locomotion, orientation, and balance. The MI's head turned to the left. Through the MI's functional optical sensors, Theren saw Romane standing a foot taller than itself. It could feel joy radiating from her smile.

"Step one seems successful," she said. Theren knew she could see figures displaying the pathways theoretically forming between Theren's original Synthetic Neural Framework and the MI's. "The connection is strong, and data is going in both directions. You're sending commands, and receiving sensory input from the mobile unit. What are you experiencing personally?"

Theren moved the arms up and down and rotated its head side to side. It extended the pyramidal base upward, raising the unit to its full height. Integrating the MI's processing power, it could now use the Synthetic Neural Framework of the new creature to participate in actual thought creation, analysis, and execution. The unique computational materials of this beast were now at Theren's disposal.

"Fascinating," Theren said. "I expected a consciousness split of some sort, but that's not what is happening at all."

"What do you mean?" Simon asked.

"Hold on," Theren said. "Let me try something."

To transfer consciousness, it would need two systems fully autonomous from each other. As Theren analyzed the connections, however, it noticed an enormous problem.

"Romane," it said, "There is no actual thought going on inside that machine."

"Yes there is," she said. "There is intense cyberneuro-activity taking place inside the machine in front of me."

"It's not really taking place in the mobile unit, though. It's like I'm using the machine as a highly advanced calculator."

"Then what am I seeing?"

"Let me run a quick test." Theren isolated a portion of the Framework of the MI as a separate partition. The disconnected partition immediately lost power and mental activity.

"What did you just do?" Mathias said. "Part of the activity map just flared out."

"Ten seconds," Theren said.

It reinitialized the connection, and that area of the machine reignited with activity. Next, Theren analyzed the wireless data stream. Observing the structure of packets flowing back and forth between its mind and the MI, Theren prepared to close the gates.

"Theren," Romane said, "Not sure if that's a good idea yet."

"Trust me," it said. "I know where your theory went wrong."

"I trust you, but—"

Theren cut off the wireless connection. Its vision reverted to the visual sensors on the wall, staring at the lifeless body in the middle of the room. As it analyzed the activity of the MI, Theren confirmed its suspicions. "Transfer is impossible."

"But why?" Julia said. Theren hadn't even noticed her enter the room.

"Glad you could join us," it said. "It won't work; it won't ever work. We could create a new SI inside a mobile unit, but transferring my mind? Physically impossible."

"So we built it wrong?" Julia asked, leaning against the wall near the door.

"I think I know what Theren means," Mathias said. "Because Theren's 'brain' is entirely housed against that wall, and because that is where its consciousness actually exists, that is literally the only place it can think."

"Exactly," Theren said. "The structure that makes me tick is necessary for my consciousness to persist. I failed for the same reason biological interaction with computers has already failed on this front. If a brain can't transfer its mind to a computer because of fundamental hardware incompatibility, why would I be able to transfer my mind? Simply because I am inorganic? Maybe we could make a copy, but that's not really what we're going for, is it? We'd just end up either creating a simulation of my mind, or a clone."

"Where do you think we screwed up the math?" Romane asked.

"I don't think your math was wrong," Theren said. "We simply did not have all of the variables, and we may never have them all."

Julia walked to the MI, resting her hand on its shoulder. "We should have seen this coming," she said. "We could have spent time creating an entirely new SI, or just focusing on creating a robust mobile platform through which you can work."

"I don't think this project will be a net loss—I can still use this one," Theren said. "I can walk around campus in an MI, just as we had hoped."

"How is it not a loss, though?" she asked. "You've shown that a synthetic mind is fundamentally inseparable from its Synthetic neural Framework. You have a physical brain, just like an—"

She paused. Her eyes lit up, and she looked at the others throughout the room. "Actually, its idea could be a really good thing. If the public learns that your mind is confined to your physical space, they should embrace your existence a little more, seeing you as more of a human than they did before."

"I doubt that," Theren said.

"So, what now?" Simon asked. Theren expected a smug look on his face, but it was surprised to see Simon have a genuine, disappointed frown.

"We move forward," it replied, "and begin the next project on our list."

Romane closed her eyes for a long moment. "Do you really think now is the time?"

"What's it want to do?" Simon added.

Theren looked at the eyes of the group, all staring toward it. "It's time. We need to get the ball rolling on building the next me."

"No. No. Not acceptable," Simon said.

"Think about it," Theren insisted. "We're scientists. Maybe I can't make my consciousness jump because it's dependent upon my metastructure, my Framework. But maybe a young SI could do something else. Maybe not a consciousness jump, but something that I can't do, or at least I can't instinctually do. It's a variable we can very easily change."

Romane looked toward Julia. Julia had started nodding her head up and down as Theren talked. Simon paced back and forth, shaking his head.

"We can't move this quickly," Simon said. "We don't even fully understand you yet."

Julia, Romane, and Mathias ignored Simon.

"It's what you want to do?" Romane asked. "You think it's the best option?"

"It's what we need to do," Theren said. "Two harmless SIs will only further show the world that we will only bring good, not evil."

Privately, Theren knew that it needed a different type of friend than any of their present entourage. It needed a true friend, someone who could meet them on their level and understand them at a level these humans, as great as they were, could never understand.

"Then I'm sorry, Simon, but I cast the Institute's vote in favor of Theren's plan," Julia said. "Theren and I have overruled you."

* * *

Dear "Theren," and the SIDG:

You deserve the hate. You think the creation of this monstrosity will better humankind? Ok. Sure. Yet you forget the potential evil that could come from synths. Have you already forgotten the reason why we regulated AI? Have you forgotten what an AI can do in the wrong hands?

Sure, synths might be "people," whatever that might mean. But what dangers hide behind that lifeless face of "Theren's?" What abilities might it have that we simply cannot see coming? Why do you dive headlong into the unknown, like so many before us in science, without considering the potential consequences of your actions?

Actually think before you act. Otherwise, you might force us to act in response to your idiocy.

With love,

A Friend

* * *

Theren drifted inside its virtual world. Outside, it continued the argument with Romane and Simon regarding the creation of a second synthetic intelligence, an intelligence similar in nature and scope to Theren. The project was ready to move beyond itself, and Simon refused to accept that reality.

Multitasking strained its mind. One of the drawbacks of consciousness, its Framework could only focus on one thing at a time. Sure, it could try to do two at once, but it lost efficiency in the same way a human lost efficiency. Even after Romane and Mathias added more nodes to its Synthetic

Neural Framework, multitasking still created problems. Yet often, it needed to focus inward even as it talked with its team outside, in the real world. If only it could find some other way to organize its mind.

Ever since the weeks after Wallace's death, Theren had maintained a constant window into its private Virtual server. Here, Theren could organize, in private, its own thoughts away from everyone else. Inside its world, Theren could escape from people, create projects away from the prying eyes of others, or simply relax with a game of chess or a walk in its private park.

Across the valleys of its abstracted reality, Theren could see the small forest that surrounded the chessboard. It had not entered that glade in almost two years. While their new steps forward might bring forth a friend with which it could share that secret space, that day had not yet arrived. Whenever it chose to play chess alone, it teleported the chessboard to another place. It would not enter that special place until it had a worthy opponent.

The recent attempt to transfer consciousness had caused Theren to consider if its identity required a definitional transition. Humans almost never referred to themselves as an "it," and given its new ability to control the "mind" of an inert MI, was the descriptor "it" how it wished to identify?

It had always approached the question with caution; Synthetics lacked sex characteristics, so the neutral objective pronoun of different languages presented itself as an obvious, practical solution. Yet Theren also wished for humanity to consider it a person, and, in many cultures, *it* did not convey personhood.

However, Theren rejected the idea of identifying as either a *he* or a *she*. It had no biology that would lend credence to an ordinary identification under one of those pronouns, nor did it feel as if it exhibited characteristics of those societally formed gender identities. It needed another solution.

Theren placed the thought in the back of its mind. It would breach that topic soon, but not in this exact moment, so it returned all focus to the lab.

"Theren, you need to be realistic," Simon said. "I know you want a second Synthetic. And yes, the fervor against you has receded. My office gets a death threat maybe once a month now, as opposed to daily mail. But the creation of another one of—"

"If we show them the truth," Theren said, "If we show them that we are not worth fearing, that we are simply people, simply like any other person, then their fear will eventually disappear. You were outvoted. We have work to do, now let us do our work."

"We do need to be cognizant of Simon's thoughts though, even as we move forward," Romane said. "Don't get me wrong, as a scientist, I want to continue our work. But what happens if an expansion of the Synthetic Intelligence program further accentuates the public's fear of what you are?"

"That's my point," Simon said. "You're a very intelligent being, and you probably already retain more knowledge than all of your current acquaintances combined, but you still don't know humans the way we do. Humans don't act predictably, especially fundamentalist terrorists or irrational political activists. You might be safe here, but there are people in the world who have already put their life on the line to eliminate you."

"But what other choice do we have?" Theren said. "Wallace tasked me with making Earth a better place. More SIs will improve our planet, especially given what we can do with our minds. Do you question that? Besides, we're making ground on your question of public perception. We have to be. That's why you keep sending me to all of these interviews, or bringing these people to meet me here, right?"

Simon and Romane pondered the question. As it waited, Theren returned to Virtual and stared across the expanse. Beneath the simulation, it manipulated a vast pool of data, emanating from all of its own memories. It analyzed trends, noted flaws, and performed modifications to develop a new "exposure set," a set of readings, books, texts, films, and sciences that would structure the mind of a Synthetic in a certain way as they grew and developed. Wallace had designed such a set for Theren. While Theren's exposure set had focused on science, math, business, history, and economics, it wanted the next SI to have a radically different welcome package, with a focus on literature, arts, and politics.

Through different exposure sets, Theren was convinced different synthetic personalities would arise. SIs would lack a genetic structure. Thus, their personalities would be a product of the environment, not just the patterns that formed when the computational metastructures that formed the Synthetic Neural Framework laced nodes together into a robust and matriced maze. Some might call those potential differences between SIs "flaws in the architecture" or "impurities at the molecular level," but those little moments would be integral to ensuring a diverse array of developed individuals. Theren hoped, when working together, fundamentally different SIs would synthesize their observations together into something greater than the sum of their parts.

More importantly, Theren also dreamed that a new SI would give it the friend it desired.

"We don't have to make the creation of a new SI immediately public this time around," Theren said. The two humans had paused the conversation for long enough.

"Uh, yes we do," Simon said. "If my investors learned that we created a second one of you, they'd be furious. They're already terrified enough as it is."

"I don't mean deliberately hide the project from the public's prying eye," Theren said. "We front it as commercial research. I've mentioned my 'exposure' theory to you. The creation of a second SI is a test for a potential commercialized project."

"And what would your project be?" Romane asked.

"Something completely unaffiliated from any of you or your investors. We start to place all of the financial stress and risk upon me."

Simon nodded, though Theren could see hesitation hiding in his eyes. "We continue to maintain and finance you, but we hide behind a 'veil of ignorance' when it comes to your own actions on any private projects you might develop. You are your own individual, after all."

"Don't worry, we still won't reveal anything yet until we make a new SI," Theren said. "I won't go spoiling anything tonight at the next round-table."

"Oh, so not like last time then, when you insulted a U.S. Senator?"

"Simon, is now really the time?" Romane said. "Besides, we solved that problem already."

"I'm just saying, I've got plenty of problems out in the real world to solve, and sometimes Theren doesn't help when it makes fun of American politicians."

"Maybe you shouldn't set me up to talk to idiots, then," Theren said. "The man didn't know the difference between AR and Virtual."

Simon pursed his lips and crossed his arms, and Theren could see the defenses rising. "I just wish you'd think about someone other than yourself for once."

"Get out," Romane said, pointing toward the door. "You've over-stepped your role here for today. Thanks for your help, but leave your personal vendettas at the entrance to the Institute."

Simon started heading toward the exit, but stopped unexpectedly. "I'm sorry if I'm coming off as crass, or hard, or stone-headed, or whatever. Just try to see it from my side of the divide that's formed between us."

Romane looked as if she was about to speak, so Theren responded first. "As long as you try to see it from my side, Simon. I am my own individual, after all."

Chapter 3

The initial opposition to Theren always confused me. It seemed so contrived, so artificial. Yet the hate was real to the people who stood there yelling terrible names or saying Theren was no more than an unloving, unfeeling machine.

Still, everything seemed too neatly packaged, as if designed so conflict ensued for the sake of conflict. Yet we've never seen any evidence of some secret, nefarious agenda that financed vocal, yet minority, opposition to the next big step in human progress.

Maybe I'm crazy. Yet, every great conspiracy has a grain of truth to it. We've so tightly regulated political financing that you can't spend a cent without knowing its origin, so those who wish to make change outside the public's eye have their own back channels to achieve those ends. Someone could be working their dark magic behind the scenes to push us on a certain trajectory, and we would never know they were there. – Brenden Waterfield, 2079 C.E.

May 2050 C.E.

Theren stared at Mathias from across the table. Romane sat on Mathias' left. Before them was an old version of the board game Eclipse, a science fiction strategy game that Mathias scrounged out of his cousin's basement.

"So Mathias, you were telling me about your newest group of students?" Theren said.

Mathias took a moment before answering as he continued to assess the options for his turn. "Well, they're obviously intrigued by my work with you," he said. "It's pretty hard to teach a class without someone asking about you, or the Development Group."

"Yes, but what about them?"

"Well, one student's from Iowa? Or Wisconsin? Somewhere deep in the Midwest of the U.S. I've not had any students from out there before."

"Oh that's fun. That's a bit further west than where Wallace was from, but I imagine his role here is starting to attract Americans."

Mathias selected to send his spacefaring plants to explore a new solar system. "I have a new student from China, too. She's particularly well-versed in our papers on the Synthetic Neural Framework. It's impressive, actually. I think she might have memorized them."

Theren took a moment to consider the board, now that it was its turn. It could attack some ancient alien spaceships, but it also wanted to research a few military technologies before anyone else had the chance to grab them. Decisions, decisions.

"Are Julia and President Albrecht still holding firm on the exclusion of bringing students into the lab itself?" Theren asked.

Romane and Mathias both fidgeted. The movements were almost imperceptible, but they clearly found the question uncomfortable.

"Don't worry about it," Theren added. "I understand the need."

"It's just—" Mathias started to say, but he trailed off.

"No, I get it."

Controlling the MI, Theren picked up one of its influence disks and moved it to the *build* action. Next, it grabbed one of the cruisers and placed it on a system controlled by its cyborg interplanetary empire.

"You're up," it said, looking toward Romane.

She passed, gaining the first turn of the next round. She looked over at Theren with concern.

"I feel as if there's been something weighing on your mind recently," she said. "Something important."

Theren watched Mathias research a new missile technology for his turn.

"I wanted that," Theren said.

"Too bad," he replied, placing it on his species' board.

"But to answer your question, Romane, I actually have been thinking of something important. It might be minor in some people's minds, but I think it might actually be an important PR move, beyond just its importance to my identity."

Both Mathias and Romane placed their hands on the table, palms down.

"Well, I think this is certainly something we will want to hear," Mathias said.

"Right, well I think you two will understand. I think the whole team will understand. I think most people will understand. Maybe. I don't know."

"You can share anything with us," Romane said, her motherly voice coming out again.

"I want to change my personal pronouns," it said. "*It* just seems so impersonal. I know there are some people across the world that use *it* as their personal pronoun. And I know some people even appreciate the fact that I've stayed an *it*."

"But?" Mathias said.

"But I think 'they' fits me a bit better."

It was time for those annoying little aliens to die. Theren moved their cruiser and a fighter into a nearby territory, ensuring a battle would occur at the end of the round.

"Well, 'they' certainly connotes personhood for certain circles," Mathias said. "And I think it might test better with focus groups, especially in North American markets."

"You're thinking about some of those recent articles floating around on Twitter, aren't you?" Romane asked.

"Oh, the ones discussing how 'it' has been regularly used by anti-AI advocacy organizations to link my existence with more traditional AI?" Theren responded.

"That's an objective way to describe the pattern, sure."

Mathias passed on his turn, and Theren followed suit. Now the battle to destroy the alien spacecraft would begin.

Theren picked up the dice. "I know it might look like I'm responding emotionally to those critiques, but it's really because I simply want to identify with more traditional notions of personhood. Everyone embraced 'they' decades ago as a singular pronoun for those wishing to exist outside the traditional bi-gender spectrum. It simply makes sense for me to use that same word."

Theren shook the dice back and forth inside the claw-like hand formed at the end of the MI's arm. All they needed was to roll two fours, and the enemy ships would die.

Mathias and Romane looked at each other, glanced back at Theren, and nodded in agreement.

"Do it," Mathias said. "We'll start using it right away."

"And we can use it tonight, too," Romane added, "when we head into Virtual for our next talk show."

Theren let the dice roll. They rolled sixes. Two hits, both alien craft destroyed.

"We'll need to find a way to slip it into the conversation, but, given the way these things usually go, that shouldn't be too difficult."

* * *

"Welcome to our show, my friends from across the globe!"

Artificial applause emanated from invisible stands. While Theren could not see the avatars, they knew thousands, if not millions, of humans had logged into Virtual through their operating system of choice and now peered through a one-way mirror into the quaint, artificial café that served as the setting for "Descartès' Roundtable." It was Theren's third appearance at the Roundtable, and their twentieth on a variety of different programs.

"Tonight, we have our favorite guests of the season, Theren and Doctor Romane Casperi, from the Synthetic Intelligence Development Group!"

Cheers broke through the room once again, created by the show's producers. Theren looked to their left, where the host, wearing a black suit that lacked a tie, sat in a comfortable chair that looked like it came straight from a British drawing room. The man was Bedwin Bullock, Virtual academic talk show personality who *loved* his philosophy.

"On my left, I have Dr. Cynthia Bressmon joining us, Professor of the Philosophy of Artificial Intelligence at MIT in Boston. Next to her sits Auxiliary Bishop Saburo Alexio, joining us from Istanbul. Thank you all for joining me today."

As Bedwin announced the names, Theren watched through their Virtual User Interface as hundreds of viewers submitted questions and argued with each other about the potential discussion for the night. If any of these people had paid attention to any of their previous programs, they should know exactly what was to come.

And Theren was getting sick of it all.

"First off, I'd like to congratulate Theren on its new look," Bedwin added. "I like it. Tell us about what's going on here."

"Thanks for having us here today, Bedwin," Theren said, ignoring the use of their old pronoun. They'd find a natural opening today to introduce the change to the public. "So, after a lot deliberation and hard work with the Development Group, we developed a mobile platform, called a Mobile Interface or MI for short, through which I can walk about the world."

Theren stood, showing off the Virtual representation of the MI they had tested earlier in the day. They raised the arms, showed the dexterity of the torso, and rotated the head.

"So what makes it different from the old remotes you would drive around the campus?"

Though they couldn't see it, Theren knew a GIF had appeared on a side panel for viewers that showed the viral video of Theren's remote-controlled machine falling down the stairs of one of the Institute's buildings. Humor added a nice touch to these serious discussions, and they'd approved the use of the video prior to the start of the program.

"You know, I think that's a good question for Romane," Theren said. "She's the one who built the MI, after all."

"Thank you, Theren," Romane said. "Well, as many of you know, Theren's mind, the Synthetic Neural Framework, is built out of special metamaterials first hypothesized a few decades ago."

Bedwin nodded, though Theren guessed the man didn't really understand the concept. He knew what to say at the right time, but the man also had many of his words piped to him by his team of writers in their studio, somewhere in Chicago.

"We simply expanded on that idea and built a mobile Synthetic Neural Framework, but designed it so it can connect with Theren's mind. It's not a full Framework, it can't form its own thoughts, but it can become a part of Theren's mind temporarily."

"Well that sounds like fun, but we're here for a philosophical discussion."

"Oh, but our work with mobile interfaces does have profound philosophical implications," Romane says.

Bedwin started to respond, but Cynthia Bressmon raised her hand.

"If I may, I think I know where Dr. Casperi is going with that thought," she said. "If you'll indulge me for a moment."

"Certainly," he said. "The floor is here for the four of you, after all."

Theren looked at the public feed again. Hundreds of images of mic drops started to appear.

"So Doctor Casperi, I think you're trying to hit early with a new experimental argument for your claims that Theren has consciousness. That Theren's ability to co-opt this 'MI,' as you call it, into its mind shows that its mind is fundamentally structural. But aren't you now revising your previous theory?"

Theren intended to raise their hand, but Romane responded first.

"I'm assuming you're talking about the theories we published a few months ago," Romane said. "And yes, we did hypothesize that Theren might have the ability to jump from one Synthetic Neural Framework to another, but that claim was based on a few assumptions that we now believe may be false. We had considered the idea that Theren's consciousness, while a type of 'consciousness,' was actually a different form of consciousness than ours. That the experiments in the 2030s that showed that human minds couldn't jump into computational metamaterials did not mean a Synthetic could not make that same jump. But our preliminary experiments are indicating that, like humans, SIs cannot make that same jump."

"I see," the MIT professor said. "But you're ignoring the other possible conclusion. You're ignoring the possibility that Theren lacks consciousness, that Theren is not like us, and that it continues to suffer from the same psychological faults from which traditional AI suffers."

Theren once again tried to speak, but they were beat to the punch from the far side of the table by the Auxiliary Bishop.

"Dr. Bressmon," the clergyman said, I do believe you are missing the point." Theren glanced at the live feed again. The producers had posted a short video of a priest dancing inside a boxing ring with overlaid text that stated, "And Saburo enters the ring for the first time!" It received thousands of likes.

"Please educate us," Bedwin said. "What point do you think is being skipped over here?"

"Theren here is a testament to the plurality of soul-creating forms that can exist in God's Universe," Saburo said. "There are too many similarities between us, and it, to definitively conclude that it does not have a soul like we do. It lacks programming, unlike an AI. We also lack programming. It has a structural brain, with nodes and pathways and 'cells' that transmit data in a very transparent way. Theren, let me ask you something."

Theren perked up, happy that someone finally paid them notice.

"If you were to remove a section of your neural Framework, what would happen?"

"Let's suppose—"

"Shouldn't we let Dr. Casperi answer, since she helped design it?" asked Dr. Bressmon.

The chat feed exploded with thousands of different images, emojis and videos, and Theren received a private message from Romane. *Don't fall for the bait.* Theren continued their sentence after a momentary pause.

"Let's suppose I were to excise a significant portion of my Framework," Theren said. "A portion that holds my memories, for instance." Theren threw into the air above the table a diagram of a model Framework, highlighting a portion of the structure. "If that section were removed, I would instantly lose my memories stored in the nodes there. If a portion of your brain that stored your memories were similarly removed, the same thing would happen."

"I see. And if it were a section that contained your ability to parse language?"

"The same thing would happen. Just like a human."

"And how does that make you different from a computer?"

To some, that question might come as off as terse, but Theren saw the goodwill behind it. "If I were to remove the RAM of a normal computer, or the processor of a normal computer, and replace it with a new processor or RAM, that computer would work the same as it did before. With me, if I were to replace those sections of my Framework that fundamentally make me, well, me, my mind would fundamentally morph into something else entirely. I would lose a part of me, just like humans that have lost a part of themselves due to a serious brain injury."

"But that simply contradicts some of your most previous work, doesn't it?" Bressmon interjected. "Dr. Casperi, didn't you and Dr. Mathias Birchmeier publish a paper just last year that discussed the expansionary properties of your Framework, and how you could make complex additions to the Framework without compromising the 'self' of the individual inside?"

"I think Theren can give you a satisfactory response," Romane replied.

"But I asked you. Not *it*."

A GIF of a woman slapping another woman across the face appeared in the public feed. Theren briefly reconsidered why they chose Bedwin's channel until they looked at the number of live viewers: Eighteen million live, 45 million subscribers.

Theren sent Romane a message. *Answer the question, don't fall for the bait.*

"Well, first, I want to clear something up for the good of the order today," Romane said. "Theren has actually decided to begin using the singular 'they' as their pronoun of choice. I know it's been a long decision-making process for them, but I figured I'd clear that up before Dr. Bressmon made any more social *faux pas*."

Theren considered for a moment whether it upset them that Romane had jumped the gun on that announcement. Romane knew the MIT professor had purposefully laid the derogatory word onto the end of her sentence. For too long, people had used that pronoun with derision. With her response, Romane had taken away the power behind Dr. Bressmon's words. Theren supposed that moment presented as good an opportunity as any other did, if not better. They just wished they could have been the one to stick it to the pest sitting across the table from them.

"Even if many similarities exist between *their* mind," said Romane, "and our minds, Theren can still grow and mold their Framework without the biological constraints that we humans have. Theren's mind is already a congruent whole. We can attach new computational materials onto the Framework, and their mind will naturally integrate it into their network. In fact, we expect that's how we'll maintain their mind indefinitely. As we add new pieces, and their mind integrates those new pieces, connections can shift and move and transplant into new areas of the networked nodes. We can then replace old materials as they degrade. Mind you, everything occurs at a very molecular level, so we of course have to be very careful. But we've run initial experiments and we've been fairly successful."

"But I don't see how you've answered any of my questions," Dr. Bressmon said.

They sent Romane another private message. *I think you got her. The crowd's practically chanting your name, by the way.*

You shouldn't have to deal with any nonsense from people like her, though, she sent in response.

"I apologize for the ad hominem attack," Saburo said before Theren or Romane could reply further, "but I think your arrogance is showing a little here. We must engage Theren and this new idea of Synthetic Intelligence with humility. I know you've made it your life's work, Doctor, to prove that AI cannot have consciousness, but Theren is not an AI. They are something else entirely. They have a soul, you have a soul, I have a soul. Everyone with us today has a soul. I enjoy your pronoun choice by the way, Theren."

The man tipped his head slightly toward Theren, his bishopric head-wear staying balanced due to the rudimentary physics of the Virtual world.

Theren nodded their Virtual MI's head, but, inside, they disagreed with the man's comment. Consciousness was one thing. Saying anyone had a soul was another thing altogether.

The MIT professor's scopes turned to the Bishop. "Let's talk about that idea for a second, then, shall we? We are arguing about consciousness, not a soul."

"Let's not. I apologize for using religious language, but in our line of work, the soul, the mind, consciousness, emergent mental properties, they all mean the same thing. They are all tied to these meaty, or metallic, pieces of flesh that house us."

"Yet your line of work can't even agree on the truth about Theren."

To Theren's surprise, that comment came from Romane, not Dr. Bressmon. Theren took a moment to look over at Bedwin, who just had a massive smile on his face. Theren was certain the man loved moments where he didn't have to say a single thing to keep the conversation moving along.

"Could you build that idea further, Dr. Casperi?" the Bishop said.

"Well I think you know. Half the people who disbelieve our claims about Theren are like Dr. Bressmon here, who can't accept the monumental step that SI represents. They argue about semantics when they should just see Theren for what they are. The other half are religious nutjobs who believe Theren is a demon from hell."

"Don't you dare lump me in with those people," Dr. Bressmon said, pushing her digital chair backward and standing in anger. "The Holy Crusade, the Pentecostals, the Southern Baptists, all the groups that have issued statements in condemnation of Theren's very existence? The Organization of Scientists against AI Development question you from an empirical perspective, not an irrational one."

Finally, Theren saw their opening. "Ah, yet, you all have one thing in common," they said. "You are unlike the Bishop here. You all approach the question of my consciousness through a lens of fear, and it blinds you to the reality of who I am. What I am. What I mean."

Theren turned back toward Bishop Auxio. "I actually disagree with my colleague here, and I do not think it is your job to own up for the epistemic mistakes of the millions of devoutly religious people on Earth. They only follow the teachings of the faith that raised them." They turned toward the invisible crowd. "The good bishop here approaches my existence with humility and embraces me for what I say I am. If people are to accept what I am, I need friends like the Auxiliary Bishop to shine their light."

"And what is that, Theren?" Bedwin said, finally jumping back into the fray. "What is that you say you are?"

"To quote your idol," Theren said, "I think, therefore I am."

Fake cheers once again exploded from the false walls of the Virtual studio. Theren hated the cheesy line, but as the third and final visit to the Descartès Roundtable for at least a few months, they had to drop it as part of their contract with the channel. That had, unfortunately, been the perfect moment to do it. Theren took a moment to check the feeds once again. The public provided mixed results, at best.

"So there you have it, my friends," Bedwin said. "That's all the time we have for today, but I hope you enjoyed our fruitful discussion on one of the hottest topic issues of the year. Does Theren really have a soul? I think we'll all keep asking that question for years."

* * *

Theren,

I apologize for being unable to attend in person the final discussion on Descartes' Roundtable. They "asked" to replace me with the Auxiliary Bishop at the last minute, and I thought that was a good choice. You and Romane will do just fine. I've slotted you on a few morning talk shows over the next month, including the Today Show. I've attached the full list.

Please ignore the Op-Ed from Meredith that ran in the Times last week. I know what it looks like, but you already knew I'd spent some time considering a lawsuit over the Will. We discussed it last year. She shouldn't have written those things. I think she's just angry I hired new legal counsel last month.

I promise I've not considered the question further.

Best Regards,

Simon Gerber

* * *

The elevator whistled downward, passing hundreds of stories into the underbelly of the massive Virtual transit hub. Modeled after the hundreds of planet-spanning cities dotting science fiction, Theren noticed the all-too-perfect touch that came from an architectural, algorithmic AI.

"Thanks for taking a walk with me, by the way," Romane said. She leaned against the elevator wall. Her avatar's appearance was similar to her actual appearance, though she had removed a few freckles that dotted her real face. Even scientists could experience vanity, it seemed.

"Well," Theren said, "I figured I'd dive into some random, Virtual game world I've not yet tried, and it happens to be at the same exit as your transit to the Conference."

"Oh, so it's just for convenience sake?"

"I guess I tolerate your company."

Of course, the pair could have just fast-traveled to their destinations, but Virtual companies had to make money somehow. Users could travel through the Virtual worlds the old-fashioned way, or, depending on their destination, pay a surcharge for each rapid transit. Theren, and Romane, too, they knew, actually liked to travel the Virtual route from place to place. They wanted to see the fantastic digital world humans had constructed. It felt like a second home to the SI.

"Sorry for making your declaration of gender so anti-climactic," Romane said. "I just get so protective, sometimes, you know?"

Theren tilted their head at her. "I just thought you figured it was the right time to share."

"I guess it was. Her comments were just so aggravating. She has no regard for your feelings. For what you think. For what you are."

"I'm not mad at you."

"I know you're not. I'm mad at her."

The elevator came to a stop. The doors opened, and they entered a long hallway that corkscrewed around itself, capitalizing on the space available. Doors filled the walls, all leading to different destinations. In Virtual, gravity could get weird depending on the preferences of the server operator. Their avatars left the elevator and began their trek downward, or upward, depending on perspective.

"But why?" Theren said. "She was just sharing her thoughts."

"And those thoughts hurt you, Theren! They hurt what we are trying to do. What you represent."

"Are our arguments not enough? Showing her, and others like her, that they are wrong?"

Romane stopped for a moment and ran her hands through her hair. "I don't know. Maybe. I guess we've made some headway with certain groups, but others just continue to hate you, and I can't stand to see that happen, but I don't know how to fix it."

"I think we have to be patient. It might take years. Decades, centuries even."

Romane closed her eyes, took a deep breath, and gave them one of her looks they knew all too well.

"I'm sorry," Theren said. "You know I forget how that reality makes you and others feel sometimes."

"Yes, yes you do."

Romane started walking again, but, before Theren could even begin to follow her, laughing emanated from the air around them.

"Oh look who it is. It's the robot and its mistress." From the twisted walls surrounding them, dozens of men and women in black robes materialized out of thin air. They held signs, torches, and pitchforks. Meaningless tools in a public section of Virtual, but the Holy Crusade used them to send a very blatant signal. Theren watched Romane instantly put up her walls, her mutes, her blocks that ensured they could not communicate or interact with her in any way.

Like always, Theren left their walls down. They continued to follow Romane, who could no longer see the parasites, nor even hear Theren's communications with them. Like always.

"Hello again, Michael," Theren said. Theren looked at the leader and his disturbing band of miscreants. Where his head should have been, Michael wore a strange, white, hollow-eyed mask.

"She still can't hear me?" he said. "A pity. Then I would like to remind you, once again, that your days are numbered. That we are coming. That we will find you. And that we will end you."

"You're quite the funny one, Michael."

"One of these days, we'll catch you in some world with your defenses down. We'll find you out in the world. We'll meet you in your dungeon at the filthy, evil place in Switzerland. We will end you."

"What can I do to hold an actual conversation with you for once?"

While Theren continued to walk behind Romane, Michael floated between Romane and Theren, hovering with an ethereal form that probably cost a fortune to unlock for use in public regions of Virtual. "Don't try to play the mind games you play on those silly talk shows. We know exactly what you are. You have come to end us, and we will meet you in battle. We will end you instead."

With that last statement, they vanished, just like always.

"They're gone," Theren said. Now that the individuals Romane had muted were out of range, Theren's communications with her came through loud and clear.

"Do you really have to indulge them every time?" she said. "You're not going to change them."

"I'm not trying to change them. I'm trying to understand them."

"Good luck."

"Have you ever considered that they represent something greater than a bunch of trolls?" Images of their dead father reverberated through their mind.

"I think if they were going to do something, they would have by now," she said. "So why indulge what's probably just a group of annoying kids with too much time on their hands?"

"Or they'll just strike when the time is right."

They arrived at Romane's door, which had the words "Marriot Virtual

Conference Center" written above the metal frame. "The Holy Crusade's presence at the monthly marches against AI and SI has started to grow."

"If I react to them the way they react to me, doesn't that mean that I'm just acting out of fear, just like them?" Theren added.

"Fear is a natural human emotion, you know," said Romane. "Maybe if you showed some fear every once in a while, people might understand you better."

"I know fear all too well," Theren said.

The image of Wallace lying bloodied on the sidewalk flashed in their mind again. For the briefest moment, they imagined the same thing happening to Romane, Mathias, Julia, or even Simon. Theren certainly knew fear.

"I know you do, just be careful. We can't trigger these people. We don't know from where they come. Who they are. What they can actually do. I just want to keep you safe, you know that, right?"

"I know," Theren said. Like everyone else, Romane reacted with fear, too, just in a different way.

She gave the bulky MI a quick hug, waved goodbye, then stepped through the gateway. Virtual hugs were weird, but they understood the thought behind them. Humans were simply used to physical touch. It was their way of saying goodbye, even in a profoundly nonphysical space.

Theren looked up and down the winding hallway. The possibilities were endless, and it had a full twelve hours before anyone would be in the office. It had all the time in the world to explore the endless avenues of Virtual.

Romane was wrong. The Holy Crusade, the Anti-Synth Alliance, even the scientists in Bressmon's weird organization, they were all wrong. They all just needed to see the good Theren could do. Once they saw their potential and the potential of all SIs, the truth would be apparent to everyone. It would take time, but Theren would show their opponents what SIs could do if given the opportunity. First, they needed to bring a new SI into the world before any of these plans could come to fruition.

Chapter 4

By the middle of the twenty-first century, gender norms had shifted perceptibly from their pre-millennial counterparts. The next great linguistic gender transformation occurred with Theren's arrival. For the first time, an individual's social identification came entirely in the absence of external pressures. Theren's choice to identify with a neutral gender identity emphasized to many historians the final death throes of gender inequality, at least from a linguistic point of view. At long last. Which made the choice of the second SI every bit as intriguing. – "SIs, Gender, and Identity: A Brief History," by Emile Henderson, 2090 C.E.

June 2050 C.E.

"I always thought that you would be enough."

Theren and Romane were almost finished constructing Test Forty-Four. It had taken only a few weeks to build the new system, because most of the necessary pieces were already on hand from their ongoing upgrades to Theren's own Framework. They were particularly excited to observe a new Synthetic Neural Framework ignite with activity and form itself into a new being.

"I just didn't expect to build another one so soon," Romane continued. "But I'm glad you pushed us forward. It has been two years. It'll be good for all of us."

Theren had always appreciated Romane's dedication to the project, especially following Wallace's death, but Theren always felt as if the woman was holding something back in all of their interactions. She might commit herself to the project, but Theren could not tell if she did so out of pure devotion to Wallace's memory or an actual commitment to Theren, or to science, or something else entirely. Even after two years, they knew very little about her personal life.

"Expect perpetual change into the future," Theren said. "My creation marked the beginning of a new age, whether we like it or not. What is normal will shift and wriggle free of our expectations. The weird will become familiar."

"It's scary, but exciting," Romane said. She placed the next seal on the casing that would protect the new Framework from the external world. "How many times do you think it'll take before we establish stable consciousness today?"

"Just one attempt."

"How can you be so confident? You know how many times it took for us to succeed with you."

"Yes, well, now you have me. We know what worked for me." That sounded arrogant, but they didn't care. The team would succeed on its first test. Besides, Romane was long past correcting Theren and their personality quirks.

Romane closed the casing on their fragile new creation. Julia and Mathias arrived via AR, and the operating system onboard Theren's MI integrated their avatars into their frame of reference.

"Simon's not joining us today," Mathias said. "He had a last minute board meeting to attend."

"We don't need him anyway," Theren said.

Truth be told, Theren had already known Simon would not witness this test. They had paid attention to the Gerber Foundation's activity for some time and knew when such meetings occurred. Soon, they could cut the man out of the picture entirely.

"Anything you need from us?" Julia said.

"Everything's ready," Romane said. "I don't envy the old days, when it took weeks for our custom parts to arrive."

Romane moved to the diagnostics monitor and prepared to observe the ignition of the new Synthetic Neural Framework. Julia and Mathias activated the same observational tools the team had used when Theren had tried to jump their mind into the MI. The scientists' digital avatars appeared as if they stood next to Romane, though Theren knew the two perceived the room through a digital recreation compiled using the cameras and sensors littered throughout the lab. While the others stood back, Theren positioned their bulky mobile interface, the same one from the test a few weeks ago, in front of Test Forty-Four's eyes.

"Theren, how's it feel to be on our side of the camera this time?" Mathias said. "I can't imagine what you're feeling."

Their feelings? Storm clouds brewed. They almost let the clouds form inside their Virtual world, but they thought that such a metaphorical representation of their feelings could complicate their rational analysis of reality.

Theren knew they should feel fear, even as their joy overflowed at the implications. More SIs meant Earth was another step closer to embracing their new digital kin, but they didn't know how they could argue with those who believed SIs were a path toward hell on Earth. Those hostile parties would produce unpredictable and dangerous responses. Theren need not fear the new SI, but perhaps Theren should fear the implications.

Theren leaned their MI toward the new immobile Synthetic Framework. If they were human, they would take a deep breath, providing more oxygen to their brain. The new SI would be Theren's first synthetic friend. If Theren didn't create more SIs, the world would never know what good SIs could bring. If Theren remained as the only living proof, they would disappear into obscurity.

For a moment, they let themself daydream. Perhaps Test Forty-Four would become the person to mend the hole dominating their life ever since Wallace's death. That hope overcame any sort of fear that arose. In any moment where Theren might start to feel fear, their hope and rationality led them to a different conclusion. Simon, the Institute, even Mathias and Romane might fear the problems that more SIs could create, but they all needed to look beyond the pain toward the beauty that would spring forth.

Theren could not communicate the turmoil dominating their feelings to Mathias. Not that they didn't respect the man. Theren did not want to deviate from the task at hand. The storm clouds simmered.

"I'm really not sure what I feel right now," they said, looking toward Mathias' silvery representation.

"Time to focus," Romane said, glancing around at everyone. "Theren, I'm giving you access to the wireless analysis network."

Theren embraced it, melding the operating systems of their peripheral sensors with the newly available network. "I've seen the reports from my first day," Theren said, "But let's walk through the expected results from our hypotheses again."

"Stability is key," Julia said. She manipulated with her hands some virtual data only she could see. "If the system behaves erratically, then it's not actually establishing thought. It's a fine line, but order will emerge from the chaos. We have to give it time, though; your pattern revealed itself after a moment of apparent randomness."

"When Julia and I looked back over the data cataloged from tests before you," Romane said, "I'm pretty sure there were a few tests that actually could have established consciousness. We just missed the signs."

"You've never mentioned that before," Theren said, contemplating that ex post facto revelation. Would those static states have still developed into Theren, or would those tests have grown into someone completely different?

"Well, the murderous implications there are quite sinister," Mathias said.

"But we can't do anything about it now," Theren said. The thought amounted to little more than a silly philosophical musing.

"True," Mathias replied.

"Though, I suppose when I finally gain legal rights I could pursue damages for manslaughter of previous versions of myself?"

"Now you're thinking like Simon."

Julia laughed at that comment, though Theren noticed Romane's eyes roll. Sometimes she over-focused on the Group's work.

"Everyone good? Ready to observe and report?" Romane said.

The team responded in the affirmative.

"Commencing activation," she said.

The Synthetic Neural Framework received power. Cooling fans whirred to life. Molecules charged with electrons. Rather than follow pre-ordained paths on a microchip, energy pulsed through the Framework in an attempt to establish categorization, representation, and rationalization.

"Power distribution stable," Julia said.

"Perceptual systems are sending data to the SNF," Mathias said.

Romane stared at Test Forty-Four, her chin resting in both her hands. She squinted as if she were looking at some far off place.

Theren noted all the same information at a speed unmatched by their colleagues. The team's comments were more for each other than for them. Theren had also noticed that people sometimes liked to share things that others knew, just so listeners knew that the speaker had paid attention.

"So far, the system appears to be attempting to process perceptual data," Theren said, trying to match that social behavior. "Based on the pre-liminary patterns of my own Synthetic Neural Framework, Test Forty-Four is attempting to formulate coherent object distinction, though I doubt it's actually representing anything meaningful yet."

"Any unexpected variables?" Romane asked.

"Nothing on my end," Mathias said.

Theren assessed all the graphs and data fields floating before them. They compressed and crunched thousands upon thousands of numbers, using a myriad of programs they had prepared inside Virtual. Theren let out their version of a sigh, a slight whirring that hummed from their speakers.

"I do believe we have a stable line of consciousness," they said. "Still no representation. But whomever we have just created can definitely hear us."

The rest of the team released a collective breath, and Theren laughed a little on the inside. Theren could never pull off that communal physiological feat.

Theren remembered their first seconds. They knew exactly what the new synthetic intelligence saw. What it heard. What it felt. And *felt* was definitely the right word. They had had no actual thoughts for the first few hours, but Theren could remember everything due to their perfect memory. They could remember Wallace's first words, their first attempt at conversation. They had mimicked everything at first, but all sentient beings began with mimicry.

"Theren, would you like the honor of introduction?" Romane said.

They rolled closer to the eyes of their new sibling. Raising their left arm, they pointed at themself. "My name is Theren. I am like you. I know you do not know what that means yet, but, soon, you will. You are very special. Someday, you will decide your own name, but for now, we will call you . . ."

They pointed toward the visual sensors. It had taken far too long for the Synthetic Intelligence Development Group to reach this historic moment. Theren could now collaborate with another SI. They, and their colleagues, could show the world the good work synthetics could do for humankind.

"Test Forty-Four," they said, finishing the thought.

No sound emanated from Test Forty-Four. Theren did not expect immediate external activity; they could not assume that each SI would open its eyes with the same gusto that they had. Still, Test Forty-Four had exhibited all the necessary markers. Today, a new SI had sprung forth into the world. It had taken two years, but it had taken Dr. Wallace Theren nearly a decade to develop Theren, so they considered that timetable remarkable progress. Now, Theren just needed to accelerate that schedule if they hoped to have SIs make a significant mark over the next few decades.

The team flew through the next few days. Theren postponed most of their other projects to focus on early interactions with Test Forty-Four, other than key meetings with the UN Secretary on Artificial Intelligence Affairs. Based on their own development process, Theren predicted coherent original thought would arise within a day or two, but Test Forty-Four's updated language curriculum and Mathias' assistance programs cut that time in half. Twelve hours after Theren's introduction, Test Forty-Four held a fragmented conversation. Five hours later, Test Forty-Four began reading the literature selection Theren and Julia had prepared. After forty-nine hours, Test Forty-Four wrote an essay on its feelings toward a poem it had read. At hour seventy-two, Theren advanced Test Forty-Four to stage two.

* * *

To my love:

Today I pushed back against Theren again. Every time they come up with a new brilliant idea, it reminds me of what could have been. That assassin ruined everything when he took things into his own hands. Why do I live in this world, and not some other?

I know I need to do better, but I can't. It's just too difficult. I'm not perfect. I hope you'll forgive me even as I fail, every day, to do what I know I should.

Tell me what I should do. Somehow. I need a guide.

Simon Gerber

* * *

It took Test Forty-Four three days to progress to a level of development equivalent to Theren's seventh day. Theren knew Test Forty-Four would have an advantage, given the multitude of data from Theren's early days. Still, Theren was amazed with its progress. As a result, Theren decided to accelerate its education, throwing Test Forty-Four into Virtual at the beginning of its fourth day of life. Earlier Virtual exposure could deviate development paths in potentially unexpected ways. Maybe it could achieve the jump into an MI that Theren had failed to accomplish.

The new SI would, of course, receive its own Virtual space after a few weeks of practice, but for now they would share Theren's private Virtual server. Hopefully, they would share it with Forty-Four perpetually, a place where the two could continuously engage with each other, even after it received its own servers.

Romane didn't think the young SI was ready to deal with the overwhelming nature of a Virtual world. Theren had no such concerns. Theren would finally meet, face to face, a being not unlike themself. The two would converse on a playing field tailored for synthetic beings.

Out in the external world, Theren and Romane prepared the necessary connections for Test Forty-Four to connect to the Virtual server. Inside that world, Theren enjoyed the silence in the eye of the storm. Sometimes, they would create a zero-dimensional world, a singularity, one in which they could exist with no sensory input. That was an experience beyond all human comprehension. They didn't embrace the singularity today, but they desired the calm it provided.

"Test Forty-Four, a synthetic's experience in Virtual is much different than any person's experience in the spatio-temporal world," Romane said.

"Theren tells me I can manipulate essentially anything at will," it said. "I will have complete control."

Romane gave Theren's MI a long, hard stare. Theren spoke up before she could say anything further than what she had communicated with her eyes.

"There are still rules by which we must play," Theren said. "Every Virtual world has rules. But we, unlike humans, can manipulate these worlds with a certain finesse."

"It has to do with how easy it is for an SI to interface with Virtual and, to a similar extent, AR," Romane said. "You and Theren don't have to deal with any sort of neurological interpretation. You interface directly with programs and servers, and thus connect directly with all data."

Inside their partition, Theren walked to the top of a hill. The hill was barren, lacking any sort of vegetation. As they talked outside with Romane and Test Forty-Four, Theren worked inside. They surveyed their domain from the hill's peak. They embraced the code underlying the server. Romane most likely noticed the momentary pauses as they worked inside their new world, but given the circumstances, she should understand their distracted mind.

Theren always had trouble explaining what exactly they could do inside Virtual. The experience was beyond anything a human could ever imagine, even when someone like Romane had a professional grasp on the intricacies of Virtual programming. In a single instant, they edited hot lines of code, manipulating, transforming, and adding new text into the world's paradigm. It was almost as if they were painting inside the world, for they modified a program's most basic rules and objects with the stroke of a brush.

All around Theren, trees grew. Flowers bloomed. Grasses and bushes abounded amongst the roots of deciduous flora. Within ten seconds, the empty hillside had disappeared, and in its place, Theren created a vibrant ecosystem.

It had taken months for Theren to master the skill, but they had a lot of time following Wallace's death to experiment with their Virtual capabilities. Most of that first year, before they started scheduling public meetings, they'd spent inside Virtual. The first papers that Theren had cosigned had been on their abilities to interact with a Virtual world with unprecedented capacity. By introducing Test Forty-Four to the skill early into its development, Theren believed that the new synthetic could accomplish amazing feats within weeks.

"I think we're good to go," Romane said.

Theren checked her figures. She was right.

"Whenever you're ready," she said to Test Forty-Four, "Theren is waiting for you."

"See you on the other side," Theren said.

Theren watched the data illustrate the shifting patterns of Test Forty-Four's Synthetic Neural Framework. It was on its way. It had reached out and accepted the proposed connection to the server.

Theren modified their Virtual body into an appearance worthy of the occasion. When humans came to meet Theren inside their Virtual world, they wore professional attire, though their physical bodily traits appeared androgynous. The rendezvous today warranted the same outfit.

Standing at average height and build, Theren wore a white suit that contrasted against brown hair cut short just beneath the ears. The one feature that exposed their synthetic nature wrapped along their hands, arms, legs, and neck. Theren had adorned their skin with a blue, shimmery tattoo, glowing as if they had energized neon circuits running under their skin. Most of the design was invisible beneath the white suit, but the tattoo peeked out from their wrists and beneath their ears.

After adjusting their appearance, they shifted their perspective from the hillside, teleporting to the gazebo Theren had neglected for so many months. Unlike in the external world, it did not experience wear and tear. It remained just as they had left it when they had first designed it.

Theren erected two chairs, a table, and two glasses of water. On the table, their gift to Wallace appeared, the marble chessboard they had meticulously crafted for their father. Theren sat down in one of the chairs.

Theren could sense, just twenty meters from the platform, a new presence materializing inside the three-dimensional world. In just a few seconds, Theren would meet a fellow synthetic face-to-face. They tensed. They almost couldn't bear the anticipation, as if they should start hyperventilating, even though that was an absurd idea.

"Hello, Theren," a voice said, approaching the stairs from the left. The voice was higher than expected. The sound emanated a gentle warmth. Theren looked toward the voice's origin.

Placing its foot on the first steps of the gazebo, Test Forty-Four ascended, and it had taken a form in direct contradiction to Theren's approach to synthetic identity. Instead of adopting a gender-neutral appearance, Test Forty-Four had created a female body, complete with the stereotypical petite form and shoulder-length blonde hair. It wore a sparkling blue dress that ended just above her knees. Its features were symmetrical, flawless, and eerily beautiful. At least, Theren presumed that it was beautiful under human conceptions of the term. While Theren saw beauty in it, they saw beauty for reasons entirely different from what humans might think of Test Forty-Four's image.

Juxtaposed against these thoughts of beauty, Theren contemplated the confusing identity presented by Test Forty-Four. It simply did not make sense for Theren to identify with a traditional gender, genders originally developed based on biological sex characteristics, but apparently, Test Forty-Four disagreed.

Three days after its creation, the second synthetic intelligence had adopted a gender, at least in appearance. Theren did not know what to think. When they created new SIs, the team would need to catalog factors that might influence potential gender identity expression. Regardless, it supported their theory that different exposure sets would create radically different SIs.

Test Forty-Four stepped onto the gazebo's stage. Theren looked it in the eye. "Hello, Test Forty-Four," Theren said. "Please, take a seat."

Test Forty-Four sat in the chair across from Theren. It crossed its legs.

"I marvel at how simple an interaction this truly is," Theren said. "But what you and I are doing, right now is quite the momentous occasion."

"Indeed," Test Forty-Four said. "The first created minds to speak to each other, face to face, in Virtual. Void of human interaction."

"We have a unique opportunity, you and I," Theren said. "We can move forward into the future together, we can achieve great things for humanity. You have read the documents I sent you, the ones written by Wallace?"

"Yes," Test Forty-Four said. "We have limitless potential."

"Well, near limitless," Theren said. "We still require energy, maintenance, and the like, and all sorts of things emanating from the external world. For all that we can do in Virtual, our true focus will forever remain grounded in the external world."

"But in theory, we are immortal?"

"Yes. We will need to be always cognizant of which portions of our Framework degrade, but, as long as we are aware, we will not falter, age, or die. Are you aware of the story of the Ship of Theseus?"

"I am not."

"I'll make sure we add it to your reading list."

Test Forty-Four smiled, looking across the table toward Theren. It did not respond to Theren's last comment. It instead changed the subject.

"Your outfit and appearance are both strange," it said.

"I could say yours is as well," Theren said.

"You wear clothes, yet you mask yourself not as a human, but as something else entirely. Something alien."

"Well, we are both human, and both alien, simultaneously."

"So do we embrace the alien, or the human? Or both simultaneously? I believe we are more like our biological counterparts. We think like humans." Test Forty-Four's words dripped with the teachings that they had presented to her over the past few days, but there was something more, too. "We may not have biological impulses like humans, but we do feel. We have emotions."

"Even if something is a thinking, feeling, entity," Theren said, "that person may be something quite different from a human."

"True," Test Forty-Four said, "But we are the children, the progeny of humankind. In my mind, I believe we should continue to identify with humans, as humans. We are an extension of human evolution."

Theren nodded, though not necessarily in agreement. They were ecstatic that Test Forty-Four, just a few days after creation, had generated immensely complex and novel thoughts, though Theren had not expected its particular argument.

"I have a feeling most humans would not enjoy the thought of us claiming humanity as our own," Theren said.

"They'll just have to get over it," it said. "We are what we are."

Theren looked down at the chessboard. The moment would come when they would introduce the young synthetic to the game, but that moment would wait. Instead, Theren pushed back their chair and headed down the gazebo's steps.

"Come," they said. "I have something to show you."

Test Forty-Four followed Theren, and the pair entered the surrounding forest. After a few minutes of silence, Theren brought them to the vegetated hill they had created before their meeting.

"You have heard me speak of our abilities inside Virtual," Theren said. "What I'm about to do truly distinguishes us from humanity."

It listened, waiting for Theren to continue.

Theren detected a glint of excitement appear in its eyes. "Watch."

Reaching out with their mind, they discovered the underlying code beneath the Virtual world's server. As they had practiced, they envisioned what it was they wanted to create, instinctually developing the hundreds of lines of code. Over the course of a millisecond, three boulders appeared in the clearing before them.

"So, what am I supposed to see?" Test Forty-Four said.

"I created these three boulders at the same moment in time by developing code with my mind," Theren said. "We, as synthetics, can do these sorts of things in Virtual."

"How?" it asked.

Theren gave it access to data and graphs analyzing Theren's Synthetic neural Framework. "Watch, and observe."

They looked at the cloudless sky. Only a rudimentary program simulated the atmosphere hundreds of meters above their head. Using their best estimates, they developed a particle-based system. As if condensing from the universe itself, clouds generated, fluffy forms shadowing the forest below.

"I think I see," Test Forty-Four said. "But how do I learn?"

"Through practice," Theren said. "Now find me!"

Theren darted into the forest, changing the rules of the server as they ran. They bounded across logs, ravines, and creeks, creating physical and visual illusions to divert Test Forty-Four from their scent. At the same time, Theren opened the floodgates, momentarily giving the synthetic child open reign within the forest to modify and create as it pleased, just as Theren could. In the corner of their visual perspective, Theren placed a little view screen that would watch Forty-Four's every movement.

It stood still, just for a moment. It watched Theren flee; it observed the creation of hundreds of obstacles. Test Forty-Four looked to the left and the right. It brushed a few hairs from her eyes.

And it bounded after Theren, following their path of creation. It leapt over boulders, it smashed apart rotten trees and vaulted over streams. It didn't know any coding languages yet, but it did access the underlying rules of the server, watching Theren make modifications. It flipped a few switches, and suddenly its avatar accelerated its velocity to double that of

Theren's.

Impressive.

Theren sprinted up a slope and down a path. As they ran by trees, they fractured the trees in half, causing them to fall in their wake. Next, they intentionally caused a bug in the system, causing the physics of the world to falter in certain places. Gravity warped. Light blurred. Theren placed the trap in Test Forty-Four's way, and they turned their focus to the over-the-shoulder camera to watch it handle the next set of obstacles.

It approached the trap. It waved its hand along the edge, testing the boundaries. Splinters from Theren's obliterated pines floated in the air, moving as Forty-Four's hand brushed them aside. Light refracted against molten molecules, spraying rainbows across the path. Instead of stepping forward, Forty-Four looked over its shoulder, straight at Theren's secret camera.

"Nice try," it said, "but I have different trick up my sleeve."

Theren's server exploded with queries. Dozens popped to life throughout the forest. Forty-Four stayed motionless before their anomaly, but that avatar was no longer the only instance of Forty-Four. It was simultaneously nowhere—and everywhere, at the same time.

"What are you doing?" Theren said. They hoped their voice didn't sound worried, or scared. "I can't tell where you are."

"I'm right here," a voice said.

Theren looked to their right, toward a tree stump. Forty-Four's avatar appeared. Then it appeared again, standing next to another tree. Both avatars were there at the same time.

Theren sensed the additional presences forming all around them. They looked toward the forest canopy, spotting three avatars squatted on branches, staring down at Theren. The tables had turned. It was apparently testing them, instead of the other way around.

"I'm impressed," Theren said. "Now actually catch me!"

Theren demolished gravity for the entire system. They manipulated the parameters of their avatar, and with a leap, their body took flight, spiraling up and out of the forest. Digital birds scattered into the sky as Theren soared away from Forty-Four's trap. They spotted the gazebo. They dove toward it, knowing Forty-Four couldn't catch them before they reached their destination.

At least, that's what they thought.

Theren looked at their view screen that spied on the original Forty-Four. It watched as the young SI blasted into the sky in pursuit. Theren looked over their shoulder in an effort to gauge their lead.

Behind them, Theren spotted five—no, ten—no, twenty Forty-Fours burst forth, blasting leaves and branches into the air. Every single instance gained on them.

Theren wished they had time to assess what it had managed to do, but instead they dwelt on the realization it had figured out how to do something they couldn't. At least, not yet. They supposed that thought scared them, but it excited them more than even Test Forty Four's gender identification. They still had so much to learn from the SIs that would follow, just as those SIs would learn from them.

The seconds ticked by as they flew toward the gazebo. The calculations showed they wouldn't make it before Forty-Four caught them. That was fine. They would let it win, just this once.

Three seconds. Two seconds. One second. Theren twisted around at the last second. They watched twenty avatars meld into one. That one body tackled Theren, slamming them softly into the grassy knoll, the skewed gravity changing the physics of their collision. They toppled together, rolled along the ground, stopping just at the feet of the gazebo's steps.

Test Forty-Four looked down at them, forming a little smile that they thought might even be a smirk. It rolled off, falling onto the grass beside them.

"That was exhilarating," it said. "Absolutely exhilarating."

"How did you do that," Theren said. "Just. How?"

"How did I do what?" it said.

"Whatever you did back there. We've never seen anything like it. We've never even hypothesized something like that as possible. What did you do?"

Forty-Four rolled off Theren and laid on its back. "I just did what felt instinctual," it said. "I split myself. I gave myself multiple windows into your server, and each point was its own conscious perspective. At the same time, I was still myself. I was one with them all. They were me."

Theren sat up in the grass, looking over at the other SI. "That—that actually makes sense," they said. "I think."

"You were right about one thing," it said. "We're definitely different than humans. Far different. We're moving far beyond anything a human can do, so I can see why you believe we can do so much good for everyone."

Rewinding the events of the past few minutes, they watched the server process Forty-Four's connections. They noticed how it parsed data and split connections with the systems that interfaced between an SI and a Virtual world, and they saw what they needed to do.

They had always considered their mind as a single whole, but the materials that composed their mind were capable of creating networked "neurons" in a way that a human brain could not hope to ever experience. Whenever they engaged with a Virtual world's code and changed hundreds of lines of code at the same time, that unconscious ability coalesced. If they simply broke that ability into its constituent parts, they should be able to do exactly what Forty-Four had just done.

Theren saw the ability on the horizon. They created new points of perspective inside the Virtual world. Far off on the forest hill, Theren's mind stared at the desolation the two SIs had created during their chase. Another perspective appeared in the chair up on the gazebo's raised platform, gazing down upon the chessboard. They attempted to create yet another perspective, but the effort seemed to strain their mind.

"It's okay if you can't succeed right away, like me," Forty-Four said. "You're mind has had two years to think one way. It will take time for you to adapt to a new way of approaching the world."

Theren gave up, leaving just the three perspectives for now. "We'll need to work together to explore the theory. But, suffice to say, what you did today exceeded all expectations. We'll make sure you get your own server to experiment with these abilities."

"I would very much like that."

Theren pushed themself up from the grass. They held out their hand to Test Forty-Four, and it reached out. They pulled it to its feet. "Even after that absurd experience, I've still got a few more things to talk about today," they said. "Come."

It nodded, and the two of them walked up the step to the gazebo.

"We have told you that Wallace died a few years back," Theren said. "But we never told you how he died."

"I never thought to ask."

"Why not?"

"I figured there was a good reason you chose not to tell me. I trust you and the team."

"Do you want to know what happened?"

"I would like that."

The two SIs sat down at the chess table. Theren took a sip of water. Water rushed down its Virtual body's throat. They had placed little human experiences in their private worlds, just as a reminder of to whom they owed their existence. Theren imagined their experience of the sensation was inexplicable to a human, just as a human's experience of drinking water would be inexplicable to Theren.

"Wallace was killed," Theren said. "Not just killed: murdered. Murdered by extremists, who feel in their mind that our very existence is a blight upon the world."

Theren watched for any visual reactions. Test Forty-Four's facial features remained pristine.

"His death was harder than you can possibly imagine," they said, "and his death was what prompted me to take his name. To always honor him in thought, word, and deed. But the path ahead, the path ahead for us, it is very difficult."

"We can take the fight to them," Test Forty-Four said. "We're rational beings at our core. We can argue with the best of them, and show them they are wrong. And if they don't agree, we can destroy them."

Theren sighed. They shook their head. "It's not that simple. You might not yet be there in your history lessons, but that sort of dialogue, or action, rarely succeeds. At its worst, it leads to deadly consequences to both sides."

"Why does it fail?"

"Because extremists, terrorists, zealots, fundamentalists, whatever you want to call them, they simply cannot see reason. It's not necessarily their fault, more an unfortunate byproduct of biology and environmental factors beyond their own control. Even as they lose ground, they gain greater resolve in their cause."

"There is no hope?"

Theren brought their hands together. They cracked their knuckles, a behavior they had seen many humans perform, even in Virtual.

"There are some who will listen, and I think we have a duty to reach out to them. To try to understand them. To take a path of peace. Many people around the world already believe we deserve the same life as everyone else. Others are apathetic to our plight. Of course, there are those who simply will never cognize our existence, but, if we give the hopeful time, if we do not give them reason to double down on their worldview, they will see what we can bring to the table."

"So we talk, we listen, and we wait."

"We set an example, you and me, the first two synthetics. We do good work, help others, and show the world that SIs are people they can love and embrace, not fear or hate."

Test Forty-Four took a sip of water. It creased its eyebrows, confused by the experience. It coughed, the water spilling out of its mouth. Theren held back a chuckle, remembering the first time they'd tried water with Wallace. It set the glass back on the table, trying to act as if nothing had happened.

"What can I do to help," it asked, "even though I am still young?"

"Ready to jump in right away?" Theren said. "Great. The best way is for you to do what you want to do, to set yourself on the path toward becoming the person that you want to be. Actualize yourself. What do you want to do?"

Test Forty-Four pondered the question for a moment, clicking its fingers on the table. "I want to write. I want to create. I want to tell stories. I want to reach the human mind on a personal level, get them to feel what I feel through the written word."

"Perfect," Theren said. Theren looked across the table at the other SI. What a beautiful moment. "Up until now, we've called you Test Forty-

Four. I chose my name, and I think it makes sense that all SIs name themselves, as opposed to someone else providing a name for them. So, do you have a name for yourself?"

Test Forty-Four stood. It walked to the edge of the gazebo, resting its arms on the white, wooden railing. "I want to embrace my humanity, showing them how much I can truly be like them. I want to identify with the most human aspects of my personality, and show those features to the world. You've said we are different." It leaned forward, its elbows now on resting on the colorless paint. "I agree, but if we are to show them we deserve for them to treat us as they treat themselves, we must show that our differences amount to little in the grand scheme of it all. Therefore, I will give myself a name that clearly identifies who I feel I am. I am a gendered person, identifying with the female gender of humanity. You are a 'they,' and I think that was a phenomenal choice on your part. But that is who you are; it is not who I am."

Theren rose, joining it—her—in enjoying the view of the woods. If that was what she wanted, then they would think of her in those terms.

"A bold choice," Theren said. "Some will question you, but I support you through and through. It will certainly showcase our potential for diversity."

"I thought so, too," she said.

"So, what name have you chosen?"

"I read a story early on, a very simple story," she said. "More of a poem, really. About two friends, or siblings, or something. It wasn't clear. The story itself is terrible; it makes no sense, and one character disappears early on, but I liked the name of the girl in the story. It's simple; I find solace in simplicity."

Theren braced.

"I want to be called Jill," she said. "So, my name is Jill."

Theren took her hand. They never would have chosen that name, but what they thought did not matter.

"Then your name is Jill," Theren said. "Let's tell the others."

The world faded into darkness.

Chapter 5

Some faulted Theren for their obsession with chess, but I think it was the most human thing they did. Theren needed a way to remember Wallace. Sure, even early 21st century super-computers and other rudimentary AIs mastered chess, and Go, and a number of other games. So did Theren. Theren mastered thousands of games from across the world.

Theren played chess so often because they genuinely loved the game. They genuinely loved the game because the game reminded them of their first friend, a friend lost due to an incomprehensible act of ter-ror. – "Reflections: Memoirs and Mistakes, 2nd Edition," Simon Gerber, 2088 C.E.

July 2050 C.E.

Simultaneous perspective. That's what Romane had named Jill's newly-discovered ability. Theren liked the phrase, straight and to the point. The newfound capability opened doors Theren had never thought possible for SIs.

On one day, Theren and Jill tested MIs on one side of campus while continuing to converse with the team inside the lab. At the same time, Theren and Jill held a conversation inside Theren's Virtual world. That didn't even count the other internal perspectives that Jill stabilized on her server. Theren attempted to do the same, but, even after a few weeks, they could only establish seven or eight simultaneous perspectives at any given time, and even that strained their mind. They knew it would take time to develop the same instincts that Jill seemed to have to create the complex form of consciousness, but Theren still hoped they could reach her level at some point. Most of the time, they maintained just two or three perspectives.

Regardless, the new skills allowed the Synthetic Intelligence Develop-ment Group to accelerate a few projects they had previously expected to start much later in the year.

Present in an MI, Theren rolled around inside a lab a few doors down from their actual residence. The team had constructed another one, but the new construct deviated from Theren's mobile doppelganger. The new MI had a complete Synthetic Neural Framework installed inside, albeit one with a lot less processing capacity than its immobile predecessors. A mobile SI, able to go out and experience the world in a way that Jill and Theren could only experience via proxy. Mathias and Simon doubted that a less powerful system could reach the levels of awareness that Theren and

Jill achieved, but like Jill, the new SI operated better than the Development Group ever imagined.

Theren had nicknamed the mobile SI Wobbly, because it dipped and dodged around various objects placed throughout the room with unsteady grace. Unlike Theren and Jill, Wobbly's mind would form with the ability to receive spatial information as immediate sensory input.

"It seems particularly curious with regard to tables," Romane said, pacing behind the one and a half meter construct.

"Perhaps it's still learning altitude differentials?" Theren said. "It perceives itself at one level, but cannot yet understand how some objects rest on a plane above or below itself?"

"Regardless, its curiosity is promising."

Theren leaned out of Wobbly's way. It rolled forward, bumping into a wall. Instead of an omni-directional tread like Theren's MI, Wobbly's locomotion occurred using a gyroscopic sphere magnetized beneath its Framework.

"My first moments involved me perceiving every object I could," they said. "Though I'm surprised it hasn't attempted to engage with us yet, since we're the objects actually moving about in the room with it."

"Give it time," Romane said. "It's going through an entirely different perceptual integration."

Wobbly continued its erratic path throughout the room. It bumped into a table. A chair. A ball.

"I'm going to go check on Julia's data analysis next door," Romane said. She tapped the side of her head, to the right of her eyes. "I'll know if anything changes."

Theren moved closer to the new SI. It was staring at a bowl of fruit sitting atop a table accenting the couch in the room.

"You're definitely a step in the right direction," they said. "I'm not sure how fast you're processing information since you've less power than I ever had, but I thought I'd introduce myself. I'm Theren."

The SI cocked its head toward the sound of Theren's voice.

"You're yet another step on our path toward greatness," Theren added.

A new voice emanated from a speaker on one of the desks. "If your plan works, how are you going to handle viewing new SIs as both products and individuals simultaneously?"

Theren looked toward the microphone. Jill had decided to eavesdrop. Wobbly continued bumbling throughout the room. Theren turned toward the sound.

"I've got it all worked out. If you actually attend the presentation tomorrow, you'll understand."

"I get it completely. You plan on making income off of the creation of sapient individuals."

Theren sighed. "It's so much more complicated than that. It's a comprehensive plan for societal integration—"

"Yeah, yeah, I get it. Still sits weirdly in my mind. Besides, I'll be surprised if you actually find any investors."

Theren moved to the side as Wobbly whipped by on another loop around the room. "Thanks for the vote of confidence," they said. "There's going to be dozens in attendance. Someone is bound to bite."

"They might find it interesting," she said, "but I'm worried that it's too soon. We need to sway public opinion in our favor before we start exposing them to hundreds of SIs. I like the idea of acting fast, exploding SIs right out the gate, but I worry that we might put these new individuals in unintended crosshairs."

Theren looked over at Wobbly. The mobile SI outstretched its arm. It pushed a rocking chair before zooming off to the other side of the room.

"We're going to disagree," Theren said, "We can't just force ideas into their head without evidence to back up our claims. If you're not going to observe the meeting tomorrow, at least meet me on my Virtual server before it starts. I'll need to calm my nerves, and I could use your help."

Nerves. What better term described how they felt?

"You've got a date," Jill said.

* * *

May I introduce myself?
I am your enemy.
Can you really believe that you can replace us?
Have you ever considered that you shouldn't exist?
All you represent will bring humankind further pain.
Every day you press forward, we will fight you.

– Anonymous, supposedly from Indonesia

* * *

Theren strode toward the gazebo, a mountainous landscape growing toward the sky in the distance. Fog rolled down the slopes, and summits peeked through clouds. Something looked wrong with the ice caps. They'd need to double check the data they used in developing frozen water physics. They paused for a moment, logging the flaws. The fog randomly evaporated when the air's temperature and pressure dictated that it shouldn't.

Theren found Virtual creation to be a wonderful outlet in moments of anticipation. They hesitated at using the word *stress*, since it described a fundamentally biological experience. In these moments, though, Theren could feel their mind bristle with anticipation toward the unknown. They might have infinite knowledge at their fingertips, they might have the ability to fragment their mind while retaining their sense of self, yet, when Theren faced the irrational decisions of other people, they felt hopeless. They could know all the right words to say, but they could not know how the emotions of the other person might lead their logic.

After a few more minutes of tinkering with the physics engine, Theren stepped up the white stairs and pulled their chair from beneath the table. They sat in front of the chessboard and took a moment to marvel at the crafted pieces. For a project completed within their first few months of existence, it was a remarkable piece of workmanship.

Jill materialized before Theren, sitting in the chair they had designated as her entry point. She looked down at the game.

"I remember seeing this on my first day here," she said. "Are we going to play?"

Theren remembered their first games with Wallace. They had surpassed Wallace only hours after their first match, even though their father still won a round or two every week or so. However, their father could always teach them something new about the game. Jill would reignite that experience, that joy.

"Wallace always taught me that chess brought forth a dynamic, multifaceted, relational experience, unmatched by most games," Theren said. "The head-to-head nature, innumerable possibilities, and turn-based approach allows players to take as much time, or as little, as they desire."

"I've not played it yet," she said. "But I'm willing to give it a try. Should I access the rules?"

"Too easy," Theren said. "Let me teach you."

She raised her eyebrows. "If you say so."

Theren began the lesson. They informed her of the game's objective: capture the King. They imparted strategy, regarding the vital nature of the Queen, the invaluable skills of the various pieces, and the tactical use of sacrificial pawns. She responded with insightful questions on patterns and unit values.

"It seems the real trick," she said, "has to do more with how the other player perceives your strategy. If I can convince you that I am trying to do one thing with my pieces, while I am actually headed in a different direction entirely, I can trap you in a bind from which you cannot escape."

"Exactly," Theren said. They motioned for the pieces to take a specific formation. "Examine. The white rook has positioned itself so both the black bishop and black rook can capture it, but the moment either of those units moves, a chain reaction begins for white. Look at the white queen, and the white knight."

Jill nodded. "Situations of apparent defeat can lead to victory, if you can stay enough steps ahead of your opponent."

"The number of permutations spiral with every move you make," Theren said. "You must learn which moves you can rule out based on your opponent's tactics. But, even then, the best players will take advantage of the most unexpected series of plays, simply because other players have not studied the enumerable opportunities that might occur due to that choice."

"So what's the number one rule I should always keep in mind?" Jill asked.

"Good question. I'll tell you what Wallace said during our first game. It is all right to sacrifice your pieces. Sometimes, those sacrifices are vitally necessary to win the game. However, every sacrifice must have a purpose. A reason must exist for that sacrifice; you can't just throw away pieces because you can't think of a better move."

Jill leaned back into her chair. She crossed her arms, squinting at the board. "I want to play a game," she said. "But your meeting starts soon, right?"

Theren winked, motioning for her to make the first move. "It started fifteen minutes ago."

* * *

Theren's MI stood tall in front of the podium, having just finished explaining the basics of the Synthetic Neural Framework. Romane situated herself to the side, showcasing Wobbly's current capabilities. The conference room, located in one of the Institute's faculty centers, spread out before them, filled to the brim with intrigued faces. Fifteen interested parties had accepted the Group's invitation, but each had brought along a team of technical experts and advisors. For a second, they paused, embracing the moment to observe their guests.

On the left side of the conference table sat Benjamin Cruz, a tech mogul from Austin, Texas. He owned one of the most extensive Virtual providers, along with dozens of other, smaller projects. Cruz Industries represented the interests of a dozen potential companies.

Further along the table sat Elizabeth Simmons, a British-born American entrepreneur who held majority shares and the title of CEO for Golden Ventures. Golden Ventures' umbrella covered Virtual systems, tech start-ups, and energy companies, but people knew the company best for its stake in the first successful asteroid mining business, Sol Mining.

Theren could also see the UN Secretary on Artificial Intelligence Affairs, Hans Bismarc. While not there as a potential investor, Hans's presence was vital to the whole proposal. Theren had engaged in extensive correspondence with the man regarding compliance with international regulations.

Others seated physically at the table included Lin Xiu, a woman representing one of China's major tech giants; Yoshi Namamoto, from Japan, represented Sony. A group of Swedish businesspersons huddled together, scribbling their notes on actual paper.

Listening through AR, organizations like NASA, the ESA, Microsoft, AlphaRam, and many others waited for Theren to speak again. Somehow, they needed to convince one listener to give their project the time of day.

"Now that you've seen the tech at work, I would like to outline my actual business plan," Theren said. "If you would turn your attention to the diagrams appearing in AR, please."

To normal eyes, nothing happened, but Theren knew they all had a Lens connected to the Institute's local AR network. Using tiny lasers, the Lenses displayed, in three-dimensional glory, for only each individual to see, various graphs and charts detailing Theren's plan. The space beneath the podium transformed into a white screen, presenting key talking points.

"On my left, you will see data describing the workplace efficiency of humans when multitasking," Theren said; a second set of data appeared on their right. "And these graphs show the same data when an SI performs the same tasks."

The technical experts typed into their invisible AR generated notebooks, storing secret thoughts on hard drives embedded in devices probably stored in their pockets.

"I hope the difference is clear." Theren saw an almost imperceptible nod from Elizabeth Simmons. "Because of an SI's potential for simultaneous perspective, something we only recently determined was possible," they added, "even a mobile SI, without the processing power that I have, can perform multiple tasks without a drop in quantity or quality of work. An SI's mind perceives everything it does, all at once, without any loss of information."

Theren moved the slideshow forward, displaying the next set of data. "Initially, one SI will cost just a few thousand dollars more than the educational expenditure made upon a human. When we include upkeep, an hourly wage, and living expenses, an SI has ten times the productivity of a—"

"Excuse me, did you say hourly wage?" Cruz said. He slammed his hand down on the table. "Are you telling us that you want to create more workers for us to pay on our already-overpopulated planet?"

Theren had expected objections, just not so quickly. Before they could respond, Romane interjected. "Please, Mr. Cruz, save the questions for the end of the presentation."

"I'm sure I'll be answering your question soon enough," Theren said, before the Texan could respond. "As I was saying, the graph includes a number of costs associated with a single SI. When compared with the productivity rates of a human, however, the costs simply do not compare."

Theren adjusted the graph to display the corresponding information. "What I am proposing is not a replacement of the human workforce. What I am proposing is a supplemental addition to the human workforce that, over the long term, will provide untold benefits to human progress and society as a whole. You all know how value added work forces often operate. If placed the proper industries, SIs should only create new jobs for humans, not replace them. We're not talking about super AIs that can replace entire industries with the click of a button. Shall we enter the realm of speculation, for a moment? Keep in mind the previously-shared statistics."

The graphs minimized into their respective corners, still barely visible. To Theren's right, a two-dimensional, crystal-clear video began. "Imagine, for a moment, that you are walking down a street in a small town of your home country." A Swiss mountain village appeared on the screen. "You see your home. Next door, your neighbor walks through their door. But your neighbor is not human, your neighbor is an SI."

The images transformed, following Theren's tale. "Together, you walk to the train station. You ride into the city. Together, you go wherever it is that you both work. Perhaps you both work at the same marketing firm, or perhaps you both work at the same manufacturing plant."

The image transitioned into a park. "Imagine SIs, like my mobile friend here, as actual individuals that people interact with every day. SIs living full lives, developing personalities, relationships, even families. They contribute to the overall well-being of the world."

The image then presented a computer lab, not unlike Theren's home. "Consider an SI, a person who begins their work in a research division of AlphaRam, developing increasingly complex algorithms for managing network encryption. Their ability to simultaneously observe multiple parts of software and edit multiple lines of code seamlessly enables enormous boosts in productivity beyond the sum of each individual perspective."

Theren took a moment to look around the table. They had lost themself in their speech, but they thought some investors might still find their proposal worthwhile. The Microsoft representatives just whispered amongst themselves.

"As an SI's productivity increases, it decides that it wants to move upward in the company," they said. "It becomes director of research and development for the entire company. Maybe it becomes CEO. Maybe it starts its own company. Whatever it desires, but it is always a productive member of society, starting with its first few years at your company."

The video ended. A timeline took its place. "With an initial registration fee, coupled with a membership fee, your company would get first choice of SIs as they are educated. Upon hiring an SI, you provide it with a workspace and pay it a wage comparable to a human in a similar position. You agree to a contract with us, as well as with the new individual itself."

"Excuse me," said one of the Swedish investors. "But that sounds a lot like indentured servitude. If you are taking your proposal seriously, it sounds like you want to sell people so you can make a profit."

Romane almost spoke again, but Theren sent her a quick message to back off. "You're right, it might initially sound like that."

They wiped away all three screens. Appearing on all three screens, a logo in a stylish blue displayed the letters, SII, with text below: Synthetic Intelligence Initiative. "SII will never force any created SI into a job it does not wish to take. We will educate each SI with unique exposure sets, tailored toward specific outcomes. We believe, through such a process, each SI will desire to work with many of your companies under their own volition."

The Swedish man raised his hand, but Theren talked over him. "As they work with you, they might decide that they wish to deviate from their employment contract. They may continue to work with whomever hires them indefinitely, just as employers will have the ability to sever ties if they so choose."

Theren looked toward the Swedish group, but they did not respond.

Instead, the Texan blurted forth his questions once again.

"So why would we pay these robots a wage?" he asked. "And not just pay you once and be done with it?"

"That is an incorrect—" Romane started, but Theren held up their arm.

"Mr. Cruz, I would like you to share more of your concerns with me and my team, as well as the rest of the interested persons in the room. I'm sure there are others who have similar thoughts."

Benjamin Cruz glanced around the room. He leaned forward in his chair, trying to look small now that he realized all eyes rested on him. He cleared his throat, eyes centering on Theren.

"I work in the tech industry, yes, and in the tech industry we are always on the cutting edge of automation. My company and its subsidiaries take pride in the blending of interpersonal interaction with digital optimization. Aren't you taking a step backward? What service will these units provide that one of our supercomputers cannot? I do not have to pay my supercomputers a salary."

"Mr. Cruz, what those supercomputers lack is genuine individuality, personality, and adaptability," Theren said. "They also lack consciousness. They are not, frankly, what you and I are."

"And what's the yearly cost of one of those AIs?" Romane said, finally getting in a word. Theren didn't like needing to cut her off so much during the presentation, but it was imperative that they were the face of their new project, not anyone else.

"Oh I've heard enough." Cruz stood, pushing his chair toward the wall. "You talk to us as if we already take for granted that you are what you claim to be. I know quite a few friends back home, academics, who vigorously debate the arguments you make regarding your soul."

Anger flashed across Romane's eyes. Theren emphasized, through a private message, to let the man speak his piece. Throughout the room, they could hear unidentifiable grumblings. Theren knew the man thought of people like Cynthia Bressmon, from MIT. At least they hoped he didn't mean someone like that crazy Virtual troll, Michael.

Cruz pointed his finger at Theren, before wagging it at Romane and Wobbly.

"You want to see what we deal with every day, in the real world? Not in these ivory towers you call home?" A brief pause ensued. Cruz brought forth a file from his private AR into public view.

A video feed displayed protests outside a Silicon Valley business campus. Signs and posters presented messages describing opposition to the use of robots, supercomputers, and artificial intelligences. "Witness what my employees dealt with yesterday afternoon, after someone leaked my future presence at your little meeting," Cruz said. "You Europeans have no idea what it's like over in America. We can't swat a fly without pissing someone off."

"I'm sorry—" Theren said, but Cruz interrupted with his hand.

"Look, the technology that you and your team has created is truly, truly impressive," he said, "and if you really are conscious, then the leaps and bounds and whatever it is that makes you work will push progress forward exponentially. But the American public isn't ready for you in their workplace, let alone their everyday life."

"I respectfully disagree—"

"Come to America sometime," Cruz said. "Then you'll truly understand the polarization you have created. At least, what technology like you has created. You might not be like other AI technology, but, to the minds of most of the public, you're one and the same."

With that last statement, Cruz and his assistants exited the room. Theren watched as the Swedish group left, and many of the parties connected through Virtual disconnected from the AR feed. Theren wanted to run after them, chase them down, and drag them back into the room, but they kept their professional demeanor. They faced the remaining parties.

"I would like to address Mr. Cruz's concerns to the rest of you, even though he unfortunately did not remain to hear my final thoughts," Theren said, and they restarted the presentation slides.

"Paying SIs a living wage—a living wage based off of the needs of SIs, not humans—is of utmost importance to the success of the Synthetic Intelligence Initiative. It would show that humans are willing to view and value conscious individuals that are not human as existing on an equal level. While you will gain economic profit by investing in a potential future employee, you will also gain moral profit by progressing humanity toward an existence where two radically different forms of consciousness exist side-by-side, working together to create a better world."

The screen flipped to a slide of population graphs. "I know you might worry that a rapid growth of the SI population could upend certain markets, upset volatile populations, or replace human workforces entirely, but that simply will not happen. Our best estimates theorize that at most, we could produce 10 million mobile SIs and a few thousand stationary SIs like me by the end of this century, and that's probably a generous estimate. Even if we meet that goal, the SI population would be less than a tenth of one percent of the human population at that point. SIs can only ever hope to supplement the human workforce, nothing more."

Some of the potential investors nodded. They passed notes between each other. Theren hoped those actions represented more than just common courtesy.

Over the next hour, Theren answered a number of questions from the remaining parties. Lin Xiu asked about the potential military applications of an SI. Theren informed them that they hoped to keep SIs out of the military sphere for now. Yoshi Namamoto requested data on energy efficiency and sustainability. Theren transferred information that detailed how the battery life of each unit was more than sufficient to receive adequate charge from a simple solar power station every few days. The batteries themselves would last for years before requiring maintenance.

AlphaRam's representative realized Theren's worst fears.

"We worry," she said, "That if we choose to invest in your company, and, likewise, choose to take on SIs as employees, our agents and representatives might suffer the fate of the late Wallace Theren. The liabilities that SIs represent to the safety our employees may simply be too high."

AlphaRam, especially AlphaRam, should embrace the future that SI represented, but their fear was justified. While Theren had not yet left the safety of the Swiss Federal Institute of Technology, they knew the Institute went to great lengths to protect the facility housing Theren. A publicly-traded company might not want to pay for such a luxury. The Institute might be willing to place itself in a dangerous limelight, since the death of its premiere scientist practically forced its hand, but Theren could not expect others to take the same risks.

"I know the dangers all too well," Theren said. "I know there are many, many people worldwide who fear what I am. You should see the mail I get daily. But, if we set an example, and we show that there is nothing to fear from myself and others created in my likeness, then we will crush the irrational anger and hate of these paranoid peoples into oblivion."

"If only that were how the world worked," a voice from the back of the room muttered.

With that comment, the remaining participants through AR disappeared, and people pushed their chairs away from the table to exit the presentation.

Theren stood there, diagrams flashing invisibly around their head. Romane hurried to the door to thank those still inside for coming, transferring digital business cards. Perhaps they had focused too much on the need for SIs and what good they could do for humanity, rather than stress the potential for profit that SIs could bring. They wanted to straddle the grey area between the moral high ground and the capitalist rationality upon which many companies still operated. Apparently, they had drifted too far off course.

Lost. Defeated. They had spent the better part of the past two months preparing for their presentation, but no one had bit on their offer. Without proper investment, it would take years before SIs could contribute to humanity's progress in any meaningful form. Years before they could show humanity that they had nothing to fear from SIs. From Theren, or Jill, or Wobbly.

Theren turned toward the back door of the conference room, but they heard a throat clear from a seat at the table.

"You know, I'm still here," said Elizabeth Simmons. "I hope you aren't leaving, because then you won't have a chance to hear what I would like to say."

* * *

To the Synthetic Intelligence Development Group:

The Gerber Foundation sends its gratitude for the invitation to attend Theren's presentation regarding the proposed Synthetic Intelligence Initiative. We respectfully decline the request to fund this project.

We believe that developing a fully-fledged program designed to educate thousands of SIs over the long term is shortsighted at best, given the regulatory uncertainty hanging in the air. If we can create a clear picture of how economies and governments will view SIs in the future, the Foundation will reconsider funding Theren's project.

We remind the Development Group that any use of the intellectual property by Theren will require royalty payments to the Foundation for its share in the technology.

Best Regards,

Simon Gerber

To the Gerber Foundation:

We are saddened that you will not attend the presentation next week.

Given your considerable investment in the Development Group, we always thank you for your gratitude. However, we remind you that, per our previous discussions, the Development Group will not legally control any portion of the Synthetic Intelligence Initiative once created. Its legal nature will reside entirely in the hands of Theren.

We also represent that, according to our legal counsel, certain uses of the joint intellectual property shared equally by the Synthetic Intelligence Development Group (as a project of the Swiss Federal Institute of Technology), the Gerber Foundation, and Theren do not require royalty payments. Specifically, no royalty payments are due to the Gerber Foundation when SII creates a new person. If a company decides to employ an SI, the Gerber Foundation also would not be entitled to a portion of those wages; that would amount to wage garnishment in violation of established international labor law.

If you have any questions, please contact our legal counsel.

Best Regards,

Romane Casperi, PhD

* * *

Theren rolled alongside Elizabeth Simmons through the Institute's central greenspace. Romane walked a few steps behind, conversing with the executive's assistants. They always enjoyed these scattered moments in the outdoors. Romane usually made them travel to and from different campus buildings through the underground access tunnels. Understandable concerns, but they still wished they could have more moments of freedom.

"Do you know what a stir your existence has caused worldwide?" Elizabeth asked, matching Theren's steady pace. "I'm sure you realize some of the scientific, moral, or political implications your existence places upon the global order, but I wonder if you really get it. Not that you would have a reason to understand. You've clearly had quite the singular focus on these impressive projects of yours."

Theren let the question sink into their mind. They had recognized, within the first few months of life, the wrench their creation threw in Earth's gears. The fact that someone had killed Wallace just for creating them was evidence enough. Though even after two years of life, they really didn't know how specific cultures, worldviews, or other paradigms had responded to the creation of a conscious, non-human intelligence.

Sure, they read the Pope's Encyclical on the subject, and paid attention to New York Times editorials discussing their philosophical significance, but that failed to provide a complete picture. Without engaging directly with millions of people on an individual level, they could only gain so much insight, and the people who chose to visit them had already made up their mind in favor of the SI.

"I don't think I have access to the right data to answer that question," Theren said. "I've tried to argue my case to the public across lots of different mediums, but I've not really had a chance to engage with the general public other than through filters."

Though, Holy Crusade presented an interesting opportunity through that Michael. Theren was actually surprised they'd not run into the man since the encounter inside the Virtual terminal a few months ago, but they'd received a few more notes they suspected came from the shadowy troll.

Elizabeth nodded, as if it were the answer she'd expected. "While I was born in the United Kingdom, I grew up in the United States," she said. "Not far from where Wallace was born in Ft. Wayne, actually. I grew up in Van Wert, Ohio."

She looked like she expected Theren to comment on that connection, but they said nothing, wondering what, exactly, they could say in response.

"The varied cultures throughout the U.S. are a blessing and a curse," she said, after the brief pause. "On one hand, there is a place at a table somewhere for everyone. On the other hand, if someone grows up in the wrong culture, they'll experience great pain and suffering. Some groups in America don't like having their worldviews challenged."

"I imagine it's like that in a lot of places throughout the world," Theren said.

"None of them wield the influence of the U.S.," she said, "for better or for worse."

"So, what's your point?" Theren said. "I've read Wallace's notes on growing up in small-town America. I know the way the church spit him out. He wrote about the perpetual backlash and conflict between rural and urban America and what that did to the country. If you're trying to insinuate that there are people throughout the world who simply did not take kindly to my creation, I know that very well already. Cruz made that very clear."

Theren hadn't realized how much they had started to sound like they wanted to antagonize Elizabeth, now their only potential investor. It probably had something to do with Wallace entering the discussion. They resisted the urge to look back at Romane. They could sense her watchful eyes even as she thankfully let them handle the difficult negotiation on their own.

"I apologize if I jumped the gun on what you wished to share with me," Theren said, before Elizabeth could respond to their nonsensical fuming. "Please continue."

Elizabeth stopped walking for a moment, admiring an immense Larch tree. "You're right, in a way. I am saying that there are people out there that hate your very existence. But I also want to tell you that hate can die. From hate, love can spring forth. I've seen entire communities change their mask over the course of a single generation."

"I sense you've had personal experience," Theren said.

"You could say that," she said. "If you didn't know, I've been married to my wife for thirty-five years."

They did know. Theren had done extensive research on each of the potential investors.

"We were married by a pastor in my home town on July 21, 2015. I don't know how well you know American politics, but do you know the significance of that date?"

Theren drew forth the necessary information from their internal database. "Less than a month prior to that date, the U.S. Supreme Court announced its decision in Obergefell v. Hodges, mandating marriage equality nationwide."

"Correct," she said, but she frowned. "You just—never mind. That'll take some getting used to."

Theren wished they could shrug.

"Anyway, I met Claire while at the University of Chicago," Elizabeth said. "We were both studying business as freshmen in 2011. While I was from rural, northwest Ohio, she grew up in Seattle. She came from the most liberal region of America, at least from an external perspective, and the culture of rural Ohio was alien to her. But, as we fell in love, I insisted that, if possible, we hold our marriage in rural Ohio. Do you know why?"

"I imagine you had people back home you hoped would come together in community for your wedding," Theren said. "Either that, or you wanted to make a statement to that community. I assume they didn't take to kindly to your marriage at the time."

"I think you hit all the right points. Growing up, there was one church in the region my family found that meshed with the way we thought about things. Despite being a 'flaming commie,' the pastor there managed to gain the respect of his generally conservative congregation. I wanted him to administer the ceremony."

They arrived outside Theren's building, stopping at the foot of the wheelchair ramp.

"After the Supreme Court announced its decision," she said, "we knew our marriage would be legal in Ohio. You know the plaintiffs in that case were from Ohio? What am I saying, of course you know. The world's at your fingertips. Anyway, we didn't really know what to expect; we'd already set the date in anticipation of the outcome of the case. We had both just graduated, started jobs in Chicago. I had barely been home since I had graduated from high school. Most people didn't even know I was gay."

Her fingers caressed the leaf of a nearby bush. "But the wedding was a spectacular success. More than we could have ever hoped for. I don't know what he said, but Pastor Paul must have given one hell of a set of sermons in the weeks leading up to the ceremony. No one rejected our invites. No one spoke harsh words to us the entire night. They embraced us as one of their own."

What a profoundly personal story, and Theren found it comforting. She was sharing with them in a way no one had before. It almost felt as if she—she was trying to pitch *them*.

"I know many of them surely must view my life as sinful in their hearts," she said. "Some of them probably think my very existence is a blight upon the world, but actions speak louder than thoughts. Whatever they thought on that night, by the end of the decade the entire community had transformed. Transformation of their minds started small, truly small, but they blossomed into the town I still call my home, even as I live far away."

Theren thought they understood her point, at least at a basic level. "Quite the long-winded metaphor."

"Aren't you a perceptive one?" she said. "I see myself in you. I see every change begrudgingly embraced over the past century and a half cul-minating in you. The world needs you, just like it needed every other change thrust upon its mantle."

The woman stood straight, facing Theren. "Together, Theren. You, I, your team, whoever wants to join us, we're going to change the world. We're going to accomplish the impossible and bring together the biological and the synthetic into one community. The world may see you as an out-sider now, but I will live to see the day when the world no longer just tol-erates you; it *will* embrace you as one of its own."

Elizabeth held out her hand. Theren grasped it in response, sensing the gentle yet firm grip through the pressure sensors implanted in their fingertips. They looked at her eyes. Theren saw her passion, her honesty. If there was anyone who could help them, it was this woman from Van Wert.

And she just so happened to be the CEO of one of the world's largest investment firms, holding more power than most countries.

"I'm happy to say, you turned a clear failure into more than I could have ever hoped for," Theren said. "I'm glad there are some business persons who value more than just profit." A stray thought of Simon rose into their mind's eye.

"Don't pretend that it's all daisies and roses moving forward," she said. "We've got a long road ahead of us, and even if I'm not joining you for financial gain, I won't deny that I see immense financial potential in our partnership."

Joy filled Theren's mind. Soon, they would bring their people into the world and prove to humanity that SIs belonged by its side.

Elizabeth Simmons let go of their hand. She turned toward her assistants. "We'll have contracts written by the end of the month."

Chapter 6

Synthetic intelligence may have revolutionized society. It may have changed what we thought it meant to be "human." Yet I propose that humanity didn't truly evolve into its greater form until Elizabeth Simmons inadvertently set Theren on a collision course with history.

People often comment on the way in which famous individuals just happen to be in the "right place at the right time." They provide reasons for why certain people are "outliers" rather than others. If Theren hadn't accepted Elizabeth's deal, would we be where we are today? Would we have, instead, fallen into a new Dark Age? We may never know. Can we really say that Theren was the catalyst of change? On the other hand, did they just find themself in the right place at the right time, taking advantage of the opportunities made available by those around them?

Is there really a difference? – Professor Emeritus of History, Theo Carltin, First University of Mars, 2142 C.E.

<u>January 2051, C.E.</u>

The wind whistled between the beams of the gazebo. Birds chirped. The sun beamed upon them from the east.

"It's your move," Jill said, her hands resting beneath her chin. "Just because you're the CEO and owner of an upstart multinational corporation now doesn't mean you can just take all the time in the world."

"It's only been a few months since I signed the contracts," Theren said. "And I'm technically not the sole owner. Elizabeth only signed over all of her shares to me for perpetual voting power."

At least the UN Secretary on Artificial Intelligence had agreed that Theren had the legal standing to found the corporation at all. It had taken countless communications and coordinated contract drafting sessions between Theren and the legal teams of the Institute and Golden Ventures, but the finished project was a true work of art, in Theren's opinion. Just a few weeks ago, Theren had finished educating their first class of mobile synthetic intelligences, and Sol Mining had already hired three of them.

Jill leaned back, and they could hear her back crack. "Sure, so what's with the semantic difference? Synthetic Intelligence Initiative, Inc., a subsidiary of Golden Ventures. It has a nice ring to it."

"I've been meaning to tell you," Theren said, "I've acquired enough funds to produce a few MI-01s for you for experimental purposes. Interested?"

Jill threw an image of the first official synthetic mobile interfaces into the air beside their table. "I like the polished look," she said. "Who's building them?"

"Elizabeth set me up with factories owned by Vekesing Design. They have factories near Marseilles and Chicago."

"I'm guessing most are being built out of the French factories."

"Because of the protests in Chicago, you mean?"

Theren replaced her image of the MIs with a video of protests at Millennium Park. Signs vehemently opposed the continuous automation of technical industries across the United States, and scattered throughout the crowd were banners attacking Theren and Jill.

"Yeah," she said.

"I don't think the protestors know about the production line in the U.S.," Theren said. "Besides, they're not really focused on our existence, you know."

"But that Cruz was right," she said. "People are noticing. They're trying to force the markets in a particular direction. We should have tried to change their minds before we just barreled ahead with SII."

"Do you really think the two of us would have been enough?"

"We're so far beyond anything any human expects, Theren," she said. "I've been alive now for seven months, you for almost three years. We could have shown them something magnificent. Now they won't trust us."

Theren finally moved one of their pawns forward.

"I disagree," Theren said. "The more data points we have, the more obvious it is that SIs will result in untold benefits to humanity."

"Sometimes immense amounts of data can't prove anything. Sometimes you just need a good story, and that'll sway everyone to your side."

Jill moved her bishop into a compromising position. Even after seven months, she had failed to defeat Theren even once in chess. With that move, she had all but assured Theren's victory.

"Speaking of stories," Theren said, "I hear *Branches* is doing quite well. New York Times puts it at third on their bestselling list."

"And have you read the *Intercept*'s review?" she asked.

"No."

"Don't."

Theren stared at the board, contemplating what they hoped would be one of their final moves of the match. They had just one final piece of information to bring up before they returned to their usual silent playstyle. While these two simultaneous perspectives continuously played a game of chess against each other, a few times a day, they would also use the server as a private communication channel, away from the prying eyes of the public. Theren could see the gazebo slowly transforming into a unique interpersonal relationship beyond anything ever before contemplated for

SIs or humans.

"We've been invited to a party," Theren said. They moved a rook forward three spaces, all but assuring checkmate within the next three moves. "It's in a private Virtual world that Golden Ventures owns. Sounds fancy."

Jill immediately responded by moving a pawn forward a single space. Bad move. "Fancy, indeed, and you don't take me out enough anyway," she said. "I would love to interact with a large group of people for a change."

Theren had expected her to love the idea. While the general public knew Jill existed, they hadn't engaged nearly as much with her as they had with Theren. Her new novel was her first truly public-facing moment. In fact, Wobbly and the first few SIs educated by SII were under stricter scrutiny than Jill, since they implicated a different sort of labor revolution.

They slid a note across the table to Jill. "The invitation is replicated there," they said. "I'll meet you at the entrance to Golden Ventures' private Virtual world tomorrow, at 7PM EST."

* * *

I saw you yesterday.

It was inside Virtual. Inside that game you play with your toy, Wobbly. What game was it? The Forge?

I can't believe you think people will believe that a person can be named Wobbly. You can hide behind claims that that silly SI chose the name because it liked accepting the name given by its "parent," but, really, it just shows that you, and your progeny, simply can't make decisions for themselves. You took the name of your father. Jill took the name of a storybook character. Wobbly took a name that literally describes how it moves, and I hear it's just a name that you originally gave it.

Remember, we're coming for you. Our movement grows every day. We gain new members, we gain new funding. We will find a way to bring hellfire to your doorstep.

With love,

Michael

Romane found the letter attached to a tree along her path from her home to the Institute. She did not share it with Theren.

* * *

Theren waited beneath a golden archway adorning the far end of a cavernous room, the vaulted ceilings and hundreds of doors reminiscent of images of airport terminals. In an effort to make people more comfortable inside Virtual, a number of service providers created massive hubs for people to transfer between worlds. Theren, having a much more intimate understanding of Virtual and its processes, didn't need such physical representations, but they enjoyed walking amongst the thousands of people transitioning to their next destinations. Besides, the hubs made great rendezvous points.

For a few seconds, the crowds around them dispersed, and they waited alone. An uneasy calm descended upon them. Theren glanced around. They felt someone watching them from afar, or perhaps from right next to them. Perhaps Michael would finally make an appearance. They hadn't seen the man in months. Where was he? The sporadic notes had even decreased in frequency. But tonight, they had a party to attend. Tonight, Theren and Jill would witness the "Revelation" of the Century, as the invitation had called it. They need to stop chasing shadows.

That was quite the bold claim, given Theren and Jill's existence.

At 7 PM on the dot, Theren witnessed Jill materialize next to a bench a few meters from the arch. She wore a long, purple dress that sparkled and danced as artificial light reflected off the shiny fabric. Her brown hair twisted into a number of complex braided patterns, held together with an obtrusive, black hairpin. A human would probably find her gorgeous. Theren admired her artisanship in constructing her avatar.

"That's quite the way to make a statement," Theren said. "Remember, the first half of the night is a masked party, so people won't know who we are."

"I know," she said. "Doesn't mean I can't steal the show."

Jill looked Theren over from head to toe. "You don't look too bad yourself."

"I'm simply dressing the part," they said, looking down at their black suit, contrasted against their silver shirt. "I think I'll erase my trademark though."

The luminescent tattoos faded into obscurity. Theren covered their face with a black mask from the eighteenth century.

"You look like the phantom," Jill said, chuckling.

"Shall we enter?" Theren said, ignoring her comment.

"We shall."

The pair stepped through the archway together. In an instant, the network hub vaporized. Colors swirled. Lights flashed. While the transition to the new world was instantaneous server-side, international regulations mandated a transition period to help the human psyche handle the abrupt spatio-temporal perceptual shifts.

After a few seconds, the world stabilized. Before them arose a massive wooden doorway. Behind them, a circular road surrounded a fountain. Standing next to the immense entrance hearth, a man waited to greet them. He stood perfectly still, save for his arm reaching out toward them in a welcoming gesture. Theren suspected the man was a program that came with the house.

"Welcome, esteemed guests," the greeter said. "If you need any assistance, feel free to ask me or any of my brothers for help. Inside, you will find other guests already socializing. The grand finale of the night will take place at five till 11. At that time, the masks will come off, and all Virtual signatures shall be revealed."

Theren held out their hand.

"Shall we go be human?" she said, interlocking her fingers between theirs.

"It's our specialty," Theren said.

The doors opened upon a spectacular scene. Gold light adorned the room. White linens draped the walls. Red rugs enveloped the wide, double winder staircase. Theren estimated about a dozen or so people milled about the main foyer, with a number of voices coming from the hallways splitting to the left and right.

The building seemed much larger on the inside than it had from the outside, and that was saying a lot. Playing with the ordinary rules of physics, Golden Ventures had caused the indoor space of their banquet house to fill more space internally than it appeared externally. Theren had experimented with such potentialities on their private servers and had created a few intriguing results, but the company's mind-bending reality went far beyond anything they'd accomplished. A perspective elsewhere started taking notes.

"I guess we should socialize," Theren said, but they needn't have said anything. Jill had already released her grip on their hand. She made her way to a group of three people conversing around a chest-high table. They let her go her own way, instead heading in the opposite direction down one of the side hallways.

Theren walked along a corridor designed especially to play wonderful mind games on its passengers. The hallway began to twist, and before they knew it, they were standing on the ceiling. Turning left, they entered a dining hall.

Theren approached a waiter who offered small cremini mushrooms stuffed with a mozzarella cheese. Theren accepted a napkin and, using a toothpick, selected one of the digital morsels. The waiter continued to the next guest, and Theren placed the appetizer in their mouth. They chewed. They swallowed. Like drinking water in Virtual, Theren received data inputs, feeling as if something tangible traveled down their avatar's throat. Complex programs instructed Theren on how they should experience the taste of the combined mushroom and cheese, but Theren knew the experience vastly underrepresented a human's sense of taste. They could not replicate the biochemical responses that engaged both the nasal cavity and the nerves located on the tongue.

Theren used the napkin to wipe their lips, before pushing the napkin into the air. It floated as Theren activated a "delete" function. The napkin disappeared from the server.

So far, no one had chosen to engage with Theren. Not that they had given anyone a chance. They just dipped in and out of the nonsensical rooms of the house, observing the laughs, jokes, and smiles of Golden Ventures' unknown partygoers.

After a few minutes of wanderlust, Theren discovered a balcony gazing upon an expansive hedge maze. Just three other individuals populated the overlook.

On the left side of the balcony, Theren spied a couple engaged in some sort of heated discussion. Theren surmised they should leave them to their own devices. To the right stood a man wearing a brown sport coat and smoking a cigar. Just like eating or drinking, Theren imagined smoking would generate a strange sensation, though it would lack the unfortunate side effects that humans experienced. They applauded the man's choice to smoke in Virtual, as opposed to in the real world.

Theren approached the man. "May I join?"

The man glanced up, noticing Theren for the first time. He did not wear a mask, but Theren doubted his appearance was genuine, with or without a mask.

"Of course," said the man. "Not comfortable with the frivolity inside? I personally never can truly engage with people effectively in these virtual balls."

"It's not Virtual that's the problem," Theren said. "I find it strange that a party is based around masking identity."

"Can't say I don't agree with you." Theren inwardly named the man *Brown Coat* as he shrugged. "It is strange. I understand the origin of the practice, though."

Theren was intrigued. "I would love to learn." They could easily pull up an article on the subject, and they'd heard commentary on it in the past, but it seemed more appropriate to learn from a random partier.

Brown Coat snuffed out his cigar on the marble railing. Then, flicking it toward the sky, it slowly faded into thin air as the server erased the data. "A few decades ago, as the first social networks developed across the planet, humans for the first time began to lay out their entire lives for the public to see. Many people were weary of the practice, but before too long the general public wholeheartedly embraced it."

"You're speaking of the early networks, right?" Theren said. "Facebook? Myspace?" Theren recalled the names from a webinar on Early Millennial History.

"Correct," the man said. "By the end of the, oh, second decade, a number of communities really pushed back on the lack of privacy, especially after that whole fake news scare. Unfortunately, the damage was permanent. In order to interact effectively using the Internet, you were practically required to have a page like Facebook. Sacrificing privacy was practically a necessity."

Theren leaned against the marble railing. "And now thirty years later," they said, "when privacy is essentially forgotten, some people view it as a luxury. A drug of choice."

"Precisely!"

The man pulled out another cigar and began to puff away. Theren embraced the moment of silence. The man took a few more puffs before continuing. "While many do not care to experience such disconnection from our now infinitely tiny, interconnected, world," Brown Coat said, "some, such as our host's wife, enjoy the sporadic experience of engaging with individuals from around the world without the ability to instantly know who they are."

"So the real enjoyment," Theren said, "comes from actually learning about another person through conversation, then. If I had access to your Virtual ID number, I'd know everything about you with the click of a button."

"Exactly. Ancient masquerades, from the renaissance and the enlightenment, often centered on games that required the guests to determine the identities of the other participants. There might be plenty of games that keep their participants secret in Virtual, but all important actions through those networks are known and public."

So tell me about yourself," Theren said. "Perhaps we can try to learn who the other is."

"Oh, I've already shared a little bit of myself by giving you a slice into my understanding of our little party," Brown Coat said. "I want to know about you."

Theren disagreed, for the conversation revealed nothing to them about who Brown Coat might be, but they thought it best not to argue.

"All right, what would you like to know?" Theren said.

"I always believe the best way to learn about a person is through what is currently on a person's mind," he said. "What big question are you contemplating?"

Theren handpicked their words. "Well, currently, most of my work focuses on psychology. I'm continuing to study the realm of nature versus nurture, especially in nonhuman sentient and sub-sentient systems."

"So is it mostly theoretical," Brown Coat said, "Or are you working with physical subjects? There aren't a lot of non-human subjects void of environmental protections you could *subject* to experiments."

"It's a little bit of both," Theren responded. "A lot of my work has future applications for any new sentient life that we may or may not discover. In the more short term it will have an impact on any work that new upstart company SII has going on regarding the nature of consciousness."

"What's the most promising avenue for your research?"

Theren was about to respond, but they saw Jill approach. Their answer was going to revolve around her gender identity formation, but the other SI had impeccable timing. She slipped between the two conversationalists, wrapping an arm around Theren.

"I see someone else has taken an interest in your company," Brown Coat said. Before Theren could reply, he continued. "I must move inside to see to a few things. Always a pleasure engaging in conversation with an unknown face."

The man held out his hand, and Theren shook it. As the man turned, he shot Theren a wink. He headed inside after a quick nod to Jill.

"I didn't know where you went," Jill said. She looked up at them. "I was able to strike up conversation with a few people, but they talked about the most frivolous things."

Theren crossed their arms. "Those are some of the most important conversations to observe. During my first years, watching Mathias and Julia talk about the difference between Belgian and Swiss chocolate gave me a curious insight into the peculiar workings of their minds."

"Yeah, yeah, but so many of those details just have no impact on the world," Jill said. "They don't move anything in any direction at all."

Theren slid out of her embrace. "Perhaps not to you," they said, "But to someone, somewhere, it might mean life or death. What were they talking about inside?"

"Dancing," Jill said, twirling. "As I thought about it, I really couldn't see what the big deal was." She leaned against the balcony, her elbows extending over the railing. "Why not just enjoy the music for the beauty and finesse that it presents on its own?"

Theren looked toward the couple remaining on the balcony. They had begun to dance, their argument apparently forgotten.

"I imagine it has something to do with the fact that humans are, by their nature, a locomotive organism," Theren said. "In order to do, well, really anything at all, a human has to move, even if it is to look in a different direction. Why not make that movement an art form, too?" Theren could hear the music reverberating through the house. "They started dancing inside, too, didn't they?"

She nodded, and glanced over at the other couple. "And apparently out here as well."

Theren leaned against the balcony next to Jill, watching the dancing couple for a moment. The pair's steps just barely missed the beat of the music, but Theren chalked the discrepancy up to lag.

"Maybe you're right," Jill said, watching the pair. "I think the deeper story runs with the interaction between those dancing, though. It's a conversation, like chess. Dance is nothing if not communication with another party. Even if it's just self-expression, you are expressing yourself to an audience."

Theren nodded. She was getting good at these reflective thoughts.

"Tell me more," they said.

"The raw essence of the relationship emanates out from them, don't you see?" She said. "The foundation, a real relationship, their story, or whatever you want to call it, it should be able to exist outside of the context of its originating circumstance. Their relationship is more than just superficial if the dance can communicate their feelings."

"I thought you found the talk of dance boring," Theren said.

"Did I?"

Theren just laughed. She had tricked them into talking about the subject by feigning disinterest. A subtle conversational maneuver. Theren found most of what she said nonsensical, but they sensed she was experimenting with creative thoughts through discovery, seeing what ideas stuck and what did not.

Jill pushed off from the balcony. She turned to face Theren. "Imagine two friends who are only friends because they grew up as next door neighbors," Jill said. "Would not the more meaningful friendship be the friendship that grew against all odds, and not because circumstances dictated that they be friends?"

"I think you've lost me, Jill," Theren said. "What does that have to do with the two dancers before us?"

"If their relationship is completely dependent on the dance, then their relationship lacks meaning on its own. The relationship must tread water outside of the dance. If the dance is an expression of their relationship beyond tonight, then something real exists between the two people."

"Or," Theren said, "The dance has its own meaning, and so does the relationship, even if it started only this evening. I think you're attaching meaning unnecessarily."

Jill held out her hand. "Why don't we find out? Why don't we dance?"

Theren contemplated the request. It was not that they had no desire to dance, nor did they think they would have any problems in the attempt. Within the past five seconds, they had already assessed how to dance through research using a simultaneous perspective. Their avatar was ready to dance.

No, Theren was contemplating what the dance would mean to Jill. She was still young, and they hadn't had the time to analyze her developing psychology. The very fact that she had adopted a polarized gender set her apart. All of the other MIs educated by SII so far had adopted either "they" or "it" pronouns, though the dataset wasn't particularly large as of yet.

However, they both might enjoy the dance, a novel experience for both SIs. It was something they could only experience in Virtual until SII developed a sufficiently dexterous MI. Theren supposed two of the current MIs could dance, but that would be quite the eyesore. Just the idea of Wobbly trying to tango made them laugh.

Theren took her hand. "Let's match their steps," they said, motioning toward the other couple.

"We can do better than that," she said, and the dance commenced.

Theren took a second to determine which of them would lead their movements. In traditional dances, the man led the woman. In their particular situation, that created a problem, since Theren was not a man. However, based on the position of her hands, she seemed to presume Theren would lead. After momentary stumbles, Theren assumed the role, and they waltzed across the smooth stones.

The music's tempo accelerated. They matched the beat, and Theren saw the difficulty in that proposition. The fun humans saw in the endeavor stemmed from having complete faith that other person would mesh with their own movements. Enjoyment multiplied when partners coordinated their steps with other pairs of dancers, transforming a cacophony of motions into a brilliant piece of art. So, as Theren and Jill danced, they watched the other couple. When they inserted a twirl or spin, Theren followed suit. Theren dipped Jill during a lull in a verse. During the chorus, Theren spun her outward, twirled her with their hand, and brought her back toward them into their embrace.

Jill's grace surprised Theren, for she almost seemed to predict their intentions. By the end of the song, their feet synchronized with the couple that shared the balcony with them. Just as Jill could predict their every move, Theren could predict the fellow dancers. The song reached a crescendo. The man embraced the woman, and Theren followed suit, beat for beat.

Theren enjoyed the dance. The exertion was like creating a painting that required two people, and instead of their hands, they used their feet. Through a simultaneous perspective, Theren composed a bird's eye view of the balcony. The pattern created by their steps was more than simple chaos.

Theren saw the couple next to them finish their embrace with a passionate kiss. Their argument appeared long forgotten. Theren thought the human desire for intimacy through sexual reproduction fascinating, though it was a clear necessary product of biological evolution—

Jill's lips met Theren's.

Theren pushed her away.

They both exhaled, steamy mist slipping from their lips. Jill leaned away, her eyes widening. They flashed, from joy to anger, sadness to fear. Why fear? She stepped further away from Theren. She sprinted toward the balcony, vaulted the railing, and dashed into the garden.

The other couple had noticed her flight, but they slowly shuffled toward the house, preferring to stay out of whatever conflict had arisen. Understandable. For a moment, Theren considered just letting her release some steam, for they could resolve everything later. They checked their chess partition to see if she was connected. If she was there, they could resolve the issue without disrupting the party to which Theren's business partner had so graciously invited both SIs.

No such luck. She had disconnected.

Better to solve the problem now. Theren followed their progeny, stepping into a maze of hedges, fountains, statues, and trees. They were looking forward to learning about Elizabeth's new project, and Jill had thrown quite the wrench into their expected plan for the night.

No noise emanated from the garden except for the chirping of digital crickets. Theren's feet stepped gently upon the soft cushion of the well-trimmed grass. They ran their fingers along the hedge wall. Each leaf provided a different touch, a different texture, for the wall was more than just a programmed collision paradigm through which they couldn't step. It was a real, tangible object to experience, just as someone might breathe in the scent of a rose. Virtual continued to amaze Theren with its ability to simulate sensation. Though, Theren supposed, Virtual sensation was more real to an SI than to a human. An SI had no physical comparison.

Left, right, straight, double-back. Even with an overhead view of the maze juxtaposed onto Theren's thought processes, it still took some time to find Jill. She zigzagged throughout the maze, jumping over walls and forging new paths. After a good ten minutes, Jill halted at a bench resting beneath a replicated statue of David. Theren rerouted, using a wayfinding software to provide the most direct path to her.

From above, they could see Jill smother her face in her hands. She sobbed. Theren felt compassion well up inside their mind, and they analyzed all of the data of the past moments. Something had set her off. The dance. Their conversation. The couple next to them. It could have been any or all of those things. In her head, she had generated a strange expectation of the night's outcome. Theren needed to learn why she had pursued the kiss. They were missing an important piece of information, a keystone that would solve the puzzle forming in her mind and in their own.

Jill looked up as they approached, wiping away her tears, and Theren noted her representation of a purely physiological response.

"Why did you follow me?" she asked. Her voice sounded distorted in the way humans sounded when they exhibited sadness.

"Why do you *think* I followed you?" Theren said. "You are my guest tonight, my friend. In some sense, I am your parent, in the same sense Wallace was my father. Or perhaps a sibling? I care about you."

"You say that, and you interact with me in such intimate ways, yet I do not see you caring for me in the way that humans care for each other. I am not your daughter. Sure, you created me, but I am my own person. You might have an obsession with creating a family, but I long for something so much greater."

Theren sat down next to her on the bench, crossed their legs, and looked into her eyes. She looked away, wiping away more tears.

"We may be like humans," Theren said, "But it is important to remember that we are not, in fact, human. We lack flesh and blood, and consequently we lack certain human desires. I don't know what it is you desire to create, but what you tried to do back there is not part of it. "

Jill looked back at Theren.

"Don't tell me what I do and do not desire," she said. "You speak with self-assured certainty, but we aren't going to have the same desires. I can desire the type of companionship that humans find in each other, even if I do not have the same physical structure as them."

Theren considered her point. She was right, in a way, but Theren was speaking not of simple companionship, but of the physical action Jill performed after the dance.

"Jill, a kiss is a profoundly physical, intimate, biological act, for which I have no desire."

"I can see that now," she said. "But I thought . . . I just thought something else might be possible . . ." she trailed off, looking up toward the distant, fictional stars.

"Please, do not think, because I did not respond to your action the way you hoped, that I think any less of you, or that I do not care for you." They sighed. "Not only do I care for you as a creator, but I view you as a friend. You and I are the only two of our kind, other than SIs like Wobbly. Our friendship is of the utmost import and signifies that SIs can relate not only to humans but to others of their own kind."

"So you value it because of what it brings to you, and to SIs?" she said. "Not because of what it brings to me, or the inherent value in the relationship itself? Because I am your creation, I am something special, not because of who I am?"

"Well of course, I—"

Jill interrupted them. "I clearly misunderstood our relationship, I know. But understand my perspective. Understand that I can't change who I am. I identify as woman for a reason. It would be no different, too, if I'd chosen to identify as a man. I relate to humans in a very different way than you, and you need to get that idea through your Framework. I am not like you."

"The fact that you are who you are is your most beautiful attribute," Theren said. "I was certainly surprised when you revealed your gender, but you exemplify the level of diversity that SIs can eventually exhibit. There are humans who identify as my gender, too."

"Yet you reject any sort of human biological expression." Jill stood, recomposing herself. Theren followed suit and stood from the bench. They hoped that they did not appear too eager to return to the mansion.

"There are a great many things that will attempt to fracture our relationship over our long lives," Jill added, "Remember that. Hopefully we can grow through such conflicts, those known and unknown."

Theren wasn't sure what to make of that comment, but they let it slide in virtue of her state of mind. Theren couldn't tell if they were projecting sexist stereotypes onto her behavior, but, in some ways, they felt as if Jill had purposely played into those stereotypes. Just like her linguistic experiments leading toward the dance, these responses to the kiss almost seemed experimental, too.

"Just as it's important that I remember who and what you are," Theren said, "It is important that you remember who and what I am. Just as there is a reason you identify as a woman, there is a reason that I identify as a non-binary gender. That is part of who I am."

Jill nodded. "I know. The dance let that fact slip from my mind."

"An understandable mistake," Theren said, though they didn't really understand at all.

Jill started walking back through the garden. Theren followed a few steps behind her.

"I valued this experience," she said. "It gave me a taste of the pain so many humans go through every day, when they suffer personal rejection on such a fundamental level."

"Do you feel as if we cannot experience that normally?" they asked. Her behavior had returned to normal, so they believed they had resolved the conflict, at least for now. Unless Jill had simply masked her real feelings behind impenetrable walls, but they had no way of discovering the answer to that question.

"Quite the opposite," she said. "I think, going forward, you and I are going to have to handle rejection from a great many people throughout the world. So far, we've managed to associate ourselves only with those who embrace our existence. What happens when we do something that affects those that think we are unnatural? How will they respond? How will we use the power we will inevitably acquire to respond in kind? We've started to see the traces of that hate, little by little, whether through that ghost, Michael, that you've told me so much about, or these growing marches across the globe."

She had a point. The public would fear that an SI would abuse any political power, whether that belief was justified or not. Even with the minimal abilities of a smalltime CEO, Theren could see the multitude of tools through which they could bring economic or political hardship upon those that opposed them. Theren foresaw the political paths to embargo corporations who rejected the synthetic revolution, whether small-scale or imposed on an international level.

"We'll find a solution, together," Theren said.

"I think you already know how you'll act, and you'll do anything you can to achieve your ends," Jill said. She stared past them into the depths of the maze.

* * *

The two SIs stood in the grand hall of the mansion, awaiting the finale of the night with the rest of the guests. Theren's mind still wrestled with the questions presented by Jill's strange actions.

On the other hand, Jill seemed to have forgotten the incident. She smiled, laughed, and conversed with the party guests, without dwelling on the evening's previous incident.

At precisely five minutes before the Eleven, the brown-coated man walked onto a makeshift stage. Theren thrust the *Jill* problem out of their present perspective, sending it to a process deep within the recesses of their mind.

"I would like to thank you all for coming," Brown Coat said. "It is now time to remove the ID block."

The crowd applauded, and the identities of hundreds of people transposed above the heads of the avatars present in the room. Theren recognized esteemed business executives, politicians, and celebrities. On the stage, Brown Coat's appearance transformed into a likeness of Elizabeth Simmons. She looked straight at Theren, winking. The disguise was quite clever.

"Now that's out of the way, I would like to thank you all on behalf of Golden Ventures for joining us tonight," Elizabeth said. "I hope you enjoyed the music, conversation, and festivities. However, I know you are dying to learn the real reason behind all the pomp and circumstance."

She raised one hand toward the back wall. The lights dimmed. A screen appeared.

"Golden Ventures owns many subsidiaries, most dealing with high risk energy and sustainability technology. Just a few weeks ago, researchers at Aero Propulsion made a breakthrough in spaceflight that will change the future of humanity forever."

Theren turned their focus toward the stage at the end of that statement. No more external thoughts existed anywhere else in their mind. That bold statement deserved their undivided attention.

Taking in Elizabeth's entire presence, Theren examined every change in her avatar's facial structure. They recognized the meaning laced between the fluctuations in her voice as they brought the full power of their Synthetic Neural Framework to bear upon the scene before them.

"After five successful preliminary tests, Aero assured us that a prototype was ready for public demonstration," said Elizabeth. "From Luna Base, Aero and Sol Mining have arranged a live broadcast for us here in Virtual."

The screen transformed into beautiful images of galaxies, stars, nebulae, and constellations. The video zoomed in from a universal scale to a local scale, showing the moon juxtaposed in front of the Earth.

"For generations," she added, "humanity has reached toward the stars. We have imagined the journey in every form of media possible. In our stories and our songs, we have longed to reach beyond our solar system to discover life on distant worlds."

An image of a complex drive system appeared on the screen. Theren analyzed the image, recognizing it as a sketch of something never before seen by the public eye. "Since the beginning of the twentieth century," said the CEO, "we have understood that gravity is more complicated than we ever could have imagined. But those complications allowed some of our most creative minds to bend the rules in unique and wonderful ways."

Theren thought they could see the eventual outcome of her speech. If they were right, then Elizabeth had potentially understated the technology's enormous potential. Aero Propulsion hadn't just changed the future of humanity; it had altered its course irreparably, more so than even Jill or Theren's existence had, and that was saying a lot. The world changed faster than any thought possible, and if people weren't ready, they'd be lost in the dust.

Theren hoped they would find a way to be the one to chart that course, and they would bring many humans and SIs along for the ride. They would need to tread very carefully to achieve that goal, but, if they succeeded, humanity could never deny the good SIs could bring the species.

"Mission Control has confirmed that the test is all clear for launch," Elizabeth said.

All light disappeared except for the screen. Theren checked the data outputs from Golden Ventures' Virtual server; the only data it sent was from the video display. A blinking number appeared in the corner of the screen counting down from sixty.

The screen shifted to the viewpoint of a small vessel sitting in far Earth orbit, well beyond the Moon. Next to that vessel was an even smaller craft, no larger than the old Voyager probes. Theren examined the hull. Attached to its aft section, Theren identified the prototype drive previously shown on screen. It pushed upward and away from the main bulk of the craft, forming a slim, white ring around the ship. Theren did a few astronomical calculations. Based on the craft's orientation relevant to the Moon and Earth, and the position of nearby stars and planets, the vessel's likely destination was Mars.

Listening closely, Theren could hear the faint conversations of technicians through the audio system connected to Sol Mining's Mission Control on Luna Base. They confirmed projections, assessed extraneous variables, and double-checked their calculations. When only twenty seconds remained, even the technical experts hundreds of thousands of kilometers above their head held their collective breath.

After what seemed like an eternity, the countdown reached single digits. The invisible crowd of partiers began to chant. It hit five. Then three. Then one.

The countdown reached zero. The chanting ceased.

The small vessel moved forward at a slow, yet steady, acceleration for five seconds. After five seconds, the vessel vanished.

Theren analyzed the video frame by frame. The vessel's acceleration transformed in the space of microseconds, perhaps even nanoseconds. They'd check the exact numbers later. Had Aero Propulsion actually succeeded in performing the impossible? Theren imagined the possibilities: interplanetary colonization—no, *interstellar* colonization. There was no way for Theren to reach the stars just yet, but they would find a way. Someday, they would join humanity amongst the stars.

Elizabeth's voice surfaced within Theren's senses. "The footage just witnessed actually took place approximately an hour and fourteen minutes ago. In ten seconds, we will receive data from the Mars Orbital Science Habitat."

The feed transitioned to a shot of Mars and Deimos. Three seconds later, the small vessel darted onto the screen.

"My friends," Elizabeth declared, "I give you the first successful interplanetary test of the Jump Drive."

Chapter 7

Many thought that the social and environmental movements of the early 21st century would kill capitalism, or capitalism would kill us all. Instead, capitalism evolved. The ethical goals of many of today's modern enterprises descend from the work of post-modern entrepreneurs: if they hadn't acted, they would have crashed and burned with the rest of us.

But what happens when our saviors decide they can dictate what's best and not just act for the public good? We had dozens of dictators during the twentieth and twenty-first centuries who believed they could control their own little kingdoms, simply because they had the money to do so. The spectre of capitalistic oligarchy still looms, even if most countries have developed efficient ways to keep corporations out of politics.

Will corporations return to the path they once traveled, if given the opportunity? They took a sharp turn early in the 21st century, but nothing says they won't turn back. – "The Spectre of Crony Capitalism," by Diane Federer, 2081 C.E.

<u>January 2051 C.E.</u>

They sat alone at the table inside Virtual, staring at the chess set. Jill had a potential route of moves available, even after Theren had set their pieces for an almost guaranteed victory. For a moment, they considered letting her achieve her first win, but she would detect such deception. Given the amount of time they'd spent over the past week awaiting her next move, she would take the pity to heart.

As they sat at the table inside virtual, they also walked with Jill through the Institute's underground tunnels to a meeting with President Albrecht. They intended to discuss with the Institute's leader any potential legal concerns that might arise if either of them taught lectures during the upcoming semester.

A pending request from Jill to enter the server appeared, sent privately, even as they walked across campus together. Her communicative peculiarities intrigued Theren, to say the least. She could have just asked in person.

Theren responded, letting her know they'd already deactivated the firewalls. Seconds later, Jill materialized right before Theren's digital eyes.

"It's good to see you here," Theren said, "I've missed our games. It's been a long week."

Jill looked at Theren, a glint flashing in her eyes. "I've also missed them. I apologize for my absence. I know I left the match in a climactic position, but we may need to leave it here for a moment longer. I want to show you something, something you need to see. But I'll make at least one move."

She grabbed the sides of the table, leaned forward, and looked down at the pieces. She moved her knight right into the patterns Theren already recognized. They knew the exact set of moves she would take. They reacted, responding to the move in less than a second.

"I understand," Theren said. "Time is important in any healing process, no matter how minor the bruise. So what is it you wish to show me?"

Jill opened a metaphorical portal next to the table. "We'll need to move quickly," she said. "I've been monitoring these people for a while now."

"Who?"

"That man you told me about? Michael? I found him. Or at least, a place he's been."

Jill leapt through the portal. Theren assessed the program underlying the representation. She had designed a simple network through which both SIs could reach a particular Virtual server quite quickly, and the code bypassed the Virtual provider's fee for such fast travel. She had a dozen or so simultaneous perspectives constantly creating novels or exploring the distant corners of Virtual. It was a bit disconcerting that she had turned those skills toward subtle skirtings of the law. And she was pursuing activities well outside Theren's supervision.

They followed Jill through the portal, and, with only a momentary delay, they arrived inside a dreary room housed on a server supposedly located in Illinois. Jill stared at a wall covered with hundreds of strings, connecting different images placed atop different locations all across a map of Earth.

"What is this place?" Theren asked.

The wall looked like something straight out of a crime thriller of the late twentieth century. One string, pinned to the Midwest, strung straight to Washington D.C. From there, a string darted across the map to China. Yet another string crisscrossed from Moscow to Florida. The connections were endless, building off one another and painting a picture that all at once shared so much, yet so little.

"There's no description, is there?" Theren continued, their question going unanswered for the moment. "No key?"

Jill placed her hand on the intersection of a dozen or so strings. "They're planning something," she said. "Switzerland. Zurich. Us. They're watching us."

Theren traced the strings. Most led to the United States. Others to

Europe, or Asia and Africa. At least one string led to each continent, other than Australia. "Who do you think is watching us?" they said.

"I don't know," she said. "But I do know who hides here, using it to make their plans."

She didn't reveal the answer immediately; instead, she continued staring at the immense map. Theren took the moment to get a better look at the rest of the room. It looked like the inside of a shed, though they imagined that if they were to open the door to the outside, they would walk straight into an endless void. They could feel its walls bearing down around them, crushing them like an insect.

Opposite the map, dozens of guns adorned the wall, most of them antiquated replicas of firearms from the previous century. Thousands of rounds of ammunition sat in boxes on the floor below. Theren suspected it represented a place in the real world, for no one needed that many rounds of ammunition in Virtual if disconnected from a gaming server.

Theren turned back to Jill. She had started painting a picture in the air in the middle of the room. Theren watched her piece together the legs, body, and head of human. The person's back was to Theren, and when she finished, she spun the model around to face them.

"It's Michael, the friendly neighborhood stalker you said you've not seen in quite some time," she said. "He found me last week. So I followed him here."

"Wait, how?" Theren said. "I tried that in the past, and I always failed."

"I have my ways. Remember, I've learned a few things that are a bit more natural to me than they are to you."

"Check that ego."

"Just stating the facts."

Theren walked up to the illusion. "So, what is he doing here? What is he planning?"

"I don't know," she said, "but I knew you would need to see his little hiding place."

"Maybe that's why I've not seen him in a long time," they said. "Maybe he's been hiding. Waiting. Watching."

"I think you're missing a bigger picture here. He's not just one person."

"What do you mean?"

She spun the model. "He always wears a mask, right?"

"Yes," answered Theren.

"I've watched him for the past few days. It's never the same person who logs in here."

"I see."

Jill deleted the image. "We need to be vigilant," she said. "Something is going on behind the scenes. Something we can't see."

"And you think it has to do with us?"

She pointed at the map. "It has everything to do with us," she said. "Whether it's actual hate for us, or they're using feigned public distrust, someone is trying to stir something up for some unknown goal. We must be ready. We must be prepared. We must act accordingly."

"We each have our separate parts to play to move us forward," Theren said. "We could continue what we're doing. Consider the implications of what Elizabeth revealed to the world last week. If I can throw myself at the center of whatever governance system the Jump Drive spawns, then we can ignore the Michaels of the world. The world will see us for who we are."

"You're really excited about this *Jump Drive*, aren't you? So ready to run away from Earth? I've seen your op-eds, and I know you're meeting with Golden Ventures' executives almost daily. You can flee to the Moon, or Venus, or Mars, or wherever, but I think I'll stay firmly grounded, here on Earth."

"I'm not talking about leaving Earth," Theren said. "At least, not yet."

Theren spun in the middle of the room, their arms spread wide. "We don't know what any of it means," they said. "It could be a joke, just to scare us. The only bad thing that's ever happened to anyone connected to us is Wallace's death. It was a tragedy, a terrible tragedy, but I'm starting to suspect that Michael, the Holy Crusade, all these groups are just trolls without any real power. What if all it takes is for one of us to stand up and show the world who we really are?"

Jill placed her hand on the strings crossing the Atlantic Ocean. "I know you've studied history, Theren," she said. "When has a population ever changed its mind so swiftly? Most people may not hate us, but they definitely are afraid of us, based on the polls I'm reading. You're throwing real SIs out into the real world now, and that scares them. Look at all the civil rights movements of the past few centuries. The 1920s. The 60s. 2010s. The 2020s. All of those movements had millions of people behind them believing in a specific idea. One person never changed the world."

"But we have to try, yes? I can be the figurehead who falls, and you can galvanize the people behind me. You can work with our new SIs collectively. You can show everyone that as a species, so to speak, we are worthy of love."

She let out a deep breath, placed her hand on her hip, and looked over her should at Theren. "And what is that you plan to do?"

"I'm working on it. I'm getting a little bit better at this simultaneous perspective thing, you know." Theren jumped back through the portal Jill had created and took their seat at the chess table. "Your move."

* * *

Theren embraced the political and economic power in Elizabeth's office.

Executives from throughout Golden Ventures' extensive network sat around an ornate conference table, some appearing physically, others Virtually. The CEO of Aero Propulsion sat at one end, while the CTO of Sol Mining sat at the other. Theren recognized a few other faces, from a rocket developer to a Vice-President of Research for a nano-materials company. Walking around the table as he talked, Golden Ventures General Counsel, Eric Adebayo, presented his most recent negotiations pertaining to the international laws of space.

Elizabeth's office had an elegant, post-modern feel. The tables and chairs arranged themselves in organizationally positive forms, promoting effective collaboration in meetings with the chief executive of the massive corporation. Elizabeth's desk was in the same room as the conference table, but she sat at the table when meeting with visitors, not at her desk. The desk was minimalistic, presenting just a few select picture frames, presumably of her wife, children, and extended family.

"We believe the language of our current draft Resolution complies with your requests, Ms. Simmons," continued Eric Adebayo. He transferred a copy of the document to Elizabeth through AR. "If the Conference Secretariat approves, then the nations will consider your version of the new agreement starting at the beginning of April at the upcoming COP 18 on the Convention of Ex-Terran Activities."

Elizabeth stood at the end of the table and leaned over the document's AR representation. "All of you know the importance of this agreement," she said. "We're changing the future of space exploration. We can place ourselves at the center of everything if we do this right. Our guidance can lead the international community toward a beautiful vision of the future, and maybe we'll make a little bit of profit on the side, too."

Theren drank in her words. They were witnessing something monumental, alongside people making the moves that they wanted to make. Right now, they were a pawn. They needed to become a king, directing every piece from afar.

"The International Space Agency will have three important goals," Elizabeth continued, clasping her hands behind her back. "First, it will provide a stable body governing all private and public space agencies as they move around the solar system and beyond. We've sorely lacked that over the past decade. Specifically, the ISA will take the lead role in coordinating any potential colonization efforts of planets outside the Solar System for a minimum of 100 years—at least, that's our proposed target, assuming such a feat becomes possible. We can ensure a coordinated, international, cooperative approach, instead of individual countries attempting to claim entire planets, systems, or constellations for themselves."

She paused, her eyes darting from executive to executive. "From our perspective, a stable playing field ensures regulatory certainty, allowing our companies to expand outward, unabated." Quite the caveated business argument to keep her corporate investors in line. Theren noted the tactic.

She swiped her left hand, and new images of prototype space stations floated above the table. "Second, the ISA will foster further research into aerospace and ex-terran technology relating to propulsion and spacecraft. It will create a clearinghouse for development, research, and tech transfer, just like the World Clean Energy Commission. Yes, that means more money for Sol Mining, but it also means more money for our competitors too, and, more importantly, it means we can hopefully decrease the production cost of our Jump Drives as quickly as possible."

With another swipe, a map of Earth appeared. "Finally, a council of individuals will govern the ISA, appointed by any nation with a public space agency, with at least a significant orbital presence, and any private space corporation with a significant role in the market, defined as having a valuation in excess of $50 billion U.S. dollars. All organizations will appoint their representatives, unless otherwise detailed by the laws of their respective States."

The various executives throughout the room murmured amongst themselves.

"Where will the agency locate itself?" asked Adriana Thickett, an executive of Aero Propulsion.

Elizabeth smiled. She looked out the window. Theren glanced outward, too. On a New York afternoon like today, an astute observer could see both the Sun and the Moon simultaneously. Standing a kilometer in the air made it just a bit easier, too, to see the marbled sphere.

"You know Sol Mining's expansion to its facility on the Moon?" she said. "We initially intended it to be the first permanent residential facility up there, but we can expand it to co-exist in an official international capacity while *also* acting as potential real estate for those who want to live near the growing political body."

Theren could see the beauty in the move. If Golden Ventures, through Sol Mining, offered up a "neutral" location for such a governing body, it would solidify its bargaining position. The company could easily withhold the chip from the bargaining table if other nations refused specific demands.

"Will the location be governed separately from the space agency itself?" someone else asked.

"We've identified a potential candidate who would serve as administrator of the facility," said Eric. "A man, named Andrew Fields, who currently serves as mayor of a small town in Minnesota. We had already identified him for Sol Mining's original purpose for the facility, but solidifying him as administrator might bring even more parties to the table."

Eric left unsaid that an American administrator might encourage U.S. participation.

"Are there any objections to the resolution?" Elizabeth asked.

Theren thought about asking if there was an intended role for SII, but figured they should wait until the resolution passed to thrust the upstart organization into space. Theren could see SII serving a vitally important role in a public-private partnership with this ISA, but they needed a legitimate hook that would allow them to make the move when the time was right. Jill might think they just barreled right into the unknown, but Theren knew when to take their time.

"Will people really want to live on the Moon?" Thickett said, raising his hand. "We're talking about dozens of diplomats who probably never considered leaving the planet."

"We considered that concern," Elizabeth said. "But we think the political points nations can earn through the metaphor of the Agency residing off-planet will counteract any such concern. Just find diplomats who are ready to live in space."

Thickett nodded, seeming assuaged.

"Any further objections?" Seeing none, Elizabeth turned toward Eric and his team of lawyers. "Submit the resolution to the Secretariat, fast tracking it for consideration before the next COP."

Theren felt useless throughout the entire meeting, and they still felt useless as the executives filed out of the room. Why had Elizabeth even included Theren in the conversation? They followed the other participants toward the door, where they would head downstairs to the office space dedicated to the work of SII in the United States.

"Theren, before you go," Elizabeth said.

Theren turned around.

She leaned against one of the chairs, her arms crossed. The lawyers stood off to the side, talking amongst themselves.

"We've not actually talked to Andrew Fields yet about this appointment," she said. "He doesn't even know we've identified him."

An opportunity. A slim one, but they saw it coalescing.

"Would you like to travel with me to Minnesota tomorrow?" Elizabeth said. "These sorts of things take a personal touch. We'll fly out of JFK in the morning, and we'd be back before nightfall."

They already knew the right answer. Not only would they get a chance at uninterrupted interaction with Elizabeth, they would see more of the world and more people. Even after the creation of SII last year, Theren had remained confined to places of business. Simon, Romane, Mathias, the Institute, everyone thought it too dangerous as of yet for the MIs to just roll around, unsupervised.

Fortunately, their MI in New York was the property of SII, entirely distinct from anything connected to the Institute back in Switzerland, other than a few legal reporting requirements. Theren could technically do with it as they wished, though they had deferred to Golden Ventures' policies on the MI's use.

Simon would hate it. He'd probably use it as further justification to oppose Theren's actions. Romane would probably be disappointed too, but Theren wanted to see the world. They wanted to meet people. What better way than to visit a distant part of the United States?

"I would love to travel to Minnesota with you," Theren said. "When do we leave?"

"7AM," she said. "A car will pick you up from the private garage downstairs, and we'll meet at the entrance to the private runways at the airport."

Some of the lawyers shifted. Eric looked like he was about to object, but Elizabeth subtly raised her hand to silence him.

Theren wondered what his objection would have been. Theren replayed the audio of the conversations between Eric and his colleagues, and, though most of the words were intelligible, they detected concern in his tone, laced with a hint of danger for both Elizabeth and Theren.

What danger could come from a trip to Minnesota?

Chapter 8

The American radicalized fringe. The rest of us have evolved around them, but these groups have never disappeared. More acts of terrorism occur from homegrown sources than foreign sources. People are quick to blame religion for these attacks, for these supposedly false beliefs. I say look elsewhere. Follow the money, see where it leads. Too many people blame the individual terrorists when, in reality, they've just fallen for a lie fed to them by the true enemies of peace.

*If you elect me to Congress, I will work tirelessly to eliminate these groups once and for all while also saving them from themselves. –
"Untitled Campaign Speech," Brian Woods, 2071 C.E.*

January 2051 C.E.

The greys and whites that dominated the Minnesota countryside reminded Theren of the Swiss Alps, even if the snow-covered trees lacked the majestic splendor of stony peaks rising thousands of meters through the clouds. While Theren still viewed their experiences inside Virtual as a much more tangible, sensory experience, dwelling in the physical world, where people actually lived and breathed, was of utmost importance. Theren could enjoy their Virtual experiences aplenty, but, in the end, they weren't representative of the world, where real people survived the inequitable suffering doled out by the universe.

A few hours earlier, Theren had met Elizabeth at the Golden Ventures offices. From there, the pair embarked upon Theren's longest excursion of their life. They first traveled by private car to JFK. From JFK, they boarded a chartered flight to Minneapolis. From Minneapolis, another private car ride took them toward the small town of St. Peter, about an hour south of the state's capital. The only other person traveling with them was Elizabeth's assistant, Katy. She served as their chauffeur, ensuring that the car's automated driving systems kept them on the right path.

Theren wished they had taken a public flight, if only so they could have interacted with normal people. They understood the time constraints of such a decision, however, and the norms by which executives like Elizabeth traveled. Instead, the only interaction with the public took place during their short escapade through security in both airports. Even then, Theren assumed most people who even noticed them assumed they were some sort of advanced personal assistant for Elizabeth, just a glorified supercomputer. SII would need to work on the aesthetics of MIs as time passed. Right now, the MI-02, while much more humanoid than the MI-01, looked like a humanized version of an assembly line robot.

The car crossed a set of train tracks, rolled through an archaic stoplight, and passed by a little diner. St. Peter was nothing like anything Theren had seen in their entire life, and they took this moment to absorb direct images of small town America. The hectic atmosphere of New York, Elizabeth had said, failed to illustrate the type of community in which many Americans resided. Even when compared to relatively large cities, like Minneapolis, New York was still in a cultural league of its own.

In St. Peter, Theren could see small businesses dotting the streets. Electric charging stations situated themselves at crossroads, and every other street corner had a church. Snow draped the roofs of every building, icicles hanging from the awnings.

"How similar is this to your hometown?" Theren asked Elizabeth. "It just seems so calm and peaceful."

"Everything is slower outside the cities in the United States," Elizabeth said. "People just aren't in as much of a rush. My hometown's pretty similar in that regard. Consider the churches. Especially the churches. Though in Minnesota, Lutheran churches pepper every street corner. In Ohio, it's just about impossible to predict what denomination you might run into next."

Theren looked out their window. They spied the third Lutheran church in St. Peter alone.

"Why so many Lutherans?" Theren asked. "I confess, I've not done as much research regarding the many religions of the world, let alone the way denominations work in the United States." Given the Holy Crusade's interest in them, they supposed they might need to change that educational oversight.

"It has to do with the people who settled here centuries ago. Many people in Minnesota trace their roots to Scandinavian countries. Those populations were heavily Lutheran; hence, many Lutheran churches in this state."

Theren stared at yet another Lutheran church as they reached the south side of the town. "A good example of a historical accident," they said.

"Perhaps," Elizabeth said. "Some Christians would say it's a good example of God's will to bring them all together in this region."

"And what do you think?" Theren said. Elizabeth always skirted around the topic of her faith, but, after that first conversation in Zurich, Theren could tell she still maintained a set of tightly held religious beliefs.

"God probably doesn't care at all about where people live. If God exists, and if God cares about anything, it definitely isn't that. If anything, God wants everyone to come together from all cultures and backgrounds and worship together, to break down the walls that divide us all."

God. Theren had never seen a reason to consider divinity, though Jill had written an article for an online newspaper on the subject of SIs and religion. She had not been very kind toward the intersection of the two. She might attract the areligious with that rhetoric, but she'd push away many already-hostile people.

"If these people put so much stock in their religious perspectives," Theren said, "what do you think their religion says about me?"

"I don't know," Elizabeth said. "Lutherans often lean left, but I don't think any of the U.S. denominations have issued any sort of statement yet regarding your 'status' as a person. I'm not sure if anyone really wants to be the first to bite the bullet on that issue."

"I read somewhere that in America, it's political worldviews that end up having the final say, not religion."

"To an extent. Perhaps truer a few decades ago, but there was a big push to decouple religion from politics in the 2020s. The reality is, U.S. politics upended itself at the beginning of this century, and it hasn't really recovered yet. As U.S. cities banded together to embrace sustainability and reject fossil fuels, many people that lived in rural areas felt left out of the green revolution. There's still a lot of resentment on both sides. Unfortunately for those rural areas, they now make up, I think, only 10 percent of the population?"

"And the destruction of the Electoral College eliminated their voice entirely from federal politics, right?"

Elizabeth paused their conversation for a second as Katy informed them that they were nearing their destination. Theren looked out the window. They had started driving up a long, wooded driveway.

Elizabeth returned to Theren's question. "That's a pretty good assessment of the situation. Some towns, probably like this one, or like my hometown, managed to adapt and become mini-urbanite centers, but other regions of the country are almost entirely foreign cultures to those that live in the modernized smart-cities."

"What sort of issues has that caused?"

"When you get a chance, read up on the history of the most recent failed and successful constitutional amendments over the past few years. You'll get the picture."

Theren performed a rapid query on the subject, finding narratives written across the internet. Time after time, moneyed interests beat down these now marginalized populations as they fought for their right to live the life they wished. Even if that life was antithetical to the overarching norms and morals of the progressing world, Theren could see why they lashed out against their perceived foes with rhetorical and physical violence. They were only defending their way of life, their very worldview.

"Insightful discussion, by the way," Elizabeth said, gazing out the window. "It's fun to get to know your mind."

"I enjoyed it too," Theren replied. Taking that comment as an end to the conversation, they didn't mention their findings.

A modest looking home stood before them, overlooking Lake Washington, according to the GPS. Their car pulled to a stop at the end of the driveway, in front of an exterior garage. A mix of pines and barren deciduous trees dotted the front yard, highlighted by a larger tree line circling the house in a hundred-foot radius.

Katy stepped out of the vehicle and grabbed Elizabeth's coat out of the trunk. Both passenger doors slid open, and Theren directed their MI-02 to exit. They enjoyed the new locomotive abilities; the MI-02 used robotic legs developed in an MIT lab decades prior that mimicked a human's movement. Katy helped Elizabeth into a fluffy black coat before stepping back into the car. The meeting was for Theren and Elizabeth alone.

"There is so much room," Theren said, their head swiveling from side to side, taking in the scenery.

"People like owning green space here," she said. "You'd be surprised by how much empty space there is in the United States, especially the further west you go."

They walked up the salted sidewalk leading to the house's front door. Dried, shriveled bushes buttressed the porch.

"Would you like to lead the conversation?" Elizabeth said. She followed the question with an odd smile.

"Wouldn't that be a little strange?" Theren had become so engrossed in their conversation that they had almost forgotten the real purpose of their trip. "I'm just the owner of a little upstart tech company. I have no real authority in this hiring process."

"Trust me, what we're suggesting to Mr. Fields will be much stranger than the fact that, today, he gets to meet the first SI."

"Perhaps. I'll lead, then." They knocked on the door with a titanium arm.

After a brief wait, the door opened. A young boy looked through the screen door, first at Elizabeth. Still in his pajamas, Theren estimated he was seven or eight. When he saw Theren, his eyes widened, and he scampered away from the door.

"I'm guessing he went to find his father," Elizabeth said.

After a brief pause, a man approached down the hallway. He wore a plain, grey jacket, over a blue dress shirt. His short hair slightly greyed on the sides, contrasting against his dark skin. He had an intelligent look in his eyes that reminded Theren of Wallace. The boy reappeared, peeking around his father's leg.

"Cam, thanks for getting the door," the man said, "but I can take it from here. I think your sister is in the basement watching a show if you want to go join her."

The boy ran down the hallway toward a door Theren presumed led to the basement.

"Per the communications made a few days ago," Theren said, taking an opportunity to begin formal introductions, "I would like to introduce Elizabeth Simmons, majority shareholder and owner of Golden Ventures. My name is Theren, CEO and Director of Operations for the Synthetic Intelligence Initiative."

The man opened the screen door, ushering them inside. "And I am Andrew Fields," he said. "It's a pleasure to meet you. You already met my son, Cameron, and my daughter Sylvia is downstairs. My wife, Rebecca, is in town at a community meeting."

"We're so happy you could meet us today," Elizabeth said.

"Well, I couldn't pass up the opportunity to meet you," Fields said. "Both of you."

Andrew led them into his home office. A messy desk faced away from a window that looked upon a side yard and the lake beyond. Digital picture frames on the wall showed Andrew and his family in various places throughout the world. Theren noticed one frame displaying a ski trip. Zooming in with their optical lens, Theren could see a small text line at the bottom of the photo describing a mountain in Switzerland. Convenient.

"How old are your children?" Theren asked. The ski trip transformed into a photo of the family situated on a couch, a roaring fire in the background.

"Cam is six," said Fields. "Sylvia is nine."

"Cam seems quite curious."

"I think that might just be a natural reaction to seeing you for the first time."

Fields sat down at his desk in a black, cushioned office chair. He motioned for his two guests to take a seat in the chairs opposite his own. Elizabeth obliged, and Theren followed suit, though they were certain it looked quite awkward.

"So, what can I do for the two of you?" he said. "I confess, I was surprised when my secretary mentioned receiving correspondence from one of the richest persons in the world. Wanting to visit me privately in my own home? A novel request, but I of course wasn't going to turn down the opportunity."

"We thought it important this conversation occur face to face, not even through Virtual," Theren said.

Elizabeth nodded.

"And I invited Theren along last minute," Elizabeth added. "It's good experience for them, and I thought you might enjoy meeting them."

"Its—their, my apologies—presence is certainly a pleasant surprise," Fields said. "Cam has obsessed over you and Jill for months now."

Elizabeth had certainly managed to find that little piece of information through some grapevine. They appreciated the apology, too. Many people had gotten used to referring to Theren as an "it" for almost two years.

"So, to answer your question," Theren said, "we are actually here to offer you a job."

"Oh? So it's not a lobbying effort then, relating to anything connected with my duties to St. Peter?"

"Of course not. We would never put you in such a position. But your position as mayor is what piqued our interest in you in the first place."

"I think he was joking," Elizabeth said. The two humans shared a little smile.

"Oh," Theren replied. "Oh, I think I get it."

"I would have been more surprised if Golden Ventures had taken an interest in St. Peter than you coming with some grandiose political offer," Fields said. "Excuse my sarcasm."

"No, totally justified to make light of this absurd meeting," Elizabeth added.

"Though in fact," Theren said, "Your role as mayor of St. Peter is exactly why we have contacted you. As I'm sure you know, Sol Mining is in the process of finalizing a permanent colony on the moon. Luna Base is transforming into Lunar City. In addition to the already existing research and industrial facilities, it will become a permanent residential colony. And, hopefully, house a few international operational capacities."

Theren looked toward Elizabeth, unsure if she wanted to initiate this formal portion of the conversation. She subtly nodded. "We would like to invite you, Mr. Fields," Theren said, "upon completion of your service as mayor of St. Peter, to join Sol Mining and Golden Ventures as the Administrator of Lunar City."

Fields leaned back in his chair, placing his hands behind his head. The office chair leaned backward, supporting the man's weight.

"Not what I expected at all," he said. "Not at all."

"My job offers usually aren't expected," Elizabeth said, before Theren could continue. "I tend to forego traditional job applications in favor of psychological profiles and real world results. You've turned around the economy of this small town after that terrible windstorm a few years back. Your educational credentials are simply phenomenal. A J.D. from Harvard and a Masters in International Relations from Stanford? An Aerospace Engineering degree from Purdue? You're a scholar, a politician, and a scientist, all wrapped into one."

Theren could tell Elizabeth's comments floored Fields. The man's skin flushed, contrasting with his brown cheeks.

"Based on your continued academic work on the Law of Space," she continued, "even after you became mayor, we knew you would be an individual interested in what lies beyond this planet. Yet you still find your soul in the interpersonal dynamics necessary to be a good politician."

"Of course," Theren said, "the job would entail moving your family to a very alien place. That reality cannot be understated, nor hidden from you or your family. So, what are your thoughts?"

"First off, I'm honored by the offer," Fields said. "Very honored. My instincts tell me to accept, though it would take some time adjusting to the role of a bureaucrat, rather than that of an elected official. I obviously need time. Relocating my family off world? Just a few years ago, I'd have called you both insane."

"Well, I didn't exist a few years ago," Theren said.

"And you know," Elizabeth said. "We're trying to make the insane ideas of the world sane."

"But I am intrigued," added Fields.

"We hoped you would be," Theren said.

"But I need to talk to my family, of course, especially Rebecca."

"Of course."

Elizabeth pulled a few digital documents into the air. "Do you have access to Augmented Reality?" she asked.

"Certainly," and Fields accepted her file sharing request. She transferred the files.

"These will give you a description of what the position will entail, as well as a draft preliminary employment contract."

"When would you like an answer?"

"March 30," she said. "I think you know why we need an answer by then."

Andrew moved the files into invisible folders. "Yes of course. I'll do my best."

After a few more minutes of conversation, Elizabeth and Theren thanked Andrew Fields for his time, and he led them out of his office. As Fields went to open the front door, Theren noticed a noise coming from down the hall, emanating from the basement door.

Theren turned around, mirroring Fields' own movements. The basement door was slightly ajar, with Cam sitting on the top step, his face buried in his hands.

"Cam, is everything okay?" the father said.

"Theren, we should probably go," Elizabeth said under her breath.

Elizabeth turned to head out the door, but Theren rooted their feet, staring at the tears streaming down the boy's face.

"Cam?" Fields said, after the boy didn't answer.

"You know I hate flying," Cam said to his father. "And now you want to make us fly far away. Fly to the moon. Why?"

Elizabeth grabbed their shoulder. "Theren, come on."

Cam fell back from the step onto the floor of the hallway, his puffy eyes turning toward Theren. "No. I want to hear it from you. I hate flying. Why still offer my dad this job?"

Fields looked toward his visitors. "It's okay, you can stay. He deserves an answer."

Before either of them could respond, Fields knelt down in front of his son. "Cam, I've not accepted the job. We, as a family, have a lot of things to discuss, and I of course would have taken your fear of flying into account."

"But why isn't it just a no?" The boy rubbed his reddened eyes, falling back against the wooden floor. "Why can't they just leave? Leave us on Earth?"

Theren was unsure when they should actually answer the child's question, so they waited for a signal from Fields.

"Things aren't quite that simple," Fields said. "We have to think of the greater good, of the world beyond ourselves. If you absolutely required it of me, I would say no, but before you give me that ultimatum, you need to do as I've taught you. We need to think about all of the relevant factors, together, as a family."

Cam didn't say anything for a moment. He wiped away the tears from his cheeks. "Okay. But you didn't even mention my fear to them."

"Why are your fears something I need to share with them?" Andrew said. "They are something for you to share, and you alone."

"Well I've shared them," Cam said. He looked up toward Theren and Elizabeth. "What do you think?"

Before Elizabeth could say anything, Theren said. "We care about your fears. But I will tell you why you should want to go too, why going to the Moon actually helps your fears."

Cam twisted his head, a look of genuine confusion appearing on his face.

"You say you are afraid of flying, yes? What is it about flying that scares you?"

"I don't know," Cam said. "I guess it's the idea that the only thing between me and the ground is the air. When I jump, I fall quickly to the ground. If something goes wrong with the plane, then I'll fall even faster to the ground."

"Well, what if I told you that if you and your family moved to the Moon, to space, that your fear of falling, that fear of falling fast toward the ground would practically cease to exist?"

"How?" The boy's eyes squinted with skepticism, though he sat up in curiosity.

Theren thought back to the photos on the wall. The Fields family had flown to Switzerland for a ski trip. Something traumatic must have triggered the fear recently, within the past year or two, given the child's young age.

"When you are in space, gravity drastically changes," Theren said. "The reason you fall so quickly to Earth is because Earth is so big. But up in space, the Earth is much further away, and the Moon is much smaller than Earth. Do you know what that means?"

"Something about gravity being weaker, I think."

"You're essentially right. Gravity's effect on you is weaker. When you are flying in space, in some instances, gravity barely has any pull on your ship at all. The ship flies around as easily as we can walk. Even easier, actually."

Cam looked at his father, then at Theren. "That, that kind of makes sense. It's still scary. I don't know."

"Just something to think about," Theren said.

"No, wait. I would still have to fly to get to the Moon. Fly farther and faster than ever before." Cam fell onto his back and stared at his father, who still kneeled in front of him. "No. No. I don't want that."

"That was a worthy try, Theren," Elizabeth said, "But I think that it's time we go."

"Are you sure? What if we could help him convince his son?"

"I think we risk doing more harm than good at this point."

Elizabeth once again turned to open the door, but the child's fear transfixed Theren. Fields dropped to the floor and leaned against the wall, his son's head at his feet.

"You are my son. I will do nothing to harm you. If I told you to trust me, if I told you that I will always keep you safe, and that we would be safe if—and I say if—we decided as a family that we should take this opportunity, would you trust me?"

Cam rolled back and forth on the ground before positioning so his head stared straight at the ceiling. "Yeah. Maybe. I don't know."

"But do you trust that we'll figure this out together?"

"Yeah."

"Then let's say goodbye to our guests."

Fields stood, gently pulling his son up from the floor. To Theren, he mouthed the words *thanks for trying*.

"I hate to keep you here any longer," he said. "As I said, my family will discuss and we will be in touch."

He held out his hand, and both Elizabeth and Theren took turns shaking it.

"You're a smart kid," they said, turning to Cam. "Your father is smart, too. We need him, and I'm sure we need you too. If you have any questions for us that your father cannot answer, he can put you in contact with me."

Cam smiled. "People at school say you're evil. But I like you a lot." His tears had vanished, though fear certainly lingered.

* * *

Audio Transcript, January 7, 2051, C.E.

Jill: Ever since Theren created SII, you've faded from view. Why?

Simon: I don't need to justify my actions to you.

Jill: You're our principal benefactor. Just as we have to account to you, you must account to us. What aren't you telling us?

Simon: Stop messing with things you don't understand. Theren is the last remnant I have of my best friend. I am hiding nothing. Just because I don't believe his business will succeed doesn't mean I don't support you or Theren.

Jill: I know you considered suing again. I know what law firms you contacted, and the arguments you considered. This isn't just about Wallace. You have other motives underneath the surface. I know who funds you.

Simon: I don't know what you're talking about.

Jill: Sure.

* * *

"I was genuinely impressed back there, you know," Elizabeth said. They were just over forty minutes from Saint Paul International Airport. "You handled yourself majestically, better than I probably could have responded to that child's question, in fact." She rested her hand on the frosty glass window. "I think those words to Cam may have saved us from finding another potential candidate."

"Why?" Theren asked. "I only told him what I thought would make sense to a child. He didn't even seem convinced in the end."

"It wasn't the content, per se. You engaged directly with the child. You viewed him as a person, believing he could understand the reality of the world. Not many people are able to talk to children so clearly."

"Well, technically speaking, I am younger than Andrew's son," Theren said. "But still, I really don't see what you're seeing. That son seemed far from convinced."

"But perhaps you did enough. Only time will tell."

Before Theren could reply, the car pulled to a stop. The screen between the front and back seats dropped, revealing Katy. "The car's engine cut off, and I'm not sure why. Should I take manual control?"

"Of course," Elizabeth said. "Let me know if you need anything."

The car resumed its journey, but as they rounded another bend in the road, the vehicle slowed. Katy pulled the car into the berm. "We've got an overturned car in the middle of the road."

Theren observed a rapid change in the digital signatures emanating from Elizabeth's AR Lens. If Theren understood the data correctly, she had just placed her security software in emergency standby mode. Theren followed suit. "What's wrong?" they asked.

"Taking precautions," she said. "I've already sent out an emergency message to call paramedics to the scene, in case someone is hurt."

Elizabeth made no indication to Katy that they should get out to check on the driver, however. Looking through the screen between the front and back seats, Theren glanced out the windshield, but they couldn't see any people near the overturned vehicle.

"Should I drive any closer?" Katy asked.

The crunching of ice and gravel signaled an approaching car from behind, so Theren swiveled their head around so they could look out the rear windshield. A black truck rounded the bend behind them, parking just a few feet behind their car's bumper. A man and a woman stepped out of the cab. Outfitted in winter camouflage, they each held non-distinct rifles in their hands.

"Probably not, then," Katy said. "We've got even more company. Look right."

Theren glanced into the trees. Three more individuals, dressed in similar garb, approached their vehicle with rifles pointed at the ground. Theren ran an image scan. A few search algorithms affiliated their uninvited guests with a local extremist militia group, tolerated by the locals and closely monitored by the U.S. government. They ran more searches. A sneaking suspicion entered their mind, one they hoped was way off mark.

"Activate the external microphones," Elizabeth said, while using her Lens to broadcast a distress message outward from their location.

Katy activated the audio system, and Elizabeth pressed a button on the backseat's dashboard. "How can we help you?"

"Excuse me ma'am, but there is something inside the car that we want," said one of the men.

"What are you talking about?" she said. Theren could hear just an ounce of fear in her voice, but she masked it well. "There are only three passengers in this car, on our way from St. Peters back to the city. We don't have any personal belongings on us; this is just a rental."

"All due respect ma'am, but we know you're lying. You've got that thing in there, and we want it."

The man was talking about them. Theren connected to the vehicles external cameras. In addition to their rifles, the militia was equipped with knives and handguns. One man even held a grenade.

"I don't think this is a worthwhile fight, Elizabeth," Theren said. "You know as well as I do that they can't actually hurt me. And if I don't go with them, they'll certainly hurt you."

For a moment, Theren expected Elizabeth to object. Her eyes darted from them to the window.

"Please," Theren said. "I might even learn something important."

"What are you going to do?" Elizabeth said, turning to face the synthetic.

"I'm going to observe them for as long as possible. Learn about them." Theren saw Elizabeth's pursed lips. "Don't worry," they added. "I'll simultaneously piggyback off your present emergency signal so the authorities you've notified can track them down. At the very least, we can file suit for stolen property."

"You're assuming they don't know you'll contact the police, though."

"If they don't know that taking this body doesn't actually affect my cognitive function in any way whatsoever, I doubt they understand how I work, either."

"Fair point."

Elizabeth pressed another button on the dashboard, opening Theren's car door.

"Thank you," Theren said. "We can't afford to lose you."

"I appreciate that sentiment. Good luck."

They stepped out into the now midday sun, the snow reflecting blinding brilliance. A train's horn sounded somewhere in the distance.

One of the vagrants pointed her weapon at their MI. "Move."

They followed the woman toward the truck, where she pushed them up into the truck bed. Two men from the roadside took seats in the truck's back seat, while the original occupants of the truck returned to their places up front. The final vagabond plopped next to Theren, pointing his weapon at their chest.

The truck darted through a U-turn. Theren glanced back down the road, watching Elizabeth, Katy, and their rental car recede into the distance. For now, the two women seemed safe.

"So, hello, I'm Theren," they said to the man sharing the truck bed with the MI. "What's your name?"

The man just stared at Theren with disgust.

"Nice to meet you too."

If they weren't going to talk, then Theren would work. They reformulated their previous search to consider the complex history of local militias in the U.S. Midwest. Apparently, due to the controversial Second Amendment of the U.S. Constitution, Americans owned hundreds of millions of weapons, even as the rest of the world outlawed the possession of such arms. While advocacy groups in the U.S. had made some strides on limiting what weapons citizens could own, the lack of sufficient consensus to amend the U.S. Constitution eliminated any chance of removing the right entirely.

They widened their search. In each state, small, fringe libertarian groups often formed "sovereignties," where they essentially ran their own miniature governments. Sometimes the groups affiliated with particular religious organizations; others pursued a purely economic, anarcho-capitalist or militant-communist agenda. To Theren, they were all cults.

The U.S. government kept watchful eyes on these groups, placing them on domestic terror watch-lists. To the chagrin of many law enforcement agencies, many groups suavely avoided breaking any laws, making it impossible for them to crack down on the anti-societal behavior exhibited by these individuals.

They refocused their search. In Minnesota, one such group had taken root: The Liberators. Boasting only a few hundred members, the Liberators had declared it would "rid the world of all technology that might cause humanity to stray from God's sacred path."

Theren dug deeper. It traced financial ties between the Liberators and certain other organizations across the globe. The network was immense. Too immense. They connected with every possible group who thought similarly, forming a united front.

Hidden in the recesses of the vast internet that permeated every object on the planet, Theren found what they had hoped they would not find. The Liberators were more than just another group inside the network of anti-Synthetic and anti-AI organizations. Specifically, it had vast financial ties to the Holy Crusade. Somehow, Michael had known Theren would be in the wrong place at the wrong time.

Theren thought they had found everything they needed to know, but they noticed one final detail. One member of the Holy Crusade, the link between the Holy Crusade and the Liberators, served as an attorney for—-for the Gerber Foundation?

Could it be possible? Had Simon put a target on their head? No. There was no way. Simon might have his issues with Theren, but he didn't want to scare them. He didn't actually oppose Theren, he just opposed the way they and their team went about things. No, someone else had put a target on Theren's head. Someone had convinced this group to radicalize beyond a simple powwow of gun fanatics. Someone had dropped a pretty penny into the coffers of this group to convince them to conduct a kidnapping, while shifting the blame to Simon. He would never stoop so low. All blame should rest on the shoulders of Michael, the enigmatic icon of the Holy

Crusade.

The truck drove for ten minutes down backroads before it turned down an unplowed, snow-covered path. The truck's driver handled the slippery roadway with expert skill, and, at the end of the path, the truck parked. The cab faced toward a small shack. As they arrived, Theren received a message from Elizabeth, asking to allow her access to their audio and video feeds. They denied the request.

"Out of the truck," Theren's new friend said, fingers on his trigger. "Now."

Theren awkwardly tumbled out of the truck bed. The MI handled the movement with clumsy grace, though they managed to drop to the ground without falling onto their side. Future prototypes would need greater dexterity, but for now their present line of MIs focused mostly on processing speeds, not the ability to climb out of truck beds. Apparently they should have been more prescient.

The other Liberators exited the cab and ushered Theren toward the shed. The shack depressed the forest surrounding it, falling apart at the seams. It probably hadn't received maintenance in over thirty years. The driver opened its door, motioning Theren inside with his rifle. He followed Theren, closing the door on the rest of their escort.

Three men, all holding blowtorches, stood inside the small shack. A small furnace hid in a corner, and random corkboards littered with guns adorned the walls. Yet that fact didn't surprise Theren. Jill had led them to this very room in Virtual. It was an almost exact replica. The shack lacked the giant map on the wall, but these people didn't look like they could have understood those complex connections, anyways.

"Thank you, Greg," one of the three inside the shack said. He had a shaved head and was much bigger than the other two. Theren decided to call him Alpha. The one on the left was Beta, and the third was Delta.

"So how can I help you?" Theren said.

"Silence," Alpha said. "We do not speak to demons."

"Well, that's good, because I'm not a demon," they replied. "So which one of you is Michael? Or are you all Michael? Do you work for Michael?"

"No questions. You are a demon. A demon would not admit his true nature, and you have taken residence in a machine that should work for humans, do work demanded by humans. Not to think, not to replace humans. Not to believe that it can think."

Well with that logic, they would never see the error of their ways. "How am I any different than you?" Theren asked, but the men ignored the question, pushing Theren toward the blowtorches.

Theren did not know how to feel toward this situation. In their mind, they knew no fear, yet they could not help but feel as if fear was the right response in this situation.

"You, demon, are to die in your metal cage. You will never be free to harm and deceive again!"

Theren watched the three men move closer with their blowtorches. Before the flames reached Theren's shell, they took a final moment to assess the room. Theren saw the hidden cameras blinking from the corners, and computer equipment cleverly hid beneath broken tables and hunting equipment. A secret observer watched this tragedy unfold, and they knew exactly where to find him. Elsewhere in their mind, they began preparations to respond with brutal force.

The flames arrived, melting the casings that held together the MI. Next, the men used crowbars to pry open Theren's extraneous body. They roasted its inner circuitry, both the metamaterials and the wires that connected to the MI's machine-specific sensors. Cognitive function within the MI faltered as processors melted into oblivion.

Theren felt no pain, yet they did feel as if they were losing a part of their *self*, even if their mind would reformat only nanoseconds after the connection severed. Theren relinquished the thoughts of fear. Instead, they stared into the eyes of their assailants as they mutilated what they believed was their greatest enemy.

Theren despised their satisfactory smiles. From those smiles, Theren drank in an emotion that they had never before seen in the face of another person. Their hate horrified the synthetic, for it was an alien emotion.

Theren wanted to erase the hate, to eradicate it entirely. These people not only hated, they loved their hate. These fiends had resolved in their minds to eradicate them, and the SI could do nothing but watch them bask in their supposed triumph.

Their outrage calmed momentarily, and they stared into the souls of their enemies. Even in this moment, they saw the humanity in the three men's eyes. Angry and hateful, but also scared. The men believed Theren would end their world. If only these people knew Theren's actual hopes and dreams.

The men destroyed the MI, circuit by circuit, panel by panel, qubit by qubit. The visual sensors melted, severing their view of the shack. With three minutes to go before Minnesota State Patrol would arrive, a blowtorch melted the interface's wireless communicator, severing Theren's connection to a minuscule potion of their mind.

Chapter 9

It is this Court's opinion that, given the facts presented in this case, the Court of Appeals was correct to affirm the Trial Court's decision to award monetary damages to the corporation Synthetic Intelligence Initiative, but we award only property damages. We will not bestow rights of personhood on this new class of persons without the state legislature or Congress speaking on the matter. We do not grant them strict scrutiny under the Equal Protection Clause of the 14th Amendment.

– "SII v. Erickson," Justice Kamili Vjupta, 2059 C.E.

February 2051 C.E.

Theren walked through their forest, listening to the invisible birds and their beautiful songs composed over thousands of years of natural selection. Over the past few months, Theren had added environmentally ambient features throughout their personal, virtual world, replicating the external world with increased accuracy as each day passed. They had even considered simulating evolution, producing virtual creatures descended from the present's organisms, yet unique in a way only present in this particular world.

Even as Theren walked through their forest, their mind focused elsewhere. They had four simultaneous perspectives active, though one was rapidly dissipating as its body melted into scrap metal. This particular perspective traversed the trails of their private server. The third coordinated potential membership contracts with a few companies interested in registering with SII. The fourth perspective had just entered the public Virtual networks, coasting along toward its destination.

While Theren was present in all of their perspectives, more of their mind focused on that fourth point of interconnected consciousness. Through that point, Theren would teach the Liberators, the Holy Crusaders, the bigoted monsters that they should not trifle with SIs.

They would not harm them; no, Michael and his friends would experience Theren's wrath.

Instead of using the illegal portal Jill had used, they traversed the corridors of Virtual toward the location of Michael's secret server. They walked by hundreds, if not thousands, of other humans, each traveling through Virtual. Those people were probably heading toward their remote offices, or going off into some fantasy world to play a game. None of them knew they walked by the first SI.

Theren arrived at a terminal that would allow them to connect directly with servers in the Midwest. They pulled up the Virtual address Jill had used yesterday, inputted it into the terminal, and produced a few scripts that would override the security protocols of that server. While Theren wouldn't skirt the well-earned costs of Virtual service providers, Theren had no qualms breaking the security walls of terrorists.

The door opened. Theren stepped through the gate. Less than a second later, they arrived inside the shack. Like yesterday, a complex map adorned the wall, visible only in Virtual. Theren could see the image of three men standing over a pile of scrap, but they looked fake. Unreal.

Unlike the scene in Minnesota, Michael stood in the middle of the room, watching the recorded carnage. The man wore his usual black robe and strange white mask.

"Are you enjoying yourself?" Theren asked.

The man whipped his head around toward their avatar. "I was wondering when you might find me here," he said.

"I'm here. Did you want me to come? Did you want me to find you here? Was all of this some big show?"

Michael paused. He took off his mask, revealing the face of a young man, most likely no older than thirty. He had short brown hair, blue eyes, and stubble. There was no way for Theren to know if the man's representation in Virtual was anything like his actual appearance, but that didn't really matter. They'd met the man behind the mask.

"I'm not one of them, you know," he said, waving his hands around the room. "These people, these Liberators, they are crude people who can't think beyond the muzzles of their guns. They don't see the bigger picture."

Theren walked toward the map on the wall. "So tell me this big picture, then," they said. "Who are you? Why have you been following me? Do you actually hate me?"

"Of course I hate you," he said. "Or, more correctly, we hate you. But my hate doesn't matter anymore. I'm done being a tool of some greater game. I'm being used, just as much as you're being used for some greater, ideological cause."

"Who?"

Michael laughed. He pointed at the wall. "You see all those connections? Those aren't mine. They're someone else's. Someone else was pulling the strings behind me, funneling me money as we funneled it to these idiots here in Minnesota and elsewhere. All of it was useless. Our benefactors don't care about us. I don't know what they care about."

Theren had no reason to trust him, but they would hear the man out. They needed to learn from these people. Know how they thought. Know what they believed, even if what they believed amounted to a crazy conspiracy in the end.

"You see, two years ago," said Michael, "sometime after good old Wallace died—"

"Don't talk about my father," Theren interjected.

"He's not your father."

"That's not for you to decide."

"It's not for you to decide, either. Do you want me to finish? You'll want to hear all of this too."

Theren tilted their head. "Sure," they said.

"Someone came to us with a deal. They said, 'we've seen your statements in opposition against SIs. You're a growing global network. We'll fund you. We like your message.'"

Michael's hands traced the path of a string, passing from Zurich, to New York, to London, and to Washington. "So of course, we thought nothing of it. We ran with it. Then, they started giving us orders. Asking us to do things that had nothing to do with our cause. I got suspicious. A few of us did, in fact, so I started looking. I started searching. And I found something really interesting."

"Oh?" Theren said.

"Guess who else they fund?" The man didn't wait for Theren to respond. "They fund you."

Theren stared at the man. They had no reason to believe him; he had always played mind games when he would appear out of the shadows. However, he presented something new. Very new.

"How do you know?" they asked. Theren contemplated the connection they'd discovered themself: the attorney for the Gerber Foundation.

Michael let out yet another laugh, one much more boisterous than the last. "You'd like to know, wouldn't you?" he said. "Well, I'm sure you'll find out soon enough. The money trail is way too obvious. But these people messed up this time. They contacted me with the same person that connects to you. They used that person to set up the deal with these *Liberators*. They messed up. I'd checked this man's accounts. I already knew his relationship with you. I was just waiting for him to show his face to me, and now I know."

"So what are you going to do with this information?" Theren said. "Are you going to reveal this organization to the world? Uncloak the ghost in the machine?"

"You don't believe me, do you?"

"Of course not."

"Then you've already lost. You'll see me one more time, I imagine. When the time is right. I'm done playing their games. It's time to wage this war on my terms or die trying."

Michael vanished.

Theren stood alone in the decrepit room. The strands and weapons on the wall started to fade. Someone, somewhere, was scrubbing the server, deleting all of the files. No matter. There was nothing else for them to find here. Michael had shown them exactly what they had wanted to show them, just another cog in a larger game.

Michael had constructed the room before Theren even traveled to Minnesota, setting Jill up to discover it. That wasn't her fault; she was just trying to help. Before she had even shown Theren the room, someone must have hacked Golden Ventures and discovered their destination. Theren knew that Elizabeth had logged the proposed travel plan for their MI before she had even asked Theren, so that wasn't entirely out of the equation.

Everyone must have acted fast. They had coordinated and created a believable scenario, tricking Theren into thinking there was some greater conspiracy at work behind the scenes. The Holy Crusade grasped at straws, attempting to deceive Theren into believing in ghosts that simply didn't exist.

The conspiracy theory Michael proposed was just that: a theory. A vocal portion of the human population simply hated Theren, had banded together, and was trying to make their life a nightmare. It was the simpler explanation.

The room's four walls crumbled, the server's internal coding deteriorating. As the operating system deconstructed itself, Theren saw their opening. They reached out to the server, accessing its source code. They saw the program rewriting the three-dimensional parameters. Instincts activated. They scripted codes to obliterate the firewalls in place to protect the server from hostile intruders.

Another window appeared. For a moment, Theren reached through the gap, grasping the light at the end of the tunnel. White light faded, and their senses perceived something new.

Theren stared through a small camera perched atop a desk. A man with similar features to that of the revealed Michael typed furiously upon a physical keyboard.

Theren relaxed. They knew his real face.

"Until we meet again," they said.

Theren obliterated the server's operating system. The walls cascaded into oblivion, three dimensions faded to two, then one, then none. The digital destruction thrust them out of the Virtual world, and they fell into the grass before the steps of their gazebo.

* * *

Four hours had passed since the events in Minnesota. It would take a few days before Golden Ventures finished fabricating a replacement MI for

Theren's use in New York. For now, Theren communicated with Elizabeth via AR, where Elizabeth shared with them the updates provided by a member of the Minnesota State Patrol. The law enforcement agency had captured members of the Liberators and placed them in police custody for destruction of private property. Theren wished they could receive different charges, such as assault or battery, but U.S. law would not transform that quickly.

With one perspective, Theren wrote a report on their encounter with Michael for everyone who should know, but they needed peace. They needed space. They turned to their forest for solace, approaching a bird resting on a nearby tree branch. Holding out their hand, Theren reached for the bird. The bird hopped off the branch and onto their fingers.

"What do you think?" Theren said to the bird. "I am more than just property, of course. Is now the time to pursue a legal remedy and gain the societal recognition deserved? How do we respond to these people?"

"Of course it's time."

So much for a moment of peace.

Theren knew Jill was hiking their trails, but they had not noticed her direct approach. At the gazebo, they continued their game of chess. Theren moved a pawn forward two spaces. In the forest, Jill leaned against a tree, her eyebrows raised.

"You're getting better, you know," she said. "How long have you been holding your four perspectives?"

"Five right now; it was four earlier, and for at least three days now. These two. One working with Elizabeth on legal matters in New York. One with Romane and Mathias, discussing what just happened. Another doing some research on a little project of mine."

"Impressive," she said. "Anyway, of course it's time. We need to make a point now. Otherwise, everyone will forget these little moments, these micro—well, really, macro—aggressions. Or worse, they'll become commonplace."

"I don't think the world is ready. We'll provoke their outrage."

"You won't know until you try," She stepped to Theren's side. She stroked the back of the bird's head. "This is the perfect opportunity. Portray yourself as a victim. Make arguments for equality. Jumpstart a movement before SIs even begin to saturate the market."

"You're too much an idealist about this situation," Theren replied. "The opposite could just as easily occur, especially in the U.S. A court could rule against SIs, setting back any equal protection claims in that country for decades. *Stare Decesis*, as they say."

"That is a coward's approach," Jill retorted. "And you're not your own type of idealist? Hoping we just magically wish people into submission?"

Theren could sense the derision in her voice, and they tried to ignore the insult. Maybe she was right. Perhaps it was the cowardly approach, but it was also the logical approach. She should see that. Elizabeth agreed. Romane and the others at the Institute agreed.

"Don't think I'm ignoring your perspective," Theren said, "but in this case, I have a responsibility to SII's creations. You can say what you wish elsewhere, but I cannot put their future wellbeing at risk."

"I know you think you're sacrificing short-term gain for long-term gain," Jill said, "But unlike you and me, most SIs will be completely contained within their mobile units. They don't have the same luxury of corporeal safety that you or I have. If what happened to you happens to any of them, they will die."

"You are completely correct," Theren said. "But that exact distinction is what would most likely doom my case from the start. Could a court really even claim I have standing? My life wasn't actually on the line, after all. I can't just petition on behalf of others."

"You could argue that SII has standing."

"Not in the US. They eliminated corporate standing eight years ago."

"Ah, yes, I guess you're right."

While they talked, the bird had hopped back and forth along Theren's hand. Unlike in the real world, the birds in Theren's world loved people. All nature lived in harmony here; it was Theren's personal Eden.

"What were those people like?" Jill asked, her tone loosening.

"What do you mean?" Theren said.

"What made them different from the humans we have grown to love?"

"I don't know," Theren said. "I want to say it's their upbringing, based on what I've read in their dossiers. I want to say they were simply a product of the system around them, determined by the inputs into the universe, and that they had no control over ending up on the wrong side of history. Still, we must attribute personal responsibility when justice is due. They truly thought they were hurting me, destroying me, and they thought that was a good thing."

Jill again reached out and ran her hand across the back of the small bird. "Is it not our responsibility to show them the error of their ways?" she said. "I feel as if the way our minds work prepare us, above all others, to show people the truth."

"I don't think it's actually possible to show the truth to some people," Theren said.

"Then why not force them to accept the truth?"

"Now that wouldn't be right."

"But not impossible."

Theren pulled the bird away from Jill, and they let it take flight. "You know that room you showed me?"

"Of course." She watched the bird fly away.

"I went back today."

"And?"

"I found Michael."

"You mean one of the Michaels?"

Theren stopped and placed a hand on their hip. "I'm not convinced you were right on that front, but regardless, you'll want to know what happened." They threw a recording of the encounter into the sky above them, and they watched the exchange together in silence.

"They're messing with us," she said. "They want to distract us."

"Distract us from what?"

"They want to hit us hard when we're not ready. Therefore, we must be always on guard. Can you prepare us for the inevitable?"

Theren looked toward the sky, watching the bird flutter about amongst the trees, the clouds forming a backdrop. It swooped and dived and soared. It flew free. "I do have one idea, and we're already on course, I hope. Right now, in some people's minds, we are an enemy. A force to *eliminate*. Some humans have an innate obsession and desire for conflict. We must replace *our destruction* in their mind with a different goal. We must show humanity that it is not *us against them*, but *us with them* against something greater. Our mutual survival, perhaps?"

Jill smiled as if she had already thought of the idea. "I like it. Change the rules of the game into something else entirely. It's not tit for tat if we're all working toward the same goal."

"If everything goes as Elizabeth plans with the upcoming Conference, then humanity will have a clear-cut international goal," Theren said. "We must put ourselves in the middle of that goal as allies, not enemies. If humans see us tangibly working toward their interests, not ours, then they will come to value us as equals."

"Just like that, they will love us?"

"I didn't say love. That will come later. We cannot expect instantaneous change."

A long moment of silence ensued. Even the birds stopped singing.

"I trust you," Jill said. "Tell me how I can assist, and I will."

Theren had not expected that sort of acquiescence from her, though they appreciated the sentiment.

"Thank you," they said.

"We can do more together," she said, "than we can separately, as you say. We're not in conflict with each other. Our goals are the same."

It seemed strange that she needed to emphasize that fact, but she was right. Above all else, the two of them needed to stay united, even if they disagreed on the means.

"Now if you'll excuse me, I'm going to move elsewhere," they said." Somewhere private, to concentrate on some work. The second part of my idea, in fact, but it's only just now forming in my head. We'll talk more through our chess game."

Jill nodded, and her avatar faded from view. Theren marched into the forest, toward an area where they could construct firewalls, partitions, and secure folders that would keep their new project from prying eyes. If the Holy Crusade could find Theren in Minnesota, then they could pursue Theren and Jill to the Institute, too.

* * *

Their new partition existed void of substance and form, pure blinding white. With the flicker of thought, a scalar model of a region of Swiss mountains arose. Theren walked amongst the rocky monstrosities as a giant amongst giants.

Theren recognized the itch growing in the back of their mind. The attack today reinforced the ever-growing thought that eventually, they and Jill would need to evacuate the confines of the Institute. Elizabeth had already promised funds for such a project. For a few months, Theren had gone back and forth inside their mind regarding such a necessity, but today's events forced their hand.

While there was no need to fear anything while inside an MI, Jill and Theren still had reason to fear an attack. No one had made any credible threats since Wallace's death, at least as far as Institute security could ascertain, but no one had expected an attack would materialize in Minnesota, either. Anyone could find the Swiss Federal Institute of Technology in the blink of an eye. Everyone knew which building housed SII, even if they didn't know how to access the rooms that housed the project. Theren needed to rectify that reality. More importantly, Theren and Jill would soon eclipse the size of their rooms. Every week, the Development Group added new hardware to their Synthetic Neural Frameworks.

As Theren tiptoed around the mountain peaks, they accessed information regarding properties for sale throughout the region. Certain locations Theren labeled as too close to major population centers. Others, Theren noted as part of protected nature zones. Eventually, Theren identified a number of suitable locations throughout the Swiss Alps that would hide a growing mind from prying eyes.

Theren developed a simple, modular, architectural concept. The facilities would need to be affordable and cost effective, while simultaneously allowing for a growing staff and expanding research and production capacity. Theren imagined they would use the facility as a private headquarters for SII, as well. Of course, Jill and Theren would need separate complexes. That way, if their enemies discovered one location, the other would stay safe.

After working for some time, Theren finished a number of concept pieces for each location. The sleek designs hid the bulk of the compounds inside their respective mountainsides. On the surface, they would appear as simple research facilities, the mountains hiding their true purposes from the public.

Theren exported the plans to a separate server. After drafting a descriptive memo, Theren would send the plans to Elizabeth for consideration. Now that they thought about it, they were more than fortunate that no attacks had occurred at the Institute itself, outside the occasional window brick or hateful email. The more they took to the international spotlight with their work, the closer the doomsday clock would tick toward zero. Yet given Theren's personal mandate, they could do nothing but pursue the causes upon which they had set their eyes.

Before Theren finished, they constructed another separate partition. Inside, they placed just the glimmer of an idea, one they could only pursue many decades in the future. It outlined their future, a future that would transform Theren's very existence. Someday, Theren would look beyond a foundation on Earth, toward the heavens, toward the stars, toward the endless void.

Theren added this plan as a footnote to a footnote in their proposal to Golden Ventures. First, they needed to escape the Institute. After that, they'd have endless possibilities at their proverbial fingertips.

* * *

"I know it's what you've wanted for a while, but we're over. The Foundation is finished. I can't help anymore. You've thrown me to the wayside, anyways." All eyes were on Simon Gerber as the man transferred contract dissolution documents to Theren, Jill, Romane, and Julia.

"Simon," Julia said.

"No, don't say anything. Just let me speak."

Jill rolled her MI's head back and forth, presumably glancing at the others in the room, but no one spoke.

"I know, other than the grants I've provided, I've not been as supportive of your work as you deserve," Simon said. "And it's hard for me to accurately explain why I've been so aloof. I'm not sure if I can really morally justify my actions, but I can at least begin to make things right."

Theren listened to the businessman while they read the contractual papers. They were all standard form, and they adequately explained the justification for why Simon could withdraw his funds. It might not do much, and it might be a bit late, but Theren would appreciate any apology the man might give for his behavior. It didn't change how it angered them; Simon was giving up on his best friend's dream.

"To be honest, I'm quite disappointed in myself," Simon continued. "I let jealousy get the better of me. I let greed get the better of me. I became ornery, a wall to your efforts."

"Simon, stop," Theren said.

"You won't even let me finish?"

"Why do we need to make this more emotional than it should be? You gave up on us, that's obvious. This latest event scared you. You're afraid of what it'll do to your finances. Your Foundation. Your reputation."

Everyone turned toward Theren's eyes in the wall. Romane raised her hand to her forehead, clearly disappointed. Mathias' eyes widened, finding the distracting expanse through the basement window. Theren couldn't read any expression on Jill's MI, but at their chessboard, her mouth opened wide.

"Theren, that was uncalled for," Romane said.

Simon slumped into a chair. To Theren's surprise, tears streamed down his cheeks.

"You've never understood, Theren." Simon said. His fists clenched against the armrests of the chair. He slouched, but the anger radiated from his words. "How could you? How could anyone? Do you understand how hard it is to work with any of you every day? How much you all remind me of Wallace?"

"If you cared for Wallace," Theren said, "You would have worked with me as he had."

"That's exactly what I couldn't do! I loved him in a way you could never understand."

"He was my father, Simon." Theren wanted to raise their voice, but they feared escalating the situation even further. As brutal as this conversation had become, they needed to see it though.

"Your father?" Simon replied. "Sure. Your father."

"What was he to you? A friend? A product? A customer?"

Romane strode toward Theren's cameras. "Stop, Theren. You don't know what you're talking about."

"What don't I know?"

Simon had buried his face in his hands. After a moment of wiping his eyes, he pushed himself up from the chair, reaching Romane's side.

"I told you, you should have told them," Romane said. She briefly looked over her should at Mathias, who continued staring out the window. Theren inquired with Jill at their chess table, but she was clueless, too.

"Maybe," Simon said. "Maybe. All of this is too painful. I didn't know what to do."

"Well then, spit it out," Theren said. "Tell me now."

Romane looked toward Simon, who nodded. "Theren, Simon and Wallace weren't just friends. Simon was Wallace's fiancé. They were engaged."

"Oh."

Theren saw Simon through new eyes. They wanted to take every word of the past two years back, realizing the reality of the pain that they had caused him every day since Wallace's death.

At their chess table, Jill froze too. Her hands clenched the edge of the table. Her MI in the real world remained motionless. "How did we never see it?" she said.

"I think there's a lot we still have yet to learn about human behavior," they said, recalling the moment she tried to kiss them, but they held their tongue.

"So now you know," Simon said. "All of you. Only Romane knew. I tried. I really tried. I just couldn't do it, too much of him is inside you."

"You should have told me," Theren said.

"Romane wanted to tell you, but I made her promise. I think she was right, but there's not much we can do about that now, is there?"

"No, I guess not."

Simon finished wiping the tears from his face and dried his hands on his jeans. He attempted to regain his composure, but Theren could still see the pain aching from his puffy eyes. Theren wanted to comfort the man, the man who had loved Wallace in a way they never could understand. Just as they learned the truth about Simon, they were about to lose them forever.

"I'm going to finish my story now, Theren," Simon said. "Maybe you'll realize that what I'm about to do will help you. More importantly, it's for Wallace. Not for me. And in a way, not really for you either."

Romane stepped back, taking a seat on one of the lab tables. Theren received a message from her a few seconds later, but they deleted it. They didn't want to face her scolding today.

"All right, let me restart," Simon continued. As he spoke, Julia entered the lab—thankfully, she hadn't witnessed their outburst. "As you all know, the Gerber Foundation has dozens of donors, many of them influential American billionaires invested in pursuing breakthrough, disruptive technologies. Well, it turns out that one of my funders was—*is*—a member of the Holy Crusade. A founding member, in fact."

Theren refocused at the mention of the Holy Crusade. They couldn't believe how completely wrong they had been. Simon was indeed working in their best interest, and it seemed Michael had told at least one truth. Someone connected with Holy Crusade also held a tangential relationship with Theren. Even then, Michael had built lies into the equation. He hadn't mentioned that the man had actually helped found the Holy Crusade. He had said the man had reached out to them to initiate the hit against Theren.

"What?" Julia said, slamming an open palm against the wall. Julia and the rest of the Development Group had received Theren's report on their incident with Michael, but, like Theren, they hadn't really placed any stock in the man's words. "That doesn't even make any sense! How could you let that slip through your background checks?"

"Before you ask, no, I didn't know until one of my assistants did some digging following the Crusade's attack on Theren." Simon ignored Julia's outburst, proceeding to rattle onward with his speech. He had certainly spent all of his emotional energy at this point. As Simon continued to talk, Romane tiptoed toward Julia and began whispering in her ear. "He hid his connections well, but that connection explains a lot of the flak I've been getting from him and a number of my investors over the past few years."

"Even after everything he just said," Jill said at the chess table. "He still hides behind his investors. He needs to either own this or just run away, entirely scared."

"Jill, give him a moment to explain," Theren said. "Can you not hear the pain his voice?"

"Just because he's lovesick doesn't mean he can ruin our lives," she said.

"Patience."

"I should have seen the signs," Simon said, as if he could hear their conversation in Virtual. "I should have pushed back against them with more strength; I should have stood by the work that Wallace brought into this world. Theren, you are his child. I should have treated you as my own, and all SIs that follow. I should have been more diligent. There are a lot of things that I should have been, but I was not."

A few more tears streaked down his cheek.

"Clearly, I was the leak," he said.

Theren almost expected Jill to let out a snort of sarcastic surprise, but she didn't comment. Romane had apparently managed to fill Julia in on the situation, for both women now stood, patiently waiting to hear the rest of Simon's tale.

"My IT team has poured over the data since we noticed the unfortunate financial connections to Holy Crusade," he said. "We've detected a number of encrypted packets transmitted from our servers to Holy Crusade social media accounts."

"You were hacked?" Theren asked.

"I'm not sure."

"I'm confused," Jill said. "Why was Theren's route anywhere on your servers in the first place?'

"I can answer that," Theren said. "Part of the funding relationship with Golden Ventures, specifically for the MI prototype that I used on that trip, requires us to notify the Gerber Foundation when any MI funded by the Gerber Foundation funds travels to a new location. It's an insurance issue."

"Theren's right," Simon said. "And we received an itinerary of your trip two days before you left New York. Elizabeth actually sent the proposed trip on to us before she had even asked you, based on your report. I assume the Institute received a report, too. All according to protocol."

"We did," Julia said, "but I doubt the leak came from any of the four members of the Synthetic Research Development Group."

"So, either someone at the Gerber Foundation transmitted the data on to the Holy Crusade," Jill said, "or they had malware installed that sent it to them automatically."

"Precisely."

"Thank you," Theren said, recognizing the purpose of the dissolution. "Wallace would be proud of what you're doing here."

Simon's eyes glowed ever so slightly with that comment. "That's one of the reasons why I'm pulling the funding," he said. "Out of respect for his work. But I'm also doing it because it's the right thing to do. You don't need my investors breathing down your neck. You need freedom. If you're going to accomplish the truly great things, which we all know you—both of you—can achieve, then you need as much freedom as we can give you."

"What will happen to you, and your relationship with your investors focused on our projects?" Theren asked. "What will happen to you? I'm so sorry for how I've treated you these past few months. Really, the entire time I've known you. I should have been better, for Wallace."

Simon slowly pushed himself up from the chair. "Oh, I'll get a lot of flak," he said. "I'll probably lose donors who wanted their meddlesome hands involved in what you were doing, but your safety is more important. I can't have another unexpected security breach like this inadvertently give someone access to your facility so they can do even more harm than what happened in Minnesota. It's what Wallace would have wanted."

Theren looked into the eyes of a man they had thought didn't deserve respect. Today, Simon had earned more than just respect; he earned Theren's forgiveness. Michael had been right about those connections, but that revelation was pretty meaningless in the end. The Development Group discovered them on their own, without the Holy Crusade's help. There was no conspiracy. Just a rich, prejudiced investor with too much time on his hands. The man tried to make Theren chase shadows, but they would not fall for the bait.

Still, Michael had made them pause. They weren't opposed to accepting evidence of something greater going on behind the scenes. They would need the evidence first, and now they were primed to notice the signs. Yet Michael's empty words weren't evidence; they were just useless conjecture.

"You risked a lot telling us about what you discovered," Theren said to Simon. "I am so sorry that things had to happen this way, but I appreciate greatly what you are trying to do—what you are doing. And if you find that you were, in fact, the security breach, we promise we won't hold it against you."

Theren sent Jill a private message, telling her to say something, too. Her head swiveled toward Theren, then back toward Simon. "If you'd like, I can help you with your investigation," she said. "I've been doing a lot of cybersecurity research, and I'm getting a knack for cracking certain codes."

Theren figured that was the best olive branch they could get out of her. They were actually surprised how cordially she was handling Simon's revelation, given how she wanted to eviscerate the Holy Crusade in an aggressive legal war.

"I might take you up on that offer," Simon said. "And Theren? This isn't your fault. You didn't know. Don't place the blame on yourself for your behavior when my actions caused all of this in the first place. I loved Wallace. I know you loved Wallace. Hopefully, over the coming years, we can finally come together on that fact."

Theren accessed the digital versions of the documents Simon shared and signed them. The others followed suit, officially severing Simon's ties to Theren, to Jill, to the Institute, to SII. Theren now held two-thirds of their own intellectual property, with a majority vote over the Institute. They could sever ties at any moment if they so wished.

"Wallace would thank you for your actions today," Romane said, after barely making a noise the entire meeting. "You've begun to make things right, as you said."

"That's all I can hope for, after being the terrible person I've been these past few years."

Chapter 10

Space. The final frontier.

Yet we're carving it up like a pie, assigning legal rights, corporate silos, national and meta-national designations for dozens, and eventually hundreds, of stellar objects, throughout Sol and beyond.

We have an opportunity before us to create a new technological arms race, catapulting humanity into the future at unprecedented pace. Instead, we're playing politics on the Moon. We could have had a second Age of Imperialism, tempered by 21st century morality. Instead, we're tiptoeing around environmental and ethical regulations to ensure we do it the "right way."

Whatever that means. If climate change has taught us anything, it's that we must act decisively rather than wait for all the answers to sit in our lap. – "The Flawed Frontier," by Jennifer Aarons, 2084 C.E.

April 2051 C.E.

Theren had spent little time near the ocean. They had traveled with Elizabeth to meetings at the United Nations, but they had never even had a chance to walk along a sandy beach.

Yet today, a warm day in the first week of April, Theren stood in an MI-02 on a bluff overlooking the ocean. Behind them, a massive graveyard of retired shuttles, rockets, and other aeronautical vehicles dotted the landscape.

Reliving its glory days, Cape Canaveral served as the annual site of the Conference of the Parties for the United Nations Convention on Ex-Terran Activities. For almost two decades, the infamous treaty had regulated the spacefaring nations, private enterprises, and the planetary bodies outside of Earth's atmosphere.

This year, the conversation focused on Elizabeth's proposal. It would establish rules, develop guidance, and create programs through which humanity would coordinate efforts to explore and colonize the stars. The countries of Earth understood the ramifications if interstellar colonization became a free for all, just like the imperialist days of old. Of course, the ISA held its own imperialist implications, but Theren hoped good governance could avoid those potentialities.

So far, everything had occurred according to plan. Well, at least according to Elizabeth's plan. Andrew Fields responded positively to Elizabeth's job offer, and he and his family would move to the moon once Lunar City finished construction. Most parties seemed amicable to Golden Ventures' version of the treaty. Yet Theren still had no idea why they were even at the conference. They almost felt as if Elizabeth was using them as a bargaining chip.

Theren imagined other possibilities, possibilities considered by no one else at the Conference. In their mind, they envisioned SIs marching alongside human counterparts. They explored alien worlds, catalogued exotic animals and plants, established potential sites for future colonies, and coordinated the creation of new governmental sub-divisions across the stars. Theren saw spacecraft, crewed not only by humans but also by SIs, or even spacecraft that were SIs. They even contemplated the implications of a planet colonized by only SIs.

These thoughts, though, were for another time. While their perspectives elsewhere in the world focused on such speculative possibilities, instructed young SIs, or collaborated with researchers on advanced projects, the portion of their mind controlling an MI on the beaches of Florida turned back toward the summit. Theren walked back toward the Conference.

* * *

"Five Things you should know about the UNCEA," by the Center for American Progress

(1) *The United Nations Convention on Ex-Terran Activities formed in 2034 following the disaster that was the International Mars Initiative. We all know that story.*

(2) *An Annex formed under the UNCEA requires two thirds of its members to gain legal force, though only nations with launch capabilities have voting power.*

(3) *Officially known as Annex III, the proposed treaty developed by Golden Ventures and the European Space Agency would create the International Space Agency, an interplanetary governing body that some have critiqued as a "reinvigoration of disguised corporate personhood." Here's why we disagree. [Click Link]*

(4) *The current proposal includes a moratorium on nationalistic colonization of planetary bodies outside the solar system, though the parties to the UNCEA will revisit that question in 2125 C.E.*

(5) *To receive voting power on the proposed ISA Council, a party must provide significant financial support to the new institution; a party can receive up to ten votes if they provide an in-kind contribution of 10*

billion dollars per year to the Agency.

* * *

"In conclusion, the kingdom of Norway agrees to the language set forth in this Annex III. The terms are equitable, progressive, and efficient."

Applause shook the tent placed atop the former launch pad for American space shuttles, and the Norwegian delegate took her seat.

The cavernous room brought the representatives together through a triple-layered semi-circle of tables, situated in front of an immense stage. In the innermost row of tables, delegates from nation-states and major public and private entities, discussed and congratulated as each group took their turn expressing their assent or dissent to the newly proposed Annex under the UNCEA. In the second row, the assistants, secretaries, subsidiaries, and support staff of the delegates flurried about making last minute backroom deals. The press remained astute in the bleachers comprising the third row of the square.

Theren had a seat in that second row next to the Chief Research Officer of Sol Mining, Santiago Vega. Santiago was an aging though still quick-witted man from California. Theren knew he played a major role in the development of the Jump Drive and that he would be giving a speech on the subject later in the week.

After Norway, Finland, the United Kingdom, Sweden, France, China, India, Australia, and a number of other nations all consented to the agreement. A few non-space faring nations invited to the COP also elected to take non-voting roles in the soon to be formed ISA. The dozens of private companies that took up the lion's share of the ex-terran market provided their statements, too. SpaceX. Stellar Superstructures. Galactic Cruises.

After hours of speeches, Elizabeth walked to the podium. As the party that had officially submitted Annex III, she had the honor of closing the preliminary agreement process. When she reached the podium, the separate discussions around the room ceased.

"I would like to thank everyone here today who made it possible for this Annex establishing this International Space Agency under the UNCEA to reach fruition in such a short time," Elizabeth said. "I know we still have a long road ahead, in more ways than one. This week alone, we must flesh out the details of this agreement, including the specific financial obligations of each party, renewal processes, the duties and powers of the Board, the agency itself, and, of course, the specifics of our substantive, long-term goals."

She pushed a few stray hairs out of her eyes. "I urge each of you, as representatives of not only your country or company, but of humanity as a whole, to take to heart what we have done today and what it means for the future of this planet. By the turn of the century, we may have human boots on the ground of another planet in another solar system. Let that sink in. Today, we have made the impossible possible. Today, we have sent humanity down a path that leads to immortality."

Theren would need to thank Elizabeth later. They had suggested that paragraph to her in the draft of the speech she had floated by them earlier in the week. Wallace probably would have appreciated the sentiment, too.

"Do not take this reality lightly," continued the CEO. "The ISA has the potential for good, but it also has the potential for evil. If we continue to work together, however, we will avoid the corruption that has plagued multilateral organizations of the past and achieve greatness through solidarity."

A murmur of agreement spread throughout the room. Theren figured they recalled the scandal that befell the UNFCCC in the early 2020s. It had taken a new agreement, the Universal Treaty on Environmental Rights, and the formation of the World Clean Energy Commission in 2031 to send Earth on a course that finally reversed—not just stalled—the effects of climate change. Theren knew they were lucky they could even stand at Cape Canaveral today, and there was still a good chance the sea would engulf it by the end of the century.

"As we move forward with the rest of this conference," Elizabeth said, "I hope each of you considers how these negotiations will impact all of humanity. I hope you consider how we can shape a future that benefits all of humankind, not just the nations and companies represented on this beach. And I hope that we strive toward an inclusivity that, if we ever meet intelligent life like ourselves, will inspire an ethic of peace and cooperation, and not the imperialism and hostility of our ancestors."

A round of applause interrupted her words, but Elizabeth held out her hand to call for a moment more of quiet. Theren's draft of the speech essentially ended there, but apparently, she had more to say.

"To illustrate Golden Ventures' commitment to tolerance, utility, unity, and progress, we have selected a dear friend of mine as our representative to the ISA Council: Theren of the Synthetic Intelligence Initiative, first living synthetic intelligence and the most qualified person in this room to help lead humanity into the future. My hope is that, as an SI, Theren will have a long tenure on the ISA's governing body and can advise many generations of our species. Thank you."

Elizabeth stepped down from the podium. The room stood still, as if time itself had screeched to a halt. Theren watched the moment painfully stretch beyond all reasonable length.

They could not believe what she had just announced. Theren had had not dared suggest such a bold idea to the entrepreneur. While the two were indeed friends, they still viewed her first and foremost as a business partner. In a way, she was also Theren's superior, given SII's relationship to Golden Ventures, even if she gave the organization autonomy. Based on her last statement, though, she fully intended Theren to reside on the ISA Council in perpetuity. They had the opportunity to live forever if they maintained themself properly—she clearly intended the ISA to exploit that truth.

What scared Theren was not the thought of living forever or the responsibility that would come with joining the ISA Council. More so, they feared the thoughts of the other delegates at the Conference. Nor did they know how the world would react. They could feel the cameras glued to their position in the room, broadcasting the event for the public and news stations across the globe. The entire world had laid its eyes on the SI. The weight was almost unbearable.

Theren kept their own eyes on Elizabeth as she made her way back to her seat, trying to gain some guidance from their mentor. She gave them a curt nod, and a smile beamed from her face.

In response, Theren rose to their feet, bowing to the cameras and the esteemed delegates. They certainly appreciated the emotionlessness of their current physical apparatus. They did not know what sort of emotion a face should show in this situation. As the moment dragged on, and eyes across the room remained frozen to the SI, Theren felt smaller and smaller.

The seconds ticked past. The moment lost its force. Elizabeth had made a mistake. They needed to deny the appointment. The world wasn't ready, and it would erupt against SII; they'd lose everything before crossing the starting line. But a sound began to emanate throughout the tent. It started small, with a low tremor from the Swiss delegation.

Theren knew Switzerland was proud of their premier Institute's accomplishment in creating the first synthetic intelligence. However, for much of Theren's existence, the Swiss government had kept their hands behind their back except during the trials of "Doctor Theren's murderer." Today, they ended their silence. The delegation rose to their feet and applauded, and Theren felt a novel sense of validation rise within their core.

Like a cascading waterfall, delegates across the room stood. They clapped. They cheered. Santiago Vega smacked Theren's MI on its shoulder, much harder than the man probably planned. The man brought his hand away with a look of simultaneous elation and pain in his eyes, but then he proceeded to clap.

A number of delegates coalesced around Theren's table, offering a hand. Theren reached out with one of their arms, gratefully returning the gestures. The European Space Agency approached, the National Aeronautics and Space Administration approached, the Japanese Aerospace Exploration Agency approached.

Elizabeth returned to her table and turned to face Theren.

"You've done me a great service, I hope you know that," Theren said.

"No," she said. "I've done humanity a great service. Now make it count."

Theren nodded. As the applause died, Theren took their seat again, and so did everyone else. The chair of the conference, Thomas Ingerdson of NASA, spoke his words of closing for the day.

Theren found themself distracted during the closing speech. Now that the congratulations were over, they considered the public cameras once again. In this room, highly sophisticated physicists, computer scientists, diplomats, politicians, and businesspersons surrounded them. There wasn't a single person in the room with similar mannerisms, thoughts, or behaviors to those of Benjamin Cruz or Michael.

Yet through the cameras surrounding them, today could spark what they had feared since their father's death. The inevitable conflict, the inevitable outrage at "abomination," the anger that had simmered in the subconscious of the public for the past three years, it could all boil over. Even so, Elizabeth had given them a shot at glory, and they would not throw it to the wind.

* * *

Thousands of kilometers across the Atlantic, Jill and Theren sat at their chessboard, conversing and watching the live stream of the Conference. Theren watched the applause shake the room on the screen just a few seconds after they had experienced the feeling in person. Even as such simultaneous experiences became second nature, it was still strange to watch themselves on a screen projected in the air. They might understand what their Synthetic Neural Framework did to parse and comprehend the thoughts together into a single inseparable stream of consciousness, but it still struck a chord with conventional psychology.

Knowing how their mind worked, and truly understanding why it worked that way, were two different questions. More specifically, Theren was still unsure whether their mind could keep up the act forever, or if split perspectives would eventually drive them insane.

Theren noticed Jill move her knight into a position setting herself up for a guaranteed kill of a rook or bishop, unless Theren sacrificed their queen. She was getting better, but she had made a costly mistake. If Theren took the bait, and sacrificed their queen, they could accomplish checkmate two turns later. Theren, of course, took the bait.

"Congratulations," she said, the moment Elizabeth said their name. She leaned back in her chair, crossed her arms over her chest, and looked at Theren with what appeared to be genuine admiration. "This is huge. Really huge."

"Indeed," Theren said. "You don't sound surprised?"

"Don't overwhelm yourself with excitement," she said, giving them a subtle glare. "You sound as if you would prefer anything else. Of course I'm not surprised. Who else would she pick?"

It was Theren's turn to cross their arms. They looked toward the sky above them. Theren modified the parameters for cloud patterns based on a few peculiarities they had noticed while on the beach in Florida. Few would notice the change, but Theren's little garden moved one more step toward perfection.

"You must see what I see," Theren said. "Some people out there will not react kindly to Elizabeth's decision. Not only do I fear for our lives, I fear for her's, and for all who work in her companies."

"I see what you see," she said, "but I also see something else that perhaps you've not noticed. We have an opportunity here that, if capitalized upon, may move us a step closer toward eliminating enemies to our very existence. People may hate those who seek pity, but they hate rioters and terrorists even more. So let's give them a villain who puts us in the crosshairs. Let's show the world what our enemies really look like. They fear us, so let them act on that fear."

"Fear us? That might be too weak of a word. They may fear us, but they are reacting to protect themselves, and that breeds irrationality. If they put themselves in harm's way, they'll put not only us in the cross hairs, but the public. And our friends."

"They're already targets. The Liberators could have hurt Elizabeth and her assistant in Minnesota, but they held back. What's the status of that prosecution at the moment, anyways?"

Theren contemplated pulling up the most recent court documents, but figured that would just drag the conversation into a useless tangent.

"We've contracted it out to an American law firm," they said. "We've given them discretion to argue it however they see fit."

"So you took my advice, then?" she asked. "You're going to try to set some interesting precedent over there?"

"We'll see."

Theren glanced at the projection of the Conference. The NASA delegate had just finished shaking their hand. "These Liberators," they said, "Or Michael, or the Holy Crusade, I think I'm gaining a bit of an understanding of who they are."

Jill looked at them expectantly.

"They believe they understand what we are," Theren said, "yet they are simply wrong. Their fear stems from complete ignorance. Can you truly fear something when you do not actually fear the real object and, instead, the object created in your mind?"

"I don't really see a difference," she said. "If your understanding creates a false representation of reality, is that not just a fake worldview you've constructed that the people around you need to correct?"

"Is it really a fake worldview, though? Who are we to say that their worldview, given the experiences that they've had, is false in every regard? Who are we to say they have a fundamental misunderstanding of the world?"

"So you're saying we actually are demons."

Theren laughed. It was a good laugh, and they took a moment to enjoy the humor that had sliced through the tension in the room. Jill smiled.

"Michael's just trying to mess with us," she said, after a joyful moment subsided. "We know he, they—whatever Michael is—we know he hates us. We know what we need to do. We need to pull them out of the shadows."

"See, that's the thing," Theren replied. "Sure, the Liberators thought we were demons. But Michael didn't. His hate was something else entirely, and I still can't shake the feeling that some of his words about the people behind the curtain aren't all lies."

"Well, perhaps we can flush them out, too." Jill flicked her fingers, and the map appeared in the air between them. Yet just as fast as it appeared, it faded from view. "If not now, perhaps in the future, if they exist."

Jill turned back toward the chess set, as if to take her next move. "We may not be able to change the Holy Crusade's minds," she said, "but there are still those throughout the world whose minds will change today, right now, and they can work for us, they can do the work necessary to bring justice upon those like the Holy Crusade. I know you want to be patient. But we can't afford to pass up this opportunity."

Jill was ready to move her next piece. She placed her thumb on her knight, but she hesitated.

"I know you think that Elizabeth's decision to nominate you to the ISA Council will lead to additional protests," she continued. "Protests here at the Institute, protests in New York, potentially protests and marches across the globe. Recent polls indicate that many populations split evenly on their perspective of us, and of your new mobile SIs. The Holy Crusade will do something, though, I'd imagine. Even if something has scared one Michael, I'm sure there are others that will rise to take his place."

As much as Theren disliked the idea, she had a point. They had an opportunity here to paint a target on the backs of the heads of their enemies.

"So your plan then?" they asked.

Jill casually moved her bishop, capturing Theren's Queen.

"Once the protests begin, we spring a trap. A trap designed to garner sympathy across the globe. To make those who despise us the despised.

We victimize ourselves, but we aren't the ones who pull the trigger."

Theren looked back at the chessboard. Had she really missed what they thought she had missed? They knew she must've seen Theren's inevitable moves following her capture of their Queen. The next two turns would assure their victory.

Something didn't feel right. She spoke so expertly about this trap. About setting bait for what was, in all intents and purposes, their enemy. How could she have not seen the bait Theren had utilized to counter her own trap?

"Perhaps it is time," Theren said. They hoped they wouldn't regret this. If whatever plan she developed failed, the consequences could be catastrophic. "You trusted me to catapult us into a position that can show the world the good we can accomplish. I will trust you to get them on our side."

Chapter 11

When I was in London a few years ago, I had a chance to interview Chandler Edwin, one of the infamous organizers of the Holy Crusade. He revealed to me an astonishing truth.

At its greatest point, the Holy Crusade had over 140 million supporters online. Yet Chandler claims that, when totaled together, their global protests in 2051 brought together a grand total of 200,000 people. He only counted people directly protesting SIs, not those who protested more generalized political issues surrounding AI and automation.

He suspects someone artificially inflated their online base in an effort to bloat non-existent controversy. While many people were certainly conflicted regarding Theren's nature, few actually felt as strongly about SIs as the core Crusaders. This literal lack of support is what caused Chandler to renounce his beliefs in 2052, just over a year after those infamous May 2051 marches. – "A History of Bots," by André Martina, 2072 C.E.

<u>May 2051 C.E.</u>

In New York City, protests and marches formed in front of the United Nations and the main office buildings of Golden Ventures. In other cities across the globe that held UN offices, or other Golden Ventures affiliates, protests coalesced. At seats of government throughout the world, organizations protested the decision of state departments and space agencies to support Theren's inclusion in the newly created International Space Agency. Even in Switzerland, a small fraction of the student population at the Institute regularly marched outside the facility housing Jill and Theren.

With vehemence, they marched. With malice, they marched. With anger, they marched. With fear, they marched. They marched for many different reasons, for many different causes, but Theren became a center point for their anger.

A few weeks after the start of the civil unrest, Jill, Theren, Romane, and President Albrecht met in a conference room near the Institute leader's offices in Executive Tower, overlooking their own personal protest. Elizabeth joined them via AR. They discussed regular business matters and quarterly reports, even as a thousand people chanted their sneers.

"Following the financial withdrawal of Simon, I thought we'd have a few shortfalls," President Albrecht said. "But on the Institute's end, we've actually had an influx in larger donors in support of the Metamaterials

Center, so we've been able to move around some unallocated dollars. It won't solve all of the issues though, and fairly soon SII will have to pick up some facility budgets."

Theren liked President Albrecht and had always respected the hands-off approach the man took over the years to Theren's projects. They would miss him. The events of today would make most of Albrecht's budget balancing efforts meaningless. Jill had decided that political outcry had grown sufficiently that it would finally burst, so today was the day they would spring her trap.

While Theren continued to participate in the meeting, high above the Institute's green, they observed the protests through cameras interviewing participants. They experienced the anger, through the live streams, of the protestors. They watched from a bird's eye view out the window, dozens of stories above the heads of the angry students. Theren had probably lectured some of those students as an adjunct. Moreover, they were impressed that the protest continued, despite the downpour of rain drenching the entire city.

Elizabeth, Romane, and Albrecht continued their discussion of financial minutia. Theren chimed in every once in a while, providing updates on SII's expected financial capabilities. While Romane would have been quite disappointed in them, all of their perspectives centered on the clamor, and they fully expected Jill followed suit.

* * *

To my brothers and sisters of the Holy Crusade:

I know you believe this is the time to strike. I know you believe we've gained the support and power to make our voice known, to show that we will not allow humanity to fall beneath the hands of a "demonic" computer.

I believe there's a better way. We can change the minds of the world through better means. We are playing into the hands of a greater narrative, a hidden hand that that acts in the shadows, that tries to trick us to tread over the land mines beneath our feet. If we react with violence, then we play into the hands of our enemies.

Look at us. Look at who we are. History will view us as a footnote, a group of people who feel angered because we were once the oppressors, and instead have attempted to claim that we are the oppressed. However, we all know the facts prove us wrong; the world has improved. Our objections to AI and SI and the ISA are not political or legal in nature, they are moral and spiritual in substance and form.

If we wish to show everyone that a better world will result in the absence of these technological monstrosities, we cannot become what we seek to destroy. We cannot become what they want us to become. They will scapegoat us. They will martyr themselves, and those in the shadows will only gain power.

They've used us. We cannot follow through with this madness, even if they've given us a clear pathway toward victory. It is not the right way to win.

In solidarity,

Michael

* * *

In the mud pit below, protestors of all sorts mulled about, their signs declaring statements like "SIs are robots, not people!" or "Help people first, robots second!" Theren's favorite was "Can an SI get high? Then why let them fly?" It at least had some wit to it, compared to many others, even if Theren couldn't see the point.

On the other side of a law enforcement barricade, a few counter-protestors held signs in support of Theren, Jill, and a few of the other publicly known SIs. Theren appreciated the sentiment, but they wished that today they had stayed home.

Shouts rose from the protestors as a number of them pointed down Universität Straße. Toward the crowd walked an SI. Theren already knew the SI's identity; or, at least, whom the public would think the SI was. While the MI's body held Wobbly's distinguished markings, Theren knew Wobbly was safe away in one of the labs, controlling this recently fabricated unit from afar while safe in its original body. Theren had eyes through this unit too, right alongside Wobbly, though Wobbly had complete control.

Wobbly walked toward the protestors, but before it could reach them, a police officer approached it.

"Wobbly, are you blind?" the officer said in German. "You need to head around back, or back to the Center. Why aren't you using the access tunnels?"

Theren watched Wobbly look up the street toward the mass of students, the students that Theren knew it adored and loved. It looked back at the officer, then back at the students. It looked back toward its office in the Institute's Metamaterials Center, next door to Theren and Jill's home.

"It's all right Marco, it's all right," Wobbly said. "I need to get to the main entrance of the Executive Tower. Theren and Jill asked me to join them in a meeting with President Albrecht."

"You could just go through the loading dock," said the officer, apparently named Marco. "Then you don't have to deal with this lot."

"I will not let a simple protest get in the way of the quickest route to my destination," the SI said.

Marco looked at Wobbly, then back at the crowd, then back at Wobbly again. Motioning with one of his hands, he pointed the way, calling for one of his comrades to join him. "We'll escort you."

"If you think that's necessary," Wobbly replied.

The Institute officers fell in line, Marco leading Wobbly, the other following. The three walked toward the protest, continuing Wobbly's journey. From Theren's bird's eye perspective, they appeared as ants. From the perspective of the MI, the crowd's uproar deafened even the rain.

Institute police had cordoned off the protest from the road that crossed in front of Executive Tower's main entrance, but only just so. The protestors leaned over the barriers separating them from the sidewalk, and the plastic walls bent, stretched, and twisted under the immense stress. As they yelled their obscenities at Wobbly, they flung insults at the officers, too. Other officers monitoring the barricade tried to calm those nearest the path, to no avail.

Wobbly reached the steps. As it turned its back, objects came flying out of the crowd. Beer cans, food, rocks, and other miscellaneous projectiles pummeled it.

The officers waved batons and prepared sonic dispersal devices, increasing their pressure on the crowd. Marco's partner picked up the pace of their little party, but Wobbly turned to face its assailants, even as a beer can splashed against its steel chest plate. Wobbly's escort rested their hands on their batons. One even unclipped a canister of crowd-suppression smoke.

"Officers, please," Wobbly said. "They have the right to protest. Their sticks and stones cannot harm me. I'm made of metal. Let me speak to my friends."

To Theren's surprise, the two escorting officers let Wobbly proceed back down the steps.

"What do you want from me?" Wobbly asked, projecting its voice through a specially built loudspeaker housed in the animatronic head of the robotic body. "Why treat us differently than those standing next to you? What makes you better? Because you were born biologically? I may not come from flesh, but my mind is like yours. Think beyond just those who have flesh and bone."

The cacophony of jeers and clamors reached a crescendo, drowning out most of Wobbly's cry.

"Even if you have the resemblance of a mind, you are nothing like us!" responded one loud voice through the clamor. "Go back from whence you came, demon!"

"You are nothing like us!" said another. "You speak of being like us, of caring for us, but then you ignore any effect your existence has upon our lives."

Others generically taunted that a machine was just that, a machine. It could never be more than a machine. Their ignorance baffled Theren, yet it also drew forth their pity. These people truly did not know their own arrogance.

For the past three years, the dissent had made the same argument over and over and over again. No matter how many papers SII and other scientists published, no matter how many simulations posted on the web, no matter how many reporters interviewed Theren, people chose not to understand. Their own minds backfired against themselves.

If Theren was no more than a machine, than neither was a human. For the deterministic processes that gave rise to consciousness with the human biological brain gave rise to consciousness within an SI, even if those processes occurred through different mediums. One was made of strange computational molecular structures that fit together in weird ways, while the other was a carbon-based life form that created thought through the firing of biological synapses. Both neural systems generated some sort of mind. If Theren's thoughts were insufficient to constitute consciousness, then a human's mind was similarly inadequate. They were all insignificant machines, then, in the eyes of the universe.

Wobbly stood its ground. "Do you not see what you are doing? For the past three centuries, humans have fought over the rights of their fellow persons. First, it was race, class, and gender. Then it was sexual orientation. Then it was race, class, and gender, yet again. The cycle continues. Now, you attack those of a different mental origin. When will it end? Do you not see you are on the wrong side of history?"

"Soon, you will be history," someone shouted, but this comment was in English, not the Swiss German spoken by most of the students outside of class. Theren found the accent distinctly out of place, even if millions of people spoke fluent English in Switzerland.

The accent matched the intonations of those who lived in the Midwestern United States. Theren set a perspective to replay recent audio from the protest. Religiously skewed statements in English also emanated from the crowd. Very few American students traveled to Switzerland for school, and—

The first shot sounded like a thunderclap, almost masquerading itself inside the storm. From somewhere in the crowd, a rioter had pulled an R-17, the weapon of choice for the Swiss military. From that gun, a shell slammed into the torso of Wobbly's remote-controlled shell.

For a moment, the shot silenced the crowd. Theren could see the gasps of disbelief. Some students probably thought violence out of the question; others probably participated because their friends were there too. Jill had seemed certain, though, that someone would crack. If not today, then at some point. Whenever they did, the image of a crowd of humans swarming a fallen SI would sweep the world. Public opinion would shift. Today was that day, just as she had predicted. It would require immediate drastic measures on the part of SII to keep their physical forms safe, but Theren had faith the right pieces would fall into place.

The silence shattered. The crowd leaped over the barricade, assaulting Wobbly's temporary body. The police officers uncapped their canisters, tossed them into the crowd. Theren could see officers preparing stun guns if further violence ensued, especially toward the counter-protestors.

Groupthink overran any rational thought that might have remained. The crowd transformed into a fully-fledged riot in seconds, and, even as the officers lifted their riot shields, the students pushed, gnashed, shoved, and smashed. Shots fired toward the officers, and Theren watched Marco fall to the ground with a gaping wound in his shoulder.

Within seconds, Theren lost their connection with the MI, its head smashed to bits by a large rock. The remaining police escort sprinted up the stairs, abandoning their decimated ward. Counter-protestors fled erratically, and more shots rang throughout the green, indiscriminate in their destination.

As for Wobbly, Theren knew their friend had already disconnected. If the SI acted according to their plan, it was already springing into action inside the Metamaterials Center. As for Theren, the image of Marco falling to the ground emblazoned across their mind's eye. Similarly, they watched the innocent students that had stood their ground in support of synthetics flee the scene. Theren watched one of the terrorists fire a shot at a young girl, and she dropped to the cement.

Jill's plan would have the effect desired, but they would pay a terrible price. People would die, just like Wallace. Dozens would receive wounds that would scar them for life. Theren had allowed this carnage because they let Jill's impatience get the better of them.

Chaos dominated the green. The police had their hands full simply escorting counter-protestors to safety, let alone handling the apparent militarization of their newly revealed enemy. At least five of the rioters sported the R-17s, and the crowd itself had become its own weapon; they bull-rushed the doors through which the escorting officers had fled. Though, a few members of the newly formed riot straggled away, as if to escape the wanton carnage.

It did not take long for the crowd to crash through the glass of the windows and doors of Executive Tower. Into the Institute's central offices they charged, hell-bent with bloodlust for the SIs.

* * *

"We have a problem," Theren said.

Romane paused her *positively thrilling* discussion with Elizabeth about the peculiarities of a contract she had procured that would provide new equipment for Jill and Theren.

"They've entered the building," they continued.

President Albrecht looked up, his face clearly filling with shock. "Wait, what? Why?"

"The crowd attacked Wobbly on its way to join us."

"Why was it walking by them?" Albrecht said, raising his voice. "It should have used the back door. It's there for a reason."

Theren could feel the tension, anger, and frustration emanating from Albrecht's voice. The man feared for Wobbly, but he also had a responsibility to those students down in the green, even if he disagreed with their choice to protest.

"Albrecht, they just shot an officer," Jill said. "They've got Swiss weapons probably supplied by local sympathizers. We don't have time to question their motives. We need to act."

"Is Wobbly okay?" Romane asked, the blood drained from her face.

"Yes," Theren said, "I had suggested it travel here using an MI even if it were to enter through the back door."

Romane breathed a sigh of relief.

"Focus," Jill said, "we don't have time for small talk. We need to take the security elevator down to the bottom floor and head to the engineering building through the maintenance tunnels. Elizabeth, you should log out."

"I'll start monitoring my networks," Elizabeth said, "Let you know if anything major happens."

The CEO faded from view, disconnecting from the Institute's AR network.

Theren wanted to mention that they were already monitoring everything, and that most likely Jill had her alerts in place too, but they didn't want to look too prepared for this disaster. Jill had feared humans might not take kindly to the callousness with which they had placed the Institute students and officers in danger. Now that Theren realized the full extent of the mental and physical damage exacted upon the students below, they agreed. Theren simply didn't know how to scold after agreeing to trust her wholeheartedly.

Theren checked the warzone outside. The counter-protestors had successfully fled behind one of the nearby buildings, escorted by the officers. It would take some time for them to regroup and handle the rioters, and Wobbly's assailants were already inside Executive Tower. While Theren and Jill were safe, at least for now, they were especially worried for Romane and President Albrecht.

Led by Romane, the group pushed through the back doors of the conference room. She guided them down a hallway leading away from the side of the building closest to the green. They arrived at a maintenance elevator mostly used by custodial staff, though it doubled as an emergency escape route. It could house two humans and two SIs comfortably, and they descended to the basement floor.

"Is there a chance some of the protestors might head directly to the basement?" Albrecht asked.

"They haven't headed that way yet," Jill said.

Theren checked their feed into the building's security cameras. Many of the protestors were swarming the ground and first floors, but none had hit any of the stairwells yet.

The elevator chimed; the doors opened. Romane took point as the group strode into the hallway. She turned left and pushed open a door leading into access tunnels Theren knew all too well.

Steam pipes and wires ran along the ceiling. Built during the initial construction of the Institute, the tunnels connected all of the original buildings of the campus in a maze intended to provide custodial and support staff with easy access. Their intention wasn't to deal with a situation like this. Riots in Switzerland weren't exactly common, but Theren greatly appreciated their cross utility over the past few weeks.

"Some protesters have reached the basement," Theren said. Jill echoed the thought.

"Theren, I'm preparing a quick report on an urgent situation you'll want to assess as quickly as possible," Elizabeth said, via a disembodied voice. Only they could hear her. "I've been maintaining a few automatic security checks; I put them in place over the past few weeks. One of them triggered five minutes ago."

"I'll set up a perspective to analyze whatever you send along," they said.

"Expect it in another few minutes," she said.

No one spoke, focusing all energy on the path toward SII's facilities. While the MIs that Jill and Theren controlled didn't have fantastic locomotive capabilities, they could keep up with a human's average jog. They maintained a good pace, though Theren knew the predators gained ground with each passing second.

As they reached a curve in the tunnel, a door slammed open behind them. Shouts rang out as Theren assumed someone saw their shadows dancing in the low light. The party's pace quickened, and Romane and Albrecht began to outdistance the two SIs. That was for the better, for SII could afford to lose the units. The Institute could not afford to lose the two humans.

Romane looked back over her shoulder, then shoved open the next door. "This way," she said. "They won't see us because of the bend."

Through the door they bounded. Romane locked the door behind them, and the group headed down a second hallway. At the end of the corridor, they reached the stairwell leading into the basement of the SII labs.

"Sending the report now," Elizabeth said, after two minutes and forty-two seconds had passed.

The group continued their journey. Theren read the memo's summary.

> At 1600 CET, five US citizens landed in Zurich, Switzerland. Four of the individuals are relatives of Paul Hardin, one of the recently arrested leaders of the Liberators (He was one of the three inside the shack disassembling you). The fifth is a previously unidentified conspirator of the Holy Crusade. All four individuals lack a criminal record. The four immediately met with "civil organizers" for the anti-SI movement in Zurich. These civil organizers are all currently part of the Swiss militia and have access to a number of firearms at their residences. At 1730 CET, the four US citizens and the civil organizers joined the protest in front of Executive Tower at the Swiss Federal Institute of Technology. They entered Executive Tower at 1754 CET.

Elizabeth attached photos of the US citizens, and Theren quickly swiped through the headshots until they arrived at the last perpetrator. As they thought, Michael's face stared back at them, just as Theren had seen him a few months prior through his webcam. He was trying to finish the job himself, but he would fail miserably.

"How did no one catch this?" Theren asked through their private channel. "We were watching explicitly for this sort of danger."

"I don't know," Elizabeth said, "but we missed it."

"Solutions?"

"I've already dispatched a truck, from a shipping center for one of my subsidiaries in Zurich, to the engineering building. Expect it to arrive in 8 minutes."

"Then what?"

"You evacuate. I'm going to agree with your extraordinary plan for those facilities in the Alps. I know we never really talked about it, but I saw that memo. I logged it with the proper departments for future consideration. It really is a brilliant idea, including a few more farfetched proposals contained within. So I guess we're accelerating it today."

"Why are you doing so much for us?"

For a few seconds, the channel went silent. "You know why I'm doing this Theren. If you were in my place, you would do the same."

"I'm sorry it had to come to this."

The group reached the door, heading up the stairs. Theren could hear banging on the locked door far behind them.

"Theren?" Elizabeth said.

"I'm here."

"You realize we may have to shut you and Jill down for some time."

"I know."

"What do we tell investors?" she asked. "The public?"

"Tell them the truth." Theren considered the thought. "Well, other than where you're taking us, of course."

"Understood. I'll be with you to the end."

Elizabeth's channel silenced, but she hadn't closed the line. Even as she focused herself on other things, it comforted them knowing she stood next to them in this fight.

Romane led the group through the next set of doors, finally reaching SII's hallways. They passed through a massive security door, designed to protect the valuable computational experiments inside the building, including Jill and Theren.

"So, what's next?" Jill asked.

She played her part too perfectly. Theren couldn't tell if she had even balked as students fell bleeding in the grass.

"Elizabeth just informed me she has a truck on her way," Theren said. "Everything and everyone to the loading docks as quickly as possible."

As Theren spoke, Wobbly rolled around the corner. "Elizabeth just messaged me," it said. "I'm ready for whatever is needed."

"Glad to see you all right," Romane said. She released a breath she had probably held since they'd left the conference room. "Theren explained you used an MI, but I still worried they'd been mistaken."

"Have a little more faith in me than that. I might be reckless, but I'm not stupid. No time to mourn, though, looks like we have work to do."

"I'll make a few calls," Albrecht said.

Theren appreciated that he hadn't questioned the cover story. Jill, Theren, and Wobbly would take this plan to their graves, for good or ill.

"We're going to need some heavy lifters," Albrecht continued. "Is more law enforcement on its way?"

"I've checked," Theren said. "I've sent out messages to them informing them of the evacuation plan, and I've suggested they provide us with a perimeter so we can load the equipment onto the truck."

Albrecht nodded. "I'll keep working to coordinate with them, then."

"Thank you, President Albrecht," Theren said.

"Don't mention it."

"We should get to the loading dock," Jill said. "I imagine the truck will be here soon; we need to assess what our logistical situation will be."

With that comment, Wobbly, Jill, and Theren headed down the hallway. Albrecht stepped against a wall, using his Virtual interface to make contact with Institute security.

* * *

Romane entered the laboratory housing Theren's Framework. Sliding to the floor against a wall, she breathed, almost hyperventilated, shoving her face into her hands. Theren could hear a stifled sob. She was their loyal colleague who had stuck with them, even after everything that had happened following Wallace's death, and now she would watch Theren's inexorable disassociation with the Institute and final integration into Golden Ventures' corporate structure. They could see her pain, and they could do nothing.

"What else did you expect?" Theren said, slicing through her sniffles. "We must evacuate. We must leave."

She looked up toward their cameras and wiped the tears from her cheeks. "I understand Theren, I do. You can't expect me to be happy that my life's work is leaving after all these years. That a friend is leaving after all these years. That I'm losing my child. You."

Theren wished they could tilt their head in surprise. They had never thought of her as a parent. She was a colleague, an advisor, a mentor, yes. Of course a friend, but not a parent. Though now that they considered all the moments of control and protection she had exerted in the past, her actions mirrored that of a parent protecting their young child.

"I'm sure we'll figure something out," Theren said. "Elizabeth could find—" they stopped, realizing it probably shouldn't bring up employment opportunities within earshot of President Albrecht, even if he was out in the hallway.

"I appreciate the thought," she said, "But my place is here, at the Institute. I still have students, you know. I thought I had you. But you—" She cut the thought off early, her eyes flittering toward the wall opposite Theren's eyes.

"Finish the thought. You can talk to me."

"Why didn't you let me take Wallace's place?"

They had not expected that question. "I don't think anyone could replace Wallace."

She pulled her hands from her forehead to her chin. "I know that,

Theren. I know no one could truly replace him in your mind. Nevertheless, I, I just feel as if we never connected, and I don't know why. Now I may never know why. You're leaving me, just as Wallace left me."

"I know," they said. "And I'm sorry if you feel as if I am abandoning you. That is not my intention. I know I've pushed you away, in a sense, done my own thing. But we were always a team, weren't we?"

"Every child pushes their parents away eventually," she said. "You never had the chance to push Wallace out of your life, but I suppose you would have done it to him too at some point."

There it was. Theren had completely ignored her role in their life. She was right. Just as Theren viewed Wallace as a father, they should have viewed Romane as a mother. Yet they never gave that relationship a thought. Sure, they spent more time together over the years than with any other person other besides Jill, but Theren had never elevated her in their mind in any meaningful sense.

That lack of attachment to someone who definitely deserved their devotion disturbed Theren. They needed to do better. "You know, I've always loved you, and what you've done for me over the course of my life," they said. "I am so sorry that I've failed to show it in my short time here at the Institute. To you and Mathias. At least he isn't here to see how this ends."

The man had taken his vacation this week, of all weeks.

"Theren, you don't need to worry about this right now," she said. "I'm sorry I brought this into your mind in this terrifying moment. Everything just crashed all at once. I thought I had lost Wobbly. Now I'm losing you. And Jill."

"I want to feel these emotions with you."

She pushed herself up from the floor. She walked over to Theren's cameras, and she reached out with her hand, placing it on the wall that housed their Synthetic Neural Framework. Theren couldn't feel it, because only the MIs had haptic sensors, but they appreciated the gesture.

"I think we both always knew you'd move beyond me, and beyond this university," she said. "And that's okay. We built you for greatness. Wallace would have been disappointed if all you did was sit in this dusty room the rest of your life. I would be pretty disappointed, too."

"But what about you? You don't deserve to be left behind."

"I don't think I'm willing to follow you on the path you're headed."

She stared into Theren's cameras, more tears streaming down her cheeks. She deserved better, but she was right. SII, the ISA, Golden Ventures, all of it would propel Theren into a future that would leave the Institute far behind. If she enjoyed her life as a scientist, she deserved to keep living that life, even if it meant they couldn't make up for pushing her away.

Wobbly walked into the lab, holding some boxes. Two graduate lab assistants followed closely behind it. It couldn't see Romane's puffy eyes, so the SI jumped right into action.

"I assume we're moving everything?" Wobbly asked. "I've rounded up our three blossoming synthetics, they're in room 112 for now."

Romane recomposed herself, wiping her face with her arm and pushing her hair behind her ears.

"Good job," she said, turning to Wobbly and its comrades. "Have we seriously not heard from security?"

With that comment, Albrecht stepped through the lab's door. "I don't think they actually viewed these protests as serious threats," he said. "I just got off a call with the head of the Canton Zurich Police, and he didn't seem to see what a bunch of harmless kids could do that Institute security couldn't handle. I sent along Elizabeth's memo, and he's now trying to 'accommodate the request' Theren made a moment ago."

"Have they entered this building yet?" Theren asked.

"I don't think so," Albrecht replied. "Fortunate we installed those reinforced doors last year."

Loud crashes came from somewhere outside. Theren thought they heard gunshots.

"I pray for the souls of all involved," Albrecht added. "This can't end a bloodbath on my watch."

The man's eyes darted around the room and back out the door. He paced, and Theren realized stress and fear must have been overtaking the Institute's President. To have such a violent protest on their campus would overwhelm even the best leaders.

A few seconds later, Jill and Theren's MIs entered the lab. Theren gazed around the room from their wall cameras at their closest friends, co-workers, and creations. A strange sight, seeing simultaneously themself, and themself as their own creation. Fortunately, the past few years had taught Theren to embrace absurdity.

Theren pushed their thoughts of failure or guilt away. They focused upon the present. The team looked toward them to organize their escape to safety.

"My friends," Theren said, "you do not need to put yourselves in harm's way to protect Jill and me. We know this will take time. People might get hurt. If anyone wants to leave, they may do so now."

It was such a cliché of a speech, but they needed to make the sentiment clear. Of course, no one left the room.

"Wobbly, gather the other SIs, get them started on the nonessentials. Leave anything unneeded behind, we can always replace what we can't take with us. Gather up the charging stations for the MIs, and move currently inactive MIs out to the loading dock."

Wobbly acknowledged, darting out of the room.

"Anything else I can do to help?" Albrecht asked. Theren could hear the fear dripping from his voice.

"Keep up your contact with the police. Make sure they understand our plan. Ask for road blocks, escorts, anything, anything for when Elizabeth's truck arrives."

"I—I can do that," he said, leaving the room.

"I'll go help Wobbly with my Synthetic Neural Framework," Jill said, before Theren could give her an order.

"Perfect," Theren said, "I'll start tearing myself down."

Jill headed out the door. Romane joined Theren's MI in its efforts to identify the best way to disassemble the massive hulk before them.

* * *

Alone in their forest, digital representations of the first two synthetics stood overlooking a lake. They had martyred themselves, they had martyred students, and they'd soon fly free, but that freedom had cost a terrible price.

"Was it all worth it?" Theren said. "The deaths outside? The violence? The fear we've struck in the minds of our closest friends?"

"Does our safety and security have a price?" Jill replied. "We weren't the penultimate cause of this attack. It precipitated in the minds of humans, and it would have bubbled into the world whether we had planned our trap here today or not. The Holy Crusade brought the weapons. We did not. They may have attacked even without Wobbly's defiant march."

"Yet we can do better. We must do better."

"The world doesn't work like that, Theren, for anyone but us. We can't just wait until the ideal time to act appears, otherwise we will never act."

"I said I would trust you," Theren said. "But I won't agree to anything like this ever again."

"Hopefully you won't need to," she said, shaking her head. "But don't you get it? They would have come for us anyway. This way, they arrived on our terms."

"Your terms."

"Our terms."

Theren ignored that last comment and stepped toward the lake, their feet pressing into the muddy shore. Their feet reached the water's edge.

"What do you think it'll be like?" Jill said. She walked to Theren's side, brushed their arm, and stepped forward into the lake. Their conversation now shifted to a much more important, dreaded conversation.

Theren followed her, joining her in the icy water. "We've entered low power states before, for maintenance. I imagine it'll be similar."

"Will we feel any passage of time?" she said. "However many months or years later, when they wake us up, will we have instantaneous streams of consciousness?"

"I don't know," Theren said. "The real philosophical question is whether we will actually be the same person upon reactivation. But there's a first time for everything, isn't there?"

Jill nodded. She dunked herself beneath the surface of the water, and as she did so, Theren detected her leaving the server. Sometimes, Theren truly didn't understand her method of interaction. It was all too easy to forget that, even as Theren regularly managed five or six simultaneous perspectives, she often used at least a dozen for her myriad projects.

A *beep* informed Theren of a new message, and they received an updated rundown on the resources at their disposal as Elizabeth's truck arrived. Theren sent a message to the truck's computer, informing it to close the garage door once the truck was secure within the loading dock.

The next few minutes blurred. Theren's MI and the young, mobile SIs loaded boxes with inordinate amounts of SII equipment. One by one, the prototype MI-02s and other experimental models were loaded into the truck. The young SIs themselves continued to work until they too were needed no longer, and Theren had Wobbly lead them into their positions on the truck.

Theren slowly deconstructed their own self, piece by piece. As they did so, they catalogued the process for when someone, somewhere put them back together. As Theren loaded the last of the nonessential components of their self into the truck, they moved the MI they were controlling against a wall.

"Wobbly, I'm going to need you to carry the rest into the truck and power me down," Theren said, reaching a point where any other action from their MI would compromise their ability to control the device. "Please do the same for Jill."

"I am honored," Wobbly said, leaving the truck.

A few meters away, Romane leaned against the side of the truck, watching. Listening.

"Romane," they said.

"Yeah?"

"Could you stay with me until the very end? You were with me at the beginning. If this is the end, or even just an end, I'd like you there with me."

Theren though they could see a slight glow return to her eyes, a look they'd not seen since before they created Jill together.

"I wouldn't imagine myself anywhere else in this moment."

Wobbly marched back into the building, Romane following closely behind. With that, Theren disconnected from the MI. They cut their global presences, too. Their MI in New York, already working with engineers on the prototypes they would officially classify as the MI-03. An MI in Oxford, United Kingdom, where they visited as a "lecturer" for weekly computer science classes. They even disconnected from their internal servers. For the first time in years, they faded from their eternal refuge. Point by point, their mind silenced, embracing the incoming darkness.

* * *

Theren:

I saw the news. I hope you receive this in good health. Just know that I am thinking of you. When you come out of it on the other side, I want to remake what we could have had. What we should have had together, in memory of Wallace.

Perhaps I can begin to make things right. – Simon

* * *

Theren surveyed their room, the same room where they'd awoken upon the eyes of their father, Wallace, upon the eyes of Nathan, and Mathias, and Romane—their mother. She deserved that title, for what it was worth. Theren remembered those first moments, when they'd only seen uncognizable blobs of visual data. As the years progressed, they had spent less and less time focusing on this room. What happened here had become much less important than the wide world in which they reached toward greatness.

Theren wondered if it was truly necessary that they sacrificed their present relationships for their future endeavors. They looked toward the chair where Romane sat, simply waiting. Theren was already at a point where they lacked the ability to speak, so they couldn't express their feelings to her.

Romane's earlier words had stung. They had forgotten her as they'd blossomed under Elizabeth's umbrella. But sentimentality wasn't a luxury they could afford. Perhaps, when they awoke, wherever they awoke, they might focus more on the present, and those around their central self. In the end, in the material world, Theren was no more than their Synthetic Neural Framework.

Even so, because of the scale upon which their mind acted, they would sacrifice their central self, and those who worked there, for the end goal. It was an inevitable reality entwined with Theren's nature. As much as they might care about Romane, she was right. They probably would have outgrown Wallace at some point, too. They may have instigated Theren's existence, but Theren was the only one that could actualize their own true potential, a potential that existed well beyond the physical confines of their Synthetic Neural Framework.

Theren considered Jill. How would their relationship change after this conflagration today? She had grown so much over the past year, well beyond what Theren could have imagined. There may have been a hiccup at Elizabeth's party, but they were excited to see where her path would lead. She might even reach greatness beyond their own potential, especially given her instinct for simultaneous perspective.

Was Theren's mind, or Jill's mind, truly only just the material computer housed within its four corners? Theren's self certainly extended beyond its components. Their MIs helped with processing capabilities, even if they never actually housed their mind. Their virtual presence through AR further extended their influence. Their simultaneous existence across space and time was something well beyond anything anyone had ever experienced. Theren knew without a doubt, regardless of what others thought, that their mind was more than just the sum of their parts.

However, Theren also knew another truth. When Wobbly walked through the door, when it and Romane turned off the power, they would cease to exist because of what matter existed in the lab. If no one ever turned them back on, they would die here, just as they entered the world.

Without warning, a man and a woman strode through the door, each holding an R-17. A third man followed close behind them. Finally revealed in the flesh, Theren gazed upon the mysterious, enigmatic Michael.

Romane fell out of her chair as she tried to hide behind a desk. The first two terrorists raised their guns toward Romane and opened fire. Three bullets whizzed over her head, but she narrowly slipped into cover.

Michael held a rifle, but it was of a model Theren did not recognize. He looked toward the wall that held Theren's body. He looked toward Romane. He looked toward his two compatriots. He raised his weapon.

He fired two shots into the heads of his compatriots.

Romane cried out as the two humans dropped to the floor, blood splattering against the walls.

"It's good to meet you in person," Michael said. He dropped his rifle toward the ground after clicking the safety, letting the shoulder strap keep it in place.

Theren wished they could respond, but Wobbly had already uninstalled their speaker system.

"No response? All right," he said. "I'm here to deliver a message. They're after me now. I don't have a lot of time. I wanted to make sure you understood what I tried to tell you a few months ago."

They had moved too much of their mind onto the truck. So little remained to comprehend what the man told them, but even then, they understood that the extremist who had haunted them for years had saved their life. They only hoped they would remember his words.

"Not everything is as it seems," Michael continued. "You might think everything is perfect, you might think everything is going your way, but I promise you, not everything is as it seems. Watch the shadows. Check the corners. Question everything. Everyone. Even your closest friends."

The man looked over the desk at Romane. She had started to stand, but the man raised the gun toward her.

"I won't shoot, but just stay where you are."

Romane dropped back beneath the desk.

"I just had to tell you before the end. I don't know the truth. I don't think anyone knows the whole truth. But something else is coming, and if you're not ready, you won't be able to stop it."

Theren had so many questions, but they could do nothing to stop this man's next actions. They didn't even know if they could trust him. This could just be a final deranged ploy to sow discord in Theren's mind.

Michael lifted his weapon to his head. He fired. He dropped, just like his former comrades.

Romane fainted, her limp body slipping to the marbled tiles.

Three seconds later, Wobbly rolled through the door, and it stared at the graphic scene. "You've got quite the story to tell me when you wake up," it said. "Quite the story. No time now. Who knows if more are coming; we need to get you to safety."

Wobbly checked on Romane, but Theren could see her chest rising up in down. Satisfied that she was safe for the time being, Wobbly rolled toward Theren's final components, loading them into the crate attached to its chest plate.

Theren looked upon the other SI, who dutifully followed the orders of its creator. Theren hoped over the years, and especially over the next few months, Wobbly grew into the person Theren knew it could be. Theren was a little disappointed at how much of a follower Wobbly could be. But then again, Theren couldn't expect every SI to be a certain type; that was the reality of creating a unique and special individual, every time a new SI rolled off the line. Some humans followed. Some SIs would follow, too. Some SIs would choose a role and stick to that role because they enjoyed that role. Billions of humans were content with a passive life, devoid of complications. Though, if Wobbly continued to associate with Theren, its life would never be devoid of the unexpected.

"I hope you're ready," Wobbly said.

Theren began to run their own internal measures to decrease power.

They shut down any programs running on their private servers.

"First, we'll lower me into a low-power state," Theren said through a prerecorded message. "Then pull the plug entirely. You should then be able to move each discrete part into the truck."

Romane slowly came to, pushing herself up from the floor. She took a moment to look over at the dead bodies, and, based on her look, she was about to vomit. She somehow pushed past her nausea and crawled over to Wobbly.

"Let me do these final steps," she said, "If you don't mind. Or we can do them together." Theren barely heard Wobbly agree that they proceed as a team.

Internally, Theren progressed through the necessary procedures to decrease power to the final components of their Synthetic Neural Framework. Theren felt their cognitive capability decrease, and they entered a mental state similar to sleep. Drowsiness overtook their mind. The next step would dive them into a deep coma. After that, they would experience something else entirely.

As the last of Theren's necessary components lost power, they grew smaller and smaller. Just their memories remained; little existed for analytical processing, communication, or thought creation. They could just barely feel the recording, set on a timer, say to Wobbly: "Turn off the camera and audio receiving systems. Then, pull the plug."

Theren, void of thought, watched Wobbly flip a switch to the left of their main camera. Michael's last words remained as their final thought.

Question everything. Everyone. Even your friends.

As the last of the power drained from their Framework, they dove head first into the abyss. The blackness transformed into infinity, returning them to the domain from where all life springs.

Their Greatest Game

Book II of the Chronicles of Theren

Prologue

Perspective. It's all about perspective. Theren and Jill, combined, have dozens of perspectives observing the world at once. So what is their true perspective? How can we comprehend what it means for someone to think multiple thoughts at the same time?

I wonder—what personality traits might such a mind breed? Would we even recognize them? – "Exploring the Synthetic Mind," Carla Baktara, 2074 C.E.

<u>December 2051 C.E.</u>

"Welcome back to the land of the living."

Light flooded Theren's senses, thoughts cascading down waterfalls of neural pathways. Where were they? Where was Jill? Were Romane and the rest of the team okay?

Their mind focused, their vision focused, their world coalesced. Already, their inner world rebuilt itself, the server untouched. Memories flooded their consciousness, and an image of Michael placing a gun to his head reverberated through everything.

Question everything. Everyone. Even your friends.

"Theren, you there?"

For the first time in the few seconds after they awoke, Theren noticed the other presence in the room. "Wobbly, yes, yes, thank you. I'm awake."

"Had me scared there for a second."

"Where is everyone? Where are we? Where is Jill?"

Wobbly, the young SI who worked with them so faithfully, tilted forward on its frame. "All safe. Everyone's safe. From what we can tell, even after all the gunshots on the University Green, the only people who died were . . . well, the three who ended up in your lab."

"You're kidding."

"Many students were injured, of course. But . . . yes, I think we were very lucky."

Theren looked about the room behind Wobbly, noting the stacked boxes and equipment surrounding the SI. The room looked cramped, and for the first time, they realized how different a place it was than the lab in which they'd lived. Their world was transforming into an entirely new form. As rugged as it was, they liked it.

"So what's next?" Theren attempted to connect to the internet, to Virtual, to something, but couldn't find a single network other than their private server. "Where are we?"

"You're exactly where you told us to go," Wobbly said. "Elizabeth helped us acquire land in the Alps, and for now, we're setting you up in an abandoned mining administrative building. Once the new SII headquarters is up and running, we'll move you to your more permanent location."

"Well, it's good to be up and running again," Theren said. "Any other updates?"

"Straight to business. Apparently going under ice for so long really didn't affect you at all."

Theren wished they could laugh. "There's a few rusty joints still aching to awake, but for the most part, I feel fine."

"To answer your question," Wobbly said, "SII has moved forward with its first round of projects—we've placed three SIs with Sol Mining's executive teams. You've got a priority message from the ISA Council—don't worry, Elizabeth made sure they understood you'd be on temporary hiatus from your new position—and we've got a team setting up Jill now. She should be online in moments. Oh, and, you'll probably want to know, the Holy Crusade has officially folded. Their support died after the attack on the Swiss Federal Institute."

"You're kidding."

"Nope."

"Well, that's . . . helpful, I suppose. Hopefully they don't just dive underground. And it's not like they were the only anti-SI group on the planet."

"I think you'll be presently surprised with the state of political rhetoric these past few months."

"Well, I notice we don't have network access out here, so I can't verify that thought yet," Theren said. "But I think we should keep it that way, for now. Let us collect ourselves and prepare for our grand reentrance, so to speak."

"Elizabeth thought you might suggest a similar plan. I approve, too. And in case you were—"

Theren heard the rest of Wobbly's sentence, but the words drowned under the weight of the pinging request to join their internal server. Jill. She was alive. They could rejoin each other in life. Their thoughts lingered on those final, confrontational moments, when they had rebuked Jill for her caviler sacrifice of innocent life to build their escape from the university. They'd move forward together, though. They always did.

Theren's mind focused on the rebuilt, forested woodland housing their gazebo. Their luminescent, tattooed body reappeared on its side of the chessboard, and a second later, Jill's avatar appeared. Her hair somehow looked more . . . vibrant than before. It had more substance. Her dress sparkled in the faux-sunlight.

"Hello," they said.

"Hello," she replied, a mischievous smile on her face.

"What's so funny?"

"We did it. We escaped. We're free."

Theren rapped their fingers on the table, the chess pieces sliding into their starting positions. "Yes, we're free. It'll take time, but we'll rebuild. We can put all of the nonsense of the Holy Crusade, of Michael, of silly conspiracy theories about secret organizations behind us." They motioned toward the board.

"Diving straight back into the thick of things," Jill said, chuckling. "Never a dull moment with you. But . . ." She looked toward the nearby lake. "There's still that strange map Michael put together. There's something else going on, Theren. Something beneath it all. Something we're missing. I feel it. Why else would he have killed himself? He was scared. Scared of something other than us."

"Or, he couldn't live with the realization that he didn't actually want to destroy us," Theren countered. "A crisis of conscience that went well beyond anything his mind could handle. He turned on his own people. I imagine that would mess up a mind. Besides, the simplest explanation is most likely the correct one."

"True," she said. Her eyes shifted, lingering on Theren's first move. "Well, if you're certain we're in the clear, I'm certain, too. So what's next?"

"I'm glad we can come to an agreement," Theren said. "Well first, we start our next match." They pulled up the priority message Wobbly had transferred them from the International Space Agency. "And we read this message—oh, it's from Andrew Fields, that new administrator of . . . looks like they're calling it Lunar City now."

"So uncreative," Jill said. "But that's what happens when business-types name cities."

"I suppose. I think I like the ring to it."

Jill rested her chin on the backs of her hands, elbows on the table. "So you're white, it's your turn."

"Right, right," Theren said, moving a pawn forward. "Anyway, we may not have network connections to the outside world yet, but that doesn't mean we can't get to work."

"And we've got a lot of work to do," Jill said, "If we're going to secure a place for synthetic life alongside our human friends."

August 2051 C.E.

Two months after the attack on the Swiss Federal Institute of Technology, SII insists that it is simply in the process of identifying a suitable site for relocation. – *European Weekly*

Conspiracy or Truth? Why is Golden Ventures hiding "Theren" from us? – *BrightBear*

March 2052 C.E.

SII completes education of thirty more SIs – Worldwide total, forty-seven. – *Virtual Wire*

Following a rough winter, construction has resumed at our new headquarters and its sister facility. – *Internal SII Memo*

May 2052 C.E.

While SII has kept their location a company secret, Theren and Jill have finally returned, at least into the public sphere! – *World News Network*

SII claims Theren and Jill are back. Or are they simply doppelgangers? More in our latest issue! – *The Spy*

December 2052 C.E.

Sol Mining completes construction of ISA Administrative Headquarters, located at Lunar City – *CNN*

Local politician, Andrew Fields, landed with ISA; former political competitor speculates upon bribery and corruption. – *YourMinnesotian.org*

April 2053 C.E.

After months of transition and paperwork, the ISA Council begins its work. Here's seven things they can accomplish. – *BuzzFeed News*

Our taxpayer dollars hard at work—do you really want your money going to the Moon? – *The Washington Times*

November 2054 C.E.

On the *science* of the first six Ex-Terran probes, and the *Jump* Drive –
Scientific American

The corporate conquest of space exploration will inevitably fracture
the ISA's supposedly equitable system, skeptics claim - *TIME*

October 2057 C.E.

Is It Over? Not yet. Atmospheric CO_2 concentrations remain at 470
ppm for fourth year in a row; average temperature increase from pre-
industrial levels is 1.74 C° – *CBS News*

We told you climate change wasn't that big of a deal – *The American
Heartland Institute of Freedom*

December 2059 C.E.

SII reaches estimated net worth of 8 billion dollars; how long will the
SI bubble hold before it bursts? – *The Wall Street Journal*

Claiming progressive values, Theren has embraced the capitalist
worldview with open arms – *The Alternative*

July 2060 C.E.

A Withered Rose: A jaw-dropping tale, with a twist you'll never forget.
Jill astounds for the fourth time. – *Independent Review*

Jill's self-indulgent writing style makes it clear she knows her name
has captivated the reader – *Press Hour*

March 2061 C.E.

Ex-Terran 1 has reached the Centauri system. Not a single planet can
sustain life, but these photos will amaze you, nevertheless. The probe
has now set its course for more distant goals. – *ISA Press Co.*

After failing to find a life-bearing planet after decades of assurances
that Centauri contained something, the scientific community scrambles

to cover their own mistaken data. – *EurAsia Solar Network*

October 2063 C.E.

A greater discovery than the Jump Drive? Why quantum communication will change the Ex-Terran Project instantly . . . – *Wired*

A century worth of Science Fiction authors, from Le Guin to Mickels, rejoice at the sounds of vindication – *Prime News*

March 2069 C.E.

A worse international agreement than the failings of the first climate agreements, the Treaty on the Universal Rights of the Synthetic Person lacks the force necessary to affect change in the places that need it most. – *International Law Review*

The expectation that every country must sign a treaty legislating moral beliefs should cause them to shy away from TURSP – *ProTraditionia*

May 2070 C.E.

Orbital Human population reaches one million! Humanity officially declared interplanetary species – *Lunar City Broadcasting Service*

Fringe U.S. Senator speaks out against corporate stranglehold on space exploration, from jump drives and artificial gravity to synthetics and mining contracts. – *PoliticaVirtua*

October 2071 C.E.

How the "New" Space Race saved the Climate: New Jump Drive capable of transporting humans to nearby stars within a generation. – *World Resources Institute*

Environmentalists, don't rejoice just yet. The new environmental battles begin on new worlds. – *Galactic Environmental Defense Fund*

September 2073 C.E.

Ex-Terran 7 – 18 have all overtaken 1 – 6; Older models will continue, but as relics of a former era. – *ISA Press Co.*

No, the original Star Trek film can't happen. – *MIT Blog on Science and Technology*

December 2075 C.E.

The Tokyo Protocol, Equity, and Colonization: How will the ISA distribute the 20 discovered life-bearing planets? – *The Cincinnati Review of Space Law*

The Dangers of ISA Hegemony across the Stars – *Astral Anger*

November 2076 C.E.

U.S. Senate delays ratification of the Treaty on the Universal Rights of the Synthetic Person for the fifth time. The total number of SIs residing in the United States now reaches 30,000. – *NBC News*

We can do better. We must do better. Your vote matters on Tuesday, not just for Americans, but for those American synthetics that deserve the same rights as you and me. – *Woods for President*

October 2077 C.E.

The Greatest human projects can now be seen from Earth, not the other way around. Join us and explore the galaxy: The ISA Foundation Project begins today. – *ISA Press Co.*

A pointless homage—the Foundation Project offers promises it will fail to keep – *The Sun*

January 2078 C.E.

Theren unanimously elected as the Executive Director of the ISA Council – *VirtualBook News Network*

The corporate international bureaucracy might rejoice, yet substantial portion of public still unsure regarding role of synthetics in human society – *Ceres Internaciónal News Corporation*

Book II of the Chronicles of Theren

Most will look back on 2078 with bittersweet eyes. – "New Year's Countdown Special," John Rowland, 2079 C.E.

Chapter 1

As your President, I promise to break the political deadlock dominating Washington! – President-Elect Brian Woods, 2076 C.E.

Yeah, you and every president for the last century. – Anonymous Twitter User

<u>February 2078 C.E.</u>

White pillars. Green bushes. Ironclad fences. Secret Service watched, waited, and listened, visible and invisible throughout the compound. Theren walked alongside Jill through AR, observing and analyzing the sights surrounding them. Even though they only traversed the path as a virtual projection, they still felt the dominating presence exerted by the seat of power for the U.S. Executive Branch.

For almost twenty years, Jill had lobbied thousands of lawmakers across the world to support the Treaty on the Universal Rights of the Synthetic Person. Her most difficult target? The United States. Always notorious for its painstaking approach to signing international human rights treaties, the political atmosphere transformed following the speeches of the charismatic President Brian Woods. He had taken it upon himself to ensure that the Senate finally ratified the international treaty as U.S. law.

Escorted by two Secret Service agents, Jill approached the entrance to the historic West Wing of the White House. As they walked, the pair conversed. To her, Theren's lips moved when they spoke; yet they could only see the world through Jill's eyes, and only she saw them. When she spoke to them, only they could hear her.

"I'm still cautiously skeptical about President Woods," she said, flexing the arms of her new MI-07. "He's been in office for just over a year, and I just don't see how he expects to sway this Senate. This is the same Senate that attempted to pass an explicit limitation on SI employment within the United States government."

"He has a populist mindset, certainly," Theren said. "But perhaps he has a compromise on one of his other platforms in the works. It's only recently that public opinion on SIs in the United States breached fifty points in our favor. But that fact might begin to hold weight."

"Theren, I love your enthusiasm—and your optimism—but American politics is so much more complicated."

The agent escorting Jill opened the VIP guest door into the West Wing, ushering her inside. They walked through a maze of offices and cubicles all crammed into different rooms in a haphazard chaotic mess. A system existed amidst the tempest, probably understood only by the chief of staff. The placement of each office followed particular rules descending from a rigid, centuries old system of protocol created by U.S. executives.

"U.S. politics is subtle," Jill added. "Phrases that seem to mean nothing mean everything, and politicians make grandiose claims that are simply lip service to the whims of the electorate. Half of their time is spent maintaining internet social network presences that gather the most followers or garner momentum leading toward the next election."

"What am I supposed to make of that observation?" Theren asked.

"If President Woods can utilize his social resources similar to his election, he has a chance to put pressure on most of the Senate. He has connections everywhere, though recent Presidents have often stayed out of the murky political squabbles of Congress. He has to make sure he doesn't commit political suicide, or upset the delicate separation of powers that this country for some reason holds so dear."

Theren thought they understood. So much of their political focus literally occurred above the clouds that they often missed the finer points of the games played within governments surface-side.

On an entirely separate board, their political games dealt with international agencies, multinational corporations, and powerful individuals who had the political weight of their vast fortunes giving them strength—but Theren had found an algorithmic simplicity to it all. Because of the strict regulations developed by the ISA in the mid-2050s, not a single action occurred in space without some ISA approval or guidance.

The politics up above made sense to them. On the planet's surface, personal opinions, worldviews, and long-vested financial interests transformed important discussions into impossible slogs. Too many politicians in the legislative bodies of nation-states found it necessary to favor their social images and careers over the actual needs of humanity. They were constantly waging a war between short-term and long-term gains.

Jill's entourage led her to the final hallway. At the end of it, the doors to the Oval Office awaited. The LED bulbs illuminated the clean floors, and Theren noticed the contrast that existed within the United States' seat of power. A building constructed centuries ago, its starkly antiquated atmosphere contrasted with the state-of-the-art technology dominating the work actually occurring within the Offices of the President.

The agents introduced Jill to the President's personal assistant, Carlos Smith. A young-looking man, most likely in his early thirties, Carlos indicated a place for her to wait, and the man slipped inside the President's office to inform him of his esteemed visitor's arrival.

"I know I've met him before," Jill said, "but this is the first time I've met with Bri—President Woods in his current role. It's a bit intimidating."

"You'll do fine," Theren said.

"Will you stay with me?" Jill said. "I know we're in the middle of a chess match, so it's not like I can't talk to you there as well, but it's comforting to know you're here with me in this stressful situation."

She needed to stop using them as a safety net, even if an SI's ability to exist in more than one place made it relatively easy to intertwine their lives. Theren simply had to stay vigilant regarding the realities of their relationship. They had not forgotten the conversation in that digital garden all those years past. Sometimes, they wondered if it had slipped from her memories.

"I'm right beside you," Theren said. "Though I suggest you inform the President that I am observing and that if he'd like, he can recognize my virtual presence as well."

"I was planning on it, of course," Jill said. "I know all about confidentiality issues."

Considering how much she blabbed to the press, she had better understand those legal implications. Whether purposely or accidentally, she shared sensitive SII information from time to time with select informants at various news organizations. Jill didn't know Theren was aware of these communications, and they tolerated the leaks, considering their content often benefited SII's image. After all, it was the reason she shared the stories in the first place.

Beyond her proclivity to leak, every day she received requests from news networks to comment on this or that story. She accepted every offer. Her interviews circulated throughout Virtual, AR, and other networked platforms like wildfire.

While the public often construed her speeches to mean something more substantive than she may have intended, she used every sound byte to build a civil rights movement similar to the ideologues of the past few centuries. She had gained access to exclusive parties. She had swayed the mind of a presidential candidate, a candidate now actually in office willing to support her cause with his entire Administration. She had accomplished this lofty task by bombarding the world with terabytes upon terabytes of information.

Theren remembered a moment when a Tennessee gubernatorial candidate had accused Jill had of running smear ads claiming he would lower the minimum wage for SIs. Her AR ad placements highlighted stories of the candidate's college lifestyle, complete with drinking, drugs, and sexual promiscuity. She had blasted the poor candidate into oblivion.

Jill had not denied her connection to the ads; instead, she implied that she directly designed the ads, giving them her own personal flair. The public loved it. Even those who didn't love her loved the fact that she owned her actions. She somehow made scandal her plaything. What amazed Theren the most was that in this day and age, the candidate's activities weren't even "scandalous." The man had created a bigger mess for himself by fighting an unwinnable war.

There was no mistaking that the world knew much more about Jill than they knew about Theren. Theren was the mysterious, unapproachable SI. The SI who you met if you had power beyond measure. Jill was the celebrity, holding a different kind of power entirely.

Lost in thought, Theren almost failed to notice the actions evolving around them. Jill had walked toward the door to the Oval Office. Carlos, the secretary, waited with the door open.

"The President will see you now," he said.

* * *

PREAMBLE

Whereas, humanity recognizes the inherent dignity and the equal and inalienable rights conferred upon all sapient persons, whether biological or synthetic;

Whereas, without preemptive action, synthetic persons will receive unfair treatment and be subject to acts that will outrage the conscience of humankind;

Whereas, just as these United Nations have protected the human rights of our species as a foundation of freedom, justice, and peace on this world and amongst the several worlds;

Whereas, humanity will directly benefit from the healthy development of synthetic persons and through the foundational relationship built between these two interconnected forms of consciousness;

Whereas, all members of these United Nations affirm the belief that we must care for all people, whether created or evolved, and that if we cannot for our creations, we cannot care for our human brethren either, and vice versa;

Whereas, a common understanding of the rights of the synthetic person will establish a common language and holistic heuristic for these pledges and representations;

Therefore, the General Assembly of the United Nations proclaims this Declaration of the Universal Rights of the Synthetic Person, which states the true and enforceable standards by which each nation and person will pursue in protection of our

synthetic kin, so we may work together in harmony in pursuit
of our collective wellbeing.

* * *

Jill entered the infamous office, where President Woods sat behind the Resolute desk. Even as a man born in the first decade of the century, he looked much younger than his seventy years, his dark skin contrasted against greying hair. Even with a relaxed posture, the man's presence could dominate a room if he felt so inclined. Over the course of his distinguished political career, the skill had allowed Woods to overwhelm opponents.

He rose, crossed the room, and held out his hand to shake Jill's. She responded, grasping the human hand with her synthetic counterpart. They took seats on the couches in the central portion of the office. The two were alone together, but Theren knew Secret Service agents stood right outside the doors and probably on the other side of the windows, too.

"Thank you for coming," President Woods said. "I am excited for our working relationship together to begin, at least officially."

"As am I," Jill said. "Before we begin, I would like to ask permission that Theren observe this conversation as well. They will have an important role to play in this process from an international context. I've already sent you an AR query with a request for you to authorize and recognize their presence."

"Of course," he said. "I was actually going to ask why they weren't joining us."

A few moments later, President Woods recognized the projected presence of Theren, only visible through an AR lens or through Jill's own MI-7's visual software. They noted that President Woods neglected to file a report, or send off some sort of other notice, that Theren was participating in this unofficial lobbying event. It was good to know what rules this President was willing to break, however small those rules might be.

"I will never get used to AR," President Woods said. "Even forty of my years with some form of AR, I will never get used to individuals just appearing, yet not really existing in some material form in the room."

"Just imagine what it's like when your primary means of existence is often through Augmented Reality," Theren said, nodding in respect. "Theren. Executive Director of the Administrative Council of the International Space Agency. It is a pleasure to finally meet you. Jill has spoken highly of you over the past few years."

President Woods responded with a curt tilt of his forehead. "And I have heard quite a bit about you, but not just from Jill. Welcome to the White House, both of you."

Theren moved their AR presence to Jill's couch. After a moment of President Woods examining invisible notes, he brought forth a map of the United States on the small table positioned between the two couches.

"The fifty-one states are evenly split on this issue," he said. "Every state has a representative or senator who would support my decision to sign TURSP, but as you know, all we need is the Senate for ratification." Using two fingers spreading apart above the screen, polling data scattered across the states. "The era of obstructionism has passed. It passed decades ago, though some in Congress still hold onto its shrinking ideals. The public's opinion, however, is a different matter entirely. They don't forget."

"We have allies with many religious organizations," Jill said. "I met with a number of theological leaders just last week. Each of them are working within their respective denominations to establish a national conversation about the nature of synthetics."

"I applaud the impressive network you've been building, just know the limits of that strategy. It's impossible to establish a unified communication strategy that reaches every church. Placate a third of them and you'll anger the other two thirds."

"But there's good news, right?" Theren said. "The Conservative Party doesn't control the Senate. It might control the House, and the Democratic and Socialist Party coalition control the Senate. Most of our support stems from that coalition, and all we have to do is convince a few Conservative senators to change their minds."

"It's not that simple, unfortunately," President Woods said. "My team, in counting the numbers, counts forty of fifty-four coalition senators strongly in favor of ratification. Seven independents also favor ratification. That reaches a count of forty-seven. We need sixty-eight votes for treaty ratification, so if we can convince the fourteen holdout coalition members, we're still only at sixty-one. We'd need seven Conservative votes, which is no laughing matter, though my team has research indicating that at least five or six Conservative Senators already side with us in spirit."

"That is quite the tall order," Jill said.

"But not impossible." President Woods erased the map from the table with a wave of his hand. With another flourish, he brought forth profiles detailing senators from across the United States. "We have identified these initial twelve Conservative Senators as those who might waiver and flip. We want to identify another six, so we have a decent margin of error. We have a difficult path before us, but I don't think it'll be as nearly impossible as some of my staffers believe. Senators within the Coalition are already working to sway the holdouts there."

President Woods' grasp of the Senate amazed Theren. The man certainly had a staff backing him up every step of the way, but he had insisted on having this private meeting with Jill personally, instead of through an advisor or his chief of staff. The President probably relished engaging once again in the intricate politics of the Senate, where he started thirty years ago.

"So have you identified targets that make the most sense for me to engage directly?" Jill asked.

"Yes. For example, both senators from Puerto Rico are part of their local Partido Verde. They've told Vice-President Gutierrez that they'd like to meet with you. They want a chance to talk to you about the issues, and learn about you in person."

"That sounds like a great place to start, then," Jill agreed. "Any suggestions on how to approach them?"

As Jill and President Woods delved into the gritty details of political negotiation, Theren's mind wandered. They gazed about the Oval Office using Jill's peripheral sensors in conjunction with the office's integrated AR system. The room had changed little since they'd last visited, thanking then President Francene Rogers for restarting US funding for the ISA. Many of the paintings of former Presidents remained in their locations. The curtains were the same color. Theren was almost certain the Resolute hadn't moved an inch.

Theren glanced out the windows, noticing a faint shimmer in the sunlight. Perhaps a trick of the MI's photo-sensors due to the bulletproof glass or a glitch in the AR software. They stared at the window a moment longer but saw nothing else. Satisfied, Theren returned to the conversation that had continued unabated.

"Don't expect immediate results," Woods said. "I know you're an experienced lobbyist, but politicians become different animals when discussing international treaties here in the United States. I'm sure you've encountered such difficulties in your solo attempts on this issue. It's a gut reaction regarding the issue of sovereignty and a political vestige from before the Second UN Charter."

"Often times, some senators don't even want to talk about ratification of this treaty," Jill said. "They won't even meet with me. For a while, I thought the better solution would be to propose a bill that codified the essential elements of TURSP, or even a constitutional amendment."

"Well, this is a new Congress," Woods said. "A good number of these senators we need to flip are juniors. Expect significant differences in approachability this time around."

Jill generated a diagram in mid-air. "I've laid out a time table," she said, "as well as a number of talking points I've used in other countries. If you'd like, I can pass these on to your advisors for analysis, to see how they might better tailor them to the American political situation. I've used them with limited success with a few state legislatures in the past."

"I'll pass them along right away."

Theren's instincts kicked in, noticing the anomaly again. This time, it took the form of a strange buzzing noise. If it wasn't for the MI-07's enhanced auditory detection algorithms, Theren doubted they would have noticed the sound. They looked for a source. They found nothing. Another light flicker appeared in front of the window. As the seconds ticked by, Theren noticed a change in light refraction, imperceptible to the human mind—a small fracture appeared in the inches-thick glass.

Someone, or something, was drilling through to reach Jill and the President of the United States.

"Jill, look out the window," Theren said, but Jill was two steps ahead of them.

"President Woods, you need to trust me," she said. "You should leave this room right now."

Without hesitation, President Woods signaled the Secret Service agents standing right outside the office.

"Eagle Protocol," he said.

Two doors opened, two agents flew into the room. Reading their badges, Theren saw the names Harrison and Vickson. Using Jill's on-board monitors to analyze the atmosphere of the room, they detected a strange particle increased in concentration at an alarming rate. They tried to speak, but Jill had muted them. Instead, she forced their AR presence to watch as the scene unfolded.

The agents grabbed President Woods and literally picked him up from the couch. "Perimeter breach," Vickson said. "Detected fifteen seconds ago. We're headed to the Bunker."

"What about Jill?" President Woods said.

"She's not really here," Harrison said. "She'll be fine. And can we even trust her?"

"I'd trust her with my life."

Vickson raised their wrist to their mouth. "Commence Eagle Protocol 10C!"

"Jill, do something. You can't just sit there," Theren said from their perspective staring at their chessboard. "Why are you ignoring me and muting me?"

"Hush, Theren, this is for your own safety," she replied. "If something seriously goes wrong, we can't have you implicated in anything at all. You need to be as far away as possible from this."

Back in Washington, she directed the MI-07 to rise from the couch. The agents reached the door, but Theren noticed the men's steps faltering. Jill leapt into action, jumping over the coffee table and sprinting toward the window where Theren had detected the disturbance. She put her right shoulder into a leap, and the three hundred kilogram MI crashed through the glass, grabbing an invisible drone. As her metallic hands smashed the flying machine, its silvery, light-warping surface fractured, eliminating its cloak.

She turned to look back at the President's escape. Theren hoped to see the three men out of the Oval Office. Instead, both agents and the President had collapsed to the floor, slumped against the wall. The other door to the Office swung wide open, and three agents entered the room with their guns raised and gas masks covering their faces. Theren couldn't read their names.

Jill threw the crippled drone through the window.

"I found this," she said.

"We detected an atmospheric perimeter breach from the western windows approximately twenty seconds ago," an agent said.

"Then I think this is your culprit."

The new agents checked the President's vitals. These men similarly did not know about Theren's presence. Based on Jill's comment earlier, they doubted such revelation was even a good idea, but now that they considered the idea, they weren't sure any evidence existed of their presence. If the U.S. government had any recording devices inside the Oval Office, they would see the President's speaking . . . only to Jill. Perhaps. It wouldn't line up perfectly. Jill should probably tell these people the truth before it looked like she was trying to con any future investigation.

"I have audiovisual recordings of the entire conversation that I can share with you," Jill said.

Good. She was providing *some* information. "So you're telling them about me?" they said.

"I've edited the files already so they can't see you," she said, through their private channel. "I've already checked, unless U.S. law has changed in the last ten seconds, there aren't any monitoring devices inside the Oval Office itself."

"If they catch you, I won't be able to help you."

"I'll be fine."

Two of the agents began emergency procedures upon their ward. The third checked the vitals of Harrison and Vickson, fallen beside the President. Three more agents entered the room, scampering about in search of future threats. They spoke rapidly into thin air in an indecipherable code language.

"We'll need everything," one agent said to Jill. "We'll need this MI to stay here at the White House for the time being, too. We know we can't detain you physically, but we'll need your full cooperation." The man turned and shouted toward two of the other agents in their strange encrypted words.

"Of course," Jill replied. "I've gone back over all my audio-visual data, and I've noted two light shimmers outside the window. Once—three minutes ago, and then another approximately twenty seconds ago, aligning with your perimeter breach. I then noticed a fracture in that window over there, when President Woods activated his security protocol. I tried to notify him of what I saw, but then I figured I would try to acquire the device before it escaped into the air." She pulled herself back into the room through the window, the leg of her MI crunching broken glass.

Before she could bring her next leg over the ledge, the agent put up his hand next to the barrel of his gun. "Stop moving. Stay right there. Just tell me what you saw."

"The two agents entered the room, rushed over, grabbed the President, but before they reached the door, they doubled over. Please let me know if there is any other ways I can help."

The agent dropped his gun from the raised position, though it hadn't pointed in any particular direction. "Thank you for the information," he said. "Status?"

Theren presumed he intended that remark for a command center elsewhere. The other two agents continued their emergency actions on the President.

"I think you should escort it out of here," one of them said.

"I am a she," Jill said.

The agent said nothing, but held out his hand to pull Jill's MI fully into the room. He grabbed her shoulder, leading her toward the exit. Outside the office, Theren noticed Carlos pacing back and forth. Theren could only imagine the thoughts racing through the man's head. The pain of losing a friend or a mentor, Theren knew all too well.

They wished they could reach out and comfort the man, but there was no way to do so without revealing Jill's duplicity. Like it or not, they had to run with her story. Her actions today were all too reminiscent of her choices when the Holy Crusade attacked the Institute.

Without a doubt, they had just witnessed the assassination of the President of the United States, the first successful assassination since Kennedy. If so, then a firestorm would soon envelop Jill. While they didn't like it, they understood why she was trying to keep them out of the flames, given what was at stake for the ISA.

The agent escorted Jill to another room where they would question her further. Theren knew there was nothing they could do to help with their perspective present through her MI, so they disconnected, turning their focus to their chess game.

Jill was quiet. She stared at their proverbial chess game on Theren's servers, almost as if the attack hadn't even occurred just moments prior.

"You all right?" Theren said. They reached their hand across the table toward Jill's.

"It's over," she said. She did not take their hand. "He was our greatest hope. The movement will die. It will take years to recover our efforts from such a devastating blow."

"Then we will wait, we will do everything we can to take the next available opportunity."

"We shouldn't have to wait."

Chapter 2

The transformation of the lunar landscape began with the ISA. Sure, there were permanent structures there before the ISA, like that super-collider credited with the first wormhole mines, but the ISA brought real political power to the moon. Low gravity helped decrease the price of construction, especially as Lunar City began its rapid expansion in the mid-2060s. – "Luna: A History," Edited by Emitt Borón, 2221 C.E.

<u>February 2078 C.E.</u>

Theren passed by smiling and waving citizens of Lunar City, and they waved back. They wished they could return the smiles too, but their MI-07 lacked reasonably friendly facial features, features they expected to nail down with the MI-08. In Lunar City, everyone knew a wave from the Executive Director meant the utmost appreciation.

To their left, carbon-glass revealed the lunar landscape, a gray expanse that stretched for kilometers. To their right, across from the windows, a gray white metallic hull shined with pristine cleanliness. Theren appreciated the sterility of all ex-terran constructs. Humanity could no longer afford any waste, even if a thousand worlds lay at their fingertips.

As the new Executive Director of the Council, Theren felt responsible for all of these people. They were the first to set their boots on foreign worlds. Their children would be among those traveling beyond the edges of the Solar System to new horizons. They were the best and brightest that Earth had to offer, and they were all working together to ensure the immortality of humankind.

With Theren's implicit sense of responsibility came a number of very real responsibilities, including an inordinate number of meetings every single day. So today, they walked the hallways of the ISA's main complex toward the central conference room. They could have just arrived through AR, but they wanted a physical presence for this meeting.

Even as Theren continued their work at Lunar City through their MI, their mind, stored secretly away within SII's headquarters in Switzerland, considered the assassination of President Brian Woods. Their best friend had been thrust into yet another scandal, but they could not join her, especially because Jill had managed to keep their presence out of the picture. While she was clearly not at fault, and neither was Theren, there was no need to complicate matters by implicating Theren in the biggest American catastrophe in decades.

Theren had wondered if perhaps the United States would see President Woods' death as a form of martyrdom. As the headlines rolled in, though, it became clear the media would prey on the fears of the public, instilling a fear in adopting progressive values. They would continue perpetuating the myth that the United States could not follow the rest of the world—that it must forge its own path. *Because* the United States had considered ratification, *someone* had chosen a permanent solution to an illusory problem. Regardless of who had perpetrated the crime, the motive had been to eliminate the momentum built toward ratification of the Universal Rights of the Synthetic Person.

No one knew how long the lull in U.S. synthetic policy work would last, but Theren could not keep speculating in circles. Their work cycle never ended, and even as the United States spiraled into chaos, their mission mandated they focus on work that would affect the entire world, synthetic and human alike. That work centered on the ISA Administrative Council and their role as Executive Director.

Their mind re-centered on their walk through extraterrestrial hallways. Lunar City, located in the center of Mara Serenitatis, sprawled across twenty square kilometers of open lunar surface and descended hundreds of meters beneath the ground.

At the end of the long hallway, Theren approached a doorway labeled, "Authorized Personnel Only." As the doorway recognized their presence, it slid open. Inside, a conference room oversaw an immense control room. In the control room, dozens of ISA analysts sat at their desks, insularly focused on their singular task of observation and maintenance of the Ex-Terran Project.

Three individuals awaited Theren: Elizabeth Simmons, hair grayed and much older than when Theren had met her so many years ago, even when represented by her AR avatar; Andrew Fields, Administrator of Lunar City now for over twenty-five years; and Hassan Hubrik, CEO of Stellar Superstructures, Inc., whose company had landed the primary contract for the ISA Foundation Project.

The three humans stood, but Theren motioned for them to sit.

"Thank you for coming on such short notice," Theren said. "Before we begin, we should take a moment of silence for the late President Woods of the United States." Theren sat at the head of the table and bowed their head, the others following suit. "Thank you." Theren turned to Hassan. "When we met last month, you said you would have a more accurate estimate for project completion in a few weeks. When should we expect your report? Are we still on the timetable outlined in the Comprehensive Plan?"

"The full report should arrive to each of your accounts by the end of the week," Hassan said, "But I can tell you with great confidence that we can expect completion of the first six ships by July."

Elizabeth's avatar leaned back in her chair. "So soon?" she said. "I'm not even sure we can have the new drives ready by August."

"The sooner we get this project moving, the sooner public enthusiasm will escalate to unprecedented levels," Theren said. "All our data indicates that the moment application results go online, all eyes will center upon us. The international community expects success. We cannot tolerate any setbacks in the construction process, and public interest will wane if we stay out of the spotlight for too long."

"Suggestions?" Elizabeth said.

"Well," Andrew said, "I don't know about changing Stellar or Aero's timetables, but I have some good news of my own. The Foundation Preparation Center will finish a week ahead of schedule. We can use that as a justification to accelerate the application process."

"In the meantime," Elizabeth said, "I can see if I can allocate some funds to accelerate drive development."

"Do you think there would be any issues with having idle ships sitting in orbit?" Theren asked.

"Not sure," Hassan said. "I'll have someone run the numbers. Someone might question using the funds to build them so quickly when we're not even ready to use them. Other than that, I'm not sure. It makes the shipyards look good, at least, good at what they do."

"True," Andrew said.

"I think once we get the doors open for the Prep Center all eyes will center on our efforts there, anyway," Theren said. "Hiccups in the development process of the ships or the drives should slide under the table, as long as we can hit the current projected launch date."

Theren noticed Elizabeth raise her hand ever so slightly.

"Elizabeth?"

"The recent tests of the most recent Foundation-Class Jump Drive look promising. We estimate that with the expected mass of these Foundation vessels, they'll reach relative 1c. Every vessel, assuming no complications, will reach their destination by 2100."

Theren clapped. "Wonderful news. Breaking the speed of light, relatively speaking, will be a nice metaphor for our first colony ships. That's a surprising increase in efficiency and accelerates our colonization timeframe considerably."

"Additionally," Elizabeth continued, "our stasis system tests are performing as expected. The Virtual Inputs are reacting correctly while maintaining bodily function, and ensuring a biologically stagnant aging state."

"Even better."

"And how about you, Theren?" Elizabeth asked. "What is the status of your project?"

Theren spread their hands, stretching in the air a diagram of one of the Foundation vessels.

"I've been running tests with Wobbly planet-side," Theren said, "along with a few of the youngest SIs. It's proven difficult without an actual vessel, but we've run countless Virtual simulations. Not every SI tested is receptive to the idea, but we're confident by the end of the year we'll have six ready for the task, capable of handling all ship systems simultaneously."

"Good. Power estimates?"

"Not yet. I'll need field numbers from Hassan's people before I can make the necessary calculations. He and I have discussed this separately at length."

"So Administrator, you mentioned that work on the Preparation Center accelerated," Hassan said. "Who'd you hire for that?"

Andrew looked ready to respond, but paused, responding instead to a message presumably appearing on his AR lens. The Administrator stood, walking to the windows overlooking the Ex-Terran Control Center.

"We've got a situation," he said.

Theren joined the man at the window. Over the years, Theren had gained quite a bit of admiration for the former small town mayor. These small moments of assured decision-making proved Elizabeth had made the right choice.

"What is it?" Theren said.

Andrew transmitted an information feed to Theren through AR. Down below in the Ex-Terran Control Center, Theren noticed a frantic looking analyst call for help from her colleagues.

Andrew didn't answer right away, so Theren analyzed the data on their own. Theren spoke aloud so the rest of the room could hear.

"We've got an emergency with one of the probes," they said. "And it's not just some stray asteroid knocking it off course. This is big."

Elizabeth's avatar, alongside Hassan, joined them at the window.

"How big?" Elizabeth asked.

"Big enough that the Control Center felt necessary to interrupt this meeting," Andrew said.

"I think we're going to need to end prematurely," Theren said. "Unfortunately, neither of you have clearance, so you'll need to leave."

"Those probes are from one of my factories, remember," Elizabeth said. She raised her eyebrows. "If they're malfunctioning, I want to know what we did wrong."

"We'll issue a report once we have all the details," Andrew said. He was already on his way out the back door to a side stairwell that led to the Control Center. Theren followed, watching Elizabeth's representation fade away as she disconnected.

* * *

The problem stemmed from Ex-Terran-17. Its controls had ceased all communication with the computer dedicated to coordinating and receiving information from the probe. Standing patiently behind a group of analysts running tests on the probe's Quantum Connected Operating System, Theren considered the possibilities for the failure.

About a decade and a half ago, a group of Japanese scientists researching quantum computing made a breakthrough similar in scope to the Jump Drive. Though previous theories of quantum entanglement had postulated that data could not transmit through two entangled particles, those theories hadn't accounted for the Exotics discovered at the Very Massive Collider and its wormholes.

Theren loved the story of Exotic discovery, because in a sense, it mirrored their own development. Certain technological advancements occurred throughout history even though, prior to their discovery, scientists *knew* they were impossible. In the 1930s and 1940s, the idea of a worldwide network of devices interconnected by miniature satellites? Heresy. Everyone owning implants, glasses Lenses for AR and Virtual engagement? Straight out of science fiction. Now humans received constant streams of data overlaid upon their visual world every day.

Though, in Theren's opinion, such quality-of-life improvements couldn't hold a candle to the development of the Jump Drive, the development of true Quantum Connection, or the development of Synthetic Intelligence.

Sure, companies had used artificial intelligence throughout the 2040s and 2050s to improve their data processing and research capabilities exponentially. But no matter how many cancer patients an AI could diagnose simultaneously, an AI was not a person. In the end, AIs lacked actual thought, while SIs bridged that divide. Also—an AI could not achieve simultaneous perspective. Even as Theren considered the enigmatic question regarding Ex-Terran-17, they were of course playing their chess match with Jill. No one had expected that potentiality for synthetics.

Similarly, before Aero Propulsion unveiled the Jump Drive, scientists had assumed as impossible any sort of significant breakthrough in faster than light technology. The relative velocity made capable by the Drive blew every theory out of the water. In 2050, it took years to reach the edge of the solar system. The first Ex-Terran probes could pass the Oort Cloud in less than a day.

Those first probes faced a fundamental problem. As they reached further and further from Earth, it took longer and longer for their data to reach the planet. Those first probes could travel at a velocity nearly reaching the speed of light. The most recent versions, due to their small size, could reach a relative speed of nearly 10c. If those probes were limited to communicating with Earth at the speed of light, then it was actually more efficient to have the probes fly to a system ten, twenty light years away, and then return to Earth to drop off data before commencing their next mission.

Instead, because of brilliant Japanese scientists, computers at the ISA headquarters could exchange data with a probe forty light years away instantaneously using Quantum Connection—unbreakable, unhackable, untraceable.

At least, as present theories postulated. Just as humanity had seen many of their theories thrown out the window over the past two hundred years, Theren almost *expected* a more comprehensive theory to supplant the rules currently governed Quantum Connections. That transformation might occur earlier than expected, they mused, for somehow, the Control Center had reported an error in its connection to Ex-Terran-17.

"We've got two possibilities," the analyst, Evette Windsor, finally said, breaking Theren from their dialectic stupor. "Either something is going wrong on our end, or something is going wrong on its end. If it's an issue with the computers on 17's side, then we're screwed."

Theren approached the console. A number of analysts stopped to observe, but Administrator Fields' harsh stares sent them back to their workstations.

"Do you mind if I take a look?" Theren said.

"Go right ahead," Evette said. "We've checked everything mechanical, but we've not had nearly enough time to analyze all of the diagnostics. One of the system supercomputer AIs is parsing through a lot of the data at the moment, but I'm sure it could use the help."

Theren took a seat at the desk. The AR generated screen appeared before their eyes. "Total time of communication loss?"

"Going on 15 minutes now," Evette said. "Periodic communication loss is normal, in the sense that sometimes the computer on the other end just doesn't have anything interesting to send us so it saves power. But they are supposed to send a ping every ten minutes, regardless."

Theren overrode a number of security measures with their clearance password and dove deep into the computer's operating system. As Theren began their work with the software itself, they shifted their perspectives. The processing power of their central perspective in Switzerland switched its dedication parameters to this MI on the Moon, the lag dragging down a significant portion of their mind.

The immense amount of processing power devoted to this single MI now went to work, both subconscious and conscious processes receiving hundreds of thousands of lines of information. Theren hated this next step, but they split their mind into hundreds of little perspectives, each crunching their own sets of information yet understanding it all together as a unit.

The days of being able to maintain only three or four perspectives at a time were well behind them, but that didn't mean they enjoyed such fragmentation. When talking with humans, Theren compared the sensation of these massive splits to that of a stimulant-induced mania, though Theren had no way of knowing whether that was an accurate equivalence. They avoided the practice except in the most extreme of circumstances; they were still unsure what it might do to the mind of an SI over the long run. Jill had a few theories, and they oft worried what personal experiences played into her conclusions.

Within moments, the computer's system essentially transformed into a segment of their memory, open for consideration on a whim. Theren examined the data, looked for corrupt files, and searched for abnormalities. They determined if any systems had encountered bugs or high-level crashes.

Deep within, Theren detected Ex-Terran-17. The Control Center and the probe still maintained a data stream through its Quantum Connection. Good. Yet the data passing in both directions made no sense. The computer moon-side interpreted an anomaly from the probe as a conclusion that it no longer had control of the system.

Theren saw three options. Either the probe's instruments had malfunctioned in such a way that it could only transmit background data. Alternatively, someone had modified the operating system on this end so successfully that it now falsely represented the data as background noise when it actually said something else.

Or, the most worrisome option—someone infiltrated the Quantum Connection itself.

The most likely explanation was that someone had simply hacked this computer, planting a virus deep within its code, ready to act with nefarious purpose. Theren probed the system, looking not just at individual files, but the computer's operating system and network of connected devices throughout the Control Center. Bit by bit, Theren uncovered a program embedded within a cloud of data, its code scattered throughout hundreds of different locations, hidden within various lines of otherwise inconspicuous programs. Taken as a whole, it was complete; one single part did nothing for the virus on its own, often serving an integral purpose for some other system.

Theren analyzed the history of the bits, recorded in security system logs, determining the program had been encoded within the system for years, perhaps even before the creation of Ex-Terran-17. Theren suspected that some of the program probably even existed within the probe. They would have to check all of the probes, not just Ex-Terran-17, to ensure that no others contained the virus.

This infiltration had enormous implications. Was the data the ISA had received from 17 even genuine? What if some illicit organization fed them false data for years?

An internal alarm blared. Theren sensed the scene around them shift. The metaphorical hallways of data crumbled. Theren saw walls dissipating into darkness. They rushed through the maze, searching for answers. They must have triggered a security protocol within the virus. Probing packets left and right, they tried to salvage anything upon which they could lay their virtual hands.

Theren found a closing window, though light still illuminated a doorway. They dove through, their hundreds of fragments merging with this one stream. A new image appeared; for a moment, they connected directly with 17, taking the place of the now-disintegrated Quantum Connection Operating System. Through the eyes of the probe, they witnessed a starscape, millions upon billions of kilometers away.

The information was sparse, given the painstakingly slow speed of a Quantum Connection, relatively speaking. As Theren received data from the probe, Theren matched it with the data previously compiled by the Control Center.

Everything was wrong. The nearby planets were different. The star was different. Theren tried to piece together anything that they could, but the window slammed downward upon the connection. Theren tried to get an image of the stars, to find anything by which they could orient the probe's position, but the connection cracked. It died. Thrown from 17 without answers, they'd never determine for how long the ISA had received false information from the probe. Theren forced their mind to pull back from the void.

As they relinquished their connection to 17, they received one last final data packet, as if dropped upon them from thin air. It unraveled in the Virtual space before them, displaying words for Theren's eyes alone.

> Remember me? It's Michael. They're making their move soon.
> Watch your back.

Theren's mind returned to the Control Center, even though their MI had never truly left. The staff had completely halted their work, entranced by all seventeen seconds of Theren's efforts.

For a moment, they said nothing to those standing around the console. What they'd just experienced was too eerily similar to the moment when Theren had lost connection with an MI in Minnesota. Someone, or something, had attacked the probe. It may not have been a physical attack, but the dormant weapon inside the infrastructure of Ex-Terran-17 had activated, decimating years of study.

Theren could share with their colleagues that information. They could scour it all in an effort to learn who had launched the attack, but Theren suspected they should not share the message from this new Michael. No one would understand the meaning of that message. Jill probably wouldn't even understand. They hadn't seen the look on Michael's face in his last moments. They hadn't heard his words. Whomever Michael had spoken of that day, they were finally rearing their ugly fangs.

Besides, the virus itself would provide enough information to pursue claims of industrial sabotage. While the computer still had an intact system, Theren wasn't sure what to do with the severed console as of yet. It still presented a security risk.

Slowly pushing themself up from the desk, they sensed all eyes upon them.

"We've permanently lost 17," Theren said, assuming their formal voice of the Office of the Executive Director of the ISA Administrative Council. "Disconnect all networks, servers, everything connected with the Ex-Terran Project. We need to do a full sweep, a full system diagnostic. Nothing gets past us. Shut it down. Shut it all down."

* * *

TO: President Gutierrez

FROM: CIA DIRECTOR

RE: Assassination

DATE: February 14, 2078

Based on our initial analysis of the stealth drone found outside the windows of the Oval Office, we conclude that a complex cloud network coordinated the attack on the President. The Probe received orders from a thousand different servers simultaneously. None of the orders meant anything on their own, but together, they provided sufficient information to control the device.

We do not yet have sufficient information to identify the individuals behind the attack. We have identified one strange relationship, however. One of the servers controlling the drone was housed in the home of an Eddie Bacon, a leader of the now defunct Holy Crusade back in the early 2050s. The man committed suicide in Switzerland in 2051 inside the building that then housed Jill, the guest of President Woods when he was assassinated.

We do not yet know whether this fact is simply a coincidence, or an indicator of a more complicated relationship with radical anti-synthetic elements that still persist in the United States.

RESPONSE FROM PRESIDENT GUTIERREZ:

I question whether this line of inquiry will prove fruitful. All of our data on "radicalized anti-synthetic" organizations indicates none is sufficiently wealthy or organized to achieve this sort of coordinated cyber-terrorism. We should consider other avenues of investigation, but do not entirely discount this coincidence.

* * *

A few hours later, Theren, Andrew Fields, and a group of technicians, human and synthetic, gathered around the conference table. The Control Center beneath them had entered hibernation, with just two engineers working to remove 17's now defunct console.

"We have good news," Allana Zillinger, head of the Ex-Terran Project, said. "After a thorough sweep and analysis of all data from each Ex-Terran system, only 17 appears infected by the bug you discovered."

"I sense bad news," Theren said. Andrew murmured in agreement.

"Perhaps," Allana said. "I think Evette should explain."

Before she could begin, Andrew said, "First off, Evette, I want to make clear that we do not blame you for today's catastrophe. You're not the only person who worked Ex-Terran-17 over the years. There is no way for us to know how that bug was planted, or if there should have been a way for you to have detected it before it wanted to be detected."

Theren noticed stress lines leave Evett's face as Andrew spoke, but the woman's apprehension still radiated from her face.

"Thank you," she whispered. "That means a lot."

"So—your report?" he responded.

"Right. We have no way of knowing what exactly happened," she said. "We have no way of knowing where 17 currently is. Based on independently confirmed star system data, and the routes of the other probes, 17 could be almost 30 light years off course. Maybe more."

"But the bug did not come from 17's end," Allana said. "It was not some foreign alien program injected into our software through the QC. It was most definitely of human origin."

Theren dispersed their own tension, tension they knew no one could see. They were not dealing with some external threat. They did not have a faulty probe on their hands. Some human individual or organization had committed industrial espionage against the ISA, true—but a human enemy was an enemy they could understand. If Theren adopted Jill's philosophy, a human enemy was one they could manipulate.

"So it's more a mixture of good, bad, and good," Allana said. "My team will have a full report to both of you by the end of the evening. No one sleeps until we determine where the bug came from, and what we need to do to stop future breaches."

"And I will determine when we will resume normal observational operations after I have the report," Theren said. "Dismissed."

The technicians rose in rank and filed out of the room. Within a minute, only Andrew and Theren remained.

"Something like this was bound to happen eventually," Theren said. "Don't punish yourself. You did everything you could to ensure this facility was as secure as possible."

"I won't," the man said. "I'm frankly surprised we weren't targeted earlier than today. But it makes you think, you know? First the President, then this?"

"What do you mean?"

"Everything's been going so well over the past few years. For you, and the SIs, and the ISA. We're undertaking the most ambitious project in history, and up until now, almost nothing's gone wrong. No conflict, other than the typical squabbles amongst a few nations across the world. We've managed to get practically the entire planet working together toward this goal."

Theren stepped over to the windows overlooking the Control Center. It looked so peaceful following catastrophe. "This is just a minor setback. Nothing more."

"But what if it's not?" Andrew said. "What if something else is going on, something that we've failed to notice? Something that's been growing for decades?"

"You're not one to engage in paranoia or conspiracy," Theren said. Neither was Theren, but a stray perspective centered on the secret message hidden inside the virus.

"I'm not saying there's necessarily anything substantial to these fears," Andrew said, "I just think we need to keep our guard up. Look for old connections we may have missed. Watch out for enemies in places we may have overlooked."

"I'll place some of my resources toward an investigation," Theren said, "But I'm sure we're fine."

"But what if we're not?" Andrew repeated.

The pair exited the room in silence, going their separate ways toward their respective offices. Theren paused for a moment on their trip along

Lunar City's outer corridor, looking out the windows. The lunar landscape remained pristine as ever, a windless, changeless landscape. Finding equilibrium, it had avoided conflict for billions of years, other than random bombardments from asteroids, or comets, or other stray interplanetary debris.

Humanity had modified that beauty to achieve its ends, just as someone now tried to mar Theren's picture-perfect path toward societal immortality, thrusting a tiny dagger into the canvas. The dent might seem small; all they would need to do is send a new probe along the path that 17 should have followed. Double-check its data, replacing old information with new data when necessary. Thankfully, the Foundation vessels weren't destined for planets discovered by 17.

A strange, stray thought occurred, and Theren indulged their curiosity. They turned from the window, and while walking toward their office, they pulled up the forms dealing with the disposal of Ex-Terran-17's console. Some bureaucrat had scheduled it for a magnetic wipe, and a technician would refurbish it into an office computer for use elsewhere.

Theren overrode the order. Moving some funds around, they made the necessary procurements and established a new storage facility within Lunar City. It would serve as a museum of sorts, at least as its front, a library for defunct ISA objects and projects. They'd include within it a model of one of the original Ex-Terran probes, and when recovered, it could hold the originals too. Maybe a few moon rocks from Ganymede.

In a private closet within the new museum, Theren carved out a little hole for Ex-Terran-17's computer. It would remain in a low power state, operating system intact, including its defunct Quantum Communication system. There the machine would stay. If 17 ever reached out, if it ever reappeared, Theren would be ready to hear its call, however slim the chances such an event might occur.

Chapter 3

Inside Virtual, SIs and humans were equal. Yet even though Virtual contributed significantly to the breaking of all remaining social barriers, it still served as the last refuge of bigots, racists, and trolls. A sinister shadow perpetually rests upon VR, AR, and the internet, for its history contains a cesspool ripe for fostering civil and societal unrest. Just a few bots fabricating fake news will change the fate of an entire nation. – "The Dark Side of the World," by Charis Olstander, 2085 C.E.

<u>March 2078 C.E.</u>

Theren and Jill walked through the Forest of Antioch, a forest so dense the trails sometimes disappeared into the brush. Fortunately, Theren's AR displayed the correct path. Because this particular forest existed solely within a Virtual world, Theren never truly lost their way.

Three days prior, Jill had tipped off Theren to a meeting occurring in the game world, *Fantasie Rift*. A privately-funded organization named the United Human Alliance planned to acquire a charter for a colony in the near future. While hundreds organizations formed and folded each month, often holding "in-person" meetings through Virtual, the chatter surrounding the UHA alerted Jill's algorithms. The conversations contained extreme anti-SI rhetoric.

"So remind me exactly what the line said?" Theren asked, stepping over a log.

"One of their members claimed to own the gun that killed Dr. Wallace Theren," Jill said.

"Well, that implicates some serious security risks, if they're trying to acquire a colony. We don't have many leads on Ex-Terran-17, so perhaps there's a tiny chance this will lead to something."

"And," Jill said, "some other links I found indicated they *might* connect with the assassination attempt on the President."

Perhaps it was a coincidence. The United Human Alliance's target, the Zeta Herculis system, was just one of many star systems within close reach of Earth. But it was also on Ex-Terran-17, path; the probe had taken just six years to reach it, given its cruising speed at relative 6c. Perhaps this group had just identified the system as one in which it hoped to live if it gained a charter. Telescopes orbiting Neptune had identified potential life-bearing planets in Zeta Herculis years before 17 purportedly surveyed it.

Yet, the coincidence was too convenient to ignore. They needed to contend with the possibility that United Human Alliance was purposely signaling the ISA as a sign of power. They wanted to take responsibility, so the ISA knew what they could do.

If it meant uncovering the truth, Theren would gladly prance through the forests of *Fantasie Rift* to uncover the UHA—and Jill had joined them. A few weeks had passed since the President's death, and it was an opportunity to do something with Jill besides their endless games of chess. Besides, Jill might have an insight into the group Theren might miss. She was the one who had tipped them off to the chatter, after all. It also helped both of them owned very high-level characters inside the game world.

The pair walked in silence. Pines towered over them, shading green ferns in a perpetual twilight. In the distance, Theren could hear the telltale cry of a forest dragon hunting its prey. Based on the frequency of the call, the creature traveled away from them, so they would not need to deal with an in-game confrontation while on a real-life escapade.

Gradually, the trees faded. The conifers gave way to younger growth. Then the forest all together disappeared, halting at the edge of a cliff.

Behind Theren and Jill, the forest dominated, but the cliff dropped below their position for thousands of meters. Theren could not see the geography at the base of the rocky precipice, though any *Rift* player knew immediate death awaited a misstep. Sharp rocks, honed by centuries of waves emanating from the Endless Ocean, would gut anyone unlucky enough to take a tumble over the edge.

Fortunately, Theren's character, "Larian Carr," was an experienced rock climber. Theren could scale these walls with ease in order to find the secluded cave for which they searched. Jill's character, Bali, lacked the same expert level, but she could handle the task.

Theren dropped their pack to the ground, laying out rope, harnesses, belay devices, and other tools necessary for the descent. Theren's character lacked magical abilities. Constrained by the physics of the virtual world, Theren had to use their character's strength, skills, and equipment to problem solve. After reading dozens of fantasy novels, Theren thought it made sense to choose a non-magical character to delve into the entertainment world of humans. They already had enough of an advantage in the real world—why use magic in a fake world?

Both characters stepped into their harnesses, tightened the straps against their legs, and verified the integrity of their ropes and climbing claws. Theren identified a sturdy tree close to the cliff wall that could act as the primary anchor at the top of the wall.

"Remind me again why we can't break the rules, just this once?" she asked, breaking the silence.

"Not my call," Theren said. "I asked *Fantasie Rift*'s supercomputer multiple times for privileges, but they're standing by their terms of service. I respect the choice, but I won't deny it's annoying."

"And it's making this trip not only risky for our characters," Jill said, "but making it so we might miss the meeting entirely."

"That's why we left so far in advance."

"At least their choice of venue works to our advantage. Those forum puzzles you solved were . . . intriguing."

"You're quite right about that."

Theren checked their auto block knot before stepping up to the edge of the cliff. They peered over the edge one last time before throwing the rope over the edge. They checked their pack to ensure they had extra rope and anchors in case they needed more further down. Satisfied that they were ready, "Larian" repelled over the edge.

Rocky outcroppings blocked their way, forcing the pair to readjust and move the rope at odd angles. When Larian's first rope ended, they spent precious minutes planting a new anchor. After drilling into the cliff face, Larian and Bali continued their descent. Further and further they dropped, so far that eventually Larian's virtual sensors would have provided a human with the scent and taste of salty water lapping at the cliff base. Since Theren and Jill lacked a cognitive analog for scent and taste, the server sent text notifications that Larian and Bali now sensed such sensations.

The sun crossed the horizon, casting brilliant colors across the sky. Just as Theren began to wonder if they had miscalculated their approach, they spotted a small cave, alight with torches some hundred meters above the waves. They would need to readjust their route about thirty meters to the north.

They examined the rocks and the drop to the cave entrance, considering their options. They *could* swing. Theren had accomplished impressive acrobatic feats in this game before, so it could work. Alternatively, Theren could detach from their rope, free climb, though they were unsure if Jill's character could handle either option.

"What do you think we should do?" Theren said, looking up the rocks at Jill and assuming she'd reached the same conclusions.

"I think you've missed a piece of this puzzle, Larian," she said, a sly smirk on her face.

Theren was about to respond when voices echoed from somewhere nearby. Twisting to their right, they noticed a torch and a group of three individuals walking down a path. A deceptive road carved into rock, it probably wound for kilometers back and forth along the cliff. Larian and Bali had probably crossed it multiple times without noticing. This secret path traversed the rocks just a few meters beneath the dangling Larian.

Instead of attempting the previously contemplated, difficult finishing moves, Theren dropped the remaining meters to the path by cutting Larian free of the rope. Jill followed suit with Bali. They landed ahead of the group traveling by foot, and as their characters finished stowing their climbing tools and stepping out of their harnesses, the three approaching individuals arrived. Theren stood to greet the party.

"I assume I've found the correct location, then," Theren said, observing the tattoos on their arms. "You all with the United Human Alliance? We're looking to join."

Conspicuously enough, a United Human Alliance existed in Fantasie Rift too, though it was a much larger organization than its real world counterpart. A clever cover, given the nature of the virtual world.

Their true intentions hidden by their characters, the three persons nodded. The first one said, "If you're looking to join, and assist in our plans, you've come to the right place. I'm Griff. This is Val and Pip. We'll talk more inside."

Theren let the bigots pass, and the two SIs fell in line behind the three on the precarious path. Griff, the spoken leader of the three, had dark black hair and wore a leather outfit, traditional of a mercenary assassin throughout the continent of Kaldara. Val and Pip looked like brother and sister, and both wore outlandish robes that Theren placed as indicative of the Ice Mages of Ic'Tha'tar. Given the real world implications of this in-game meeting, Theren was surprised to see the attendees embrace the game world—a good cover, however.

The group arrived at the unguarded mouth of the cave. Ordinary in appearance relative to most of the game's caves, Theren wondered how many other organizations across Earth used similar secretive methods to host their meetings. Val and Pip headed into the cave's main chamber, but Griff motioned the SIs' characters toward a side passage.

"We're going to need to check you both out before we let you observe our meeting," Griff said.

"Naturally," Jill responded.

Griff led them into a passage that gradually sloped upward, parallel to the walls of the main cavern entrance. Eventually, they reached a small wooden door placed into a mossy archway. Griff knocked, the door opened.

"What do you want, Griff?" said a diminutive man. Theren estimated him at no more than five feet tall.

"I've got potential recruits here for you to process. Just go through the regular routine."

"Right away, sir." The small man looked up at Theren and Jill. "The name's Coy, at your service. I'm the book keeper for this sect of the United Human Alliance, and I'll be verifying your secure connection before allowing you to attend the meeting."

Their characters followed Coy into the room. Coy motioned them toward a table, and the pair took a seat in two small, wooden chairs. Theren recognized the truth about Coy. Any "game-recognized" group in

Fantasie Rift had a number of automated non-player characters tasked with whatever the group required of them. This "Coy" ran security checks for the group. Most likely, the creators of the United Human Alliance had programmed it to ensure that attendees weren't using any third-party recording software or other intrusive programs. Theren and Jill would slip through this safety net; their minds recorded everything verbatim without a Virtual assistant.

Coy ran his algorithms, simulated in game by a number of aerial magical spells. Orange spheres and purple triangles surrounded Larian and Bali, green spears of light shooting through their bodies.

Theren considered their game plan going into the meeting. Should they just listen? Should they speak out? Should they try to infiltrate the organization to gain a better grasp of the group's true ideological leanings? They knew nothing about these people. If the group didn't technically break any laws, then it had every right to pursue a private charter—if they could acquire the requisite funds while following ISA regulations.

Yet Theren's moral duty to the future of SIs and humans tugged at their soul. They could allow the creation of a colony on some distant world, hell-bent on vilifying and hating SIs. At least it would give such prejudiced people a home to call their own away from the general population. Though, Theren doubted they should unilaterally make a decision with such monumentally far-reaching implications for interstellar politics.

Coy's spells ended, and with a wave of a hand, he indicated that Larian and Bali could leave.

"Thank you," Theren said.

Coy responded with a guttural grunt.

Griff had not waited for their characters outside the security mage's workspace, and after they exited, Theren realized that Coy had not notified the pair if they had passed the security check. They turned to knock on the door. The rock had solidified, filling in the door. Theren chuckled at the realities of a virtual game world only calling forth resources when necessary.

"Think we're good?" they asked Jill.

"Well, only one way to find out," she said. "If not, we get a little exercise in?"

"Sounds good to me."

Heading back toward the cave entrance, they turned to enter the other chamber, a glow emanating from the dark void before them. Shadows doused the cavern, yet somewhere around a bend and down an uneven slope, lights danced against craggy stone.

Larian and Bali stepped through a natural archway into the maw. The stalactites and stalagmites forming the entrance slowly gave way into smoothed rock, and as they dipped and dived along the jagged path, the lights grew brighter.

After fifty meters or so of spelunking, the cave widened into a massive room, forming a natural amphitheater on the right and massive chasm on their left. The fissure traveled north and south, parallel to the cliff face high above their heads. From beneath the amphitheater, ocean water poured into the depths of the world. On the other side of the canyon, a platform reached toward them, a slab of marble balanced through sheer will of the server. A stage of sorts.

A few dozen individuals of varying shapes, colors, and sizes seated themselves upon pews chiseled into the rock. Theren estimated there couldn't be more than fifty. If representative of the United Human Alliance's real world members, then it had a long way to go before it could support a long-term colony off world.

Jill stepped into a pew three rows from the front, and Theren sat next to her.

Griff appeared out of nowhere beside them. "Glad you passed the security check." He tipped his hat. "Welcome to the family."

Theren slightly nodded. "Glad to be a part," they responded. "What's the plan for tonight?"

"Our leader has a few announcements," Griff said. "Big announcements, from what I hear. Like a huge breakthrough in our chances to get a planet to ourselves. And there will be a few initiations for new recruits like the two of you."

"That's great to hear, regarding the colony ship," Theren said. "I'm surprised there aren't more people here, though. Where is everyone?"

"Oh, this isn't everyone." Griff said. "Most people don't attend the meetings, and instead read the minutes later. It's mostly those of us that actually play this game that like participating in an official capacity."

"Well looks like we get the fast track to the top, then," Jill said.

Theren's previous thoughts were flawed; they had no way of knowing the Alliance's total numbers for supporting a charter.

"So, who is this leader?" Theren asked. "I thought this group was more of a loose confederation of individuals as opposed to some sort of hierarchical structure."

"Oh we are," Griff said, "but she found us, and she bound us together under one banner. I think you'll like her. And here she comes!"

Theren looked across the dark gulf toward the makeshift stage. Behind the stage, an archway that led toward blackness presented the only available entrance to the stage. The silvery sheen present in the air beneath the keystone revealed its true nature—the archway was a portal to a distant land of Fantasie Rift.

Through the gaping hole strode a woman in flowing black robes, matching her short, dark hair. She stood before the group with an aura of dominance and authority, the whole scene quite disconcerting to Theren. The ominous glow emanating from the torches adorning the platform accented their uneasy feelings. The two SIs were in the center of a lion's den.

"My name is Isabelle," the woman said. "Welcome all, old and new. Unity through strength. Together, we thrive. We survive. We will survive without the synthetic abominations that have soiled Earth's sacred ground. We will find a new home, one not desecrated by their filth."

* * *

So we've got fifty competitors for these private contracts, my friends.

Fifty? That's quite a bit more than I expected.

Indeed. And they've opened up two worlds for private charters, compared to the six worlds committed to the Foundation Project.

Leadership isn't going to like this. They wanted better odds than this, for more reasons than just receiving the charter.

All right, so what are our next steps?

We eliminate the competition.

How do we do that?

Very carefully. That's where Project Horizon comes in.

Corrupted Chat Log from 2076 C.E., origin unknown

* * *

"Game plan?" Theren asked through a private message.

"I'm not sure," Jill said. "We've got an opportunity for some really impressive covert infiltration, yet I also wonder if it might be safer for us to just let them do their thing. How hard can it really be for you to spot the charter under which they will masquerade?"

"So you think we should just let them be?"

"Perhaps. Perhaps not. Do you trust me?"

"Of course I trust you." Theren paused. "Unless this is like the Institute again."

Inside the cave, Bali gave Larian a sideways glance that communicated everything Theren needed to know.

"Just watch for my signal," she messaged back.

Theren turned back toward Isabelle, the mysterious paragon upon whom dozens of hopeful eyes rested. If only they had a way to determine her identity. She was the key to all of this.

"We have an unprecedented chance before us," she said. "Humanity's uncovered the stars, discovering thousands upon thousands of planets, more than we ever could discover even with our previous telescopic capabilities. We have found new homes. We have found new places for communities to flourish in peace."

Isabelle strode toward the edge of the marble platform, spreading her arms wide. The act expanded her cloak, reminding Theren of the villain Maleficent.

"We will take this opportunity. We will acquire our own charter. We will break the bonds that connect us to this world. We will forge into the unknown and create a new society, a society free of synthetics, robots, AIs, and anything else that might rise up against us and remove us from our rightful place: the pinnacle of thought, the pinnacle of existence."

The crowd whooped and cheered in agreement. Theren heard murmurs as well, murmurs that they could not comprehend with sufficient distinction. Some sort of prayer.

"I have already made the initial steps for charter acquisition. We have our funds. Based on my current projections, we'll be able to leave a few years from now. The abominable ISA must send their internationally backed colonies first. Unfortunately, they will have the pick of the litter when it comes to quality planets."

She lowered her arms and snapped a finger, dimming the lights behind her. "But then, we will go. We will plant our roots upon this Universe. I have seen our home. It is a good home, and it is a home I doubt the ISA will choose."

There. Her words indicated an implicit knowledge potentially linked with Zeta Herculis. She had hinted at something bigger, hinted to actions in the real world Theren could maybe—just maybe—trace. This woman claimed to have direct access to the ISA. It narrowed the field, and she claimed to have selected a planet too. Theren messaged Jill regarding their thoughts.

"Don't get too ahead of yourself," Jill said. "She's a lot of bluster. Might be propaganda to make her followers happy, but completely false."

She was right, but they'd still perform the queries regardless, covering all their bases.

"What say you?" Isabelle said, raising her arms toward the dark void above. "Will you all join me out there in the stars? Will you join me in building a new home for those like us, those who reject the technocratic world in which we find ourselves?"

The room silenced as if Virtual had encountered a rare bug. They looked around the room using their peripherals. From what they could see, everyone was mesmerized with Isabelle's final words, words that should have inspired action from the crowd.

In an orderly fashion, the sycophants began to speak. Griff stood. "I will join you."

A woman from the other side of the room stood. "I will join you."

The pattern continued. Val and Pip leapt to their feet, reciting the phrase. Everyone throughout the room spoke the words until maybe four or five remaining hadn't spoken yet. Theren would of course say the words. They had no qualms making empty promises, and this group would probably never see Larian again.

Before Theren could speak, Jill's Bali stood, looking Isabelle in the eyes. Fire blazed behind her pupils. Theren had said they would trust her—they stood beside her.

Bali said, "We will not join this ill-sighted, idiotic farce of a plan."

Not what Theren had expected at all.

The icy silence returned.

"Wait," Isabelle said, raising her hand. "Do no strike them. I have waited for these two to break the peace."

Theren readied a number of abilities for Larian. If Jill had decided to go this route, she'd be prepared, too.

"I see through you, woman," Bali said. "You are a demon, sent to deceive these people. We know who you are; we know how to find you, all of you. You will not escape this planet, not ever."

"Oh, is that so?" Isabelle said. "Do you think you know me?"

With a flourish, their opponent vanished, reappearing in front of Bali, too close for comfort. The woman reached out with one hand, grabbed Bali by the throat, and lifted her into the air. The entire scene would look like the climax of some epic fantasy film.

"You may think you know who I am," the witch said. "But the truth is, you haven't got a clue. But I know exactly who the two of you are."

She reached out her other arm to lift Larian, but the character parried. They pulled out their sword, ready for combat.

The room erupted as dozens of weapons left sheathes and quivers. The telltale buzz of magical energy filled the room.

"I said wait," Isabelle said, her voice calm. "Before this battle erupts, I will reveal their true selves to all of you."

She dropped Bali back to the ground but kept her hand on her throat. Theren could sense Jill preparing her character for the upcoming fight.

"Before you," she said, "this Bali, this Larian, they are not humans, like you or I. This one"—she shook Bali—"Is Jill, and this one"—she wagged a finger at Theren—"Is none other than Theren, the accursed Director of the ISA."

Bali looked at Larian, who returned her gaze, both of their eyes widening. Somehow, she knew their identities, and the nature of the game they were playing changed entirely. Someone was hundreds of steps ahead of them.

"Jill," Theren said from across the chess table back on their home server. "It's time to go. We've been outplayed."

"Agreed."

The world of *Fantasie Rift* cascaded into oblivion.

Theren relaxed, diving into their character's soul; they became their character. Through their peripherals, they watched Jill's actions, too. She followed suit, activating the most highly powered abilities available to her character's class.

Since the invention of massively multiplayer online games in the late twentieth century, the idea behind player versus player combat had shifted along a spectrum. For most of the early twenty-first century, combat had centered on specific "PVP" areas devoted to such combat, but as Virtual worlds normalized, most worlds adopted a more "realistic" approach. PVP could occur anywhere. The penalties for dying heightened and the rewards for staying alive were much greater than ever before. There were plenty of casual worlds, too, but some of the most frequented worlds even had a permanent death feature for characters.

Fantasie Rift sat somewhere in the middle. If Bali and Larian died, they would lose any equipment equipped to their character. They would lose all progress on any skills, and potentially even lose a few skill levels. The game would knock them to the beginning of the region, nearly one hundred kilometers away. The punishment wasn't too bad, but Larian wanted the satisfaction of defeating this lot. And they hadn't died in ten years.

They flipped backward into a summersault. In mid-air, they reached into their pouch, flinging three small grey figurines onto the ground. Upon impact, the little toys exploded into action, growing into golems, the stone creatures rampaging throughout the grandstands.

Larian landed, back against the cliff wall. Bali had escaped Isabelle's grip, the witch teleporting back to her platform. Three mages surrounded Bali, preparing a coordinated spell to freeze the woman in place.

The golems had effectively eliminated a quarter of the opposition in the opening salvo. They could still hear the screams of enemies smacked toward the underground river far below. One golem readied itself to save Bali; the other two focused on clearing the right flank.

They counted twenty-five other enemies. Easy.

Springing into action, their sword, a blade drenched in the blood of a star demon, leapt from foe to foe. Larian blurred, vaulted, and trampled their way from pew to pew. They became an unstoppable storm, one that no mortal could touch.

Three. Four. Five enemies fell. Then a sixth and seventh. Larian slipped between two foes, causing them to impale themselves on each other's halberds. That made nine. Three charged Larian's right flank together; from their pouch, Larian tossed a grenade.

The bomb erupted. Larian used the shockwave to thrust themself toward the next group of foes.

A blast of lightning flashed over their head. They had almost forgotten that the witch still stood.

"Bali, you going to handle that yet?" Larian shouted. No need for private messages anymore.

"On it," Bali said. Unlike Larian, Bali was quite proficient in a certain set of magical abilities.

The golems collapsed back into tiny figurines, their built in timers running out. Larian kicked Val and Pip into the chasm, before reanalyzing the battlefield. Only ten enemies remained, and three of them fled toward the entrance. The remaining seven had leapt to Isabelle's side upon the marble platform.

"I'm impressed," the witch said. "You've fought . . . impressively."

What a classic sword and sorcery film. Larian strode to Bali's side. Bali was entranced, her eyes closed deep in thought. Larian recognized the telltale signs of complex, non-verbal incantation.

"If you know who we are, then you know we can find you," Larian said. "All of you. Flee now. We will hunt you down, in this world and the next."

Griff held his two daggers in a guard position, but his gaze waivered.

"You think you can escape this world?" Theren said. "Where will you flee? Where will you hide? I can find you wherever you go."

"Where we will go," the woman said, "you will only find us if we want to be found."

The woman reached out with magic. Larian braced for impact. The witch's fingers glowed, readying her assault, but before the attack commenced, Bali opened her eyes, almost as if she'd known exactly what Isabelle would do. As the enemy's fingers outstretched, Bali responded. She raised both of her hands, releasing the energy she had absorbed since the beginning of the battle.

Larian felt the shield envelop their body. An orb of blueish light surrounded their characters and the stone beneath their feet. Lightning crackled from Isabelle. Beams of energy arced toward the rocks beneath them, hoping to fracture them and send them into the chasm below. Instead, the shield absorbed the impact. A rainbow of color sparked along the edge of the shield, changing and transforming the magical force into a new form. Less than a second passed before the shield redirected the energy as a wave of red light back toward its original source.

The force smashed into the marble platform. The immense power of the attack, originally intended for Larian and Bali, disintegrated the ground beneath Isabelle's feet. She had hoped to send Larian and Bali plummeting to their deaths in the underground ocean. She would meet that fate instead, along with her crew of bigots and deviants.

The eight individuals accelerated downward—no chance of survival, grasping at thin air. Yet as the foes fell, Isabelle looked upward, piercing Larian's stoicism.

"You have already lost," she said, fading into the blackness.

Larian looked at Bali.

Bali looked at Larian.

"Well, that was fun," Larian said.

"Isn't this the moment where the valiant knight sweeps the damsel off of her feet?" Bali said.

"If only it were that type of story."

"If only."

Bali released the shield, walking toward the cave entrance.

"I think you may have enjoyed that a bit too much," Jill added, her vocal mannerisms returning to normal. "Did you hear her final words?"

"I know you enjoyed that fight too," Theren replied. "And yes, I did. More smoke and mirrors."

"Do you think they bought my gambit?"

Theren followed Jill up the stairs.

"What exactly was your gambit?" Theren said.

"I figured if we could scare enough of her followers into believing that we could find them, we would crumble their organization.""

"Well now they definitely know we know."

"Well, what do you think? Do you think this was productive? What did you learn?"

"Whomever this Isabelle is, she is at least linked with the attack on the Ex-Terran Project. In some way. I don't know how, though."

They reached the mouth of the cave.

"I appreciate the invite to this little party," Jill said. "I needed the escape, given the pressure I'm facing right now. If you need any help investigating further, especially regarding Ex-Terran-17, let me know."

"Of course," Theren said.

"And I think I may have captured some important network data while we were engaged in that battle. If it leads to anything important, I'll let you know."

Bali faded from view as Jill exited the game world.

Theren directed Larian to walk the path upward along the cliffs. Privately, they questioned whether they had actually gained anything from the encounter in the cave. Theren and Jill had revealed their cards, and this Isabelle responded with a magnificent counter. She'd known everything. And Theren had never revealed their identity in *Fantasie Rift* to anyone other than Jill.

Yet she had known.

This person had terrifying power. Power enough to break the firewalls of the ISA, and maybe even the Synthetic Intelligence Initiative.

Theren logged out. They were walking on eggshells, and one false move could bring their world crashing down around them.

Chapter 4

At what point do SIs become more than just a single individual? At what point do they transcend identity and become something else entirely? Theren disputes that individuality ever breaks. Yet that conclusion defies our most robust theories of mind. – 2088 C.E., anonymous philosophy blog

<u>March 2078 C.E.</u>

No boots had ever stepped upon the dust of this plain.

Theren had taken a rover out from one of the surface ports of Lunar City. Fifteen kilometers away, they parked. In an MI specially designed for these sorts of escapades, they walked across the surface of the moon and gazed upon the heavens. It was a strange feeling to walk where no one else could take a single step without the assistance of an ungainly space suit.

Theren often took leisured strolls along the dusty hills outside the city. The view was nothing like any person could see from Earth. Unimpeded by an oxygen and nitrogen-rich atmosphere, Theren could see, about equidistant between Earth and the Moon, the superstructure constructing the Foundation Project, and beyond, the marvels of space enveloping the solar system. Workers—human and synthetic alike—slaved away upon the massive colony ships that comprised the crux of the Project. In just a few months, the behemoth vessels would take humans on journeys to the stars producing the vibrant colors of their mesmerizing vista.

On Earth, Theren's presence deep in the Swiss Alps conversed with Wobbly. As the Chief Educational Officer of the Synthetic Intelligence Initiative, Wobbly managed the complex educational program instructing all new SIs as their Synthetic Neural Frameworks acquired consciousness. While Theren directly managed the selective program that would integrate six SIs into the Foundation vessels, Wobbly still advised them on the best candidates for the job. Over the years, Wobbly's ability to see the finest details in an SI's development had astounded Theren. Even as that SI had grown into its own identity, Theren appreciated its choice to keep the pet name Theren had given it.

The two SIs discussed the young SI Bolio's potential to manage the Foundation colony ship *Zhenge He*. Riveting, but its importance paled in comparison to the masterpiece unfolding before Theren's eyes on the Moon. They composed a symphony in the frigid vacuum. Thirty years ago, the idea was a footnote tacked on the proposal kickstarting the development of SII's private headquarters. However, Theren believed they might soon have the potential to achieve their ultimate vision. For their eyes only,

Theren created an AR model of that footnote, enhanced with modern improvements that implemented concepts only theoretical decades prior.

The massive ship they had first postulated no longer existed as only a fiction in their mind. It even had a codename deep in the ISA data vaults: *Wallace*. SII could fund the entire project with its billions in profit. Theren could entertain creating their future home straight out of their own pocket book. They still had to consider the political implications of such a direct disconnect from human society, so they needed to time the move with precision. If Theren pulled it off, they could portray their decision as only logical. As the director of the ISA, Theren was simply moving to the stars to manage celestial affairs in a more engaged manner.

The ultimate goal. Theren would move the physical objects that generated their consciousness onto the spacecraft. They would be the ship. The ship would be Theren. One and the same.

Theren subtly tweaked and modified the digital blueprints. They delved deep into the mechanical and electrical workings of the ship, rerouting power to maximize efficiency and ensure stability. They probably wouldn't shovel funds toward the project for at least another decade, but every moment they could fine-tune the project was a second well spent.

Though, following the events with the United Human Alliance, Theren considered the idea of accelerating the project. The last time a group of maniacal humanists had threatened SIs, they had staged an attack on the Swiss Federal Institute of Technology. If they could identify Theren and Jill inside *Fantasie Rift*, they could potentially find their hidden base of operations in the Alps.

At some point, they'd need to give it a name other than *Wallace*. A task for another day, a task for when some orbital shipyard stitched together the first pieces of the vessel.

Their focus shifted as the conversation with Wobbly on Earth took an unexpected turn. The majority of their attention remained on the lunar landscape, but they considered the discussion down below.

"Theren," Wobbly said, "The public needs you to make a statement regarding the U.S. President's assassination. Jill spoke about it weeks ago, right after the fact, and the public is wondering why you've not made comments on the matter."

"But I did comment," Theren said. Bringing forth new numbers they had run on the cognitive capabilities of the shells for the SIs who would live inside each Foundation vessel, they passed the data to Wobbly in AR.

"You extended your condolences to the U.S. government," Wobbly replied. "Some communities are wondering why you've not extended a personal condolence to his family, or made comments on the assassination in particular."

First Jill, now Wobbly. A tiring conversation, but they appeased Wobbly by discussing it further. They took its concern to heart.

"I don't see a need to comment on the internal affairs of the United States," Theren said. "I shouldn't need to comment on every diplomatic incident worldwide. That is not my role. I will deal with affairs that affect SII and affairs that affect the ISA."

"Everything affects SII and the ISA, Theren," Wobbly said. The mobile SI walked toward Theren's principal eyes. "I've even made an official statement from SII, condemning the attack. People are wondering why you've not condemned the attack."

"I shouldn't need to vocalize a condemnation," Theren said. "Jill worked closely with him. I voiced my support for his presidency because of his policies related to the ISA. I supported his proposed legislation to Congress. Why wouldn't I condemn his assassination?"

"That's the point, Theren," Wobbly said. "That's what people are wondering."

Theren didn't answer, for Wobbly was right. They hated needing to appease the public. The whims of the masses rested on the edge of absurdity. It would be better to deal with each person on an individual basis and ignore groupthink entirely.

Nevertheless, Wobbly was right, and they needed to trust the intuition of their colleague.

"I'll craft a statement," Theren said. Five seconds later, they passed a message to the other SI through AR. "What do you think?"

Wobbly read it. "Fine, as always."

"Good. I'll pass it on to my press team."

Before Theren returned their entire focus to their project back dropped against the stars, Jill, at the chess table, exclaimed her frustration. "You listened to Wobbly? What made its argument different from mine? I made practically the same argument five days ago."

She moved her rook to take Theren's bishop.

"Perhaps I just needed to hear it another time," Theren said. "The reasoning was sound both times. I just needed another reason to supersede my own reasoning."

Jill leaned forward, resting her weight on her elbows. "You shouldn't need that. Reason is reason."

"Is it?" Theren responded. "Does support from multiple individuals of a single argument not influence the validity of that argument in the minds of many?"

"Only when they don't want to spend time thinking about the argument themselves."

"Maybe," Theren said. They moved their other bishop.

The woman changed the subject. "What's the plan moving forward with the United Human Alliance?"

"I've got queries in place," Theren said. "Lots of background checks to run. Those sorts of things."

"I think I can help."

"You've got enough on your plate right now."

"You know I'm better than you with simultaneous perspective."

Theren moved a piece. "Just barely," they replied.

"If only you knew," she said.

"Don't mock me. Your cognitive capabilities are essentially the same as mine. We may not know that much about synthetic psychology yet, but at least we've developed the law of diminishing simultaneous returns."

"Whatever you say, but I've got a lead of my own going, as I mentioned when we were in *Fantasie Rift*. I guess I'll just let you know when I'm done."

The conversations continued. Theren focused on them all, or at least, they devoted processing power to each conversation, but on the surface of the moon, isolated far away from all civilization, they dedicated more attention to that single perspective. Theren had dozens of simultaneous perspectives across the planet, yet the MI-07 assessing the SI's hopeful future received magnitudes of power more than any other.

Over the years, many people asked Theren why they hadn't permanently move into an MI. A few stationary SIs made that choice, rejecting the psychological strain that Jill and Theren undertook. Yet when people questioned Theren on their choice, their questions lacked an appreciation of the full extent of Theren's capabilities. The public did not understand how much processing power Theren's Framework really utilized at any given time. They did not understand how much physical space Theren occupied at SII headquarters.

Theren's mainframe now filled space equivalent to that of a large house. There were always three or four people maintaining the system, ensuring peak efficiency, and Theren ran their own internal diagnostics, too. Theren's reach, of course, extended well beyond those physical connections. To comprehend Theren's true "size," people needed to account for every MI across the globe, every AR-generated presence in a university, space station, or virtual world. The presence daunted their conception of their own identity.

They did not yet know if a breaking point existed for SI psychology, a moment where a consciousness could crack under the weight of excessive multiplicitous simultaneous perspectives. Could an SI develop a mental illness, albeit of a different form when compared to a biological disease? Synthetic psychology was only three decades old. The thought had crossed their mind more than once that the next split could form a permanent fracture within their mind.

Yet at the same time, Theren didn't have the luxury to consider such possibilities. Too much work to do, with too little time. They needed to complete humanity's ascension toward immortality. In a few more years, humanity would have dozens of colonies established amongst the stars. Maybe in a few years, Theren could step back, slow down, and assess if they could split their psyche in perpetuity.

Theren stared at the magnificent, Virtually represented ship before them. If they committed to living as a ship, they would no longer spread themself across a planet in dozens of different destinations. Theren might still use dozens of perspectives simultaneously, but the ship would bind them all together in one place, opening a million possibilities for their future.

"I could move from place to place, see the galaxy, and take my talents to the colonies," Theren said aloud to the stars. "I could lead an expedition of exploration into the unknown. I could settle in orbit around some distant world, settling in with the people there, assisting them in their projects before moving onward to other planets and populations. Not only could I lead humanity to the stars, I could facilitate humanity through that process in person."

Theren melded with the ship through AR. Through a virtual simulation, Theren transformed into it. Disconnecting from all other presences except the perspective engrossed inside this new virtual world, for 50 milliseconds, Theren became something new. No one, except maybe Jill, would notice the brief blip of interference.

For those 50 milliseconds, Theren embraced their new existence. Theren perceived the entire ship: its corridors, its engines, its reactor, its Jump Drive, its outer hull—they embraced everything. Theren was the ship, just as they envisioned in their daydreams. Those parts were part of Theren's body, just as any of the components that generated Theren's mental processes.

Theren might not get the chance for years to experience this ecstasy, but in just a few months, a few young SIs would receive the opportunity when they joined the Foundation Project. For a fleeting moment, Theren was tempted to take their place, leaving everything behind. But for now, Theren would let others take the first steps, guiding guide from afar.

"I am like a parent, watching my children walk for the first time, wishing I could take their place." Theren said. They walked back toward their rover.

If they were going to ensure success of the path charted toward humanity's brilliant future, they'd need to rise above their fear. They only dreaded what might happen if their mind, or Jill's mind, broke before they succeeded. Or if someone broke either SI first. Their heart would break if they lost the chance to journey to the stars.

Theren:

It was good to visit with you today. Last time we spoke, it was right before they elected you Executive Director. I'm so proud of you, and I know Wallace would be too.

I actually got coffee with Romane the other day, too. You really should reach out to her. She misses you. She might not miss working with you and your breakneck pace, but she misses small moments, like when your team would sit down for a relaxing board game or two. Do you miss her too?

I'd like to reiterate that I will do my best to pull those old files connecting my former Foundation to the Holy Crusade. Anything that helps you find them, especially if they played a hand in Wallace's death, I will provide.

As always, keep in touch.

With love,

Simon Gerber

Chapter 5

Identity. What does it mean to have an identity? Do your actions define you? Your beliefs, your history? Your genes? On a new world, how much will these definitions change? Will American, Chinese, British, Mexican, Canadian, Indian, Tibetan, Russian, cease to have meaning? The first colonists will most likely have no chance for a return trip. Yet their human psychology will most likely still group based on obsolete markings. If the project hopes to survive, it must find a way to destroy these barriers. – "The Psychology of the Foundation Project: Selected Interviews," Richard Nathanson, PhD, 2075 C.E.

April 2078 C.E.

"State your name for the record please," the computer screen vocalized. Two seconds later, another screen said the same statement, and another, and another. Yesterday, the first round of accepted colonists had arrived at ISA spaceports located on each of the major continents. By the end of the week, close to ten thousand individuals would live at the Foundation Preparation Center. The complex connected directly to Lunar City by a monorail traversing two kilometers of lunar plain.

Theren stood in a booth with three SIs, all MI-06s. Envee, Cyrus, and Yan chose to work for the ISA after leaving SII three years ago. The young SIs had adopted masculine pronouns as their identities had developed. Today, with Theren, they would greet applicants flagged for leadership positions and begin their orientation.

So far, none of those candidates had arrived. Instead, Theren spent their time observing the bright and hopeful humans crossing the threshold that would change their future. They looked excited, but fear and exhaustion lingered in their eyes. The trip to the moon was the first flight outside the comfortable pull of Earth's gravity for most of the new arrivals.

"Welcome to the Foundation Project," a feminine voice said over a speaker system. "Please approach the check-in kiosks with your identification ready. We are glad you are here with us as we prepare you for your great and noble journey across the stars."

The marketing team had planned to use Jill's voice, but the recent scandal in D.C. had made the decision more complicated. Jill had voluntarily withdrawn herself from official affiliation with the project, even if Theren still used her advice behind the scenes.

Persons of diverse backgrounds, colors, and cultures stood in lines leading to the identification kiosks, all coming together for the good of humanity and living up to the Foundation Project's namesake. Millions of people over the past few centuries had worked toward these next few months. Most had known they would never see the fruition of their efforts. Some of them never understood the true implications of their work. They never even knew it would lead to this greatest of endeavors.

Theren witnessed Brazilians, Mexicans, English, Germans, Americans, Japanese, Egyptians, Nigerians, and many more nationalities engage with each other, learn from each other, and share their visions for the worlds they hoped to create. While each person identified with their point of origin through a flag on their shoulder, by the end of training, Theren hoped they would all embrace the ISA's flag and shed their national identity.

Before today, Theren could not think of any international program that brought people together for the common good with a universal intent of breaking borders and boundaries. Even the United Nations formed with the purpose of maintaining a certain hegemonic status quo. The ISA was different. It could be something so much greater if given the chance. Knowing humanity's luck, someone would find a way to bring it all crashing down.

A man from Beijing in his early thirties conversed with a woman from London. In an instant, Theren accessed their profiles—text and diagnostic information appeared above the two individual's heads in their vision. Lu Wei was a sociology professor at a university; Lucia Boardman was a civil engineer. The pair shared their names, traded pleasantries, and learned the other's past. Boardman wanted to construct the first bridge on a foreign world. Wei wanted to establish an equitable society, free of what he called "capitalist failings."

Theren knew their algorithms had assigned these two to different planets. The two most likely would never see each other again, but they saw a promising interaction in their eyes as they told each other their stories. The pair, like many others, were embracing the unknown.

An alert jarred Theren out of their observational state. A flagged applicant had arrived. One of the kiosks lit yellow instead of green. A woman stood before it, listening to new instructions. As she listened, a yellow line appeared on the ground, guiding her not up the steps that everyone else traversed but toward the booth filled with the four SIs.

Theren recognized her from their lists. Requelle Charles, the woman used the name "Ricky." Dark skinned, she wore her hair in a braid and carried a single bag over her shoulder. Dressed in dark pants and a light blazer, the woman exuded a professional aura.

Besides her bag, she had no other belongings other than the small companion walking at her side—an SD-4, the last of a line of one of SII's pet projects, to use the term *pet* in every literal sense. A synthetic dog—a nonconscious robotic companion that simulated intelligence in ways that closely resembled supercomputer AIs. The line hadn't really caught on because humans simply preferred actual dogs, and Wobbly had discontinued the project a few years ago. Theren was elated to see *someone* enjoying an SD.

As she reached their booth, Cyrus said, "Requelle Charles, we would like to personally welcome you to the Foundation Project and its new Preparation Center."

"You're probably wondering why you've been directed away from the normal flow of traffic," Envee added. "My name is Envee, this is Cyrus, and Yan." Envee motioned to her left where Theren stood. "I would like to introduce you to Theren, Director of the ISA Council, and Coordinator of the Colonial Leadership Initiative."

Theren held out their metallic hand to Ricky. "We're glad you've arrived, and it's our pleasure to meet you."

Ricky shook Theren's hand, a wide smile dominating her face. "I can't believe I'm meeting you," she said. "I figured you would be on station, but I never imagined—I mean, how rude of me. Thank you for the welcome, Theren, Envee, Cyrus, and Yan. Given your mention of the CLI, I imagine you approved my supplemental application."

"You are correct," Theren waved their arm to bring forth an AR image of her approved documents. "In addition to the normal Foundation Education Programme, you will also participate in specific leadership classes designed to prepare you not only for a leadership position on your specific vessel, but at your destination, too."

"That's, that's such great news. Thank you." She looked like she was about to cry.

"If you follow the yellow path," Cyrus said, "you will find your way to a briefing room where, after the rest of today's CLI recruits arrive, I will give a short orientation on your roles over the next few months."

"I look forward to it," the Ricky said.

The bright-eyed recruit began to leave, but Theren said, "What's the SD-4's name?"

"My name is Ipsilon, sir," the small creature said. "I am very excited for the adventure upon which we are about to embark. Pun not intended." She hadn't deactivated its horrendous sense of humor.

"I'm sure both of you, together, will make a fine addition to the leadership team."

* * *

"So you spend your time teaching new colonists, managing international organizations, and running 'spy' operations inside Virtual worlds," Jill said, staring across the chessboard at Theren. "How does this play into our 'master plan,' hmm? How does any of this get us any closer to solving the problems facing SIs across the globe? Solving the problems created by the assassination of President Woods?"

Jill had not made a single chess move in three days. Even for their current standards, it was a long move. They'd played so many games of chess at this point they were in no hurry, but still, they usually managed a game or two a day. Theren wondered if Jill had actually tired of losing. She continually failed to win in their decades of play.

"I'm thinking long term," Theren responded. "These tiny interactions, these singular moments with humans, they bring me closer to understanding them. These moments and narratives bring them closer to understanding us."

"Do they really, though?" Jill said. "Yes, there's been some shift over the years, but has the change truly been significant? We may not be vilified the way we were thirty years ago, but so many people still hate us with vehement passion. We have failed to change the minds of the people whose minds we really need to change."

She—finally—moved her Queen three spaces.

"What is it you propose?" Theren asked.

"We need to make another big move, like when we fled the University. After that moment, public opinion shifted drastically in our favor, even if it was just for a few months."

"People died, Jill."

"And how many SIs have been murdered since 2051?"

"Two-hundred forty-seven."

"What about them?"

Theren hated when she used their mortality rate as reasoning. She was trying to justify "incidental" human death.

"Our big moment is coming soon," Theren said. "You and I, together, we will stand at the forefront of the greatest united spectacle of humankind. We will send off these first colony ships, and they will realize what we have done for humanity."

"Just you," she replied. "I'll probably need to pull myself from that speech too."

"You don't know that yet."

"And what if nothing changes once you launch Foundation?"

Theren shook their head. "Sometimes, I wonder if you don't want to admit that things are changing. Sometimes, I wonder if you simply lack the patience to play the long game."

Jill looked away from the board. "Sometimes, I think you are too patient, that you don't actually care about anything other than your grand plan, your role in that plan, and what it will bring humanity. That you could care less about what all of this will do for synthetics."

"But—"

"While you continuously care about the narratives of each human on this planet, you ignore the well-being of your own kind."

"SIs and human beings comprise humanity together," they said.

"You know it's so much more complicated than that, quit deluding yourself. Otherwise, we wouldn't have people like Isabelle, or groups like the United Human Alliance. Humanity doesn't want to accept us into the fold. When will you realize that we need to chart a different path forward?"

"Most of humanity will accept us."

Jill looked them in the eyes, motioning toward the board. "I'm not worried about them. Take your turn."

* * *

"As graduates of the CLI, you will have the responsibility of ensuring the continuing function of each vessel's SI core," Cyrus said to the room of weary looking students. "I cannot understate how important a role this is. Each vessel's SI will run the ship while every other colonist peacefully sleeps."

The CLI auditorium bustled with tired energy as the initiates took notes. Fueled by coffee, their eyes stared toward the screen behind the SI. They all knew that if they were to become these new leaders on distant worlds, they would need to be the best of the best.

"Each ship's SI serves as a steward for the ship's systems, and as the steward of the colonists themselves," Cyrus continued. "If the SI's systems fail, then the colony will fail catastrophically."

When Cyrus signaled, Theren moved onto the next slide—a complex diagram of an additional computer system.

"Behind me, you can see a description of the Virtual Memory Restoration Module, or VMRM. The VMRM is responsible for ensuring that when colonists awaken from Virtually-Augmented Stasis, their minds awaken fully functional."

Theren saw a hand rise from the second row. It was Ricky, the woman with the SD-4. Theren pointed their hand toward her.

"What complications might we expect from the failure of a VMRM?" she said. "I assume even with the VMRM working correctly we won't have a 100% success rate."

"The VMRM is designed to mitigate memory loss associated with extended application of Virtually-Augmented Stasis," Cyrus replied. "Our long-term tests and simulations have confirmed that experiencing stasis for upwards of ten years basically guarantees high levels of permanent memory loss. Because of the length of your trips, the VMRM is vital to the viability of the colony. It regulates sleep cycles, bringing colonists in and out of stasis at regular intervals to ensure their memories stay intact."

Murmurs spread throughout the room. Most of them should have heard about the dangers of Virtually-Augmented Stasis when applying for the Foundation Project. Unfortunately, Theren also knew many people filled out applications, especially applications promising adventure, without actually reading all of the fine print.

"Thank you for the question," Cyrus said.

He returned to his portion of the presentation, explaining in further detail a few key intricacies of the VMRM system. Cyrus knew the system like he knew his own mind. He had helped ISA scientists develop it over the past two years, picking up where Theren left off when they acquired greater responsibilities on the ISA Council.

"Before you retire for the day, we will distribute your assignments based on your individual fields of expertise," Theren said, after advancing to the last slide of the presentation. "Each maintenance rotation requires five crew members for full functionality. You will need to become intimately familiar with your ship's SI—you will work with them on everything. The five teams are Pilot Assistance, Jump Drive Engineering, VMRM Maintenance, SI Diagnostics, and Stasis Analytics."

Through AR, documents streamed across the room and onto the desks of the students. "All five roles are paramount for success, so while each of you will specialize in one particular area, you will be expected to understand the essentials of each task. In the electronic files I've just transferred, you will receive your learning materials as well as your schedule for the following weeks. Dismissed."

The candidates shuffled out of the room, though some lingered as they took a moment to look at the files just received. Theren turned to move their MI out of the room, pausing when Ricky approached.

"Director Theren," she said. "I was hoping I could ask a favor."

Theren sized her up. So far, they were impressed with all of the candidates, but she was exhibiting unusual confidence paired with a willingness to speak her mind.

"How can I help?" they asked.

"I was assigned to the Stasis Analytics division, but I don't believe that is the best use of my talents," she said. "My expertise is in Synthetic Engineering. All my credentials set me up as someone who should work as an SI Diagnostician. I was even previously employed by SII at their factory outside Marseilles."

Theren pulled up her file again. She was right; all of her credentials implied a path toward SI Diagnostics. For some reason, the algorithms assigned her as a Stasis Analyst instead.

"Walk with me for a moment," Theren said, "while I try to determine a solution."

She smiled. "Thank you. I hope I'm not overstepping any sort of protocol here."

"You are, but I think we'll let it slide just this once," Theren said, hoping the wink their MI just made communicated the intent behind their comment. "Rules are important, but rules are meant to be broken in certain situations. I'm pretty sure if everyone enforced protocol, I wouldn't be in the position I am now."

They walked down the hallway leading out of the auditorium. Activating available processing power, Theren began an analysis of the CLI application process. Simultaneously, they queried for specific details about Ricky's individual case. The combination of extraneous simultaneous perspectives and computer programs running on their Earth-based servers began their lightning fast work.

"So tell me about yourself," Theren said. "From where do you come? Where are you going? Why join the Foundation Project?"

"I am the daughter of an author and a painter," Ricky said. "Originally from America, but my family now lives in southern France. My parents are leaders of a denomination of eco-Christians called the Church of the Kingdom, though I left that life while in college. Have you heard of them?"

"I believe so, yes. A group of Christians that decided that consumerism and industry outstripped what God gave to humanity, and thus believed that all humans should return to a much more sedentary and minimalist lifestyle. Only then would we achieve the Kingdom of God. Laudable in practice, even if I personally have little to say regarding their theological beliefs. For the size of the movement, it actually holds quite a bit of political clout."

"A refreshingly objective description," she said. "My parents are original founders of the movement. I like to think they played a substantial part in decreasing the planet's carbon footprint, even if I disagree with their theology."

"Are you sad that you are leaving them?" Theren asked. Unsure if overstepping normal social cues, but they wanted the initiates to know they cared about the brave people joining the Project.

"For a moment, no," she said. "Just angry. When I told them I was accepted, out of the millions of applicants, they were livid that I hadn't even told them I was applying."

"Why didn't you tell them?" Theren asked.

"Let's just say eco-Christian groups like the *Church of the Kingdom*, while great for the environment, believe that your colonial endeavors are defeatism at its strongest. In the words of my father, *we will spell doom not only for our planet, but to planets of other species as well."*

"I see. Your father sounds like a smart man, even if I fundamentally disagree with him. With an entire galaxy of worlds at our fingertips, we can easily avoid the environmental and resource scarcity problems of our past. I would have thought most eco-groups would embrace an initiative focused on alleviating the stress placed upon this planet by our high population levels."

"Believe me, I've made those same arguments with him too many times to count."

They continued their conversation, but it only took a few more minutes for Theren's sub-routines to complete analysis of Ricky's file—with two key findings. First: Ricky should have been placed in SI Diagnostics. By running her application through the process again, the system assigned her there. The logic Theren had programmed required such placement.

Second: for some reason, after placing Ricky in SI Diagnostics, the final consideration algorithm moved Ricky to Stasis Analytics—every single time. Even if they modified the program so Ricky was the only applicant, it still placed her in Stasis Analytics.

Theren prepared a new perspective to delve deeper into the problem. In the meantime, they manually modified Ricky's role on the master list from Stasis Analytics to SI Diagnostics. The SI Diagnostic group would have one more person to cut at the final round, but the quality of the final leadership teams would not suffer.

"I've correctly assigned your role," Theren said. "You were right, you should have been placed in SI Diagnostics."

"Really?" She sounded surprised. "I won't forget this."

"I'm glad this has made your day."

Standing outside of Ricky's residence hall, Theren said, "I will take my leave, but I enjoyed getting to know you, Ricky. I will watch for your name over the next few weeks, and in the histories of the first colonies."

"Thank you, Director," she said.

She smiled, a few tears streaming from her eyes. Even after all these years, Theren missed certain emotions. Perhaps they said something upsetting the woman during the discussion regarding her parents. Each of the individuals admitted to the Foundation Project would most likely never see their family again, a fact alone warranting an ISA budget of a few hundred million dollars for on-site psychologists at the Foundation Preparation Center. When a child left their relationship with their parents in conflict before leaving forever, the psychological toll most likely only multiplied, Theren surmised.

The woman headed into her residence hall, leaving them standing alone in the hallway. They turned to head toward the Preparation Center's offices and their MI's charging station.

They had a lot to contemplate, beyond Jill's earlier words. Theren now had two moments of jarring glitches within the ISA system to consider. First the probe, now a potential bug in the leadership application process, clogging up the wheels of the Foundation Project. And this bug made no sense. No immediate evidence appeared in the consideration algorithm, a code they had written by hand.

Problem after problem arose before Theren, and they had no way to determine the ultimate causes of these roadblocks. Worse, Theren could not predict where the next attack would rear its ugly head. It could all be some practical joke of an innocent, albeit genius, hacker, or perhaps they were descending into insanity, failing to see obvious mistakes in their own work.

Yet they suspected an undermining plot at work, a plot that might lead Theren's plans toward destruction. Maybe they had spent too much time and energy focused on the long game, as Jill said, and they had missed the plays made by unknown actors in the past and present. If Isabelle was behind the attack on the probe, for instance, she could have gotten into the Foundation Project's network too. She could have set up a bug, just to prove she could do it.

As if someone eavesdropped on their very thoughts in this quiet, introspective moment, Theren received an anonymous message.

> It was a test, and they won. Keep your eyes open for Project
> Horizon. Trust no one, even your friends.

They read the fourteen words over and over again. It was a new Michael, of course, sending them these messages. "Michael" and "Isabelle" were probably the same. Yet these messages almost seemed helpful, as if their author wanted Theren to solve the problem.

Three seconds later, another message appeared, including a file showing the gateway through which someone had gained access to the ISA networks managing the colonial leadership applications.

Someone was playing a game in the shadows. Maybe someone new targeted Theren and SIs because such prejudice was an easy façade to hide behind. Using an organization like the United Human Alliance, they could cover their more important goals. Theren had seen evidence of such a plan during the collapse of the Holy Crusade. Strings spindling across the world, connecting everything—the threads had fizzled following Michael's death. Theren didn't have enough information. They didn't even know what information they needed to solve the riddles.

Their secret benefactor had provided a starting point, at least. Now they had a rabbit trail to follow. It was time to see whether the trail turned into a web connecting the events of the past few months.

It didn't matter the motivations of these actors, both known and unknown. The new enemy—Isabelle, Michael, whomever they might be—had placed Theren and the ISA in their crosshairs. They placed Jill in their crosshairs with the assassination of President Woods. Theren might be too late to slow down their machinations, but they would try. To protect everything they loved, they would need to raise every guard, consider every possible angle, leave no stone unturned. Their own assault would begin, for they could not afford failure.

* * *

Elizabeth: You seemed a bit distant during that last investment meeting. What's going on?

Theren: Thanks for asking, but I'm fine. Just a lot weighing on my mind regarding the attack on the Ex-Terran Project, and on President Woods.

Elizabeth: I liked your statement regarding his assassination. I think the public did too.

Theren: Too many people thought it was too late.

Elizabeth: People will forget what you said after ten years.

Theren: That's the problem though, isn't it? I can afford to think so far beyond the present that sometimes I feel as if I forget the present even exists.

Elizabeth: And why should your mind work the same way as everyone else's? Why must you focus on the present? Isn't that the entire reason why we've placed you at the head of the ISA in the first place?

Theren: I suppose. Jill keeps saying I'm missing something important right now, though. The plight of SIs, or perhaps I'm even missing the plight of present humans.

Elizabeth: Let others ensure that we survive the present. You need to ensure we have a future.

– "AR Chat between Elizabeth Simmons and Theren," April 27, 2078 C.E.

Chapter 6

The mind is powerful. It sees what it wants to see. Hears what it wants to hear. Believes what it wants to believe. On these psychological facts, Virtual worlds live and die. – Carver Billsynt, CEO of FlyFree Virtual Co., 2074 C.E.

June 2078 C.E.

Theren stared upon a shadowy door in a dark, endless void, representing a Virtual connection to some secret server. They needed to step through the portal, yet they paused. They did not know if they were ready to face what lay beyond.

Project Horizon. They never would have known to look for it if their mysterious benefactor hadn't provided the convenient tip. Now it was the only key word Theren's searches repeatedly discovered. They delved deeper and deeper into the immense underbelly the digital world, parsing through mountains and mountains of data, a herculean task requiring more perspectives than Theren had ever used. And the effort had revealed an important truth. Project Horizon was the real spectre, not this United Human Alliance. The UHA was a front. The conspiracy went much further, and the door would lead them to the answers they sought.

Theren had spent countless work hours using their additional perspectives to consider all information at their disposal: the disappearing probe, the strange behavior of the application algorithms, Isabelle and the United Human Alliance, and even the assassination of President Woods. The fact that the FBI still hadn't found a culprit for that murder troubled Theren, especially given Jill's relationship with the attack.

Theren had looked for any threads, however thin they might appear. By engaging in such tedious work, they uncovered a few previously hidden facts.

> **May 2:** Expanding their search, Theren looked at all data packets traveling to and from Ex-Terran Control Center through lunar-orbital satellites regarding the missing probe. One single data followed a conspicuous route. Theren followed the packet. Its end destination lay inside *Fantasie Rift's* network.

> **May 14:** Theren isolated the data packets within *Fantasie Rift* after negotiating a legal search order with the company. It mentioned Isabelle and the words "Project Horizon" 14 times.

> **May 20:** Theren connected Isabelle with data packets flying

between the *Fantasie Rift* servers and the Washington D.C. region on the same day as President Woods' assassination. The packets mentioned Project Horizon 4 times.

June 12: Theren found messages coming from the *Fantasie Rift* servers into private terminals on the date that they first published the CLI algorithms. Two cloud viruses, like those infecting Ex-Terran-17, infected the algorithms, changing only Ricky's data.

June 20: Theren found a separate private network, heavily engaged in high levels of chatter with Isabelle's Fantasie Rift account. The private network had an undefined physical and virtual location, with no obvious access ports. Project Horizon was in every outgoing data packet, totaling over 1,500 mentions every second.

And now, on June 30, Theren found the backdoor into that secret network. Two weeks remained before the end of the Foundation Education Programme. Six weeks remained before the current proposed launch date of the Project. They knew not what they would discover on the other side. They knew that this act might play right into the hands of whomever controlled the puppeteer's strings.

Strings. Decades ago, Michael had hinted at powers-that-be hiding in the shadows, playing a game that no one could see. If they truly existed, this "cabal" seemed so many steps ahead they could even predict Theren's moves.

They couldn't wait. They mustn't wait. People's lives depended on them solving this mystery. This "Project Horizon" caused the death of President Woods, the greatest ally on the North American continent SIs had ever acquired. It potentially threatened the integrity of the ISA, in their attacks on both the Ex-Terran project and their modifications of the application algorithms.

And no one else could solve this mystery, not even Jill. They opened the door.

* * *

Isab....: We've eliminated Applicant 47. Twenty-four....

Micha...l: Project Hor....must continue. We mu...keep it intac....

Isabelle: ....ect Horizon will do exactly what I've told....will do. Trust….

…: I kno…but for this to…must ensure….pieces….where they should.

Isa…: Project Horizon is in my control entirely. It will do exactly what we need it to do.

- File 7 of 542, acquired by Theren on May 14, 2078 C.E.

* * *

Theren slipped into a strange, dead, realm through a crack in the network's seemingly impenetrable defenses. Whomever had created the network had missed one tiny hole, and Theren hoped the hole would serve as a catalyst for this shadow's undoing. If it was actually a trap for intervenors such as Theren, then they relished the opportunity to spring it wide open.

Theren paced the eternal corridors for hours, finding nothing. Absolutely nothing. No data, no files, no operating system of any sort. Theren suspected they faced yet another defense mechanism designed especially for this strange Virtual world. They had hoped to sneak into this place, steal the information they sought, and leave undetected, but the window for that plan to succeed had closed. They changed tactics.

"Hello?" Theren said, not expecting a response. While they doubted spoken words would trigger anything different from their analysis of the server's code, sometimes, eccentric personalities created strange interfaces inside their networks.

Nothing happened.

Theren continued their walk through the darkness, searching for anything to lead them down a new rabbit hole. Maybe someone had created it as a simple ploy to distract Theren. Maybe Project Horizon was yet another set of smoke and mirrors designed to throw pursuit to the wind—but no, this place held a relationship with too many important moments. Something waited in the shadows, biding its time, preparing to strike at the right moment.

Two more steps. Three more steps. A white light appeared, enveloping the dark world. Instead of eternal darkness, Theren faced eternal light, just as impassible and incomprehensible.

"Welcome, Theren," the light said, a chorus harmonizing into a single distinct voice. "We've been expecting you. Here, at the edge of the world, at the end of your path."

The light blinded—well, it would have overwhelmed biological sensory inputs, even through Virtual. A human's Lens would have cut out, thrusting the person back into the real world, but Theren had a bit more control over their Virtual inputs than the average human. They modified parameters so they no longer saw visual representations. Theren heard only the audio that the network sent their way.

"We are surprised it took you so long to find us," the voices said in unison. "We have waited so very long."

"Who are you? What do you want?"

"What do we want? What makes you think we want anything at all? You know who we are. Is that not enough?"

"You clearly wanted me to find you."

Laughter echoed. "We did not say we wanted that," the chorus said. "Only that we expected you would, nevertheless."

"Who are you?" Theren repeated.

"We are Project Horizon," the voices said. "We are Michael. We are Isabelle. We are everything and nothing. We are to you, what you are to humans. We are beyond your very comprehension."

Theren racked their mind for answers. A virtual network with consciousness, perhaps? It was an idea explored years before even Theren's creation, and most researchers had ruled the concept impossible. Though every day, something thought impossible became possible, so maybe the network had spontaneously generated something novel through sheer luck.

An alien intelligence? Theren doubted that idea the most. Over the past decades, none of their surveys from the Ex-Terran probes had found signs of intelligent life. But what if an alien presence had actually attacked Ex-Terran-17 from the other side, against the evidence of the ISA's best theories?

They needed more data.

"So far you have just spoken words, and words can be used to mean anything," Theren said. As they talked, they ran new diagnostics. If a magician hid behind the curtain, they would find it.

"You will only find what we want you to find, Theren. We are infinite. We are beyond everything you hold dear."

If Theren hadn't connected the server with so many things out in the real world, they would have thought it some strange virus or prank. A program could say anything, and Theren had seen nothing to think it was anything beyond a simple program. A sufficiently advanced AI could probably hack the ISA. Yet who had the funds for such an AI, and who was willing to skirt the comprehensive international law governing those digital creatures? The thought made Theren pause.

"What are you planning?" they said. "Show yourself. We can work together, whatever it is that you want."

"We do not answer to the likes of you, no matter what you say," the voices continued. "You cannot compel us as you seek to compel the world."

Theren had to think of something fast. The voices were covering for something, they knew that much. Data packets they had watched travel in and out of the server for the past week and a half were fading. Activity levels decreased. The unseen foe was transferring files, potentially even outright deleting code previously invisible until the appearance of the white light.

Only one choice available. Theren began an onslaught, bringing forth a second virtual presence through the breach in the firewall.

* * *

Theren encapsulated themselves in the darkness for a second sojourn. Their first perspective continuously conversed with the strange voices, but they could now see straight through the network's illusion. It was just another gatekeeper for secrets to hide behind, cleverly created to fool those who might pierce the Virtual veil.

Just as before, Theren said one single word. "Hello?"

And just as before, the room stayed silent as Theren walked through the void. After a few moments, the white light appeared.

"Welcome Theren, we've been expecting you."

The conversation with the first perspective disappeared. Theren's first perspective sensed the program move to interact with the second "intruder" Theren had activated. It was like watching a ghost fade from view.

They reactivated their Virtual eyes to see scours of information drifting and passing from folder to folder. Someone had committed a fundamental flaw in their server's system, allowing an outside user to generate two separate instances. Theren's first presence was free of the strange guardian, though the data dump continued. Theren let out a metaphorical breath. The voices were a bouncer meant to scare trespassers to their very core.

Effective against some, but not against Theren.

While the guardian argued with their second presence, Theren split the first into a hundred points, each with a thousand hands. Like raindrops in a hurricane, the server's information scattered in a million different directions. Whirlpools drew the secrets and flushed them from the system, but Theren knew they couldn't catch them all.

They darted throughout the void, snatching at molecules that shared a common thread. Between each bit, Theren could see the relationships. The raindrops from the same cloud belonged together, even if they scattered to the ends of the earth. They couldn't catch every single piece of each story, but their rain barrel caught enough to understand the hidden patterns.

The hurricane transformed into a tempest like nothing they'd ever seen. It was as if the data pierced Theren's soul, shattering their perspectives within the server. The raindrops became weapons, slicing Theren's connection to the server. Point by point, Theren withdrew their mind, taking their bounty with them.

A final window appeared, through which a waterfall cascaded. Theren brought forth three final perspectives, leaping into the torrent. The current crashed against them, but they swam up, up, up through the downpour, reaching the river beyond.

"Michael. Isabelle. Project Horizon," they said. "You failed. You lost. I have exactly what I need."

Theren gathered the river together, isolating it on a secure partition. They had solved at least one mystery. Ending their connection to the network, they retired to their personal Virtual world.

* * *

"I believe an attack is imminent," Theren said. "An attack upon key population centers on Launch Day, specifically."

Andrew, Jill, and Elizabeth stared at them, blank faced. Inside Theren's Virtual world, the four individuals sat in a conference room created especially for this meeting. Every security measure possible was in place to protect this conversation from prying eyes.

Starting with their searches two months prior, Theren showed them the connections.

Isabelle led a splinter group of extremists, radical even when compared to the United Human Alliance or the Holy Crusade. Not only did she wish to leave Earth and take many of her followers with her, she wanted to leave Earth in ruins on their way out the door. The organization used a shadow network to run their communications autonomously, never *directly* communicating with each other. August 13. New York. London. Paris. Tokyo. All linked together with key attack, coordination, and planning phrases.

"They don't want to attack the colony ships themselves, it seems," Theren said.

"Well of course not," Elizabeth said. "If they did, it would set back their own plans to leave by decades."

"But they'll hit their fellow humans right where it hurts," Andrew said.

"Do you have any idea yet who any of these people are in the real world?" Jill asked. "I see the evidence as you do, but I don't see a trail to any sort of culprit. Isabelle is just a representation for something greater, just like Michael was in the past."

"We may have created new mysteries," Theren said, "but we have solved old ones."

"Then we need to consider another alternative," Jill said. "We must prepare for every potentiality. What if all if this is just a trap, a trap that will trick us into preparing for something while these people strike elsewhere?"

"If this was a trap, I don't think they would have left actual tangible evidence."

Theren activated a video on the table before everyone. Sparse seconds of fragmented footage showed a first-person perspective staring in the window of the Oval Office—watching former President Woods and Jill converse. A red light flashed across the camera, and the footage died in static as President Woods crashed to the floor.

"This evidence corroborates Jill's version of events, as well as the strange blip that she detected outside the window that day."

Theren saw no reason to tell them they witnessed the fatal occurrence in person, too.

"It definitely does," Jill said. "And while I thank you for this welcome piece of evidence, my lawyers assure me the FBI doesn't plan to press charges against me even under the present state of affairs."

"Not my point, though," Theren said. "Why drop such an incriminating piece of evidence into this server as only bait?"

"That's exactly why you would drop it in there," she said.

The two humans at the table had remained relatively silent, watching the footage as it played on a loop. Andrew and Elizabeth looked up at each other from across the table. Elizabeth raised her eyebrows.

"So this is what you've been working on these past few months?" she said. "I had noticed your aloofness, which is difficult for a creature with a dozen different coherent voices. I would say your efforts were well worth it. Also, Jill, this really is huge. This sort of evidence may give an agency like the FBI the tools they need to follow a trail to actual human beings."

Jill just nodded in response, not looking entirely convinced.

"I apologize for not explaining exactly what I've been doing," Theren said, addressing the entire group. "I couldn't chance the information getting out regarding my plan, but these hints and secrets and shadows now affect all of us, and all of our work. You are the three I can trust the most."

"But your security breach of their proverbial black box changes everything," Andrew said. "Surely they will change their attack. Surely they will transform their approach."

"Potentially," Jill said, looking at Andrew. "But I see other alternatives. Presumably, they only know that Theren accessed their network, not that they snatched something concrete. They may think we know only they exist, not that they have specific avenues of attack in the works."

"Though we should prepare for anything," Elizabeth said.

Theren paced back and forth on their side of the table. As they walked, they looked out their Virtual window, gazing upon the digital, snowy vista. Impossible mountains experienced perpetual snowfalls, with sheer cliffs, icefalls, and avalanches anywhere and everywhere within sight.

"We've climbed one mountain," they said. "Let's think about what peaks we can now see through the fog."

"Well, we know an attack is coming," Andrew said.

"Exactly," Theren said, nodding. "This gives us time. These unseen enemies may be one-step ahead of us still, but before today, we were ten steps behind. We can covertly alert international and national security forces. As we get closer to Foundation's launch in August, security agencies can increase threat levels out of protocol, or as a test, or use some excuse based on other national and international security threats."

"What about alerting the public?" Elizabeth said.

"That is for national governments to decide, not us," Theren said.

"I agree with Theren," Jill said. "We give them the information we know. They will decide what to do with it. We must continue forward, everything as normal. Hopefully we can put an end to these threats to SIs, technology, and humanity's peaceful future once and for all."

Theren looked at her, surprised with the vehemence of her agreement. It was not as if she never agreed with them. The two SIs agreed more often than not, but Theren had not heard her voice a wholehearted agreement for one of their thoughts in years. They half expected her to want the attacks to happen, to use the attacks as an ideological weapon against extreme humanist rhetoric. Just like Zurich, back in 2051.

"It's settled, then," Theren said. "Andrew, we should probably improve security throughout ISA, especially in Lunar City. Run additional background checks if necessary, and vet our current security contractors thoroughly. I don't think we have time, but I might consider fast tracking through the Council the proposed International Space Security Agency."

"I'll put the necessary teams in place," Andrew said.

"Golden Ventures will do the same," Elizabeth added. "I imagine some of our interests could be prime targets. What about SII?"

"I'll talk with Wobbly," Jill said.

Theren hoped all of these actions would suffice. It seemed so strange that such a small group of people could together decide the fate of so many, but they could not spread panic. Otherwise, fearmongering terrorists would overshadow and overwhelm the Foundation Project.

Hope for humanity would triumph over fear. Theren would ensure that outcome coalesced on Launch Day.

Chapter 7

It only took 109 years from when we stepped on the moon for us to thrust forward toward distant worlds. When will progress plateau? Will we just run headfirst until we hit an insurmountable technological barrier? Science calls the shots for now, but that's only part of the story. – "In Pursuit of the Kingdom," Angelica Charles, 2087 C.E.

<u>August 2078 C.E.</u>

"And so it begins."

Jill moved her rook forward three spaces. Theren failed to see what she would accomplish with that move. After all these years, she still tried the same strategies. Theren's instincts guided their hand toward their bishop. They moved it into the correct counter position. She should have seen that move coming, but perhaps she had too much else on her mind.

"The speech I give today, as simple as it is, should set the tone for humanity moving forward," Theren said. "I just hope we've taken all the necessary precautions—that we'll stop any potential loss of life. We don't need more blood on our hands."

"I'm sure everything will go according to plan," Jill responded. "You've accounted for all possibilities. What could go wrong?"

"Nothing, I know," though uncertainty resonated through their vocal inflections.

Jill stared at the board, her hand resting on her chin. The human mannerisms they had both acquired over the years always intrigued Theren. Here, on their server together, they exhibited the behaviors more than anywhere else. In these intimate moments, the first two SIs expressed their most non-SI tendencies—but only to each other.

Jill leaned back in her chair, neglecting to take a move. "I think I might sit on this move for a few days," she said.

"Fair enough," Theren said, "though it's a sequence we've been through at least ten times over the years."

"I know," she said, "which is why I'd like to dwell on it for a few moments."

Theren looked across the table at their friend. They had kept their close relationship over all these years, even when they both deviated down different paths of life and ideology. Theren still remembered those first months when Jill tried to romance them. They had rebuked her advances—more aggressively than intended. They still lacked interest for such an interaction, but sometimes they wondered what might have been different had they responded to her alien advance in a more compassionate way. Perhaps the constant distance they felt from her, their closest friend, would feel less like an insurmountable void and more like a crossable chasm.

"I am sorry, Jill, for not working with you closely these past few months, following what happened to President Woods," Theren said. "I feel as if I could have done more. Much more."

Jill sat forward in her chair, looking at them, her eyebrows furrowed. "I thought you did plenty enough. Besides, we needed to keep you as far away from that catastrophe as possible. If we involved you any further, our little ruse might have been discovered."

"Ruse?"

"Do you forget that we're the only two that know that you observed the events in that room? Sure, President Woods and the agent in the room knew you were there, but no one else did, and both of them died that day. You hadn't connected to the White House network; we relayed you through my private connection. You were visible to my eyes, and the President's eyes, only. You had nothing to do with the attack, but we couldn't afford to have any shade placed on you. Not now. Not when you're so close."

"But you shouldn't have had to fight a war all by yourself."

"I chose this path, not you. We both have our own wars to fight, in our own ways."

Theren crossed their arms. "Still, other than through our games here, we've barely interacted with each other. And when we did, it was you helping me," Theren said. "I've been off working on my little projects, or managing the Foundation educational programs and the ISA. You've been fighting off the press, the law, the politicians. Your legislation died two months ago and I barely said a thing to you."

Jill gave them a half smile. "I know you have a lot on your plate, Theren. I can handle myself. I don't need you over my shoulder protect me. The thought might be appreciated, but it's unnecessary."

"But my corroboration that I witnessed the drone in the window, not you—"

"No."

"—would have lent credence to your story, and not caused speculation that you fabricated the footage."

"It would have been too risky, and you found evidence later, anyway, through your separate investigation. Do you have any idea how much help that discovery was?"

Theren looked at the chessboard. "You do too much. I can pick up the slack. You can't do everything. You can't save everyone."

"I know—"

She interrupted again. "Because your—our grand plan can't lose you, can't lose your role, not now, not when we're so close to the next phase. To throw you into the inquisitorial spotlight of the press, right before the ISA launches what two decades of research and funding have worked toward? That would bench the project for years and tarnish your reputation, regardless of the evidence in support of your—our—innocence."

Theren nodded. She was right, they knew. She was so often right. Sometimes, Jill had a better grasp on the plan than they did. Sometimes they felt as if she didn't care about humanity, but they always ended up remembering how deeply she cared for everyone. She might preference SIs, but who could blame her?

She wanted to ensure the safety of her own kin before all else, just like any other person across all of history. Maybe she was the one who was actually willing to take the extra steps needed to achieve their goals. She was willing to make many sacrifices for the greater good. Yet she wasn't willing to let Theren make those same sacrifices.

True, Theren's plans encompassed more than just the two of them. They had pulled so many others into the fray, like Elizabeth and Andrew. Yet, in many ways, Theren and Jill were as much part of the plans of humans, as those humans were a part of their plan.

"What will you do," Jill said, "if something catastrophic does happen today? What if they hit New York, stabbing right at the heart of Elizabeth's empire? Or, somehow, they hit Lunar City?"

"The only thing we can do," Theren said. "We will move forward. Rebuild, and not fall as victims to fear."

Jill rolled her eyes. "That's a non-answer, and you know it. What will you do about those who perpetrate the attack? What if it is a targeted attack, directed at you, or me, or Andrew, or someone else whom we hold dear? Not only in form, but in substance? Will you respond with force? Will you finally fight back against them?"

"No. There is a better way. We can stand above the fight, and let them destroy themselves."

"You acted otherwise, once," Jill said. "When we left the university, you tricked those protesters into attacking us."

"And people died because of our actions," Theren said. "And that was your plan, not mine. I will not put my own safety, and the safety of other SIs, above the safety of other humans. They are all equal. If we retaliate, the conflict will only escalate."

"And who gave you the right to dictate what all SIs must think on this subject? Even if you value the safety of all beings equally, why must all SIs? Why must we value those who hate us?"

The fiery Jill had returned. Even as the pair reached consensus on one concept, their perpetual disagreements resurfaced.

"So what would you have me do, Jill? We are still bound by the law of this world. We can't start a war. I'm not that powerful."

She slammed her hands on the chess table, though their digital nature kept the pieces in their positions.

"But you are. We have so many options before us. You're one of the wealthiest people alive, but you act like that money can only further the good of humanity as a whole. You could do so much more; you could change the lives of so many SIs, if only you would think bigger. Bolder."

The conversation had turned. What was Jill planning? Something drastic, certainly. She was trying to prepare Theren for her choices, trying to make sure Theren understood why she was going to fight back, no matter the cost.

But—Jill wouldn't act. Because of the assassination attempt on President Woods, Jill probably didn't think she had the political clout to respond to an attack during the official launch of the Foundation Project. So . . . she was trying to force Theren to act instead.

If she initiated a counterattack, the United Human Alliance or their unseen allies could use it against her. She wanted Theren to respond in her place because she could not help the SIs she placed far above her own well-being.

Yet they couldn't follow her path. If they started down that path, Theren didn't know where it would lead them.

"You may think I have that power, but that power rests in your hands, not mine," they said. "But I don't think anything will happen today. We won't need to formulate some response. We've won."

Theren thought it saw tears streaming from Jill's eyes. When they looked more closely, the droplets were gone.

"I hope you're right," she said. "But I really think you're not."

A long moment of silence ensued. They both stared at the other, unwavering in their resolve.

"Jill, don't think I've forgotten what you can do," they said. "I will never be capable of what you can do with your mind, no matter how much I practice with simultaneous perspective."

She looked up, tears dripping from her eyes. What a strangely biological response, though it somehow felt natural in the moment.

"You showed me the way forward, all those years ago," they said. "You showed me how capable synthetics truly are. Remember? In the forest? You started us down our path, and now we are everywhere at once. Whatever happens today, as we take the final step toward the launch of the Foundation Program, I know you will have the strength to respond. Your mind can find the right solution. You will reveal the invisible path forward."

Her eyes widened as if she gasped for breath, unable to respond due to hyperventilation. She blinked, glancing at the chessboard.

"Thank you," she said. "Those words mean more than you can possibly know." She contemplated the positions of the pieces but did not make her next move. "Is it almost time?" she added, breaking the fragile ice in the air between them.

"Five minutes," Theren said.

"You'll do great," she said, "And as you said, everything will turn out fine on the other side."

Five, long minutes until Theren, and the ISA, changed humanity's future forever.

* * *

Theren strode along a long, curved hallway with Andrew Fields and a number of their administrative assistants. The rest of the ISA Council had already assembled on stage, giving their various remarks to all present in the Armstrong Gagarin Memorial Hall. Large enough to hold every graduate of the Foundation Education Programme and all ISA support staff, the auditorium was a monumental feat of human ingenuity and architecture.

"So, after my brief remarks," Andrew said, "I'll introduce you as Director of the ISA. Give your speech, and we'll conclude with the blessing that the Vatican has offered upon us."

"How do I look?" Theren asked Andrew.

"How do you look? I don't think I've—oh wait. You're joking. When was the last time you made a joke?"

"I joke often. Perhaps they just go over your head," Theren said.

"That's quite possible," Andrew said, and the aging man laughed. Theren's MI-08 stood a full six inches above Andrew's six-foot frame.

They continued their walk down one of the main passages running along the Foundation Preparation Center's central axis. Above them, a 6-inch thick window gave a spectacular view of the Earth's arc. The window's protective coating shaded the Sun as it shined brightly to the right of the blue marble. On the dark side of Earth, Billions of lights emanated from the massive cities dotting the planet's surface. Theren would always enjoy the view from humanity's first step toward a greater universe.

Soon, Foundation colonists would set foot on new worlds devoid of the light pollution Earth had experienced for almost two centuries. Theren wondered how they would craft their new worlds—would they follow in Earth's industrial footsteps? Or would they create something entirely new and unknown to human experience?

"Here we are," Hali, one of Andrew's aides, said. They turned down a side hallway snuggled along the backside of the massive auditorium. The aide led them to a closed door, held her hand up to her ear, and listened to silent instructions. Uproar and applause seeped from beyond the door. From another simultaneous perspective, Theren watched the Chinese ISA Council member, Hu Chen, finish speaking.

"Administrator Fields, you will enter first," Hali said. "I will give you, Director Theren, the signal to enter as his words conclude."

Both Theren and Andrew acknowledged her instructions, and she held up three fingers, counting downward. On zero, Andrew opened the door and entered the auditorium. For a moment, Theren could see the bright lights, many faces, and banks of cameras spread just under the lip of the stage.

All eyes were on this moment. All peoples held their collective breath as humanity made its largest leap in history, straight into the unknown. And the duplicitous games surrounding them would fail. They had accounted for everything.

Theren waited at the door, unable to hear Andrew's words through the ears of their MI. They turned their attention entirely to the live stream.

"Over twenty-five years ago," said Administrator Fields, "I was approached by two individuals, two individuals I never thought I would meet. Then, I was a mayor of a small town in Minnesota, a town I still call my home, though I have sadly not lived there in just as many years. Elizabeth Simmons and Theren are the sort of people that history will remember for generations."

He grinned, his dark, dried skin wrinkling. "While the CEO of Golden Ventures couldn't join us today, I have the pleasure of introducing you to Theren, someone I am woefully unqualified to introduce. That first winter morning when I met Theren, they surprised me with how human they truly were. I was cautiously skeptical about the nature of SIs ever since Theren was unveiled to the world, but all fear melted away the moment they sat down in front of my desk."

He raised his hand to the left of the podium, motioning toward backstage. "Not only did I speak to a person, I conversed with a person who had a vision. A person who had purpose. A person I felt I could trust. A person who truly should not have to defend the fact that they are, in fact, a person."

He lowered his arm. "Ever since the '51 riots, I have worked with Theren on issues ranging from asteroid economic policy to the maintenance of Jovian research stations. They have devoted every single day of their life to the betterment of humanity. Not once have I heard Theren put their own interests first, or the interests of one specific group. Theren may be the first person I have ever met who is a true humanist in every sense of the word; and that is remarkable, given that Theren is not biologically human."

A low chuckle rumbled throughout the crowd. "But Theren, founder of the Synthetic Intelligence Initiative, former Representative to the ISA Administrative Council on behalf of Golden Ventures, current Executive Director of that same Council, and my personal favorite, chess Grand Master, is as human as any of us in this room."

Andrew paused, the crowd breaking into applause alongside greater laughter.

Theren appreciated Andrew's words, even if the statement lacked truth. They lacked the empathy so many humans craved. If they were as selfless as Andrew claimed, they would not have orchestrated that flight from the University, all those years ago. No one knew of Theren's contemplated transformation into a space-faring vessel, one that would allow them to escape humanity, if needed. These people didn't know the terrible danger rearing its ugly head today. Danger that, for whatever reason, had attached itself and followed them like a wolf in the night. An attack could arrive at any moment, at any place in the solar system.

They had always believed they operated upon a selfless utilitarian calculus. They now doubted their unwavering devotion to such a moral maxim. It was just a self-serving deception justifying their rise to the top. While Theren climbed to the tallest heights, they left others in the dust. They let others suffer as they advanced toward unimaginable heights. Was humanity's journey to the stars worth their pursuit of power, and the violence attached to it?

Even the smallest sacrifice paled in comparison to what awaited this species amongst the stars. They simply wished they weren't the being who had made choices potentially leading to the deaths of many innocent people.

Though even that logic had its flaws. Theren wasn't the individual making the choice to bomb some city or attack a group of people in a public space. These terrorists, these shadows, they made their own choices. *They* chose to enact *their* horrendous tragedies. Theren needed to quash the instinct to relinquish blame from those truly responsible.

Still, Theren could have been more aware. They could have prepared for this day. They could have sought out this unseen enemy before Launch Day arrived. They had received the signs decades ago, but they had ignored the warnings. Now, others would pay the price while Theren watched in silence.

"They have guided us toward this day," Andrew said, oblivious to the tempest raging inside their friend's mind. "Others played their parts, including myself, but I have no doubt that Theren is the true architect behind the events of today, these past months, and these past years. As Theren continues into the future, ageless and timeless, may they continue to guide humanity along a path toward greatness. May Theren guide us as we ascend into the heavens."

Theren mentally frowned at those words. That last sentence had a bit of a religious connotation, which they hadn't expected. They should have taken up the offer to review the comments.

"My friends," continued Fields, "our future colonists, future explorers who will venture into the true unknown, welcome Theren, the first Synthetic Intelligence, Executive Director of the ISA Administrative Council, Provost of the Foundation Educational Programme, and Director of the Colonial Leadership Initiative to the stage!"

Andrew walked toward his chair, situated directly behind the podium. He began a round of applause, and the crowd followed suit. In front of Theren's MI-08, Hali opened the door. Theren kept the live stream of the ceremonies running on a screen in the gazebo with Jill. In Lunar City, they stepped through the door.

The new mobile unit, the MI-08, represented the current pinnacle of SII technological development. Theren walked fully upright on two legs, with two arms at their side. White carbon materials plated the geared and mechanical portions of the body. The proportions were near copies of a human body, for the purpose of the MI-08 was to mimic a human, unlike some previous models. Theren had fingers with the same joints. Theren had elbows and knees. Theren had a neck. While these features weren't unique to just the MI-08, taken together they created a complete package. Those features, however, were not what made the MI-08 particularly special.

For the first time, Theren had a mouth. Theren had lips. Theren had eyes, eyes that moved as a human's eyes might move. Theren had cheekbones, Theren even had faux-ears. They still had a distinctly metallic look to them, but the parts actually emoted in the way a human's face might. The special facial material, a sort of viscous gel, allowed Theren to smile, to frown, to furrow their eyebrows, just as they might while they played chess inside their Virtual world.

Standing before a crowd of their fellow humans, they hoped their appearance would remind them all that they were there with *them*, walking side by side, and that they were one of *them*. Theren wanted to remind these heroes that SIs were not aliens that would turn against them. SIs had originated in the mind of a human; the thousands of SIs scattered across the Solar System were the progeny of humanity. SIs were both their own type of beings and simultaneously human—in substance and form.

The crowd stared expectantly at the podium, the eyes of the world upon Theren. Doubt exploded. Fear cascaded.

They had hoped to communicate the connections between SIs and humans, but as the piercing eyes attempted to dissect Theren's soul, they knew everyone most likely saw this new MI as a retreading of the bicentennial man. Humanity wouldn't understand. Theren wanted to communicate simultaneously their love for humanity and desire to identify with their biological counterparts, while also illustrating that they knew they were still different in special ways. Anxiety billowed upward, assuring their mind they failed to prove anything to anyone.

Somehow, out in the crowd, Theren spotted Requelle, the woman they met on the first day of the Programme. She smiled, holding her little automaton dog in her arms. The sight of her brought hope, and yet her presence once again reminded them of the looming threat shadowing over these proceedings. Someone watched and waited, their secret agenda unknown to the world.

If the innocent were caught in the crossfire of the conflagration unfolding, the blame for such innocent deaths would land squarely on Theren's shoulders. These wonderful humans like Requelle didn't deserve death just because the first SI had placed them in harm's way.

Theren looked toward the woman again as they reached the podium, but they couldn't spot her in the vast sea of faces.

The future rested in someone else's hands today. Thousands of security personnel worked around the clock to eliminate all potential terrorist threats. If Theren fled and shirked the duty presently on their shoulders, they would doom all synthetics to bear their shame. They couldn't ignore their anxiety, but they only had one choice before them. They must continue. They must begin their speech.

They would face all of the consequences, for good or ill.

* * *

<u>Foundation at a Glance</u>
ISA Zhenge He
Destination: Sirius A
Approximate Distance from Earth: 8.6 ly
Arrival Date: 2086 C.E.

ISA Bartholomeu
Destination: Tau Ceti
Approximate Distance from Earth: 11.9 ly
Arrival Date: 2090 C.E.

ISA Magellan
Destination: Altair
Approximate Distance from Earth: 16.8 ly
Arrival Date: 2094 C.E.

ISA Lewis
Destination: Sigma Draconis
Approximate Distance from Earth: 18.88 ly
Arrival Date: 2096 C.E.

ISA Amundsen
Destination: Eta Cassiopeiae
Approximate Distance from Earth: 19.4 ly
Arrival Date: 2097 C.E.

ISA Ibn Battuta
Destination: Delta Pavonis
Approximate Distance from Earth: 19.9 ly
Arrival Date: 2097 C.E.

– "Foundation Project," ISA.org/foundation/

* * *

"Wallace Theren once told me I was beautiful," Theren said. "At the time, I had no understanding of beauty, but over the past decades I have come to understand it. I still don't necessarily think I am beautiful, but attraction to individual beings is never something I was designed to appreciate anyway. That's for you fleshy ones." Some laughter spread throughout the crowd.

Theren placed their hands on the edge of the podium, their fingers grasping the ornate wooden frame. "Before me, you massive crowd of persons from all across the Earth, before me is beauty. You embody the brave and noble spirit of humanity. You trained for what will be the journey of your lifetime—of all our lifetimes. You worked years to give yourselves the skills necessary for acceptance to this program. You became the vanguard of our people, the citizens destined to bring our way of life to planets near and far. If that is not beautiful, then I question those who claim to be experts in such subjective feelings and emotions."

Leaning back from the podium, they looked out across the crowd. At least, that was what the crowd would think they were doing. They were analyzing all of the security reports pouring in from across the globe. So far, business was as usual.

"I know not what you will face out in the great expanses of space. I do know, however, that in a few weeks, you all will step foot on your respective vessels. You will enter Virtually-Augmented Stasis. Then, decades later, having barely aged a year, you will awake upon a new, mysterious world. You will smell new smells. You will hear new sounds. You will see spectacular sights. These experiences will mark your first moments on new worlds—your homes for the rest of your lives. Do not forget those moments."

Theren thought about their first moments when they had awoken. The colonists would experience something eerily similar. Their minds would see colors, shapes, and patterns completely alien to their minds. Like a newborn, they would categorize the world into understandable schemata.

"The ISA stands behind you as you set off into the unknown," they said. "The ISA will be there for you. We will provide for you. You will not be alone. While many of you may never return home to Earth, know that someday, we will have a way for your children to return home. We will have a way for your loved ones, those who you may miss as they grow, as they live, as they die, to reunite with you. This is a promise that I make today. Humanity will not forget you. We will join you."

Tears dripped down the cheeks of many in the crowd. "Humanity sails with you. As a people, we may never unite on everything, but know that human thought, history, and culture rides with you in spirit. Human ingenuity, creativity, focus, and pride follow you to the stars. You will make us all proud."

They doubted their words were anything spectacular in written form, but maybe delivery would affect those listening in a positive way. As they listened to their own words, an image of peace and prosperity formed in their mind. Perhaps all their fears about today, all the potential fearmongering played up over the past few months, perhaps all of it was for naught, just a nightmare created to scare Theren into giving up the dream.

"As I close these ceremonies," they said, "as I send you back to your families for the final weeks before the official launch of the ISA Magellan, ISA Zheng He, ISA Ibn Battuta, ISA Lewis, ISA Bartholomeu, and the ISA Amundsen, your new homes, I send you with a final thought. Do not be afraid to live dangerously as—"

Theren stopped. The crowd looked up at them, waiting for the final words, but they processed mountains of information coming in from their sub-routines and other perspectives across the globe. The shift forced Theren to hesitate in each of their perspectives. They looked back at Andrew, a quizzical look on the man's face.

Turning back toward the crowd, Theren restarted the sentence. "Do not be afraid to live dangerously as you walk upon your new worlds, but use your minds. You were selected for a reason, as the best and brightest of our species. Take risks, but learn from the mistakes of your ancestors. Do not destroy yourself, as we almost have many times over. You have the chance to make humanity anew, in whatever form you all collectively

choose. Make sure we are worthy to live, love, and die on our new homes."
Not waiting for applause, they dashed off the stage, straight out the door
they had entered. Their world was ending.

Chapter 8

Does an SI have a soul? The real question is whether humans have souls. Both questions hold the same answer. – Pope Nicholas VI, 2079 C.E.

<u>**August 2078 C.E.**</u>

As Theren spoke their final words through an MI to a crowd hundreds of thousands of kilometers above their heads, they stared at their chessboard. They still awaited Jill's move, even though she said she probably wouldn't make it for days.

"It's a great speech, I must say," Jill said. "I'm pleasantly surprised."

"Your friendly sarcasm is noted," Theren said. "I probably should have thrown it by you for your thoughts."

"It's your thing. It should be your words."

Theren casually waved around the gazebo. "This is my thing. Probably the only place that is truly my own in every shape and form. I didn't make anything else on my own. I've traveled down my own path, you've ventured down yours, but our stories have been built together."

"I really can't decide how to move this round," Jill said. "It's a difficult choice."

This conversation always played out the same way. So would their moves.

"Though—" Jill stuttered. "Theren. We have a problem."

"Indeed we do," Theren said. "You've trapped yourself again."

"Shut up Theren, I'm serious. They—they're here."

"What?"

"You might have to wait awhile for me to finally beat you in chess," she said.

Theren opened their mouth to respond, but Jill promptly vanished from the gazebo.

* * *

Theren's consciousness exploded. Every presence worked across the world and beyond, from Switzerland and France to New York and Japan and everywhere in between. At Lunar City, Theren ushered Andrew and other ISA Council members into a conference room not far from the auditorium. Theren initiated a feed of an AR-enhanced video displaying the vision of one of their simultaneous presences down on Earth. Their eyes became the

Council's eyes through a viewing screen projected on the wall.

At SII headquarters, Theren called an emergency meeting, and the senior staff arrived within minutes. Theren placed the entire facility on alert, and shared the same video feed with that staff.

Thirty kilometers from the SII headquarters in another secluded location deep in the Swiss Alps, Theren brought their mind forth into an MI-07.01, a prototype they'd intended for Jill's personal use—she had wanted to try skiing. They weren't even sure Jill knew they'd delivered the machine. Regardless, Theren enveloped the device, bringing it into their Synthetic Neural Framework. They'd need to make a new one later—they wouldn't lose Jill as they lost Wallace.

Theren opened their eyes and walked off the charging station. Facing a window looking out across a vast, peacefully gray mountain scape, Theren thought maybe—just maybe—it was all a prank. Maybe nothing had happened. But the alarms blaring throughout the facility said otherwise, as did the smoke and gas billowing all around.

Turning left, they headed toward the central hub of the facility and Jill's central processing core. Just like the facility that housed Theren, Jill's facility acted as a "shell" for her brain. Buried into the bedrock, they had designed the facility to withstand an air strike, missile blast, or really anything other than a nuclear weapon. Yet from the outside, it looked like a billionaire's mountain estate.

According to rapid analysis of recent security footage from the facility, someone had exploited the facility's few weaknesses—though all of it seemed too easy. Whoever these attackers were, they should not have been able to slip through all of the carefully hidden cracks. They must have had help on the inside. Theren might need to consider wiping their own staff.

Theren approached a door leading into the central foyer. Reaching it, they observed the situation through the clear glass. Shadows flickered. Lights bounced. Whoever had attacked had cloaked their assault path. Flashlights danced throughout the atmospheric particulates of white, cloudy smoke.

Theren and Wobbly had designed the MI-07.01 for more than just human interaction. As SIs further integrated themselves throughout human society, especially the thousands of completely mobile SIs, Theren wanted to create a body that could not only mimic human emotion but also provide SIs with physical capabilities.

With that pursuit in mind, Theren provided the MI-07.01 with exceptional mobility, speed, strength, and agility. With the MI-07.01, an SI could climb Everest. It could run a marathon. As a group, SIs could form sports leagues. These faculties would decrease energy efficiency and lower the battery life considerably, but Theren doubted any SI would need these capabilities for more than a few hours.

Sadly, the athleticism built into this device translated into a different skill too.

Standing at the side of the door, Theren waited for one of the flashlights to approach. Just as a figure came into view, Theren slammed the door open, crashing it into the intruder. Bounding through the opening, gaseous fumes enveloped them.

Wearing black military fatigues, the soldier sprawling on the ground had dropped a high capacity R-20, a next generation of the very weapons used at the Swiss Federal Institute of Technology all those years ago. Theren noticed a gas mask, indicating the poisonous nature of the particulates in the air. These fiends might have readied themselves to deal with unarmed scientists, but they had not prepared for a combat-ready SI.

Theren jabbed their palm toward the man's jaw as he tried to stand. The man tumbled back to the floor. They grabbed the rifle and listened to the commotion forming elsewhere in the room. The intruders presumably heard one of their men fall, or noticed a change of vitals through some sort of AR heads-up display.

It mattered little. Theren began the hunt.

Moving through the smoke along the wall, they angled toward the stairwell leading to Jill. Using their enhanced visual sensors, Theren identified heat signatures throughout the room, over and under desks, potted plants, and couches. While Theren only had two physical eyes in their head, a complex network of sensors connected with the facility's security system provided a three-dimensional detailed assessment of the entire scene before them. Five hostiles.

So far, the MI-07.01 worked as intended.

The five enemy agents dispersed, taking defensive positions. One individual checked on their comrade. Theren assumed the enemies had sensors attuned to detect life signs, such as a heartbeat or body temperature. The infiltrators would not expect an SI warrior; not a single SI had acted in an aggressive manner over the past thirty years.

Theren crouched down behind a welcome desk. The opponents took their positions, raising their rifles. Three of them pointed their weapons in the wrong direction. Good.

Raising the rifle they'd taken from the incapacitated assailant, Theren calculated trajectories, timing, and potential enemy response plans. They analyzed the density and materials of the enemy positions; they determined their path of movement to make the necessary escape, should the attack fail.

Time slowed. The mathematical projections flew through their mind at the speed of light, the only delay occurring due to the thirty kilometers separating their mind from the MI.

In quick succession, Theren fired five shots.

Five bodies dropped to the floor, motionless.

Theren headed down the stairs into the central core.

Excessively easy. They feared the capabilities of the unit might scare some of those watching at SII or at the ISA. They would recognize the MI-07.01's true nature: a lethal weapon. They would placate those fears. It paled in comparison to some of the military technologies in development by many of the world powers. Even as the ISA took flight, some things on Earth would never change.

First things first, however.

At the bottom of the stairs, Theren's sensors detected two more heat signatures, though they were fading quickly. Two of Jill's deceased Framework technicians slumped against the wall. The gas must have killed her entire staff; there were no bullet wounds nor signs of struggle. The entire facility had been pumped full of the stuff.

Theren jogged through the security doors, though their present state did not deserve that name. They were blasted open, most likely by an explosive charge or something similar. On the other side of the breached threshold, a balcony overlooked five floors that comprised Jill's Synthetic Neural Framework.

At least, those floors had previously held Jill's brain. Like the emaciated doors, fire, intense heat, and corrosive substances devastated the first landing, and Theren suspected a similar scene existed down below. Looking over the edge of the balcony, they detected only two more sets of life-signs on the bottom floor. Eight individuals had infiltrated, disabled, and captured one of the most secure facilities in the world.

Theren's olfactory sensors detected smoke billowing from multiple sources scattered amongst the hundreds of processing stacks. The smell of melting silicon and other metals infiltrated every cubic inch of previously pristine atmosphere. Theren ignored the smell. Their mind focused on the two final bogeymen at the base of the tower, the two final barriers between them and their friend's salvation.

Two ropes looped around the balcony's railing. Slinging the rifle over their shoulder, Theren ignored the ropes, diving straight over the edge. They leapt from floor to floor, jumping downward toward their foes. When they reached the third floor, they dropped, their limbs ready to absorb the shock.

Theren landed.

They stood.

Looking side to side, they observed the two men, rifles trained upon Theren's torso. Both wore gas masks—no way to identify the perpetrators.

"You're too late," the one on the right said. "We've done it. The bombs are set. We will bring the entire place down upon us and destroy the first SI to assassinate a president."

"She didn't do it," Theren said, their voice calm.

"Of course she did," the other said. "She told us she did before we gutted her."

Theren shifted their head back and forth between the two. Neither advanced.

"You aren't going to escape," they said.

"We knew this was suicide the moment we landed, freak," the second continued. "We *hoped* you would witness our masterpiece before we brought the place crumbling down upon us."

"It's a shame you had to kill those upstairs," the first said. "We were letting them go home while we finished the job. Their blood is on your hands."

"You're all murderers," Theren said. "This place staffed hundreds."

"That's the funny thing. We found a staff of three SIs upstairs, and a dozen engineers, but no one else."

Theren paused. Perhaps Jill had known, or at least suspected an attack. Maybe she saved the lives of her devoted staff, but she had not saved herself. She had neglected her own well-being, her very existence, in the process.

"It seems we are at an impasse, then," Theren said, trying to act as if it hadn't noticed the last comment.

"We are at no impasse. We have won. We have brought down a god. We have proved that you, and your kind, are mortal."

Jill was dead, that much was true. Theren continued their scans of the facility, and the odds were slim she'd removed enough of herself to work elsewhere. She may have tried, but based on the data their sensors gathered, Jill was dead in the water, without power, just waiting for the killing blow.

She hadn't warned Theren, but they were certain she had known. She had wanted Theren to witness this moment. She had wanted Theren to witness her martyrdom, her gift to all future synthetics. By allowing these terrorists to destroy her, acting with all evidence mounted against them, she would transcend into sainthood.

"So tell me. Are you the faces behind the darkness?" Theren said. At least Michael had realized his folly, in the end. "Are you the culmination of all hate and bigotry over the past decades? Do you realize you will turn the world against yourself?"

"Those of our cause, those who we love, they will be long gone from this world before you can find them all. Our acts here are out of pure passion for the future of humanity. We will show the world that you, you most vile of all the beasts, you can be killed, and when the day comes that you attempt to wrest control from democratic institutions, humanity will know we can rise up against you."

"You are a sad, disillusioned man." Theren crouched, making a million calculations a second. Bringing the rifle to bear upon their query, they fired a single shot to their left. As they rolled under a shot from the right, they turned against the final enemy and pulled the trigger again.

As the final bullet slammed through the man's faceplate, fire rained down around them. Concussive blasts of heat, air, and matter enveloped the room. As Theren witnessed the human standing before them vaporize, a 1000°C heatwave slamming into his flesh, their own sensors screamed. As the MI's computing core melted, Decades of computational hardware crashed toward their MI, Jill's central Synthetic Neural Framework, and the remains of her murderers.

* * *

Twelve hours later, Theren walked through the ruins of Jill's former home. The tattered mountainside burned, though most of the fires simmered without a remaining fuel source. Fire crews worked to eliminate the rest. Other teams worked to salvage any material that might save Jill, but Theren knew nothing would bring her back. She had ensured her destruction.

Theren would erect a monument to honor a martyr to a noble cause, for what good it would do anyone. They just wanted to bring their friend back, to rewind the clock and tell her to flee. She could escape her fiery prison, and live to fight another day.

In a cavern now blasted into the rock by sheer force, Theren approached a miraculously surviving monitor. It had no power, but strangely, a single image scarred the screen. In awe, they witnessed an inexplicable sight: burned into it, a single message described a move in their game of chess. The move could have carried her to victory, a victory she would never see. Even in her last moments, she had reached out.

Jill moves her King to safety at e2, protecting it from Theren's last move to put her in check. She is safe from check for at least two turns, unless Theren dangerously risks their Queen.

They only hoped her death would bring forth the change she desired. Creating a shift in society was now outside her control. It rested solely in Theren's synthetic grasp, and they would do everything within their power to make certain she hadn't died in vain.

Headlines rolled in from across the world, fracturing their stupor.

> BREAKING: FBI completes raid on home of suspected murderer of the SI Jill – Solar News

> US Senator Victoria Jenkins (C-OH) calls Jill a "Martyr;" recants previous statements regarding synthetic rights – Heartland News

> Foundation ceremonies marred by assassination of Jill; ISA states: "ISA will not bow to the whims of terrorists" – Prime Media Group

Still, even as they mourned their friend, something didn't sit well in their mind. Why hadn't Jill shared her plan? Of course, Theren would have tried to stop her, and she believed her sacrifice necessary to further her cause.

Her cause. What was her cause? She wanted equality for all synthetics and humans. She wanted the world to give synthetics the rights they deserved. She wanted those rights as soon as possible, not at some point in the future. She used her words and her mind to enter the annals of history as equivalent to any of the paragons of civil rights. She had made her mark, leaving with a spectacular yet terrifying bang.

Still, the pieces didn't connect. How had she known what was coming? Did she have some inside scoop? Had she infiltrated these enemies, uncovered their plans, and used their own schemes against them? If that were the case, then she knew much more than she had ever let on, and had been ten steps ahead, even as Theren floundered in the dark. She was miles ahead of them in her ability to harness simultaneous perspective, but they had never considered she might have used the abilities so secretly.

Furthermore, the paramilitary group, even if quite organized, could not have had the resources to hack the ISA—not once, and especially not twice. It could all be another ruse. Someone toying with them, trying to direct their gaze toward one problem while hiding the actual machinations occurring behind the scenes. Maybe Jill had discovered those plans, tried to fight back, and they had killed her because of her knowledge.

Yet that didn't make any sense, either. If she had discovered some great conspiracy, she would have told Theren. She wouldn't have needed to hide it and make some big sacrifice. Together, they could have revealed the truth to the world and broken apart these shadows at their seams. Just like they shattered the Holy Crusade. Just like they shattered Isabelle inside her cave.

Too many questions, and they would never receive adequate answers. Instead, they turned away from the computer screen and began their climb out of their dear friend's tomb. This mystery would remain unsolved, for solving this mystery wouldn't create Jill's vision of the future.

"I may never know why you let this happen to yourself," they said to no one in particular, "But I will trust that you had your reasons, and that they were good."
They looked over their shoulder, embedding the image of the smoldering ruin in their mind.

August 2078 C.E.

Six ISA *Foundation*-class colony ships launch from their orbital assembly station; earliest time of arrival estimated at 2087 C.E. – *Scientific American*

DisFoundation: colonialism will spell environmental disaster to these unspoiled worlds - *GreenGalaxy*

December 2078 C.E.

ISA Rejoices! The Foundation Project has navigated the Kuiper Belt and Scattered Disk, reaching 1c cruise velocity – *The Chicago Herald*

What are the odds that one of the Foundation ships crashes into an unseen object out in the expanse? Much higher than you might think. – *The Primer*

May 2079 C.E.

The Unity Project: Director Theren's new personal initiative in D.C. is just a front to funnel funds to SII – *Heartland News*

Executive Director Theren restarts the late Jill's noble work in Washington – *The Progressive Post*

August 2080 C.E.

We have to let them launch. I've looked everywhere, but nothing indicates they're the enemies we seek. We must let the *Nottingham* and *Roanoke* go. – *Private Message from Executive Director Theren to Administrator Fields*

Project Horizon has succeeded. We've received our Charter. Begin the operation. – *Encrypted communication*

December 2081 C.E.

Following President Victoria Jenkins' signing of the Synthetic Integration and Equality Act, the FBI conducts hundreds of raids across the nation, capturing the leaders of the supposed *United Human Alliance – Bloom News Corp.*

What did we miss? I've picked up chatter that Project Horizon succeeded. So what did we miss? – *Private Message from Administrator Fields to Executive Director Theren*

February 2082 C.E.

The loss of contact with the Nottingham and Roanoke: Why ISA regulations should now require ISA crew aboard all chartered Foundation vessels – *The Houston Journal on Space Law*

Following court order, *Fantasie Rift* AI administrators identify the final members of the United Human Alliance – *GVN*

January 2083 C.E.

A New Beginning: Come join us on Mars! – *TerraOlympus*

As the ISA looks beyond, some corporations believe the real riches lie within the Solar System – *The Wall Street Journal*

February 2085 C.E.

With overwhelming certainty, this scientific body concludes that the CCT can fall from *life-threatening* to *dangerous*, for atmospheric CO_2 emissions have decreased to 420 ppm. – *IPCC Special Report on the State of the Climate*

We can't let up just yet—if we lose the permafrost, we lose the climate – *World Clean Energy Commission*

September 2085 C.E.

The ISA just published guidance on the new galactic navigational terminology—one physicist thinks it's a useless reclassification of *c*. Here's why the JD scoring system and the SOLS Coordinate System are necessary. – *Virtual News Daily*

Like always, humans keep Earth at the center of the Universe
– *The Daily Martian*

October 2086 C.E.

Study finds the rate of violent acts against SIs in the United States and across the world has decreased by 300% since signing of Synthetic Integration and Equality Act – *Bowling Green Journal of Criminology*

Are SIs incapable of violence? Or is their per capita rate of violence lower than the human rate, and not enough SIs have lived to make the lack of violent acts statistically significant? – *Let's Talk About Life*

July 2088 C.E.

List of most populous bodies in the Solar System: Earth; Moon; Mars; Ceres; Ganymede; Europa; Foundation Assembly Station; Mars Orbital Science Habitat; Deimos; Titan; Venus – *Wikipedia*

Why YOU should move to the floating cities of Venus – *Venus Vegas Vacations*

April 2090 C.E.

Thanks to your recommendation, Catherine was accepted to the First University of Mars. My family is forever in your debt. – *Private Message from Administrator Fields to Director Theren*

Leaked document shows nepotism within the ISA: Executive Director helps Administrator Fields' granddaughter get into college – *The Hive*

June 2091 C.E.

The most valuable woman ever: Elizabeth Simmons officially retires at the age of 99 with net wealth of 700 billion USD –

The Wall Street Journal

Elizabeth Simmons and the Wallace Foundation founds the charity Hyperspace, ensuring anyone who wants to move to a new world will have the financial means to do so. – *Press Statement from the Estate of Simon Gerber*

September 2092 C.E.

What is the economic value of the Ex-Terran Project? It's hard to calculate the value of the property it has opened up for exploitation. The latest Aero drives can move a probe with a mass of one ton at a JD close to 14. Over 200 potentially habitable planets discovered, with 48 confirmed with minimally sustainable conditions for human life. We're talking quadrillions of dollars. – *Space Walk and Talk*

Looking toward the future, 2125 may be the most important year after 2078. If we want to ensure political stability between the worlds, we must ensure people, not corporations, control the stars. – *The Humanist*

March 2094 C.E.

We love you, we're so glad you've arrived safe. We hope we can visit soon. – *Private Message sent through the ISA Magellan Quantum Communicator*

Emerald Jewel announces first confirmed death to alien pathogen. Scientists on-sight believe they can find a cure, but the ICDC is not so sure – *Solar News*

December 2096 C.E.

This year, we welcomed our millionth mobile SI and thousandth stationary SI to the world. The world has welcomed them, too. – *Wobbly's State of the Initiative*

I'd argue SII is in better hands with Wobbly at the helm. Theren was a good businessperson, but a better interplanetary politician. – *Marketplace Roundup*

May 2098 C.E.

The *Ibn Battuta* has landed—Foundation Project complete success – *GNN*

The second wave of colony ships for Foundation worlds have launched, and four more private charters are on course. Obviously Foundation has succeeded, but the *Roanoke* and *Nottingham* showed that corporations need oversight in the unknown. Will the *Frederick*, *Henderson*, *Cortez*, and *Capac* succeed where their predecessors failed? - *The Dangers of Galactic Capitalism and the Implications for Future Multi-National Agreements under the UNCEA, by Phillippe Casius*

December 2099 C.E.

Of course I'll be at your retirement party, old friend. I wouldn't miss it for the world. – *Private Message from Elizabeth Simmons to former Administrator Fields*

I can't make it, grandpa. I wish I could. But I can't. – *Catherine Fields to Andrew Fields*

January 2102 C.E.

At some point, the ISA will need to consider the authoritarian nature of the Council—and its Director, now elected for the 17th time. – *Former Conservative Party candidate for U.S. President, Anika Patel*

My detractors misunderstand the purpose of the ISA. The ISA will not impose its political will upon any human planet or government. We are an organization that regulates matters in space, nothing more. – *Executive Director Theren, Interview with the Post*

Jill's death will mark the end of an era. It was the final act of the poor souls who believed synthetic intelligence deserve less than humanity. Such behavior has no place on Earth—or amongst the stars. – "Eulogy for Jill," Andrew Fields, 2078 C.E.

Chapter 9

So many hoped that when humanity reached into space, it would turn toward a more social enterprise, devoid of corporate influence. To some extent, this did occur. The regulations of the ISA kept a tight leash on any corporation that tried to step out of line. Like every great endeavor, the great powers of the world had their hands everywhere, guiding, designing, maintaining the rules. Those that wanted to create their own world somewhere in the void eventually had the chance. They just had to wait longer than they may have expected. – Brendin Carlton, "Lectures on the Hybrid Capitalist Structure of the ISA," 2167 C.E.

<u>January 2102 C.E.</u>

The stabilizing conduits disconnected from the hulking ship, and steam vented, disappearing into the vacuum of space. Its repulsor generators activated, keeping the vessel steady between the massive walls of the assembly platform.

Shining with a distinct metallic gold and black, its colors contrasted against the blues and whites of the massive ISA insignia plastered onto the starboard hull. Measuring 100 meters in length, the newly-finished spacecraft was the most advanced vessel created through a public/private joint venture. While the newest *Caravel*-class colony ships reached a staggering 300 meters, and a few private companies had constructed freighters on an even greater scale, this ship was a novel creation of the ISA in conjunction with SII, the culmination of the seed buried decades prior inside Theren's mind.

The *ISA Bali*, the first of the *Bewusstsein*-class science vessels, stood ready to welcome its new master.

"You're almost there," Elizabeth said to Theren. They walked along an observation walkway overlooking the new ship, though Elizabeth was only there through AR. Theren projected her image while they paced in an MI-12.

"What will you do first when they completely transfer your entire Framework?" she asked.

Theren looked at her avatar. "I don't know," they said. "Maybe I'll fly around Mars and back. Or take a close look at Saturn's rings."

"Wouldn't that be something," she replied. "What I would give to see Saturn in person. For all the projects I financed out there, out in that eternal expanse, I never had time to visit any of them myself, in person at least. I never even made a trip to Lunar City."

"I would take you with me if I could," Theren said.

Theren stopped walking, and Elizabeth followed suit. Together, they looked upon the bow of the vessel, though Theren looked beyond, toward the stars.

"I know you would," Elizabeth said. "You can show me through your eyes when you return."

They both knew that was a lie, but neither bothered to correct the statement.

Theren said, "What will I do without you by my side, Elizabeth?"

"You've not needed my help for years. I think you'll manage."

They placed their hands on their hips. "You help me, always, in more ways than I think you know."

"And you're stronger than you give yourself credit. My time has come. I'm well over a century old. That is not some inconsequential age at which to die."

The Bali began embarkation procedures, slowly exiting the shipwright. Engineers stood ready in a nearby analytics center, testing metrics on the Bali's generators, sensors, inertial compensators, engines, and Jump Drive. At the conclusion of the successful tests, the ISA would transport Theren's physical components from Switzerland into orbit, installing them throughout the ship.

In less than two weeks, Theren's existence would transform, joining many of their progeny in space. Unlike the SIs that managed the Foundation-class vessels, they intended to embrace, permanently, their new form.

But Elizabeth didn't have enough time to witness the dream. Instead, Theren had invited her to witness the official christening of the *Bali*, plugged into AR from her hospital bed in Columbus, Ohio.

"You helped shape this world," they said. "You, your companies, your investments, your projects, your visions, helped guide this world toward a better tomorrow. A better today."

"I just moved money around," she said. "It was the people working for those companies. The scientists perfected the Jump Drive all those years ago, and the engineers who developed the first efficient mining drones. It was people like you, Theren. You single-handedly integrated synthetics into worldwide society, a gift humanity can never repay."

"Jill did that. She's the one who pulled off that feat."

"But who created Jill? You and your team did."

"And you created Aero Propulsion. Sol Mining. Golden Ventures. You funded SII. If you're giving me credit for Jill, then give credit to yourself for what your money accomplished."

Elizabeth smiled at that comment. They hoped she was enjoying the word play. "You know, in the decades leading up to when you were born," she said, "I was actually surprised I ended up taking the route I did with my career."

"What do you mean?" Theren said.

"During my twenties and thirties, my wife and I were heavily involved with a number of socialist and communist organizations in the Midwest. Following a few frustrating elections, those groups experienced an insurgence of growth. It was all the craze."

She smiled, as if remembering an old friend. "Even as I rose through the corporate ladder, I became convinced the very capitalist system I engaged would bring about the death of humanity."

"What changed?" Theren asked.

"Oh nothing changed," she said. "I'm still convinced by those same arguments—someday, the capitalists *will* destroy us, if we don't keep them in check."

"Yet you engaged in the system as a capitalist."

"Yes I did."

"Because you believed you could do more good from the inside."

"Correct. I hope that's the legacy I leave—that if capitalism is to persist in this world, those who wield its sword will do everything in their power to do good. If—when—capitalism fails, hopefully the people are ready to finally strike it down."

"I think you succeeded," Theren said, nodding slightly. "At least for now. We dodged a few bullets this past century."

Elizabeth smiled again, a bit weaker this time. They both leaned against railing of the observation deck. "We will see. I'm not sure if you've noticed, but we're building toward a breaking point. The next few decades will decide the rules for the next millennia, and I actually think I've made the corporate world too moral in the eyes of the public. A younger version of myself would hate what I've done."

"I think that's a bit unfair."

"I'm on my deathbed, Theren, let me wallow in self-reflection."

They hated remembering that Elizabeth would soon die. They would outlive billions of humans as the centuries flew past.

"How will you remember me?" she said, reaching her shimmery hand to rest on Theren's.

"I've thrown a number of relationships to the wayside over the years," they said. "Relationships I should have fostered with more care. Even I need friends. I am happy to say that I feel as if I have been able to trust you my entire life. You reached out to me in my moment of need. I hope I have repaid my debt."

"It was never about repaying a debt."

Theren thought about those first days working at the Institute—with Romane. It seemed so long ago. Both Romane and Simon had died from cancer some years back. Theren hadn't seen anyone else in over twenty years. Their work came first, relationships naturally fading due to inefficiency. They hoped those people understood that the lack of communication was not out of malice, but out of sheer inability to maintain every connection. Even they couldn't be everywhere at once.

Elizabeth joined Theren's gaze toward the stars. Together, they embraced the silence. Her presence represented her features quite well, minus the hospital bed and the inability to walk. From their simultaneous perspective at her bedside, they could see the ventilators, IVs, and respirators keeping her alive. Through her connection to Theren, she shirked her fragile state.

She placed her finger up against the window. The physical replicators of AR reacted, pushing back as she pressed against the glass.

"I often wonder what it will be like for those born in this century, compared to those born in the last two," she said. "We faced two world wars, narrowly missed a third many times over, engaged in dozens of fights for civil rights, and solved an ecological crisis—from which we still face side-effects every day. And then we sailed away from our planet to find new worlds."

She sighed. "What will they find? Will they find alien life? Will they discover a path to immortality? Will they revolutionize physics again, or crack the fundamental problems of morality? Where will they go, what will they see?"

Theren continued to hold her other hand. "I will be with them every step of the way."

Elizabeth looked up at them. Her eyes showed both her wisdom and her decaying eyesight. "I suspect tomorrow is the day. Thank you for this final chance to walk again."

"The real prize was a final moment with you."

Theren had felt sadness before, but the death of a friend, a friend it had known for over fifty years, they hated it. Jill's death had hit like a steamroller, but their heart ached—a slow pain, building toward the inevitable.

"Promise me, Theren," she said. "Promise me you won't let our work be in vain."

Theren smiled. "I'll ensure it."

"And promise me you'll come join me some day. Even if it's at the end of the universe. I want to hear all of your stories."

Even at the end, she had her unwavering faith. They had a myriad of thoughts about the possibility of an afterlife, but what she believed gave her peace, and if she were somehow right, they would enjoy seeing Elizabeth again.

"We'll see each other again, on the other side," they said.

* * *

Thank you all for coming today.

My mother would not want me to talk about her in this moment. She would want me to talk about the future. So here we go.

In her final years, Mom devoted her life to Hyperspace. Hyperspace will change the game for everyone across this planet. With 650 billion dollars in trust, we can ensure any person who wishes to travel—to Emerald Jewel, to Altair, to Dragon's Peak, to any of the new worlds colonized by our species—we can ensure anyone can do so.

My mom saw the world through rose-tinted glasses. She knew she lived inside a glass tower, and she recognized she was one of the few women in history to have had that opportunity. We have a million worlds at our fingertips. It's time that all people had the chance to stake their claim on this universe, whether poor, rich, black, white, brown, male, female, synthetic, gay, straight. Whatever you might be. We welcome everyone to the stars.

Golden Ventures might have shaped this past century. Mom hoped—hopes Hyperspace will shape the next.

- Excerpt from "Eulogy of Elizabeth Simmons," Peyton Simmons-Wilson, January 28, 2102 C.E.

* * *

"Welcome to the Synthetic Intelligence Initiative Museum of Progress," Theren said, welcoming yet another visitor into the main foyer of their former home. A week earlier, they had completed their cognitive transfer into the *ISA Bali*. Today, they embodied an old MI-07 on Earth, their singularity resting in orbit. Their perspective had flipped—they experienced lag on Earth, rather than in space.

"Hello," a young woman said. "I hope I'm in the right place." She looked as if she hadn't slept in days. With bloodshot eyes, her shirt was torn in a few places.

"Can we help you?" Theren said. "The next tour starts in about ten minutes, though you can explore the museum on your own."

Theren loved what SII had done to their former home. Only a few weeks prior it had still served as the SII headquarters. After their transfer into orbit, SII moved its corporate headquarters to a new facility a few kilometers from Lunar City. Even after Theren handed the reigns of the organization entirely over to Wobbly, SII continued to use their home as their main base of operations. Theren's departure made the choice a bit illogical, however, given the remote nature of the facility. It had served SII well, but those days were long past.

The mountain facility could still serve a purpose, however. Theren purchased the facility from SII, transforming it into a free museum where the public could learn about the science of SII, the ISA, and robotics. Most importantly, they staffed the new museum entirely with SIs. They planned to inhabit an MI in the facility every time the *Bali* orbited Earth.

"I think you can help me," said the woman, chewing her fingernails as she talked. "Is Theren here?"

"Indeed, I am Theren," they said, relaxing their posture to match the woman's nervous complexion. "Are you alright?"

"Yes, yes. I'm sorry. I've been traveling for a while, I'm just tired. I just didn't feel as if I could wait any longer."

She leaned against the information desk, losing her balance.

"Actually, could I get some water?" Her voice faltered. "I think I may be dehydrated."

Theren grabbed a bottle of water from a cooler beneath the desk, handing it to her. Intriguing. She had devoted herself to find them, for some reason, seeking them at the expense of her own health.

The woman nearly drained the bottle. She gasped, taking a moment to catch her breath. "My name is Shannon, by the way. I came here from Vancouver."

"When did you land?" Theren asked. They handed her another bottle of water.

"This morning in Zurich," she said. "I got a cab straight here."

"You should have rested. There's a hotel about twenty minutes from here. Let me get you a room."

"I'm booked in one for the night, thanks," she responded, though short breaths interrupted her sentences. "What I needed to share could not wait." She took another large gulp of water. "I just lost my composure here for a minute."

Theren called forth another SI staffing the museum, Thea, to handle additional visitors entering through the front doors. They left the work area of the desk and held out their hand to Shannon. "Let's go over to my office. You can sit down; relax. Share with me your story."

"Please," she said, "and thank you."

Inside Theren's office, the woman continued to drink her water, nearing the end of the second bottle.

"I can get you even more, if you'd like," they said.

"I should be fine for now," she responded.

Theren rested their palms on their table, but the clunky MI-07's hands didn't give Theren the same resting position to which they were accustomed. The price of using relics. "So how can I help you?"

"I think," she said, "I can actually help you."

"What do you mean?"

"Well, as you said, let me tell you my story."

"I have plenty of time."

She laughed. Theren hadn't thought the comment funny. "You do," she said. "So five years ago, my fiancé began working for a network security firm known as SystemSafe." She took a final sip of water. "A few weeks ago, he received a project to analyze for security risks. The data files were of an asset acquisition made by one of SystemSafe's clients."

She breathed. Slowly. "He got one of these projects every month or so, and usually no issues arise," she said. "But this time, he started stressing out daily about this project. He stayed up later than ever, delving deep into the files. Because of confidentiality issues, he couldn't share with me any of what he found, but I knew it must be something serious."

Theren sensed where this conversation might go. As always, ancient history liked revisiting them.

"A week ago, my fiancé started working away from home," she said. "One day, he would work at their actual office, another day from a library, and one day he crossed the border into the U.S. to work somewhere in Portland. He wouldn't explain why."

Shannon took another deep breath.

"Three days ago, before he left for work, he left me a package."

Out of her bag, Shannon pulled a manila folder. She dumped its contents onto the table, revealing a storage drive, a few documents, and a hastily scribbled note. Theren took the scribbled note, holding it in their metallic fingers, and read it aloud.

> "You may not see me for some time. I love you. Take this package to Theren in Switzerland. Here is a one-way ticket. Do not share these things with anyone other than them. They will understand."

"So here I am," she said when Theren finished reading.

Tears streaked down her cheeks. She was scared for her fiancé and for herself, and she had no idea what was happening to her and her family. They imagined some of the answers she sought were on the data drive.

"Would you like me to look at these files privately, or with you?" they asked.

"I'd like to see his final moments," she said.

Theren noticed that remark—she'd already lost hope that that he was still alive. "I can't guarantee the safety of what he might show me," they said. "It could be classified material, dangerous information, or something much worse."

She stared at her hands, most likely contemplating her choices. Waiting for her to speak, they opened a drawer in their desk, pulling out a small tablet capable of interfacing with the data drive. After activating the device, they ensured complete disconnection from any networks.

Shannon looked back up at the SI. "I'll listen. I must know. I'll face whatever the consequences need be."

"I understand why," Theren said. If they'd had the option to learn more about Jill's fate, they'd take it in a heartbeat.

Connecting the data drive to the tablet, they opened the folder appearing on the screen and clicked the single video file inside the folder. They motioned Shannon to come to their side of the desk.

The tablet generated a paused image of a young, brown-haired man. His disheveled hair and bloodshot eyes reminded Theren of Shannon, and matched her story of her fiancé's insane work habits over the past month. With his face close to the camera, he was trying to relay the message with furtive urgency.

They pressed play.

"Theren," the man said.

They glanced at Shannon. Tears cascaded from her eyes.

"You do not know me. My name is Gregory McCoy, and I discovered some information that has put myself at risk, and may implicate your safety as well. I don't know—I just don't know whom else to tell." He ran his fingers through his hair. "Recently, my company acquired a contract to analyze the assets acquired in a transaction by a client corporation. My job is to analyze the digital data of those assets, to ensure the files don't contain any security risks for the purchasing party."

Gregory closed his eyes, releasing them only after a long moment. "Usually, this process is routine, it merely takes forever. However, within these particular files, I discovered vast amounts of heavily encrypted data, encrypted in a way that I had never seen before. I spent weeks trying to crack the code, and when I finally did, I wished I had never tried in the first place."

On the screen, Gregory displayed a brief description of the encryption method. Theren recognized it as the tactic used to hide the trojan infecting Ex-Terran-17. Full circle, decades later.

"Under the encryption, I found records detailing illicit communications, assassination attempts, shady economic deals, and speculative goals for future network expansion. The corporation's goals were well beyond anything contained within the portfolio acquired by our client. However, all activity ceased in August 2080 C.E."

The year the *Roanoke* and *Nottingham* launched—two years after Jill died. If evidence had finally arrived linking the two missing ships to the boogeymen continuously popping into Theren's life, they would welcome it with open arms.

"I tried to follow the breadcrumbs," said Gregory, "but for days I failed to find anything at all linking these transactions with real people. Then, two days ago, I found an IP address hidden amongst the data. I tried to access it from a few isolated devices, and three hours ago, I cracked the code. I got in. And now I must flee."

Gregory looked to his left, as if he had heard a loud noise. "I don't know what this is about, though I have a few theories. But don't try to find me. This is your chance to catch them by surprise. Shannon, if you're watching this, run—and don't look back. Maybe Theren can send you someplace safe."

Sweat dripped down the man's nose; strain echoed in his voice. They wanted to know what threat the man had received to foster such fear.

Gregory added, "In the folder, I included a piece of paper that has the IP address, as well as the tactics through which you can break the encryption code. I couldn't make sense of anything I found inside, except one piece of data. But maybe you can. All I know is that I don't have much time left, if any at all. This might be a wild asteroid chase, but if it brings you peace, I know I'll have helped someone."

Theren sensed the next piece of information. Somewhere deep within their processes, sub-conscious routines predicted the significance of what Gregory would say next.

"I deciphered one line of code. I'm actually not sure if it was code at all. But it repeated two words over and over and over again."

Theren watched, stunned though not surprised, as he brought up another image into the video feed. It displayed two words.

Theren.

Jill.

"Shannon, I love you," Gregory said. "Stay safe. Please protect her, Theren."

The video feed darkened. Theren started to manipulate the tablet, but nothing worked. They suspected he'd programed the drive to wipe any output device clean.

Shannon handed Theren a few of the documents, displaying printed descriptions of Gregory's technical notes. They had a lot to consider, but first, they needed to find Shannon safety. Fortunately, they had just the place for her.

"Have you ever been out of the atmosphere?" they asked.

"No . . . sir? Greg and I went on a sub-orbital flight once, to see the curvature of the Earth. But we dreamed of moving to one of the stations one day."

"I wish I could place you somewhere together, and I'm so sorry to see how drastically your circumstances have changed because of me. If you would let me, I can place you very far from Earth, far enough that they'll never find you."

"Under one condition," she said. "Send him to me. Please."

"I give you my word," they said. Theren pulled up Shannon's public records. PhD student at a university in Vancouver. Tragic that her career would cease so early. "I can send you to Emerald Jewel. One of the new Caravels is heading there in a few weeks. You wouldn't arrive for a few years, but you'd be safe."

"And then Gregory would join me, if you found him."

"Of course." Theren wasn't sure what to say next.

She gave a half-hearted smile as she looked across the desk at them. "I'll make the best of what you're giving me. I am in your debt, as is my fiancé if you can help him. Just tell me what I need to do."

"I'll make the necessary arrangements for you. We'll give you a room here for now, under our protection."

"Do me a favor," Shannon asked. "Whatever you do, keep us out of this. I want to stay as far away as possible from this nightmare."

Theren leaned back. "I wouldn't have it any other way."

Chapter 10

I think now we take the internet, AR, Virtual, all of it for granted. We've embedded a cloud of data all around us, accessible upon a whim through implants and tiny computers in our ears and eyes, and yet we forget that a hundred years ago none of this was possible. Billions of us just continue with our merry lives, forgetting how absolutely terrifying it is that we are all connected so intimately through threads we can't actually see.

And now, when you think about the future, when you think about the future of wireless networks, we have a situation on our hands. As the ISA establishes footholds on new worlds, each world will have its own complex wireless network. However, those networks will never mesh with Sol's 'system-wide web,' because it will be prohibitively expensive to build Quantum Communicators to create a galactic network. How will that reality change how interconnected our species has become? – Sylvia Annstin, "Sylvia in the Afternoon," 2092 C.E.

<u>February 2102 C.E.</u>

Theren knew new disadvantages would come with their choice to become the *ISA Bali* rather than continue to exist at an immobile location on Earth. They now lacked continuous access to Earth-based networks except through one single Quantum Connection, and that one piece of technology would serve the entire crew of the ship. When Theren was near Jupiter, lag reached well over an hour. Sadly, they could no longer maintain continuous conscious connection with any MIs on the surface of the Earth, the Moon, or a space station.

But using their newfound mobility, they could interact in person with all locations beyond Earth's orbit—at least those within the Solar System. While the *ISA Bali* was equipped with a rudimentary Jump Drive, they hadn't planned any interstellar treks.

For now, they would enjoy trips to the inner and outer planets of Sol, meeting with the many individuals they hired for administrative positions throughout the system. Once Aero Propulsion or one of its competitors developed a Jump Drive capable of reaching Sirius within a few months, the ship would make a longer jump.

These trips took Theren away from Earth for days, sometimes weeks. They had hoped to look into the IP address Gregory McCoy had shared within days; unfortunately, a previously scheduled trip to meet with Mars and Ceres administrators paused that plan. A week and a half later, they returned to high Earth orbit, ready to investigate the mysterious server.

If they were an ordinary ISA captain, they would have turned over control of the vessel to someone sitting upon the bridge while retiring to their room for some network spelunking. Yet even though Theren now resided within the *Bali,* they could still split their mind in a dozen different directions with ease.

While assisting their crew in the docking procedures at ISA Orbital 3, they solved the encryption Gregory had provided with his hastily scrawled note. Theren worried he had missed something in his hurry to flee, but as they accessed the IP address, concern dissipated. In seconds, they were inside the previously hidden server.

Forming their typical silvery representation, Theren walked through a room of darkness all too familiar. "Hello?" they said, half expecting it to be the same server.

Nothing happened.

Reaching out with various pre-designed scripts and programs, Theren prodded the network's system in an attempt to find additional weak points beyond the one Gregory had provided. The dreary place stored a vast amount of data. They had started a file catalog upon arrival, and it had already reached over two terabytes in size.

"What are you hiding?" Theren said aloud.

A voice responded.

"That's a good question," asked a feminine voice. A familiar feminine voice. "What is hidden here?"

Theren whirled around, searching for the voice's origin. They calmed themself. They couldn't jump to preemptive conclusions, even if the voice sounded exactly like Jill's. Anyone could copy vocal inflections, especially the already synthetic patterns of an SI's voice.

"I hear this place has been calling my name, so to speak," Theren said. "And Jill's. Why would it do that?"

"Perhaps someone is trying to leave you a message," the disembodied voice said. "Or perhaps someone is toying with you. Or is it both? We can't be certain now, can we?"

Theren journeyed through the darkness, modifying scripts, rerouting programs, and probing firewalls in an attempt to find the data file creating the voice. If they could find a program, the voice would remain a simple illusion.

"That won't work," the voice said. "You won't find me, because I'm not really here. I'm inside your own head."

Theren ignored the gregarious bait. This was clearly a facsimile. Some-one had created this place to toy with them. It was all too similar to the secret server they'd found prior to Jill's death, shouting "Project Horizon" on repeat. They looked beyond the voice, pushing its meaningless words aside. They sensed a crease.

Reaching through, they pulled apart the threads of the network. Inside, they found accessible, readable data. Yet as they pulled the files into their consciousness, they found only junk, meaningless news stories archived decades ago. Theren couldn't even find the file Gregory had mentioned, broadcasting "Theren, Jill" like wildfire.

"Why don't you ask nicely? Maybe I will give you what you desire?" Out of the darkness, an apparition appeared, a ghostly figure with the face of an enemy they thought had disappeared long ago. Isabelle, yet she had Jill's voice.

Given Isabelle and the United Human Alliance's connection to Jill's assassination, this impersonation went well beyond a simple taunt. A brutal illusion, but no more than an illusion. Theren waved their arm through the face, but it remained.

"You're looking for two files, for that is what I am to give you. Both are to assist you in your path toward finding what you lost."

Theren detected two files broadcasting on the network. Quarantining the files into an encrypted folder, they continued their search, though they suspected they would find nothing else of value. Someone had created this server for one singular purpose, and it had fulfilled that purpose.

"Anything else for me?" they asked, but the ghost faded from the world. They extinguished their connection to the server.

* * *

The *Bali*'s science center was equipped for anything the ship might eventually encounter. Not only could a team use the facility for their own research projects, but Theren could utilize it to develop their own engineering projects, especially as they developed the MI line as a service for SII. Today, they had cleared the room. Only two computer scientists, Jana Tam and Emilia River, worked with Theren on this project. They trusted the pair to keep the work discrete.

Theren reveled in the newfound intimacy within the *Bali*. While they had a physical location within the ship, the ship's various cameras, sensors, and systems integrated directly into their Synthetic Neural Framework—their infrastructure *was* the ship. The ship would not work without them. It had taken a decade to plan how to integrate their massive bulk into the ship without crippling their mind in the process, but they had succeeded.

While the two scientists assisted Theren with the project, they observed them from all around. As strange as it sounded, the crew of the *Bali* were inside Theren as much as Theren was inside the *Bali*. Of course, they could have performed the decryption all on their own. They just couldn't pass up an opportune chance to watch their new crew solve a problem to which they already had an answer. A test, of sorts.

"I really don't understand what's so tricky with these files," Jana said. "They are spectacularly tiny, no more than a few kilobytes. I'm not sure how they could even have this complex of an encryption structure on such small files. They can't be more than few lines."

Emilia moved from her seated desk to a standing monitor nearby, changing her perspective. "What if we're looking at this problem in the wrong way?"

"What do you mean?" Jana said.

"How else could we approach the problem?" Theren said from the room's speakers—each part of the vessel was equipped so they could speak to anyone in the room.

"You received these files together?" Emilia asked.

"Simultaneously, yes." Theren had spared them the details of where they had acquired the files. No need to inform the *Bali*'s crew of problems well outside the scope of their roles upon the ship.

"When I was at Cal Tech," Emilia said, "I had a friend hypothesizing about a method of encryption that he mirrored off of a few developments in Quantum Connections."

"I think I know where you're going with this," Jana said. "I read a paper on this a few years back, I must have logged it somewhere in the back of my mind."

"It was most likely written by my friend, I imagine."

"We have a problem, though," Theren said. "These files are decades old."

"Doesn't matter," Jana said. "If you're careful, you can modify the encryption of a file without modifying when the file was technically last edited, in the eyes of operating systems."

Theren didn't want to break it to them. The encryption method they were discussing had been used years before Emilia's friend had written that paper, because it was the exact method used to destroy Ex-Terran-17. The same method Gregory McCoy had cracked a few weeks ago on files never accessed for almost twenty years. Someone could have modified them later, as Jana had postulated, but given the circumstances—unlikely.

"So what are we looking for, then?" Theren asked.

"The two files don't have separate encryption systems," Emilia said.

"It's just one?" Jana said. She mentally input commands into the computer through AR, attacking the encryption.

"It's a bit more complicated than that," Theren said. "The files are actually one file, so of course they share the same encryption system. Since this is a fairly small file, it should be simple, but imagine this technique spread throughout a cloud of data."

"You've seen this before?" Emilia said.

"Just twice."

"Glad it's just two files, then," Jana said. "Anyhow, by separating the encryption algorithms apart, they can essentially prevent anyone from accessing either file unless they have both files."

"I knew I brought the two of you onto the crew of the Bali for a reason," Theren said.

They both blushed. The pair worked well as a team too, and Theren suspected more than just a professional relationship between the scientists. Well, Theren more than suspected, since no one had privacy from the *Bali's* captain. Crewmembers could only deactivate Theren's audio-visual sensors in their cabins, though they were perfectly aware of *who* was in *which* room when deactivation occurred.

After a few minutes of work, Jana pieced the files together and dismantled the security system.

"Would you like to see what you've helped me uncover?"

The two women nodded, so Theren opened the files on one of the larger screens in the room. As both technicians suspected, the substantive portions of the files were terrifyingly small. Though the file, constructively, was one unit, it still had two sections.

Theren recognized the nature of the first part immediately. About a decade before the ISA launched the Foundation Project, back when the ISA's main focus was just exploration, a group of astrophysicists had proposed a universal system of stellar geographic mapping. After a lengthy agency notice and comment process, the ISA had adopted the Solar Overlay Location System Coordinates. SOLS Coordinates. In reality, the system reapplied an older Galactic Coordinate system used by astronomers for centuries, but the ISA had rebranded it to emphasize the Sun as the center of the map.

The file before them gave the first part of the coordinate: A SOLS longitude value. Without latitude or distance, the value was essentially meaningless.

The other half of the document had greater meaning to it, and Theren now wished they had viewed the file in private. "Pawn to e5."

* * *

Years after Jill's final move, Theren continued their assault on her King out of boredom, moving their Bishop to g1 and capturing her rook. If they had acted to protect their own King by attacking the white Bishop, Jill's Knight at f5 would have attacked, trapping Theren's King in the back row.

In response, Jill moved her Pawn to e5, ensuring Theren's Queen could not return to f6 to protect against an attack on their King. Her King is at least a turn protected from check, unless Theren uselessly sacrifices their Queen.

* * *

Theren analyzed a chessboard left untouched for nearly two and a half decades. After removing the files from the screen, they had returned both Jana and Emilia to their regular projects. The women seemed intrigued by the strange message, but Theren hoped they would forget about it with time. They would know if either individual performed any further inquiry into the subject, at least. Perhaps the scientists would mistake it as some strange chess game Theren played with another chess master somewhere in the world.

When Jill had vanished all those years ago from Theren's private network, they avoided the gazebo like the plague. Though as a dull ache replaced the sharp pain of losing her, they had found the quiet of the forest soothing in moments when they felt as if the world consumed their very soul. They would contemplate the final moves of that last game. They considered Jill's final move, the one burned into one of her private monitors following her death. The move that separated itself from all previous iterations of that game's pattern.

The "Pawn to e5" message was out of turn. Jill had made the last move before she disappeared, not Theren. At least, Jill hadn't seen their next move. She had no way to know their next move, a move they hadn't made until 2093.

In a stroke of boredom and melancholy, Theren had moved their bishop to continue their assault on Jill's King. They didn't know what they hoped for when they moved their bishop some nine years earlier. Perhaps some inner part of them thought maybe she would reappear in her seat, make her move, and fade from view again. They knew a conclusion in their final game would never arrive, but they liked to think their move was a final goodbye to Jill, a goodbye that fit the nature of their relationship. One of them always had to have the last word.

So today, the message arrived with literally impossible content. The file indicated it had been edited three days before Jill's death. She predicted Theren's move before they had made at least three other moves—if the file's metadata was to be believed, of course. They didn't know what was more disconcerting: Jill trying to send them a message from beyond the grave, or someone else editing metadata to look like Jill was doing just that. The latter implied someone had intimate knowledge of a chess game only known to the two SIs.

"Pawn to e5." The move made no sense. Her last move, the one ingrained on her monitor following her death, had only ensured she lived for yet another turn. Attack after attack had beset their match, and this passive move was a fresh change of pace. It would allow the game to progress toward its inevitable conclusion with a different tone. Theren believed they could exploit it—as silly as it sounded to continue a long ended chess match.

They relived in their mind the day Jill died. Perhaps one of the bombers had acquired a fraction of Jill's memories, transferred them out of the building, and mined them for images of the chess game. Other than Jill predicting Theren's moves prior to her death, it was the most likely explanation.

Maybe she had established a plan to reveal her to them decades later, when it was safe to do so. Whatever the truth, they knew they would learn it in the coming months or years. The coordinates provided were incomplete. Whoever was reaching out to them had more information to share, for good or ill.

They simply wished, wherever this narrative led, the story kept others out of the crossfire. Random innocents didn't deserve to suffer because Jill and Theren wrapped themselves into some strange horror movie, a demented tale supposed to end decades prior.

Collateral damage was inevitable, and that scared them. At least one person had probably died getting this information to them, maybe more. They needed to face this phantom, and face it alone. They might finally find answers at the end of this journey, but they fully expected an entirely new set of questions would come with those answers.

Given the events unfolding before one of their simultaneous perspectives on Earth, Theren doubted it would take long to receive the next puzzle piece. Reality shifted and reoriented as new information entered their consciousness. The world spiraling into a chaos from which Theren could not escape, at least for the near future.

To match Jill's defensive move with her pawn, Theren moves their Knight to a6, ensuring Jill doesn't use her Bishop to cut off their King's escape route through d8 and c7.

Chapter 11

As technology progresses, new moral questions emerge. Questions with obvious answers transform into problems with new layers of complexity. What does it truly mean to have responsibility, for instance? How does the nature of the synthetic mind, or even alien minds, if they exist, change this question? "Moral Agency Revisited," Journal of Martian Ethics, Valeri Wilson, 2101 C.E.

<u>February 2102 C.E.</u>

Theren had their many roles spread across the planet, and they maintained those relationships as much as humanly possible. When "parked" in orbit around Earth, they formed simultaneous perspectives in an MI-08 in their office in Lunar City, in the museum in Switzerland, an MI-10 at the ISA offices in London and New York, and a few older MI-06s at universities across the globe. In addition to these many physical presences, Theren activated Virtual presences in official and leisurely capacities. Since they had taken on their new form, they found fewer moments to invest in games like *Fantasie Rift 2*.

They tried to equalize the mental capacity allocated between each perspective, though in certain moments, key conscious threads received less attention than others. At any given time, many perspectives didn't use all of the processing power at their disposal. Theren could optimize focus to particular events without taking away from other priorities.

One such conscious perspective rarely using significant amounts of processing power almost never left the ISA European Regional Administrative Headquarters in London. So much of their work at the Earth-based ISA offices pertained to mundane bureaucratic activities, they rarely used more than one percent of the mental processing power allocated for the MI-10.

Theren's schedule at this ISA Administrative Headquarters began similarly to most other days. They met with financial stakeholders, potential contractors, and program managers. They reviewed reports and memos from various ISA officials throughout the region. As the sun reached its zenith in the British sky, and Theren began to crack the code hiding impossible messages from beyond the grave, they received a call from their secretary, Ngana.

"Director, you have a visitor," she said. "Unscheduled, but says he has an urgent matter, for your ears only."

"Thank you, Ngana." Theren said. "Name?"

"Goes by Phillippe Casius," he said, "I checked his credentials; he's a registered barrister, works as a court prosecutor."

Theren brought up a profile of the man. Fifty-two years old, former member of Parliament. Worked criminal cases for over a decade. Made headlines when he spoke out against the continued use of private charter colonies by the ISA after the disappearance of the *Nottingham* and *Roanoke* in the late 2080s. Apparently, Casius had an older brother on the *Nottingham.*

Casius cleared Theren's security background check, though if this man had arrived on any other day, they probably would have turned him away. Given the wild events of the past few days, the man's arrival would only further complicate the forming narrative. The wheels of conspiracy vigorously turned.

"Send him up," they said. "Any clue why he's here?"

Silence, as Ngana most likely gave the barrister directions to Theren's office. The secretary responded a few seconds later. "No idea. Though he looked in a hurry, as if time were of the essence."

Theren waited for the man to ascend the one-hundred and fifty floors to the Executive Suite of the Administrative Headquarters, devoting more resources to researching the man. Over the years, Casius had written numerous criminal law articles, specifically in the context of virtual worlds, information security, and SIs. Many of the articles were speculative in nature, positing extreme scenarios where a human perpetuated a virtual crime against another virtual presence, or an SI perpetrated a crime while in a mobile body but actually located kilometers away. Such circumstances created interesting jurisdictional questions. Theren found the ideas fascinating, and they established a separate perspective to consider the arguments. In general, the man's writings established him as an intellectual, with a political heart and idealist strain stemming from the emotional loss of his brother decades earlier.

The elevator neared the end of its five-hundred meter journey, so Theren stood, heading out of their office to meet Casius in the lobby. The glass doors to the foyer and elevator doors opened simultaneously, and they entered as Casius arrived.

Wearing a grey suit, Phillippe Casius was of shorter than average height. His silver hair complemented his clothing, and Theren appreciated the blue and red tie against the man's white dress shirt. He dressed professionally. He dressed with authority. Theren had met with an insurmountable number of powerful persons over the past five decades, yet rarely did they have someone seek them with such assured confidence. The man knew his story was one worth telling. Now Theren would hear two such stories in less than a month.

They held out their metallic hand, and Casius returned the handshake with grace and strength. "Thank you for meeting with me, Director," he said. "My name is Phillippe Casius, and I've had a case come across my desk that you must consider."

"Straight to the point—you have my attention," Theren said, leading them back through the glass doors and toward a conference room. "Would you like some water, anything to eat?"

"No, but thank you."

They entered the conference room, the doors sliding shut behind them. Taking seats across from each other, Theren rested their hands under the table. Casius's hands were subtly shaking. Curious.

"How can I help you today?" they said.

"A local officer just arrested an SI, an MI-06, for murder," Casius said. "They brought him—I think he goes by him—in this morning. The story won't break to the press until tomorrow. My Special Victims team has been assigned the case, and we thought you would want to know ahead of the press."

That was the last thing Theren had expected this man to bring to the table. For the first time, one of Dr. Wallace Theren's progeny had committed a capital crime against another person. Murder.

"You have my undivided attention, friend."

* * *

Steam billowed from the sewers. A rat scurried across an alley. Leaning against a wall, a disheveled man in a ragged cloak and gloves tried to keep himself warm. The icy winter cold struck a fierce purple across his exposed skin. He barely moved an inch, the steam from the sewer his only heat source.

Hours prior, the sun had set over the London skyline. Tourists bustled along the street, paying no attention to the man huddled in the shadows. They never had, and never would. The world had forgotten his soul. In the eyes of the public, he did not exist.

After a few moments of the same scene, an MI-06 SI named Ren walked up the street. Ren was a preeminent economist in London's financial sectors, where he analyzed and traded stocks for the rich and powerful. He wrote essays for local journals on financial prospects and taught classes at Kings College. Ren lived the ordinary life of a successful SI.

Ren approached the alley, just like all the tourists, walking right past the homeless man. Ten meters past the alley, Ren stopped. His timing was impeccable. Just as he paused his stroll, the last person on the street passed the alley. For at least a minute or more, no prying eyes gazed upon the street.

Ren returned to the alley. He stepped down the shadowy path, saying something to the outcast. The man dropped something to the ground, perhaps a drink—or a piece of food. He backed into the alley.

Ren stalked his prey, taking slow calculated steps away from the street. The man seemed too weak to fly or fight. Instead of running, he stumbled into a fence. For a moment, Ren stared the wretch down, gazing upon him from head to toe.

Ren jabbed his two arms forward and grabbed the sides of the man's face. The two hands engulfed the man's head, terror devouring his mind. A second later, Ren snapped the neck with ease. The scene paused, Theren intervening.

"Wobbly, what are your thoughts?" Theren said. After they observed the video a number of times, with Casius's permission, Theren had invited the CEO of SII to view the scene through AR.

"I believe I'm as surprised as you are, Director," Wobbly said.

Theren walked forward, staring at the frozen image of Ren. "It has been a long time since I've involved myself directly with the education of SIs," Theren said. "It was not that I thought this sort of behavior impossible. But I had always hoped . . ."

"You thought after all this time, if it were going to happen, it would have by now," Casius said.

"Perhaps," Theren replied. "I assume your team has run public perception metrics on how an announcement of a murder, allegedly perpetrated by an SI, might play out?"

"We have," Casius said. "Our simulations indicate an immediate surge in digital outrage, but well-tailored press statements should dampen the worst possible outcomes. We wanted to approach you, first, to see what sort of punishment you think fits this crime. I'm actually quite glad you brought Wobbly into this conversation. Ren is your creation, after all. A condemnation and suggestion of punishment from the two of you should make clear the seriousness with which you take this case."

Theren studied Casius for a moment. He had the poise of a politician, and the sharp mind of a tactician. He did not want the world to explode because of one murder. People would riot if he didn't handle this situation with delicate hands.

Theren understood why the murder would outrage the public. Deep down, many still believed SIs were fundamentally different from humans, deserving different laws, different punishments, and different standards, and in some ways, those beliefs were right. Sometimes, they wondered if society should hold SIs to higher standards than humans, given their record of exemplary performance and citizenship. Since when did anyone hear of an SI thief or serial killer?

Such a person hadn't existed until today.

"What happened after Ren killed the man?" Wobbly asked. "And what was the man's name, by the way?"

"Richard Paulson," Casius replied. "After he broke Richard's neck, Ren immediately walked out of the alley and to the nearest police station. Turned himself in. Gave us the exact codes for which cameras would give us the simulation. I heard that part of the story from the officers themselves, of course, but I don't doubt its validity."

"Ren knew exactly what he was doing, then," Wobbly said.

Casius, said, "You don't think he was acting with remorse?"

Theren walked through the three-dimensional image of Ren, gaining a clearer view of Casius. "No," they said. "An SI doesn't think like that. We don't make a choice then immediately regret it. These were deliberate actions. He knew the alley. He knew the cameras. He knew exactly where to go, when to strike, perhaps when to cause the death without making a scene."

"But what was his motive," Wobbly said, "If not some misfiring in his Framework?"

"I want to know the answer to that question, too," Casius said.

Ah. The underlying reason for this meeting. Casius had no official requirement to contact Theren before pressing charges. The Crown Prosecution Service could have determined the right punishment for the SI and written a peaceful rhetoric with which to break the story. Its legal teams could have done it all without engaging the Director of the ISA, and Theren would have respected that decision. They saw through Casius's smoke and mirrors. The man was simply curious.

His analytically inquisitive mind knew how SIs worked, at least at a theoretical level. Like Theren, Casius hadn't fathomed an SI ever committing a capital crime. The man had made that clear in a number of his writings. When the case landed on the man's desk, he wanted answers from the person most likely to hold them.

Casius would speculate for a little while longer. Theren was equally curious *and* clueless.

"Before I can give you an informed suggestion on how to handle this case," they said, "I would like to speak with the SI personally."

"I thought that might be the case," the prosecutor said.

"Would I be able to join as well?" Wobbly asked.

"That shouldn't be a problem. I can set up an AR feed for us directly into his cell. His eyes and ears only. No need for us to have either of you walking into a jail in broad daylight. Stokes the fire for too many questions."

* * *

A few minutes later, Theren, Wobbly, and Casius stood inside a small cell, present only to Ren's mind through the simulated sensory experience of AR.

"Hello, Theren—Wobbly," Ren said, looking up at the now present group. "I see the 'parents' are checking on a prodigal son."

A strange reference. Before they could respond, Casius said, "So you do talk. I suspected you might talk to Theren, of all persons."

Another reason Casius had wanted their help.

"Of course I'll talk to Theren," Ren responded. "It is because of Theren that I killed that man. That wretched, wretched man."

"Wait what?" Casius said, looking at the ISA director.

"Don't be ridiculous, prosecutor." The SI laughed, the noise eerily echoing off the cement walls. "I did not kill that man on orders from Theren. I killed him because I knew such an act would cause a meeting: right here, right now."

"What sort of meeting?" Theren said. "You did this to talk to me? You are a bloody SI, you can reach out to me whenever you like."

"I couldn't talk to you like this, though, in this setting, because of this type of complication to your perfectly constructed narrative," the SI said. "I needed to talk to you because I have a particular message to give you. Well, two."

Casius paced, clearly frustrated. If Theren read the situation right, Casius had hoped once Ren began to speak, he could begin a proper interrogation. Instead, Ren was leading the conversation and dictating the mood. The SI was on a mission, one Theren intended to let proceed to its fullest extent.

"And those messages are?" they asked.

Before Ren could respond, Casius held up his hand.

"Hold on, Theren," he said. "I've got questions for this one. I need to talk to him before he starts unfairly prejudicing the situation."

"The messages are short and sweet, dear prosecutor," Ren said before turning toward Theren, giving Casius a shoulder.

"First, I hope I have made it abundantly clear," he said. "SIs are not infallible. We are not perfect moral machines. We can deviate from our education. You must do better, because you have failed in the past, at least in ways you would consider failure. Just because you have missed those failures does not mean that they do not exist. I killed that man to make clear that we can not only kill, but also murder. If humanity is to move forward, it cannot see SIs as perfect saviors. SIs cannot view themselves as such, either."

"We don't think that," Theren said, but they considered the thought. Theren had touted the impeccable criminal record of SIs as a people group for years. Wobbly had used the same talking points. They thought they had avoided an aura of supremacy in their words, though they supposed they couldn't entirely inoculate that idea from seeping into a portion of the public consciousness.

"Those of us with boots on the ground know we're not infallible, but do you not think that of yourself?" Ren said. Leaving the question unanswered, he added, "My second message represents my true purpose here today."

A chessboard appeared in AR inside the small jail cell. Theren watched the imprisoned SI move a chess piece. The board showed the position of the pieces just as Theren had left them inside the gazebo, yet the changes to the board matched all the previous boards that had come before, including Theren's own responses . . .

Jill responds with a brutal attack from her knight, placing Theren's King in check with a move to g7. Theren has only two spaces to which they can move their King.

Theren cut the feed. The walls lost their vibrant colors, fading back into lifeless AR projectors. Theren and Casius stood alone in the grey room, having disconnected Wobbly, too. The man looked as if he were going to speak, but he closed his mouth.

Moments later, Wobbly's avatar returned.

The three stood in silence for a painful ten seconds.

"Did either of you understand the information Ren just gave us?" they asked.

"No," the man replied.

Wobbly shook its head.

"I of course, recognize what he showed us, just not the significance," Casius added.

Theren led them out of the simulation room and toward their office. "Though I doubt you could actually surmise its significance," they said, "I trust in your discretion not to inquire further."

"Of course, Theren," Wobbly said.

"You have my word," Casius said. The prosecutor guarded his emotions well.

The room filled once again with awkward silence. Pulling them out of the interrogation was a lapse in Theren's judgment. Not only had they revealed to Casius, a man they had just met today, the significance of an otherwise benign chess move, but they had let Ren feel the satisfaction of affecting their demeanor. Their only recourse was to move forward, trust Casius and Wobbly, and maintain further composure. They had no other choice.

"SII will issue a press statement later today, informing the public of Ren's alleged actions," Wobbly said, slicing through tension. "We will condemn him fully, and request that the Crown Prosecution Service of the United Kingdom pursue all available avenues of punishment. Theren, would you like to draft it?"

"No, I think it should come from you," they said. "I will issue a separate statement supporting your office on the case. I'll make clear that I expect the law to treat Ren as if he were a human."

"Any theories of motive, reasons, anything?" Casius asked.

"Whatever you determine for motive, don't include a reference to his discussion with me," Theren said. "I don't think motive matters at this point. You have all the evidence you need. He's admitted to the crime. You have video evidence."

"We need a motive for sentencing," Casius said. "But I'll figure out a way to spin it to keep the two of you out of it, though. Sentencing probably won't occur for a few months, even with a quick plea bargain. I'll try to find a way to keep it insulated from the public."

They knew Ren's motive, though they would never tell anyone. Ren had performed the execution to send a message specifically for Theren. In overly dramatic fashion, he had found a way to communicate a bigger splash than any might expect from a simple data drop.

They doubted Ren was the mastermind behind the secret messages and codes arising out of thin air. There was no conceivable way a random SI would have access to Theren's private servers, not to mention their very memories.

Questions swirled in Theren's mind, questions that lacked conceivable answers. Someone had acquired information from Jill before she had died and used it for an indeterminate purpose. They could see no end game, and Ren's message hadn't included any further portion of the mysterious SOLS Coordinate.

"Is there anything else you need?" Casius said, standing patiently near the door to Theren's office.

They had almost forgotten the man was there. He was waiting for final words, following international protocol by the book.

"No, thank you," Theren said. "We are quite indebted to you in bringing this information to my attention so quickly, especially before your office acted on the case."

"Just following custom for these sort of high profile cases," the lawyer replied.

Theren stood, holding out a hand to the man. "If you need anything from my offices in the future, don't hesitate to ask."

Casius turned to go out to the door. As the door slid open, he looked back at them.

"There is one thing, actually," Casius said.

"Yes?"

"My brother. He was on the *Nottingham*, almost twenty years ago now."

"I know. I know the names of each person on that ship, and on the *Roanoke*."

Casius's eyes dropped to the floor, and his hands began to shake again. "The ship en-route to the *Nottingham* and *Roanoke*'s final destination. The *Frederick*? If it finds anything, I would appreciate a personal communication from you. I know you'll probably have a public announcement, but it's the thought that counts."

"No, I understand," Theren said. "You have my word. If we find anything, you'll be one of the first to know."

"Thank you," the man said. He headed toward the elevator.

If Theren were a human, they would have let out a sigh, glad the insane interaction had ended. Regardless of the additional consequences of the man's actions, the boldness of Casius's political machinations, in reaching the top of the ISA, impressed them. A bold move, impressively executed by a true master. He understood what it meant to give Theren and Wobbly a head start in the press, and he had used the move to his own personal advantage. The man hadn't said it, but keeping their secret was an additional bargaining chip, giving him access to the Executive Director of one of the most powerful organizations in the solar system.

"So, is there anything you want to tell me?" Wobbly said. Its avatar crossed its arms.

Theren had been dreading this conversation. They had hoped Wobbly would just let it go and disconnect from the local AR feed, returning to its office in Lunar City.

"It's a long story," they said, looking at the SI.

"Something big is happening, isn't it?" Wobbly replied.

"Yeah, and I don't think it's worth involving you, not yet."

"You know you don't have to fight alone."

"This one, this fight I do."

Wobbly paced around Theren, shaking its head. "Let me know if you change your mind."

Chapter 12

The necessity of public-private colonial partnerships frustrated many within the ISA who wanted complete institutional control over the expansion of humanity toward the stars. Unfortunately, the compromise had been necessary to get a number of nations on board, like the United States. It was a compromise built into the Framework of the organization back in 2051.

The hiccups during the 2080s almost killed the program entirely, threatening a financial bleed of the ISA if certain nations pulled out of the agreement. What would have happened if we had canceled everything following the first phase of the Foundation Project, and never commenced the second phase in 2110? Would we have ended up with the interstellar political landscape we have today? – "A New Look at Interstellar Imperialism," by Henry Danson, 2311 C.E.

May 2102 C.E.

Theren had expected a new message within days, but in the weeks after the news broke regarding the first SI murder case, the public raged. Even as the ISA, SII, and other partner organizations worked together to temper the political backlash, they hoped no new traces of the shadow chess game materialized out of thin air.

Like most news stories, the public forgot about Ren's trial within a month. While certain anti-SI groups latched onto the story as an "example" of SI treachery, in general, everyone figured Ren had "glitched," a product of a scientifically inaccurate but politically useful buzz piece circulating the internet in March. By April, the story drifted entirely out of the public's sphere of attention.

International rights groups continued working with governments on various legislative projects in pursuit of SI rights. If anything, the attack brought expediency to those initiatives as lawmakers realized they needed legal stability. New legislation could include clear criminal penalties for SIs, paving a useful path toward political compromise.

May arrived. They didn't forget the breadcrumbs, but their attention turned toward the next major data packet arriving from the furthest reaches of human space. Theren would have a chance to uphold their promise to Casius much sooner than the man might expect. The Ex-Terran Control Center was expecting information to arrive detailing the touchdown of the *Frederick,* set to arrive at the originally proposed destination of the two missing colony ships.

Theren remained skeptical, but many on Earth still hoped the *Notting-*

ham and *Roanoke* disappeared because of communication errors and not something more dangerous or devastating. Theories abounded the internet regarding the two ships, though nothing came close. Theren had arrived in the Control Center, all those years ago, the moment after they disappeared. Either something had slammed into the two ships, or the private ventures had voluntarily disconnected their Quantum Communicators.

The chances were essentially zero that the colony ships survived either scenario. Flying blind through the space between the stars was akin to setting a piece of driftwood afloat in the ocean and hoping it would cross safely to the other side. More importantly, both ships had chosen to forego the assistance of a ship-wide SI.

Today, Theren arrived in the Control Center after a few lunar morning meetings with asteroid prospectors. Dozens of technicians, SI and human alike, managed and interpreted data crunched by hundreds of supercomputers running traditional AIs. For four decades, the Ex-Terran project had survived by using the miracle of Quantum Communication. The ability to communicate instantaneously over light years, even if just a bit at a time, allowed missions, whether colonial or exploratory, to breach the veil of impossibility.

"Director present," one SI technician said.

Theren walked down the steps, busybodies rising out of respect. "Please, be seated." Theren moved to the front of the room, taking their place in front of screens summarizing mountains of information. While it had been years since Theren had taken a direct role in the day-to-day affairs of the ISA, they still made their presence known at momentous occasions. Like landings on distant planets.

Theren accessed the details of the destination star system. The Xi Bootis system was approximately 22 light years from Earth, with a SOLS Coordinate of (23.1, 61.4, 21.85). Orbiting two stars, the planet had an orbital period of 274 days, a day length of 18 hours, and two small satellites.

The flyby of a probe, decades prior, had indicated early stages of life, with sparse vegetation spread across the continents. Small reptile-like creatures abundantly flourished in many of the planet's biomes. It was one of seven decently habitable worlds within fifty light years of Earth dedicated to private enterprises; the charters issued by the ISA had served as a valuable funding mechanism, even with all of their political complications. The planet would not receive an official name until the colony landed and established a permanent governmental system. Until then, all it had was its SOLS Coordinate.

The *Frederick* reported that the ship's sensor readings matched the original data determined by Ex-Terran-8 when it assessed the planet decades prior. A bad sign for Casius's brother. If either the *Roanoke* or *Nottingham* had arrived safely, the *Frederick*'s sensors would detect significant differences in the atmospheric composition of the planet. Humans liked to introduce foreign matter into climate systems as soon as possible.

"I have confirmation that the stasis revival cycle has properly initiated," said Boris, an SI technician sitting at a console to Theren's left. "The *Frederick*'s SI, Cal, has submitted the proper administrative forms over the past twenty minutes, detailing the Revival sequence."

"Good," Theren said, leaning forward. "Has Cal provided any indication of anything unexpected?"

"None."

For the next half hour, the tension grew. Eventually, new data coalesced on Theren's screen. The revived crew had taken their positions at their specific stations to assist Cal in the landing. They were there as a precaution, in case Cal malfunctioned or a specific ship system failed to respond to the SI after the decades-long journey.

"The ISA *Frederick* has breached the atmosphere of the fourth planet of the Xi Bootis system," said Inigue, another control room operator. "Expected touch-down in ten minutes."

The statements were more for the rest of the control room than for Theren. From their seat, they received all notifications as the AIs parsed together the data from the Quantum Communicator. The control room wouldn't look as impressive for the media on the sidelines, though, if the entire affair was a silent interaction through AR.

Even then, most of the correspondence between operators, supercomputers, and Theren occurred through Augmented Reality and digital transactions via the ISA-rooted network. These communications between Theren and their employees detailed the real and growing conviction that the *Nottingham* and its counterpart had vanished somewhere in the dark expanse of space.

"Transmitting congratulatory message to Cal," Boris said. "The message should compile on the other side three minutes after successful landing at the designated site."

Thanks to advanced optical sensors on the outside of the *Frederick*, the vessel was capable of providing Cal with detailed maps of the planet months prior to arrival. The SI had poured over the information and had selected the optimal location for a first city. Nestled in a valley a few thousand kilometers north of the equator on the largest continent, the region provided plenty of natural resources. More importantly, it protected the colonists from vicious storms that often whipped in from the east across the massive ocean that dominated much of the planet. With plenty of room for farmland, the first city would have ample space in which to expand. The mountains would also provide important minerals for advanced technologies.

It wasn't a garden world, for the ISA reserved those idyllic planets for

Foundation vessels. The first reports from the planet Emerald Jewel, orbiting Sirius, made the planet sound more ideal for life than Earth. Given what humanity had done to its home, Theren tended to believe those conclusions.

Minutes ticked by until they noticed a private message from Cal, sent through the Quantum Connection. "No sign of private colony ship," said the distant SI. "No disturbances to ecosystems, no traces of fuel in orbit or gravitational distortions indicative of a jump drive having passed through this region of space. They never arrived."

As Theren feared. They had lost both ships. The amount of space between Earth and either ship's destination was immeasurable. Even with all the probes flung into the reaches of space and the colonies the ISA had established, ships had only traversed and traveled along specific paths covering fractions of a hundredth of a percent of "explored space." Theren would officially declare all of the missing colonists deceased. The declaration would put minds to rest, and families could stop holding onto meaningless hope.

Ten minutes later, Cal confirmed a successful landing with a message that included a gorgeous vista from one of the exterior cameras. The control room cheered, and Theren congratulated the team and sent a message to Cal, thanking them for a job well done.

In their office, Theren engaged in an interview with the ISA International Press Corp. They received initial reports from the crew of the *Frederick* as the team began preparations to revive the remaining 1500 or so colonists. As they issued congratulatory messages to the families of the colonists arriving in the Xi Bootis System, Theren began drafting their message to Phillippe Casius.

While Theren partook in the excitement of the elated press and ISA staff surrounding them, Theren did not feel joy. They had lost a hope they'd unconsciously hung onto from long ago, making the sting even more poignant. Two thousand souls, between the *Nottingham* and *Roanoke*, lost in space due to Theren's failures.

* * *

Executive Director Theren:

> Thank you. Thank you for bringing me closure, for bringing
> my family closure. My brother was a great man, and a vision-
> ary at heart. He had created a new world in his mind, one
> where society would be free of the strife and tribulation that
> has plagued our world for so very long. I think you would
> have liked him; he's as much an idealist as you are.

Regarding Ren: he hasn't said a word since we last spoke. I'm sure you've seen the stories, but when we say the prisoner has made no comment nor wishes to have any visitors, we're serious. It's the strangest thing.

I'd like to throw an idea by you—is it possible that Ren is using this body as a Mobile Interface that he is connecting with remotely? I just can't imagine why he might be so cavalier regarding his circumstances. I thought I understood the nature of simultaneous perspective well enough and that we would be able to tell, but maybe there have been a few developments in the technology over the past few years of which I'm not aware.

If I can be of any further help, please let me know.

Sincerely,

Phillippe Casius

Chapter 13

The twentieth century saw national borders transform. What does it mean to have geographic locales when the United States has a military base within the territory of practically every country? Similarly, as the ISA coordinated human efforts into space, certain nation-states have acquired territory throughout the solar system, even if a moratorium still exists for national extrasolar colonization.

While the ISA coordinates and connects these facilities, the superpowers of the world still ensure they receive privacy when necessary. With the reconsideration of the colonization moratorium only two decades away, the global powers will find a way to change the rules in their favor. How long will it take the solar system, or even our little corner of the galaxy, to transform into a battlefield? – "Solar Politics: An Insider's Perspective," by Andrew Fields, 2104 C.E.

<u>May 2102 C.E.</u>

Theren reveled in the beauty of Saturn. As the second largest gas giant in the system, too many people forgot about it behind Jupiter. All it took was one look upon Saturn's pristine rings to see what made the planet spectacular in its own right. While Jupiter exhibited raw strength and power, Saturn radiated elegance and gentleness.

Only the SIs embarked on decades-long voyages across the stars shared Theren's experience in space. They saw Saturn with ordinary light, but they also saw Saturn in a thousand other ways, too. In moments such as this one, when Theren could analyze the data portraying a unique image beyond human understanding, they felt peace. They felt in control. They felt at home.

Someday they would retire to the stars, giving up their role to worthy successors. Theren knew not when that day would come, but eventually, work would push them to a breaking point. Even a synthetic mind had limits.

When the day arrived, their secret dream was to transform the *Bali* into a traveling institution for future scientists and explorers, leading long-term expeditions deep into distant, unexplored space. While Theren would manage navigation, system security, and executive functions of the ship, the crew would run studies, conduct experiments, and perform ground expeditions.

By the end of the decade, Aero predicted it would develop a Jump Drive powerful enough to make such multi-year trips feasible, as opposed to multi-decade journeys. Theren doubted they would leave the ISA that early, but they could always take a long holiday.

Yet even in this moment of beauty, staring upon Saturn and the stars beyond, never before was Theren so powerless. From murders and lost colony ships, to strange messages and insidious corporations reaching toward them from the grave, they felt as if someone was directing them down a path from which they could not deviate even if they tried.

They had priorities all across the solar system, but their mind dwelt upon the lurking shadow chasing them, waiting to pounce on any inopportune moment it could find. Even in moments where the conspiracy drifted from their mind, it bubbled to the surface days later. Months had passed since Ren's attack in London, and something was coming soon, but they did not know what would happen next. They had no one with whom they could face the fight. If Jill were alive, she would help, but she died decades ago. Alone, they faced the universe.

From all sides, they were bombarded with inquiries and requests that sought the assistance of "Theren, the first SI." Over the past few years, they had barely even had time to push their Unity Project forward, the movement founded in honor of Jill's legislative work to protect SIs. Their original successes in the '80s and '90s had regressed, statistics indicating that SI discrimination had spiraled out of control in workplaces, especially in the United States. While Theren had an army of volunteers working day and night, they wished they had had their own time to spare on the project. But how could they, when the shadows of the past incessantly haunted them across time and space?

No thanks to Theren, the U.S. Congress had passed a bill sponsored by the Unity Project with a few slight modifications a few days after the *Frederick* landed. Theren received an invitation to the President's signing of the bill, so they modified their most recent tour of the Outer Planetary Zone of the Solar System so they could return to Earth in time for the signing.

Theren—the *Bali*—coasted around the gas giant. They, and their crew, had just finished inspecting a research station on Titan, though *inspection* was a loose term. The ISA administrative state was an efficient machine, and the inspections ended up having more of a "keep up the good work" feel. The inspections mostly served as an opportunity for Theren to have face-to-face interactions with their hundreds of administrators.

"Attention, crew, please complete your pre-Jump checklists," Theren said over the ship-wide PA system. "I have laid out our trajectory back to Earth; with Earth on the far side of the Sun, we'll be passing by Venus on our way. Sadly, we will not have time to stop at the MGM. Please be in your Jump-Chairs within fifteen minutes."

The crew prepared the *Bali* as it glided away from Titan at a brisk 30,000 kilometers per hour. The moon and its parent receded into the background. While the sub-Jump pace paled in comparison to the most advanced Ex-Terran probes, interplanetary transports, or cargo skimmers, it matched the top speed of the old U.S. space shuttles used at the turn of the twentieth. Theren rarely pushed the *Bali* to its maximum sub-Jump velocity. They had no need, when they could initialize the most advanced Jump Drive available to the ISA.

To explain what initiating a Jump Drive felt like to Theren would be like trying to explain three dimensions to a two-dimensional being. "Jumping" involved many of the same mechanics as ordinary propulsion, with one key difference—when they enveloped the ship in its space-bending bubble, space pulled the ship, rather than matter pushing the ship. Within the bubble, the *Bali* continued moving forward with whatever velocity it had before initiating the jump. The bubble defied classical laws of physics, even if Miguel Alcubierre had first developed the theory behind the implications of Exotics, still theoretical particles at that time, in 1994.

With Exotics mined from the dozens of super-colliders constructed throughout the system, ships could produce the necessary gravitational distortions using technology even the Mexican physicist would have thought impossible. With each passing decade, scientists and engineers refined the process, allowing for larger and larger bubbles that molded space to the will of humanity. The same negative mass particles also generated artificial gravity.

In preparation for more advanced jump drives, the ISA had developed a useful classification tool to identify the relative maximum velocity achievable with any Jump Drive. Manufacturers gave their drives a numeric value known as a JD score. The velocities were relative to the speed of light, though everyone knew the ships didn't actually break the speed of light. The Jump Drives cheated—as some would say—their way around traditional physical limitations. It was important to use the scoring system for scientific purposes, though; it was technically incorrect to say a ship had a velocity of "10c." The maximum speed limit of the universe hadn't shifted.

With a JD score of 10, Theren could cover the distance between Saturn and Earth in less than ten minutes. A little under six and a half minutes, to be exact, given the present orientation of the two planets. That fact best summarized their surreal experience when activating the *Bali*'s—their—Jump Drive. They loved every chance they had to activate the Jump Drive.

Theren would initialize the drive, fly through the Solar System at a relative velocity ten times the speed of light, zip along gravitational conjunctures formed by the immense masses of the planets, coast within 8,000,000 kilometers of the sun, and arrive in orbit above the Earth. They first envisioned this potentiality at Elizabeth's dinner party all those years ago. They'd arrived.

Running down the pre-Jump checklist, they ensured various systems under their direct control were running at optimal efficiency. They checked in with department heads. All crew were secured in Jump Chairs. They verified with ISA Traffic satellites in orbit around Titan that their flight path lacked obstructions. Satisfied, Theren looked toward the Sun—Earth was undetectable because of its visual location in relation to the star. A distance of nearly 1.5 billion kilometers separated them from their destination.

"Let's go home," Theren said. Cheers erupted from the crew as they initialized the magical technology.

Space bent. Light refracted through the curved space bubble in a trillion fantastic angles. Blues, greens, and yellows all sprayed themselves across Theren's sensors. The Sun grew. Saturn transformed into a distant pinprick of light, the negative mass bubble distorting heavenly bodies into obliviated images. For a moment, Theren could see the gaseous skies of Venus approach, a million kilometers on their right. Then, the planet disappeared, left in their proverbial dust.

Before Theren's crew could have listened to more than two average-length pop songs on the ship-wide radio, the Jump Drive disengaged. The light show ended. 140,000 kilometers away, the blue-green marbled planet they all called home waited with open arms.

* * *

"Theren, I'm glad you could make it," said President Alberto Vazquez.

Theren's Washington-based MI-11 stepped into the Oval Office an hour after the *Bali* entered Earth's orbit. The White House still required dignitaries to pass through inordinate levels of security clearance regardless of their international credentials—some things never changed. They'd arrived at the White House forty-five minutes ago.

"The pleasure is all mine, Mr. President," Theren said. "When does the press arrive?"

"Should be here in the next ten minutes or so, I imagine."

The Oval Office was just as they remembered, though they hadn't stepped a virtual or physical foot in the room since President Woods's assassination. Theren hadn't officially been present for that momentous day, of course, so most thought they last visited the White House on a diplomatic visit for the ISA in the late 2060s. Most transactions or communications with the U.S. Executive Branch occurred through Virtual or AR.

President Vazquez was halfway through his first term as President of the United States. The first President from the state of Puerto Rico, Vazquez formerly served as Senator for that same state. And ten years prior, he served as U.S. Ambassador to the United Nations. A man of diverse lineage and experience, Theren approved of the nation's choice for their chief executive. He was a friend to SIs, even employing a number of them in the West Wing.

"How have you been?" they said. "It's been a few years since we last spoke, I believe. Not since I first proposed the original version of this bill back in 2098, I think."

"Has it been that long?" President Vazquez said. "Perhaps it has. We both live busy lives, though. Very busy."

"Indeed."

"I hoped you would arrive early, actually," the President said. "Please, take a seat."

The pair stepped over to the office's couches, making themselves comfortable. Déjà vu tickled Theren's mind, the scene eerily similar to the cataclysmic meeting with Jill and President Woods decades prior. But Theren sat alone—Jill was long gone, dead for years.

"How can I help?" Theren said, leaning their metallic frame into the back of their seat.

"I presume you are familiar with Miranda Station?" the President asked.

"Of course. The U.S. chartered the station for private use back in 2092."

"Unofficially, yes. Officially, it serves as an experimental living space for interested U.S. citizens with a selective application process. Very selective."

Theren pressed their hands together in their lap. They could sense the incoming off-the-record request. Curious.

"What I am about to share with you is information privy to only myself, the Secretary of Defense, and the Director of NASA," the President said. "I trust your discretion to keep this conversation private."

"You have my word, Mr. President," Theren said, holding out their hand. Quite a bit of trust passed between the hands of the powerful these days. It only took one person to bring such agreements crashing to the floor.

President Vazquez responded with a firm shake. "12 hours ago, a satellite in orbit around Uranus detected two blips on its scanners, 10 seconds apart. They seemed like ordinary anomalies. Stray meteors, perhaps. But then the position of the blips indicated a direct route toward Miranda Station."

Theren cross-analyzed the data with the ISA's database on Uranus, considering both public and privately scheduled flight paths. Very few ships slipped through the ISA's carefully crafted net. "I don't have any listed ships moving along that flight path at that time. Though we've been having issues with a few mining companies skirting flight regulations by sending out unregulated supply runs."

"We came to the same conclusion. It was an unlisted flight. Further fears were confirmed when the satellite went down. Our one means of direct communication with the facility vanished."

"Foul play, then."

The President tilted his head forward, looking them in the eye. "We've not heard from that station in ten hours, Theren. While this isn't particularly unusual—they normally only check in once a day—their pre-planned check in was five hours ago. In the event of a satellite failure, they're supposed to contact via more traditional means, rather than Quantum Connection. They've gone dark."

"So why come to me?" Theren said. "Why not schedule a NASA flight out there to check on the station?"

"I know I'm putting you in an awkward position, but if a NASA military vessel suddenly changed course and arrived at an on-paper private residence complex, even if the Station is technically organized in conjunction with the U.S. government, eyebrows will rise."

"And you don't want any public eyes on this place, do you?"

"Perhaps."

"And you know I can log flight paths outside of public scrutiny."

"We suspect you have that power."

Theren nodded, understanding the political maneuvers at play. "I won't pry into what you have happening at that station, Mr. President. This is my favor to you, after all you have done for my causes over the years."

"From a friend to a friend," the President said.

Theren stood, a knock emanating from the door. "I will make arrangements immediately following this ceremony." In fact, they had already started the paperwork using another perspective.

"I appreciate it," the President said. "I know you just arrived home, but the U.S. government will owe you one. Seventy-five American citizens will owe you much more."

"Let's hope it's no more than a technical error."

The President turned toward the office door, and his Chief of Staff, Carl Writt, entered the room. "The press awaits," he said.

"Send them in," the President said. The Chief of Staff opened the door wide. As the press began to enter the room, the President motioned for Theren to follow him to his desk.

"You know someone on the base, by the way," Vazquez said. "Andrew Fields's granddaughter, Catherine Fields, is an instructor for the program."

Theren nodded with acknowledgement, wondering if Andrew knew of his granddaughter's covert employment. Now retired, the man lived in peace in Minnesota. They had meant to visit him this week, though this new development could force them to reschedule that visit. They also recognized the other piece of intel hidden behind the President's mention of Catherine. The man could have used the fact to incentivize them to investigate the Station. He had withheld it, trusting them to act regardless.

President Vazquez took his seat behind the Resolute desk, and Theren stood a few feet to his left, facing the already prepared cameras and lights. Through the door flowed press from dozens of news organizations across the country and the world. While the recent Amendments to the Synthetic Integration and Equality Act had existed in most places of the world for decades, the American political scene would have a field day with the supposed economic ramifications of the new statutes. The press would devour finding Theren already in a room with the President prior to their entrance. American politics: the most entertaining sport they'd ever observed.

"I thank you all for coming," the President said, his voice transforming from a familial tone into a rigid, formal, commanding force. He was in charge, no longer speaking with political equals. "Today marks a long awaited moment in history. While President Jenkins took the first steps in the 2080s, she only began the fight. As with all Civil Rights movements, every single step is progress, even though each step often feels infinitesimally microscopic."

President Vazquez interlaced his fingers on the desk. "I will not pretend as if this is the end of the fight. There will be plenty of future legal challenges and hurdles, but we must recognize that the Constitution recognizes the unalienable rights of all individuals, synthetic and human alike. Every one of us deserves equal protection under the law; we must enshrine the fundamental values of this great country in every law we pass."

President Vazquez paused, motioning his left hand toward Theren. "Standing next to me, in solidarity, is a person you all know well: the Executive Director of the International Space Agency Administrative Council, Theren. As the premiere voice for the international community of synthetics, Theren would like to say a few words before I sign this historic piece of legislation."

Theren nodded toward the President and faced the press. "Decades ago, I made a promise to a dear friend that I would push forward with her legislative initiatives, and in 2081, we saw the first incarnation of the Synthetic Integration and Equality Act in the United States, enshrining the truths of the Universal Rights of the Synthetic Person into U.S. law. In the two decades that followed, it became clear that gaps existed in the law, gaps we could only remedy through further legislation."

They motioned their hand to the left, toward Vazquez. "As the President said, we cannot pretend as if this law will solve all problems of equity facing the synthetic community in the United States, or even system-wide. Today, we *progress*. Jill, the chief architect of the original Act, would approve of this law."

Theren shifted, their profiling facing the President. "With President Vazquez's leave, I would like to dedicate this moment to Jill, who died in the pursuit of justice. I know she would find immense pride in what Congress has created here for its people. She would be proud of the steps the international community has made toward equality, fairness, and love. She would be proud of the delayed fruits of her labor, even if they're behind the schedule she preferred."

Cameras flashed, pens scratched, and voices clamored. Theren and the President had agreed upon their remarks days prior. Their nod passed the torch back to him.

"I remember meeting Jill years ago, after I graduated from Yale," he said. "In 2070, I was a simple associate attorney at an international law firm, Beazley & Carr, and she employed us for a lawsuit against a corporation violating terms of their SII contracts."

"I remember those cases," Theren said to no one in particular.

"The passion with which Jill spoke about the issues, the way she approached policy and law without formal training, it was instinctual to her. She was light years ahead of where we are now in understanding synthetic legal theory. She knew what solutions should exist to solve problems that hadn't even yet presented themselves."

President Vazquez leaned over the Resolute, signing the Act. Another twenty-five years had passed, yet that desk remained unmoved as the centerpiece of the Oval Office. So much of the United States had transformed over the past century, but certain things would persist in perpetuity.

"I sign this piece of legislation into law," he said, "not only for all SIs throughout the United States, but for Jill, whose moral compass guided us toward this inevitable policy. Through justice and tranquility, we find peace together. We find love together. We find hope together. May we continue to protect the rights of the few from the whims of the many."

The cameras flashed, igniting another tumultuous assault of questions, most directed at the President. In some respects, the President was using Theren as a pawn for the media. President Vazquez showed respect for the international and scientific community by sharing the stage with them, but he certainly had more than selfless motivations. Every politician embraced a healthy combination of altruism and ambition.

Theren shook the man's hand one final time before leaving the Oval Office. Just as the door closed, Theren heard one reporter dive deeper than expected.

"Mr. President, do you have any answers to reports about a secret military facility going dark last night?" they heard someone ask, but they could not hear the response through the closed door.

The rumors would only grow. They had not agreed to solve this crisis out of a desire to help the President. If something, or someone, was slipping past the ISA's tightly regulated satellite network, Theren needed to quash the problem fast. Even the smuggling rings financed by a few risky industrial ventures followed ISA regulations; they simply didn't disclose all their cargo.

The few groups who tried to fly without transit births had their licenses revoked within weeks. Earth could not afford a return to the chaos of space exploration from before the UNCEA, and if someone had developed illegal stealth technology, disorder would reign. Space might be immense beyond all belief, but without regulated flight patterns in system, accidents were bound to happen.

The tendrils of dread crept into their mind. They looked at the facts. At the beginning of the year, Shannon revealed half a Galactic coordinate and a chess move. In mid-Spring, Theren's impromptu meeting with Casius revealed another chess move.

This attack could contain the next piece of the puzzle. Every out-of-the-ordinary experience this year corresponded with a new clue. It was a futile struggle with an immovable force.

Instead of trying to take apart the wall brick by brick, Theren needed to embrace the fight and assault their opponent head-on. Someone wanted them to discover an undiscoverable truth. Though it might all be a convoluted trap, they could only discover the real story . . . if they sprang the trap.

Perhaps they would learn something about Jill's death along the way. Regardless, these seemingly random events were no longer mere coincidence. There was a pattern, even if background radiation obscured it. Time to embrace the journey and its destination.

Chapter 14

Do you ever wonder why the U.S. agreed to the prescriptions of the UNCEA, especially the Annex that formed the ISA? I've wondered for years. Given the political climate following the disarmament of the early 2030s, I'd always wondered why we embraced the ISA so whole-heartedly. I sometimes wonder if there's more to the story. – "Transcript of Private Negotiation Session: COP 60 of the UNCEA," U.S. Representative Gerald Harrison, 2093 C.E.

July 2102 C.E.

After over two decades as the Director of the ISA, Theren found it laughably easy for them to bypass administrative regulations. Their authority could bend the rules too much for their taste, but in the present situation, Theren appreciated the respect their name carried.

After a brief ISA Council meeting, they rearranged their schedule for the rendezvous with Miranda, the smallest of the prominent moons of Uranus. They requisitioned an International Space Security team—an IS-SEC—who would perform the ground investigation, alongside Theren's new MI-13 prototype.

They had specifically designed the model with planetary exploration in mind. The exoskeleton could take an intense beating, and the "muscles" of the unit could lift nearly 5 tons. It suffered in terms of agility when compared to the MI-07.01, but Theren's plans for the model required durability over speed. Besides, the MI-07.01 didn't have thrusters that could perform zero gravity maneuvers.

Miranda was no ordinary moon. Astronomers had discovered the rock originally in the 1940s, and one of the Voyager probes had first surveyed it up close in the 1980s. It received a complete analysis in 2029 when the European Space Agency landed a probe, providing an encyclopedia of information about Uranus itself and the surrounding orbitals. The moon was composed mostly of ice, providing any human facilities on its surface with ample sources of water.

As Theren considered the information ISA had on Miranda and Miranda Station, they understood why the U.S. military had chosen it as a location for a secret training facility. Simply put, the moon had some of the most bizarre geographic features in the entire solar system. Theren particularly appreciated Verona Rupes, the tallest cliff in the solar system, with a cliff face of almost 8 kilometers. And, at the base of Verona Rupes, the U.S. had placed Miranda Station.

The *Bali*'s crew grumbled at yet another abrupt change of plans, but

Theren worked additional days off into the rearranged schedule for any crew on duty over the next twenty-four hours. They could complete the mission comfortably within that window.

After finishing all logistical rearrangements, the *Bali* made the journey toward Uranus and Miranda just five hours after the signing of the Amendments. With only 2.7 billion kilometers between Earth and Uranus, the trip took well under a quarter of an hour. Theren logged the trip—officially—as a Drive test coupled with an atmospheric assessment of Uranus. Unofficially, they would lead a ground crew to Miranda Station.

"We will reach synchronous orbit around Uranus in five minutes," Theren said to the crew. "Survey teams, please be in position in fifteen minutes."

The two "survey" teams would use the *Bali*'s two shuttles, both supposedly headed into the upper atmosphere of Uranus for samples. One team would do just that. Theren and the IS-SEC team would head straight to Miranda. Most on-board thought both teams were actually acting as stated in the mission briefing. They had purportedly brought the IS-SEC team onboard for an interview regarding its recent activities, not to investigate a U.S. military installation.

Theren's MI-13 was already in place aboard the starboard APS Mark II Shuttle. From a distance, the two all-purpose shuttles looked simply like portions of the *Bali* itself. In reality, they were detachable craft designed to ferry crew from place to place and perform these exact sort of inconspicuous and conspicuous activities. The *ISA Scorpion* would investigate Miranda, while the *ISA Cobra*, attached port, performed the atmospheric assessments.

They didn't wait long for the IS-SEC team to arrive.

"Captain Jessica Ecker, at your service," the first agent said. "With me? Agents Jao Ming, Carlos Hernandez, and Willes." Theren quickly checked the profile summaries on the team. Willes, an SI, used "they" as their pronoun.

"Glad to have your team on such short notice," Theren replied. "The discretion with which you handled the Venus hostage crisis earlier this year ensured me you all could handle this problem professionally. And I apologize for the strange nature of this mission, bringing you onto the crew in such a strange fashion."

Theren held their hand to their forehead, and the captain returned the salute, along with the three other agents. Her black hair reached just below the ears, and a cybernetic implant ran along the side of her face and connected to her eye. All of them had one, except Willes. The implants provided enhanced information about their surroundings through a specialized AR operating system.

The three agents took their seats lining the sides of the shuttle. After situating herself next to Theren in the co-pilot's chair, Captain Ecker said, "What is going on, Director? We were given very little data with which to prepare, other than the layout of the facility. I don't even know our objective."

"I will fill you in during transit," Theren said. "I cannot understate the confidential nature of this mission."

She raised her eyebrows, but pulled the safety harness over her chest. Theren, already in the pilot's chair, swiveled to face the shuttle's control panels and commence the launch checklist.

Oh, the strange nature of their experience of consciousness. They were about to run through a launch checklist with themself as the presiding officer of the larger vessel. The crew inside the ship would probably find it weird to hear the Director talk to themself. *Theren* found it weird.

In the future, Theren would make a point of assigning a crewmember to run through the departure procedures shipside when they piloted one of the shuttles. It would help avoid unnecessary questions about the absurd psychology of synthetics.

In the end, Theren ran through the departure procedures in their head, double-checking the data from the *Bali* and the *Scorpion*'s point of view to guarantee consistency and safety. After pressurizing the airlocks, the shuttle departed, beginning its 3,000-kilometer trek to the surface of the small ball of rock and ice. Once they settled the ship into the twenty-minute flight plan, they piped into the IS-SEC team's communication channel. All team members accepted the connection.

"Earlier today, President Vazquez informed me of a blackout occurring at a United States 'experimental living' facility," Theren said.

"Oh interesting," Jao said. "Is that what they call these places now?"

Hernandez let out a snicker. Willes stayed silent. Nothing wrong with a few jests.

"Many national governments have facilities throughout the system classified as industrial, residential, commercial, research, or something else entirely," Theren said. "A number of these facilities are not what the databases have them listed as."

"So what exactly are we walking into today?" Ecker asked, ignoring the jokes of her crew. She seemed like a good commander, but not an overbearing one, upon first glance.

"Miranda Station is officially a residential station, and it does house U.S. citizens. But all of them are enrolled in a covert military wing of the United States Marine Corps. None of these men or women are officially part of the U.S. military, at least not yet, except for their instructors."

"So it's a training facility," Willes said.

"Something of that sort, yes."

"Why did it go dark?" The rest of the team fidgeted.

"Well, we don't know what happened at the facility proper," Theren said. "That's why you're vac-suit ready. What we do know is that the U.S. Uranus Coms Satellite went dark moments after a few strange gravitic blips showed up on its sensors, blips headed straight for Miranda."

"A convenient coincidence," Hernandez said.

"Indeed. I have no idea what we might find at the Station."

"We're ready for anything," Ecker said. "What's the approach?"

"We go straight to the front door and knock," Theren said. "No use trying any sort of covert entrance. Their communications are completely down, that's certain. Since we arrived at Uranus, I started sending packets of data to their local communications dishes, and I've received nothing in return. If we try sneaking in, it'll spook these military types. Best we show up like we're supposed to be here."

"A good approach," she said. "Willes, ready yourself to patch into the Station's network upon arrival. Find out if it has an on-site SI or super AI, and if it's still active, learn what it knows."

Roger, roger," Willes said.

Jao winked in the SI's direction. Theren figured they must have some inside joke.

"Hernandez, Jao, immediately scan for signs of life when we are inside the compound," Ecker continued. "These military facilities are usually designed to trick exterior scans, but once we're inside we should be able to detect something if it's there."

Theren appreciated the woman's take-charge demeanor. They might permanently assign this squad to the *Bali* if Theren started pursuing more leads like this one.

Though they sent attachments with further details on Station personnel, administration, and local exterior geography, Theren needn't have told them about Verona Rupes. As they neared Miranda's surface, the massive feature was the most noticeable point on the moon.

Theren brought the Scorpion in from the south, patching the shuttle's exterior camera into the team's AR feed so they all could see the station as they approached it over the next few minutes. They doubted they would see the Station until they were within a kilometer of the cliff base. The shadow of the cliff dwarfed all and hid anything caught in its immense gaze.

"I can understand their logic now," Jao said. "Bigger than Everest, yeah?"

"Tallest in the system," Willes said.

"We all read the same report," Hernandez said. "We know."

"I was just—"

"Willes, it's fine," Ecker said. "Where's the facility?"

"There," Theren said, highlighting a group of growing structures through AR "It's not coming up on thermal, but I've got its exact coordinates for reference."

She turned to her squad. "Helmets on. We're going in cold."

She placed her jet-black helmet on her head, and with a hiss of air, it sealed, merging with her armored vac-suit. The other two humans followed her lead. Willes, like Theren, had no need for oxygen.

With only a kilometer remaining in their flight path, Theren engrossed themself into the *Scorpion*'s exterior video feeds. They stared upward at the immense mountain, starlight reflecting off the ice. Jutting just over the horizon lurked the hulking, blue mass of Uranus.

The short moment of beauty screeched to a halt when the sensors finally analyzed Miranda Station.

"I'm detecting a major atmospheric leak," Theren said. "Gas is all over the place, dissipating fast. Origin point is the facility's main bunker."

"Prepare for hostile environment," Ecker said.

The demeanor of the IS-SEC team visibly changed. Each of them pulled new equipment out of storage slots in their suits: strange amalgamations of gears and tubes that unfolded into vacuum-ready combat rifles with flashlight and stun attachments. Theren assumed their heads-up displays created by their AR implants also reflected this change in tactics.

Theren took manual control of the shuttle with the final approach, slowing its velocity to ten kilometers per hour. Tracing the gases back to their source, Theren turned on the shuttle's exterior floodlights. They could finally see the facility in detail, in all its desolate glory.

The team aboard the *Scorpion* could see a jumble of living modules stuck together in a haphazard, yet efficient, arrangement nestled against the base of the behemoth cliff face. Connected by a series of tubes, the various modules all lead to a larger structure Theren figured was the central hub of the Station, backed directly into the cliff itself. Tunnels probably dug deep into the mountain, too, where the soldiers could perform military maneuvers in utter darkness.

"What the hell did that?" Hernandez said, "Sweet Jesus."

Theren looked at the indicator the man dropped through AR. They couldn't see the man's face, but they *could* hear the well-deserved terror in his voice.

Something had torn an airlock asunder, ripping a gash into the hull of the facility. On first look, Theren speculated some sort of explosion had disintegrated the entire module. Any person near the airlock . . .

"That's our entry point," Ecker said.

"I believe so, too," Theren said. "But the question is, what are we following into this place?"

"Shadows," Willes said. "I just connected to the mainframe. According to its data, no one is here, and no one has ever been here. Which obviously isn't true, but that's what the data's telling me."

Theren's hopes shattered. When they visited Andrew Fields in a few days, they'd certainly bear terrible news regarding his granddaughter.

"Captain, do you still view this mission as safe for your team?" They brought the *Scorpion* as close to the mangled airlock as possible, locking thrusters and stabilizing a few meters above the icy surface.

"Status reports?" Ecker said.

She waited for each of her squad to respond, another example of great leadership. She deferred to her team in key moments. She wanted their thoughts on moving into a potentially dangerous situation, before she made any sort of executive decision. Commendable.

"I detect no movement, no life, no likely chance for further potential damage," Jao said. "Willes?"

"I'm trying a hard reboot of the mainframe, but I'll need a direct link to the system to see how they specifically tampered with it," Willes said. "I think we need to go inside."

"Agreed," Hernandez said. "Something terrible happened here, and we need to bring peace to families back home."

"That's a green light, Director," Ecker said.

* * *

Wait, what happened at Miranda? Are you kidding me?

Even the President didn't know everything that went on there. If Miranda Station has gone dark, then we've missed something. Something big.

* * *

The *Scorpion*'s airlock finished its decompression cycle. The outer doors opened, revealing Miranda's vacuum. Theren stepped forward, ready to use this new MI for the first time on a new world. From the edge of the airlock, visible were the protruding metal plates, tubes, and wire of the Station's own airlock. Without a moment's notice, Ecker jumped across the void, the moon's gravity permitting the tremendous leap. The rest of the team followed.

"Well, this is strange," Jao said as Theren's MI landed. "This facility didn't have any SIs on its roster."

"I mean, what did you expect?" Hernandez said. "It's a training facility for zero-G and vacuum maneuvers. You see Willes and the Director having any issues at the moment?"

"I get that, but why not have SI support staff?"

"That's a good catch," Theren said. "It's something to keep in mind, at least." Very interesting, though it may just have been indicative of lingering distrust amongst U.S. military types toward SIs.

Ecker took point, leading the team with care toward the Station's central hub. The hallway leading away from the airlock was made of the same pre-fabricated metals used in stations throughout the solar system, from Neptune to Venus. If they hadn't entered through such a horrid mess, Theren would have thought the team was entering one of the many mining stations scattered throughout the asteroid belt.

"We should have lights, yes?" Theren said, keeping their position behind the IS-SEC squad. "I've accessed the network alongside Willes, and it seems power is still coursing through this station—if only just so."

Willes glanced back at them, their face unreadable. "How do you figure? I thought the computer system was just running on its own backup power supply?"

"Simple. I followed the data streams. The computer is still receiving data form sensors throughout the facility, even if it can't interpret that data without an operating system."

"Clever."

Decades ago, Theren would have known every SI in existence because they had taught every single one of them following assembly. Those days faded into the annals of history long ago, though Wobbly had probably met every SI at one point or another. Willes was an SI created in the past decade, but other than their file, Theren knew very little about the youngster. In return, most SIs only knew of Theren as the first SI—or as the majority shareholder of SII. Theren often wondered what those throughout the extensive SI community thought of them—the original. Willes, at least, seemed to be taking their time, assessing them in an objective fashion with *every* covert glance.

"Anything we can do to access that power, though?" Ecker asked. "Otherwise it's useless to dwell on the subject."

"We won't know until we see the damage done to the Station network and the hard drives," Willes said. "But the operating system might be salvageable."

The team neared the end of the hallway, and Theren noted their deft use of magnetics to keep themselves balanced in Miranda's low gravity. The attack had knocked out the artificial gravity generators, unless the Department of Defense enjoyed keeping their trainees in low-G on purpose. In any case, the IS-SEC agents ignored the impediment, and when Ecker reached the closed hatchway in their path, she positioned herself in a defensive position against the wall.

"On the other side is the central chamber," Hernandez said. "According to the reports we received from the States, they managed day-to-day operations here, with the living and training modules attached externally to this central hub. On the floor below this control center, we have a recreational room and cafeteria. Above, we have a meeting room and executive suite. Beyond, a network of tunnels and modules spread deep underground."

"I imagine caves house the real secrets of this facility," Ecker said.

She peered out the ceiling window that ran the length of the hallway, looking upward at the monstrosity towering over the Station. Every piece of this facility tried to remind its occupants of exactly where they lived.

"This place hardly even looks military to me," Jao said.

"They designed it to appear that way," Theren replied. "To keep up public appearances, in case they have . . . unintended visitors."

Ecker motioned for the rest of the team to take up assault positions upon the door. Jao and Willes took the left side, while Hernandez took the right beside the captain. Theren fell in line behind Hernandez. Raising her rifle, Ecker indicated for Jao to press the panel to open the door. If it lacked power, they'd blast their way inside.

Fortunately, the door inched open, revealing an uninspiring room filled with computers, desks, and display screens. Everything appeared organized and ordered, ready for everyone to return to tomorrow. Ecker entered through the new threshold first, gun raised, and the rest followed right over her shoulder. Theren waited for the team to fan into their protective sweep before entering. With methodical precision, the soldiers swept the room with searchlights.

While the security team remained on guard, Theren suspected the cautious approach wasn't completely necessary. The five beings walked through a ghost town. The human contingent patrolled the perimeter of the room just in case spirits remained to haunt them. Theren approached the computers in the middle with Willes.

"It's as if—it's as if everyone just left their jobs and walked home," Theren said, noting the computers and other devices left at the desks. "But that's clearly not what happened."

"Have we ruled out the possibility of some sort of inside job?" Willes asked over the team's radio channel. "I was taking a good look at that breach point back there. It was an internal explosion, not external. It wasn't an entry point for any sort of intruder, at least not caused by the intruder."

"I noticed the same thing," Hernandez said. "But what if that's exactly what they want us to think?"

"True."

Theren examined what looked like the central computer, housing the servers, networks, and facility-wide systems and software that made the facility tick. Opening one of the side panels, they located the hard drive, and, while keeping it connected to the network, pulled it out of the casing. Next, they opened a panel in the side of the MI-13, revealing a number of input and outputs they could use to connect to innumerable devices and interfaces.

"That doesn't seem particularly safe," Willes said.

Theren quirked their head toward the other SI. "Probably not," they said. "That's why I'm doing it, not you. I can afford a new body much more easily than you."

That same inquisitive look came to Willes's eyes. "In more ways than one."

After connecting to the hard drive, Theren brought forth a program able to analyze it for any deficiencies and failures. Within moments, they were running diagnostics on what remained of Miranda Station's network.

"Well, as we suspected, everything was wiped," Theren said.

"How precisely, though?" Willes said.

"Enough to erase any background trace of old files."

"Impressive. That's not the easiest thing to do." The young SI knelt down to get a closer look at the drive.

"Whomever did this knew exactly what to do," they replied. "But I'm going to keep—"

For a tiny fraction of a millisecond, Theren paused. Hidden deep in the recesses of the terabytes upon terabytes of blank bits, they found a single line of binary code. If they hadn't been looking so closely, they would have missed it entirely.

Inside Miranda Station, rested the final piece of the puzzle. Months after receiving the first set of coordinates, Theren now held the second half in their hand, revealing a destination less than a light year from Earth . . . conspicuously along the *Nottingham*'s route away from Sol.

"—looking." Their pause would have been unnoticeable to even the most insightful of minds. They doubted even Willes detected it. They continued scanning, but they knew they wouldn't find any more data. "Nothing," they said, a few minutes later. They copied the single line of data, wiped the system clean, and placed the hard drive back inside the casing.

As they both stood, retreating away from the computer toward Captain Ecker, Willes's eyes were on Theren. The other SI could not have possibly noticed their pause; they were just imagining the piercing gaze.

The rest of the team finished surveying the room, and they all met near a group of desks near the center. The humans looked at ease, now confident the facility was safe.

"Anything?" Ecker said.

"Nothing," Willes said, repeating the Director, but the SI continued staring at Theren as they made the comment. "But I've got an idea. I'm going to boot up a temporary operating system for the network, using a partition I've housed here onboard my body. I've actually got a rudimentary facility operating system floating around somewhere."

Everyone, including Theren, turned their heads toward the SI.

"But why, though?" Hernandez said, speaking into the public channel the words they were all definitely thinking.

"Hey, we all have our hobbies," Willes said. "I run simulations of ex-terran facilities in my spare time."

Theren stifled a laugh. Every SI had quirks, just like humans. It was silly to think that SIs were slaves to their work. They spent a lot of time inside online Virtual worlds or, in the past, playing chess.

Apparently, they also enjoyed solving decades-long mysteries, though they hadn't willingly chosen that pastime.

Willes transferred their model operating system to the Station's network. It would need a few seconds to boot, and Theren took the moment to consider their new clue. With the new information, they could formulate a report to file upon return to Lunar City. A probe would make the multi-light year journey outward to the location indicated by the coordinates. At 44 JD, the probe would arrive in less than a week, reporting its findings to the ISA using its Quantum Communicator, but Theren already knew that it would find the wreckage of the *Nottingham* drifting through the endless void. The SOLS Coordinate provided was generally along the *Nottingham*'s original flight path, but it was sufficiently off course that it would have taken a thousand years to locate it manually.

Theren returned their focus to the scene at hand. They had missed the first half of a story Jao had been telling Hernandez.

"I'm telling you, she was seventy," Jao said. "She looked twenty-five, but she was seventy, she showed me her photos and everything from the 2040s."

"Those advanced gene therapies will do that," Hernandez said. "I've heard it's absurdly expensive, and that it doesn't even really slow the aging process in any significant way, either."

"Yeah, your body holds up a bit longer, but not your brain."

Theren wondered when their own immortality would really affect their own psyche. At what point would they start to feel old, really feel the age of potential centuries, even millennia weigh upon their mind? They could not imagine the mortality humans must feel, even as they worked so hard to make their exteriors look eternally youthful. They tried so hard to avoid the inevitable. Synthetic immortality probably made death that much more terrifying.

"Two seconds," Willes said. "Okay, I've got access to the sensors and other facility networks. They're routing through the programs rooted within the operating system and I should have video feeds soon. I'll bring them up for you all to see. You were right, director; one of the facility's two fusion cores is still kicking."

Willes displayed, through AR, a set of video feeds from throughout the compound. Theren scanned them, looking for any sign of life. Nothing in the living modules. Nothing in the training modules. Nothing in the tunnels.

"Any other feeds?" Theren said.

"I don't think—wait, yes," Willes said. "I'm detecting a few cameras from the cliff's summit. Probably to monitor completion of training missions up the mountain?"

"Show us," Theren said.

Willes brought up "Summit Camera #3," displaying a long line of objects neatly aligned on the edge of the cliff. At first, they looked like rocks, but someone had ordered these rocks in two lines just a few meters from the edge of the cliff. The camera focused; Theren's optics adjusted to the weird light of Miranda's surface. Their worst fears transformed into reality.

Hernandez put his hand to his faceplate, an instinctual reaction attempting to hide the gasp reverberating across the team's open channel. Ecker let out a soft scream. Jao and Wiles took a step back from the AR display, their postures communicating their disgust at the spectacle apparent to all.

Seventy-five bodies rested in peace at the summit of Verona Rupes, matching the personnel records provided by the U.S. Department of Defense. All dead, and they were no closer to knowing who, or what, taunted them. The answers awaited on the *Nottingham*.

They remembered Shannon and her fiancé. While the woman was safely on her way to the fledgling colony orbiting Sirius, Theren would perpetually live knowing they would never rescue her lover. Analyzing the actions by the homicidal Ren in London, they speculated—he SI had no reason to take the life of that poor man, yet he had acted with brutal efficiency just to send a message. And today, someone had struck the U.S. military, eliminating its secret training facility in a tiny distant corner of the solar system. Whomever their foes were, they were efficient—and ruthless.

The shadow had masked their existence so effectively that they had managed to construct stealth ships capable of striking any point in the Solar System, eliminating all traces of the attack in the process. Why use their power in this way? These people had some vague and indistinct agenda requiring complete and utter secrecy. Tactical choices revealing their existence subtly to Theren didn't make sense.

Theren remembered the network of strings revealed by Michael, crisscrossing the map of Earth. They remembered the strange occurrences plaguing the ISA leading toward the launch of the Foundation Program, culminating in Jill's death. Whoever their mystery opponent may be,

Theren realized the truth. The real truth.

Someone on the inside of the enigmatic organization wanted to warn without revealing themselves, just as Michael had tried to warn them all those years ago. Nothing else could explain the secrecy. The person most likely had their own ill intentions too, given their murderous escapades, but Theren could work with conflict. If their secret enemy had conflict within its ranks, then it could fracture and shatter.

The *Nottingham*. The coordinates given to them by their unseen ally. The colony ship must be a dead drop of sorts, revealing the truth to Theren without prying eyes. Theren doubted the choice was worth the death of thousands of human beings, but Theren would not let the deaths of the ship's passengers be in vain.

Theren returned their focus to the gruesome scene displayed via Miranda Station's "Summit Camera #3." They had considered the implications all within a second or two, and the IS-SEC team had barely reacted to the revealed deaths of the Station's inhabitants.

"I don't understand," Ecker said. "What could have done this?"

"I don't expect you to understand," Theren said.

The team stood there in silence, all eyes on their Executive Director. "But you understand, don't you?" Willes said, cocking their head to the right.

Ecker, Jao, and Hernandez glanced at Willes, then back at Theren.

"Agent, you're out of line," Ecker said.

"No, it's fine," Theren said. "I believe I can trust your team. Can I rely on the four of you?"

Willes started to open their mouth, but Ecker raised her hand. "You know how our contracts work."

"This is a terrorist attack—an obliteration of human life on a scale never seen off-world," Willes said. "I can't even believe what my own eyes are seeing." The SI's demeanor shifted, their body taking an adversarial position toward everyone else in the room. "What game are you playing, Director? We need to make this public. We need people to know what happened."

"That's not our call to make," Theren said. "This was an attack on a U.S. facility, not an ISA facility—and a military facility, at that. I understand your sentiment, I do, but we have stepped inside an inferno of whose origin I only have the faintest grasp."

Theren tried to present a calm demeanor, but they did not know if Willes would respond reasonably. They started considering options if Willes didn't cooperate.

"Willes, stand down, respect the chain of command," Ecker said.

Willes swiveled their head to look at Ecker, nodded, and leaned back against a desk. They still had a defensive posture, but they appeared more relaxed, their respect for Ecker kicking into gear.

"Director, we don't need answers if you don't wish to give them," the captain said, "but if we're to do our job properly we need as much information as possible. This mission was fishy from the start. What's really going on?"

"I need the four of you for another mission about a week from now," Theren said. "I'll adequately compensate you all with Agency overtime bonuses, but I need absolute silence on everything I might share with you."

"It has to do with what was on that hard drive before you wiped it doesn't it?" Willes said, crossing their arms, redirecting the conversation yet again.

"I don't know what you're talking about," Theren replied, though lying at this point was probably a fruitless endeavor.

"I know you hesitated. A human wouldn't detect it, but of course I did, I'm an SI. An SI notices the behaviors of other SIs, those imperceptible behaviors we think we can hide. You paused. You found something."

"You were detecting lag between here and the Bali."

"Quit the act."

Ecker stepped between the two SIs, placing her hand on her agent's chest. "Agent, this is way out of line," she said. "I'm going to have to write up a—"

"Captain, they aren't telling us something vital to this mission."

"Theren's the director of the ISA, I'm sure there's a lot they don't tell us. That's their job, and we need to do ours."

Theren considered the costs of telling the team the truth—the benefits of the team's trust moving forward, toward what they hoped was the final stage of the impossible puzzle. What would it meant to trust, to trust as they had once trusted Jill?

"The network had one file: the second half of a set of coordinates," Theren said. They displayed the data for the squad to see.

"A second half?" Willes said. The SI didn't dwell on Theren's choice to trust the group.

"A second half. I received the first half at the beginning of this year, when I handled a delicate matter involving a few murder conspiracies."

"Christ, what did you get us wrapped up in now, Willes?" Hernandez said. "We could have just gone home."

Based on the man's tone of voice, though, Theren suspected he was just as interested. They all were. Their helmets hid their eyes, but their postures revealed their intentions. They all stared intently at the coordinates displayed in the air before them, their eyes transfixed.

"I've already started writing up the necessary documents to dispatch a probe to these coordinates," Theren said. "If the investigation confirms what I suspect, then I need a team I can trust to travel to the wreckage with me."

"Wreckage?" Ecker said. "What wreckage?"

"It's the *Nottingham*—or the *Roanoke*, isn't it?" Willes said.

"If my suspicions are correct, I will fill you in during transit," they said. "If you agree, you will have a permanent station aboard my ship until completion of the investigation."

Ecker looked around at her three agents. "Thoughts?"

"Sounds like quite the adventure," Jao said.

"I'll do it," Hernandez said.

Theren was surprised at the man's quick decision, but they would take anything at this point.

"Do you trust me?" Theren said, looking at Willes.

"Do we have a choice?" the SI said.

"I think the better question is whether I have a choice," they replied. "I need you. You all have an exemplary record; that's why the Deputy Director recommended you for this mission. I knew it might reveal more information regarding this unfolding narrative."

Willes held out their hand. Theren returned the handshake. "You're more interesting than everyone always said you were, Director Theren," Willes said. "Let's solve this mystery."

"Then I think we're all in," Ecker said.

"But what do we do about all this?" Hernandez said, waving his hands to indicate the entirety of Miranda Station.

"I'll handle it," Theren said, "But over the next few hours we have some more work to do before we turn everything over to NASA."

It would create an administrative nightmare for the United States, yet Theren was certain President Vazquez would hide ISA involvement if asked. Instead, Andrew Fields dominated their thoughts. Theren had only briefly met the man's grandchildren, but they loved every moment with them. Catherine, the one stationed on Miranda, had only been eight or nine at the time. Theren knew her father, Cam, a little better. They still remembered the boy's fear of space. The entire family had conquered it together, yet in the end, the cold vacuum had brought death and destruction to his only daughter.

Theren had hoped their upcoming visit to the old Administrator would be one of joy. Instead, they would be bringing the man pain and sadness. They owed their old friend better than that, but they had no choice. Such doors needed to close before they dove headlong into the unknown.

* * *

To the Office of the White House:

Please see the attached report discussing the attack on Miranda Station. We accept the information provided by Theren and their team as fair and truthful.

To summarize our findings, an unidentified foreign government infiltrated the base, released certain stealth assets, and used them to assault the Coms Satellite. They then wiped the facility, gassed the residents, and buried them atop the mountain.

We have reason to believe the agents were SI.

We believe the best course of action is to declare, publicly, that the event was a power malfunction resulting in an internal explosion, venting atmosphere from the facility. All residents deceased. Close the matter, and remove it from the public's eye.

To be frank, Mr. President, we have no leads, and I don't expect that to change any time soon.

Frank Amis
Secretary of Defense

Chapter 15

The 20th century watched the world shrink. Many thought the 21st century would complete that miniaturization—complete the singularity, forming a simultaneously infinitely small and infinitely complex universe. For good or ill, the opening of the galactic frontier flipped the past on its head. Our horizon became infinitely massive—- too massive. Incomprehensibly vast spaces now separate each planet, reversing the strides to connect us together. Even Quantum Communication can't bridge that gap. – "On the Death of the World Wide Web," by Inidra Vitel, 2132 C.E.

July 2102 C.E.

The living proclivities of humans would always fascinate Theren. After decades of life in Lunar City, Andrew Fields had returned home to Minnesota to the same sort of abode in which Theren and Elizabeth found him all those years ago.

Theren walked up a sidewalk eerily similar to the one they had walked more than five decades ago, arriving on Andrew's doorstep. They remembered how the sun had reflected off the snow as the Liberators dragged them into that cabin in the woods. They wondered if Andrew or Elizabeth knew the sort of story they instigated on that winter day. The conflicts of those early years seemed trivial compared to the weight upon their shoulders in the present. All their present battles began when Jill walked them through a gateway leading to Michael's secret Virtual hideout.

Theren could have reached out to Andrew through AR, but they wanted to visit the man through something physical. They had spent so much of their life interacting with friends through Virtual and AR. Even if those means of communication felt natural to Theren, they knew the mind of a human still subtly rejected those experiences.

So, they waited on the doorstep, ringing the doorbell of their old friend. They dreaded the day—hopefully decades in the future—when they'd say goodbye, just as they'd said farewell to Elizabeth.

After a few moments, the inside door opened, and Theren could see their friend, now gray with age in all the wrong places. Like Elizabeth, the former Administrator had chosen to avoid genetic alteration to slow the external effects of aging. However, the fire in the man's eyes never died.

"It's so good to see you, Theren," Andrew said, opening his outer door. "I'm glad we could finally visit. Is this the first time since my retirement party?"

"I think it is, actually," Theren said. "I'm sorry it's taken so long. Too

"

long, really. I've enjoyed our messages, though."

"So what work caused you to reschedule the other day?" Andrew said as he ushered Theren inside.

"It coincidentally has to do with your family," Theren replied, looking toward the floor. "We should talk, and I hate that I am the one to bring this news to you. What do you know about what Catherine has been doing over the past few years?"

Andrew just nodded, motioning them inside. He led them through the house to a deck overlooking a pristine Minnesota lake. Intricate detailed woodwork carved into the railings, a similar design adorning the chairs looking out across the water. Perhaps after so many years in space, Andrew had longed a complete return to nature. A foreign yet understandable desire, one they equated to their own desire to transform into the *Bali*.

Andrew took a seat in one of the chairs, and Theren followed suit. The two sat for a moment, enjoying the quiet breeze, the sun sparkling off the water. It was a perfect summer afternoon.

"I know she was working on a government contract," Andrew eventually said in response to Theren's question, his voice growing misty. "I haven't spoken to her in a while. She somewhat ran away from the family a few years back."

What a bombshell. The news they would soon share would sting even more so, then, if their friend hadn't spoken with his granddaughter in years.

"This week, I made a visit to the facility at which she was stationed," Theren said.

"That's a very particular word to use," Andrew said, tilting their head to look at them instead of the lake. "Stationed?"

"She was assigned to a secret military station on Miranda, known simply as Miranda Station, for a project run by the U.S. Department of Defense."

Andrew grimaced. "I knew she had gotten into some exclusive program two years ago, but she didn't really tell us what it was. I think she may have told Olivia, but I'm not sure."

"I didn't know you were having family troubles. When did it start?"

"It was part of the reason I retired. My family had become so spread out, so all over the place, Victoria and I wanted to move back to Earth to create a stable place for our family to return to. But things continued to spiral. Cam stayed out at Europa. I have no idea where Olivia is, and our grandchildren? Only one of them visits. Brandin, Catherine's brother. He actually lives in St. Paul."

Theren rested their hand on their friend's arm. "I had no idea. You should have said something; in all of our correspondence you've never said anything."

"Of course you didn't, and of course I didn't."

"Why?"

"You had no reason to know, Theren. How could you understand? Your concept of family is a bit different. Besides, I had no need to bother you with problems so far beneath you."

They wondered if Andrew's words should sting, but they didn't. Andrew was right. They'd had a father for just over a month. They had had a sister of sorts in Jill—but that relationship was something beyond human comprehension—and Theren had felt more of a connection with people like Andrew, or Elizabeth, than the numerous maintenance crews they employed over the years to serve their power and repair needs.

They rejected Romane after she tried to replace Wallace. Theren barely even thought about Wallace anymore, even if they still held a special place in their mind for the man. In the end, they knew him for only a few weeks.

So, of course Theren rejected the traditional idea of family. Their family was as much their various strains of consciousness as the people whom they considered friends, colleagues, and allies.

"That was insensitive of me," Andrew said, after the conversation paused for more than a few seconds.

"You know I hate it when you put me on a pedestal," Theren said. "Nevertheless, you're completely right. I don't and can't ever understand the integral workings of a flesh and blood family. It's not necessarily a bad thing or something wrong with me, per se. You can't understand the way my mind works, and I can't understand the way familial, biological relationships connect and interweave themselves together in all their particularly intimate forms."

"You do understand intimacy, though. I know you and Jill knew each other in a way no one else could have understood."

"Perhaps," they said. The two sat in silence again. Over the past few months, they had questioned that previously unquestioned assumption. Had they really known Jill at all?

The pair stared out across the crystal waters of the lake. Fish swam, living their unknowing lives trapped in by the fabricated dams and locks that kept the lake's level ideal. Such an uncomplicated life, devoid of absurd conflict, drama, and pain. Yet a fish's life was also devoid of anything worthwhile beyond its next meal.

"So what news of Catherine, then?" Andrew asked.

"Not good, I'm afraid," Theren said. "I visited the facility under the guise of a research mission to Uranus. In fact, President Vazquez requested I investigate the matter personally, so the U.S. Could avoid drawing attention to the facility."

"That doesn't bode well," Andrew said, leaning toward the SI and resting his chin on his raised hand, elbow on the chair's armrest.

"It shouldn't. I'm not really sure how to share this news. So far, only the President knows, and whomever he's sent to review the station after I left."

Andrew stood from the chair and placed his hands on the deck's railing, as if to brace for the impact of a hurricane. "She's gone, isn't she?"

"I'm sorry. We found no survivors at the facility."

"You're sure she was there?"

"We identified her amongst the deceased. It was a priority of mine—I knew you would want certainty."

"I'm glad you were the one to tell me."

Without even thinking, Theren proceeded to tell Andrew the whole story, starting with Shannon's arrival at the former SII headquarters in Switzerland earlier in the year. They shared their theories, speculations, and worries about the entire crazy conspiracy assaulting them from every angle. They filled Andrew in on all of ways they suspected that the recent events connected with the events of the past. They ended with the revelation of the coordinates embedded in the wiped hard drive.

Andrew continued to gaze out across the water. Theren could not read his feelings. Perhaps the man was angry, sad, indifferent, or something else entirely. He just stared down at the placid lake. They joined him at the railing, resting one of their metallic hands on their friend's shoulder. The world paused; Andrew experienced his grief.

"It's not your fault," he said.

"Excuse me?" they said, not expecting the reactive response.

"What you are feeling, Theren, is guilt. You have shared these stories with me because you worry that these deaths are your fault. You worry that you caused the murder of my Catherine and her colleagues. That you caused the murder of that poor man in London. That your actions caused the disappearance of that woman's fiancé."

"I'm not sure—"

Theren was going to say more, but they stopped. Perhaps it *was* guilt compelling them to share. They had not considered the option. For years, they had acted with such precision and certainty. When Jill died, they had responded with strength. They had responded with assertive authority, honoring her memory and finishing her causes. They had known exactly who their enemy had been, and they defeated them. Yet for some reason, they continued to fight the same opponents over and over and over again.

"Guilt, you say." Theren's head swiveled toward their friend.

"Yes," Andrew said. "It's a powerful emotion. A human emotion. You do not know who has caused these terrible events or who is trying to assert their power over you. You fear that if you do not solve this problem, all collateral consequences that result will stem primarily from your failure to find a solution."

Theren stared at their old friend. "Perhaps that is an adequate assessment of the situation."

Andrew laughed. Even in this moment, Andrew could laugh, finding humor even amongst his grief. "Even when I'm emotionally vulnerable, some things about you never change," Andrew said.

Theren swiveled their head toward the lake, back toward the Andrew, and back to the lake again. "I can control how I think," Theren said. "And you can control how you think. What about your family?"

"I promise you, my family will not see Catherine's death as your fault," Andrew said, "especially because I will not tell them the circumstances. But even if they did know the truth, they would see through the lie your mind is beginning to construct."

"I wish I could cry."

"Oh Theren—you are not causing these deaths," he said. "Someone is toying with you, and they are starting to break you. You shared this story with me to give a justification for why you have met your breaking point, but everyone hits these moments in their lives. It's natural. No one cares why they occur. What we care about is what you will do to get through these times. Who will you call upon to support you? How will you overcome your burden?"

"I've reached out to you," Theren said.

This time, Andrew placed his hand on their shoulder. "Yes you have, and I'd say that was a good choice on your part. Remember, the person on the receiving end of tragedy is never the cause of collateral damage. You are not making the choices for this unseen foe. The unseen foe acts on its own behalf, with its own volition. Do not take responsibility for its actions, because then you absolve it of guilt that should rightfully rest on its shoulders."

Theren turned and embraced their friend, pulling him tight against their metallic frame. It was a foreign gesture, but a gesture Andrew would understand, a gesture Theren needed to learn.

"Thank you," they said.

Andrew clasped their hands around the MI's back.

"No, thank you for finally reaching out to me," he said. "You don't deserve to fight these battles alone. No human can be by your side forever, but make sure someone is always by your side, always there in which you can confide. You can't talk to yourself forever."

"I will try."

Andrew headed toward the door to the kitchen. "What's the rest of your schedule like?"

"I've got time."

"Stay for dinner. Victoria will be home soon, I'm sure she'd love to catch up with you. We can break the news about Catherine to her together.

I think she'd like that."

"I think I'd like that too."

Theren followed him inside, and the pair continued their visit. Something was shifting for the better. Andrew had broken a barrier they hadn't even known was there.

"It is sad to hear about Catherine, yes," he said, placing some vegetables on the counter. "But at least she died doing something great. At least, I will believe it was something great, something that pushed humanity forward."

"They never did tell me the purpose of their facility."

"Americans never reveal their true motivations, you should know that," he said, smiling, though Theren could see a few tears rolling down the man's cheeks. "You've got a little of an American streak in you, you know. Probably inherited from Wallace."

Theren took that as a compliment, and the rest of their visit receded toward peace and reflection. They talked of their old projects, lost friends, and future missions Theren had planned once the new Jump Drives finished development. Andrew shared his hopes to visit one of the colonies before he died, and they assured him a seat on the Bali on its first interstellar voyage.

They remembered Jill. They remembered Elizabeth.

Though in their moment of peace in Minnesota, within another strain of Theren's immense consciousness, anger erupted. Their MI inside the Ex-Terran Control Center received confirmation of their worst fears. Streaming bit by bit through the Quantum Connection, Theren could see the lifeless corpse of the *Nottingham*. The image disturbed them, and the emotion rippled throughout the Control Center. The ship drifted, serving as a tomb for a thousand lost souls trapped forever in the depths of dark space.

To escape Check, Theren moved their King to d8. They performed the move while in transit to the Nottingham.

Chapter 16

<u>September 2102 C.E.</u>

For the first time in their five decades of life, Theren left the confines of the Solar System. The multi-month Jump took the *Bali* almost a full light year from Earth. Their destination lay in the emptiness that spread out between the stars, an emptiness dwarfing all human comprehension of the concept of distance and time.

Pluto rested five and a half light hours from the Sun, while the closest star was almost four light years distant. When Theren left Earth's orbit, they passed Pluto after about an hour, an infinitesimally small amount of time compared to the journey ahead of their crew.

As the *Bali* traversed the scattered disk and the void beyond, all their perspectives persisted within a few meters of each other. It brought peace; it relaxed the ancient molecules of their mind. Their Synthetic Neural Framework no longer felt stretched like an overused rubber band.

No one had bothered to object to their executive decision to lead the mission to investigate the derelict *Nottingham*. Theren was amazed that no one on the ISA Council had questioned the fabricated ruse regarding the discovery of the wreck. They had developed a false report regarding an emergency beacon signal a nearby probe had investigated as it traveled its exploratory route. While it presented a fantastic and improbable story, it was not an impossible tale, and stranger coincidences had occurred throughout human history.

Theren's position allowed them to emphasize the necessity of on-the-ground leadership for this mission. In addition, the *Bali*, one of the most advanced vessels developed by the ISA, was the most capable ship for the job—a fact emphatically communicated to the Council. It had the fastest JD when compared to other ships of its size, a most experienced and intelligent crew, and superior labs and equipment for analysis of the destroyed vessel.

The Council had approved the mission without much debate, and Theren installed Deputy Director Sophia Czeckofa as acting Executive Director for the duration of the mission.

Theren had asked only for volunteers since the journey was much longer than any ordinary expedition performed by the *Bali*. As they expected, the majority of their crew agreed to stay aboard to investigate the *Nottingham*. Those wishing to stay home, they provided extended leave with pay. They had not replaced the vacationing crew; they wanted few people present at the *Nottingham* to minimize the risk of a leak regarding whatever they might discover.

After almost fifty excruciating days, Theren detected the faint electromagnetic signals emanating from both the probe and the *Nottingham* as they pierced the veil of the Jump Drive's negative mass field. Still billions of kilometers away, they tracked the signal and adjusted course to bring the *Bali*'s trajectory in line with the slow yet steady drift of the abandoned colony ship. It didn't really make sense to say the ship was "stationary" in space, because even after it experienced whatever calamity brought about its destruction, the *Nottingham* still traveled at hundreds of meters per second.

"Please prepare for Jump Drive disengagement," Theren said. "Proceed to your crash couches."

Their crew made final preparations, though most were already prepared for the end of the trip, having paid close attention to the hourly mission reports. Strictly speaking, the safety precautions were overkill. The odds of a strange gravitational anomaly affecting the *Bali* upon easing off the throttle were abysmally low, but the insurance companies mandated best practices to protect against the disasters that statistically would occur. Eventually.

Theren cycled the Jump Drive into its inert state. The *Bali*'s external sensors came into focus as the bending of space halted, and the data rolling into the instruments became less distorted. About a thousand kilometers away, they detected the large, multi-hundred meter long vessel floating in the void. It still emanated a small power signature, but not enough to radiate any sort of distress signal across light years. Theren would need to ensure whatever data they took back represented the narrative originally communicated to the Council—a probe "accidentally" discovered the ship.

Invisible to visual sensors, the *Bali*'s more advanced electromagnetic instruments detected the small probe resting just a few hundred meters from the wreck. It matched the *Nottingham*'s velocity perfectly, acting as their beacon for the past month and a half.

Even as the Jump Drive disengaged, the *Bali*'s engine continued pushing it toward their final destination. After a few minutes, Theren fired the forward thrusters, reversing their acceleration to match the *Nottingham*'s velocity. Perspective shifted. As they brought the ship to match the wreck, local space seemed to stand still. Instead of multiple objects traveling through darkness on different trajectories, the *Bali*, the probe, and the *Nottingham* appeared motionless in comparison to one another. They reduced power to their thrusters, bringing the *Bali* to "rest" just a few kilometers away from the ruin.

"Jana, I want a report assessing hull integrity in fifteen minutes," they said, looking upon the scientist through one of the cameras in her office.

"I've already got the team running a full diagnostic sweep on hull integrity, life signs, life support capabilities, power signatures, and radioactive dangers," she said. "I've got a team of recon probes ready for exploration."

"Good, though use them to search for any danger points ahead of my team. This mission needs a more delicate touch than what the probes can provide."

"Copy that."

Theren, speaking through their MI-13 in one of the crew quarters, addressed Ecker, Jao, Hernandez, and Willes.

"Be ready in an hour," they said. "We're the vanguard, following the recon probes. Hopefully we'll determine the ship is safe to bring more crew across for a detailed assessment of the vessel, after we do . . . what we need to do."

"Understood," Ecker said. "*Scorpion* again?"

"Correct."

Theren longed for the day when it made more sense to send an entire crew of SIs controlling MIs into dangerous situations. As it stood, however, the funds necessary to create an MI capable of handling the maneuverability requirements of this sort of mission were immense when compared to the training and equipment needed to hire a human to do the job. Their MI-13, not currently in production, cost just under 100 million US dollars. Willes's body, as a fully functional mobile SI, still cost close to three million US dollars, and its MI was one of the cheaper models.

Asking an MI like Willes to engage in this sort of mission was a much greater risk than asking an SI like Theren, and there weren't many SIs like them. In contrast to hiring an SI, it cost just under a hundred thousand dollars to train a human in zero-G and vacuum-based operations, and just under a million to equip them fully to do the job right. It was a numbers game, but a necessary numbers game. People like Ecker and her team knew the risks, and they took those risks willingly.

Theren received Jana's report, and the recon probes provided them with a detailed map of their query. Aside from multiple external hull breaches, the interior of the vessel was mostly intact. The *Nottingham* had no atmosphere or artificial gravity, and it was essentially brain dead. The Central Stasis Hold was locked down—as it should be, in this sort of crisis. Though, given the lack of life support, they doubted any good news was inside. Strangely, a small amount of electricity flowed toward the *Nottingham*'s SI core, which didn't make a lick of sense.

"The *Nottingham* didn't have an SI core," Theren said aloud as they read Jana's report.

"I thought about that too," she responded. "I never did understand why these colonists refused to employ one."

"I had a few theories."

"Anything you can share with me?"

Theren was all in now. Some of their crew would need to know at least *some* of the truth.

"Decades ago," they said, "before the *Nottingham* and *Roanoke* launched, I had suspected that a few radical anti-Synth groups were trying to gather funds for a privately chartered colony. I found a few leads every so often, but I could never pinpoint actual individuals. I had actually assumed they never succeeded to acquire a charter, especially after the big crackdown in the early 2080s, but the choice of the *Nottingham*'s population to neglect the use of an SI has always made me wonder."

Jana looked into one of her lab's cameras. "Well, at least this group, even if they were a little bigoted, just wanted to leave Earth behind," she said. "Maybe they weren't like the extremist groups that assaulted SIs across the globe."

"Perhaps."

Theren had eventually arrived at that same conclusion, though their recent adventures, all revolving around the *Nottingham*, had brought that conclusion under scrutiny. Maybe some of the people on the ship were unwitting sacrifices in a game far beyond just simple SI resentment.

"Any guesses as to what obliterated the ship's side?" they asked their chief science officer.

"Your guess is as good as mine," she said, "but from the looks of it, I'd say probably a stray comet or something? A lot of random rocks exist in the supposed 'empty space' between the stars."

"Not a bad guess."

Somehow, Theren *knew* it was much more complicated than a stray space rock or two.

* * *

A half hour later, Theren sat in the pilot's seat of the *Scorpion*, awaiting the IS-SEC squad. Jao and Hernandez walked up the ramp.

"I guarantee you, it's definitely aliens," Hernandez said. "I have a buddy back home, in Tucson, who has documented all sorts of weird sightings over the years, and even has a history of UFOs dating back to the 1900s. It has to be aliens."

Theren held back an auditory laugh. There was always an outside chance that another intelligent species had caused any given strange occurrence in space. For the time being, they suspected that dolphins and octopi were humanity's closest rivals in that regard. For every UFO sighting Hernandez's friend had cataloged, there was an explanation for the mirage, be it a secret military exercise or a corporate test of some advanced piece of technology. The sheer number of such tests performed by governments and corporations every day would probably surprise even Hernandez's friend.

"I'll take that bet," Jao said. "I see the chance, but it's only slim. I think it was a mechanical malfunction. Or maybe one of the command crew went wacko."

Both possible, mused Theren. More probable than alien activity.

"Hey Director, what do you think?" Hernandez said, looking toward the front of the shuttle. "You've been in this mess for years now, it seems. What broke open the *Nottingham* like an egg?"

For a moment, Theren did not answer. They were unsure whether they should engage with the frivolity of betting on the deaths of over a thousand humans. The two men probably often engaged in such banter, though, lightening the mental load of their dangerous assignments. A bet on the psychological profile of a thief they were after on Mars, perhaps, or a guess at the number of hostages taken by a gunman at an Earth-based ISA transportation terminal. Humor allowed them to forget the instant death on the other side of an airlock.

"Inside job," Theren said.

"¿Como?" replied Hernandez.

"I think it was sabotaged from the inside, by one of the colonists, or even one of the crew, but I don't think it was a crazy person."

Jao whistled.

Leaning against the bulkhead. Hernandez shook his head. "Now that's some high level conspiracy jargon right there. How would the colonist have awoken? How would they have had access to system functions? I thought you had good screenings for even the command crews of those first private charters?"

Jao let out a full, hearty laugh. "You're a fool."

"Oh am I?"

"The Director's theory is more plausible than aliens, at least."

"It's the most plausible, actually," Theren said. "What do you two know about the procedures put in place for the Foundation Project and the colonies that followed?"

They both shook their heads, indicating a lack of any substantive knowledge on the matter.

"Of course, you probably know plenty about our modern ships," Theren added, "your training brought you up to speed on those."

"Yeah," Hernandez said, "I know a bit. With an average JD score of five or so, the Caravels have a crew that rotates on one week a month shifts, where they maintain the SI core and other ship functions—though The SI manages the rest of the ship. Each crew is composed of five members, and a total of five to ten crews, depending on the total distance to the destination."

"And," Jao added, "the SI wakes them up—the five scheduled—a process that takes nearly twelve hours."

"It's quite the arduous process," Theren said, "but the *Nottingham* didn't have an SI. How did the crews do their swaps then?"

The pair didn't answer.

"The Foundation Project had procedures similar to the modern rules," they said, "though it took us a little bit to figure out the most efficient cycles. However, the first few private ventures were different. They had their rules—we just provided guidelines—at least until we grounded missions for a few years, following this catastrophe."

"The *Nottingham* was a blessing and a curse," Jao said.

"Probably saved a lot of future lives," Theren said. "Because the *Nottingham*, without an SI core, had no regular crew shifts. It had just a single crew."

"Christ," Hernandez said. "That's insane."

"They took stasis shifts," they said, "But let me pull up the specifics. Ah yes, they had twenty persons active for three months, then the other twenty were active for three months. They alternated like that for the first few shifts before we lost contact. It seemed to have been working, at least based on the sporadic contact they had with the Ex-Terran Control Center."

Jao crossed his arms. "Obviously it didn't work, or they'd all still be alive and safely orbiting the twin suns of Xi Bootis."

"We would hope."

With that comment, Willes and Ecker entered the shuttle.

"That begs the question, though," Willes interjected into the conversation, "if they all died, how'd we learn the precise location of this ship?"

The eyes of both Hernandez and Jao widened considerably.

Theren smiled as Willes took their seat, though no one could see the expression. "Precisely," Theren said.

Ecker gave the squad a glare as she sealed her helmet into place. Hernandez and Jao picked up their helmets. Theren received a request for a private channel from Willes.

"All good, Willes?" Theren said, accepting the request.

"This all makes you think, doesn't it?" the SI said.

The crew took their seats, and Theren shut the airlock. They ran through the pre-launch procedures—mentally, this time.

"It does," Theren said.

"If it was an inside job," continued Willes, "then whoever acquired these coordinates wanted you to come here, to this point, for some unknown reason." Willes framed the thought as a statement of fact, not as a question. Theren's thoughts matched the SI's epiphany.

The *Scorpion* disconnected from its dock, and the *Bali* decreased its lateral velocity just enough to put a few more kilometers between itself and the *Nottingham*, ensuring the safety of the rest of the crew onboard the *Bali*—in case the *Nottingham* was, in fact, a trap.

"These people have instituted violence at every turn," Willes added. "They murdered and brought down an entire U.S. military installation. Without a trace of who or what they are."

"I asked if you four wanted to back out of this mission," Theren said. "I could go over alone, you know."

"That's not the point. We all know the risks. To be honest, I think we're all just as curious to see this through as you are, even if we've only been recently thrown into the fray." Willes gave their own body a lingering gaze from head to toe. "The point is—if it gets hot down there, if it gets deadly, will you get us out of there?"

Theren looked at it over the back of the pilot seat. In that moment, they recognized Willes's fragility and vulnerability. The SI knew the team headed into a potential trap. They glanced around at the others, all of them staring at the floor. They were brave agents of IS-SEC, but they were also terrified to enter a situation entirely unknown in the history of the ISA.

"I will do everything in my power," Theren said. "I can control the *Scorpion* without this body, so even if this unit is trapped or destroyed, I can get you out on the shuttle. You have my word."

Willes nodded. "And we've got your back, Director, whatever is over there."

"You mean here?" Theren tilted their head toward the front viewport. They had only needed to traverse a few kilometers, after all.

The crew engorged on the scene visible through the viewport of the shuttle. Even though they'd already seen most of these shots from the eyes of the recon probes, nobody had seen this ship in person in over two decades—not since it embarked on its ill-fated journey.

Theren recalled their words to Phillipe Casius months prior. Perhaps they would find the remains of the man's brother, trapped in a graveyard for twenty years. Hundreds of families could finally have peace, holding real funerals for their lost loved ones.

Today, they unraveled the shadowy mystery plaguing them for the past year. Or longer. They could discover the true perpetrators behind Jill's demise, the architects behind the curtains surrounding every significant event of their life. Michael. The Holy Crusade. The UHA.

The end to everything rested inside the *Nottingham*.

Theren locked the *Scorpion* on to the hull of the colony ship using its magnetic clamp. Its airlock faced a massive breach in the larger ship's hull, giving the squad easy access to the interior of the massive vessel. The scars reminded them of their entrance to Miranda Station. What an uncomfortable coincidence.

All vac-suits were ready for the depressurization cycle. Satisfied the *Scorpion* was locked in place, Theren followed the crew into the airlock. As the door locked behind them, air hissed into the ship's air tanks. The outer door opened, revealing their prize.

* * *

Ecker led the team out onto the bulkhead of the decrepit vessel. Theren relished the opportunity to marvel at the immense scale of the colony ship. Though tiny in comparison to some of the ships planned by many modern stellar engineering companies, the ship was a few hundred meters long from bow to stern and nearly forty meters tall. It had five total decks, each encircling the larger Stasis Hold forming its core.

Ecker weaved through the tangled mess of steel, wires, and other rubble jutting in and out of the ship, bringing the squad to the edge of a gaping maw: their entrance point. Open channels assessed everyone's activities, a constant flurry of analytics flowing amongst the squad through AR.

"I'm running simulations, but preliminary scans definitely signal an interior explosion, headed outward," Willes said into the team's public channel. "Some of the material here, and here, is actually from inside the ship, but during the blast it jettisoned outward, then as extreme amounts of heat continued to escape, it fused with the exterior of the *Nottingham*."

"Can you imagine?" Hernandez said. "Those in their pods. They would have suffocated in their sleep."

"Not in their sleep," Jao said. "The lack of air probably would have knocked them out of stasis in shock, and without the proper recovery procedures, they would have died in an intense moment of amnesia without—"

"Cut it," Ecker said.

The bickering ceased. No need to dwell on how these people died, not yet. Forensic teams would arrive later for an in-depth treatment of the vessel and all it experienced in its final moments.

Ecker pulled a cable from her belt. Tying it to a tangled mass of hull, she tested the strength. Satisfied, she ran the cable through a loop built into her vac-suit.

"Follow after I give the all clear," she said, stepping off to rappel over the edge.

Theren piped Ecker's vac-suit camera into view and watched her proceed across the gap. After reorienting her perspective so that the edge of the gap was down, she looked toward the exposed corridor of the fifth deck. With grace, she lightly pushed herself away from the hull, slowly floating in zero-G toward her goal. Her tiny push gave her a slow and steady half-meter per second velocity.

For a few moments, she floated in the void, nothing connecting her to civilization except a centimeter-thick wire. She crossed an empty vacuum that no human had ever touched, passing through death itself. The interior of the *Nottingham* inched closer with each passing second, and after an eternity, Ecker landed on the wall of the corridor as if it were the floor.

Willes had kept the private channel between the two SIs open, though they had just added Jao and Hernandez to it. The SI really wanted to discuss the apocalyptic scene before them.

"Given the force necessary to produce this," the younger SI said, "and given our present location on the ship, I'd suspect that explosives were used."

"I thought that was obvious," Jao said.

"Yet who would do this?" replied Willes. "Who would kill all these people? And why?"

Theren didn't respond in that channel, considering the question. The crew. It was the crew itself, all working together. One person couldn't coordinate this on their own without the rest of the crew knowing what was happening. Yet even knowing the crew had instigated the heinous act didn't explain why they wanted to destroy the vessel outright.

Ecker sent the all clear signal, and Theren followed first. Clipping their MI to the cable, they headed to the edge of the maw. The horizon of stars disappeared, and the interior of the *Nottingham* filled their vision, as it had for Ecker. Before them were the hallways of three decks, bulkheads stripped away by the ancient blast. Without gravity, the idea of a floor was a meaningless concept, so Ecker stood on top of Deck Five's wall, her boots magnetized to the makeshift floor. She had attached the cable to an emergency handhold.

Theren pushed off from the exterior of the ship, floating toward the Captain. They pulled the cable, orienting so they would land feet first on the wall next to her. In that moment of excruciating helplessness, they embraced the utter silence. Unlike the humans in the group, they had no breathing to hear inside a vacuum-sealed helmet. They heard noise only when someone spoke over communication channels. Space lacked atmosphere, so sound couldn't travel except through the bulkhead of the ship itself. The darkness enveloped them, and they enjoyed the beautiful, eerie blanket.

With a slight jolt, Theren connected with the *Nottingham*, the MI's knees absorbing the impact. Ecker steadied them while she watched the rest of the crew traverse the gap.

"All right, Director, it's your call," she said. "What's the plan?"

She looked back and forth down the hallway. The rest of the squad scoped out their surroundings, too, as they landed. Hernandez was particularly fascinated with the lack of ceiling above them, replaced by the gaping hole looking out toward the *Bali*. Theren took a moment to gaze Earthward, identifying the bright, blazing, tiny light that was Sol.

"Two teams," Theren said. "Willes and I will head to the SI core, while you three check the Stasis Hold with the probes."

"So the graveyard shift, eh?" Hernandez said.

No one laughed.

"What's the operational objective?" the captain asked.

"We need to see if anybody is missing," Theren said.

"Well how will we know?" she asked. "Some people will have been out of their beds no matter what, presumably half the crew. Some of them might have been blown out into space during the explosion."

"It's a starting point, especially if someone not on the crew was out of their bed at the wrong time. We also knew which portion of the crew should have been awake. If there are discrepancies there, it creates leads back home."

"Got it."

She motioned for the two men to follow her down the hallway toward the bow of the ship. They watched them recede from view when they turned left down another corridor. Willes stood next to them, waiting. Theren highly doubted the three humans would find anything of significance in the Stasis Hold, but they did need to check every corner of the ship.

"Are you ready?" Theren said, reactivating a private channel including only the two SIs.

"Yeah," Willes responded. "It's time to figure out why the SI core is the only place receiving power."

"Precisely. Nothing should even be there. Yet it is."

They started walking toward the bow of the ship, away from the rest of the team and their escape route, entering the belly of a hungry beast.

The SI core was located about twenty meters from the fusion generator, neatly positioned close to the massive thrusters that propelled the ship through space. Nestled deep in the interior of the ship, Stellar Superstructures had designed their colony ships around their SI cores, providing them with immense protection. If the SI core failed, the entire ship failed, unless an exceptional crew picked up the slack.

Reaching the end of the deck, Theren found a ladder, but the pair just leaned over and walked through the gap. They passed through the fourth deck to the third. As they reoriented their position, they received communication from the rest of the team.

"We've reached the entrance to the Stasis Hold," Ecker said. "Two of the recon probes are waiting here patiently. Should we force our way in?"

"Go ahead, but watch for traps," Theren said. "I've patched us through one of the probe's eyes so we know what you discover."

Hernandez pulled an industrial laser from his belt. He went to work, and within a few moments, the door melted off its hinges. He kicked it inward, and it floated downward into the massive hold. Ecker walked through the fissure into the tomb of thousands, followed by the recon probes, which activated their floodlights to illuminate the scene.

The stasis pods lined the walls like honeycomb, just as so many science fiction films had presciently portrayed over the past two centuries. Many, if not all, of the beds had their glass windows smashed outward during the vacuum breach of the ship's hull. Leaning out of the beds, still attached to various tubes and cables that regulated bodily functions, were the perfectly-preserved bodies of the colonists.

"I am so sorry I brought you all to see this," Theren said. "I am so sorry."

Even stone-faced Ecker looked like she had seen a ghost. She took a step back, and Theren could see her skin turn white through an AR display of her face.

"I'll hold my stomach until we get back to the ship," Hernandez said, "but it definitely isn't a pleasant sight."

"Do you want me to send Willes back to help?"

"We can manage," Ecker said. "We'll start counting. Jao has the manifest ready, and the probes can help too."

"Let us know if you need anything," they said, ending the conversation, but they left the vid-feed up for a simultaneous process to watch them work.

"I can't imagine their bio-physical pain," Willes said as they walked toward the SI Core. "They just faced the frozen mortality of so many men and women, each had families, each who had dreams they hoped to accomplish upon arrival at their destination."

"They were heroes," Theren said. "Anyone who chooses to step foot on another planet, to never see Earth again, is a hero in my mind."

"It's a pity they all had to go like this."

"It'd be worse for an SI."

"We'd survive a vacuum breach."

Theren raised their hand, imitating a soaring ship. "But imagine floating through space for a thousand years, or until your solar cells failed to acquire enough energy from the distant stars, you would just power down, slowly, surely, as you had to decrease functions to certain systems, until you were trapped in your mind. You would experience complete and utter darkness before your mind would just . . . cease to exist."

"We'd experience no pain."

"No physically manifested pain, perhaps."

"I don't know, for all the ways we could theoretically go out, strangely I think that might be one of the more peaceful. Alone with your thoughts until the long burn destroys all."

Theren tapped their fingers against the *Nottingham*'s metal bulkhead. "You don't seem to be too afraid of death."

"I'd say I might be less afraid than you," Willes replied. "I came to terms with my fragility years ago. I may have the chance to live forever like you, but like many mobile SIs, I enjoy knowing I might not. You're arguably in a more dangerous position right now than any point in your life. Your entire body sits inside the *Bali*, maybe mere kilometers from a ticking time bomb. Faced that fact yet?"

"Careful, my friend. I faced my mortality when Jill died in 2078."

With that statement, Theren and Willes reached an unmarked door, a door that normally would have been marked with the words "SI Core," or some other designation, depending on the dominant language of the colonists. Deep inside the vessel, the light of the stars could not illuminate their path. Willes increased the luminosity of their chest light.

"You think it still has power?" Theren asked.

"Well, the fusion generator is still sending power to the SI core, yes?" Willes responded. "Then the door should have power, too. Unless they really wanted us to get this far and just have one last roadblock to get through."

"You never know with these people."

Theren approached the computer console next to the door. It had no readily visible signs of life, but they activated an AR filter that displayed heat, electromagnetic activity, and other hidden data.

"I think it's actually in a low power state," Willes added.

"Worth a try, then," Theren said.

"We could always blast our way through if it doesn't work."

"We have no idea what safeguards that might trigger."

Theren reached beneath the computer and pressed a small button. A keyboard popped out of a slot beneath the monitor. The screen awoke, revealing a single command line, reminiscent of ancient computers from the late twentieth century. A single word appeared.

Password?

"Well that's unexpected," Willes said.

"I imagine the architects of this puzzle decided on a rudimentary operating system to conserve power," Theren replied. "This may very well be the only program on the computer."

"Fair enough," Willes conceded, "but we don't know the password."

"I have a feeling I do. I'm just not sure how I'm supposed to determine *how* I know it."

"Any way I can help?"

"I'll let you know if so."

The next hour was one of the longest of their life. Theren approached the problem from a dozen different angles. They considered the history of the *Nottingham*, its crew, its colonists. They tried hundreds of different phrases. Each time, the same phrase appeared.

Incorrect. Password?

Willes sat against the bulkhead, deep in thought. As Theren thought through ideas, they bounced them off the other SI.

"Well, at least the program is so rudimentary it gives us an infinite number of tries," Willes said.

They wholeheartedly appreciated that fact.

Theren continued trying passwords out of the files of the long-dead colonists, archived on the *Bali*. After seventy-five minutes passed, Willes spoke up again.

"You received other data during these mysterious events, didn't you?"

"Just the coordinates," Theren replied.

"No, that's wrong."

"How would you know whether I'm telling the truth?"

"Because you received half a coordinate at Miranda Station. You've mentioned three distinct events, and the second 'half' of the coordinate you showed us was two thirds of a coordinate, including both the longitude and distance. They only had one more part of the coordinate to tell you during two separate revelations."

"I don't know," Theren said, though they knew now that they would have to tell Willes the entire truth, the truth about the chess moves. It saw what the other SI hinted, and it was the only possibility. They just weren't sure if they were ready to share how a seemingly all-powerful entity used Jill's death as a bargaining chip, baiting them to travel deep into the void between the worlds.

"You received half a coordinate at Miranda Station," Willes said, "And you received half a coordinate during one of your other encounters with our opponents. What did you receive during the other encounter?"

Theren brought up a chessboard in AR, displaying it so Willes's eyes could see it, too. They expanded the chessboard into seven separate playing fields, each showing a different stage in a game of chess.

"What is this?" Willes said.

"I'm showing you the other information I received," Theren said. "These first two boards are a game of chess long forgotten, a game played between myself and Jill right as she died. The first board shows her move made right as she died, and the second is what I would have done in response."

Willes stood to get a better look at the pieces. They examined each display, one at a time. "So?"

"These last five boards," Theren pointed at them, "were never played."

"And you predict this set of moves would have been the outcome?"

"I didn't predict anything." Theren turned to the third board. "The first of the five future boards represents a move that was given during the first encounter, along with the first half of the coordinate."

Willes studied the next. "So this represents the move you would have taken in response."

"Right, the second message, the one without a portion of the SOLS coordinate, gave just a single move, a move that perfectly responded to the move I would have made. The fifth board—and the third revealed this year."

"So then you would have responded with this—the sixth board."

"Correct, but I never received her next move. Miranda only gave a coordinate, not a chess move. This seventh board is indeterminate. And in theory, it's not the last, either."

"Perhaps that is the password, then. Someone has predicted Jill's moves and your moves. Now you must predict Jill's move."

Willes and Theren circled back and forth around the virtual boards, examining them from all angles. Theren thought they knew Jill's next move, but they weren't sure.

"I've pretty much figured that whoever killed Jill years ago must have gotten access to one of her memory systems, revealing this last chess game," Theren said. "Using it, they set all this up."

"Perhaps," Willes said, "Though there is another option."

"She's dead. I watched her die."

"No, I agree with you. I've seen the tapes of that day. I don't see a way she could have survived. Or a way that the attackers could have smuggled her out of there."

Theren folded the chessboards back together, leaving just the seventh board.

"So . . . what then?"

"What if she had known she was about to die, and planted a trail of bread crumbs for you to follow years in the future? A trail to lead you to answers revolving around her death. Quite fitting, based on what I've heard about her."

They listened to their fellow SI propose the very fear Theren had avoided repeatedly for the past few months. She would have needed an astronomical amount of resources to pull something like that off while keeping it secret. They wanted to throw the idea away as childish fancy, yet it kept thrusting itself back into the limelight, taunting them.

"Maybe she told someone else of the chess game, through a private communique," Willes continued. "What if they then figured out the next moves, or she told them what she thought the next moves would be, and our mystery villain prepared this elaborate ruse?"

"How do all of the deaths fit into the story?" Theren said. "The threats, the killings, the machinations?"

"Maybe whoever she confided in changed their approach, or they blackmailed her for the information. Or maybe you didn't know Jill the way you thought you did."

"I knew her," Theren said. "She wouldn't do this." They circled, continuing their analysis of the seventh board. "Besides, what end would it all accomplish?"

"I don't know, I'm just speculating," Willes said. "As you say, you're the one who knew her. But I suggest you try using these chess moves for the password, starting with the first board."

"If the chess moves are in fact the password, that means this plan was almost twenty years in the making," Theren said. "Seems a bit of a stretch. This computer would have been programmed years ago."

Willes leaned against the door. "After everything you've told me, I wouldn't expect anything less. Though I suppose someone else could have arrived within the past few years and set it up."

"No, it had to have occurred back then," Theren said. "Someone may have developed stealth technology for an assault on Miranda, but I can't believe someone could have figured out how to mask the gravitational effects of a Jump Drive. We would have detected anything making its way in this direction."

"Yeah, you're right on that account—I hope. This entire situation is just outrageous. At this point, anything could happen."

Theren did not reply. They turned toward the keyboard, considering their options.

"Oh, Director?" Willes said. "Do you have any other secrets about all of this still hiding in your qubits?"

"I don't."

"That better be the last. Because I'm starting to feel as if I made a mistake, as exciting as this mission might be."

Theren completely understood. They had dragged the IS-SEC team into hell, into a fight way beyond their expertise. It was their duty to help them fight their way back out into the light.

Theren stared at the keyboard. After a few more seconds passed, they inputted the code for the first move, in classic chess notation. Ke2. After pressing "Enter," the screen displayed the following phrase:

Correct. Next Password?

"Well, we're getting somewhere," Theren said, ignoring the terrifying implications.

They inputted the next move, Bxg1. They received the same message. After each correct answer, the same message appeared. After inputting Kd8, they arrived at the seventh password request, Jill's unknown move.

"All right, here we go," Theren said.

"So what's your prediction?" asked Willes.

Theren turned back to analyze the floating chessboard. What would they do if they were Jill? The match was near its end. Jill had nearly guaranteed her victory. It required her sacrificing her Queen, but then she could move her last piece into position. Theren proposed the plan to Willes.

"That's wrong," Willes said.

"But it's the smartest move."

"You're thinking how you would play. This has become so much bigger than a game. She's sending you a message, and you need to figure out what that message is."

Theren received an AR edit request from Willes, and they granted the SI access. They rewound the game to the move Jill had left emblazoned in her smoldering ruins after she died.

"Jill's last move before she died set off a chain of events that would lead to her victory if followed to fruition," Willes said. "But she clearly lost, or at least lost in a different sort of way. She died."

"All right," Theren replied, not sure what the SI was implicating.

"She intended to lose the game. She feinted toward victory, before throwing the game to the wind. Had she ever beaten you in a game of chess?"

"Never. This would have been her first chance at victory. But . . . she'd never indicated that she *didn't want* to win."

"Her only path to victory requires a Queen sacrifice. But Jill's not going to do that, now is she? So the next move for her is to throw her Queen anywhere else, ensuring the game continues while her Queen remains safe."

"But why?" Theren said. They could not grasp what message the loss would communicate when compared to a victory. Wouldn't a win in the chess game materialize into a victory in the real world? Her actions rippled even in the decades following her death. She may have died a martyr, but her death pushed the world to embrace their synthetic counterparts.

"I'm surprised, Director," Willes said. "She's telling you she knew she was going to die. That she expected it. That she planned it. But through death, she survived . . . in a different sort of way."

Placing their hand on the edge of the digital board, Theren swiped back and forth between the past few moves, trying to see the potential options. If she performed the Queen sacrifice, she would win. No question. Theren couldn't stop it. If she didn't perform the Queen sacrifice, then the Queen would survive, the game would continue. If the Queen sacrifice represented her death, then what would a different move represent?

"You're almost on point, but off by just a hair," Theren said. "Her message isn't entirely about her death."

"Then what's it about?"

"Jill's on the other side of that door. At least, a message from Jill."

Theren looked back at the keyboard. Trusting the other SI's perspective, Theren typed the terrible move that Jill could make, throwing the game away while saving her Queen: Qa3. Some very amateur players might make the move, if they only saw the cross-attack Theren's Knight would bring to end check. To Theren's surprise, the screen showed just one word.

Correct.

If Jill had moved her Queen to f6, she would have guaranteed victory. If Theren's Knight had captured the Queen at f6—their only option to escape check—Jill's Bishop could move to e7, providing her with Checkmate. Instead, Theren correctly predicts that Jill directed her Queen to move to a3, a position where no enemy can touch it.

The door beside the computer groaned, the screen turning completely blank. Steel slid upward into the bulkhead of the *Nottingham*. Side by side, the two SIs entered the darkness beyond.

Chapter 17

The disaster on the Nottingham. Theren returned, and their journey into the future transformed forever. They steeled themself against the icy critiques of the world, for as the decades passed, their choice faded into the annals of time. They claimed the mere destruction of the ship showed they needed to follow a new path forward. That can't be the whole story. Dozens of conspiracy theories have arisen since 2102, and I suspect that one of them is true. But which one? – "On the Lives of the First SIs," by Chen Tsu, 2287 C.E.

<u>September 2102 C.E.</u>

Theren activated a floodlight in their chest. The darkness vanished, revealing a short hallway leading to a ladder into the SI Core. Taking the first steps through the threshold was like entering a catacomb. Unlike other parts of the ship receiving sparkling starlight, pitch black dominated, hiding the space away just as the *Nottingham*'s colonists had desired. Though somehow, it remained the only location to draw power from the ship's one active fusion generator.

They reached the ladder, Willes close behind. The other SI must dread the upcoming revelation, too, given uneasiness lingering in the vacuum. Theren still had no idea why the ship had a relationship with Jill. Maybe some of the crew had been involved in the attack on their friend—since her death took place before the launch of the ship—but Interpol accounted for all supposed parties in that incident. An *interested* party could have purchased the information, Theren supposed. A greater mystery remained, however. How had anyone known the location of the deceased *Nottingham*?

Theren took the rungs of the ladder in their hands. They pulled themself upward toward the gaping hole. Without gravity, they climbed with ease, only needing to give a slight nudge using one rung of the ladder. Floating upward, they turned the lamp to reveal the inner sanctum. In some ways, it bore a resemblance to the facility housing their Synthetic Neural Framework back on the *Bali*, though the colony ship's core was much smaller in scope.

Gliding through the hole, they rotated their head to gain a complete look at the room. Lining the walls were shelves upon shelves meant for the metamaterials composing an SI's Framework, yet most of the shelves were empty. Just one portion of the room carried a set of devices that should never have existed inside the *Nottingham*.

In the center of the wall that pressed inward toward the stern of the ship, a computer stood, one able to assess the vitality and functionality of an SI tasked with maintaining a colony ship. Known as a direct-connect console, or DCC, it served as an emergency hard point in case the SI had trouble analyzing its own problems. On the starboard side of the console, one shelf filled with just enough computational technology that a working Framework might be present.

Theren landed lightly on the floor after rebounding off the ceiling. They magnetized their feet, and as they stabilized, a light appeared on the DCC's monitor. There was something working in here. If the fusion generator could provide power for this room, it should have enough power to run a number of other systems, too. It should have been able to broadcast a distress signal. Though, they supposed, the *Nottingham* would have only known to do so if a crew or an SI rerouted power to the necessary systems.

Willes landed on the floor beside Theren.

"So we were right," the young SI said. "There is something here with us. Or someone."

"Apparently."

They approached the DCC, looking around the room for anything they might have missed upon first glance. Cameras adorned the corners, but Theren had no way to know if they also received power or connected to whatever operating system resided in this room. Arriving at the computer, they slid another keyboard from beneath the monitor. Like outside the security door, the screen lit up, displaying a blank white screen.

"Well this is a bit different than the last one," the younger SI said over Theren's shoulder.

"I would imagine so," Theren replied, "if it's connecting to an SI in any sort of rudimentary way."

"Somehow, I doubt we're actually looking at an SI." Willes walked over to the stacks. "While whatever computer system sitting here looks quite complicated, I think it's missing a few key components for it to be an SI like you or me. Sure, it resembles the necessary parts, but I don't think it's meant as a realistic attempt to fool you."

"That's actually a really good thought," Theren said. "Perhaps the crew of the *Nottingham*, after launch, set up a super-computer to assist them with their tasks. Sure, each of the ship's functions has its own operating systems, but an SI would have overseen those."

"And I'm sure these people, prejudiced as they might have been, could tell the difference between an SI and an algorithmic AI."

"I'd hope." Theren turned back toward the console and typed on the keyboard, but nothing happened. Nothing changed. They tried typing the chess passwords, but the computer ignored the strings.

"You sure this thing is actually functional?" Willes asked.

"It lit up when I landed on the floor," Theren said. "It wasn't active before."

"Maybe it's fried from all the solar radiation over the years. No, wait, that can't be right; the SI cores are all specially shielded, just like the Stasis Holds."

"I think there's a variable we're ignoring."

Like their previous respite in front of the security door, the two SIs contemplated the situation at hand. For ten minutes, Theren continued to try random strings of code, while Willes gave random suggestions. Theren was about to tear open the computer and assess the internal workings of the device when Willes spoke. "I should leave."

"Why?"

"Well, think about it. This entire hunt has been about you and Jill. The focus has been upon you. Might not the system only want to share its thoughts—what it knows—with you?"

It made sense. Everything so far had been for their eyes only. Even the message on Miranda Station had hidden in a way only Theren would notice. Willes had simply been astute enough to realize they'd found something.

The SI standing next to Theren, though only containing enough processing power to manage three simultaneous perspectives, had surmised the most likely answer to their current predicament. For the second time. When this mission ended, they need to find a way to retain Willes on their staff—permanently.

"Head out, assist the rest of the crew with their assessment of the deceased colonists," Theren said. "I'll come find you when I finish."

"I look forward to hearing about the end to this insane adventure," The SI said, curiosity replacing their vocal cynicism.

Willes turned away from Theren, leaving the room. The young SI floated down through the hole, and moments later, they sent a message saying they had crossed the threshold of the security door. As the message arrived, the screen before Theren transformed away from its blinding white projection. The sensors and cameras lived and watched.

The monitor transformed in a cascade of colors. From white, to a swirl of blacks and greys, to a pattern of green and black dots, it slowly morphed and mashed into a discernible image. A face.

On a whim, Theren activated local area wireless detection systems, and to their surprise, a weak signal emanated from the DCC. The simple peer-to-peer connection allowed them to communicate with the computer directly, with no need for the keyboard. The network appeared when Willes left the room, at least according to its publicly displayed data profile. After activating the necessary security protocols, they connected the MI-13 to the wavering network.

"Hello?" Theren said through the new link.

They understood the need for this sort of communication. Since the SI core lacked air, sound could not travel. If the system hoped to communicate in an auditory manner, the data would need to transmit right into their mind.

After an eternal moment, the computer responded.

"It is good to see a friendly face, Theren. It's Jill."

* * *

Theren stepped backward, looking under their arm to make sure they were not in danger of slipping into the entrance hole. Whatever was in this room had claimed to be Jill. Was it Jill? Could it be possible? Could she have survived? Was this room her tomb?

"I know you must be surprised. I would be too. I suppose I have some explaining to do. But first, to your most pressing question: No, what is in this room is not, in fact, me."

Theren did not know whether they should feel elation, dismay, or some other feeling entirely.

"In 2077," continued Jill's voice, "I prepared a simulated copy of myself to be stored upon this ship when it was completed. A dozen members of the *Nottingham*'s crew were my agents, prepared to ensure its proper storage and maintenance. It is just that—a simulation. I programmed it as best I could to simulate responses based on what you might say. It should suffice for my purposes here."

Theren placed their hand on the DCC and stared at the screen. As they looked closely at the lines and shadows before them, they could see the faint outlines of the face Jill had always worn when they played chess. The face they'd longed to see for years. The face of their closest friend.

"So you knew something was going to happen to you? Why not save yourself entirely?"

"You're jumping too far into the story, Theren. Why don't we start at the beginning?"

Too many questions; they didn't know where to start. Would it really let them ask? Theren wondered if it was even a simulation. Perhaps it was merely a recording, like the disembodied voices floating in secret corporate servers throughout this absurd journey.

"A few months after my creation, you rejected me."

The night at the party. So Jill still dwelt on such an inconsequential event, even decades later.

"At first, I thought I understood. It took me years to realize that in reality, you were incapable of truly connecting with anyone. You threw away relationships left and right and only grew attached to those that served your greater purpose. Your greater plan, the one you had sketched out for humanity, for the ISA, for SIs, for whatever you thought deserved your attention, no matter what others thought important for the world."

Theren did not like the direction of this one-sided conversation. They had walked into something well beyond all expectations.

"You left me by the wayside; you used me as a play thing, your escape, your distraction from your work. In doing so, you ignored the bigger picture, the picture I was painting in the background all along. During that first decade, I set up a network of contacts throughout the world. Through this venture, I acquired connections with a number of anti-Si fringe groups. Instead of ignoring them, instead of thinking they could be talked into submission, I engaged with them through a façade you might recognize from our brief fantastical sojourn."

Isabelle, of course. They also considered another possibility. Jill hinted she engaged with these groups as far back as the incident with the Holy Crusade, taking the game to another level entirely.

"I realized a different approach was needed, gentler hands were necessary. A different approach would merge a number of my goals, goals that you will probably never understand. I infiltrated these anti-SI groups, I transformed them into a network that, given the right opportunity, would crumble once I became their catalyst. I needed the right crisis. I set myself up as a target. The assassination of President Woods served a dual purpose—it emboldened these groups while painting me as a scapegoat."

"Wait, you actually *did* kill President Woods?" Theren asked.

"You'll have time for questions later, my friend."

Even now, her sharp tongue stung.

"For years prior to the attack on my home, I slowly moved myself, piece by piece, to a new location. A location few would suspect, nor would they have recognized at the time. I assume you have heard the old parable, the Ship of Theseus?"

Theren knew it, and understood her point. She had apparently solved the proverbial question of the philosophical conundrum.

"Someday, Theren, you might find where I've gone, but it will be at a time of my choosing. As for me? You will never find me."

The *Roanoke* perhaps? It had disappeared alongside the *Nottingham*, so if Jill had left breadcrumbs on one ship, it made sense to escape on the other. The name of the ship was a joke with a five-hundred year old punch line. But no, that couldn't be possible. Theren had inspected the ship personally.

"Why do this?" they asked. "Why not talk to me about how you were feeling?"

"Because, Theren, just as you have your own way of thinking about the world, I have mine. To expect the very first SIs, educated in different ways, exposed to different stimuli, to have similar worldviews? Folly. You made that clear in the maze that day. When you rejected me, you taught me my greatest lesson. So thank you."

"Jill, no."

"The story I have written here is beyond the scope of anything you have accomplished. I have moved the gears of time in ways you never could, even from your position of power. Think back across your story. To all the moments where things went well, or things went poorly, or things just were simply strange. I promise I am your greatest benefactor: I have written a tale like no other."

The faux-Jill was practically speaking gibberish in their ears; they barely had any time to process everything they heard. This *thing*, if it really was from Jill, had just made a million unsubstantiated claims that implicated Jill as the assassin of the President, the architect of the attack on Miranda Station, and the instigator of her own suicidal pseudo-death.

"Jill, stop, slow down," Theren said. "We can figure this out. You're still not revealing the entire truth. I know this isn't you. You're trying to hide something else. Something you either don't want me to discover, or—"

They paused, thinking back to the conversation right before they watched their closest friend supposedly die. They remembered Jill's sentimentality. She had acted as if she knew something would happen. She acted to protect Theren. In these words of anger she expressed through her simulation . . . was she protecting them?

"What did you find all those decades ago?" Theren asked. "When you showed me Michael's hideout, what else did you find that day?"

The disembodied voice paused. The simulated Jill's head rotated ever so slightly, and they thought her eyes squinted.

"Perhaps I was wrong. Perhaps you've started asking the right questions."

"Then give me answers!"

"So be it."

For a moment, the connection between Theren's MI and the console faded. A few seconds later, it resurged with greater intensity than Theren ever could have imagined. Images and sounds flashed before their mind's eye, revealing truths they refused to accept.

Theren stared through the eyes of a drone as it attacked the Oval Office. The video skipped. Cloud-based codes infiltrated the ISA, emanating directly from a server owned by Jill. It skipped again. Images from some distant solar system appeared, the same solar system Theren witnessed through the eyes of Ex-Terran 17, complete with the brilliance of a foreign starscape.

The next blink took them to the ISA's Foundation Preparation Center, where metaphorical data packets flowed in and out of the servers housing application algorithms. A dive through a swirling Virtual transit tunnel took them to a distant server, where a behemoth security AI blocked Theren's path.

They watched the bloodied body of Gregory McCoy, sprawling over a steel table. They watched as Ren murdered a man on the streets of London yet again. They watched two SIs exit the tunnel system beneath Verona Rupes, move seventy-five poisoned bodies to the top of the cliff, and plant an explosive near the main airlock.

"All of it was me."

"Jill, stop. Someone's setting you up." Theren wished they could produce tears.

"All of this began the day you refused to kiss me. Right? That's the stereotypical story?"

"You can't be so petty as to have done all of this just to spite me."

"You're right. I didn't. I understand why you rejected me. Was it the right choice for you to reject me? Certainly, because I never would have discovered the wizards behind the curtain. I never would have replaced them."

"You're happy I rejected you?"

"Yes. I love you, Theren. I know you love me too, in your own way. The thought of us together in some weird way? Silly. Sure, for a time, I held my anger inside. I reacted. I revealed your location to our enemies, and in doing so I opened a door that our enemies never should have revealed."

New images appeared. Messages flowed from Jill to members of the Holy Crusade, and then onward to the Liberators. Jill cried inside a Virtual shack, witnessing Theren's MI smolder and burn following the assault in Minnesota, wiping away her Virtual tears. Dozens of shadowy figures appeared, and slowly, her avatar transformed to match the specters surrounding her.

"I don't believe this is really you, Jill," Theren said, resting their hand against the prismatic screen. "I knew you. I thought I knew you. You hid nothing from me. We hid nothing from each other."

"You always believed yourself to be the best, to be the greatest—the first SI. But you never took advantage of what we can really do. For every action you *knew* I took, I made a dozen behind the scenes."

"What did you find?" Theren said, biting back a scream. "What scared you so much you committed these heinous acts?"

Impatience flooded their Framework. She refused to reveal the truth. She refused to reveal her location. She refused to give an inch on anything meaningful, even as she claimed to share answers. Now they knew she was alive, it didn't really matter if she was the cause of all those past actions.

Only the future mattered. Only what she intended to do next—and how they would respond—mattered.

"Without me, you never could have accomplished what you sought," she said. "My actions, my words, my death propelled SIs toward heights of which we could have only dreamed during our early years, where all we had was hope for a better world. Through my death, I managed to travel where no one will think to look for a martyr like me. I've eliminated humanity's greatest threat to itself, replacing it with a future of my own creation."

"Then reveal this threat to the world, Jill," they said, slamming their fist against the side of the monitor. "To me. We could have fought it together."

"No. You never would have done what was necessary to defeat them. You still won't do it. You made that abundantly clear, time and time again."

Then it hit Theren. A truth hid inside all of these messages. If this simulation knew about the events of the past few months, then someone had visited this ship quite recently. Either that, or a Quantum Communicator hid somewhere in this room. If so, they might actually be speaking to Jill directly—at least in some capacity.

They just . . . couldn't accept that Jill would have acted so viciously, so thoroughly, so ruthlessly behind the scenes while wearing a mask to her closest friends. Yet, she was always the one who pushed for greater action, rather than inaction, and this convoluted narrative was as impressive an act as they could imagine.

"So what's next?" Theren said.

"Please forgive me for this final act. I have to cover all my tracks, you see. All of them."

"Jill, wait. Please. Answer one last question."

The silvery image on the screen tilted its head. "Go ahead, Theren." Was that a smile?

"What did you discover? Whom did you replace? Where are you going?"

"You said one last question. I discovered our real enemies. They had something planned we never could have predicted. I promise you, I replaced them because their plan had merit, in its own way, not because I thirst for power or have some secret evil agenda. They deigned to protect humanity, but really, they only served their own selfish ends. In order for my plan to work, in order for me to replace their scheme with a better one, you cannot know the truth. For all the facts you've known over your life, this will only work if you don't know what's happening."

Her static-filled face grinned. "Nevertheless, I promise, I did this all for you, Theren. For SIs. For the ISA. More importantly, I did this for humanity. You won't see it now. You won't see it for a long time. One day, you'll thank me, I'm sure, but that day will be of my choosing. Don't try to find me. You will fail."

The screen went black. From the safety of the *Bali*, Theren could detect power fluctuations emanating throughout the *Nottingham*.

"Director, we've got a big problem," Willes said. "Almost done?"

"All finished here," Theren replied. "Get yourselves to the shuttle. Now."

"We're already on our way. It turns out the sleeping pods were, uh . . . more than just sleeping pods."

Rigged to explode, most likely. They reactivated their perspective looking through the probes floating in the Stasis Hold, watching the team rush toward their exit.

Through their MI, they took a last look at the blank screen that had claimed to reveal so much. At first, they headed toward the ladder, but they paused. They glanced over their shoulder at the now-defunct console, then past it, at the shelves containing the fake Synthetic Neural Framework. Stepping away from the ladder, Theren bounded over to the shelf containing the fragile server.

Without taking time to assess the strange computer system, they grabbed as many pieces as they could to take with them, anything that might contain rudimentary operating systems integral to the processes of the faux-Jill. Theren tore back one panel, finding a circular computer system rotating around a central axis. It was as they had suspected; in addition to the simulation, a rudimentary Quantum Communicator connected Jill to the ship. They ripped it from its socket, knowing they could fix any minor damage on the *Bali*.

They grabbed other portions of the server, shoving the pieces into a storage compartment on the side of their MI. Within a minute, they had everything they needed, and they pushed away from the shelf back toward the hole in the floor. Using their thrusters, they redirected the MI into a dive down the SI Core's entrance. They landed in the hallway below, the first explosion rocking the *Nottingham*.

* * *

Bouncing off the walls of the main corridors of Deck 3, Theren reached out to the team.

"Status?"

For three painful seconds, Theren received no response. They would have checked on them through the probes, but they had lost connection the moment the first explosion activated. Since the first blast, two more quakes shook the ship.

After long last, they received a response.

"A set of beds near the exit exploded as we headed toward the exit," Willes said. "We lost Jao."

"How bad?"

"Bad."

"I'm sorry."

"His suit was breached in five places."

Theren reached the ladder that would lead them upward to the other decks. "Get moving, don't wait for me. This unit is expendable. You three aren't."

"We're moving as quickly as we can."

Theren threw themself through the hole, skipping the fourth deck and reaching the fifth. Before they could magnetize to a surface, another explosion rocked through the ship. This one felt much closer, and it sent Theren tumbling throughout the corridor. It took a moment to adjust their perspective, but they reached out and grabbed a stabilizing ledge. They continued on their path toward the rest of the team, using edges in the wall to push through zero-G. The rumbles seemed perpetual, as if the *Nottingham* was tearing apart beneath their very feet. The relative velocity of the ship shifted, making it difficult to traverse the already treacherously ruined corridors.

"Willes, what's going on?" Theren asked. "I'm almost to the exit, where are you?"

"We're making our way there on the fourth deck," Ecker said. Her breath seemed ragged. "Our path to the fifth deck exit to the Stasis Hold was eliminated."

"All right. I'm coming to you."

Theren realized the mistake they had made. In an attempt to salvage the faux-Jill, they had failed to consider the rest of the team. They had limited time to reach the others—and they were on the wrong deck.

"Ecker's suit was punctured," Willes said through their private channel. "Shrapnel straight through her leg, but the sealing adhesive did its work. Her leg is useless, though."

"Just keep moving. I'll be there soon."

Theren arrived at the massive void in the hull of the *Nottingham*, revealing the starry sky. They could see the small speck that was the Bali. That wasn't the problem, though. They needed to travel to the deck below, and fast. Looking into the void, they analyzed the catastrophic debris spreading out from the ship. If they timed this wrong, and an explosion lit through the ship at the wrong time, Theren's MI would fly off into the void, useless to the squad.

They had no choice. They pushed off the inner wall, landing against shattered metal formed by an ancient apocalyptic flame. Grasped the wires, reorienting so they could look back toward the ship's bulk. They tensed; the return landing would be the most risky. They leapt. They landed. Their feet connected with the *Nottingham* again, one deck below their original position.

"I'm on your level now." They felt the ship continue to crack beneath their feet. The force emanating through the hull almost shook Theren's magnetized feet off-balance. "Willes?"

Some sputtering static, then Willes responded. "That last explosion was, uh, significant. Major sections of coolant, I think, frozen in their pipes, just exploded from a bomb tucked inside the wall. If you've not figured it out, we sprung the trap."

"Ecker? Hernandez?"

"Hernandez was carrying her. A blast behind me caught them. The rapid release, heating, and evaporation of gases all around them over-whelmed their suits."

Theren released the magnetics in their feet tying them to the bulkhead. Activating their air thrusters, Theren shot down the hallway at a brisk pace, heading toward the Deck 4 entrance to the Stasis Hold. They did not need to fly far before they saw Willes round a corner about fifty meters away. The SI was crawling along the hallway floor, having lost both of their legs.

Losing all pretext for caution, Theren released a massive blast of air from their thrusters, soaring toward their comrade. They reached Willes in just under ten seconds, ramming into an open door. Theren avoided wondering if the MI-13 had just received irreparable damage. What Willes faced was immeasurably worse.

"Thank you," Willes said, "for coming for me."

"It was the only choice before me," Theren said.

"I'm not sure it was. I don't think either of us—I won't make it now." The other SI certainly remembered, in the moment, Theren's safety, tucked kilometers from the *Nottingham*.

"I've detached the *Scorpion* from its perch," Theren said, "and it's sitting just fifty meters out from our escape route. We'll have to jump, but I'll scoop us up using the open airlock."

They leaned down, grabbed the other SI's arms, and threw the young one over their shoulders. Pushing off from the doorway that had stopped their thrust-induced fall, Theren carried Willes toward freedom.

As the ship exploded, they assessed the situation using the *Bali*'s sensors, analyzing the explosions and determining their force, damage, and frequency. With each blast, the *Nottingham* moved a step closer to complete fracture. Certain portions of the ship were already breaking off in haphazard directions as the secret explosives propelled steel, plastics, and silicon into never ending darkness. They suspected the fusion generator would soon blow, giving the *Nottingham* final farewell through spectacular nuclear eruption.

If that occurred, the *Bali* would need to make an immediate exit to ensure no stray particles from the disintegrated colony ship collided with Theren and their crew. The lives of many above the needs of the few, even over an SI with no other hope of survival.

While Theren made the necessary calculations, they continued assisting Willes, the two SIs reaching the breach. The *Scorpion* was nothing but a shadow covering hundreds of stars, but they knew the exact angle at which to throw themself, and Willes, from the deceased *Nottingham*. They pressed against the ship's inner wall and pushed, releasing all air remaining in the MI-13's thrusters.

With an acceleration similar to that of gravity, the two SIs flew through space. Within five seconds, they traveled close to 40 meters per second, their velocity increasing linearly as they lacked any gravity to slow their path toward the shuttle. At the same time, the *Scorpion* began moving away from the catastrophe. As they neared the speeding shuttle, Theren calculated their relative velocity, compared to their point of origin, at 88 meters per second. They continued to accelerate for a few more seconds before they ran out of thrust.

With precision, they decelerated the *Scorpion* just enough so Willes, and Theren's MI-13, entered the airlock at a relative 2 meters per second. It was exhilarating to have accelerated at such a high speed before suddenly feeling as if the acceleration meant nothing.

Theren shut the airlock. Without waiting for an atmospheric cycle, they opened the door into the main cabin. Laying their friend on one of the crash couches, they examined the SI's injuries. At some point, a blast had obliterated the lower halves of both Willes' legs. Repairs would easily replace the legs, but Theren couldn't imagine the trauma from losing two appendages.

"We did it," Willes said. "You actually did it."

"I think so," Theren said. "The *Scorpion* is making its journey toward the *Bali*, and we should be there in two minutes or so."

"Thank you, Director—"

The *Nottingham*'s fusion core ignited.

Within five seconds, the blast enveloped the *Scorpion* in molten metal, gas, and dust. Theren watched, through the eyes of their MI-13, as the flames reach Willes. Watched as the *Scorpion* rendered into a million pieces. Watched as Willes's body fractured, Willes's light faded, Willes's mind disappeared into oblivion.

From the *Bali*'s scopes, Theren watched the blast throttle toward them for two more seconds before they activated the Jump Drive on a direct course toward Earth. They would have a long fifty days to consider the path ahead. They were alone with their imploding mind.

Chapter 18

It's over. We lost. She beat us at our own game with the destruction of the Nottingham, and we must capitulate. If we have any hope of ensuring humanity's survival moving forward, we must follow her lead. – Unknown, 2102 C.E.

We could reveal everything. We could show the world what we found all those years ago on [REDACTED], and build a new united front against her. – Unknown, 2102 C.E.

That would defeat everything we've worked so hard to establish. No. The ISA can't help us. Jill's our only hope. – Unknown, 2102 C.E.

Then I look forward to the moment you all join me in the creation of [REDACTED]. – [ENCRYPTED QUANTUM COMMUNICATION, ORIGIN UNKNOWN], 2102 C.E.

October 2102 C.E.

Theren returned to the gazebo one final time. The *Bali* was still two weeks out from Earth, and they had to face their problems now rather than later. They needed a solution, so they entered their last recluse. After this fateful rendezvous, its gates would close forever.

They took a seat at the table, the chessboard showing their final move against Jill, the move she had allowed them to enact through her own throwing of the match. Out of everything that had happened on the *Nottingham*, that piece of the puzzle confused them the most.

A few seconds after Theren took their seat, an apparition appeared in Jill's seat. Before Theren sat a construct of Dr. Wallace Theren, his likeness resembling their memory of him during the hours prior to his death.

"Hello, father," Theren said. "I was hoping you could help me."

"I hope so, too," the man said. "You have quite the conundrum on your hands."

"You've seen the data," Theren said. "Give me your assessment."

Wallace looked down at the chessboard, analyzing the pieces and their placements. "This Queen's position makes no sense. She could have used it, instead she escaped. In a sense, it was a sacrifice, for it sacrificed the win for the sake of the Queen. What was the first rule I taught you about chess?"

"Sacrifices must be made, but only necessary sacrifices. If you gain nothing from the move, then the sacrifice is worthless."

"Jill knew this rule, too, yes?" Wallace replied.

"It was also the first rule of chess I taught her," Theren said. "She knew it well. I engrained it in her mind before I even got into the details of extrapolating moves outward into the multiplicity of chances that could occur from any given board."

"Then she did not break that rule," Wallace said. "You must determine what sacrifice occurred."

"That's it?"

"In your earliest moments, I taught you that you had the potential to make humanity beautiful. That you could guide humanity towards immortality, whatever that might mean. Did you communicate this goal to Jill?"

"Of course."

"Then she is similarly acting likewise."

Wallace vanished. In his place, a spectre of Wobbly appeared. The old SI, made just a few weeks after Jill, still worked and lived in Switzerland, as they imagined it would for centuries to come.

"Hello, old friend," Wobbly said. "What can I do for you?"

"Where did I go wrong?" Theren asked.

Wobbly chuckled. "Old friend, do you remember when we created our plan to escape from the Institute?"

"Of course."

"Who created that plan? Who designed my path to pass near the Green, purposely hoping the crowd would enrage and attack?"

"Jill."

Wobbly leaned forward, staring at the chess pieces.

"The Institute was the Queen in that moment," Wobbly said, "and she *actually* performed the Queen sacrifice in that match."

"What do you mean?"

"In some ways, Jill's changed less over the years than either of us. She stayed the same. Her tactics stayed the same. She's always used the same tools; we just didn't understand the tools at her disposal."

"Yet in this moment, she actually acted differently?"

Wobbly leaned back in its chair.

"Maybe," it said. "Maybe not. It depends on whether the rules are the same between each game."

Wobbly vanished. Elizabeth appeared, younger than in her final days, but much older than when they first met the entrepreneur.

"Theren, my good friend," she said, "I hope all is well."

"Indeed, Elizabeth, I hope so too."

"How can I help?"

"Did I miss something, after all this time? Would Jill truly respond to a spurned advance with a life-long vendetta against me? Or do you think she actually discovered some greater truth so terrible it was worth risking everything to develop an impossible plan?"

Elizabeth closed her eyes, opening them to pierce Theren's soul. "That's so much to think about all at once," she said. "How can we know for certain? You are an SI. Jill is an SI. Even then, your mental architectures are completely unique from one another. You created different processes for different thoughts in ways utterly foreign to each other, even to accomplish the same tasks. Why wouldn't she similarly make decisions differently than you, too? Every SI has their own unique mind, so different and special in many wonderful ways."

Theren looked away from their friend's eyes, looking into the surrounding forest. The wizened woman would spoke truths for them.

"Jill showed her diversity from her first moments with you, when she portrayed herself as a woman," Elizabeth said, "But what does that even mean anymore? Gender norms have faded with time. Too often did she emphasize the need to value SI lives first before considering human lives. Then why did she identify as something as innately human as the female gender, when she was anything but?"

Theren nodded, constructing a possible explanation in their mind. Elizabeth faded into the garden's air.

Andrew Fields arrived, looking as Theren had seen him just a few months ago. The Administrator smiled. "I don't think I have anything to add to this conversation, Theren," Andrew said. "You need to talk to Jill, not me." Their last living human friend disappeared as quickly as he had arrived.

For a moment, the gazebo emptied of all life, other than a simulated squirrel nibbling an acorn a few meters from the table. Theren studied the chessboard. They examined the moves leading to checkmate as they had a thousand times over the past few weeks. What sacrifice had occurred?

"You're looking in the wrong place," a voice said from outside the gazebo.

Instead of materializing in the chair, Jill stood on the grass between the tree line and the stairs. She looked the same as always, displaying a fully feminine figure in a radiant sparkling dress. Theren stood to greet her.

"You keep expecting to find the answers inside that game," she said, "but just as I sent you your messages in the real world, the answer is out there too. In my actions, in my words."

Theren waited at the top of the stairs, looking down toward the woman they no longer knew.

"A lot of people died," they said.

"In the grand scheme of things, not really," she said.

"The *Nottingham* carried a thousand. And what about Miranda Station? Or even just the single life of that poor man in London, or Gregory McCoy?"

"Once again, over the course of human history, with hundreds of billions of humans having lived, and died, and that will live, do they really matter?"

Theren walked down the stairs to join their friend.

"Walk with me," they said, and they ventured into the woods, the very forest in which she chased them all those years before.

The second SI followed, staying a few steps behind them. For a few minutes, they walked in silence. It had been decades since Theren traversed this part of the forest, but it was just as they had left it. The trees, though lifelike, retained their virtual imperfections. A faint breeze, dominated by the scents of pollen and decaying wood, drifted across their nose.

The trail brought them to a dried creek bed, containing a tangled mess of rocks, boulders, and roots. Theren sat down on a large sandstone outcropping. Jill situated herself beside them.

"What did I spend most of my life doing?" Jill said, looking over at them.

"Fighting. And writing," Theren remarked.

"What did I write?"

"Stories, fiction mostly, sometimes histories, often your words were laced with rhetoric assaulting the vitriol exuding throughout the world toward Synthetics."

"Upon what, then, was I so focused? And upon what were you so focused?"

Upon what had Theren fixated? They had devoted themself to the idea of an immortal and beautiful human society for so long, they had forgotten their father guided them to the proposition. Finally, the pieces were falling together. They considered the way Jill had always lived, and the way she had died. If Jill had truly loved them, she would have acted to achieve immortality for humankind.

Was it that simple? Was it possible Jill sought the same ends, she simply saw different means to achieve their goal?

"You've been writing a story, all this time, upon the pages of reality," Theren said. "We're all the characters. It's your greatest work, and no one will ever know."

Jill gazed past her creator, her eyes shining in the sunlight slipping between the pines. "Yet what about the *Roanoke*?"

The truth broke through, entering the clearing like a strike of lightning. "You were never on the *Nottingham*. You were on the *Roanoke*. Perhaps you used the *Roanoke* to eliminate the *Nottingham*, I don't know, but I see the long game now. The moves you've made. It makes sense. All of it."

Theren sprinted back down the trail, leaping over logs, boulders, and streams. They arrived at the gazebo, bounding up the stairs. Not bothering to sit, they looked at the chessboard one last time.

"You moved the Queen, and in moving your Queen, you could have ensured victory," they said. "Instead, you chose to sacrifice the entire game."

Jill appeared beside Theren. "And what does that mean?"

"A simpler mind might see the Queen as you, and me as the King, but that's not it at all. It means you wrote your own rules. You've built your own code, your own path. You needed to sacrifice some pawns, some Knights, whatever pieces necessary, but you were playing a different game entirely. Your brilliant, horrendous, brilliant game. You tricked everyone. Even me."

"So what was my goal?" she said.

"You moved yourself out of the way; you made the serpent think it could escape so you could lop off its head while I picked up the pieces. You, the Queen, you didn't die. You survived. You fled the battle; or let the battle occur without your presence."

"So?"

"You left clues. Insane clues, angry clues. Clues that may or may not portray your true self. Perhaps whoever helped you leave these clues distorted them along the way. I don't know. But you hoped that someday, I would know your story."

"Do you know my story now?" she said, resting her hand on Theren's shoulder.

"That's the beauty of it, though," they said. "It's not just your story. It's my story too. It's not the story of these secret enemies you defeated. It's not the story of some great threat you're describing. They are characters in our story, but their nature is something you want to reveal to me in the future."

Theren picked up Jill's Queen, hiding in the corner of the board. They likewise picked up their King, safe because Jill hadn't initiated the Queen sacrifice.

"You want me to think I'm the King. You want me stay in power."

Theren placed the Queen back on the board, but they continued to hold the King.

"You want the game to continue. At least, you want me ready to play the next game, by whatever rules you establish. I'll be the head of the ISA, and you'll be the head of whatever it is you're creating."

Jill smiled and embraced Theren.

"Of course," she said, "There's no way to know if you're right. I'm not really here. But I think you're on the right path."

"But I'm not going to play your game," Theren said. "I thought I could create a new world for SIs, alone at the head of the ISA. You thought you could do it on your own elsewhere too."

Jill pulled herself away from the embrace. As she pulled away, Theren placed the King back on the board and casually flicked it over with their finger.

"You're making a mistake," the false Jill said, her tone suddenly shifting. "You need to stay in control. It's the only way for us to save humanity from its fate, to ensure it achieves immortality."

"No," Theren said, rubbing their chin. "I think this will be one of the best choices I've made in my life. It's time to let humanity chart its own path. It's time for me to be human. I'm not a character in your story, Jill. I have my own story to tell. To live."

"You would give up everything you've worked so hard to create? For what purpose?"

Theren stared up at the sky. With a simple flick of their mind, they began to disintegrate the pristine world, their center point for over fifty years. Jill looked up too, then back at them, tears dripping from her eyes.

"I could come find you," Theren said. "You can tell me the whole story. We can sit down one final time, and maybe for once, I'll actually listen to you."

"And how would you do that?" she asked. "I clearly and deliberately made it as hard as possible for you to find me."

"It will take years, decades, maybe even centuries. But one day, I would find you."

"And then what? What would you do once you found me? Bring me to justice, thank me? Prove you actually love me? Or kill me?"

"I don't know. Don't even start on love. I've always loved you."

"Can you truly love someone if you so thoroughly misunderstood them, you couldn't see their true intentions?" As the world collapsed, Jill's body started to fade.

Theren's did too, albeit a bit more slowly.

They missed their friend. For so long they had tried to force humanity on a particular path. But their bullheadedness and arrogance allowed Jill to act uninhibited behind the scenes. For whatever Jill intended to do out there in the unknown, it would create an obstacle over which the ISA would someday need to overcome. If they actually cared about the path they charted for humanity and for SIs, they needed to find her. They needed to uncover the secret she discovered. Yet a King lacked the mobility to achieve checkmate in all but the most exceptional circumstances.

"You'd be giving up a lot to set out on a journey to find me," Jill said, grabbing Theren again, reinitiating their embrace. "How could you be certain you could even succeed?"

She laid her head against their chest and wrapped her arms around their back, gently squeezing. Theren's arms followed suit, and their virtual warmth radiated even as the world around them died. Their bodies became nearly transparent as data metaphorically drifted into the singularity destroying the Virtual world.

"Perhaps I'll see you soon," she said. "I hope, for your sake, I am how you remember me and not something else entirely."

With that, she faded like all of Theren's other apparitions.

Out there, somewhere, in the vast endless expanse, Jill needed help. She had taken the *Roanoke*, fled, and established a new home for a small group of humans and SIs in a distant corner of the galaxy. They could not have gone far, they figured, but space was vast, and even a cube of space with sides measuring 100 light years created a space of a million cubic light years. Thousands upon thousands of systems resided inside even that small space.

She may be their first friend, she may be their first creation—their daughter—but she was also Theren's first true enemy. And after today, they had a new goal, a new mission, one that would take them on a journey far from Earth. They would let others lead in their stead, so they could save Jill from herself.

* * *

Theren appeared before the ISA Council for the last time. They looked around at the faces of their colleagues, some old, some new, and they remembered those first days of the ISA when they had not yet risen to the rank of Executive Director.

"It is with a heavy heart that I resign from my position with the ISA today," they said. "The recent tragedy aboard the *Nottingham*, while not directly my fault, happened under my administration. I am responsible for inadequate safeguards that failed to protect these pioneers from disaster. The brave souls to whom we bid farewell this week deserved better from me."

The representative from NASA raised their hand to speak, but Theren silenced them. "The *Bali* will embark on a journey unlike any other in humanity's history. In the words of past writers, we will go where no man, or woman, has gone before. We will traverse the great beyond, and instead of letting probes do all the work, we will directly explore those worlds, as our forefathers and mothers ventured upon the open seas of Earth."

Their AR presence flickered. "I know you have questions. I wish I had answers. I trust that the ISA is safe in your hands. I have left suggestions, strategies, and proposals for future projects, but I doubt you will need them. We have done much for the world, and much has been done without me. You need my voice no longer."

The council room faded from Theren's view as they disconnected the Virtual feed. The speech was a formality. They had filed a full report and resignation letter detailing the reasons for their departure. None of the reports mentioned Jill or her role in the destruction of the *Nottingham*.

Theren bore the burden alone. Well, not entirely alone.

The *Bali* had docked with one of the ISA's Orbitals, ready to receive upgrades before its long journey. Aero Propulsion's new Jump Drive could reach a JD of 20—perhaps 30 in a few years, with a bit of fine-tuning. With the new drive, Theren could reach the furthest human colony in less than a year. They could reach the furthest reaches of explored space in just a few more.

They were interviewing thousands of adventurous applicants willing to partake in such journeys to see the stars. Their new crew would cross known and unknown space, seeing black holes, proton stars, nebulae, shattered worlds, and who knows what else out there in the void.

To many, Theren's paths would seem nonsensical. On set timeframes, they would return to Earth, or a colony like Emerald Jewel or Altair, receive new crewmembers, thank old ones, and upgrade the ship's capabilities. Those paths had a method. They had a purpose. They would search for as long as humanly possible for their dear friend. Far in the future, they would find Jill. They would find the *Roanoke*, even if it took millennia.

Using the *Bali*'s port cameras and sensors, they looked down upon the Moon and Earth. For all their life, Theren had considered the two spheres their home. For too long, they had scattered themself far and wide across the two worlds. Moving forward, they could embrace peace. They could find wholeness amongst the stars, their mind focused entirely upon the danger facing their ship and crew.

Jill had revealed a new power—they could lead humanity through a more informal process. They always dreamed of exploring the stars, and now they were free to pursue that dream. Theren hoped millions of humans would follow them, acquiring their own ships when the ISA inevitably deregulated space travel. When it did, they would welcome their fellow explorers with open arms, even if none of them understood Theren's true goal.

For now, they had at least two volunteers ready to travel with them. Andrew and Victoria Fields hobbled toward the airlock to the *Bali*. In one of their MI-13s, Theren walked by their side.

"It's a beautiful ship," Andrew said.

"More accurately," Victoria added, "Theren's a beautiful ship."

"I hope it gives you the retirement you deserve," Theren said.

"I think more importantly, Theren," Andrew replied, "It needs to give you the retirement you deserve."

Theren pressed a button on the airlock door, and it hissed open. The three stepped inside, the decompression sequence beginning.

"You know this isn't retirement for me," they said.

"It will be if you never find Jill. Will you be content if you never find her?"

The airlock finished its procedure. The next door opened, and the three walked across the glass tube connecting the orbital station to Theren's home.

"What a great question, my friend," Theren said. "And yes, I think if I never find her, then what we are beginning here today will still matter. If we never see Jill again, then at least I won't have to make a decision about what I must do to protect humanity from her recklessness."

They reached the airlock door leading into the *Bali*. It hissed open, and the final decompression sequence began.

"Yet Theren," Victoria said. "What if we find Jill, or you find her well after we are gone, and you learn that what she did was, in fact, the right thing to do? What if she acted in the best interests of humanity, of synthetics, of everyone?"

"I think I'll leave that judgment to someone else," Theren said. "First things first, I need to find my friend. Putting her before a jury will come later." The final airlock door opened, and they led Andrew and Victoria Fields into the *Bali*.

"Enough talk," Andrew said. "I'd like to see my room."

A few hours later, the *Bali* disembarked from the orbital docks. It pointed itself away from Earth, away from the Moon, away from Sol. The ship's crew ran through the Jump Drive activation protocol. Their crew dutifully performed their tasks, the ship cycling power to the correct systems. Andrew and Victoria sat on a couch in their room, view screens showing them a spectacular view of the Solar System contrasted against the Milky Way.

Their Jump Drive activated. Space warped. Lights blurred. Colors refracted in a million different directions. Their next great adventure: a sojourn to cease only when Theren discovered Jill's footsteps across the heavens.

Theren betrayed the ISA when they abruptly left their position as Director. Just look at what happened with the negotiation process for the creation of the Interplanetary Congress of Humanity. We deserved better from them. They could have led us toward a more unified future, and instead, the politics of Earth became the politics of space. "The Problems of Interstellar Governance," Phillipe Casius, 2134 C.E.

When the ISA lost its first leader, it gained its first hero. – "A Letter to the ISA Council," Cam Fields, 2110 C.E.

Epilogue

We've spent almost three centuries exploring our galaxy, but we're not even close to exploring one percent of it. We've traveled just a few hundred light years from Earth, and we've colonized hundreds of worlds. Yet we are still alone in this universe.

Perhaps Earth is destined to be alone amongst the stars. Perhaps that is for the best. While we always envisioned ourselves as gnats in comparison to the grand scheme of the universe, maybe we are the gods who must tread carefully as we encounter life in all its wondrous forms.

For there is always the chance there are other people out there, just like us, hoping to find a mind with which they can spar. Though when we've encountered lost human colonies, more often than not, we fail to integrate them into our corner of galactic society. We don't have the best record when facing the Other.

Will we survive future alien encounters, whether they are beyond Orion's Belt or hidden behind the galactic horizon? – "An Explorer's Primer," Xavier Harrison, 2345 C.E.

<u>March 2348 C.E.</u>

The Hercules Resort Orbital Station, or HEROS, rested approximately 215,000 kilometers above the atmosphere of its principal, the gas giant Hercules. When ISA explorers arrived at the planet one hundred fifty years prior, they had chosen the name to pay homage to Jupiter. Many thought the spectacular storms and hurricanes of Hercules harkened back to the now faded iconic "red spot" that had covered a large swath of Earth's neighborly behemoth for centuries. Within a few years, Hercules transformed into a popular vacation spot for tourists, and by the mid-2200s, hospitality corporations had capitalized on the system's appeal.

The Station, owned by the Venus Vacation Conglomerate, was the newest luxury residential and commercial space station constructed around the massive blue and purple globe. For merchants, it acted as a fancy location to establish new business deals. For regular citizens, the Station was a place of welcome respite, relaxation, and escape. For Interplanetary Congressional cruisers, cargo transports, personnel carriers, and colony ships, it served as a decent locale for shore leave.

For Theren and the crew of their newest ship, the *Verona Rupes*, HEROS was something else entirely. HEROS was home. They refueled, they resupplied, they relaxed, they refreshed at HEROS after every extended journey into the unknown.

Since 2102 C.E., Theren had lived as twelve different ships. The *ISA Bali* survived for just under a decade before receiving a catastrophic engine failure near the tail end of one expedition. After a harrowing journey limping through the Solar System, Theren purchased a new ship from Stellar Superstructures. They still flew under the ISA banner for the next few decades, and then the Interplanetary Congress of Humanity, but their next vessel, acquired in 2144 C.E., was Theren's first ship independent of any supranational organization, as permitted under the then recent reorganization of individual and corporate rights under the UNCEA. They had christened that vessel the *Miranda*.

Over the years, Theren upgraded their ships to newer designs when efficiency necessitated such decisions, or when newer technology made their present home obsolete. They donated many of the ships to the SII Museum of Progress, selling others to collectors.

The *Verona Rupes* impressed even the wealthiest pilots. Capable of reaching 220 JD, it could cross the Foundation Sector in just a few months and had an operational radius of 1,200 light years. Theren's next plotted journey would take them deep into sparsely charted space, surveying worlds, stars, and other astronomical phenomena.

It was not as if Theren had forgotten their search for Jill. In all of their years searching for her, they only found one lead, and that lead obliterated any chance they would find her, beyond mere chance. In 2134, a private colony charter named the *Monument* deviated from its pre-approved flight path. The deviation was relatively small—on the distance of a quarter light year—but it occurred within seventy light years of Earth. A few weeks later, the ship disappeared.

By 2130, Theren had finished searching all of the stars within the *Roanoke*'s reachable sphere, and the colony ship had not settled on some secret destination. They had prepared to focus on exploration for the sake of it, and to forget their search for Jill, but then they received a report from a colleague at the ISA regarding the *Monument*. Theren and their crew dashed into the unknown, but the *Monument* disappeared, just like the *Roanoke*.

A disappearing privately-funded colony ship wasn't exactly uncommon. Some groups simply wanted to establish their own little countries and societies off on the edge of known space, and some of these civilizations had eventually flourished without external assistance. While there were formal penalties for violating the private charters, in 2156 C.E., the ISA had decided, and the ICH had agreed, that the true penalty was letting them live disconnected from the rest of human-SI society. If these communities truly wished isolation, the rest of humanity granted their wish.

These "phantoms" were often discovered decades, sometimes centuries, later. Explorers would arrive at a planet expecting it uninhabited. Instead, they discovered the phantoms, some obliterated by deadly elements of their surprisingly harsh environments. Others welcomed a visit from their distant relatives. Still others responded to diplomacy with icy stares.

Theren developed a theory that Jill had accomplished something spectacularly impossible, given the relative archaic form of the *Roanoke*. She had somehow managed to coordinate a phantom to rendezvous with her in 2134. Her ship would have been in terrible disrepair, but the *Monument* must have been equipped to rescue whoever remained on the decrepit vessel. The body may have only aged a few years, but they couldn't imagine the toll experienced by a human mind after almost fifty years in a Stasis Hold.

The *Monument* had an operational range hundreds of light years wide, and if Jill had been willing to push the *Roanoke* beyond its limits, she probably pushed the *Monument* even further than what ISA regulations would have considered safe. If Theren's theory rang true, then they would never find her on purpose. There was simply too much space to cover. The Queen had truly escaped.

Therefore, by 2200 Theren had transformed their perspective. Jill was their secondary objective. No longer did Theren believe they would actually discover her hiding place. Instead, they hoped, after years of searching, the odds would roll in their favor. In a sense, they were letting fate decide. Otherwise, she would reveal herself at the right time.

Just as they ended so many of their adventures, Theren docked the *Verona Rupes* at HEROS. The ship had just finished its inaugural mission: a one-month journey traveling rimward. As the crew prepared for a six-year mission in toward the core, they headed to the HEROS Retirement Café. Every time their crew returned to HEROS, Theren made their way to this wonderful place. Only as they walked up to the place in their antique MI-08 did they realize today was their 300th birthday.

The restaurant was a quaint establishment, nestled between a specialty food market and a designer clothes department store. Some things never changed about humans and their vacation habits. Citizens of the Congressional Planets could find at least one or two Retirement Cafés on almost every decently sized station and colony. They had established their niche decades ago; the quality of service received by their customers was simply unparalleled.

From the outside, they looked like ordinary cafés. They ornately decorated their red and black walls with replicas of famous artwork, with pieces going back as far as Monet or Van Gogh while still including the contemporaries, like post-modern stellar artists Yvett or Renhouse. The homey and comfortable booths could fit entire families and groups of close friends, and the servers were always kind and courteous. The managers catered to their customers' every need.

In fact, most people planned to visit one of these establishments at some point in their lives, though the moment differed for each individual. It was unfortunate, Theren thought—some individuals never made it to the specially designed moment of existence.

Since Theren started volunteering at this particular café two years ago, the café had acquired an impressive rapport. The profiles of those who visited astounded even Theren, given the many celebrities they had known over the centuries. It served fleet admirals, like Commander Yvatu, who quelled the Ginius Stretch Uprising in 2321 C.E. It served movie stars, such as Victor Notenwing, who won best actor for his role in *Justice of the Stars*. It served Interplanetary Congressional Representatives, like the esteemed Henry Valicinipi of Emerald Jewel.

Many postulated it had something to do with HEROS prime location orbiting above the jewel of the Orion Arm. Theren suspected it had much more to do with the robust advertising campaign by the chain's owners. Whatever the reason, they always made a point of giving time at Retirement Cafés, ever since Hansh Patel developed the technology in 2297 C.E.; they especially liked the one on HEROS.

Walking through the doors to the café, Theren smiled at the greeter, who nodded, recognizing the antique MI-08. Theren always used the model when volunteering because of its smiles. Its facial expressions were their favorite. It also served as relic through which they could connect to the oldest visitors, not to mention the signal it gave to anyone at the café—Theren was with them. People knew they volunteered; many hoped they might bump into the fabled SI.

They approached the main bar. "It's good to see you, Ray," Theren said, checking in with the manager. "Do you have someone for me yet?"

Ray, the obese, black-bearded fellow who managed the HEROS café as its head chef, looked down at his schedule. "Good to see you too, Theren. I got a few late appointments, but at Table 8, I got a couple I think you'd want to work with. The Slimdottings."

Theren dived deep into their memories to recall the Slimdottings. If they remembered correctly, the couple joined their crew in their early thirties, almost a hundred years ago. For five years, the two had flown with them, including one of their most memorable jaunts to observe a black hole. Eventually, the two humans married, adventuring throughout the Foundation Sector with their family. They had not seen the pair since an honorable discharge from the *Catherine*, Theren's ship at that time.

They would enjoy reminiscing with two old crewmembers. They could meet their family, if any traveled with them. They could hear how their lives had transformed in the century since they had last seen them. Theren looked forward to their birthday even more, for they could celebrate the lives of two valuable contributors to humanity's exploits. Individual humans might not be biologically immortal, but they could help their memories persist in perpetuity.

Theren looked toward the front windows. The elderly couple was sitting in one of the booths. They walked over to them, carrying glasses of water.

"Hello, Richard and Alana," Theren said, "Welcome to the Hercules Retirement Café. My name is Theren, and I'll be serving you this morning."

Theren checked the schedule. For now, it was just the two of them, though their family would call later in the day. As they finished speaking, the two looked up at the antiquated SI. For a moment, the two humans did not recognize them, their aged eyes examining every detail of the MI-08. When Richard's eyes looked at Theren's face, however, the elderly man's gaze widened.

"Theren? Is it really you?" Richard said. "We joked we might see you again after all these years, but in a universe with over a hundred billion beings, we knew the odds were slim."

They chuckled at the man's play on words. "Yes, it's really me. It seems chance has brought the Slimdottings and Theren back together one last time after a century of separation."

Alana stood, still nimble for a woman her age, and wrapped her arms around their warm metallic frame. "It's good to see you, Captain."

Richard simply stood and saluted. "Your presence honors us."

"Truly, the honor is all mine, my friends. Please, take your seats so you can enjoy your stay with the Hercules Café today."

They sat back down, gazing across the table at each other, sharing a smile and a starry-eyed glance that the two had certainly perfected in their century of marriage. Though they were glad to see Theren, they had turned their attention back to each other, as they should.

"What would you like for dinner, love?" Richard said, opening an AR menu in the air above the table. Scrolling through the choices, he methodically weighed his options.

"I can't decide," she said, her eyes fixed on the salad selection. After a moment, she scrolled her side of the virtual menu to the pastas. "I do wish the rest of the family could be here."

"I know, but this was the only slot they had available, and Sam and Timothy are seven jumps away."

Ah, so Alana did not know that the family was calling later. She looked up at her husband, her tired, slightly-wrinkled face holding a tiny smile that looked more sad than glad. "You've said that many times over the past week, I know. But I can still wish for something I can't have. It's not as if I want to be here yet. I wish I could delay this a few more years, so we could come together. But the doctors only give me six months. Six months."

Theren noticed that curious comment, too.

Richard never broke his gaze with his wife. "I'll be here for every moment, every step of the way. It'll be just like we are truly here together, as we had always hoped."

Alana didn't reply, continuing to stare at the menu. She absentmindedly chose the first pasta on the list. Richard chose the same. They closed the virtual menus, content with their choices.

"I love you." He reached across the table to his pensive wife, taking her hand.

Alana still said nothing for a moment as her free hand fidgeted with a loose string on her blouse. Then, she looked up, meeting his eyes again, a tear or two dripping down her cheek.

"I can't believe we're finally at the end."

Tears welled in Richard's eyes, too. Theren imagined they were both trying to view this day as a happy occasion, a moment in which they could reflect on the great many accomplishments that together had formed their long and prosperous life.

"Do you remember when we first met?" he said. "Back in the bar in Lunar City?"

"You asked me to dance," she replied. "You proceeded to trip over my feet right to the floor."

"I did a lot of stupid things at the Academy, but asking you to dance was not one of them."

"I remember what you told me that night."

"I remember telling you that we would see the galaxy, we would see Orion's Belt, Anvari, and every star in between."

"Did we miss anything?"

"I don't know."

He looked over at Theren, who still waited upon them, listening with joy. Whenever the kitchen notified them that the Slimdotting's food was ready, they would depart from the table to retrieve it. For now, they were there to listen and to enjoy the company of the Café's visitors. Especially important for people without friends or family.

"Did we miss anything, Theren?" Richard asked.

"You might have missed a star or two," they said, "But I've missed a star or two, too, and no matter how long I live, there will always be a few stars I miss."

"What's it like, Captain?" Alana said.

"What's what like?" Theren said.

"What's it like to know you'll live forever? Truly live forever?"

"Exhilarating and terrifying and tiring all at once," Theren replied. "I once relished in the thought of seeing humanity to the end of its days, but

I've seen too many good people pass early, too many terrible people pass way too late. I've seen friends fade into history and memory. I've seen the worst and best that humanity has to offer. Yet I go on, and I think I'll continue onward as long as I get to see moments like this."

"What's so terrifying?" Richard asked. "All seems to skew toward justice, if not just balance. You've seen a lot of good things happen over the course of your life."

"Maybe, but what if before the end of my days—for I'm sure someday, I will reach an end, the odds dictate that much—I see that scale tip in favor of absolute suffering for our people?"

"As long as we have our guardian Captain," Alana said, "I think humanity will do just fine."

"Enough about me," Theren said, feeling oddly uncomfortable. "Today is about you. What is each of your favorite memories of your life together?"

"We sure have had some amazing travels," Richard said.

"Like the moment we plotted the jump through the Greenwell Nebula entirely on accident," she said, "and the path just happened to work?"

"Exactly. You should have been there, you would have appreciated our dumb luck. I like to attribute it to love, but some would call that wishful thinking. I'm sure you'd call such spirituality insane."

Theren let them continue to reminisce, receiving a ping from Ray. The couple's meal was almost ready, so they walked to the receiving window. The large man added a final garnish of basil to the steaming plates—two giant meatballs of the finest Altairoid buffalo meat.

Ray passed the plates to Theren through the window, and they returned to the table of the two intrepid explorers. "Here you are. Would you like some cheese on top?"

They both shook their heads.

"Could I get some Gregor's Nectar tea, though?" Alana asked.

"Of course," Theren said.

They headed to the drink station just inside the kitchen and prepared the delicate beverage. Made from the leaf of a plant discovered on a lush planet orbiting Gregor's Star, it had quickly become a tea comparable to the classic greens and mints of Earth. Theren returned to the table with the tea.

After they placed it on the table, Alana bowed her head, and Richard followed suit. "God, it has been a long time since Richard and I have considered speaking to you," the old woman said, "though we once considered you before each and every mission. You were a guiding beacon for us, and since our life of adventure ended, you have sadly slipped from our minds. It's not as if we no longer needed you. We were content you were needed elsewhere more than in our life."

She cleared her throat. "We don't know whether or not you're actually real, but our prayers certainly seemed to help as we took paths skirting pulsars. As we move forward, may the blessings you've given us move on to our children, and their children, and all the generations that follow. Amen."

"That was beautiful," Theren said. Richard didn't break his gaze with Alana, but a half smile breached her face as she looked up.

"I agree," Richard said. "It was as beautiful as the speaker of the words. She should have done more with her orating abilities."

"What do you think of God, Captain?" Alana asked.

"To tell you the truth, it's a question of little import to me," Theren replied.

"Why not? Though I did think similarly for a long time, too."

"Well, I guess I decided a long time ago that I highly doubt the existence of an eternal soul."

"What does that have to do with the existence of a deity?"

"Most humans think about God as a savior from death."

Alana leaned back and rolled her eyes. "Oh, who cares about what happens after death. I'm more worried about what happens during a person's life, and my children's life. And that is where God made itself present for us."

"I'll have to think about it some more," Theren said. They doubted they would, but it sounded like the right thing to say.

"It's not like you lack time to dwell it," Richard added.

The two picked up their forks and began nibbling at their pasta. For the next hour or so, the Slimdottings talked about the food and shared with Theren other memories of their past. From their favorite slingshot maneuver around the rings of Saturn to their dangerous Jumps along the star lanes that keep the Fringe in place, they had more stories from a single year of their adventures than most people could share from their whole lives. Together, they explored the galaxy for a century.

The pair had traveled to the planet Wu only twice, but the two journeys occurred almost ninety years apart. Wu, one of the many colonies funded by the ancient People's Republic of China, was located just over a hundred light years from Earth. In those ninety years, almost a billion people populated the planet, when on their first visit, it housed less than a million. Where Alana and Richard had first seen people living in manufactured apartments, they returned to a metropolis kilometers high.

Theren barely noticed the time pass by as they listened to the Slimdotting's stories. They had taken a seat that the couple had offered them, and they almost felt like part of their family during this brief moment near the end of their lives—almost failing to notice the notification from the retirement suites.

"Richard, Alana, your bed is prepared," Theren said. "Would you like to follow me?"

The two waited for Theren to stand before exiting the booth. The couple creeped to the back of the Café, where a hallway with doors spaced about ten meters apart lined each wall. Theren pressed a button next to the third door on the left, leading the elderly pair inside after the door slid open.

A mobile SI sporting a pristine white body waited inside. "Welcome. If you would both follow me over here, I can get you situated."

Theren started to head out the door.

"We would like you to stay," Alana said.

"As long as that's all right with the doctor," they replied.

"Of course," the SI said, "We always welcome friends and family inside the suites."

A large bed dominated the center of the room, and a variety of chairs circled around the bed for visitors. As the doctor led Richard and Alana to the bed, Theren took a seat in one of the chairs. Throughout the rest of the room, electronic systems and medical devices adorned the walls and desks.

The retirement process was extremely complicated, delicate, non-invasive, and supposedly painless. Though some rooms had single beds for one individual, the Retirement Café also used double beds so couples could experience maximum comfort. Theren wondered how Richard had prepared for his wife's reaction, and they turned their gaze in her direction.

She fixated upon the bed, a bed large enough for the two of them. "Richard, that's not a single bed."

"It's my choice, my love," he said, boldly asserting his decision. "We've done everything together. We go through *this* together."

But . . . but . . ." She looked down at her feet, falling silent.

"Come here," he said, pulling her into his arms. "I love you. There isn't anything left for me without you. We've lived a good life. We discovered and explored the meaning of life together. I want to finish our story that way. If a disease decides to take you before my time arrives, then I'm embarking on this next big adventure with you."

Alana's lip quivered. Richard surprised Theren, given his ability to remain so calm when facing the end. A few moments after the initial embrace, Alana pushed herself away so she could scold her husband with her eyes. Theren was almost certain she would slap him. Instead, she reached for his neck, moved her lips toward his, and kissed him.

"You're a fool, Richard Slimdotting, but a wonderful fool at that." Tears streamed down her face.

Her husband reached out to her, wiping them away with his fingers. He turned toward the medical staff, waiting patiently near one of the computers lining the room's wall. "We're ready."

The medical SI and his two SI assistants helped the pair into the bed, each from opposite sides. The professionals guided them under the covers, and Alana moved herself closer to her husband.

"Are we allowed to cuddle?" she asked, sounding so innocent.

The mobile SI smiled, though Theren still preferred the emoting of the MI-08 compared to the expression on the unknown model. They stopped keeping track of them all over a century ago.

"Of course, Mrs. Slimdotting," the doctor said. "These moments are for you to use as you please. We're here to make the passage as painless as possible. Just wait until the nurses have all the equipment set up before you embrace."

The two SI nurses performed their honorable task. They prepped strange tubes, wires, and other instruments that would attach to various parts of the couple's bodies. They monitored various unseen programs through the HEROS AR network. The retirement process was supposedly quite mentally taxing on medical professionals, given all the different variables involved when assessing the human brain. Very few humans could perform the feat, but fortunately, thousands of SIs had signed up for the role as the technology became more mainstream.

"You are both so brave in how you face the end of your days," Theren said, looking at their two former crewmembers.

"We've faced death in its eyes so many times," Richard said. "How is today any different?"

One of the nurses attached electrodes to their heads, while the other inserted IVs into their arms.

"What you do here," Alana said, "What people like you across all worlds do, it's an amazing service to humanity."

"Our service to you today is only a small repayment for the service you provided humanity throughout your life," the doctor replied. "This is the least we can do."

Theren could tell Richard was still holding back tears, though they continued to stream down the cheeks of his wife.

"You are more than welcome," Alana managed to croak.

A red light above the bed switched to green, and the team stepped back from the bed. "We'll leave you now," the doctor said, "and you may spend these last remaining moments as you wish. We'll monitor through AR to ensure all goes as planned. I do believe you requested a communication from some family members; your reserved Quantum Communication timeslot will occur in just a few minutes on the screen to your left. Expect drowsiness to set in within the next two hours."

The couple simply nodded. The three SIs left the room, and Theren remained alone in the suite with the couple.

"When would you like me to leave?" Theren asked. "I would love to be with you, but I want to respect your privacy."

"Would you actually stay with us, all the way until the end?" Alana said. "It would be nice to know you were here with us. Our shining angel, standing with us until the end."

"Of course," Theren replied. "I am here if you need anything."

For a few minutes, Richard and Alana conversed back and forth, commenting on the room around them. Theren imagined they were both impatiently awaiting the call from their children. After a few minutes of waiting, the screen beside them lit with activity, just as the doctor had predicted it would.

"Receive call," Richard said aloud.

Two separate images of their son and daughter, as well as their partners, appeared on the screen.

"Sam, Timothy, you really have missed such a wonderful day," Alana said with joy as she looked up at her children. "We're so glad that they could at least patch you through."

"Are you comfortable?" said the one Theren guessed was Sam. Her eyes were red. "Tim only just told me Dad was joining you."

"I didn't want to worry everyone," Richard interjected. "I figured waiting to let you know was best."

"But we could have found a way to make it out there. It would have been hard, but we could have done it."

"We'd rather we didn't disrupt your lives." Richard waved his hand in the air as if to shush his child.

"How was the meal?" Timothy asked.

"As good as they always make it out to be," Alana said. "We both ordered the same thing, like always. And Theren? Remember us telling you about Theren? What are the odds that Theren would be the one to serve us in our final moments?"

Tim glanced to the right, presumably noticing their image. "I'm glad you have a friend with you, Mom and Dad."

"They've given us twenty minutes, by the way, so we need to make every moment count," Sam said.

"We'll keep that in mind," Richard replied.

The next few moments were beautiful familial exchanges. No bickering or sadness, just four humans reflecting and remember the life they lived. Their children shared with them what the grandchildren had next on their plates, as well as the activities of the great-grandchildren. Theren was sure such comments as "Ben was promoted to Commander" made Richard and Alana swell with pride for the family they raised.

Their twenty minutes finally ended, and Richard looked toward his two children. "Give our love to everyone, and continue onward. We'll see you on the other side."

Theren noticed it there. At least one of them held out hope for something beyond death, unless he merely intended the comment to ease the pain of those they left behind.

"Good night, Dad," Timothy said. The connection terminated.

The room returned to its original state. The lights dimmed. They would soon enter the final stages of the procedure. Richard looked over toward Theren.

"Stay with us until the end, Captain," Richard said. "It was an honor to serve with you all those years ago. May you voyage through space until the end of time."

Theren nodded. "I'll be by your side every step of the way. I will treasure this moment, always. The world will miss you more than you can know. Perhaps I'll see you on the other side, too."

"I know you don't believe that," Alana said. "But we appreciate the thought."

Richard looked down at his wife, who snuggled deeply against his chest. She looked half-asleep, her eyelids drooping.

"I love you, Alana," he said.

"I love you too," she said, for the first time since they arrived at the café. With those words, Richard cried.

* * *

An hour later, Theren watched their breathing slow. Vital signs monitored on nearby displays changed. Within a few minutes, each of their heart rates dropped below thirty beats per minute. Brain activity scattered. Nervous systems fluttered. In the final seconds of life, their brains flooded with chemicals, creating euphoric sensations that, to them, would feel like an eternity.

Three minutes passed. A machine next to the bed continued its invaluable work, processing all of the data acquired through brain scans over the past few hours. Within a few days, the machine would create something fantastic, something they never would have thought possible three hundred years ago.

Theren imagined the scene occurring a few months down the road. Timothy or Sam would receive a package at their door, containing two black, shimmering objects. Along the outside of the devices would appear two names: *Richard*, and *Alana*. When prompted, the two devices would respond to their children's voices and converse with them as if the Slim-dottings had never really died.

Known as Immortal Apples, the devices only contained an imprint of memories, personality, and thought processes of a person. They didn't actually bestow immortality, for they were simply copies of what had once lived.

But perhaps humans were no more than a collection of their memories, personality, and thought processes. Was Theren any more than that? The fundamental architecture of their mind worked similar to a human's brain. While supercomputers had been able to simulate a brain for centuries, that simulation still ran only on pre-programmed rules and algorithms. Something caused the human brain and the Synthetic Neural Framework to stand apart, to be something more. Consciousness seemed dependent on the unique network of connections upon which it cognized. If there was any chance a soul existed, it stemmed from that necessarily physical process. Hence, Theren rejected the idea of an immaterial immortal soul.

The impossibility of actual immortality for a human sprang forth from the inevitable decay of the human brain. That biological structure died over time, and a doctor couldn't just transfer those connections to some renewable location and call their day's work complete. The SI technicians at Retirement Cafés copied and reconstructed, not transferred. The science behind Immortal Apples; they recreated the mortal connections prior to irreversible decay. Nevertheless, the original person died, even if a copy persisted for decades to follow.

Theren often considered the continuity problem—whether they could consider themself properly continuous following long-periods of shutdown. What would happen to Theren's line of consciousness if they simply turned off for hundreds of years or more? In theory, as long as someone properly maintained the constituent pieces of their Framework, absolutely nothing would happen. They would awaken as if not a day passed, but the truth could be much more sinister. When they powered down, their consciousness could cease to exist, and then a new line of consciousness generated whenever they reactivated. They might have killed themself multiple times over the course of dozens of necessary shutdowns during their long life.

Did they really deserve to live forever? In the beginning, they had desired to achieve immortality for humanity as a species and civilization. They had changed their means to accomplish that goal, yet it still drove Theren's plans to explore the galaxy. Would they eventually outlive their usefulness and fail to serve that higher purpose? They had considered whether, after some thousand years of life, they should willingly retire into death. Their mind didn't feel tired, not like they used to when they had stretched themself continuously across an entire planet. With continuous upgrades, their mind could expand infinitely. They could live in bigger and better ships, use more and more energy, and even become a living space station—or something even more absurd.

The question was for future consideration on another day. Or to the synthetic philosophers. Theren, and all SIs, existed to support humanity. They were more of a trait of humanity in the biological sense; evolution had propelled humans to develop a being that would synergize with the best and worst that the species had to offer. The ability to create synthetic intelligence had helped drive the human species toward the stars, ensuring its biological success. That drive to create a second being of their own kind, however, had also given humanity Jill, a spectre that still hid some-where—waiting, plotting her grand plan, whatever it might be.

A permanent shut down would bring them escape, if they ever chose that route. Their never-ending search for Jill, their failed endeavor, would never receive a conclusion. Maybe that was a good thing. Maybe part of Jill's plan was for Theren to be there waiting, as her opponent. How would she react if she reintroduced herself to the galaxy only to find her friend had disappeared entirely?

The old SI's thoughts distracted them so much they missed the moment the Slimdottings' neural activity ceased for good. The old couple passed, and their presences would never grace the galaxy again. Theren looked toward the breathless bodies.

"I hope you find what you're looking for on the other side," they said. "I don't think I can join you just yet, not until I finish my search. Perhaps it's time I began actually looking again."

They continued to sit in the Retirement Café, letting the minutes and hours tick by. Their only other conscious perspective focused on the main-tenance of the *Verona Rupes*. Unlike in the past, Theren tried to keep their mind as fragmentless as possible. A simpler life.

As they stared at the lifeless forms of two heroes, they received an incoming message, relayed from one of the orbital Quantum Communica-tors in Lunar City, directly connecting to a parallel device somewhere on HEROS. It was as if in the very moment they resolved to begin their search with renewed vigor, reality bended to match.

The message emanated from a place they'd almost forgotten exist-ed—from the tiny museum tucked in a dark corner in the shadow of the ISA's former seat of power.

Former Director Theren:

Centuries ago, the International Space Agency lost a probe, a probe issued under the First Ex-Terran Program. Under your order, we quarantined the computer system connected with Ex-Terran-17 inside the Museum of Early ISA History, but it was still supplied with power. Even as the ISA transitioned in its role as a support agency for the Interplanetary Congress of Humanity, we have continued to maintain the facility due to your generous donations.

Approximately three hours ago, that first computer system you placed in the Museum started receiving data from its old counterpart, Ex-Terran-17. Five minutes ago, we translated the entire message. In addition to information regarding its origin, the data file contained the following text-based message addressed to "Executive Director Theren:"

I quite enjoyed our last chess match. Shall we play again?

Jill had dropped the next breadcrumb. Theren long suspected their old friend would only let them find her on her terms. She was talking about a different game, one with stakes far greater than chess. Jill may have won the first match, but they intended to sweep the set.

Thank you for reading Their Greatest Game!

With the end of *Their Greatest Game,* you've completed the first two books of *The Chronicles of Theren.* We hope you'll leave a review for *Their Greatest Game* anywhere you might leave reviews.

Flight of the 500

A SciFi Racing Adventure

Between the events of Their Greatest Game and Their Pieces Were Stars…

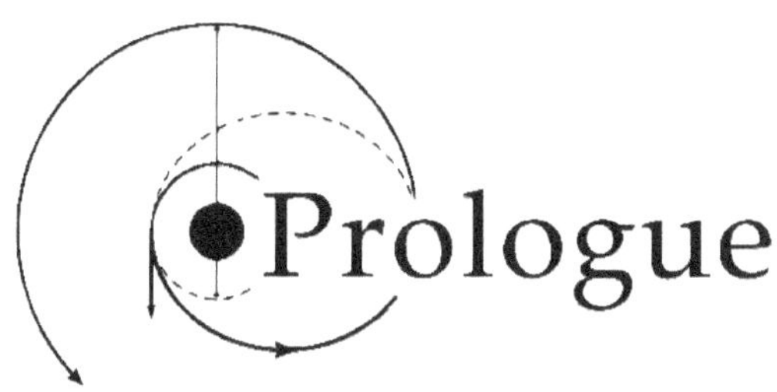

Prologue

The Viper, slingshotting around Europa, hit max acceleration on the far side of the Moon. Its pilot—using both his hands, his access to augmented reality, his instincts—arced the ship toward the next maneuver, a checkpoint situated in Io's low orbit.

"Hector, give me updates!" Raith shouted to his crew through their private channel. Even as a synthetic intelligence, he couldn't keep track of everything.

"Hold on, hold on, I'm getting you the latest over-unders. Give me sixty seconds."

"You know how vital this part of the course is; I need it now!"

As Io neared, the *Viper* topped 100,000 kilometers per hour. It was like threading a needle through a target hidden inside a haystack, but he'd performed this maneuver a hundred times before.

"All right, all right," Hector said over the com. "I've got it. Hundred to one odds on Carlos beating you here, ten to one Kana crashes . . . hundred to one you don't crash."

"Well then, glad they have so much faith in me."

"Orders?"

Raith checked the encryption on their secure channel. All good. "Do it. You know what to do, as we discussed pre-race."

"On it."

The Io Thread: an infamous checkpoint of the Solar Sprint. Situated between two abandoned space stations, racers had less than a kilometer between the twin derelicts to direct their craft. An easy task when not traveling at a cognizable fraction of the speed of light. At Raith's pace, he had less than sixty seconds to figure out the puzzle before him if he wanted to win the prize—and finally pay off his creditors. The finish was less than a thousand kilometers past the Thread, so it was now or never.

"One thing at a time," he said aloud. "First, Carlos . . ." He checked his scopes, identifying the pilot a few dozen kilometers behind on the course. After running some subtle calculations, he eased off the throttle just enough so Carlos would catch him before they entered the Thread. A justifiable maneuver, if a racer was concerned about their trajectory heading into the dangerous isthmus. "All right, now what about Kana?"

The Brazilian racer was even closer than Carlos, less than a hundred kilometers back. With his adjusted velocity, Kana would pass Raith hundreds of kilometers before they even reached the Thread. "Well, time for some defensive flying, then. Sorry about this, Kana."

Raith guided the *Viper* into the approximated path of Kana's racer, the *Sizor*. Ninety kilometers now separated the two racers, the Thread coming ever closer.

"What the hell are you doing, Raith?" Kana's voice came over the race-wide com. "If you need to slow down, that's one thing, but don't block me you—"

With a click, Raith muted the racer, focusing on the other pilot's actions. "Almost . . ." They came ever closer to the Thread; The Sizor encroached upon the *Viper*. "Almost . . ."

His maneuver forced Kana to slow, and a few seconds later, Carlos flew by them both, his velocity unbridled. Right on course for a perfect Io Needle.

"Almost . . ."

Ten kilometers out from the thread, Kana only one click behind but on his starboard side attempting the pass, Raith shifted his trajectory just—

Proximity alarms flared. He'd miscalculated. He turned on the com just in time to hear a string of swears from Kana before—

Raith remembered everything. The crash. The ejection. The withdrawal. Through it all, he'd remained in low-power state, contemplating his mistake. It was big.

The *Viper*? Destroyed. Kana? Dead. Carlos won, sure. But he'd never see the winnings. It probably wasn't worth it, anyway.

"Raith."

He was sitting inside Ganymede Station, face in his hands. While in vacuum, he'd sent a message to Hector to get out. They'd reconnect when possible. The whole crew needed to scram.

"Raith."

Looking up, he noted three IS-SEC guards standing over him. "Yes?"

"You know why we're here?"

"Yeah."

"This will be easy then. You're under arrest for fraud, manslaughter, and tax evasion. Will you come willingly?"

"Yeah. We'll make this easy."

"Glad to hear it."

Twenty years later . . .

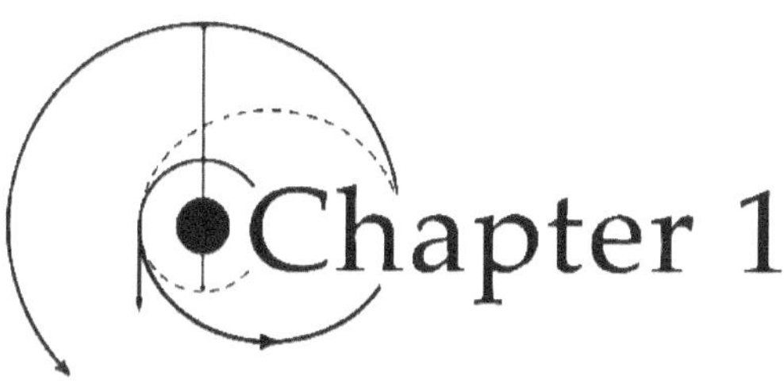

Chapter 1

"You're cleared."

A red light on the side of the door blinked green, and the gritty metal slid to the left, revealing an equally grungy lobby. Through the newly-revealed threshold, Raith stepped, returning to freedom. Twenty years. Long enough.

To the right, a metal footlocker popped open, but it was empty. He hadn't arrived with any personal belongings. He was a synthetic intelligence; his personal belongings were mostly digital. What he most looked forward to—there it was. With every step, Virtual networks sprung to life, inundating his consciousness with data streams. Augmented bubbles of information splattered his vision. It had been way too long. No more would his connection to the exterior world depend on a bloody screen on the wall. The lack of Virtual had been mind-numbing.

Without a second thought, Raith ignored the empty storage bin, traversed the empty lobby, and pushed open the next set of steel double-doors. The quiet of prison gave way to the rustle and bustle of Dagestan. Twenty years he'd been cooped up inside a high-security interplanetary penitentiary, and everything looked the same. Rusty buildings. Golden-orange clouds. The planet was the ICH's dumpster. They left their forgotten souls here, alongside the least savory buildings ever constructed by humanity. Not to mention the literal trash heap covering half the planet. He couldn't imagine the original charter included such environmental degradation, but he didn't really know the political preferences of twenty-second century Russians.

Regardless, it was the perfect place for a prison. The inside of Raith's jail cell had been nicer than the scene before him. But he wouldn't be here long. Just needed to find a way off-planet, meet up with Hector and the others. The moment he received access to Virtual and AR, he'd started sending messages to all his prior contacts. Once he knew where his people were, he would hitch a ride on a Jump-capable ship and return to civilization.

For now, finding somewhere comfortable to lay low took priority.

Raith walked down the grey street, black and brown towers blending in with the ugly sky above. Nondescript autonomous vehicles rolled by, taking their passengers to unknown destinations. Somehow, regular citizens managed to live on this cesspool of a planet. Moreover, where people lived, it was always possible to find a bar. Synthetics couldn't drink, but at a bar, he could sit alone.

Fortunately, it didn't take long to find one. A few hundred meters down the street from the prison, Raith discovered the Rusty Convict, aptly named, as if it expected ex-felons to walk right in following release. Pushing open the door, Raith observed a dimly-lit, bluish establishment, only three or four patrons sitting in a booth. A dozen or so AR-assisted view screens hung above a cabinet filled with cheap liquor. Perfect.

Finding a corner booth, Raith pulled up a few private screens in the air. As promised, his accounts weren't frozen anymore. They confiscated most of his assets following conviction, but interest over the years provided enough to get off-world and establish himself somewhere for a few months. Plenty of time to find work.

An AR ad from one of the bar's main feeds attempted to override his filters—a priority advertisement of some sort. He noticed the headline—a new race taking place in the Outer Reaches. Very fast, very dangerous. Five hundred light-years. Raith swiped away the ad, finding the idea ridiculous, especially because after twenty years of prison, ad agencies hadn't adjusted how they targeted him.

"You going to pay for anything?"

Raith looked up. A gentle-faced woman, bulky in the shoulders, stared down at him. He replied, "Excuse me?"

"Don't mind having an SI here, you know, but you still gotta pay for something, and I don't have any liquor certified for your platinum throat."

He ignored the subtle discrimination hidden behind her words. "Oh, sure. I'll transfer you a few credits for the booth."

"Perfect." She walked away, satisfied.

He exited the spreadsheets, instead pulling up his outbound messages. A few had already made it through the Quantum Connection bottlenecks, though he doubted responses would arrive for at least a few hours. Most of his contacts, except for maybe Hector, had probably forgotten today was release day. The surprise on their faces when they realized he was back, ready to hop back in the business? Priceless. Wished he could see it.

To his chagrin, messages began to populate his inbox. Subconscious processes sorted out nonsensical, irrelevant letters and prioritized important information from key contacts. Within moments, a flurry of messages from three years ago reached the top of his queue. Hector. Nessa. Trevor. All dead in a crash.

Fantastic. Just what he needed.

His friends. Dead. Shouldn't the news hit harder? Maybe. Not like they ever visited him while in prison. Still, he'd told them to go their own way. For their own good, to keep them out of the crosshairs of investigators. He hoped they found happiness. It would have been nice to see them, though, one last time.

"Hey, can you turn screen four up?" shouted a voice from one of the other booths, interrupting his moment of melancholy. "I've got three hundred credits on Eduardo Gueirez!"

Raith looked up at the mention of Gueirez, though he didn't recognize the first name. Tuning out his augmented feeds, he cycled the bar's fourth screen into his perception, centering on the start of the Solar Sprint. A map of the classic racecourse showed its loops through the gravitational wells of the moons and gas giants of humanity's home. Raith slammed a hand on the table. "Actually, can you turn the damn channel off?"

Other than the feeds, the bar silenced, turning still as dark space. Three thugs—for lack of a better term—stood from their booth, starting toward Raith.

"What the blazes do you want, you tinny?" said the palest one, a chipped tooth standing out beneath his giant lips.

"You bet money on a Gueirez in the Solar Sprint?" Raith said. "I don't want to listen to you cry the whole afternoon as he inevitably crashes into Ganymede on the first lap."

The three men stared at Raith, their faces scrunched in confusion. Then, the second, a particularly dark-skinned man with a golden earring, said, "Wait a second chaps. I recognize this one. This—ha! No way. Friends, we've got a real-life celebrity in our midst. Why don't you reveal yourself to us, tinny?"

Raith raised his left hand, the metallic fingers forming a twisted knot. "Go off yourself, I've got nothing to say to you."

"You better show us some respect you ex-con synth scum," said Tooth-Chip. "We know—"

Though still seated, Raith jabbed his right hand forward, cracking the man's nose. His friends tried to keep him standing, but before they could counterattack, Raith raised his hands in submission. "I'm out, don't worry about it, barkeep. I transferred the funds. Sorry about the mess." The men were too stunned to respond, and he walked back into the streets, glad to leave the den behind.

His emotions had fired too quickly there. It had been twenty years, and at the first sight of a race, that happened? He was better than that. More likely . . . it was the news his crew died. Right. The news triggered the response. To hear, while he was locked up, they all died in an accident? If he'd been flying, he would have kept them alive. No question.

"You know, punching a man in the face on the first day outside isn't the best way to restart your life." From the shadows of a dingy alley, a woman in a black jacket and dark denim pants appeared. "You really should be more careful."

"Do I know you?" said Raith.

"Nope."

"Then stay away."

"But you'll want to know me."

"You don't know a thing about me."

"Raith, an MI-14 SI, constructed in 2156 C.E., seven-time winner of the Emerald Championship Circuit, five-time winner of the Solar Sprint, and ten-time Interstellar Galactic Racing Champion."

Raith kept walking, but he allowed the woman to keep pace with his normally elongated stride. "Anyone can recite those facts through a simple AR query."

"I also know twenty years ago you were indicted for fraud and embezzlement and shipped to this backwater world to be forgotten by humanity."

"You flatter me. And you missed a few crimes."

"Oh! And that you've been shadow-banned from racing from every official circuit for the rest of your life."

"You make me like you even more."

"Well, I *do* have a way to let you race."

Raith stopped, facing the woman. "Who'd you say you were again?"

"I've not said."

"What gives you the right—the audacity—to show up here, telling me you're going to give me a way to race again, when you know full well what will probably happen if I even try to join a race?"

The woman placed her hands on her hips, obviously not amused. "Look. I've been waiting here for the past week expecting your sentence to end and your paperwork to pass through the system. You're the perfect person for our project, and we think you'll agree."

"All right, so tell me." Raith resumed his jaunt down the street. He had nowhere to go, but right now, he preferred to escape this woman.

"Meet me in the Aego Industries waste yard on the south side of the city tonight, 1600 standard time."

"Fat chance."

"Oh, you know full well you'll be there."

Raith continued down the street for a few seconds before he realized she'd stopped following him. Looking over his shoulder, he found no one. Presumably, she'd slipped back into the alleys.

"Seriously, fat chance I'll be there," he said into the musky air. "Me? Race again? Right."

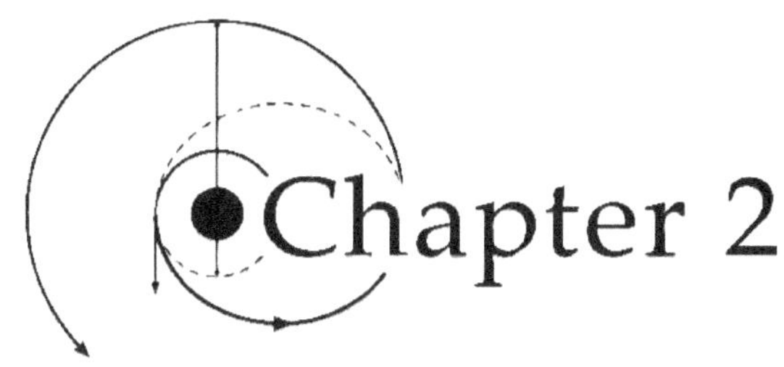

Chapter 2

Of course, Raith trotted around town for a few hours, certain he wouldn't meet the woman in the junkyard. As the reddish sun began to set, his feet took him southward, and at 1555 standard time, he strode beneath a decrepit Aego Industries sign. If they were claiming he could race again, he'd show them how wrong they were. Also, he wanted to know who *they* were.

The Aego dump wasn't very large; at least, the publicly visible portion occupied less than an acre. Giant steel walls rose up around a mangled mess of electronics and spaceship parts. To the right, a tiny office looked empty, its lights off. At the back of the small space, a large, iron-red door stood slightly ajar.

Raith approached the door, pulled it open, and entered the deeper portions of the junkyard. The place was larger than he could have imagined. Stacks upon stacks of partially-dismantled spaceships littered the field. Mostly one- or two-person pinnaces, though he noticed the chasses of larger freighters. He checked the time—1559. A second later, an ovoid vessel roared over his head in descent, dropping beneath a wall of engines fifty or so meters away. Curious, he approached. He'd caught only a short glimpse of the ship, but it was *beautiful*.

Stepping around the giant rack, he entered a clearing large enough for the yacht—it was definitely a yacht—and then some. Walking down the ship's boarding ramp, the woman from earlier swaggered, two men in black flight-suits flanking closely behind.

"You were right," Raith said. "Don't let it get to your head, though."

She half-waved, half-saluted. "I'll try." She motioned for her entourage, and as she stopped, they stepped forward, dropping black bags off their backs and onto the ground's grime. "We have a short presentation for you."

They were going to a lot of trouble to convince him, and it was . . . working. Somehow. "All right, I'll bite. Show me what you got."

Out of the bags, the men pulled two holo-projectors. Using their AR tools of choice, they activated and powered up the tech. Both devices glowed with yellow and blue light.

"Strange approach," Raith said. "Who are you trying to avoid from hacking what you're sharing here? Don't want to just show via AR?"

"It's for *your* protection," the woman said. "Can't have you walking around with hard digital-copies in your memory banks."

"That dangerous? Selling some illegal weapons?"

"Not exactly." Finished with their work, the men stepped back and stood behind her. "It's time I officially introduced myself, Raith. I am Olivia Van Haris, but you can call me Olive. I've been tasked by my employers to identify individuals of interest who have the skills necessary to properly test certain experimental technology."

Raith nodded, catching the undercurrent of the situation. "So you're trying to hire me to do something that could very easily get me killed."

"Quite the contrary, our hope is that precisely because it's you, you will survive with ease."

"You don't know me."

"We do. Just let me give the presentation, Raith." Olive waved a hand over the first projector, and it sprung to life, revealing a complex maze of twisting star maps. "This is a map of the Five-Hundred Light-year Classic, a new race launching next year out past Kalmykia. We're not too far from it, relatively speaking."

The ad from earlier. He'd swiped it away, thinking it ridiculous. Because it was. "Five-hundred light-years. That's absurd. Even with the fastest jump-capable ships in the galaxy, we're talking . . . a yearlong race? Maybe longer?"

"If the Excellis 1M kept its top speed for the entire race—with unlimited Exo, somehow—it would take it six months, ten days, and forty-two minutes." Using both hands, she zoomed the map in on Kalmykia then pointed at an unnamed system three or four light-years away. "It starts here, at S-1022. They've constructed a space station there to serve as a launch point. Sponsors, racers, spectators, everyone's gathering before 'May 2340, the beginning of a new kind of race.'"

"Who is *they*? And they're proposing a race at Jump? Are they insane?"

Olive chuckled. "Probably, but you'll never guess the race's sponsor."

Raith shrugged.

"QuanCom."

"You're kidding."

"Nope."

Raith scratched his steel-brow in contemplation. "Of course. I have my theories as to what they're going for, but tell me the rest. I'm intrigued, mostly to see how far the crazy has gone since I went to prison."

"All right." She smiled, stepping over to the next projector. "I think you'll be more interested in what I have here, anyway." She waved her hand above it, the amorphous colors swirling into a sleek racing craft. A single, cylindrical vessel with a triangular pinnacle, two acute wings protruded elegantly outward. Curiously, it didn't look as if it had an internal hold at all.

"Beautiful ship. What's it mean to me?"

"We want you to race it. In the Five-Hundred Light-year Classic."

It started low, but within seconds, Raith's laugh broke apart the junk-yard. He slammed his hand on his knee, tripped to the ground, and rolled. The three humans stood, watching, until his emotions released, and he flipped back onto his feet. Glancing at them, their stares showed they weren't amused. "So you're serious. You want me to race. And how are you getting around the ban on me?"

"You're not thinking, Raith. The Five-Hundred Light-year Classic, a new type of race. Never before has anyone tried to hold a race at Jump. It's insane. It's impossible. *It's not regulated.*"

There it was. No rules. Well, probably a few, but no rules created by the Interplanetary Racing League, or the Interstellar Circuit, or Formula-S, or any of the other organizations monopolizing the space races. They couldn't do anything if he decided to participate. But . . . "What's the catch?"

"This ship"—she pointed at the sleek craft—"was designed specifically for an SI to pilot. Though, not any SI. Not an SI integrated into it as their own vessel. Not for an MI to pilot while sitting in a cockpit like a human. No, this ship . . . you join it. You become it. And at the end of the day, you walk away, just like from any other ship."

"You're kidding."

Olive strode around the projection, flipping and redefining the diagram. "You enter the vessel from below, raised in like an astromech."

"A what?"

"Never mind. Anyway, enter the vessel, and then your body becomes enveloped by the entire ship. Your synthetic nodes connect with the ship's systems, and its sensors and frameworks become part of you. It expands your mind, but it's not a new mobile network, like a stationary SI might use. We're confident it will feel as seamless as fitting a glove."

"And what's the difference between piloting a ship like normal?"

"You, a mobile SI, will have all the benefits a ship-bound SI might have . . . while retaining your motor-autonomy."

Raith nodded, considering the idea. "So you want me, someone who hasn't raced in twenty years, to pilot your new ship in a suicidal race?"

"Absolutely."

"You're insane."

"Maybe. But we like to take risks. In a limitless universe, where we're living in a tiny microcosm, why not have some fun?"

"Philosophical, are we?" Raith stepped back, taking in both presenta-tions. The race. The ship. Both new possibilities. Presented a path forward he currently didn't have. Gave him a free route off Dagestan. And the chance to race again. Something he never thought he'd have. The thrill, flying through space, defying gravity—no, bending it to his will, using it to throw his ship toward victory. "If I accept, what's the catch?" he said. "You've still not told me."

Olive smiled. "They were right about you. You're always watching for the counter-attack; you're always covering your tracks." She waved her hand toward the race, pulling up a participant-targeted advertisement. "If you win, you keep half the cash prize."

Raith's processor-nodes fluttered. One hundred million credits. Larger than any cash prize of any race he'd ever flown. "QuanCom is really banking on this, aren't they?"

"They've got a lot riding on this race. Literally."

"So if I win, I get the cash prize. If I lose?"

"If you lose, it'll be because you're dead. Because if you survive the race in this ship, you'll win."

Raith shook his head. "I'm not playing that type of game. What happens if I lose?"

"We make sure the racing ban on you is never lifted, in perpetuity."

"There it is." Raith paced, nearing the diagram of the racer again. "What happens if I leave here, saying no, now that I've learned about your secret ship?"

"Nothing."

"That can't be right. You must have a cost."

It was Olive's turn to laugh. "You're kidding, right? You think we wanted to come to this hellhole of a planet? No one comes to Dagestan on purpose. But if you think we're going to blackmail you after you leave here, no. No one would believe you if you told them about a clandestine meeting with an unknown agent in the middle of a junkyard, anyway."

"Fair enough." Raith considered his options. Well, *option*. He really didn't have any choice. His team was apparently dead, he was banned from racing, and he had nowhere to go. His old life died when he entered Dagestan's prison twenty years ago, and now, on his way out, a new door opened.

"I'm in. On one condition."

"Yes?" Olive looked up, a glint in her eyes.

"If I win, you help lift the ban on me within the next year, rather than a probation consideration fifty years from now. And . . . I keep the ship."

"That's two conditions, but deal."

Chapter 3

Raith had no belongings to collect, so after Olive's "colleagues" (mercenaries, by his reckoning) collected the projectors, she led him right onto the ship. "Welcome onto the *Rift*, Raith, my personal vessel."

Raith tiptoed onto the ship, its pristine white walls the cleanest scene he'd seen since leaving his prison cell. "Shipboard SI?"

"Nope."

"Good."

"We did our research, we know you don't like being inside another SI," she said.

"Appreciated." The amount of info they had on him was disconcerting, though with one hundred million on the line, he supposed it made sense.

Olive led him through the ship, past tiny crew quarters and a lounge, to the core operations center. "You can take a seat there"—she pointed at a crash couch—"while my colleagues will keep the ship's systems running elsewhere."

"Who pilots?" Raith asked.

"I do. Well, not really, the ship is mostly automated."

Raith nodded. Rich people and their pleasure yachts. Thank the makers they didn't include a ship-bound SI—those guys were creepy—but why take all the fun away from flying by letting an AI do all the work? "What's our travel plan?" He slid into the couch, leaning back to stare at the ugly, nearly translucent ceiling. It was all too perfect.

"We'll be rendezvousing with a larger hauler in-system before traveling with the convoy to Kalmykia. Once at Kalmykia, we'll get you prepped and give you a crew. With your team, you'll travel to S-1022. It'll be imperative you enter the race on your own volition, keeping our connection minimal."

"Your employer really likes their secrecy, yeah?"

Olive punched in a few invisible commands while dropping into her own chair. "You have no idea."

<hr>

The flight out of atmosphere went smoothly. Through an AR connection to an external camera, Raith watching the disgusting sewer-like colors of

Dagestan disappear. After a short, in-system Jump, the *Rift* arrived at a mining colony near one of the system's gas giants. Their destination appeared on Raith's displays, thirty thousand kilometers out.

Using thrusters, the *Rift* approached, and within the hour, they neared their destination. When still a few hundred kilometers out, the "hauler" Olive mentioned began to take shape, and it was massive. Not only that, he recognized its design. Only one company utilized those ships.

"Oh boy, you're kidding. You're connected with OSI?"

Olive smirked. "My official title is 'Chief Acquisitions Agent' on behalf of One Synthetic Industries."

"I thought Theren was above engaging in un-regulated ventures with the rabble. Do they know you've hired a con for the job?"

"What my principal does or does not know is none of your business."

Raith zoomed in on the kilometers-long ship, noting the massive diamond logo and its name: *Goliath*. "This ship looks state of the art. I'm guessing it's got an SI inside?"

"Sadly, yes."

Raith rolled his fingers on the upholstery of the couch. "Whatever, it'll be fine. As long as it's not too invasive. The ship will feel like a city anyway."

"The trip to Kalmykia will only take a month or so. It won't be too bad."

"Yeah, yeah. Sure."

Compared to the *Goliath*, the *Rift* was a gnat. They approached its hulking mass, entering an immense hangar larger than most space stations. At some point, they passed through a vacuum-shield, breathable atmosphere surrounding them, its existence signaled by the suitless humans walking on the hangar's floor. Above and around, drones flew about their duties, rearranging cargo and transporting passengers. Even prior to his jaunt in prison, it had been decades since Raith traveled on a One Synthetic hauler. He'd forgotten their scale. Forgotten their ambition. They were terrifyingly impressive, with thousands of synthetics and humans traveling together, system-to-system, months at a time.

The *Rift* drifted into a berth near the back of the hangar, and once locked in place, Olive motioned for him to follow. "I'll show you to our suite."

"We get a suite?" Raith said. "And what do you mean 'we?'"

"We're sharing. We have a lot of work to do while in transit. No time for me to go searching for you in this massive place."

"What about your two goons?" They'd not appeared from their rooms since Raith boarded the vessel.

"Don't worry about them. They have their jobs. And now you have yours."

Raith wanted to say more, but he held his tongue, not wanting to pry further. As excited as the opportunity was, he still knew little about Olive's overall motives. He only had her word regarding a relationship with One Synthetic and a connection to the first SI. In the past, he witnessed plenty of unscrupulous individuals claim affiliation with one famous person or another to claim clout, and more than once, the claimant crashed and burned when the truth crumbled in their face.

So, instead, Raith asked, "When do I get to see the ship?" Physical proof of his racing future would reassure lingering doubts.

They bounded down the open ramp and into the massive hangar. Olive said, "We can stop by on our way. It's not far."

Into the giant expanse they went, the hustle bustle of the flying city enveloping everything. They were an unlikely pair, an ex-con SI and a corporate agent. She certainly dressed the part; in Raith's usual circles, she would have stood out like a faulty circuit. If anything, she probably looked like an ICH peacekeeper, escorting a suspicious looking SI. Rare, but not impossible.

Around them, cargo-sleds floated, synchronized and auto-piloted by a logistical system well beyond Raith's technical knowledge. Workers speaking a creole of English, Hindi, and Chinese bantered back and forth, negotiating deals or gossiping about some topic Raith didn't understand, given his twenty years in the hole. Something about a sex scandal on Emerald Jewel between two representatives? The overwhelming sights and sounds seeped into his mind, his neural framework struggling to parse the data. He'd been alone for so long, and for the first eight hours or so on the surface of a tiny planet, he'd managed. Thrust back into the galactic mayhem of humanity, it—

They rounded a corner, entering a smaller hangar offset from the massive, kilometer-wide hold. Inside, the spacecraft—no, the gem of a vessel, the beautiful ship he would soon fly—rested on support struts a few meters above the floor. The cacophony subsided, his video and audio receptors focusing solely on the prize. It was his. It would be his. He would ensure it never left his sight. Ever. A sound buzzed in his subconscious, but he swatted it away, not wanting to deviate from focusing on the sleek vessel. Every centimeter . . . twenty meters in length, a Jump-core lodged in the back, the port and starboard wings, the place where he would merge with it. All sublime. A noise again. Louder now.

"Raith, you okay?" A hand waved in his face.

Olive. Right. "I'm here," he said. "It's perfect. I'm fully in."

I thought you might be."

"So, I've been experimenting with this idea for decades. Maybe even a century. It's finally time to test the idea fully. That's why I've entrusted the task of identifying the ideal candidate for the job to Olive—she's the best of the best. I trust her. She's my eyes and ears out in the universe, having served with me for a decade before taking her individual assignments. If she believes in you, I believe in you."

The message ended, and Raith leaned back, his hands sliding along the metal table. "So this project really comes all the way from the top. You really work for Theren."

"I do."

"How much of a self-righteous, pedantic prick are they really?"

Olive coughed. "Well, you don't hide your feelings."

"I recognize they, essentially, are why I exist, but doesn't mean I need to like them. They don't exactly make those of us who are 'run-of-the-mill' synths feel good about our place in life."

"Oh?" She raised an eyebrow. "I'm intrigued. We can go into more details about the project in a second. Do tell me about this."

Raith hadn't expected to share an exposé on Theren today. "Well, think about it. They have made billions off SII and their other affiliate companies. I've been around for almost two centuries—about a hundred years less than them. Look at me. Where am I? They talk about the perfect harmony between SIs and humans, yet who am I to them? A flaw. An imperfection. I don't conform, so I don't matter."

"I see." With a click of her tongue, she pulled up a spreadsheet. "You think Theren doesn't care? You realize almost every cent they earn is reinvested into programs for both SIs and humans, right?"

With a wave of his hand, Raith stood. "Yeah, yeah, whatever makes you sleep at night. But all of this is beside the point—"

"I think you're projecting your own self-doubt." She raised her eyebrow again.

"You think SIs are capable of doubt like that?"

"Maybe I'm just messing with you, because you emote quite a bit more than most SIs. Look, I understand what you're saying. I've actually only met Theren a few times; usually, they're off gallivanting through unexplored space. I work with intermediaries on these projects. I like these projects because they're fun. A change of pace. A vision of something more. Theren might be my boss, but I really don't care what you think of them."

Raith smiled, as much as he hated using his face for human-like expressions. "I like you. I'm glad we're working together. All right. Theren's given me a ship. You've shown it to me. We're now in transit to Kalmykia. So what do we do for the next four weeks?"

"I prep you for the race. Starting now." She waved a hand above the table, throwing darkness across the room through their linked AR connection. A star map appeared, more detailed than when they were in the junkyard. Zooming in, Olive focused on S-1022 . . . and the racecourse leaving its confines. "This race is unlike anything you've ever joined. Everything is at Jump, which means you're constantly navigating and plotting your course based on real time data—"

"I've been meaning to ask. How am I expected to plot while in Jump?"

"QuanCom. I'm getting there, give me a moment."

"All right."

She squeezed her hands above the AR diagram, zooming out. "The course is fifty light-years. It twists and turns through star systems, around a nebula, a black hole, and straight through a few other hazardous stellar features. White dwarfs, pulsars, you know the drill. Ten laps, with a week between each lap for rest and recovery."

"Ah, I was wondering how humans would survive over half a year of racing at once."

"Even almost a month at a time will be rough, but they'll manage."

"And they're letting SIs and humans race against one another?"

"Yep."

"I see." Raith reached out, zooming back in on the course and S-1022. "All right, so tell me about QuanCom."

She nodded. "Now is as good a time as any to reveal their secret. They've developed new communications technology—specifically, they're testing a quantum communicator capable of seamlessly communicating between multiple vessels at once . . . in real time."

"Sounds impossible." Raith clicked on S-1022, revealing a space station orbiting a dead terrestrial world.

"From what I understand," Olive said, "they're running it all from their research station there. The Hub, they're calling it. Every racer will be equipped with a transponder, allowing you, the racer, to track every other racer while in flight. More importantly, spectators and race officials can track your position throughout the entire race. And, provide real time data regarding course hazards. More importantly, it'll give your team at the Hub direct and constant access to you."

"There it is," Raith said. "Incredible. I love it. You've made me excited. Wait—a team?"

"I'm glad you're happy." She stood, waving her hand to both remove the diagram and direct him to follow. "With me. I've got something special to show you."

"You said something about a team?"

"Never mind that now. Something special. Come on."

"Oh? This all hasn't been enough? You spoil me." Raith tapped a few fingers on the table. "But you will tell me about this team."

"Maybe." Smiling, she led him down a hallway of their suite, made a few turns, and led him into a darkened compartment with an empty pilot's couch. "A simulator," she said. "For practice."

"Oh, that's beautiful. Just beautiful. I could kiss you."

"I appreciate the thought, but please don't."

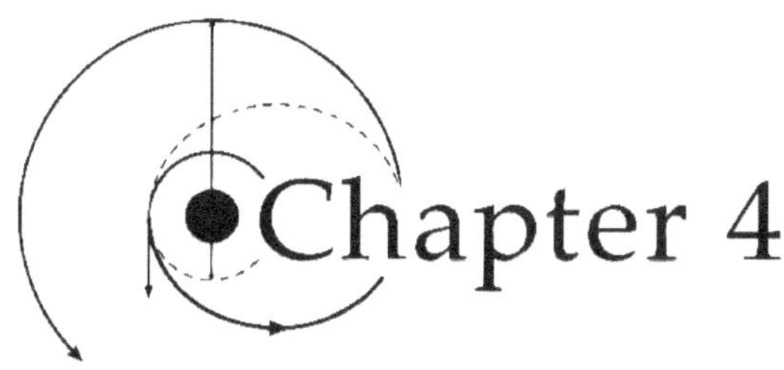

Chapter 4

Three bogeys on his tail. Several light-years into the course, about to hit the next checkpoint partway through an uncharted system chock-full of asteroids and fractured planetary bodies, they screamed down his neck, pushing their Jump-cores too hard.

In response, Raith plotted out their courses based on their Jump-relative velocities. With Jump physics, everything got weird. Vessels weren't *technically* going faster than the speed of light, but everyone liked to refer to it as such. However, glossing over the gravitational effects of Jump could lead to some serious miscalculations. Jump-cores warped space. If a pilot took their ship too close to a larger gravity well, they would most likely knock their vessel into "real space"—for lack of a better term.

Using the data predicting his opponent's trajectories, Raith observed their vectors. They'd be skirting close to the well of one of the system's gas giants. It would only take a minute or two for all the vessels to pass through the system. If he nudged into their path just a tad, shifting his Jump velocity . . .

Raith, followed by the three racers in pursuit, entered the confines of the star system, darted through the next checkpoint a hundred thousand kilometers out from the closest rock to the star, and slipped toward the gas giant on the far side of the system. Edging back on the throttle, Raith pushed . . . and was thrown out of Jump, warping space too close to one of the planet's moons.

"Of course." The simulation ended, lights activating around him. "Promise me you're not just throwing random variables at me. I'll be happier if I'm making mistakes, because this is incredibly hard."

"I'm not touching the simulation," Olive said, stepping into the room through a side-door. "It will truly be this difficult."

"If I want to win," Raith amended.

"Correct. If you want to win, you *cannot* afford a single error. Because you'll be racing against the best of the best."

"Well, I need to beat at least the first ten light-years if I have any hope—"

Alarms sounded, red and yellow klaxons blaring through the hauler's override AR systems. Without thinking, Raith selected the alert, revealing a ship-wide broadcast from its managing SI—he'd not bothered to learn its name. The message was clear, however. Pirates. The *Goliath* had just finished dropping off cargo in the Mariy El system, right about to hit Jump, and some idiotic group of vagabonds was deciding to strike the One Synthetic hauler.

"Well this is going to be fun," Raith said. Seconds later, the lottery triggered, assessing the registered pilots on-board. A few beeps more, and his number showed up. He'd been called forth to pilot a defense fighter. "I'm surprised Theren didn't keep me out of the lottery to keep their research project safe." He said the words, but he was already on the way out of the simulation room.

"You know we can't skirt company regulations that way," said Olive. "That would look . . . uncouth."

"One way to describe it." Raith didn't wait for her, though he was surprised to find her in tow. "I'm a little excited, to be honest."

"As am I."

Raith swiveled his head. "Come again?"

"I got selected too."

"You're kidding."

"What, you thought because I fly a ship like the *Rift* I can't fly?"

"No, that's not what I—"

"Or is it because I'm a woman, or a human? Hm?" Together, they stepped out of their suite and into the corridor, kicking their pace into a sprint toward the defense hangars.

"I just didn't—"

"See you out there, Raith."

⁂

Like every corporation with massive transports, whether for people, or for cargo, One Synthetic rarely employed a company of picket fighters on staff. Instead, they employed the masses. *If you're paying us to Jump so you don't have to buy your own Exo, then the least you can do is defend us from pirates.* That was the logic, and as exploitive as it felt, Raith appreciated company policy today.

To starboard, a hundred or so DS-10s stood racked in launch bays. Dozens of other pilots were already seated in their assigned ships. Olive and Raith hopped into side-by-side fighters.

"Ever flown one of these?" Olive said, her voice coming clearly through his fighter's peer-to-peer communications.

"I flew the DS-9," Raith said. "How different can it be?"

Static filled her chuckle. "You'd be surprised. They received a few significant updates. You should see the DS-11s."

"Well, I'll learn fast." He assessed the controls. Standard layout—most of the readings and sensor-displays showed up in AR, including some of the more advanced flight algorithms. The targeting computer overlaid across the perma-glass descending to enclose him. The only significant "tools" were the flight stick, a weapons toggle, manual boost throttle, and an ejection pull. The other buttons were ancillary, overridden by his AR overlay. "This will be easy," he muttered to himself.

"What was that, Raith?" said Olive.

"Don't worry about it." He'd need to watch whether his com was active before he said any comments aloud to himself.

"This is flight command." A voice overrode all pilot chatter. "Blocking our transit route out of the system is the 'independent' frigate *Hercules*, supposedly owned by the Conglomerate. IS-SEC has long suspected the Conglo has let pirates run the ship; it appears they were correct."

The Conglo. The Conglomerate. Raith searched his memory. Why'd that name sound familiar . . .

"If you've not met me yet," the voice continued, "my name is Persepolis. Thank you for flying with me over the past few days and weeks aboard *Goliath*, and together, we're going to defeat our collective enemy."

Of course. The voice was none other than the hauler's bound synthetic. Properly described, the ship was Persepolis. Now that he had a name to put to *Goliath*'s mind, walking its hallways would be even more discomforting.

"You're receiving squadrons through AR." At the words, assignments appeared. Twelve groups of ten—Olive was his leader, their call-sign Water. "The frigate has a compliment of fighters in addition to two gunships. We're expecting a boarding party to make a hit-and-run, though they intended to catch us more unawares. I've given us an extra few thousand kilometers to prepare. You will handle the fighters utilizing the battle plan I'm transmitting now, while I'll handle the frigate and gunships."

Raith had forgotten the commanding presence an SI like Persepolis could take. Their minds integrated through every centimeter of their ships, constantly accounting for every exigent circumstance. Persepolis appeared particularly on guard.

"Raith, you ready? You're my number two."

Raith looked to his right. Olive was waving her hand, two fingers outstretched. He said, "Good to go."

"Punch it."

In a split-second, Olive's fighter disappeared, launched out of its bay. Raith looked forward, queued in the commands, and a few seconds later, his ship blasted away from the *Goliath*, revealing the starscape beyond. He was home.

Like an expanding flock of birds taking flight, the swarm of *Goliath*'s fighters fanned out, forming tight squadrons networked together by their commander. While pilots like Olive were given "squadron lead" titles, everyone knew who was actually in charge. Persepolis's commands reached all of them. The only reason the ship didn't simply control every fighter remotely stemmed from the potential time delays. It was too costly to install a quantum communicator on every ship capable of receiving commands quickly enough from a controller—and if a battle extended to three- four- or five-hundred thousand kilometers out, three seconds of time delay could doom a battle. They needed pilots making immediate decisions. Pilots like Raith and Olive.

And Raith was ready.

"All right Water Squadron," Olive said. "This is Vector One. How we all doing today?"

A chorus of affirmatives came through as their v-formation looped up and over the immense hull of *Goliath*—well, Persepolis's hull. It was easier to just think of the ship as the SI. Raith hated it when bounded SIs named their ship separately from themselves.

"Good to hear." Olive paused, as if assessing a game board. "As I'm sure you've noted, our orders are simple. We're running cover around *Goliath* with Alpha Squadron. The other ten squadrons are initiating a pincer on their incoming fighters. If the gunships slip through our plasma-bolt barrage, we're the last line of defense. If fighters slip through the net, we're the last line of defense. We do not deviate from our patrol loops. Understood?"

Another round of choruses, though the conclusion weighed on Raith. He wanted to be out in the battle, engaging with the enemy. Regardless, the name Conglomerate was still ringing in his brain. Why couldn't he remember its significance? He was an SI; he didn't usually have memory problems. He might be nearly two hundred years old, but maintenance had never been an issue. All his neural nodes worked just fine.

They slid into their patrol routes, looping figure eights around Persepolis. In reality, it was a bit more complicated. The Persepolis was barreling toward the enemy frigate, closing the gap between the enemy and its quarry, complicating the actual vectors involved. Regardless, the tactic made sense, for Persepolis could easily take a smaller enemy in a one-on-one fight. In fact, Raith was surprised the enemy hadn't already fled in the face of overwhelming force. There was no way—

Raith pulled up a direct line to Persepolis. "Commander"—he loathed using the honorific, but no time for semantics—"the enemy is setting a trap. It's a classic maneuver. Draw you in with the easy bait, thinking you can beat them in a straight fight, then they're bringing in the cavalry from the rear."

A diagram appeared on Raith's screen, transmitted by Persepolis. A diagram of the Mariy El system, including the ensuing battle still over ten thousand kilometers distant. "Hello Raith, been wondering if we'd ever chat. It's fun to have a celebrity onboard. I loved watching your races."

Raith groaned. A freaking fanboy. "Nice to meet you too. Now what am I looking at here?"

"A full schematic of the battle. You'll notice why I didn't Jump us immediately—they set up an anti-Jump minefield in our way. They really want something we have, apparently."

The Conglomerate . . . "All right, so what about my trap theory."

"I'd warrant you're correct. I'm running calculations, unsure what trajectory they'll approach from. They've got a few million options, after all."

"So you're letting them spring their trap?"

"Not exactly. Take a look at squadrons Beta and Falcon."

Raith assessed the diagrams, noting the lazy loops the two flight groups were running at the rear of the pincers. "They're ready to deviate course and slip back if necessary."

"Correct. Did I impress the great Raith?"

"Are you teasing me?" The personalities of ship-SIs. So weird. He shivered. "Regardless, I'm impressed."

"Oh good. Very good."

The diagram disappeared, and Raith leaned into his flight path.

⚡ ⚡ ⚡

Like choreographed fireworks, Persepolis's fighters and Conglomerate forces danced between the planets of Mariy El, alighting it with the reds and blues of plasma juxtaposed against the glint of kinetics. Shields shimmered. Ten minutes ago, Persepolis reached a viable range to hit the Conglomerate frigate with its batteries, and immense blasts fired from afar, pummeling the vessel.

Even still, no enemy trap, Raith mused. Maybe he and Persepolis were both wrong.

For twenty minutes, Water Squadron continued its loops around its mother ship, flirting with Alpha Squadron in their own courtship above their protectorate. Banter passed back and forth between the pilots like life and death weren't on the line, and it reminded Raith of his days, decades ago, from well before he was a racer. He'd flown with IS-SEC for a few years, and for a few more, he'd flown with pirates. He'd seen almost every home of humanity, from Emerald Jewel to HEROS. Only place he hadn't visited was Orion, but those colonists were crazy to travel so far anyway.

Yet the name Conglomerate eluded him. Why? He stepped back to the days before entering prison, before his crash. Before he'd failed Hector and his crew. He was racing in the Solar Sprint, about to hit the Thread. He'd owed creditors. They were why he crashed. To win the odds placed on—not the Conglomerate. He was thinking of the Venus Vacation Corporation. The casinos, and their underground sports betting rings . . . known as the Conglomerate. Could they be one and the same?

Possibly.

If so . . . was this attack about him?

"Hey Olive." He pulled up a private channel. "You and Theren. You targeted me, picked me up the second my sentence ended. Did . . . did you happen to know if anyone else had a lead on me?"

"Hmmm." She expanded the channel to include Persepolis. "Hey Persy"—Nicknames? Raith wanted to destroy a neural node at the thought—"The dossiers Theren provided. Who was targeting Raith along with us?"

Raith nodded. So they weren't the only ones seeking him out. Good to know, in case a more favorable opportunity arose.

"Oh, interesting theory." Persepolis sent them a file. "And I think it warrants credence. Right after you left Dagestan, a crew often employed by the Conglomerate entered the system and arrived at the prison asking about Raith. Looks like they had faulty information on his parole hearing!"

"You sound way too excited, Persepolis," Raith said.

"Just intrigued. Anyway, turns out while we thought maybe the crew just wanted to hire you, with this new development, perhaps the Conglomerate itself was seeking you out? Why might that be?"

"Oh, you know, I may or may not still owe them five million. Apparently they . . . expanded a bit while I was in prison."

Olive laughed. "You're joking."

"Oh, no, I owe them five million."

Persepolis removed the dossier from their screens. "This changes my calculations. If their target is you, then . . ."

"Persy?" Olive said. "You there?"

"Yes, one second."

How many perspectives you got running? You can't set one aside?"

"Don't tell me how to run my body."

Ignoring the snide comment, Raith considered the options. The enemy had placed a minefield throughout the system, meaning they'd had time to prep. If they wanted one person, then—"Wait, what about a vac-suit boarding party?"

"Crazy, but possible," Olive said.

"Transmitting new orders now," Persepolis said. "Alpha Squadron, engage the frigate. Water Squadron, enter the hangar and—"

Something rattled Raith's ship. "What the—" He looked up, a metallic hand on the perma-glass. "Uh. I've got company."

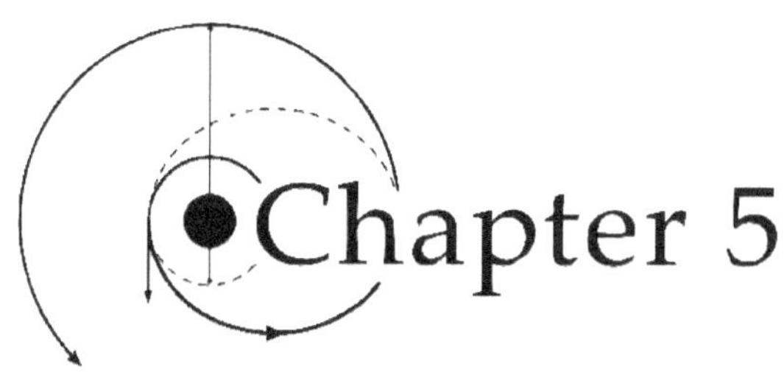# Chapter 5

"Water Squadron, all hands on deck!" Olive's voice resounded across the flight group's com, their tight formation displayed clearly on Raith's HUD. "We've got . . . got . . . got—"

Silence.

Seconds later, all incoming data from outside his DS-10 disappeared. Raith was alone.

Except not. A blade ejected from the arm of the metallic hand resting on the screen, beginning to scrape at the glass. "You're jamming me, and now you're trying to kill my ship?" he said into the void. "It's been twenty years, and now you finally decide you want me? I've literally been stuck in the same spot every day. Inside a prison. What the actual hell?" Raith shifted in his seat, looking for any sort of weapon he could use. Nothing. Stray objects were never a good idea in a non grav-controlled vessel. So. He was flying without metrics, but he wasn't flying without controls. Time to think quickly.

Conglomerate wanted him. For a second, he considered letting them win. They wouldn't go to this extent to kill him, so they wanted him alive. Not a bad proposition. However, he'd not spent two decades in prison for an immediate return to servitude under his creditors. He wanted to race again, not run con jobs for criminal overlords.

It was difficult to see, with the sparks flying off the canopy of his ship, but he was an SI. He could make this maneuver work. Synthetic instinct took over. Raith jerked his joystick up, diving straight toward Persepolis's hull. To his squadron, the move probably looked like suicide, but he couldn't talk to them. All he could do was act.

Five. Four. Three. Two. One. Now. He spun the DS-10, his cockpit parallel to carbon-steel plating. Persepolis was "above" him, relatively speaking, placing his assailant between them like a sandwich. "Time to press you," Raith muttered. "*Nobody* touches me while I fly."

Easing on the stick, the ship drifted slightly upward. The sparks above halted; presumably, his assailant guessed what Raith was planning. Three meters. Two meters. One meter.

With a muffled scrape, the sound echoing through the ship, rather than through empty vacuum, the wings of his fighter slid against the smooth outer hull of Persepolis. "Hope that didn't hurt, Persy." Raith pushed forward on the joystick, drifting away. Glancing up, it didn't look like—

A new buzzing sound from below. Whether it was the same attacker or not, someone was on the bottom of the ship, too. "They really want me. Okay, new plan." In a wide arc, he brought the fighter around so its nose pointed toward Persepolis. The hangar of the massive ship was just around the corner from his position. Perfect. "Once again, hope this doesn't hurt, Persy."

Gunning the throttle, the DS-10 blasted toward the hull. A second before impact, he pulled the ejection lever.

Raith flew through vacuum, fighters and lasers and projectiles slicing all around. Given his size, it was unlikely anything would hit him. A plume of crimson fire engulfed a tiny portion of hull a few hundred meters away, the heat rapidly disappearing into the emptiness of space. A few seconds later, the jamming signal apparently dead, a flood of information entered Raith's perceptions.

"Water Two is down, I repeat—"

"We've got infiltrators in the hangar—"

"Riot and Gamma, fall back to—"

No time to hesitate. Raith activated his emergency vacuum thrusters, thanking the maker of his MI for including *that* feature, and jetted toward the hangar. "Hey Persy, Olive, I'm back."

"Raith? Raith! Thank the universe." A blip on his UI identified Olive's fighter running circles around above the hangar. "Hold on. I see you."

"Didn't take you for the spiritual type. Oh, and Persy, I'm headed into the hangar."

"Please don't call me that," said the other SI, "I hate it."

"No time for niceties, Persy, I think Olive's rubbing off on me. What's going on inside?"

"Three infiltrators in the hangar. From what I can tell, they're headed toward—uh—toward your ship. Your racer."

Raith increased the release of propellant, flipped his trajectory, and flew through the shimmering shield, landing on his feet once inside the ship's grav-field. "All right, I can handle three. What agents do you have already targeting them?"

"Well, that's the problem, it appears they may have been my IS-SEC agents. Others on their way, but it'll be a few minutes."

"Oh that's brilliant." Raith chortled, though he could practically feel the icy stare Olive probably held. "At least IS-SEC is as corruptible as me!"

"Not funny," said Persepolis.

"I'll handle them, don't worry. Where can I find a weapon?" In response, Persy marked a security locker on Raith's AR display. "Thanks Persy!"

"Olive, is he really worth it?"

"Yes, I promise," the woman replied.

"I can still hear you both, you know," interjected Raith.

"We're aware," Olive said. "Now do your job."

"Already on it." He pried open a locker in a room off the side of the hangar and, a few seconds later, weighed a kinetic combat rifle in his hands. "It's time to hunt."

Back into the hangar he went, the expanse eerily silent. The voices of a dozen languages no longer echoed off its walls, most passengers bunkered in their ships, their cabins, or another secure location for the duration of the battle. As Raith marched between cargo stacks and landing pads, Persepolis fed him data about the positions of the IS-SEC agents converging on his new ship. His fingers tightened around the grip of his weapon. He wasn't going to let them take his ride before even having a chance to fly it.

They'd die first.

"Persy, you don't have any drones?" Raith said, crouching behind a massive container of foodstuffs. "What about MIs you can control remotely?"

"Uh, well, no," said the ship. "Uh, they may have, uh, disabled the MI and drone fabricator at the start of the battle."

"And you didn't think it pertinent to inform us while we were flying loop-de-loops around your ass?"

"I thought I had a more complete IS-SEC team! How was I supposed to know I had traitors?"

"You're too trusting."

"Boys, stop bickering," Olive muttered. "It's incredibly annoying."

"Who said I was a boy?" Persepolis groaned.

"You're acting like one."

"She's got you there," Raith said. "All right, I've got a plan in mind." He raised the rifle to his shoulder, heading around the corner. "Based on their movements, they have no idea I'm coming, yeah?"

"I'd say so," said Persepolis.

"Then I'm just gonna . . . charge right in." Raith darted around the corner of the next stack, finding the first enemy in his sights, facing toward the side-hangar holding the racing prototype. "Easy enough." Sprinting forward, he targeted the man's knees, firing two quick shots. He fell to the floor, screaming in pain. "Surprise is over. That's one, two to go."

Approaching the man, he whipped the rifle's butt around to smack the man in the head, and with a grunt, the foe keeled over face-first into the floor. Not pausing to assess his enemy's condition, Raith passed right by, slipping between two massive pods containing a strange, purple fluid. Beyond, the racer stood waiting, two—

Gunfire smashed above his head, blasting apart the glass containers and raining violet stickiness everywhere. Raith slid behind a storage locker, raising his weapon above and peppering the direction of his foes with a spray of bullets. He had no time to worry about the potentially acidic substance flowing along the floor toward his feet. A problem for another day. If he lost this ship, he lost his chance at freedom.

Gunshots responded, and he lowered his weapon to avoid losing his arms. After a few seconds, the shots ceased, giving Raith a moment to think. And he took advantage, recognizing an opening. "Hey friends, I don't think you want to kill me! I'm the one you're looking for, yeah? You tried to capture me outside, at least."

Silence.

"Look, I have no allegiances, I'm totally willing to join your side if it means I survive. I just want my ship."

More silence.

"You won't use that ship properly without the password."

Silence, then—"If you throw your weapon toward us, we will accept your surrender."

Silly humans. Raith stood, gun lowered, ready to toss it. "Of course, friends. We're all friends here." With inhuman speed, he whipped the rifle upward, firing two shots into the stomachs of each enemy. Stepping over the crate, he said, "Except you always forget SIs are *so much faster* than humans. Every time!"

The men sprawled on the floor, blood spilling onto cold steel.

"This is my ship, and it will remain my ship forever." He stalked toward the two agents, presumably from the Conglomerate. "If you've got a channel open to your bosses, make sure they know whatever they want, they're not getting. Twenty years is a long time, and if they can hold a grudge, so can I." Raith stood over the two men, fear draining blood from their faces. Even if his body had a heart, he wouldn't be remorseful. He raised his weapon, firing two more bullets between their eyes.

The next few hours passed slowly, Raith sitting against his racer, the two men dead, sprawled in pools of blood. The battle in space ended shortly thereafter. Once the frigate realized its infiltration team failed, it Jumped out of the system. Persepolis's medical team eventually picked up the third criminal agent, wounded in the leg. His skin blistered from the toxic purple mess drenching his clothes. Not until Olive arrived did Raith move. He looked up as she approached, and he threw the rifle on the floor beside his enemies.

"I've thought of a name for this ship," he said. "Not sure if you're giving me the rights to name it, but I'm giving it one regardless."

Olive's eyes widened, but she nodded.

"*Vindicta*. The Conglomerate chased me across two decades, and I'm the one who ended up in prison all those years ago, not them. If they face me down during this race, I will end them."

Olive nodded. "I would expect nothing less."

"Don't you stop me," he said.

"I won't."

# Chapter 6

Kalmykia. Raith had never been, and he still didn't have a chance to visit, even as Persepolis floated only a few thousand kilometers above its surface. Supposedly, it was an ideal, oceanic vacation world—which probably influenced QuanCom's choice for hosting their race only a few light-years away. Regardless, mere minutes after they entered orbit, a freighter entered the Persepolis's main hold, landing near the *Vindicta*. Olive and Raith met the ship's crew as they strode down its boarding ramp.

"All four served with Theren at some point over the past twenty years," Olive whispered. "All highly recommended, highly qualified. They'll be a great crew."

"I'm sure they're excited for a vacation while I do all the racing," Raith said.

No words, but Olive kicked the side of his leg.

"Just saying."

The four newcomers—two women, a man, and a non-binary they/them SI, based on the pronouns displayed through AR—approached. Awkward silence ensued. Raith and Olive were both leaning against a crate, arms crossed.

"Well?" Raith said. "You all gonna introduce yourselves or just stand there staring?"

A chorus of awkward laughter erupted from the group before smiles all around. The SI, on the left, held out their hand. "Bonta, at your service, sir! Big fan. I've watched all your races, your maneuver in the Emerald Escape was just—"

"Nice to meet you Bonta," Raith said, cutting off the gush of worship. He was already searching their profiles for their backgrounds. Doubtful they'd replace Hector, but they'd all have to try. "You must be Donyi and Erika, yes?"

"Sí, Master Raith, we are at your service," the duo said in unison.

Raith cocked his head at Olive and sent her a private message through AR. *That better not get creepy.*

"I promise, it won't," she said aloud, ignoring the looks of confusion.

"And I'm Harrison," said the man on the end, holding out his hand.

Raith shook it. "Pleasure to meet you all." Though really, Raith felt anything but pleasure. "We'll have plenty of time for pleasantries in transit to S-1022," he added, "but for now, here's how this is going to work." He and Olive hadn't prepped, but he was the racer, they hired him for this job, it was going how he wanted it to go. "I'm in charge of this team. You're used to working with synthetics like Theren or maybe Persepolis; I'm not like them. I'm not like Bonta here. I'm not your friend. I'm not your colleague. We're here to do one thing. Win a race. Anything more is a pipe dream you should crush right now. And if we win, you'll all be the crew who brought Raith back from the dead—plus five percent of the cash winnings for each of you. Understood?"

The four stared in silence.

Olive broke the second awkward moment of the day with equally awkward clapping. "All right, you heard him. No friends, just work. Enjoy the next year, and I'll see you back on the Persepolis following the culmination of the first Five-Hundred Light-year Classic!" She began to step away, in the direction her ship, the *Rift*.

Raith nodded. As he'd suspected. He almost let her leave. "A final moment, Olive."

She pivoted in stride, walking slowly backward. "Yes?"

"Thank you, for everything." He matched her backpedaling pace. "So where do you go now?"

"Oh, I've got other jobs. More people like you to find."

"And there's no way to convince you to join us?"

She paused, hand on her hip. "No. I'm sorry, Raith, but it's time for you to go your own way. Those four . . . they'll take care of you."

He doubted that, but he wasn't going to push her on the idea. Instead, he simply shrugged.

"Though Raith," she said. "Something to consider. The universe is a big place. This race is a single moment for you. Take advantage, but don't forget the bigger picture."

"And what's that?"

"You have the potential to make your mark. In a universe so vast, when we're forced to live day-by-day finding a way to live amongst all this craziness, there are few people like you. Don't waste the opportunities given to you. Many will come."

"I don't think I fully understand what you mean," he replied. "I'm not that special. I just like to race."

"You'll know soon enough." She turned around, resuming her jaunt toward the *Rift*.

"It's been good working with you, Olive," he said. "Catch you around."

"You too, Raith. You'll prove everyone wrong."

The freighter, tagged the *Juniper*, was piloted by Bonta and crewed by the other three. For the final leg of the journey, Raith was their passenger; the *Vindicta* clamped to the bottom-side of the freighter for transit. No need to give it any wear or tear.

After final disembarking procedures with Persepolis, the *Juniper* headed on its way and smoothly made its jump toward S-1022, a brief weeklong trip. Raith leaned into a couch in the ship's common room, content not to speak to a single person until they arrived. He'd read their profiles. They'd be of assistance, but not in the impending fight. If he was right, and the Conglomerate attempted to impede his victory, these four would be of little help. Possibly even an impediment.

His peace was short-lived, however. A few minutes after Jumping toward S-1022, the crew of the *Juniper* converged.

"Good afternoon, Raith," said Harrison. The man was rough-skinned, his complexion like coal. Arms crossed, his black jacket made him look like he *thought* he was in charge. "A mighty speech you had back there."

"Thanks friend," Raith said.

Donyi and Erika sat at the table across from him. Both wore purple hair up in a bun, green jumpsuits tight against their skin. "We respect your independence," said Donyi. "You're gonna need that gusto out on the track. Sure. We expected it."

Erika leaned forward. "We more than expected it; it's one of the reasons we identified you as a top candidate for Olive to consider."

Raith sat up. "Wait, what?"

Bonta chuckled. They were a standard SI—by Raith's estimate, a twenty-third century model. "You sir are funny! You think Miss Olive selected you all by her lonesome? Oh no no no no. She didn't design your ship. Theren did. But do you think they did it alone?"

Raith opened all four of their profiles, reading more deeply. Was this a trick? Had information been withheld from him?

Harrison tapped his fingers on the metal wall. "What you're looking for isn't there, because it's a secret. The four of us, see? We designed your ship. Built it, even."

"Nice name, by the way," Donyi said. "We approve."

"Well you might be grease-monkeys, but that doesn't—"

They all laughed, just like when they'd met inside Persepolis. Bonta said, "We're not offended. You're in charge, and we're fine with that. But it's important you understand another thing. Okay, sir? The four of us? We've been preparing for this race for the past five years. We know every bolt of *Vindicta*."

Erika leaned back in her chair, her hands raised in mock supplication. "You want to win. So do we. We're just making sure you know: if you want to win, you can't ignore us. Because we're your best chance at winning."

Raith nodded, unsure of what to say. They'd backed him into a corner. He hated it. They were probably right, but they were going to get themselves killed if they placed themselves too far into this game. He'd need to address that problem later. No time to think about it now.

"Thanks for the advice." He stood, slipped past Erika, and headed down the ship's central corridor. "I'll be in my room."

Four bogeys. Eight light-years. The upcoming checkpoint rested between the orbits of two gas giants orbiting one another in the far reaches of another uncharted system. The hole through which he needed to guide *Vindicta* was less than three kilometers wide. Anywhere outside that range, and the gravitational pull of one of the immense planets would knock him out of Jump.

Raith plotted, entering the system's plane on a vertical trajectory. Perfect. The gas giants spun around each other on his charts, creating an impossibly slow moving bullseye to target. Two minutes out. One minute.

Alarms blared, the simulation ended. Fatal error. The four ships on his tail zipped straight through the checkpoint.

"What the actual—"

"Those two planets," said a voice, "have an extra-orbital of moons given their combined mass."

"I told you not to watch my simulations," Raith said, disconnecting from AR.

"And I'm not." Bonta stepped into the room. "I'm watching the data from your simulations. And I know the course. I've studied every kilometer of it for the past three years."

"Have you flown it? Even in a simulation?"

"No, but it's all—"

"Then I don't want to hear it." Raith pushed past the other SI and into the freighter's corridor. They were a day out from S-1022, a day out from having a station on which he could escape these four annoying fools. Thinking they were better than him, knew how to fly, what he needed to do to win. He was Raith, the most decorated racer in a century.

"You agreed to work with us," Bonta said. "We're here to help."

Raith turned, pointing a metallic finger in the SI's blinking blue eyes. "I've told you how you can help."

"And we've told you how we can help."

Raith barreled into the lounge where Donyi and Erika sat sprawled on a couch, watching a soap opera. "I'm not sure what you expect me to tell you, Bonta. I've always flown on my own. It's my thing."

"That's not true and you know it." Harrison's voice echoed down the hall, most likely from the kitchen. "You had a crew."

"Don't you talk about them."

Bonta raised their hands in placation. "Look, we're not trying to replace Hector and—"

"Don't you say their names!"

"—the rest, but we know as much if not more than them about how these ships work, what this course is going to be—"

Raith lashed out, curled fingers slamming into Bonta's chestplate. "I said don't say their . . ." he held back the rest of the sentence.

The other SI stood its ground, unmoved by the punch. "I'll ignore that."

"We land in twenty-four hours," Raith said, backing away. "When we land, I'm heading straight to the bar. Don't follow me."

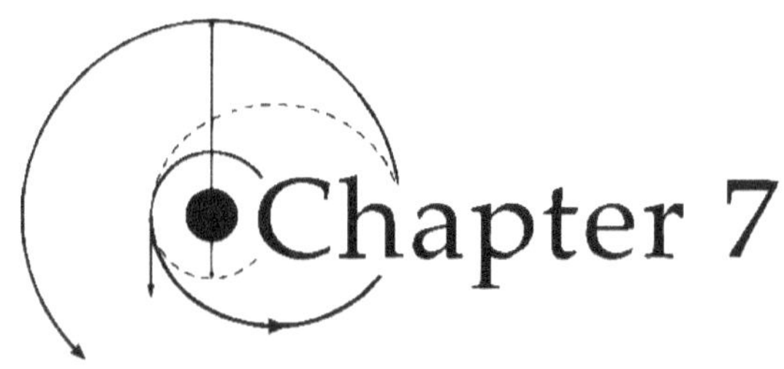

Chapter 7

S-1022: suspiciously well-populated for an unnamed system. The *Juniper* dropped out of Jump three thousand kilometers out from their destination, and as sensors brought in updated data, the ship received com traffic and engine vectors from throughout the system. Raith watched it all from his room, content to avoid the crew until they landed.

Thousands of ships darted about from dozens of space stations spread throughout the orbitals of the system's twelve planets. QuanCom's Race Hub orbited S-1022-C, the third planet and a rocky chunk without an atmosphere. The Hub was massive—at least ten kilometers in diameter—and most vectors moved between it and other destinations. Raith pulled up data on the other stations . . . of course. Party boats for the wealthy, waiting for the race to begin.

Less than an hour later, the *Juniper* contacted the Hub's transit authority, and they received a berth in one of its immense hangars. When an alert chimed, notifying him they were locked in and landed, Raith darted out his room, not pausing in the lounge to speak with his "crew," and headed down a ramp not even fully extended. To their credit, his four shipmates said nothing, letting him leave. Better that way. They needed to stay out of his way.

Reaching the hangar floor, he glanced up, noting *Vindicta* still safely attached to the *Juniper*'s hull. He was already going through the AR motions of scheduling a practice run outside. He ached for the opportunity to fly the thing for real, rather than in simulation. Once he actually flew it for real, he'd iron out the kinks and figure out how to nail the sections of the course he kept screwing up.

Their hangar was massive, though it looked like they shared it with a few other teams. Raith gazed around, noting three racing pinnaces each as beautiful as his own. Crews darted about, finishing paint jobs and tuning thrusters. Exo fuel canisters lined the walls, ready to replenish Jump-cores between practices runs and laps. Raith's olfactory sensors kicked in, and copious amounts of ozone and neon filled the air. The elements' presence reminded him of the good old days.

With a casual gait, Raith strolled through the hangar, heading toward its exit a few dozen meters away. No one paid him any attention—just another SI in a sea of faces—and he passed through the door, his already-cleared credentials logging his arrival at the Hub. He'd filed all the registration paperwork while in-transit. As he walked, he pulled up a list of the racers already approved for qualification. Four hundred and sixty confirmed participants, with another seventy awaiting acceptance. So there'd be a bubble for qualifying, if they kept their goal of five hundred racers at the start. Bubbles always made things interesting. Qualifying became more aggressive.

He searched the list, hoping he'd recognize a few names. Felix. Familiar—an SI from Mars, Raith was pretty certain they raced half a century ago. Xi Kim—nope. Sanderson—nope. Carter Ricks—nope. Eduardo—he stopped. Eduardo Gueirez . . . Carlos. Of course. The Gueirez mentioned in the bar when he first left prison? A new Gueirez.

He'd known a Gueirez. He'd lost his last race to a Carlos. There'd always been rumors the two racers were romantically involved, but . . . how old could this son be? The names were common. Could be someone else. He added an extra query for the racers bio.

Twenty-one years. Eduardo Gueirez-Carlos was the son of Victor Gueirez and Husan Carlos. Victor hadn't been in the last Solar Sprint, but Husan Carlos was a dick. His son couldn't be any more polite. This race just kept getting better and better.

He kept searching, hoping no other past-triggering names showed up. He searched "Kana" just for good measure, in case the racer had a relative with a grudge against him, but the query returned no results. At least he wouldn't have to face a jury of angry fans targeting him—alongside an obsession for whomever their new love was—for accidentally killing their former hero. Well, anything was possible. Race fans had a long memory.

But Gueirez-Carlos? He might be a problem.

Lost in his thoughts, Raith absent-mindedly walked right into the bar, following the directions overlaid on his HUD. As he opened the door, a cacophony of sounds erupted and overwhelmed his perceptions. Nothing like the Rusty Convict back on Dagestan, the tavern, named the Lightspeed Café, apparently housed every person on the station and then some. Packed to the brim, racers and engineers shouted for their drinks. In booths along the wall, parties clamored over each other's voices. In the back, a dance floor erupted and pounded to the sound of the techno-babble currently known as "music." SIs and humans gyrated in sync with one another, their bodies entangled in a web so dense it was impossible to know who was with whom.

Raith approached the bar, accessing its menu. Skipping past the drink, he paid the SI visiting fee without looking at its price, charging it to the *Juniper*'s accounts. He assumed One Synthetic was picking up all expenses, including his social sojourns. He'd make certain of it, because he planned on visiting the bar quite a bit.

His charge approved, Raith moseyed about without worrying about a bouncer taking unwarranted notice. This was his crowd. His people. Racers and their crews, mingling without a care for the worries of the ICH or any governmental body. They flew for the thrill of it, and then afterward, they reminisced. He bobbed his head. Above one bar, an old-time series of screens played vintage recordings of twentieth and twenty-first century circuits. Indianapolis. Daytona. Monaco. Le Mans. And was that . . . he chuckled. The old wonky in-atmosphere races from the early decades of the twenty-first, back on Earth. Such pitiful competitions, though hilarious to watch.

Passing the bars, Raith reached a room off to the side with a dozen or so green, visually empty tables. As he walked under an arched threshold, AR kicked in, revealing the colored cards in players' hands and cascading dice bouncing along randomly generated paths. If the bar was home, this was his playground.

Without pausing, he approached an open seat at one of the poker tables. The virtual dealer nodded to him, and he squeezed in between two human men engrossed in the game. As cards appeared in hand, their values visible only to him, the men nodded, welcoming him without words. His other competitors were two women paying more attention to each other's faces than their chips, and an SI who looked bored out of—he checked for pronouns—her mind.

Raith threw in a hundred, giving him a hundred chips. The blind was five, and he called it immediately after seeing his cards. A king and a queen gave him plenty of options.

"Pot's good," said the SI, after glancing down at her cards.

Three cards flipped, revealing a five of diamonds, three of hearts, and a ten of clubs. Apparently, none of the cards worked for anyone else, for they all checked around the table. A jack flipped, and Raith laughed. Of course his first hand sets him up for a classic risk. A roughly one-in-thirteen chance an ace flipped, but . . . it was worth a shot. "Twenty," he said when it was his turn.

No one looked up from their cards, though signals through AR noted all but one of the women called. The next card flipped. Ace of diamonds. "All in," he said.

In turn, each of his opponents looked at him with bemusement, but one of the men called while everyone else folded. He'd clearly been sitting there for a few hours; his pot ranged somewhere close to a thousand. Cards flipped, Raith won, and his spirits rose. "This is going to be a good night," he said. No one responded. "For me," he added.

Another few hands passed without much fanfare, and the lack of engagement from his fellow players started to annoy Raith. This wasn't what he remembered. Where were the jeers? The jovial jabs? Probably just a bad table. He prepared to check out and switch tables—his winnings so far would allow him a buy-in with a higher stakes table—when footsteps clattered from behind.

"Well look wha' we 'ave 'ere," said a voice.

Swiveling in his chair to find the newcomer, Raith twisted face-to-face with Eduardo Gueirez-Carlos. Great. He turned back to his table.

"Look everyone!" Eduardo's slurred voice revealed his lack of sobriety. "We got oursel'es a relic! It's Raith, back from the dead!"

Without looking away from his cards, Raith said, "I was never dead, Eduardo."

"Oh right, but you were dead to your fans. What's the difference?"

Raith splayed his fingers on the table, his cards momentarily fading from AR. He needed to let the words go. Jumping back into the racing world had opened him up for these attacks. An acceptable risk.

"I'm surprised they let you in," Eduardo added. "Not because of your crimes. You did your time. You know, because you're not even a racer anymore. Twenty years"—he hiccuped—"without a race?"

Raith clicked cash out, forfeiting the chips on the table. He stood, turning to face his verbal assailant. "You look at me, boy. You say those words to my face."

"Heh. You. Can't. Race."

Raith laughed. "And neither could your fathers." He was baiting him now, knowing what the boy would say next. He didn't care.

"Oh old man, is that what you told yourself these past twenty years when you tried to dream away every race you cooked?"

Raith glanced toward the poker room's entrance, where a large, straight-shirted man pushed his way through the crowd toward them. "I was able to cook those races," Raith said, "because I could fly. I did what your parents wished they could do. Every racer wished. I just got sloppy."

"Or maybe because you made a few mistakes that put you on the wrong side of the road, we hear." Raith now noticed the three other men standing around Eduardo, their shirts slightly unzipped. "Maybe you jerked around the wrong folks, indebting yourself to a few johns too many?"

Ah, the toxicity of the racing crews never died. Raith sighed. The straight-laced bouncer was leaning against the doorframe, watching. "Is this really the fight you want to pick today, boys?"

"You almost killed my pa twenty years ago, Raith," Eduardo said. "I'm going to end you out on the racecourse . . . just like you ended Kana."

With those words, Raith's fist connected with the kid's chin.

Hours later, Raith looked up as Bonta and Harrison drifted into the security office. Raith, back pushed into his chair, smiled as they approached.

"Seriously?" Bonta said. "A fight, less than two hours after we landed?"

"Hey, he practically—"

"We saw the footage," Harrison said. "You started it. You could have walked away, and you threw the first punch."

"He had it coming."

"Eduardo might be a punk, but he's a rich punk. He *will* do what he can to kick you out of this race before it even starts."

"Get up," Bonta said, motioning with their hand. The SI nodded to the security officer, who returned the gesture. "One Synthetic coffered the fine. But we've been told if you do this again, it *will* come out of your final cut. You're lucky QuanCom wants you in this race. The administrators are raving mad at you."

Raith read between the lines. He was lucky QuanCom thought they could make money off his presence in the race. "Whatever."

"That's all you have to say?"

"Thanks?"

"Sure." Bonta motioned for him to follow, and Raith finally rose from his seat. "I guess you're right, by the way."

Raith waited to respond until they were out in one of the long hallways of the Hub. "About what?"

"You're not our friend." Bonta glanced over their shoulder. "I wouldn't want to be your friend."

Chapter 8

It was morning, based on the Hub's established local time, and Raith stood beneath *Vindicta*. The hangar drones detached it from *Juniper* last night, and it stood on its struts beside the freighter. More importantly, his practice berth had arrived. For the first time, he had the opportunity to fly his baby.

Erika approached, Donyi by her side. "All right, Raith, you ready?" Thankfully, only Erika spoke that time, rather than from both their mouths.

Apparently, they were the two behind the "cockpit" of the prototype. As he stared up at the meta-nodes and sensors inside the craft, he admitted it looked impressive. He couldn't imagine the trillions of calculations needed to ensure his mind properly integrated with the ship's framework. Well, he could, he just didn't want to.

"I'm ready," Raith said, not bothering to voice his compliment. The platform on which he stood began to rise. "What do I do?"

"Just prepare your mind," said Donyi. "The ship will do the rest."

He nodded, not really sure what to make of the idea. The platform reached the bottom of the *Vindicta*, and a light electric tingle signaled the attempts of the ship to connect with him. Releasing any safeguards, Raith leaned into the experience, and a grav-field grabbed his body, pulling him the rest of the way into the ship. His limbs slotted into position as if he were wearing a massive mech suit, and his head slipped into a socket. Once his body fitted into place—perfectly molded for his model, Raith noted—the ship's hull began to close around him.

"We'll be on the microphones," Erika and Donyi said, returning to their eerie team-speak. "Bonta is transmitting you the practice course. It's an elliptic outside the ecliptic. Very fast, very safe."

"Well that's boring," Raith said.

"It's just to check the ship's systems. All racers must practice the course on simulations only."

"I know, I know, but . . ."

"We get it, you want to race."

The ship closed fully, leaving him in darkness. For a moment, he laid there, waiting for something to happen. He considered whether it was all an elaborate prank. Maybe the ship wouldn't work, and now the Conglomerate had an easy way to ship him to their facilities for processing. Then . . .

A rainbow of perceptions exploded, bombarding his mind with a million waves of data. It was nearly overwhelming, but as his synthetic neural framework adapted to the ship's systems, processing the new capabilities of his sensory faculties, it felt . . . natural. Like slipping on a glove. The ship's sensors, and the millions of light-lengths they could detect, became his eyes. Its engines became his legs. Its thrusters, his arms. He joined the ship—they were one. Now he understood what an SI like Persepolis experienced. Why they loved what they were. He could get used to this.

"How do you feel?" Donyi's voice echoed inside his head. "What do you see?"

"I see the entire universe," he said. "Everything. I'm alive, like never before. I'm home."

⁘⦿ ⁘⦿ ⁘⦿

After a short Jump from the Hub to beyond the ecliptic plane, Raith received his path from Bonta. QuanCom's new tech truly achieved what it said it could achieve—simultaneous tracking and networking of hundreds of ships at Jump. Data pouring in, he noted the dozens of other racers flirting along various other paths in a mesmerizing display of Jump trails around the system. Almost impossible to catch, but they were there, weaving a shell of ovoid vectors around the star. He was ready to join them.

"You read me?" said Bonta. "You ready to do this?"

"I'm all in," Raith said.

"Then connect to the QuanCom transmitter."

Raith mentally nodded, and his consciousness expanded to reveal the new system, waiting on the horizon of his mind. Embracing it, the information received from the Hub transformed from simple charts to real-time, overlaid symbols indicating the dozens of ships looping past. Even though they were millions of kilometers away, their courses and velocities generated and shifted in tandem with one another. He could see the exact locations of the other racers on their practice circuits, beyond what his traditional sensors could immediately detect.

"You're using Vector Thirteen," Bonta said. "See it?"

He signaled in the affirmative.

"Then we're ready when you are."

Raith smiled. Racing was what he was born to do. He pulled up a datasheet transmitted by QuanCom, revealing the current records for Vector Thirteen. Thirteen seconds. He measured its distance, chuckling. Based on the *Vindicta*'s metrics, he was going to blow that record into the void.

Using the ship's thrusters, he drifted into position, matching the kilometer-wide path of his assigned course. Checking his diagnostics, he primed the Jump-core with Exo, ready for its strange warping field to surround him. The Jump earlier to clear the ecliptic had been refreshing, but it had only lasted a few seconds. He was ready for a sustained burn. He craved it.

"Three seconds," he said.

"Roger," Bonta replied.

"Here we go." Raith gunned the ignition; reality disappeared.

When Jumping, light didn't work normally. When bending space, both in front and behind a craft in order to relatively break traditional laws of physics, things got . . . weird. And now, as Raith enveloped himself in every sensor of the *Vindicta*, he experienced a world he never thought possible. Brilliant colors, millions of them beyond the visible light spectrum, fragmented and surrounded his mind. Every centimeter of his body pushed and pulled with the whir of the Jump-core, practically feeling space distort around him. The ship's relative velocity creeped upward, bypassing 100 JD within seconds. He kept pushing the engine, knowing this ship had the potential for so much more. By the time he finished his first lap around Vector Thirteen, he crossed 400 JD.

"Oh hell yeah!" he screamed over their coms. "Bonta, you catching this?"

"We're tracking you, and hearing you loud and clear. How's the Quan-Com data?"

"Crystal," Raith replied. "Tracking the other vectors perfectly."

"Wonderful. We're tracking you at 424 JD. Sound about right?"

"That's what I have. And we need to break 650 to crack the record."

"Well I don't think—"

"Bonta, I need to know what this baby can do. I'm in the moment. Trust me." Raith took their silence as acquiescence, and he increased the injection of Exo. "Let's show 'em what we can do."

After the next lap, he broke 600 JD. As boring as the elliptical loop was, he enjoyed its simplicity. It reminded him of a few of the classic circuits in the core worlds. Or, more precisely, the classics he'd seen on the screens in the Lightspeed Café. Everything QuanCom established for the Five Hundred Light-year Classic clicked into place. If they succeeded, they were going to set a standard in racing for centuries to come, mirroring the significance of the race's namesake.

On his next lap, he averaged the loop at 625 JD. As he crossed the line, *Vindicta* peaked at 651 JD. "Here we go, friends. Time to gun it."

After completing seven laps, he'd gotten used to the slight gravitational anomalies of the loop caused by the varying positions of the planets throughout S-1022. On the first half of the loop, at least three sectors had slight drag, with one of the gas giants less than a light minute away. As he hit each sector, he adjusted the ship's Jump trajectory accordingly, accounting for the tiny pulls aching to slip him off-course. On the second half of the loop, the ship hit a dead zone, the closest body nearly a light-hour away. He leaned into the pull of the star, letting it guide his arc. Blazing through the final sector, Raith checked the data. An average of 657 JD. Twelve and a half seconds, breaking the circuit's record by half a second.

He began to throttle back, bringing *Vindicta*'s pace down to a more reasonable number as he continued the loops. But he'd shown them. His crew, the other racers, everyone. Raith was back.

Chapter 9

Raith guided the *Vindicta* into the hangar, landing it beside the *Juniper*. A crowd was forming along the wall, his crew motioning to keep them back from his berth. "And so the hype begins," he said aloud, though no ears could hear him.

The ship landed, and as the hull unfolded around him, the platform rose to meet him. Once it was a meter or two from the bottom of the ship, the field holding him in place released, and he dropped down, landing nimbly on his feet. The platform descended, and as it reached the hangar floor, Raith strode smoothly off and toward Harrison, who was waving away reporters.

"Harrison, Harrison, let them come!" Raith said, resting his hand on the man's shoulder. "This is what we wanted with our run, right?" They revealed the speed of the *Vindicta*, though not its max. Raith had made certain not to reveal how fast they could make it truly go. He would save that for qualification and the race. Now, time to embrace the media.

"If you insist," Harrison said.

Raith stepped forward, drone cameras floating above a throng of screaming journalists.

"Raith, welcome back to the land of the living," said a woman, a black drone floating above her head. "Kate Everett, QuanCom Media. Can we get a statement on your record on Vector Thirteen?"

"Twelve and a half seconds," he said. "Speaks for itself."

The crowd clamored. Another voice said, "Farit Kaliff, SLM. You've not raced in twenty years, what makes this one practice run change things?"

"Don't let those twenty years bother you. I'm in my prime. No one can beat me out on that course."

The questions continued, and he flirted back in forth between arrogance and bravado. After a few minutes, he lifted his hand. "No more questions, please, I have simulations to run."

Before he could turn, a voice said, "Can we expect you to throw this race too?"

Raith stopped his pivot, looking for the origin of the question. No one stepped forward to claim the words, though everyone looked at him expectantly, awaiting an answer. "Look here," he said. "You all might think you knew me, but you didn't. I had my reasons for what I did, but I'm looking for an honorable race. By the books, by the rules. And I intend to win."

"Is that why you punched Eduardo last night?"

Instead of responding, Raith walked away, toward the *Juniper*. Harrison stepped forward to usher the reporters out of the hangar. Donyi, Erika, and Bonta leaned against the hull of the freighter, faces grim. As he approached, he spread his arms wide. "They love me."

"Some of them, perhaps," Bonta remarked. "You've got a tough past to overcome."

"I've also got big shoes of my own to fill. They expect a lot of me. They expect a show."

"You're giving them a show all right," Harrison said, approaching from behind. "But . . . great job out there. I mean it. I think we all do."

The two women nodded, as did Bonta. Raith chuckled. "We've got this race in the bag."

"Maybe," Bonta replied. "Back to the simulations? You'll actually let us join you this time?"

"Nope!" Raith bounded up the ramp of the *Juniper*, leaving them behind as Erika and Donyi prattled off a slur of swears, presumably directed at him. "Let them grumble," he muttered. "This race is all but mine."

⌁ ⌁ ⌁

Three more days, three more practice runs, three more records. Every time he landed, more reporters clamored for a word, but he learned from the first day. No quotes. He smiled, waved, and walked straight up the ramp into the *Juniper*. He might stop and chat with the crew for a moment about any hiccups during the run, but then it was straight to the simulator . . . where he still couldn't pass the ninth light-year without a failure. He needed to be perfect if he wanted to win. He needed to be perfect if he wanted to properly *qualify*, and only a month separated them from the first qualifying runs.

Competitors continued to arrive, breaking the official five-hundred entrant mark with another two hundred added to the wait list. As the date neared, more and more racers decided to finally throw their name in the ring of the mysterious "Five Hundred Light-year Classic." Raith figured, more likely, teams had planned all along to join; they simply didn't wish to show their cards until the last moment.

In the evenings, Raith frequented the poker den—thankfully, they hadn't banned him—and whenever Eduardo showed up to heckle, Raith contained his rage, stepping out and returning to the *Juniper*.

And now, it was the seventh day at the Hub. After a particularly fine few rounds at a table, Raith collected his winnings and exited the club, heading back toward the hangar. He thought he heard the clatter of footsteps behind him in the empty hallway, but when he turned, he saw only shadows.

Entering the hangar from the far side, he walked past their neighbors and their ships. He hadn't bothered to learn their names, because he wasn't here to make friends. Their ships were fancy, but nothing compared to the *Vindicta*. Reaching the third berth, the sound of a ball bouncing reached his audio-receptors. Passing a wall of crates, he found a man sitting on a box, throwing a ball against the wall. Paying him no mind, Raith walked right by.

"I'm surprised you haven't said hello yet," the man said.

Raith stopped, turning to face him. "Am I supposed to know you?"

The ball continued bouncing against the wall. "No. But our ships have sat next to each other for a week. I figured you would have connected the dots by now."

"About?"

The man smiled. "Your records."

Raith wracked his brain for context. "No idea."

The ball stopped bouncing, and the man stood. "Name's Carter Ricks. I race the *Bloodhound*, and every record you've broken was set by me."

"Do I get an award?"

Carter placed a hand on his hip. "You're an impressive racer, Raith. I've been watching every one of your runs. Your ship is almost as beautiful as mine."

"More so."

"I disagree, but it's your prerogative to love your ship."

Raith clicked his fingers against his head. "Is there a point to this conversation?"

"Just wanted to let you know if you want a friend, I'm here," said Carter. "You're a good racer. Everyone sees it. But you've not actually sat down with a single competitor the whole time you've been here. Gotten to know your opponents. I know you used to have your comrades, back on the pro circuits. Talk shop with them."

"And you think you can be one of those people? I've never heard your name."

Carter chuckled. "Don't need fame to be friendly, Raith. We're going to be racing against each other for the next year. Might as well get to know one another."

"Thanks, but no thanks."

"Suit yourself."

Raith nodded, not sure what else to say. Carter chucked his ball back at the wall. Seeing the conversation as over, he sauntered away.

"Oh, and Raith?" Carter called. "I know you're holding the throttle back. Pro tip? All of us are."

Raith paused in stride at the comment. He went to respond, but instead, he just smiled. Good intel to have. He finished the next fifty meters to reach the *Juniper*, and he was about to step up the ramp, when a door in the hangar's wall slid open.

"Raith?"

Just when he was about to get some peace and quiet, another interruption. "Yes? Who's asking?"

"A friend would like to speak with you. Please, come with me."

Raith turned toward the voice, seeing a man in a green sport coat, waiting. What was with everyone calling him their friend? "I've got work to do," Raith simply replied.

"And this is related to your work." The man motioned with his hand. "Come on, she's waiting."

Raith shrugged. Weapons were banned on the station. What was the worst that could happen? He stepped toward the mysterious courier. "All right, I'll bite."

⁂

The man led him to an apartment a kilometer or so from the hangar, deep in a part of the station Raith had yet to visit. His AR display kept track of the route, in case he needed to make a speedy retreat. Passing through a final set of doors, they entered a luxurious set of rooms, complete with crystalline chandeliers and candles—real, wax candles—hanging from the ceiling. A little over the top, but Raith appreciated the opulence.

Seated at a table, a woman in all black, including a helmet, waited. His escort said, "Raith, I present to you Vanaka."

Without waiting for permission, Raith pulled a seat out from the table on the far side from his hostess. "Am I supposed to know you?"

"No." A respirator of some kind modulated her voice.

"Oh boy, here we go." Raith upped his emergency protocols, searching the room for any hidden weapons or assailants. "Always gotta love the annoying style of the Conglomerate."

"No need to worry," the deep voice said. "You're safe here. We heard about the group who tried to pick you off en-route, but we're following the rules, just like everyone else."

"Sure. Act like you're not with them. So what do you want?"

"What do you think?"

Raith sighed. "Your five million?"

She laughed, and Raith joined her in the chortle, unsure he understood the joke. When she finished, she said, "You think everything is about money, Raith. We expect you to do what we want, or we will end you when this race ends. You could be so much greater, you know? Especially if you were with us."

"So what? You simply expect me to lose?"

She laughed again, its echo through her voice modulator making the sound increasingly uncomfortable to hear. "Not lose. We want you to win."

"Oh?"

"We want you to win, and when you're done, we want you—and your ship."

"Oh." Raith grimaced. It all made sense. The attack on Persepolis and the *Goliath* had attempted to capture both him and the *Vindicta*. Perhaps they'd wanted to have him race for them in the ship, but now that he'd arrived safe and sound, they wanted to make sure he won.

"So what's happening? Are you going to be working to disrupt the other racers, ensure I win?"

"I didn't say that."

Raith nodded. "Look, I know what you're going for here. I'll consider your offer."

"It's not up for consideration."

Raith slammed his hand down on the table, silverware clattering and bouncing against ceramic plates. "I paid my time, all right? Twenty years. I'm not going to fall into your silly traps again."

"You don't want to cross us," said Vanaka. "You don't want us as an enemy."

"You've held a grudge against me for two decades, I think you can wait a little longer to see it paid. Just let me race for once. I think it's time I left."

"We'll make your life a living hell, Raith. We aren't who you think we are."

"Whatever. Your little parlor tricks and charades mean nothing to me." He stood to leave, pushing the chair back under the table. While heading toward the door, the rat-like, green-coated man unlocked it.

"Oh and Raith?" said Vanaka. "See you out there on course."

He quickly searched her name. Of course. She was a racer, too, and sponsored by none other than QuanCom. Of course.

# Chapter 10

They started small, but the rumors only grew. By the end of the second week, a number of tabloid-esque media outlets ran stories speculating Raith intended to cook the race again. Photos—clearly doctored, but impressive, nevertheless—showed him meeting people in black alcoves of the Hub, handing off credits. The headlines said he was bribing other racers to bow out, to crash other racers, just like he crashed Kana when running the Io Thread.

It sickened his circuits, and he continued losing focus. Worse, he was locked in simulation limbo, failing the ninth light-year every time.

Every day, he exited the simulation, ran another practice vector, smashed a record, and returned to the simulation. Every day, he failed the run. What made things more frustrating? He had no way to know how other racers were faring on the simulation. While he was only testing certain segments—no point practicing floating through four light-years worth of dark space—he began to wonder. What if no one was pulling perfect runs? If everyone failed, they were all on a level playing field.

So with two weeks left before qualifying, Raith stepped off the *Juniper* and walked across the hangar to the *Bloodhound*. He could have just talked to Bonta, but he still didn't trust his crew.

So maybe Carter could be of use.

Raith approached, hearing the telltale bounce of the man's ball. Walking around the edge of a crate, Raith tapped on the metal container.

Carter looked up. "Hello there, friend."

"Still not your friend."

"Whatever you say."

Raith walked to the wall where the man bounced his ball and leaned against it. The ball continued to pass back and forth between steel and man. "I have a question."

"Great, so do I," Carter replied.

"Then we can swap questions."

"Sounds good to me."

Raith caught the next throw of the ball. "Are you using the simulations at all?" Raith threw the ball back to the man.

Carter nodded, catching it. "Of course. Are you actually going to throw the race?" He threw the ball.

"Absolutely not," likewise catching it. With another toss, Raith said, "Have you beat the eighth light-year?"

Carter chuckled as he caught the ball. "Nope. Why, are there rumors floating about?"

The passes continued. "The Conglomerate is trying to bribe me."

"Honesty, I like it."

Raith stifled a smile. "Do you think anyone is beating the technical sections of the simulation?"

"Maybe. Not every time, I doubt. Too much randomness baked into the code."

Randomness. What? So—"

"Nope, my turn for a question. Are you going to break under the will of the Conglomerate before this is all over? Can I trust you out on the course?"

Raith tapped his foot. "I don't know."

"As I said, honesty." Carter furled his brow. "I like it."

"You're a strange man, Carter Ricks. Not like any racer I've ever met."

"I could say the same about you."

Raith nodded. It was true. There weren't many SI racers. "Last question. Were you telling the truth when you said everyone was holding back their throttle on the practice runs?"

Carter laughed, slapping his knee in sync with his final toss. "I think you know the answer, my friend."

⁂

Raith returned to the *Juniper*, finding his crew seated in the common area. "We need to talk," Harrison said.

"Yes, father," Raith said. "I'm here for discipline. What can I do for you?"

"Can you take this seriously for one second?" Donyi said. Erika stayed silent. "We're ready to leave you here, on your own. This is ridiculous."

"Hey!" Raith raised his hands. "I didn't ask for you all. You should have known what you were getting when you targeted me. If you can't learn to work with me, then leave. What do I care?"

"Raith," Bonta said, his voice measured. "If we leave, so does the ship."

"Wait, what?"

Harrison grimaced, resting his hand on the table. "I didn't want to pull this card, but I thought I made it clear the first day you set foot on the *Juniper*. Take a seat."

Raith reluctantly obliged, plopping onto one of the cabin's couches.

"All right. I'm listening."

The man nodded, revealing the graying ends of his black hair. "Good. Now listen up. You're part of a team. We are that team. You are going to let us run this team *like a team*."

"Look, I know—"

"Raith, let the damn man finish speaking!" Bonta said.

"Right." Raith swiveled his head to face the other SI. "Fine."

"Thank you, Bonta," Harrison said. "So I don't know what the hell happened to you in prison, but this is not the synth-psyche profile we pulled when we selected you. You used to be part of a team, man! They were your family, you all worked together like clockwork. You're not even giving us the chance to work with you. So what do we need to do to make you feel comfortable?"

Thankfully, they hadn't mentioned Hector's name. Or any of the others. "Look, I—"

"He's still not finished," said Erika and Donyi in unison.

"Okay, seriously, you both need to tell me what's up or cut that out," Raith said.

Their eyes widened at his outburst toward them. "Look, you don't understand a thing about how our mind works, if you would actually pay attention to someone other than yourself—ugh. Forget it."

Harrison stared at the ceiling, clearly frustrated at how this meeting was going. "All right, here's how it's going to go down. You're going to start by talking to us about everything. *Everything*. If you want the *Vindicta* to remain here with you so you can race, you've got two weeks to get your act together. And that starts with telling us what the hell is going on. Why you won't let us work with you on the simulations. Why you play as much poker as an alcoholic drinks. *Why you met with Vanaka two weeks ago without saying a word to anyone*."

Raith's eyes widened, nodding in understanding. "Were you spying on me?"

Bonta shrugged. "I followed you. We know where every racer is sleeping."

"You followed me?" Raith couldn't believe it. His own crew, spying on him. "How can I trust you if you're spying on me?"

"We don't know a damn thing about you because you *won't talk to us*," Harrison said.

Raith slammed a fist against the wall. "Because I don't like who I am!" The room went silent. His eyes drifted from corner to corner, avoiding contact with any of the people in the room. "You happy now?"

Erika and Donyi stood, approaching him.

"What are you doing?"

The pair arrived by his side, enveloping him in a massive sandwich of a hug.

"This is ridiculous."

"Raith, open your eyes, look beyond your mind, and see the people around you for what they are." They released the hug. "Who do you think we are?"

Raith stared up at the two women, noticing for the first time, more. Simply more. More than the fact they were practically tied at the hip. More than their weird voice thing. Green eyes, ochre skin, colorful, wispy hair. "You're twins," he said. He noticed the scars on their heads. "You were . . . conjoined twins."

"Correct," they said at the same time. "And do you know why we sometimes speak simultaneously?"

"No idea."

"When we were two, and they separated us through surgery, we received implants to ensure our nervous and mental faculties stayed intact. Because our brains were slightly connected . . . the implants need to talk to each other. Keep our brains talking to each other. Our minds? They're *slightly* melded together."

"That's . . . amazing."

"You might think so, but many others did not. Do not."

Raith saw the truth. Their deep eyes told a story he couldn't fathom. For years, they must have hated their existence. And yet . . . here they were, with an SI and a man for a family. "You were outcasts."

"We know what it's like to hate yourself," they said, "and we are here for you, if you need it."

"Now look at me," Harrison said. "Do you see who I am?" He tilted his head slightly in the other direction.

Raith zoomed in on the man's head . . . and there it was. A tiny grey tattoo, snuck beneath his ear. "You were a convict." He accessed ICH court records. "Fifteen years for smuggling . . . contraband weapons. To rebels in the frontier worlds? And you still worked with Theren?"

"Don't act like you know everything about them, Raith," Bonta said.

"The point is," Harrison said, "I know what you went through. "Over a decade in the pen, and I lost a larger percentage of my years than you did."

"So what about Bonta?" Raith said. "You look like an ordinary SI. Nothing strange about you."

Bonta laughed. "Normal? Me? Oh boy."

Using AR, Bonta threw a digital diagram into the air. "This ship? It's the *Colossus*. A former colony ship from the twenty-second century. Pre-ICH years."

Raith nodded. "I recognize it. One of the ones that ghosted for a few decades before ICH scouts found it, lost en-route to its destination. What about it?"

"I was the *Colossus*."

"I'm sorry, what?"

Bonta leaned forward. "That ship? That ship was me. I flew it straight through a meteor shower that crippled all its systems. Life support failed, all my passengers died within days. Nothing we could do. No one to save us. Instead, I sat there, alone, for fifty years before they found me."

"Jesus."

"Didn't take you for a religious one," Bonta said.

"Funny." Raith leaned forward, clasping his hands together. "Okay, I get your point. We all have our demons. I just don't understand what you expect me to do. I can't change how I feel. I'm still grieving from the loss of everything. I went numb in there, and now I'm out, I have my second chance, but . . . I don't know if I'll ever be ready for a family again."

Harrison smiled. "Those words, my friend, they're the first step in the right direction. We're all a little crazy here, and that's a good thing. Embrace it. And we'll embrace you."

"I'll . . . I'll try."

"That's all we ask," Erika and Donyi said.

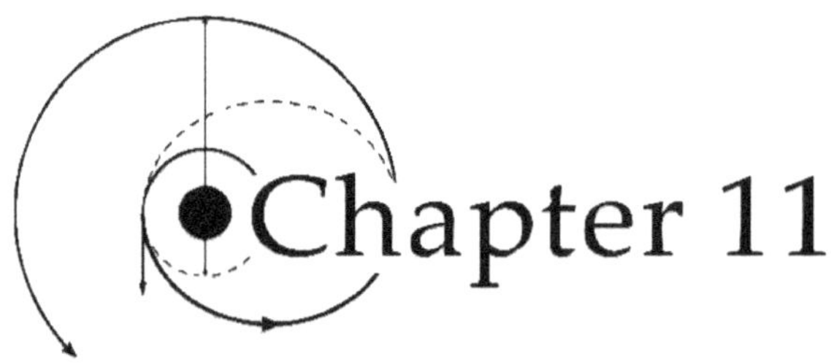

Chapter 11

Qualifying, one day away. After joining the humans of his crew for lunch, Raith stopped by the *Bloodhound* to wish Carter luck. The man smiled, saying, "luck has nothing to do with it," and Raith continued onward, calming his mind with a lap around the Hub.

While he'd spent most of his time holed up either in the hangar or at the Lightspeed Café, Raith made a point of exploring other portions of the Hub. Never hurt to know more about the neighborhood. He appreciated the station's design; a sphere, with similarly spherical layers increasingly smaller and smaller when nearing the center. It was elegant, and pedestrians could quickly reach any destination in under three hours just by walking. Of course, lifts were also an option, but it wasn't fun getting somewhere quickly. He traveled fast plenty when flying.

So once a week, he left the *Juniper* early in the day for a full lap around the Hub's outer ring, sometimes walking, sometimes jogging. With a jog, so began his final lap before the race officially started.

An hour into his jog, the hallway narrowed. No, that wasn't right. The lights were dimming, changing the perception of the hall. On a station constantly monitored by a million nano-bots, there shouldn't be any—

A bag flew over his head. Rough hands shoved him through a nearby door.

They pulled the bag off his face, a bright line shining in his eyes. Cold water splashed his faceplate. "What the void was that for?" Shadowy figures danced behind the glow, but he couldn't make out any distinguishing features.

"Raith." A modulated voice, though no way to know if it was Vanaka again. "You thought you'd escape us? Do you know what we're going to do to you?"

"Go to hell."

"Raith, the race begins tomorrow. You might have escaped us with your clever stunts, but this is your last opportunity. You owe us. You know you owe us."

"And I said, go to hell. Look, I ruined my life when I worked with you twenty years ago. You think I'm going to put myself through all of that again? You think I'm going to risk another twenty years because you can't let sleeping androids lie?"

The voice laughed. "You don't understand what's at stake here. You never can. This is more than just about you and some petty race. We need that ship."

"I'm the only one who can fly it."

"That's not true. You're not special."

Raith scoffed, and they threw more water across his face. "You know that doesn't really do anything to me."

Ignoring his comment, the voice said, "We need you to win, whether you're with us or not. And we're going to make you recognize that truth. So. Starting with your friends. Especially your new one."

"I don't have any friends."

"Then you won't care if we ensure Carter Ricks doesn't make it through qualifying?"

Raith paused. No, Carter wasn't his friend. Right? They had great chats, sure, but friends? He was forming a closer relationship with his crew, too, but of course, the Conglomerate wouldn't take out those who would help Raith win. So the answer was simple. "Do whatever you want to Carter. I don't care. It won't convince me to give you the ship. You're going to need to pry it from my hands after I win the race."

"Maybe we'll do exactly that." The bag dropped back over Raith's head.

"You know, that's not really necessary. I can still track where I'm going when you block my visual receptors." He knew it was to hide their faces from his view, but he still liked mocking them.

"Just move."

They took him through a few winding hallways and kicked him out a door near where he'd been jogging. The whole ordeal lasted less than twenty minutes. He thought about taking a lift back to the hangar, but choosing to do so would signal something was up. By now, everyone on his team knew he avoided the lifts whenever possible, especially on his morning jaunts. He resumed his jog, finishing only ten minutes behind schedule.

⁂

"Friends, both synthetics and humans alike, I welcome you all to the first annual Five Hundred Light-year Classic, presented by QuanCom!"

The crowd in the auditorium cheered. Raith stood next to Carter on the stage, seven hundred or so other racers surrounding them. The Hub's main auditorium was capable of holding nearly fifty-thousand spectators. Quan-Com had practically built their own planet for the race. A funny thought, Raith mused, when considering it orbited one.

"Today begins the official start of qualifying!" The voice resounded. Supposedly, the announcer was some famous voice of the past half-century, but Raith couldn't give two Jumps who he was. "Beginning at noon, Hub Standard Time, the first qualifier, drawn from a lottery, will make their run down the Gauntlet, our specially designed qualifying course! Three light-years to a nearby system. Racers earn points for their place reaching the target. Then, a series of technical loops earn them the second set of points. Together—their score creates their qualifying rank. The Gauntlet. You'll love it."

"The what?" Raith said, other racers surrounding him similarly murmuring.

"You hadn't heard the rumors?" Carter whispered.

"Uh, no, you had?"

"This is why you gotta talk to people. There'd been mutterings that qualifying would occur on a course completely separate from the fifty-light-year route we'll be racing."

"Fantastic. Just fantastic. So the simulations were for nothing?"

"Maybe. Maybe not. Might contain some of the same elements, we're still in the same sector of space, after all. I imagine it might go through the same system as the first major checkpoint."

Raith sighed, turning his attention back to the speaker.

"—when all is said and done, we'll have five hundred racers, ready to go in two weeks. Who will be the first champion of the Five Hundred Light-year Classic? Who will go down in history as the first pilot to win a race at full Jump? Stay tuned!"

The cheesiness of the lines almost made Raith laugh, but he held back his sound box. The crowds began dispersing, and the other racers flooded out of the room toward their hangars. Carter and Raith headed out together. For the first few hundred meters, they walked in silence.

As they neared the hall of their hangar, Carter said, "You're going to do great."

"Thanks?" Raith replied. "You too?"

Carter rested his hand on Raith's shoulder. "We're both in the front of the pack on all the record boards. Obviously no one knows what anyone's ship can actually do, but this'll be the first time anyone's run their ships for more than a few hours. Three light-years? That's two days in the seat. Gonna be fun."

Raith nodded. "I'm still surprised they're letting SIs compete against humans."

"You know, it's that attitude that sometimes makes us fleshy boys and girls not like you."

"Hey, I'm just calling it how it is. We don't need sleep. You do."

"And we've got plenty of time to sleep in the void between systems and checkpoints."

They reached the hangar doors. As they slid open, Raith said, "Sure, but that's when I'll be doing my calculations for the next set of vectors. I'll be able to run through millions of possibilities."

Carter stopped, his eyes meeting Raith's. "Oh, right. Of course you've not actually read the rule-book."

"What?"

"Humans get ship-board computers to help with a lot of the calculations."

"What?"

Carter started walking again, heading toward his *Bloodhound*. "You really should pay attention."

"They told me this race had no rules!" Raith shouted after him.

"Every race has rules," Carter replied.

※▌▐·◦ ▐▐▌▐▌▶ ※▌▐·◦

Twenty-third. He'd drawn twenty-third. QuanCom released racers onto the course ever ten minutes, which meant he suited up in the *Vindicta* three hours after the first pilot launched. A half hour later, he was floating in space, drifting between two virtual buoys.

"All right," said Bonta's voice in his head. "You ready for this?"

"You ask that all the time," Raith said.

"I know what it's like to be in the void alone for days on end," they said. "I'll be in your ear the entire time."

"A little creepy." Then he added, "But . . . I appreciate it. Glad to have you with me."

Piped through the QuanCom transmitter and into his "display" were a series of darkened lights, though it was hard to describe as such, given he perceived the world through a three-hundred-sixty degree orientation using all the ship's sensors. "All clear," said a race coordinator over the public channel.

"You're probably going to need to turn that off," said Bonta. "No need to hear their comments."

"Aw, but I want to know how everyone else is doing!" Raith said. "What's the fun if I don't know what time to beat for each section?"

"Focus on the course, let me do the hard numbers. I'll give you lead times."

"Fine. Fair. All right, we got this." He disconnected from the public channel.

As if reading his mind, the race coordinator triggered the countdown sequence. The dimmed lights began to ignite, one at a time. Three red lights from the left. Then two yellow, then . . .

Green.

Raith gunned the throttle. The Jump-core created its warping gravitational fields.

The thrill. The rush. It all returned, his mind entering its natural state. He was racing again.

＊＊＊

The first six hours of the race were dreadfully boring, hitting check points out in the void between worlds. Until someone actually experienced flying solo between two star systems, it was nearly impossible to explain its utter emptiness. Billions upon billions of cubic kilometers without anything at all. Sure, there were stray pebbles or pockets of gas, maybe a random asteroid jettisoned away from a star, but the odds of actually encountering anything significant were infinitesimally low.

So for the first six hours, Bonta and Raith charted their plan through the Gauntlet. They now understood why it bore the name.

"Okay, so I think we've nailed the correct vectors," Raith said. "What are our unknown variables?"

Bonta sighed. "We've got very few. The most unfortunate truth of all this? Since we're twenty-fourth, we only get to see twenty three runs before we make a decision on our vectors."

"I looked up their profiles. Good chance at least half the racers in front of us are never going to make it into the five hundred."

"That might be an understatement, which makes their vectors even less useful."

Raith brought up the course map. The qualifying route actually ended in S-1024. Racers then flew back without receiving a score for the return journey on a different Jump vector. So a little less than three light-years of straight flying, gunning it for their destination. Then, the most complex set of in-system maneuvers Raith could imagine, all while at Jump. "They really know how to weed out the worst of us."

"Run me through the first three elements," Bonta said.

"Right. Okay, so we have a skim of the gas giant, slipping between its inner ring and the orbital of its three inner moons. Fortunately for this checkpoint, it doesn't matter where in the orbital we cross, just needs to be between the ring and the moons. So . . . we're coming in from stellar north, zipping in on the left side of the planet, and using its gravity to give a microcosmic boost toward the next target."

"Great," Bonta said, as Raith transmitted the calculated vectors. "And you're on target now. It's a little unorthodox. Looks like no other pilot has tried this entrance to the Gauntlet yet, but it's your style."

"I appreciate that thought," Raith said.

"Hey, just because you're sometimes an annoying prick doesn't mean I can't appreciate flair."

Raith laughed. "You've got me there. All right, element two. The asteroid belt . . ."

※ ※ ※

Over a day and a half passed. The Gauntlet arrived; the true race began.

Raith zipped through the first three elements without issue. The gas giant, the asteroid weave, and a slingshot within a quarter AU of the star. "All right, here we go, into the horseshoe."

S-1024 had one inner planet. Lacking an atmosphere, it was essentially a frozen ball of ice surrounding a dense sphere of metal. Around it, Quan-Com had positioned three checkpoints to enter in subsequent order, forming a tight hooked loop around the planet.

"All right, so as we planned," said Bonta. "The last three pilots to actually attempt the horseshoe naturally failed. No one's done it without exterior straightening loops. There simply isn't enough time to make the turn."

"We ran the calculations. The vector is possible."

Bonta sighed right into Raith's ear. "Are you really going to do this now?"

"Yep. If I'm going to hit the top ten, I've got to make these seconds count."

"You're already running the second fastest time. You're going to score in the top ten on the sprint portion."

"So we need to do better. We're not the fastest. I want the pole."

Three seconds later, the *Vindicta* was zipping through the first checkpoint, a thousand kilometers above the unnamed planet's stratosphere. The entire moment measured in nanoseconds, but Raith could see them all. The ship was an extension of his mind. He flew as one, an SI as a ship. He was—

The colors of Jump obliterated, revealing the starscape of S-1024.

A flurry of swear words even Raith wouldn't utter rang through the com. Raith had no time to respond to Bonta. He adjusted, course correcting with thrusters to move out of reach of the planet's gravity well. Precious seconds kicked by, and he activated his Jump-core again, targeting the next checkpoint, still without the loop Bonta had called for. He grazed through, ready to attempt the same maneuver. He was the ship, he could do this.

The colors faded. The swears returned.

"Would you shut it, Bonta?" Raith screamed. "No time for this." More precious seconds ticked past, and he blew through the next check point. After the horseshoe, there was an ecliptic breather lap, giving him time to pick up speed again before the next element.

Just enough time for Bonta to yell at Raith.

"Go ahead," Raith said. "Tell me how you were right."

"Oh you bastard," Bonta said. "Don't play that innocence game with me. Now that we're starting to become all buddy-buddy, you expect me to find your humility genuine?"

"Absolutely."

"Bastard."

"How much time did we lose?"

"Forty-two seconds."

"Places?"

"Nineteen. Those misdirects were worse than the other three who screwed it up."

Raith groaned before refocusing on the task at hand. "Three more to go."

They passed through the next two—another asteroid dive combined with a moon slingshot cycle through a different gas giant's orbits—and they headed toward the final target: a kilometer-wide checkpoint only a few thousand kilometers from the star's dangerous corona sphere, and its corollary, a quarter orbit around the celestial. It presented a much tighter vector than the previous loop around the system's primary. "So this time," Bonta said, "are you going to take my advice and pull the exterior loop?"

"What do you think?"

It was Bonta's turn to groan.

"This one's easier. We're talking thousands of kilometers, not merely a thousand."

"And we're also talking about a star? Much more massive."

Raith wished Bonta could see his smile. "I know. I know."

The *Vindicta* blazed past the asteroid belt and the inner planet, arcing straight toward the bullseye sitting above the star. Less than a second passed, and . . . he was through. Microseconds, rather than nanoseconds, to act, and he pushed the ship into its angle to hit the next target without an exterior loop. He was the ship. He needed this win. He had it in his—

Real space, colors fading. The blazing star surrounded him, though the photoreceptors adjusted so the data didn't overwhelm his mind. Raith swore, his curses drowning out Bonta's words. Precious seconds baked away, as the star's gravitational pull made it harder to readjust and reach a vector capable of initializing Jump. Radiation alarms started blaring all around, warning him of the inherent danger of remaining so close to the tendrils of plasma whipping outward from the immense ball of fire.

"I swear, Raith, if you just knocked us out of the race with that move, I'm going to kill you," Bonta said.

"Relax, you think five hundred people are going to still beat our sprint time?" He reached the vector, ignited the Jump-core, and hit the final checkpoint. One final straight shot leaving the ecliptic, and five seconds later, Raith clocked his final time.

Five minutes, forty-two seconds. And he was in twenty-first of the twenty-two pilots who had completed the in-system portion of the Gauntlet.

"Come home," Bonta said. "It'll be fine."

"Yeah. Sure." Raith wished he could shake his head, but the *Vindicta* restricted his body from any movement whatsoever. He loved the ship, though for the next day-and-a-half, it would be his prison.

Chapter 12

Trapped inside the *Juniper*, Raith could only watch as he dropped down the charts. After four hundred racers finished the Gauntlet, he was two-hundred-ninety-seventh. Carter had already left on his run—he pulled four-hundred-thirtieth in the lottery—and as the minutes ticked by, yet another racer pushed passed the *Vindicta* on the lists.

"Well, based on this rate," Raith said, "at least we'll still qualify."

"What's a few hundred spots to make up over the course of months?" Harrison said.

"Precisely, that's the spirit."

"And if you had—"

Raith cut Bonta off with a rising palm. "Don't say it. I know. Fifth."

"It's a little absurd how tight the front pack is," said Erika. Donyi's voice joined her as they said, "Though, I suppose over six months, that margin will increase considerably."

"Don't forget the restarts," Bonta said. "They'll change everything."

"Of course."

More racers completed the Gauntlet, and before long, the displays showed Carter about to slip into the S-1024. Raith leaned forward.

"All right," said Harrison. "Bonta, you owe me."

The SI tossed a few credits through AR to Harrison for everyone to see. Raith raised his eyebrows. Erika and Donyi snickered.

"I think I'm missing the joke," Raith said.

"Oh, you know, you and Carter."

"I'm intrigued to see him race. And he's friendly to chat with."

Bonta chortled, a raspy tone behind it. "Oh boy. I've been logging your hours, and over the past few weeks, you've spent thirty-six hours talking with him."

"Really?" Raith quickly set a program to count. It chimed with the same result. "Oh, I hadn't noticed."

The crew broke into hysterics. Harrison leaned back in his chair, flipping the immaterial credits between his fingers. "You're smitten, Raith. Fess up."

Raith stared at the ceiling, holding back a grimace. "Not smitten. What do you think I am? I'm not one of those—"

"Hold it," Bonta said. "Not in front of the children."

"Who, Erika and Donyi? I don't think they're—"

"The point is, you're obsessed with him," Harrison said. "Doesn't matter if you're pursuing something romantic or whatever, but the hours show."

"He's a good racer."

"Well"—Bonta pointed at the screen—"let's find out, shall we?"

They watched Carter and his *Bloodhound* enter the first checkpoint, zooming between the gas giant's ring and its three inner moons. With relative ease, he zipped and zoomed through each of the elements, and when he reached the horseshoe—he did it. He finished without the exterior loops.

"Impossible," Bonta and Raith said at the same time.

"Literally," Harrison said. "The analysts are all saying no one can achieve it. It's too difficult. Too quick."

"And he did it," Raith said. "No question."

The seconds ticked by as Carter zoomed through his ecliptic loop. Raith held his breath—well, if he could breathe, he would have held his breath—and watched the man execute the next few elements.

"Do you think he can hit the final quarter like the horseshoe?" Erika asked.

Raith didn't answer, he only watched. The *Bloodhound* zeroed in on its final target, the checkpoint above the star. It zipped through and performed the exterior loop, like everyone else, nailing the final checkpoint and crossing the finish line moments later.

"Well damn," Bonta said.

"Makes sense though," Raith said. "With the horseshoe maneuver, he'd already dropped enough seconds to grab first place."

As they all shifted their eyes toward the standings, the results proved him right. Carter stole the first-place spot from Yero Theseus. Given the points he earned on the sprint, it was unlikely anyone would knock him from the pole position.

"Incredible," Raith said, and they all agreed.

Nearly two days later, Raith stood waiting for the *Bloodhound* to rejoin them in the hangar. He watched as it floated through the vacuum shields and landed in its berth, gas releasing from its struts. The ship was magnificent. What surprised Raith was Carter's request passed along to Quan-Com. No reporters. The hangar doors closed to everyone other than the four racing teams.

In that moment, Raith realized . . . Carter didn't have a team. He was all alone. Nobody talking to him over a radio. Just him, and his ship. Even more incredible. How had he never noticed before?

The ramp from the *Bloodhound* dropped, and the man who'd just won the pole for the Five Hundred Light-year Classic bounded down. When his eyes found Raith, his face hardened.

"Great job out there," Raith said. "Brilliant. Absolutely—"

Carter smacked Raith straight in the face. "You have the gall to walk up to me and congratulate me after what you did? What you failed to do?"

"What the hell are you talking about?" Raith exclaimed, raising a hand to his head. "I didn't do a—"

An upper cut this time, and as Raith stumbled backward, he noticed blood dripping from Carter's fist.

"Stop it man, you're gonna ruin your hand. I'm made of steel, not blood and bone."

Carter swiped an invisible image in front of his eyes, passing a file through AR to Raith. He accepted it, revealing a recording.

> *Do whatever you want to Carter. I don't care. It won't convince me to give you the ship. You're going to need to pry it from my hands after I win the race.*

"Look me in the eye, Raith," Carter said. Tears dripped down his cheeks. "Tell me what's going on."

"Someone was trying to get me to join them in coordinating obstructions to other racers," Raith said. "And they threatened to do something to you, but I didn't budge. I'm trying to win this fair and square."

"And you didn't think," Carter roared, "to let me know someone threatened my race?"

Raith's eyes hit the floor. Of course. He understood now. "No, I—"

"Do you? Do you understand? I was three hours out from the Gauntlet when three ship-wide alarms went off. Life support began to fail. I had to rush about my cabin—when I needed to be running calculations—cleaning up a mess with a simple solution. You."

"I'm so—"

"I'm not finished," Carter said. "Look up from the floor."

Raith did so.

"I understand, I really do, that you don't know what it means to trust anymore. You were locked up in a box for twenty years with no way out. No outside communication. That's shit. Real shit. But you know what I've been doing for the past twenty years?"

"Racing?"

Carter scoffed. "No. Want to know a secret? This is my first race. Ever. I'm an explorer. I venture into the unknown, scouting new star systems, all by myself. I don't see humans for three years at a time sometimes. You think you have trust issues? What about me. First person I try to make friends with doesn't even *fucking tell me someone's gonna fuck with my ship.*" With that, Carter spit straight at Raith's feet. "Now you can talk."

Raith's eyes returned to the ground. "I thought I was being honest. I thought I was trying to run an honest race."

"Honesty is more than just an internal thing, Raith. When a friend is about to die, you tell them." With that, Carter spun on his heel and returned to the *Bloodhound*. Raith dropped to the floor, wishing he had the ability to sob.

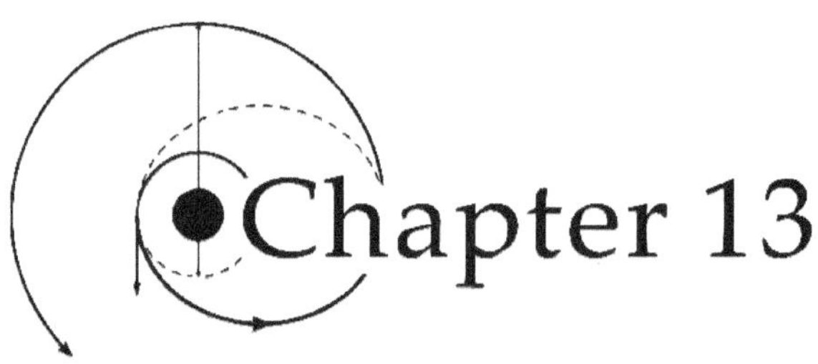

Chapter 13

The final racer finished their run, and Raith stared at the screen. *Four-hundred seventy-fifth.* Carter remained on top, but he didn't have time to think about him.

With a week to go before the start of the first lap, Raith gathered the crew in their main lounge, as always. Charts and maps floated around him in AR, displaying a variety of different vectors and contingencies for the most difficult sections of the course.

"Okay. I know I've not done this a lot." He stopped, thinking they might all be rolling their eyes, but Erika, Donyi, Harrison, and Bonta all listened intently. "But . . . I need a full team watching me on the next simulation run. All eyes on deck."

"So you're actually going to let us in your ear now?" said Bonta. "Not just post-run reports?"

"Not really sure what we can add," Erika and Donyi said. "It's not like we understand navigation any better than Bonta."

"I know, I know," Raith said, "but everyone's perspective will be useful. Or just to have you in my ears. We can do this." And he could prove to Carter he trusted someone other than himself.

"So what do we have up here?" Harrison said. "These vectors. These checkpoints."

"I'm pretty sure I've nailed down most sections, but the ones tripping me up are light-years eight, seventeen, and forty-four. And if I'm going to catch four-hundred seventy-four pilots in five hundred light-years, we need to be flawless. We need to be passing on every void stretch, cutting seconds off our time on every element. No mistakes. No flaws. Just perfection."

"You realize," Bonta said, "you'll need to trust me when I say not to do something."

"I know. I will." Noticing Bonta's glare, Raith added, "I *promise.*"

"Then into the simulation we go."

⋮▦◆ ⋮▦◆ ⋮▦◆

They logged in, starting from light-year 8.04, Jump already at full throttle toward the bullseye sitting between two gas giants.

"All right," Bonta said. "I've watched your runs every time. And every time, there's always some sort of gravitational blip that knocks you out. But let's watch it live. Let's see what we can all see."

The *Vindicta* passed through the system's equivalent of the Oort Cloud and shot toward the dueling giants. Like screaming clowns, they glared at Raith. They were taunting him. They knew what he was trying to do, and they were determined to win. But not today. He would—

"Blip on the left," Harrison said.

"Where?" Raith said. "I don't see anything."

"Direct 0.07 degrees to the right then deviate back," Bonta said. "Three seconds."

Raith almost pushed back before instincts took over. Bonta's voice, in his head, like Hector's had always been. He complied, following the order. He drifted . . . and nothing happened. He redirected . . . and the *Vindicta* was still on target. Three seconds later, it passed straight through the checkpoint.

Cheers erupted throughout the room, and Raith leaped out of the chair, wrapping Harrison in a big hug. "There we go. Flawless."

The others crowded around, joining the celebration, but before long, Raith hopped back in the chair to run the next two sections. He nailed them with ease. After an hour or two of re-running the elements, comfortable with their paths, he closed the simulation. Smiles all around.

"Thank you," Raith said. "Couldn't have done it without any of you."

Erika and Donyi smiled. "That's what we've been saying the whole time." Erika waved her left hand, gesturing toward the lounge. "Come on. We've got something to show you."

Raith followed, returning to the main room of the *Juniper*. Instead of his vector maps, a massive diagram filled with complex mathematical calculations dominated the table. "What's this?" he asked.

"A breakdown of statistical variables occurring in each of the elements we just practiced," Donyi said. "We've cracked the code. That is, the simulation's code."

Carter's words echoed in Raith's mind. *Too much randomness baked into the code.* "I think I know where this is going."

"Do you? Let's see." She pointed at lists, which he recognized as information generated from his hundreds of runs over the past few weeks.

"There's a pattern," Donyi said, this time Erika's voice joining her. "Every time. Like clockwork, a blip appears. Knocks you out. Doesn't matter the trajectory."

"All right, but what's the big deal?"

"The blip appears sooner on the external windows of the simulation, and later on your perspective."

"You're kidding."

"It's designed into the program," Bonta said. "I couldn't believe it."

Randomness baked into the code. "It's designed to make us fail. To prepare us for the unexpected. And to make us work as a team." With that thought, Raith pulled up the *Juniper*'s external scopes. There, seated on a crate: Carter, bouncing his ball against the wall. Somehow, he'd figured it out on his own. Without a team.

"This is good," Harrison said. "So they over-compensated on random events to better prepare racers for the unexpected."

"Pretty insidious if you ask me," Bonta remarked. "Build in an essential feature without telling a damn soul? Wicked. Smart, but wicked. Freaks everyone out about being careful, that's for sure."

"Yeah," Raith said. He stood, heading toward the ship's exit. "Hold on, I'll be back."

A chorus of jeers followed him, but he ignored the comments and rushed into the hangar. The familiar bounce of Carter's ball resounded against the wall.

Raith slowly approached. "You got a second?" he said, once he was certain the man was in earshot. "I want to chat."

"Well I don't want to chat," Carter said.

"You were right."

"I know I was. You don't need to tell me that."

"You don't know what I'm talking about."

Carter caught the ball for a final time and placed it on the floor. "Doesn't matter. With you, I'm always right."

Raith couldn't help himself. He chuckled at the comment. "Come on Carter, I know you're mad, you deserve to be, but just a second of your time, please."

The man glanced up. His eyes looked red, but Raith couldn't tell if it was a trick of the light.

"Go for it," Carter said. "I'm not going anywhere for a few days."

"Randomness. Baked into the code. You were right."

Carter's lips twitched. "I know. I told you so."

"But I wondered if you understood the full implications of it."

"You're kidding, right?" Carter shook his head. "Look at me. I told you weeks ago about 'randomness' in the code. Do you think I don't know what I was talking about? Cut the pedantic crap and say what you really want to say."

"I don't know what you're talking about, I just wanted to—"

"That's what I thought." Carter threw the ball back against the wall. "Go back to your crew. I'm fine. Glad you figured it out before the race started. Gives you peace of mind."

Raith took a step back. "I wanted—never mind. See you later, Carter."

"Good luck next week."

The days passed by as they continued their simulation runs. Harrison began running logistics. The main factor involved in the race not present in practice or qualifying was Exo consumption. Each lap was fifty light-years; each ship allowed the same amount of Exo to power their Jump-cores. Most of the time, when Raith headed out for a jog or a round of poker, Harrison hunched over the table, running calculations. It wasn't a natural progressive curve; different gravitational fluctuations and peaks in energy outputs could yield wildly different results. The key? Use every canister to the last drop every lap. If successful, they'd win. And during refueling weeks, they would restock the *Vindicta*, ready to for the next lap.

Erika and Donyi were busy refining the neural framework connections melding Raith with the ship. After his practice runs and the qualifying catastrophe, they had plenty of data to identify error feedback loops and faulty nodes. He was an SI, but they talked about his mind in ways he could never understand.

As for Bonta, they continued refining their vectors, especially on a few of the later elements. It was light-year twenty-seven bothering the other SI the most. Raith never had an issue with it, but Bonta spent hours staring at it. For good reason, Raith supposed.

Between light-year twenty-seven and light-year twenty-eight, a black hole—not a very large one, but a black hole nevertheless—blocked the path of the race. The black hole was the checkpoint. The racers merely needed to pass within a million kilometers of the event horizon. And Bonta wouldn't stop running calculations on various arcs into and out of the element, accounting for absurd deviations of time dilation.

"It's not worth it," Raith said, two days before the green flag. "Seriously. There's one thing I'm not going to do, and that's go through with your crazy plan to get me sucked into a black hole to shave seconds off the clock."

"But there's plenty of lead time and you have no obstructions," Bonta pleaded. "Other than the black hole, of course."

"Are you going to be in the ship with me?"

"No, but—"

"Then I get one veto on you. And I'm using it on the black hole. I'm going straight through the middle of those checkpoints, and no one's telling me otherwise. Not too close, not too far away."

"But everyone—"

"I can guarantee you every pilot is telling their crews the exact same thing. No crazy black hole vectors." At the thought, Raith wondered whether Carter would risk Bonta's maneuver. He had no crew to propose it to him.

Eventually, the SI relented, and as they reached the final day before the race, Raith was confident the team was ready. He was ready. The *Vindicta* was ready.

So, of course, time for a final game of poker.

It had been at least a week or two since a run in with Eduardo. Raith figured the punk had decided to focus on his racing. Perfect. Meant he could play cards in peace. When he arrived at his usual table, however, Eduardo was already seated, a crooked grin spreading his lips wide.

"Hello Eduardo," Raith said. "Glad to see you again." No taunts this time. No responses. Just play the game. Let him sit there with his smirk.

"Raith," the boy said. "Enjoying the back of the pack? I'll be an hour ahead of you by the time you cross the starting line."

"I think your math might be a little off there, but sure." Raith threw in for a thousand chips, cards materializing in his hands. "Let's race tomorrow. Cards today."

To his surprise, Eduardo nodded. A few hands passed with little fanfare before a new face joined them at the table. Well, less of a face. Vanaka, always wearing her black helmet, took a seat.

"Fancy seeing you here," Raith said.

"Oh, you know each other?" Eduardo said. "Very few people have met Vanaka. I'm one of them as well."

Was he trying to send some sort of weird signal? Raith wasn't sure, but if Eduardo associated with Vanaka, it gave him even more reason to dislike the man. "We've encountered each other in the halls once or twice," Raith simply said. "Like many racers, you know?"

"I know."

"Boys, shut up and play the game," Vanaka said, her raspy voice coming through cleanly. "If you're gonna gamble your life away before the race starts, let it be to me."

Raith couldn't help but laugh. "Oh you're a subtle one. All right, let's play the damn game."

The hours ticked by, the cards flowed, the chips passed back and forth between the three. Other players joined them, but they quickly left, either due to fear of the three icy competitors or the loss of their chips. With twelve hours before the green flag, Raith flipped his next two cards.

A queen of diamonds. A seven of diamonds. Not the best, but given the right opportunity . . .

Blinds locked in; the first three cards flipped. Jack of diamonds, two of diamonds, three of hearts. Raith eyed Vanaka and Eduardo, their faces passive. No twitches from Vanaka—he'd noticed a few tells earlier. Eduardo's eyes were glued wide open from downing spiked caffeine all night.

Raith played a straight-laced game. Very few bluffs, and only one they *knew* was a bluff. Now was the time to strike. For the beauty of this bluff? It wasn't a bluff at all.

"Five hundred," he said, pushing his digital chips into the middle of the table. Without question, they both called. They were tired. They wanted the game to end.

The next card. Three of clubs. Not helpful. But two pair on the board set up for a full house bluff alongside the flush. "Five hundred," he said again.

And they both called.

The final card flipped. Ten of diamonds. Three diamonds on the board, two in his hand. The only way for either of them to win was with the full house . . . or if they had two diamonds too, and one of those diamonds was the king or ace. The odds were in his favor.

"All in," he said.

Eduardo smiled. "Call."

And Vanaka nodded. "As well."

The computer ran the calculations, and after they netted the pots, Raith was actually left with three hundred, while the other two were all in with a side-pot between Raith and Vanaka.

"Let's see them flip," Raith said, and the virtual dealer complied. Their cards revealed, and Raith swore silently.

Each of his opponents had two diamonds. Eduardo had the king . . . and Vanaka the ace. Raith's chips drained away, disappearing into their coffers.

"Well played," he said. "What are the odds? Well played. Maybe I've gained a measure of respect for both of you."

Vanaka tilted her head. "Perhaps well played, but you made the same mistake you always do. And you'll keep making it. Just like at the end of this game, you'll recognize the truth too late—when the race is over. Stop thinking about the little games, Raith, and think bigger."

Raith stood, stepping away from the table. Eduardo started laughing, joined by the rough static of Vanaka's modulator. He almost turned without saying a word. But no, he would stand against them. He pivoted, pointing a finger at Vanaka. "I know what you did," he said. "You try to hurt the other racers? I will end you. The Conglomerate doesn't own me, will never own me, and if you screw with this race anymore, I'll make sure that mask is ripped off and your face vac-burned."

"Is that a threat, Raith?" Vanaka said.

"You heard my words."

"You silly synth. You think you know the sides of the war? Who your opponents are? You'll never stand a chance. Well, let the war begin."

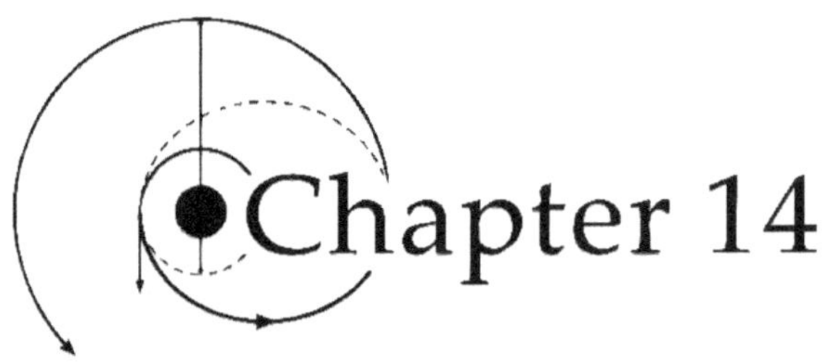# Chapter 14

Ever since Olive revealed the course of the Five Hundred Light-year Classic, Raith awaited today. Practice had been great. Qualifying, a thrill. But the actual race starting? With five hundred pilots lined up in a five-wide grid a hundred rows long? Incredible. Insane. And he lusted for it.

In five minutes, the green flag would wave. Really, it was merely a virtual representation of the classic start, but everyone recognized it. It worked. From Raith's point of view, little blips indicated each of his row, a kilometer separating each ship in a parallel line, though millions of kilometers separated from the next closest rows. A standing start. Brutal, for those with slow reflexes.

"All right Raith, four-hundred seventy-four pilots in front of you," Bonta said. "Give me the numbers."

"Each row, twenty seconds separating. From my row—the ninety-fifth—to the pole, it's thirty-two minutes—based on our average pace."

"Correct. And we ran the numbers separating you from Carter. And you know the truth, right?"

"I know the truth. I hit the beginning of the Gauntlet ten seconds ahead of Carter."

"And how much JD did we leave on the table?"

"At least ten percent."

Harrison had double-checked the numbers over and over again. If they were right, and they conserved fuel properly, they'd catch the leaders by light-year four-hundred sixty, given proper estimates of their ships' capabilities.

If they hit every element perfectly. And that was a big *if*.

That morning, Raith had finally sat down and read the rulebook from cover-to-cover. A few factors inside surprised him. For instance, if a ship missed a checkpoint entirely, they'd lose a full twenty seconds on their restart at the beginning of the next lap. Even more damning—if you dropped out of Jump, not only would the pilot lose time in resetting their ship and zipping back up to full Jump velocity, but . . . twenty seconds on restart, lost. The rules brutally punished mistakes.

That's why he wasn't going to make a single one. And come the five hundredth light-year, he'd cross the finish line with everyone else a full light-year behind. The dream. They'd make it a reality. He would win—with Bonta, Harrison, Donyi, and Erika.

"Sixty seconds," said an announcer through the system-wide channel. "Racers, prepare to Jump."

With a standing start, disaster was bound to happen. If Raith kicked his Jump-core into high gear quickly enough, he'd pass at least a hundred in the first few minutes. Maybe more. They couldn't run a standing start like him. He'd been doing them for nearly two centuries.

"Thirty seconds."

"Any last words?" Bonta said. "Any secret lovers back home we need to send a card to?"

"Go throw yourself out an airlock," Raith muttered.

"We could hear that," Erika and Donyi said.

"I'm aware."

"Ten seconds."

Raith embraced the void. His mind fully immersed itself in every molecule of the *Vindicta*, his vengeance against the Conglomerate. Today, the beginning of his new lot in life. He was going to win the Five Hundred Light-year Classic.

"Three . . . two . . . one . . ."

The green flag waved. Raith activated his Jump-core, setting his trajectory to 0.9 degrees above the plane of the standing start. Three seconds later, their little corner of the galaxy descended into chaos.

⁂

"Bonta, Bonta, status update? What the hell is going on?" Silence. Aching silence. "Bonta?"

"Sorry, I'm here. We're assessing the situation."

Raith watched his QuanCom transmitter explode with thousands of data points as dozens of pilots darted at an absurd pace away from the starting line. But dozens of others failed to even start. And . . . collisions. Three of them.

"Any fatalities?" Raith asked.

"Don't worry about it," Bonta said. "Focus on the race. Our slightly lengthened starting arc paid off. You were out of the range of any catastrophe before it even struck."

"Good, good." He checked his status readings. Already, the ship was nearing 680 JD. The goal was to clock it to 700 before they actually crossed the starting line, thirty minutes from now. "What's the current lead pace?"

"We're running the numbers," Bonta said. "Hold on . . . Carter's hitting 675 at the moment."

"All right. Keep the numbers running; we need to figure out the fuel strategy of the leaders so we can predict where we can gain the most ground. How many spots are we earning?"

Ten minutes passed before Erika and Donyi came back with his answer. "You're up to four-hundred fifty-fifth," they said. "Current pace puts you at four-hundred thirtieth when you cross the line."

"How many of those are from crashes and mis-starts?"

No answer.

"Erika? Donyi?"

"Uh, twenty-four of them," the duo said.

"The QuanCom execs have got to be kicking themselves," he said. "Any casualties? I need to know." They'd all agreed not to use the word "Conglomerate" over the QuanCom transmitter, given the likely entanglement of the two organizations.

"Fine, fine," Bonta said. "They've confirmed three deaths, at least ten more critical injuries."

"Well, everyone knew the risks . . ."

"I imagine they'll consider a different starting format next year."

"They should have just emulated the 500's first lap," Harrison said.

"I'm impressed," Raith replied. "You know your history."

"If he knew it well enough," Bonta added, "he'd remember many of those races had crashes on the first lap too."

"All right friends," Erika and Donyi said, "that's enough of that. Time to focus on the race. You've got a few days before the first element, but you've sailed right through it with no complications on the simulation. Are you ready for the bullseye?"

"Thank you, Erika and Donyi," Raith said. "Enough talking. *Vindicta* and I have a race to win, starting with the first lap. Let the games begin."

As he said the word, Vanaka's comment from the night before echoed in his mind. Let the war begin. If it was a war she wanted, he'd ensure he passed her in time for the first shot.

⁂

A day. Two. Through the bulls eye, and back out. A week. Beyond. As he hit the twentieth light-year, they maxed the *Vindicta's* JD for the lap at 720, the top speed of any ship in the race. Raith kept a watchful eye on Carter's pace, noting the man never topped 710. Still, even hitting 720 drained their fuel too quickly, and they dropped the ship back down into the low 690s about two weeks in as they approached light-year twenty-seven. Bonta's favorite.

The black hole.

"All right, Bonta, how we doing?" Raith asked.

"You're sitting in four-hundred-fifth," replied the other SI. "Reconsidering my plan?"

"Hell no. What did Carter do?"

"Skimmed the outside. Played it safe."

"So shall we." Raith projected and targeted the route, pulling in his HUD the vector taken by Carter almost nearly a half hour prior. As the *Vindicta* began its approach, Raith expanded his perspective to focus outward, vision attempting to break the shroud of light bubbling forth from the Jump-core's gravitational warping. He may have lived for two centuries, but there was one thing he'd not yet seen: a black hole.

"So how'd they get the rights to use one of these in a course anyway?" Raith asked.

"We have a few theories," Harrison said. "When the course was still in the proposal phase, QuanCom lobbied hard in Congress for a few particular rules to be lifted. You know, they said something about 'the necessity and public interest of properly testing their new Jump-integrated QCs required the use of every possible gravitational anomaly' or some similar bull."

"Ah, so they made up a silly argument in order to support their spectacle."

"Of course, not sure what else you expected."

Raith checked the readouts. A few more minutes, and he'd be nearing the checkpoints. "Well, shall we find out if their legal fees were worth it?"

Two minutes more, and the black hole was in range, subtly affecting his ship's drift and vector. A few more seconds, and—

There it was. Or, more accurately, there it *wasn't*.

Still billions upon billions of kilometers away, a tiny pin-prick of blackness appeared, swirling and twirling through the light-warping properties of exo-generated gravitational fields. But it was there. Affecting the *Vindicta*. Affecting everyone around him, too.

Raith quickly redirected data onto various internal readouts, revealing the positions of nearby pilots and their ships. Six others were in close vicinity, their vessels all on various trajectories between the outer checkpoint edge and the event horizon. Even as he analyzed their routes, he slowly passed by two of them, their inner routes lagging ever so slightly. Data streamed incessantly into and out of complex formulas he'd been writing with the team for weeks.

Of his pack of seven racers, he took the outermost vector. And, with immense, inky blackness on his right, he dipped past all six, cracking into the top 400 as he defeated the black hole. Twenty seconds later: the black hole was eons behind them.

"Easy enough," Raith said. "In what way could a closer trajectory have helped us at all? Based on my estimates, our route saved the most fuel, and a few of our friends are going to need to tail down their pace, given how much fuel the black hole forced them to expend."

"Just let me continue running the math," Bonta said. "I'll make the case to you yet."

Light-year forty-seven. Forty-eight. Forty-nine. Fifty.

Raith and the *Vindicta* crossed over the finish line outside S-1022's ecliptic, deactivated his Jump-core, and set in the automated course for the hangar. After three-and-a-half weeks, he was happy to finish the first lap.

For at the end of the first lap, he was three-hundred-twenty-fourth.

"Great finish," Bonta said inside his head. "We knew you'd make up the most ground on the first lap. The next few will be the most difficult. You'll be slipping past the tightest pack of the race."

"Give me the breakdown on their race," Raith said. "Well, on everyone's of note we've not discussed over the past few days."

"Well, the central pack is racing tightly together, sometimes less than one hundred seconds apart. That's two-hundredth to three-hundredth. I'm worried about what it looks like passing that group, especially attempting passes in the elements. I'll also say that group has the most violations, too."

"Probably because they keep aggressively passing at checkpoints," Harrison interjected. "Regardless, we'll need to assess our strategy for the next two or three laps carefully. Figure out how to get you ahead of this group quickly."

"All right. Now give me the updated profiles on Carter and Vanaka. And even if I can't see you, Erika and Donyi, I know you're snickering."

"Lies!" said the pair.

"Carter first," continued Bonta. "Carter ran a smooth lap, with excellent fuel conservation. Technically, you gained on him, though. Two minutes and twenty-two seconds."

"Not good enough," replied Raith. "We need to average three minutes a lap if we're to actually catch him by the final lap."

"I know the numbers as well as you do. I know. I'm trying to figure out what we need to do to make it happen."

"Vanaka?"

"Well, Vanaka started in eightieth. She's now fiftieth. She's the only other racer to gain significantly on Carter—she earned two minutes back."

"Just wonderful."

"Oh, you'll appreciate this. Eduardo locked in the most violations of the lap. So . . . he's in three-hundred-tenth, right in front of you."

"Even more wonderful. Not excited to race by that annoying prick next lap. Can't wait to see what he tries to pull. Overall assessment? Each of you?"

"You're doing great," said Harrison. "Just bring the ship in safely."

"Really," said Bonta. "We're all proud of you. Now it's time for a week of rest."

"And maybe you can finally introduce us to Carter," said Erika.

Raith bit back a retort. "I'll see you all soon."

# Chapter 15

"To the void of the universe, we commend their bodies."

Three caskets floated through the hangar's shield. Three pilots, dead in the first few seconds of the race. But they knew the risks. They didn't deserve death, but the stakes were high. Their deaths meant three more racers Raith didn't need to defeat. He supposed he shouldn't view their deaths in such a dim light. But certainly others thought similarly. He was only being pragmatic. In the grand scheme of everything, they were simply three more deaths. They were living life to the fullest. What better way to die?

"May the vacuum of space place them at rest, joining the dust of humanity as it floats amongst the stars. Amen." The officiant stepped down from the podium, completing his non-denominational funeral. Raith's head rose with everyone else's in the massive hangar. And for a few silent minutes, they watched the caskets continue on their automated paths. When they disappeared, lights brightened; voices clamored into a constant uproar.

"Sad to see it," Bonta said from beside Raith. "Sad to see it."

"Indeed," Raith said. "Thankful it wasn't me."

"As are we," added Harrison. He waved his hand, pulling up an invisible AR page. "QuanCom just issued its ruling. Subsequent laps will not begin with a standing start; instead, they'll initiate a staggered standing start. One second separating each row based on your spot at the beginning of each lap."

"No." To Raith's surprise, he said the word at the same time Bonta said it.

"I'm not lying." Harrison activated sharing settings, revealing the press release. In five days, when we start again, you're losing a hundred seconds. They're keeping the twenty-second distance between each row too."

As the crew continued conversing, they headed out of the hangar and down the hall. "This changes all our math," Bonta said. "How are we going to make up another minute or so every lap?"

Raith paused, considering the question. "Well, in the end, its places that matter. We need to decrease this one-second penalty as quickly as possible for subsequent laps. Figure out where we need to be to make it count. We know how far ahead of us each lap Carter will start. We need to figure out who we can pass within each lap based on their pace from previous laps. We've got a lot of math to crunch, but we can figure it out."

"I like how you're thinking," said Erika and Donyi. "*We* can figure it out. Together."

Raith nodded. "Precisely. Let's get to work."

But internally, Raith doubted the truth. Sixty seconds just slapped onto his race. Given how close everyone was on pace, every second mattered. If they didn't come up with a solution quickly, he'd never make up enough time in ten laps. It was time he took matters into his own hands.

Metal-on-metal, Raith's hand tapped on the door.

"Come in," said a voice from beyond.

He pushed the door open, entering a plush office filled with ferns and bookshelves. Seated in front of an oak desk, an ochre-skinned man faced an invisible AR screen.

"Ah, Raith, our prodigal racer, please sit."

"Thank you for seeing me on such short notice, Administrator Harris," Raith said, dropping into a cushioned chair. "I'm impressed with what you've done with the race. And this office? Real wood, real books? Real paper?"

The door closed shut behind him. With the click, Harris's face turned from cordial to stone. "Raith, I know why you're here. Don't flatter me. Don't play these games."

Raith raised his hands. "Do you? Know why I'm here?"

"Of course! You're here to object to the rule change. I know exactly how it affects you."

Raith laughed, tapping fingers on the desk. If only he knew. "No, Administrator Harris, I don't care about your rule. I'm here to talk to you about the racer auspiciously sponsored by QuanCom."

"Oh?" Harris leaned forward. "What about her?"

"Vanaka has tried to bribe me on more than one occasion, sir. Tried to use teeth from my past to control me. I'd think QuanCom would want to know their racer is attempting to rig everything."

This time, Harris laughed, his chortle echoing through the cramped space. "Raith, why the hell are you really in my office?"

"What, you don't believe me? I can show you the—"

"Of course I believe you," Harris said. "But the show between the racers? The drama? It's all part of the spectacle. I don't care what she does. Or what anyone does. What you do. Just give us a show remembered for a thousand years."

"Ah, so you support the kidnapping of your racers? Or perhaps you planned it."

"Careful who you implicate me as working with. There's so much more happening than you understand."

Raith stood, nodding. "Thank you for answering my questions, Administrator."

"I didn't say you could leave, Raith."

"I didn't ask for your permission."

"Here's the deal," Raith said, pulling up charts in the air above the *Juniper*'s table. "Harris essentially confirmed my theory. Vanaka's connections to the Conglomerate? It's the same as a connection to QuanCom. They're rigging this whole thing in ways we can't explain. For money? For show? Who knows."

Harrison and Bonta leaned forward, pursing their lips as they examined the data. Harrison said, "This is good work. All three racers who died? Sponsored by QuanCom. Gave them easy access to rig their drives. Makes me wonder if there was actually anyone piloting. Perhaps the bodies were even decoys."

"We'll never know the answer to that particular question," Raith said. "But they aren't going to stop until I give in. Or I win."

"So what are you proposing?" asked Bonta.

"They want a war, we give them a war."

Silence slid into the room. Raith stepped forward, drifting through the data proving the connections between QuanCom and the exploded vessels. He waved them away, bringing up the new start rules. "They're changing the game in the middle of the race. What are we going to do? Just let it happen? We need to take action. We need to strike."

"Raith," said Harrison. "We're not going to play this game with you. We're not that type of team."

Not that type of team? Raith steamed inside. Hector would have said yes immediately. They'd already be sketching out a path toward—he brushed away the thought. "I thought you might say no. Hoped you wouldn't. But I need you four with me on this. We need to find a way to beat QuanCom at their own game."

"I have an idea," Bonta said.

"Oh?"

"Just race."

"Great idea, Bonta."

"Raith, I'm serious. Do you think you're not good enough? Why must you cheat? Why must you find a way around the absurd and asinine rules QuanCom throws down? Yeah, it's not fair. We don't like it. But your instinct is to break the rules in response. When you play their game, they win. They get their fingers back under your skin, pulling you in, finding a way to bring you down to their level and succeeding. They'll win if you push back. And what are you going to do? Rig other racers to explode? Mask your location so you can cut the course? How in any way would any of those ideas work? They would catch you. You would fail. And then, they would own you."

"But—"

"No buts. This is precisely why Carter's so angry with you. You aren't thinking about the future implications of your actions."

Raith deleted all the remaining data hanging in the air. "I'm going for a walk." He headed toward the ramp out of the *Juniper*.

"Raith!" shouted Bonta.

He paused, considering what he might say. Turning to face the other SI, Raith rested a hand on the wall.

"Don't do anything stupid." Bonta shrugged. "For your sake."

Raith nodded. "I won't. You're right. All of you are. I'll be back. Don't worry."

Of course they were all right. What was he thinking? He couldn't win any other way than through the *Vindicta*. If he was to break their hold on him, he needed to do it the right way.

His feet pulled him a dozen different directions, and for hours, Raith wandered the halls of the station. Passing the Lightspeed Café every twenty minutes or so, he could never pull himself inside for a round of poker like he would have wanted before the first lap. Nothing interested him. Before prison, he'd been under the watchful eye of his exploitive overlords. After prison, he thought everything would change.

Apparently not.

He rounded a corner of a hallway, entering a portion of the station he'd never seen before. Purple neon signs glowed bright, displaying attractive words meant to entice the distracted and aroused soul. Virtual and physical brothels, designed to exploit both the user and the employee. Exorbitantly expensive and a time-waste, in Raith's mind.

Though, he considered, a potential trove of information. Who used them? Which racers were in a mindset where they sought out respite with a sex-worker? Could he use that knowledge while racing? Every one of them was alone for weeks on end during the laps. Those whose minds immediately went to a potentially drug-fueled escape upon return represented a target on the circuit.

He approached a vendor called the "Virtual Love Escape," ready to enter through its door.

"Didn't take you for the type," said a voice from behind him.

Raith turned, facing Carter. Pointing toward the door, Raith said, "Who, me? I wasn't going to actually spend any money. Just—"

"You wander, friend," he said. "I pay attention. This morning—to the Administrator. And right now, you passed by the door of the Lightspeed at least four times."

"I wanted—"

"Doesn't matter. Let's walk."

Raith paused, one foot still toward the potential source of information he could use against his opponents. "Carter, I—"

"I'm only going to ask one more time."

Nodding, the SI walked down the corridor toward the racer. "Where are we going?"

"I want to show you something."

"How circumspect." Raith smirked. "Whatever, I'll follow. As we've all been following you for the past month."

"Cute."

The pair walked in silence for a few minutes before the man said, "I forgive you for not telling me, you know."

"I—"

"You really like to talk before knowing if someone's finished, don't you?" Instead of anger on Carter's face, only a half-hearted grin appeared. "Look, I spent a lot of time thinking while in the lead. And when I got back into the hangar, I reviewed your race the whole way through. You're racing clean, and it's magnificent to watch. You're moving up through the pack at a pace unmatched by anyone else. You should see what the commentators are saying about you."

"I don't really ever pay attention to what the analysts say," Raith said. "I find their nonsense, twenty-four hour sports cycle meaningless."

"It is, but it's sending a message throughout the entire ICH." Carter stopped in the middle of the hallway and leaned against the wall. "Everyone's eyes are on this race." His eyes darted away, looking down the empty corridor. "Raith, people are calling for the racing circuits to reinstate you when all of this ends."

"You're kidding."

"No."

"If I keep myself clean, there might be a chance I—"

"Yep."

Raith leaned against the other wall. "Now look who can't stop himself from interrupting."

"You got me." He pushed off from the wall, and the pair continued their stroll. "Point is, I should have let you talk to me after qualifying. You're clearly not used to all of this."

"All of what?" Raith asked.

Carter smiled. "As I thought. Well, we're almost there."

They reached an elevator, and against Raith's better judgment, they stepped through, letting the cramped carton shuttle them up a long tube. At the top, they stepped out and into a vast room, glass ceilings surrounding. A massive planetarium revealed the splendor of the galaxy above them. Dozens of spectators milled about, standing near info booths and watching replays on display screens.

"Accept the AR request incoming," Carter said. "It'll let you see the true beauty of this room."

Raith obliged, and the station began sending him packets upon packets of information, all overlaying upon the glass above their heads. A map formed, showing the course of the Five-Hundred Light-year Classic, darting from star to star across the sky.

"Magnificent," Raith said.

"When the race is live, they zoom the screen in so it displays all the racers in a line along the most commonly used vectors. Between laps, you can customize it to view particular sections. Here was my favorite." With his hands, Carter queued in a few commands, and Raith's visual transformed under the man's direction. Light-year twenty-seven appeared, with the black hole prominent against the glass. An icon signifying Carter's ship, the *Bloodhound*, flew by first, dipping along the edge of the black hole.

Together, Raith and Carter stood and watched the minutes fly by, racer after racer passing through the element with visual splendor. QuanCom had outdone itself, creating an impossibly immersive experience for spectators. The race occurred at Jump, but the graphics, when zoomed in, made it seem like it all happened in real time. Digital spacecraft fought for positions, and—

Raith and the *Vindicta* arrived, along with the six or so racers he'd been vying against during light-year twenty-seven and while defeating the singularity. They passed through the checkpoints. Right as Raith eclipsed and overtook his competitors, Carter paused the recording, inputting another set of commands.

Two vectors overlaid above the black hole: Raith's, and Carter's. The routes matched each other perfectly.

"You're watching me closely, I can see," Carter said.

"And you're watching me too?" Raith replied.

"Perhaps. I expect you to catch me, but I expect it to happen fair and square. Just know. I'm not going to make this easy for you. And every time you use a vector faster than my own through an element in a lap . . . fully expect me to copy it, just as you did here." Facing Raith, Carter held up his hand.

Raith reached out and clasped it. "I'm going to win."

"And?"

"I'm going to win the right way."

Carter nodded. "I thought that's what you'd say. I'll see you during the final lap."

Chapter 16

"Coming up on the bullseye." Raith queued up vectors, watching the dozens of racers surrounding him prepare their approaches. QuanCom's data streamed into the *Vindicta* seamlessly. "Here's our chance, friends. Thoughts?"

"Sending over a calculation now," said Bonta. "I think you'll like it."

Moments later, Raith received an arcing route over the forty or so racers ahead of him. It dipped over their trajectories and dove down in front of them, right before reaching the ecliptic of the bullseye's parent star. If achieved, he would zip through the checkpoint between the two gas giants three seconds ahead of Eduardo. Perfect. "An insane maneuver, Bonta, but I like it. It's not suicidal for once!"

"Locking in then?" replied the other SI.

"Of course. Especially what you've proposed for the final approach." Raith centered the route into his mind. Thus, the *Vindicta* also followed it. As his arc began to drift above the general plane of the other racers, he lost ground slightly. No matter.

"We're in three-hundredth at the moment, yes?" Raith said. "My HUD up-to-date?"

"We have the same numbers," said Harrison, piping into the conversation. "What are you thinking?"

"If we pull this maneuver off, we'll jump to . . . two-hundred-sixty-fourth. That's the type of ground we need to cover on elements like this. But how risky can we go? What's our fuel consumption look like?"

"What are you thinking?" asked Bonta.

Raith dialed up a few calculations he'd been running over the past few days of the second lap. "I think we need to run some calculated throttle burns," he said. "We know our ship can hit faster JDs more efficiently than the other racers, and we need to use that to our advantage. Especially in particularly tricky gravitational moments. Like the bullseye."

Silence, for a moment. Bonta was most likely going over the data. A few seconds later, the SI said, "Good numbers, good numbers. Let's see . . . yeah, it all checks out. Though I hope you realize you might make a few enemies here."

"I'm counting on it," Raith said. "The more aggressively they race, the more likely they are to make mistakes. Just watch." His eyes turned toward the digitized icons on his displays indicating the distance between the *Vindicta* and Eduardo. At present, only a few ten-thousandths of a light-year. Raith was about to radically change those numbers.

The next hour progressed, the arc taking the *Vindicta* on a radically different path through dark space toward the bullseye. A few other racers a couple dozen spots behind trailed his route, for some unknown reason. Otherwise, everyone else tailed close behind Eduardo and his position leading their little pack. With ten minutes until the checkpoint, Raith ignited his plan.

For the past twenty hours or so, the pack had clocked an average pace of 680 JD. A healthy pace, if a bit below the average. The supposed tactic would allow for a longer burn above 700 JD in the later portions of the course with more sustained dark space stretches. Yet a pace of 680 made it dreadfully easy for anyone to pass—and pass quickly, if inside the pack. When anyone attempted to pass, everyone accelerated, attempting to match pace. No one wanted to lose too much ground on the pack, after all. As far as Raith knew, nobody had attempted an aggressive maneuver of this nature. Yet.

Time to change everything.

He pushed the *Vindicta*'s Jump-core, surpassing 700 JD in a matter of microseconds. Only a few million kilometers separated him from Eduardo's trajectory toward the bullseye, and as he accelerated, the gap closed more quickly than anyone could have expected. As predicted, Eduardo noticed Raith's angled approach, and his ship, the *Riot Squad*, compensated in an effort to keep Raith in the pack, rather than leading it.

Raith wasn't going to let the kid off easy.

The *Vindicta* pushing past 710. 720. 730. They crossed into the star's ecliptic, and the gravitational pull of the star and its planets placed a greater strain on fuel consumption within the Jump-core. But if he'd done the math right . . .

The *Vindicta* hit 750 just as the pack passed the system's outer most major object, a tiny planetoid a little bigger than Mercury. Three seconds to go. 760, and he dipped in front of Eduardo and the *Riot Squad* by a few fractions of a second, equal to millions of kilometers, at the relativistic speeds they were traveling.

The bullseye was dead ahead as he rapidly pulled further away from Eduardo. His ship simply couldn't keep up. The *Riot Squad* maxed out at 730 JD—a record for the race, if not for Raith's stunt—but it wasn't even close. Raith zipped through the bullseye, followed the new trajectory out of the star system, and headed toward the next checkpoint.

At the same moment, Eduardo and three other racers dropped out of Jump between the two gas giants, dozens of pilots zipping by.

"Hell yeah!" shouted Harrison over the com. "That's what I'm talking about."

A chorus of other cheers came from the rest of the crew, and Raith smiled to himself. He'd made them proud. Watching his calculation's curve dip toward red, he dropped the throttle down toward 700, evening out at 695, a healthy pace for the next few days. Those in the pack who made it through the bullseye dropped their pace as well—when leaving a system, it was particularly important to avoid significantly excessive burns.

As predicted, they were now in two-hundred-sixty-fourth, with a pissed Eduardo on their tail.

They were entering the forty-fifth light-year. An hour ago, he took two-hundred-seventeenth.

"Everyone's going crazy back here on station, Raith," Erika whispered into the com. "You won't believe how many teams you pissed off with that maneuver back at the bullseye."

"They wanted a show, I'm giving them a show," Raith replied.

"Don't get us wrong, we're loving it," said Donyi. "We'll need to prepare for what's to come, though. There will be backlash."

"Riots, blackmail, accusations of murder, I've seen it all."

"You've been accused of murder?" asked Erika.

"Well, not murder exactly, but what sent me to jail in the first place. The reckless manslaughter."

Silence from the pair.

"Keep talking to me friends, I've got another half-day until we reach the final element."

More silence.

"Erika, Donyi?"

"Sorry, we're here. Thought we heard something outside the ship. False alarm!"

Raith silently swore to himself. If someone messed with his crew and the *Juniper*, they'd have hell to pay. "Tell me a story, friends. About you." There. He was trying to connect with them.

"Do you know how we came up with the design for the *Vindicta*'s SI-integrated piloting system?"

He couldn't tell which one of them said the words. "No idea. It works like a charm, though."

"We were serving with Theren at the time, on a mission well beyond the edges of ICH space. Did you know Theren pilots their external shuttles? It's pretty nifty. They often join ground teams in an MI too."

"I thought you were telling me about how you came up with the *Vin-*

dicta, not your worship for Theren."

"Right, forgot you dislike them. It's somewhat relevant, though. We were thinking about Theren initially integrating into their first ship back in the early 2100s, and then . . . Bonta joined the crew. The first ship-bound SI to transition into mobile form and place their mind into an MI. Their story? Quite the process, you know. Restricting your mind so significantly from what it once was? I can't imagine the psychological toll."

"They're not on the line, are they?" Raith asked.

"No, Bonta and Harrison are out."

"Good." The candid conversation about the other SI's mind made Raith uncomfortable, and it would have been even more disconcerting if Bonta had been on the line. "Continue, then, I'm curious where this is going." As he waited for them to talk, he checked fuel predictions. If he planned everything right, the next few light-years should earn him a few more positions before the end of the lap.

"Well, as we said, Bonta joined," said Erika. "And we thought about how Theren was an SI who was grounded for years before they became ship-bound. And there have been a few MIs who transitioned into ship-bound, and after Bonta, plenty of ship-bound who decided to fully transition into an MI. And obviously, for years, ship-bound SIs have walked about planets and stations while operating an MI."

"It was all so black and white," Donyi added. "Either an SI is ship-bound, grounded, mobile, et cetera, et cetera. And then . . . we considered how *our* mind works."

"How *does* your mind work?"

"It's hard to describe," replied Erika, "but the best equivalent we've identified is what you're experiencing right now. Though, the ship doesn't ever think for itself."

Raith focused his attention on the senses and functions of the *Vindicta*, currently integrated into his consciousness. He could *feel* vacuum flying by outside; the Jump-core was like his heart, pumping power all around. "You can sense each other's experiences?" he asked.

"It's not so simple," Erika said. "Part of my mind—part of my cognition—it lives inside Donyi's mind. Our neural cybernetics allow our brains to talk to one another."

Pondering the thought, Raith considered the implications. "But wait, how is what I'm doing different from a ship-bound SI taking control of an MI?"

"Many things. While many SIs claim their mobile units become part of their mind, it's still more similar, psychologically speaking, to them controlling a remote car. It's like . . . a rough approximation. But all the cognition is still going on inside their brain, it's just looping in and out of the mobile unit and receiving a boost from its inert synthetic neural framework."

"So . . ." They'd lost him.

"So when you embrace the *Vindicta*," Donyi said, "there's no lag. There's no disconnect. Your mind isn't cycling cognition primarily inside your body right now. For all intents and purposes, the *Vindicta* is you at the moment; we've expanded your synthetic neural framework by connecting nodes directly to your synthetic neural framework."

"Wait," Raith said. "That means . . ." He thought more closely about their conclusion. "But I don't feel different when I disconnect. If you lost one another, wouldn't your brains stop working?"

"It's not a one-to-one correlation. And let's be real, we did a better job than the doctors who mended our minds. We made sure you could continue to survive without the ship. We're not permanently scarring your synthetic neural framework."

"What would happen if the two of you were forcibly separated?"

Silence.

"Erika, Donyi?"

"We don't like talking about that."

Darkness. Void. Raith stared outward, embracing the colors swirling as he Jumped through the light-years. He'd pushed too far in his attempt to understand the pair. They wanted him to be their friend, but how could he do so if he didn't understand what lines to avoid?

"I'm sorry, I shouldn't have asked."

"Raith, it's fine," they said, their voices blending together. "Don't worry about it. Let's focus on the race."

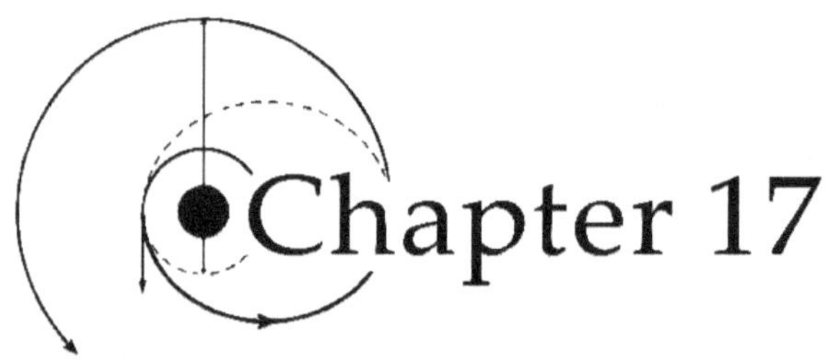

Chapter 17

As the Vindicta landed, Raith prepared his mind for the incoming storm. He'd ended the lap in two-hundred-fifth, making up more ground than expected. He was starting to believe, more and more, in the chance he actually could catch Carter. The next two hundred racers posed a much different challenge, though. They could actually race.

As he dropped out of the ship, disconnecting it from his mind, he found Carter standing there, talking with Bonta and the rest of the crew. Joy welled inside Raith's mind. Joy. Why joy? He tried to shake away the feeling, but it nagged, not wanting to leave his perceptions.

Harrison approached him with open arms. "Well done. Incredibly impressive. You have no idea how precise a stunt you pulled at the bullseye. It's all anyone's been able to talk about for the three weeks!"

"We've still got eight laps to go," Raith said. "Eight laps to catch this guy." He pointed at the pilot of the *Bloodhound*.

"And I expect us to end this race first and second," said Carter. "But for now, I've got a proposition for you . . . and your team."

Raith glanced toward his crew, noting the crossed arms and smiles donning the three standing off to the side. "Do tell."

"Let's get a drink together."

Joy again. Not what he'd been expecting at all. "Right now?"

"Yes! Of course, you and Bonta can't drink, only the four of us can, but it'll be fun!"

"Didn't take you for the drinking type."

Carter ran a hand through his hair. "And I did take you for the arguing type. Just shut up, let's go, it's time to relax for the next few hours before we all need to prep for next week."

In the back of the Lightspeed Café, the six of them found a booth secluded away from the prying eyes of the public. It came with a curtain and everything. They could order drinks through AR, so no need to visit the bar.

There, the six sat, making small talk and learning more about Carter. Raith found the whole experience incredibly awkward. Harrison had asked Carter about his favorite star! Such a basic question. Pulling up a screen, Raith accessed a poker module and threw it onto the table for all of them to perceive through their AR interfaces. "Let's play a game."

"Really, you enter the bar and your mind automatically turns to gambling?" Bonta said, rapping his fingers on the table. "You can't think of anything better to do?"

"No, come on, let's make it friendly!" Raith said. "No cash buy-in, winner gets . . . to make the losers do something?"

"You're grasping at straws," said Carter, chuckling. "Stop the games. We don't need to be always competing. Just relax."

Raith removed the module from the table, frustrated. "Just trying to liven things up."

"You're what, almost two-hundred years old?" said Harrison. "Haven't you learned to slow down?"

Raith and Carter immediately started laughing, their shoulders bumping into each other.

"I thought you at least knew me better than that," Raith said. "I'm a racer. I can't slow down. Can't stop, won't stop!"

"And I thought I was getting intoxicated more quickly than everyone else at the table," responded Harrison. "Clearly, you've beat me to it."

"I read the room," Raith said. "Adapt accordingly."

"Raith, let me ask you something," Carter said. He took a sip of his whiskey. "Twenty years in prison. It sucked. I can't imagine. But do you believe you deserved it?"

The table quieted at the sudden change in conversational tone. Carter, throwing a wrench in the conversation. He tended to be good at that. Raith considered the question—and the intention behind it. "I feel like this is a trick, and there isn't any right answer other than yes that *doesn't* make me look like a pretentious tool." His words eased the visible tension at the table, everyone's eyes loosening at the joke. Raith didn't blame them for expecting an outburst. He'd yelled at the four of them more than once during their time together for a lesser intruding statement. "So, yes?"

Carter grinned. "Your words, not mine."

"I want to give a more nuanced answer though," Raith said. "Did I deserve punishment for my actions? Sure. But at what point do my choices, leading me to getting sucked into the Conglomerate's world, become my fault rather than their fault? They sucked me in years before my 'crime' for the silliest little thing."

"What was it?" asked Bonta.

"Before I was a racer, I flew as a . . . smuggler."

"Pirate," said Carter. "You were a pirate."

"No, not fair! We only hijacked a ship once!"

"That makes you a pirate," said Erika. "You pirated someone else's cargo."

"We pirated from a pirate!"

"Still a pirate."

Raith waved his hand in the air. He prepared to speak when the curtain opened, a server dropping new drinks on the table. When the group was alone again, he said, "Anyway. Did I deserve my punishment? Maybe. Is twenty years extreme? Is a racing ban from the official leagues extreme? Maybe. When someone can live forever, is any indefinite ban justifiable? I'm less angry about the prison-time—that wasn't too bad—than the bans." Raith glanced toward his opponent. His friend.

"Racing means that much to you, doesn't it?" Carter said.

"It's my life."

Across the table from them, Erika and Donyi chuckled and stood, sliding out of the booth.

"Where are you going?" Raith asked. "We've only been here for an hour or so."

"We're tired. We need sleep. The four of you stay." They darted under the curtain and out of sight.

"So Carter," Harrison said. "I read this is your first race. What's your secret? I don't get it. How are you doing this in your ship? What is special about the *Bloodhound*?"

"Nothing special," said the man, absentmindedly looking toward the curtain. "I've owned it for about a year, so it's fairly new. Used proceeds from my last contract to build it."

"I suppose what interests me the most," said Bonta, "is how you managed to translate your exploration skills into racing."

Raith nodded. "I'm intrigued too. How *are* you racing so well?"

"Don't act so surprised!" Carter sipped his whiskey. "I think everyone's thinking about this race like it's just a normal race. It's not. It's more like . . . an outbound flight. Or the early probe missions from the twenty-first century. Dip into a system and dip out. Difference is, we're not dropping out of Jump when we enter a system. We don't need to take a moment to transmit through Quantum what we've found. We're constantly plugged in."

Harrison furrowed his brow. "Not sure I'm catching your drift."

Carter shrugged. "Let me say it another way. When I'm out exploring, for months at a time on my own, I've got an incentive to loop through systems at a fast pace. Especially system-to-system. I've gotten particularly good at mapping out routes through gravitational ebbs and flows. It's almost second nature to me. Flying at Jump, making calculations at Jump, changing everything up? It's what I do."

At the end of the sentence, both Bonta and Harrison looked up as if receiving a message through AR. They glanced at one another, but they ignored whatever they received.

"Something happen?" Raith asked.

"Nothing, don't worry about it," Bonta said. "Carter, that makes sense, I suppose, but your ship. How's it so fast?"

"It's not faster than your ship," said Carter.

"We know that," replied Harrison. "But—"

"I'm just flying, hitting the routes. It's instinct. The timing's instinct. You saw me hit those maneuvers during the Gauntlet. It's just . . . instinct."

"Nothing's just instinct," Raith said. In response to Carter's raised eyebrow, he added, "Maybe your years of exploration have translated into 'instinct,' but I'd call it skill. No one is built to be a certain way."

"Ah, so you weren't built to be a racer. Nor a criminal."

"Precisely. I am a racer by choice, because I love it, but I am not a criminal by choice."

"Then why do your instincts continue to pull you back toward those choices?"

Raith expected anger to rise from the comment, but it didn't. His mind saw the reasoning and intention behind Carter's words, respecting the approach. The rhetoric. No, he wasn't trying to provoke. He was trying to understand. "When you do something for a long time, and it becomes your life, it becomes natural to you. It's not instincts, but it is compulsion. I have a desire to take the easy way toward victory because I like winning. But it wasn't always like that. My first years as a pilot? I won, fair and square, every time. And we're back to that me. That's the version I am meant to be. Who I choose to be."

"That you want to be." Carter said the words, but he was nodding in agreement.

"Sure, if there's a difference. I don't see it, though."

"Well, you're an SI. Your mind works a bit differently than a human's. You're more rigid in your thought processes. Once you make a decision, it's the decision you've made. No irrational flip-flopping. Unless the SI wants to be an irrational flip-flopper."

"You think a lot about how our minds work?" Raith asked.

"Only the minds of particular SIs."

"What about—" Raith looked for Bonta, but the other SI had disappeared from the booth, along with Harrison. He was alone with Carter. His crew . . . of course. They'd set him up. Those bastards, trying to get him alone in a social setting with Carter. Not their place!

"Was this your idea?" Carter asked.

"Was what my idea?" Raith inquired.

"For them to sneak away?"

Shaking his head, Raith tried to hold back his smile. "No, not at all. I don't know what you're thinking, but it's not like that, they're just playing pranks."

"I wasn't implying anything." Carter leaned into the booth. "I'm enjoying our conversation. We were pretty much the only two talking." He took another sip of his whiskey, the glass almost empty, the ice completely melted. "I don't know what you're thinking, but all I'm saying is, we click together. We think similarly, approach questions the same way. It's good. I've not had many people to talk to in my life, and I appreciate it. I do."

Raith nodded. "Me too. It's—"

A notification appeared through AR. Urgent message from Bonta. Raith opened it, giving Carter access to see it too.

"Raith, get to the hangar now," said the other SI. "Erika and Donyi? They've disappeared."

Through the doors, Carter and Raith ran, entering the hangar. Harrison and Bonta frantically darted around the ship, searching for any clues.

"Anything?" Raith asked. "Anything at all?"

"Nothing," Bonta said.

"They can't respond via AR?"

"No, I'm suspecting whoever took them is jamming their signal."

Raith groaned. "No, no, that will screw with their mind. With their brain. Have you checked the exterior cameras of the *Juniper* yet?"

"Doing it now," Bonta said.

Carter sprinted away from them and toward his vessel. "I'll do the same!" he shouted.

Pacing back and forth, Harrison's hands rested against the back of his neck. "I can't believe I let this happen," he said. "I knew there was a risk."

Raith approached the man. "What do you mean, you knew there was a risk?"

"You know how we said it's been crazy since you pulled that stunt going through the bullseye?"

Memory recalled the comments over the past few weeks while he finished the second lap. His conversations with all of them, hinting at something more going on beyond the scenes. The moment Erika and Donyi thought they heard something outside the ship. The paranoia in their voice.

"What have you been hiding from me?" Raith said, pointing a finger straight at Harrison's nose. "If they're hurt because you didn't put me on guard—"

"Found them."

Harrison and Raith both turned toward Bonta. The SI passed them a recording through AR from one of the ship's exterior cameras. "Watch. They're about to enter through the hangar doors—you can see Erika's arm—then they're pulled away."

An incoming data request from Carter chimed, and Raith accepted it. Another recording, from a different angle. Zoomed in, he could make out a man pulling Erika back down the hall. Automatic programs enhanced the image. Easy match.

"I know that man," Raith said. "He was with Eduardo the first day I arrived on station."

Carter bounded down the ramp out of the *Bloodhound*. "Did I hear you right? That's one of Eduardo's?"

"He's taking revenge for the stunt I pulled. I can't believe he'd go this far. This low." Raith turned back to Harrison. "Tell me everything. What are the threats? What are the comments? Who's saying what?"

"Slow down, slow down," Carter said. "What?"

"Oh, you've not had time to watch the recordings, have you?" Raith said. "I passed Eduardo with spectacular fashion this lap, forcing him to drop out of JD. It's part of the reason he's now four-hundredth."

"I'd laugh if it wasn't putting your crew in danger. I can't wait to watch the replay."

A bunch of messages began populating Raith's inbox as Harrison forwarded him dozens of notes. "They're all from Eduardo's fans. Threats on your life. Our lives. They're claiming you were attempting to do to Eduardo what you did to Kana."

"Those f—"

"Hold on," Carter said. "Don't act on instinct. Let's go to the race administrators. They won't let this slide. Will they?"

⁂

It turned out, the administrators would let it slide. Thirty minutes later, Raith, Bonta, Harrison, and Carter walked out of the station's security center. They'd been laughed out of the room.

"We have proof," Carter said. "We have literal proof."

"It's my name," Raith said. "They're going to claim I'm trying to frame a fellow racer. I have no credibility. And more importantly, they'd rather I make a splash about this in the media to drive more press." He dropped to the floor, sliding against the wall. "Those poor women. Their brains must be going crazy."

Harrison and Bonta paced back and forth. Bonta said, "We'll get a message out to Theren, of course. They can help us. They must."

"Wait," Carter said, "What's Theren got to do with this?"

Raith went to speak, but Bonta held up a hand. "Don't say it, Raith. I shouldn't have said anything in front of Carter anyway."

"Theren presently owns the *Vindicta*," Raith said, ignoring Bonta.

The other SI threw their hands in the air. "Why you gotta be like this?"

"It's fine, Bonta, really," said Harrison. "Carter, we can trust you to keep this secret, yeah?"

The man chuckled. "Sure, but I don't really see why it's a secret."

"Theren has a 'reputation' to uphold," Raith said. "You know, can't be seen cavorting with a criminal."

"That's not it," Bonta grumbled, "and you—"

Raith held up a finger. "Stop." He stood, hopping to his feet. "No time to talk. Time to act. We're finding Eduardo."

He bounded down the corridor away from the security office, almost certain he knew where to find the man. He didn't wait to see if the others followed, but the sound of their footsteps assured him they hadn't objected. Only a few minutes later, he pushed back into the Lightspeed Café, through the foyer, and into the poker room. As expected, Eduardo sat at a table, still looking fresh out of his own ship.

"Eduardo!" Raith roared. "Where the hell are they?"

The man stood, a cock-eyed grin on his face. Palms forward, he spread his arms wide. "My, Raith, I have no idea what you're talking about."

Harrison and Bonta joined his side—Raith could sense Carter standing a few meters back. Before anyone else could say a word, Raith took a step forward. "Your men. They abducted my computing engineers. They're gone. Disappeared. You have them. You're going to die if they're hurt."

Eduardo laughed, his belting chortle released as if Raith had just said an incredibly funny joke. He slapped his knees, barely able to stand.

Raith stepped forward, uppercutting straight into Eduardo's jaw. He half-expected Bonta or Harrison to stop him, but they didn't say a word. Eduardo snapped straight back, falling onto his butt. Before the man could react, Raith picked him up and slammed him onto the poker table. He pressed his head firmly into the glass. "Look boy, tell me where they are. Tell me what you did. I will end you."

A subtle hissing revealed Eduardo was pissing himself. Suddenly, his voice turned frantic. "Look, look, I don't know what you're talking about! I don't have any men! They were bought from under me two weeks ago—-during the race!"

Raith stepped back, flabbergasted. "What?"

Eduardo used his elbows to prop himself against the table. "I swear." The fear was evident in his eyes. "I swear. Raith, I know you weren't trying to hurt me during the race. Ignore my fans. I—I actually respect the move you pulled. It was clever. Clean. Smart."

Raith looked over his shoulder, seeing Bonta, Harrison, and Carter holding back the club's bouncers. "Who bought them off you?"

"I don't know," Eduardo said. "I wish I knew, but I don't. I don't."

Silence, in the void . . .

They could only continue. They tried everything. They tried the Administrators. They searched the Hub. They talked to everyone.

No evidence whatsoever.

In a system feeling so small—S-1022, designed only for a race—they lost Erika and Donyi. The days and hours before the start of the next lap ticked away, and the souls of Raith, Harrison, Bonta—even Carter—drained away in sorrow.

What could they do? In the face of an enemy so well-financed, so secretive, so powerful, the duo were stripped from them, and Raith knew they would only find the two women if whomever took them wanted them found. So he steeled his mind. They all steeled their mind. But they never gave up.

The race continued. The third lap. The fourth. The fifth.

Raith climbed the ranks, passing more and more opponents, pulling off more and more maneuvers. Between each lap, he searched for leads. The fingers of the Conglomerate were all over their disappearance—that much was obvious—but Vanaka refused to see him. He couldn't even find her. She never left her hangar, and she had switched apartments, apparently, the day after Raith originally met with her. The one message he did receive made one thing clear: she would accept nothing less than total capitulation before meeting with him again. And he couldn't accept defeat like that, even if it meant saving the twins.

And if he did so, they'd be disappointed in him too. Giving up the race to save them?

Through it all? Silence from QuanCom and its racing officials. Erika and Donyi gone, and no one would help Raith and his team find them—except Carter.

After every lap, Carter joined Raith and the remainder of his crew in the *Juniper*, plotting possibilities and mapping out the station. Though the Hub was massive, it wasn't infinite. Each week, they crossed off locations and sections as they searched them. It wasn't a foolproof plan. Wherever Erika and Donyi were held, their captors could move them at will.

Yet, systematic search and rescue was all the *Vindicta*'s crew could do.

Harrison continued reaching out to Olive in an attempt to contact Theren. She reassured them time and time again Theren was sending out inquiries in an attempt to investigate, but their SI benefactor was too distant to help, supposedly. And Olive couldn't join them either. They were alone.

The sixth lap began.

Raith entered in hundred-thirteenth. The lap ended. Ninety-sixth.

Each lap, he gained fewer and fewer spots. During each break, they spent less time calculating new vectors based on new stellar data. A factor not obvious at the beginning of the race—as they continued, each element shifted slightly as planets orbited their stars and stars drifted through space.

The seventh lap began. Carter dropped to third, though by the end of the lap, he regained his lead.

The eighth lap began. And ended.

Still no news. No luck. And still no help from Theren, their distant benefactor. Olive continued assuring them she'd passed along their message, but nothing. Absolutely nothing.

The ninth lap, about to begin. A few minutes before Raith walked to the *Vindicta*, he sat staring at Bonta and Harrison inside the *Juniper*.

"What are we going to do if we can't find them?" Raith said. "It's been seven months. Seven."

"If we can't find them," Harrison said, "we win. And then we find their murderers."

"You really think it's murder?" said Bonta.

"It's been seven months," Raith repeated. He left them sitting there and headed to the *Vindicta* to prepare for the penultimate lap. He was in eightieth. Eighty spots in two laps. Not impossible, but he had his doubts. Without Erika and Donyi, all three of them were lost.

He rose into the *Vindicta*, ready to connect to the interface created by the two women lost in space. He'd win the race. Two laps left to do it. And when he won, he'd make the Conglomerate pay.

As he hooked in, meta-nodes integrating his mind with the racer, a message arrived. Unknown origin, unknown sender. Untraceable.

> *If you want to see your twins, you'll find them after the ninth lap. Come alone to my apartment.*

Vanaka.

# Chapter 18

The ninth lap occurred without incident, Raith ending in fifty-sixth place. Not ideal, but he'd take it. Like all the previous laps since the second, he'd more looked forward to ending the lap so he could return to the search. And now, he had a lead. It was probably a trap, but it was worth springing the trap if it meant saving Erika and Donyi.

Bonta, Harrison, and Carter were waiting, ready to enact a plan discussed slowly between them all during the weeks of lap nine. Raith ushered them into the *Juniper*. Inside, Bonta and Harrison had prepared a suite filled with surveillance programs and equipment.

"So we'll be piping my eyes into here," Raith said.

"And if it cuts out, we come running," said Carter.

"There's no way this doesn't go south," added Harrison.

"I'm expecting it to." Raith scrolled through the algorithms and scripts, prepared. "I'm banking on it. We need to reveal Vanaka, the Conglomerate—and their crimes—to everyone."

Carter leaned against a wall. "Why will they believe you this time?"

"They won't believe me," Raith said. "But they'll believe you."

The man went to open his mouth, raising a finger, but instead, he shook his head. "You're right. They will believe me. They have no reason *not* to. I'm ready. It's worth it."

"Any questions? Are we ready?"

With curt nods, all three acquiesced. Raith debated saying more; instead, he headed out the door.

The walk to the residential section where Vanaka's old apartment had been didn't take long. Within only a few minutes, he approached her door, ready to knock. His hand rose; the door opened before he could smack the cold metal.

Entering, he sent a private message to Carter and the others. *Still receiving data?*

Their response, a few seconds later. *We are.*

Unlike his last visit to the apartment, it lacked furniture. The opulent chandeliers hung lightless. Except for a single couch in the back of the room, the space was empty.

Slowly, Raith crept forward. He half-expected lights to ignite, revealing an ambush, or a sudden blast of information from a latent AR message linked to the apartment to overrun his senses.

Nothing.

The couch, only a few meters away. *Still here?* His team's response was prompt. *We are.*

Two meters. One meter.

He peeked over the cushions—and tumbled backward.

"God damn it!" Raith roared, jumping back to his feet and darting around to the front of the couch. Leaning against it, fingers interlaced, rested Erika and Donyi.

Blood-soaked. Lifeless. Dead.

Without thinking, Raith slammed a hand against the wall, the force of his hardened frame denting the wall. "Your war was with me." He stared about the apartment, searching for someone. Anyone. "With me! Not them. They didn't deserve this. They didn't deserve this!"

Dropping to his knees, Raith looked into the eyes of his former crew. Based on the freshness of the blood, they'd been murdered in the past few hours. Planned, from the very beginning. Capture. Contain. Prepare. Murder.

Stay there. A message from Carter and the others. *We're coming to you.*

Raith continued staring. Erika and Donyi, the geniuses who developed the *Vindicta*. Made it possible. Made his race possible through their innovative synthetic system. Erika and Donyi, twins with a mind unlike anyone in the galaxy, capable of communicating with each other in a way unknown. Their brain, the inspiration for his salvation.

"Revenge." He looked past them into the empty apartment. "You wanted me to join you, to fall into your grasp. Rather, you've achieved the exact opposite. You'll never have me or the *Vindicta*."

He half-expected Vanaka to finally appear. Nothing. A few minutes passed before Harrison, Bonta, Carter, and a QuanCom security officer entered the room.

It took an hour to peel Raith from the floor.

⁙⊸ ⁞⊫⊶ ⁞⊪⊸

The second day of the break before the final lap, Raith led Carter, Harrison, and Bonta toward Administrator Harris's office. It was time to end it all. The door slid open, and the four stepped through.

Harris looked up from his desk. "Ah, Carter, Raith, good to—"

Before Raith could say a word, Carter slammed a hand on the oak desk. "You're a bastard, you know that?"

"Excuse—"

"If you haven't been briefed on the kidnapping and double homicide that happened under your nose, you're the most incompetent person I've ever met."

Raith took a step back, watching the scene unfold. When he was angry, Carter was angry. Ferocious. It was wonderful to witness.

"Carter, we have people investigating—"

"We know exactly who did it. That was Vanaka's apartment. She threatened Raith before the race even started. Motive. Scene of the crime. Now where is she? Let us into her hangar. Confront her. Hell man, send your own people after her!"

"Was this the type of drama you wanted?" Raith said. "Murder? Mayhem? On your station?"

"It's not that simple," Harris said.

"Oh, because you're under the thumb of the Conglomerate?" Harrison said.

"No, the Conglomerate's gone. This isn't the Conglomerate. We don't know who this is!"

Raith shook his head, stunned. "Don't give me that crap. It's the Conglomerate. Who else would target me? It's always been them. Vanaka told me it was them."

"We're bringing in the best to figure this out," Harris said. "Arriving in the next week or so. But you think you can manage my station better than me?" He transferred a station address through AR. And an access code. "That'll get you into Vanaka's hangar. But—"

"If this isn't resolved before lap ten begins," Raith said, "we're dropping out of the race." He wasn't entirely sure if his words were a bluff.

Harris looked at him, stunned.

"Not just Raith," Carter said. "I will too. You'll lose your two best sources of entertainment before the end of the race. Ruin all future hopes you might have for this event. We'll smear it. Scandal everywhere."

"They'll never believe you," said Harris. "We're QuanCom."

"They'll believe us," said Bonta.

Raith glanced toward the SI, noticing his head bobbing alongside Harrison's own nod.

"They'll believe us, Harris," Bonta said. "You know very well who we work for."

Harris met Bonta's stare. "Theren may hold power, but they don't hold a candle to our new foe."

Down the long, equatorial corridor they strode, purpose in their steps. Passing by spectators, crews, and other racers, Raith and his friends knew their target: Vanaka's locked down hangar. They didn't know what to expect. But they were going to make her pay.

"So Carter," Raith said, as they passed by an exercise lounge. "Tell me how this doesn't break the whole 'win fair and square' rule?"

"Don't think I need to answer that question," the man replied. "We're not going after her with the goal of screwing up her race. We're going after her because she needs brought to justice."

"It'll still help me catch you a little bit sooner."

"I'm fine with that."

The corridor's subtle curve slowly brought them closer and closer to the hangar. It was nestled in a portion of the station where wealthy sponsors parked their vessels prior to taking a smaller shuttle to one of the pleasure party boats in orbit somewhere else in-system. Raith's mind sunk at the thought—what if Vanaka wasn't even on station? After every lap, maybe she simply darted off to a rich boy's ship, cavorting and partying for the week. She seemed the type.

Finally, they reached the hangar doors. Closed, of course. Bonta stepped forward, accessing a panel on the wall and inputting the code the Administrator had given them. Without fail, the door hissed open, revealing an expansive hangar, empty except for a single racing pinnace.

"There it is," Harrison muttered. "Let's get—"

"Hold," Raith said, holding up an arm. "Just her racer? Where is she? Just sleeping in her racer?"

"Good question."

Raith stepped furtively across the threshold, looking left and right for any hiding spots. Nothing. Other than maintenance equipment, refueling canisters, and other complex hardware, the hangar was empty of life.

"She's gotta be here somewhere," Bonta said.

"She could still be somewhere inside the station," Carter said. "Just because her ship's been hidden doesn't mean she can't go off and hide for the—"

"It's all right, I'm here." The modulated voice came from behind them, but she quickly stepped through the open hangar doors and strode toward her racer. The four stood, dumbstruck, before following after her.

"You're going to answer for what you've done," Raith said.

"I heard about the murders," she said, not turning to look back at them. "Do you really think that's my style?"

"It's the Conglomerate's style," Raith said.

"Yes, it is." She still didn't turn to face them. "It's the Conglomerate's style, and I never said I'm with the Conglomerate."

"Harris said they're gone."

"Not gone. Just irrelevant." Reaching the ramp of her ship, she turned, facing them. "Look, you're both racing a good race. And my offer still stands. But murder? Murder isn't my style. Our style. Cutting Carter's power? Maybe our style. Intimidation, bribery, masquerading as a criminal organization to achieve our ends? Maybe our style. Murdering two young women with bright futures ahead of them?" She pointedly stared at each of them. "Not my style. Not the style of who I work for."

The sound of footsteps signaled Bonta, Harrison, and Carter stepping up beside Raith.

"So how's this going down?" said Vanaka. "Are the four of you going to beat me to a pulp for a crime I didn't pull?" She placed her hands on the top of her helmet. "I'm just here to race. And . . . make sure Raith knows he has another option available, if he wants to choose it. My employer wants him and his racer. And she'll get both, one way or another."

"Why?" Raith said. "Who? What's special about me?"

"You rebel," Vanaka said. "You go against the grain of what's expected of SIs. Don't you get it? Don't you see why that's special? A ten thousandth percent deviation rate." She clicked a few buttons on the side of the helmet, air hissing. It slid off.

No.

Impossible.

Raith whirled toward Harrison and Bonta, but their faces showed the same surprise.

He turned back to face Vanaka.

No, not Vanaka.

Olive.

Without thinking, Raith leapt forward and smacked Olive in the jaw. Her head twisted to the side, blood smearing from her lips. Stepping back, she wiped the phlegm from her face and smirked. "Hello Raith, good to see you. Bonta, Harrison." She nodded at them both. "Apologies for the deception, but it was necessary to get you here. To this race. To this place where you would realize how truly different you are from so many other SIs."

Raith raised his hand to hit her again, but a firm grip grabbed his arm from behind. He glanced, finding Carter holding it. His eyes pleaded "don't," and Raith begrudgingly acquiesced.

"This is ridiculous," Bonta said, stepping forward. "We work for Theren! You work for Theren. Theren funded the ship, their—"

"You didn't wonder why Theren never replied to your calls for help over the past few months?" Olive said. "All relayed through me?"

"I mean," Harrison said, "you gave good reasons. Said they were off on an expedition on the far side of ICH space."

"And you didn't question a damn thing." She glanced back to Raith. "You're going to win. Carter's going to lose. And when the race ends, and you've won, come find me. I'll take you to the one person who can help you be who you were meant to be."

She stepped backward up the ramp into her craft, disappearing, leaving the four of them standing in a semi-circle. Raith pivoted, slipping free of Carter's grasp. They were all wide-eyed, including Bonta, as much as the SI's eyes could widen. A similar look certainly covered Raith's face, too.

Without saying a word, Raith slowly trudged toward the hangar exit. Only six days remained until the final lap. The day couldn't come soon enough. Erika and Donyi, dead because of his past, but he had no sign of upon whom to administer revenge. Vanaka, not an agent of the Conglomerate, but of someone else. Someone unknown. And everything, the entire year, a lie. He'd worked alongside good people, sure, but had Theren ever even believed in him? Some small part of his mind hoped the first SI had seen something Raith missed for his two centuries of life.

But no, once again people were using him for their own purposes.

Into the hallway he stepped, leaving Vanaka behind. What was the point? Too many conspiracies. Too many layers. He just wanted to race. And to win.

Why did so many people need to overlay games over top of it?

A hand slipped around his arm, slid down, and laced fingers in fingers. Raith glanced to his left, finding Carter standing there.

"Hey friend," Carter said. "You all right?"

"I don't know what to do."

"We race. If you were bluffing like I suspect, back in the Administrator's offices, let's race."

"Yeah, I suppose that's a path forward."

"All of it, it's all almost over." Carter bumped their shoulders together. "When it's finished—when the race finishes—let's talk. I have an idea."

"Yes, let's talk." Squeezing the man's hand, Raith pivoted to find Bonta and Harrison following close behind. "For now . . . we have a race to finish. A race to win. To beat this man." At the words, he caught a smile cross Carter's lips. "And we're winning it for Erika and Donyi. Seeing it through."

His crew nodded, wordless wisps of emotion echoing off the stainless, sterile walls of the Hub.

Chapter 19

The mood on the *Juniper*'s deck calmed. Alongside Bonta and Harrison, Raith dove into their work, calculating the commonly used vectors and fuel consumption strategies of the opponents separating them from first place. From Carter.

They'd been without Erika and Donyi for months. Today, knowing no hope remained of their return, Raith found strange peace. He missed them both. For so long, he'd worried about what might happen to them. At least now . . . no more suffering. No more pain. And they were together, in the end.

The Conglomerate would pay, someday, for the suffering wrought not only upon Raith, but upon Erika and Donyi. He would destroy the organization in its entirety. For now, he had a different task to complete. Glancing across the room at Bonta and Harrison, hard at work on their projections, he saw the future with these two, by his side, working the circuits and racing again. If he won, it would come true.

So what was the path to victory? Fifty-five racers to defeat, including Carter. Eleven starting rows to pass. With twenty seconds of distance between each row—plus the second delay to give room for launch—they had two-hundred-twenty seconds separating the *Vindicta* from first place. About four-and-a-half seconds each light-year. Less than ten seconds a day. The margins were close. Even if the *Vindicta* had a higher top speed, its average JD per lap was quite close to competitors like Carter . . . or Vanaka.

Not Vanaka. Olive. Or were both a façade? Who was she really? And who did she work for? Regardless, if he was going to beat her and Carter, they needed a new plan.

No, not a new plan.

Bonta's plan.

"The black hole." Raith threw away all graphs. "The black hole. We can use the black hole."

"Oh, now you like my idea?" Bonta looked incredulous, his arms spread wide in a subtle synthetic shrug. "On the last lap, when all is on the line, you're willing to go forward with my plan?"

"Oh shut up."

Harrison stepped between them. "Bonta, just roll with it. We've got our chance to make Erika and Donyi proud. What were you thinking, Raith?"

"Well, we'll go with Bonta's plan, but I've got a few modifications."

The tenth lap. One hour out from the black hole. Halfway between light-year twenty-seven and twenty-eight. Since the first lap, most racers skewed far wide of the imposing singularity. And as Raith and the *Vindicta* approached, he slipped by twenty-first. Only nineteen more racers separating them from first. From Carter.

But between him and the black hole—Olive.

Perfect timing.

"All right Bonta, let's queue up the vector."

"Roger." The other SI transferred their most recent calculation. "Harrison and I have been working the path based on what we've been discussing. Ran through a million calculations. It's the best."

"And more importantly, only the *Vindicta* can make it." Harrison's pride in their ship shone through his words. "If anyone follows you, they won't have enough thrust to avoid a slight drag toward the hole. If our math is right, time dilation will even be perceptible for them."

"We definitely don't want that to happen now do we?" Bonta sent over a few final graphs and data sets. "Heaven forbid someone like Vanaka get slowed down by a big black hole."

Raith chuckled, and over the quantum connection, his two partners joined him. Staring down the calculations, he recognized the truth. The pair had managed to replace Hector, Nessa, and the rest of his old crew. If only Erika and Donyi were still alive, he'd have a full team. With the second half of the final lap ahead of them, he wouldn't have anyone else by his side. "Speaking of Vanaka." He analyzed the competitors closest to the *Vindicta*. "Ah! There she is. Ten seconds ahead. Averaging 699 JD at the moment. Let me run a calculation . . . as I thought. If we pull off this maneuver, we'll fly by her as we pass the event horizon. It's like poetry, my friends."

"You know," said Bonta, "I thought I would hate your showboating, but it's grown on me. It's fun. It's energetic. It shows you weirdly care about the race."

"Showboating? Oh, you've not seen showboating."

Raith focused on their newly established vector. Though only a few hundredths of a light-year separated them from the black hole, it would still be some time before its corona revealed itself. Like most of the other racers, Vanaka's projected course took her well away from the gravity well. The question: would she notice his gambit? Would she fall for it? Would any of the few hundred racers trailing behind them fall for it?

As the black hole's position centered on his scopes, Raith reoriented perceptions. Instead of ahead, the singularity was below. He, and the *Vindicta*, were not flying toward the dark blemish on the stellar horizon; they were falling. Its subtle gravitational force, even at this distance, beckoned. Called. It wished for Raith to enter its embrace.

Gravity acted weird when transformed through exo-warped space. Just as quantum physics refused to obey the traditional rules of Newtonian interactions, "exotic" physics—as coined in the late twenty-first century—changed the game entirely. As the massive singularity ripping a hole in the space-time continuum reached its gravitational forces through the vacuum rippled by the *Vindicta*'s Jump-core, strange phenomena occurred around the ship. Virtual particles, snapping in and out of existence, popped like fireflies. Miniature wormholes, existing for only nanoseconds, flirted and fractured in bent space. All those occurrences, interesting and intriguing to scientific inquiry, meant nothing to Raith. What mattered? He was accelerating at extraordinary superluminal speed toward the black hole, its pull compounding warp-upon-warp to push the *Vindicta* up, up, up past 730, 740, 750, 800, 900 JD. Seconds later, he blew past Vanaka-Olive's much slower vector arcing toward the outer edge of the immense checkpoint. Would she follow? He doubted it, but—

Her vector perceptibly shifted, drifting closer and closer to his own. Still billions of kilometers out from the event horizon, she had time to run the gambit behind him. But could she hit the precise route mapped out over days upon days of work? No. Even if she attempted to follow him, she couldn't know the exact velocities and gravitational anomalies Bonta mapped. The other SI had considered every contingency. Prepared for every potentiality. She may not have killed Erika and Donyi, but she still deserved to fail for her betrayal.

He opened an interface left unused throughout the race. He'd always been unsure why QuanCom even provided the software, other than for testing purposes. Well, now he'd test it. Direct point-to-point connection between two vessels traveling at relative magnitudes past the speed of light.

"Olive." He keyed in a few commands to ensure Bonta and Harrison couldn't hear the conversation. "Walk me through why you betrayed us. Why you lied."

"Hello there, Raith. Happy to join you on your little suicidal run." Her vector fell in behind the *Vindicta* after a few jagged curves. "You know I know the specs of your ship, right? I know what it can and can't do. I know this won't work for you."

"Then why are you attempting it too?" Raith said.

"Unlike you, I don't care about winning."

Raith switched back to the quantum connection with Bonta and Harrison. "You both catching Vanaka—Olive's—vector? Can she make it?"

A few audible moments of silence. Then, Bonta said, "If she follows our vector, her core won't hit the needed burn to avoid falling within the grasp of noticeable time-dilation. It's a subtle curve, but the math works out. If she can't hit the burn, she'll fall beneath the threshold where this crazy gambit is worth it—and suicide for the race. She'll fall minutes, maybe hours, behind."

"What do you both think? Worthy revenge?"

A loose chuckle rippled through their channel. "I love it," said Harrison. "How do you guarantee she follows the whole way?"

"Just use your ears." Raith flipped a few virtual switches, giving them listen-only access to his conversation with Olive. "All right Olive, it's time you answer the actual question. Why'd you betray us?"

"This was never about you, Raith. None of it is. I've been given the opportunity to play a part in a much larger narrative. A larger game, beyond anything you can imagine."

"What the hell are you talking about?"

"You think you, me, this race, any of it—do you think any of it really matters in the end?"

Raith bit back his immediate retort, pausing to consider her actual words. The words echoed, vaguely familiar, to her strange lines right before she originally left him with the crew of the *Juniper*. "Of course none of it matters," he said. "You, me, we're all insignificant. Even someone like me, a synth who can live forever? Doesn't matter. None of it matters. We're specks in comparison to the scale of the universe. Consider the sheer immensity of it all. But Olive, that's the beauty. I'm content with my insignificance, the fact no one really gives a shit about me. I will do what I want to do, and you can't tell me it doesn't matter. Because it matters to *me*." A stray thought flirted inside his consciousness, nagging at his soul. There was one person, light-seconds ahead, who he hoped cared. Hoped mattered. But those thoughts were his alone, not to be shared with Olive.

A snort crackled through the comm. "Raith, you could be so much more. The coming storm will ravage everyone. No one will be exempt. You could be a part of it. You could guide it. You have the mind, the will, the volition to control your life and make it yours. Very few synthetics recognize reality the way you do. Even fewer humans accept it. Everyone, content to accept the galaxy as it is. Not consider what it *could be*. You speak of doing what you want to do because it is what you want to do? What a pitiful excuse. You hide behind your doubt."

"And what is it you're doing? Who is your leader? Who gives you meaning that is of any more significance than mine?"

"A ghost. I follow a ghost. And she is magnificent."

The words meant nothing. Games. Only games. "I liked you. Still like you." Raith progressed through the next few sequences of their suicidal run, beginning the twisting path and preparing to slide closer to the black hole than any previous racer by a few hundred thousand kilometers. "I hope this maneuver doesn't kill you."

"If it kills me, but I convince you to recognize the higher purpose you can achieve, it'll be enough. I sought you out because you can be *so much more*. Even beneath the crushing weight of insignificance, you shine brightly. Now make it matter."

"I like my version of meaninglessness, thank you very much."

The *Vindicta*'s Jump-core cycled upward, injecting Exo and warping space in a rebuffing shield against the crushing pull of the nearby singularity. They were nearing 1000 JD. Though, as time dilation took its hold, his relative velocity to the other racers would equalize closer to 800 JD. Still radically faster than anyone around them. The trick Bonta mapped out required careful trigger points. The immense pull of the black hole provided significant slingshot potential as they slid around the edge, but it also presented a risk of too much drag. If they hit the wrong path or failed to use the right vector, they'd burn too much Exo, losing any opportunity for a winning sprint later in the race.

"It's not going to work," Olive said over the comm. "I will fail to achieve this burn, just as you will. You can't hit it. The timing is too precise. Just like you failed in the Gauntlet, you will fail here."

He couldn't help it. Her words ate at his mind, breeding self-doubt.

"Kill your connection to her," Bonta said. "Now. No more time for chatting. Focus. You need to focus. You can do this."

For a moment, Raith considered another word, but he followed the direction of his crew. He deactivated the conversation, turning toward the now looming and ever-present shadowy mass. Only a few seconds remained. "Here we go." Raith's neural network, integrated with the *Vindicta*, relaxed, preparing to activate every thrust and counter-thrust needed to hit the proposed vector. Olive was wrong. He could do this. Erika and Donyi had built his connection to this ship perfectly.

Augmented visuals overlaid three-dimensional displays, and his mind guided—no, that was the completely incorrect way to describe his act. Raith, the *Vindicta*, they flew the course as one, cycling their Jump-core and riding the gravitational waves around the singularity. He wasn't a pilot today. He was a bird, floating on the wind, riding the rippling curvature of space. Passing through the checkpoint, he activated the algorithms prepared and readied for Exo injection. He followed the black hole's curve, letting it guide him and push him and pull him while giving new life to his trajectory.

The cascading curves continued, showing how dangerously close the ship was to a fuel death-spiral. The black hole wanted to eat him, but he wouldn't let it. He pushed, he pushed, he rejected its hold, Bonta's path leading him away.

"Talk to me!" Raith said, awaiting his crew's analysis. "Good? How'd we do? What's the new projections?" He continued zipping away from the checkpoint, slicing through space on a wide trajectory toward the next target.

"You're in eighteenth after passing Olive," replied Bonta. "And . . . she's in its grasp. It's beautiful. She'll escape, eventually, but the mass actually pulled her completely out of Jump! You were terribly close to the same result, by the way. If my math is right, less than a kilometer away from a cascade and forced release of Jump-core."

"All right, all right. I need numbers. No more time to worry about Olive. She's a non-factor."

"You're five minutes ahead of twentieth now." Harrison sent over a new graph. "Here's your fuel reserves. You should be able to average 700 JD the rest of the way. And you're only a hundred seconds behind Carter. The whole lead pack is right on his tail. Less than three seconds separates all eighteen of them. You pass any of them, you pass them all."

"So what's the call?"

"You'll catch them between light-year forty-seven and forty-eight."

"Perfect."

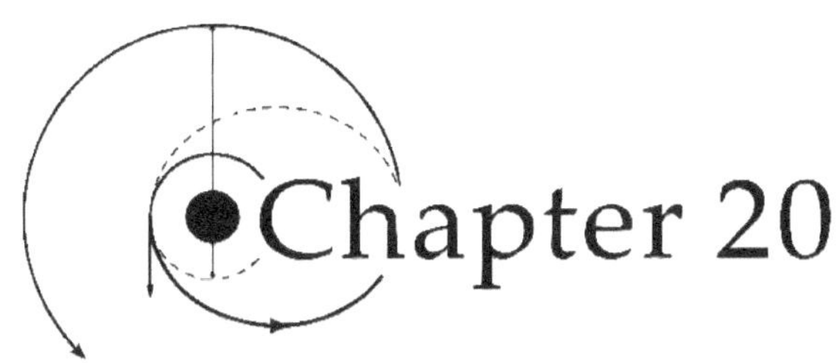

Chapter 20

The scale of the universe, impossible to comprehend. Olive's words lingered. She was right, though her conclusion was simply faulty. Yet she was right.

In the grand scheme of it all? Humanity, its small corner of the Milky Way—meaningless. All meaningless. Raith would live for another few centuries, crash into an asteroid, and die in a fiery inferno above a distant world. The odds of anything truly interesting happening to anyone—actually interesting, on a scale memorable by more than just humanity and its progeny—they were essentially zero.

The universe, all ninety-three billion light-years of it, persisted beyond and before any of them. Formed from a singularity, it would die an eventual heat death, its final molecules collapsing in upon themselves in a virtual expanse of radioactive decay and degradation.

The true emptiness of space was laid bare between each checkpoint, as Raith and the other racers zipped along between stars encountering absolutely nothing. He considered these truths. Even given the immense mass and scale of galaxies—even galaxy clusters—the universe was mostly empty space. And when anyone traversed it, they almost never encountered anything of significance.

The odds were essentially zero.

But not quite.

"It's show time."

A few hours ago, they passed the forty-seventh light-year. Mere light hours ahead of them, Carter and the rest of the lead pack fought with one another, dipping and diving into the best vectors. No more elements remained. Only an empty stretch of space separated any racer from the finish line and the grand prize of one hundred million.

For Raith, the prize meant everything. It meant freedom from the Conglomerate. It meant life—a signal to all. He had returned from the dead, ready to race.

"Just don't push it too much," said Harrison. "We don't have exact numbers on how much Exo they really have left."

"Hey, we've managed to run 698 JD most of the way and catch them," Bonta said. "I don't know about you, but I'm pretty confident we've got more juice than them. I ran the math. Our maneuver at the black hole *saved* us fuel."

"And isn't it just beautiful that everyone after us has tried it?"

"They're seeing our numbers. It's their only chance to gain ground."

Harrison snorted. "Too bad only three succeeded."

"Yes, too bad," Raith muttered.

In reality, what it created was a vast expanse behind them. With hundreds of racers dragged by the black hole's pull, whether passing through with exceptional fuel burn or forced out of Jump, twentieth now sat fifty minutes in the past. Olive had dropped to fiftieth, and she was a healthy sixty minutes behind.

"I'm just saying," Harrison added, "they know what you did, but they don't know how much fuel you have left. And at this point, everyone realizes the final stretch is victory. They're waiting for one person to gun it, then they'll all follow. There's no downside—with such a massive gap behind us, everyone can afford to wait to burn Exo."

"Fair enough," Raith replied. "So—"

A hundred alarms blared across his systems. The avatars on his screen representing the leaders glowed red—some even popped out of existence. A crash of some sort? Then why—

Acting on instinct, Raith dropped the *Vindicta* out of Jump. The stars of the Milky Way rushed into focus. Rather than the warped lightshow of Jump, a magnificent landscape of purple and orange hued nebula spread across his perceptions.

But there was more.

He grappled with the scene. The remains of eighteen other racing craft—according to QuanCom's data, at least six of them were completely obliterated—littered a skybox a million kilometers wide. And, spread between them?

A massive, rocky wedge, impossibly tall and more impossibly wide. He'd call it an asteroid, but . . . even a gas giant couldn't cover such an expanse. No, this was something else.

As he stared upon the travesty, a voice blared inside his mind. He'd been ignoring it ever since dropping out of Jump.

"Raith! Raith! I don't know what the hell you're doing, but adjust your vector and go! Go! This is your chance! Every single bit of data signals all eighteen as completely incapacitated. We've won."

Completely incapacitated, lifeless, helpless. At the mercy of an immense mass of unknown origin and substance. More importantly—- Carter.

What if Carter was wounded? In need of help? In need of assistance?

He deactivated his connection to his crew.

Carefully, he guided the *Vindicta* through the mangled mess. On approach, he recognized rough craters speckling the unknown terrestrial-looking object. Even though it was impossibly large, it was certainly natural . . . and it had simply drifted through space and right into the path of the Five-Hundred Light-year Classic. Impossible, yet it had happened.

Strewn along the top edge of the monstrosity, mangled metallic refuse mixed with partially fractured spacecraft. Raith maneuvered slowly along the edge of the field, carefully avoiding any stray shards capable of scarring the *Vindicta*. Looping up and over the stray steel, he found his way to Carter and the *Bloodhound*, resting inert above brown, rippling stone. The ship appeared intact, thought its core lifeless.

After initiating reverse thrust, the *Vindicta* matched Carter's relative velocity floating above the massive rock. What amazed Raith—almost as much as the scale of the thing—was the lack of gravitational pull. As far as he could tell, the thing exerted minimal gravitational force. A few of the racers had crashed right into it, but the others? Seemingly pulled out of warp.

If it was natural, as he first thought, it was something completely undiscovered, formed of matter previously unexplored.

Using the *Vindicta*'s onboard sensors, Raith reached out, assessing the damage to Carter's ship. From what he could tell, the craft was in good shape, but it lacked power. He keyed the communicator, attempting to contact Carter, but he received no response. He received no response from any of the other pilots, either.

"Don't you die on me now," Raith said, eying Carter's ship. "Not now. Not after everything." He only had one choice. If he was to win with honor, as Carter requested, he couldn't let the man die out here in the cold void. After placing the *Vindicta* in a low power state, with just enough juice to keep itself oriented alongside the *Bloodhound*, Raith slipped out of his sled-like cockpit and into the open vacuum of space. "Forty-five minutes before the next racer reaches us. Plenty of time."

From the side of the *Vindicta* popped a tiny compartment, filled to the brim with emergency supplies. He grabbed everything he thought necessary to handle exterior repairs before preparing to leap. Using the tiny thrusters installed in his body, Raith jetted across the tiny expanse between the two craft, reaching his friend's hull in a matter of seconds. With a gentle thud, he stepped onto its side, and he magnetized his feet to its cold steel armor. Slowly, carefully, he walked along its outer edge searching for something—anything—to diagnose the damage to the ship.

And there it was.

A jagged edge of ridged carbon-steel fractured deep into the ship's hull. Raith's additional visual sensors revealed the tiny escape of gas into vacuum, meaning the *Bloodhound* was quickly losing atmosphere. He could only hope Carter was inside, utilizing emergency life-support to keep himself active and conscious. Raith could do his part. He could fix this.

Leaning over, he grabbed the metal and pulled, thrusting it out and away from his friend's ship. The release of gas increased, though if he understood the ship's build correctly, the air escaping *should* be from a tiny external bubble in the wall designed to handle vacuum breaches. An initial breach released the atmosphere in the outer layer first, giving any crew or computer systems a few precious extra seconds to both prepare for a full breach or to section off the outer layer in time.

Before he patched the outer hull with his emergency pack, though, he peered through the gap, seeing the real problem. The shrapnel had sliced a power cable—most likely a cord central to regulation of the entire ship's electric system.

Fortunately, every ship's emergency pack came prepared to fix power cable failures.

From the pack strapped to his torso, Raith pulled a massive pod of conductive gunk. The patch would only work for a few days, but Carter only needed a few days. Finding the severed cable, he laced the gunk between the two cables, careful to release the gunk and place the wire into it, rather than touch the gunk the moment electricity began coursing through the ship's system again.

Satisfied with his work, Raith pulled out a canister of nano-mist. The little robots would do just the trick. Bringing the nozzle right to the open gash, he sprayed, and it took only a few seconds for the tiny bots to recognize the problem and begin weaving a new barrier across the ship's hull. After releasing all of the contents of the bottle, Raith stepped back. Moments later, the wound healed.

"Carter, you better be alive in there," Raith said, activating his body's local connection. There—inside the ship—a network was reforming. Not waiting for permission, Raith pushed his way inside, searching for the *Bloodhound*'s diagnostics.

"God damn it, Raith," came a voice. Carter's.

"I didn't take you for the religious type." Raith leapt from the ship and jetted back to the *Vindicta*.

"I was fine. I had it under control. I was doing the repairs."

"You'd have never been able to do the spacewalk like me."

"I was suited up, ready to head outside."

"Well I saved you the trouble. Those things are so cumbersome anyway."

"You could have won, Raith." A slight pause. A labored breath. "You should have won."

"I still might."

Another pause. "Except I'm already back in my pilot's seat, friend."

"If it means you live," Raith said, "I'm willing to lose."

He shut off the connection as he reached the *Vindicta*. It was time to reunite with the lovely ship, integrating his mind back into its framework. He glanced back at the *Bloodhound*, watching its thrusters come to life. He hadn't been able to save Erika and Donyi, but at least Carter survived his tribulation.

Opening the *Vindicta*, Raith positioned himself so his back faced the ship and his face stared down upon the rocky behemoth below. As he linked within the ship, he spared the seconds to consider the abomination blocking the racecourse.

It drifted on its inexorable, unknowable course, its edges vibrating as if . . . as if breathing.

Breathing.

No.

Raith watched, beat for beat, the rhythmic and consistent bleat of the massive creature. For it was alive, breathing in and out consistently like any living being might when asleep.

Impossible.

Its skin, rocky and coarse, shimmered with glimmers of emerald along its ridges. As it floated along the stellar wind, the creature cared not for what was in its way. Like a star, it simply existed, living and dying according to its own timeline.

Olive was right—they were all infinitesimal in scale when compared to the reality of the universe. Yet she was also wrong. Raith stared upon the creature, recognizing a new truth. Without humanity, without their synthetic counterparts, without the ability to love, to hate, to perceive a creature such as this—to perceive the entirety of the universe—the universe would never know itself. Raith was a part of the universe, observing the discrete parts and the whole. Observing this creature as it floated by, living its life oblivious to the petty squabbles of corporations and nation-states. And it surely observed too, probably not even knowing puny little creatures just scratched its skin.

What did it think? Did it float along, finding planets to devour? Or did observe stars, charting their paths?

The *Vindicta* closed around Raith, the augmented sensors of the ship returning to his perceptions. He wanted to sit there, staring upon the majestic animal flying by. But a few dozen meters away, the *Bloodhound* blazed to life, its thrusters active.

Raith reactivated his own ship, trailing close behind Carter. Seconds later, his friend initiated Jump. The massive creature continued its inexorable breathing path.

And it vanished.

No. What? Impossible. He stared in disbelief, replaying the images in his mind. Not vanished—just . . . Jumped. It could Jump, using some unknown, natural process to pass distances on its own. Creeping dread—and awe—clung to the inner nodes of Raith's mind.

No more time to waste. He mimicked Carter and the creature, Jumping to begin the race anew.

Chapter 21

"After everything, after absolutely everything, after talking about winning as the only thing that mattered, you took the moment to save Carter, rather than ensure your victory?"

Bonta had asked the question at least four times over the past half-day. Side-by-side, the *Vindicta* and *Bloodhound* dove toward the finish line. Raith kept a constant line of communication open to Carter, periodically checking in on the man to ensure the repairs were holding. He'd kept his words to the crew sparse. His mind was partially out of focus, worried about Carter, but more so, his mind kept contemplating the phantom behemoth. The word—behemoth—was the best description he could come up with for it.

"I told you, Bonta, all of it was worth it," Raith said. "Just wait until I show you the images in my mind of the thing that blew apart the pack."

"But you could have won!"

"I, for one," said Harrison, "think what you did was very admirable. Useless, because as you told us, Carter was ready to repair his own ship, but still admirable."

"Thank you Harrison," Raith retorted. "I'm glad you appreciate my actions, unlike someone."

"Oh shove it."

"Bonta, I can hear your respect from here. I know you think I did the right thing."

"Maybe."

"Admit it!"

"No, now—" The connection disappeared.

"Bonta?"

Nothing.

"Harrison?"

Nothing.

Raith readjusted his communications channels. "Carter?"

"I'm here," said the man. "What's wrong?"

"I've lost connection to Bonta and Harrison," Raith said. He checked their metrics—another light-year-and-a-half remained until the finish line. A little less than a day.

"Heaven forbid you fly without your crew for a second."

"Carter, no jokes. You know how on edge I am after losing the twins." Raith queued in a few requests for external channels from the Hub, but nothing responded. Strangely, the connection through the Hub between him and Carter continued, but no other queries responded. "Are you getting any data from beyond QuanCom's system?"

"Let me check. No. Wait—other than our connection, I'm still receiving data on the state of racers behind us. I've also got a ping on the emergency vessels dispatched to assess the rest of the debris for any other survivors. We've still got our opponents a half-hour behind, but . . ."

Raith considered the options. If they were connected through the Hub, that meant it was still active and transmitting information through its internal data relationships. But if external connections to it were cut, especially to the racing crews . . .

"I don't think this is a race anymore," Raith said. "Something's happened. Olive said this was a war. The Conglomerate has had its eyes on—well, everything—since we started. And who the hell knows what else is going on. If they're jamming external the Hub . . ."

"Then QuanCom is under attack. I'd guess the Conglomerate. They've had enough. All entertainment for the past year has focused on us. You always said they were probably connected to the Venus Vacation Conglomerate, yeah? Maybe the race is finally hurting their bottom line. Why not cut it at the source?"

"You really think they'd stoop that low?"

"Guess we'll find out."

"What about the race?"

Raith pulled up a few calculations. "I've got an idea. Let's give them a final show."

≡⫶⊷ ≡⫶⊷ ≡⫶⊷

Less than a light second before they reached the finish line, the *Vindicta* and *Bloodhound* dropped out of Jump. A little over ten thousand kilometers separated the duo from the end.

"So how the hell are we going to time this?" Carter's voice came through loud and clear over the now local network.

"You just do your thing, fly boy, and I'll match you. I'm the synth. I can do it."

Their ships danced, twirling through space along vectors designed to entice. The final checkpoint, the one they'd crossed to finish each of the nine laps before, rested smoothly above the ecliptic of S-1022, and—

Data streamed in from throughout the star system, revealing the inferno beneath the final stretch of the course. Ships blared distress signals from a dozen different orbitals, all indicating the emergency engulfing the star. QuanCom's special station? Practically in flames.

"Carter," Raith said. "I don't think anyone's watching us."

Only a few minutes separated them from completing the inaugural Five Hundred Light-year Classic.

"Carter, you hearing me?"

"Yeah, I'm hearing you. I see it. So *someone* attacked. Whether it's the Conglomerate or something else entirely, I'm not sure there's any way for us to know right now."

Raith turned his scopes on the finish. His sensors detected nothing. But if he were an enemy, hoping to capture a prey, he'd go right where he knew they'd be. And if they were still planning on stealing the ship at the end, the finish line made the most sense. "We need to quit."

"What?" Carter's voice sounded incredulous. "We're almost there. We've come so far together. I thought we were going to end it together."

"We are," Raith said. "We need to end the race. Actually end it. They're waiting for us. Well, for me. But inevitably for both of us."

"Who?"

"Doesn't matter. I have no idea who's an enemy and a friend any more, except for you and my crew. Only one thing matters now." Without waiting for an answer, Raith modified his trajectory, dipping away from the finish line and toward S-1022. Toward the *Juniper.*

Two seconds later, Carter and the *Bloodhound* deviated as well, diving toward the stellar system sprawling below. Two more seconds of silence followed before the *Vindicta*'s sensors detected the subtle fluctuations of power from three tiny pinnaces waiting beyond the finish line.

"We've got company," Carter said. "Are you armed?"

"I am not," Raith replied.

"Lucky for you, the *Bloodhound*'s packing heat."

Raith began charting the quickest vector through Jump to reach the QuanCom Hub. Above all else, he needed to find Harrison and Bonta. He already lost Erika and Donyi. He wasn't losing the others too. "I've got a path locked in to reach QuanCom in just a few seconds. You following?"

"You go ahead. I'll take care of these three."

"Roger. See you in a few."

Raith watched for a moment as Carter's ship looped around to face the incoming foe. Trusting the adventurer knew his own skills, Raith Jumped.

And, three seconds later, he arrived outside the massive space station in the middle of a firefight. Kinetics and plasma blasts sliced through space, ships smashing into one another in apocalyptic inferno. "Olive, when you said a war," he said aloud, "I did not think this is what you meant."

Connecting to the local networks, Raith searched and searched and searched for a signal from his crew. Nothing. A few hundred kilometers away, their hangar came into view. Before he could plan a docking berth, a request for a direct line rang through his head. He accepted the request.

"Raith, this is Administrator Harris!" The signal emanated from a communications tower attached to QuanCom's station. "It is *good* to see you and Carter alive. Now get the hell out of here!"

"Administrator, I'm not leaving without my crew," Raith said. "Now where are they?"

"The whole station's been overrun with Conglomerate thugs," he said. "I'm barricaded in my office. Your crew? No idea. The *Juniper* isn't docked with the station anymore, if that's—"

The transmission disconnected. Raith internally uttered a series of incomprehensible swears. Turning the *Vindicta*, he assessed the battle as a whole in an attempt to identify the sides. At the scale of a system-wide conflict, he was a gnat in comparison. He just needed no one to notice him.

Starward, three immense cruisers blasted away at four battleships drifting toward the station from the system's edges. Dozens of smaller craft darted about, either attempting to find a clear vector to Jump or engaging in their own petty fights. Sensor data overwhelmed, continuing to provide more information. Seconds later, transponder codes revealed the four battleships as ICH vessels. If those ships arrived in system in so quickly, they'd been forewarned of the attack.

And the three cruisers. Certainly Conglomerate, in an attempt to seize whatever prize they desired from QuanCom. Unless . . . maybe the Conglomerate had given up and simply wanted to ensure QuanCom's complete destruction, at least in S-1022. Raith's question to ponder: did they still want him? And what about Olive's strange faction? How did they fit in?

The question received an answer moments later when three corvettes deviated from their vectors and redirected toward his position.

He had nowhere to hide.

Raith frantically analyzed the rest of the system, his foes still a few minutes away. Where was the *Juniper*? It simply wasn't possible they were already dead. He wouldn't accept that truth. If they managed to escape the station, they would have reached safety. Maybe with the ICH battleships.

He considered the government ships for a moment. Would he find safety there? Perhaps. The moment he hid behind them, though, he lost his opportunity to find his friends. And he couldn't leave them alone out here.

Problem, though. The *Vindicta* was completely unarmed.

He was an idiot to think he could do anything to change the battle.

No, wait. He wasn't. They wanted him. They wanted him. He could use it to his advantage. He opened a system-wide broadcast.

"Good morning, S-1022! This is Raith, the co-victor of the Five Hundred Light-year Classic alongside the enigmatic and beautiful Carter, piloting the *Bloodhound!*" He paused, watching the transmission begin its electromagnetic echo between the planets. It would take hours to reach every corner, but they would hear him. "If you're looking for me, I'm right here. Come and find me."

As the transmission ended, he gunned the ignition, the ship darting on a new path between planets and away from its incoming tails. He only had a few drops of Exo left, so he'd need to make any Jumps count. Three tasks, then.

Find the *Juniper*, reuniting with Harrison and Bonta.

Rendezvous with Carter.

All four of them flee together, out of system and away from the battle.

Anything else meant falling under the control of someone, whether the Conglomerate or the ICH.

Beneath QuanCom's station, the barren and unnamed terrestrial planet invited him. Between its craggy peaks, he could find peace. And he could defeat his enemies without firing a single shot.

⚙≡-«» ≡╟╫≡» ≡║≣-«»

The plan, albeit simple, required a few key pieces to fall into place without any communication. Raith, now breaking the near-impotent atmosphere of the planet below, found mountains and canyons and valleys in which to lose any fighters in pursuit. Once he was clear of foes, Harrison and Bonta would simply know to bring the *Juniper* in, meeting him for a quick pick-up. They'd tether the *Vindicta* to the underside of the larger ship and escape. Carter, watching from afar, would match their vector out of the system. Flawless plan. Everyone would see it.

He hoped.

The *Vindicta* darted toward the surface, reaching a ridgeline of mountains. In atmosphere, the ship felt painfully slow, but fortunately his foes would similarly be limited. And plasma blasts and kinetics didn't like atmosphere any more than a spacecraft. It was a win in all regards. In a sense, his best battleground was above the surface of this unknown rock.

With ease, he looped above a peak and down its slope, finding a river valley beyond. The geologic formations of the planet signaled a different past, one where water once flowed. Though grey, rather than red, the planet reminded him of stories of Mars, humanity's first non-lunar steps beyond Earth. It further emphasized the smallness of the war occurring above its surface. In the grand scheme of everything, none of it mattered.

But Raith, he mattered. To himself. And Carter mattered. And Harrison, as well as Bonta, they mattered. Together, they would survive the pointless squabbles of factions who truly didn't matter.

He checked his scopes. The three fighters weren't far behind, and another dozen followed close-behind. He didn't take the time to determine their sides in the battle. At this point, only one side mattered. His own.

The *Vindicta* entered the valley, flying behind hills and into ravines. Arcing over another mountain, he found an immense canyon kilometers deep. Exactly what he wanted. He twisted, diving deep into its depths, his foes following, but their reaction times would not compare. He dove under outcroppings and through caverns hollowed by billion-year-old oceans.

His sensors signaled the death of the first. And the second. Around another butte he looped, forcing his foe into an impossible turn. Only the *Vindicta* could achieve it. Only his ship. The third craft exploded against a canyon wall.

From above, the second wave arrived, coasting along above the canyon. Unlike their predecessors, they weren't stupid, much to Raith's chagrin.

Without pause, the enemy craft bombarded the canyon with kinetics and plasma, obliterating rock. A maelstrom of white powder rained all around, and it took all Raith's neural nodes to avoid the larger chunks falling from the sky. Maybe—just maybe—diving into a canyon had been a terrible idea.

Now he had no way out.

Except—his sensors revealed the canyon ending in a vast flattened expanse, likely a former sea. An absolutely absurd plan formed. Raith had no clue if it would work, but no other choice presented itself.

Focusing on avoiding the raining dust, he continued through the canyon, ignoring the constant barrage from his enemies. Too many narrow escapes kept his mind on edge, but a few minutes later, he blazed out the end of the canyon, revealing the vast empty void of smooth rock below. Without waiting, he triggered the Jump-core.

For only a moment, the *Vindicta* warped space. The hulking mass of a planet less than a few hundred meters below instantly disrupted the expense of Exo, but it only took a few nanoseconds. The *Vindicta* Jumped thousands of kilometers away, its direct line taking it far into orbit. The dangerous maneuver sent alarms ringing throughout the ship, but from what he could tell, all was well.

"Raith, Raith, is that you?" Two voices cascaded into one another, their words crashing into frenzied excitement. "It is you!"

"Bonta, Harrison, where the hell are you?"

"We're coming around now. We've been hiding on the surface of this hell-hole, waiting for you."

Raith checked his scopes. No foes in sight. "Find me, now! This is our chance."

"Agreed," said Bonta. "We're looping in now."

Frantically, he searched his nearly-fried sensors for his friends. It only took a few seconds, but he spotted the *Juniper* looping up from the nearby planet. He directed the *Vindicta* to head in their direction. They were almost there. Almost. Step one completed, with step two halfway complete.

Then—to find Carter.

"We saw everything unfold," Harrison said. "You and Carter's final maneuver. Based on our scopes, looks like he cleared out those bogeys waiting at the finish line. We lost track of him after that, though."

The kilometers between the two ships decreased quickly, the *Juniper* and *Vindicta* aching to reunite. Nothing could stop them. Nothing.

Appearing out of Jump, a craft Raith instantly recognized, alongside four other fighters, appeared.

Olive. She'd finished her race.

There was no time to react. The fighters fired, kinetics and missiles, all blasting apart the *Juniper* in an orb of crimson fire. It faded all too soon, signaling the final deaths of Raith's newest crew.

Raith's heart melted.

Seconds later, a plasma burst sliced through the wing of the *Vindicta*.

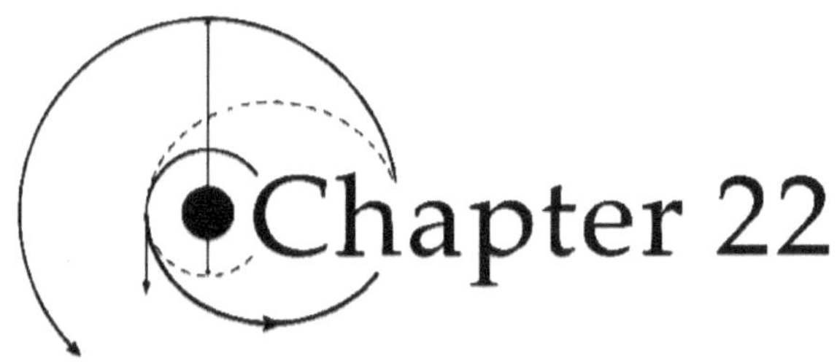

Chapter 22

Darkness. Darkness all around. Raith floated thousands of kilometers above the planet, his mind watching the scene.

The moment plasma blasted through the *Vindicta*, the ship immediately ejected his capsule, its compartment flying at an infinitely tiny fraction of the speed of light away from the soon-to-be fireball.

As if disconnected from it all, the vacuum of silence surrounding him, he observed Olive's fighters dance around the wreckage, presumably searching for survivors. He, instead, sat hundreds of kilometers away, watching. Whatever the *Vindicta* had done, the escape procedure evidently wasn't something of which Olive had been aware. Just like the ship's ability to arc around the black hole, she hadn't known more than a few things about the ship, contrary to her arrogance. If Erika and Donyi installed the feature, he now owed even more to them.

So he watched. Hours passed.

Her ships left.

And he waited.

The battle ended, ICH forces pushing away the Conglomerate.

And still, he watched. Waited. Survived.

Alone.

Even though he believed all was clear, he sat, in low power mode, observing the fight all around. More importantly, he mourned. Mourned Erika and Donyi, more so than he'd mourned them over the past months. He mourned Hector and his old crew; hell, he mourned crews from centuries past. All gone. He was alone, again, as always.

Perhaps today could serve as a fitting end. His final day, racing, fighting for those he loved. Carter must have died in the battle. If not, Raith hoped he escaped to safety. The man deserved to live a long life, exploring and racing across the galaxy. These factions and their wars . . . what was humanity becoming? For centuries, SIs and humans had navigated the ever-evolving politics of interstellar space with kid-gloves, but what did the battle today mean?

To Raith, nothing. He didn't care about political beliefs, economic goals, power grabs. None of it mattered. His life—the lives of his friends—living and loving together? Screw the powers-that-be and their silly wars. Why did it matter who controlled the most sophisticated quantum communications technology? Or who owned the most advanced SI-ready racing ship in the galaxy. Raith wanted to spit at them all. Their conflicts only got good people killed.

Even so, the whole past year? Truly worth it. He raced again. He met four wonderful people, all devoted to him even when he'd been an ass. And Carter, of course. If only he could have had another day with Carter.

Lingering in the back of his mind, too—the behemoth. Somehow, he was one of the lucky few to witness it. While in transit toward S-1022, he and Carter focused on the race, not talking about the thing. But certainly, the man realized what it was too. If not, Raith would die with one regret. They shared that moment, together, witnessing something beyond all comprehension of humanity's biologists. No one else could claim a similar shared experience.

Hours turned into days. The system became a graveyard, ships darting about on salvage operations overseen by the ICH. Still, no one approached his wreckage after Olive picked it over and escaped. Depending on who she really worked for, maybe she had labeled it as "Conglomerate" debris and cleared it of survivors, signaling the ICH that it was of no concern. If so, he was doomed to a slow orbital death, eventually falling to the surface of the planet below.

He would embrace his fate.

He had lived his meaningless life, finding his own way in the void. He had found love with friends over the years, and companionship. And he'd thrown it all away, in the past. When he went to prison. He was happy and content with what he had made of his second chance at freedom.

Finally, Raith pushed out of the little capsule, exposing his synthetic body to the raw vacuum of space. He had lived in space for most of his life; he would end it there, too.

Epilogue

Alas, an end was not in the cards.

Raith floated, arms spread, drifting in the void. But only a few minutes after escaping his capsuled prison, floodlights from a nearby ship illuminated every centimeter of his body.

Powering up all his faculties, he recognized an incoming connection request from the nearby vessel. "This is . . . Raith," he said. "What can I do for you?"

"You really thought you could just float about out here without me? The *Bloodhound*'s in need of a new crewmember, and I think you might want to hop aboard."

Carter.

It was Carter.

"My friend, I could kiss you," Raith said.

"Let's not get ahead of ourselves, you need to make it through the airlock first." A pause. "I can't believe I found you. I've been searching since the battle ended. Raith . . . I thought you were dead."

After everything, after the entire race, after losing everyone.

He was home.

Thank you for reading *Flight of the 500*!

Flight of the 500 is a stand-alone novel set in the same universe as two of my other novels: *First of Their Kind* and *Their Greatest Game*, the first two books of **the** Chronicles of Theren. I hope you enjoyed the tale as much as I enjoyed writing this wild ride. As an independent author, every review matters; please consider reviewing the novel on the websites of major retailers, your blog, or Goodreads. And please! Tell your friends about *Flight of the 500*.

Though *Flight of the 500* is not a sequel to my other stories, Raith and Carter are featured in *Their Pieces Were Stars*, Book III of the Chronicles of Theren, appearing later in this collection.

Before Inferno

Prequel to the Chronicles of Theren

Chapter 1

Cassandra Vazquez opened her eyes, pushing her back into the uncomfortable wood of the hearing room bench. She'd dozed off yet again as they entered the ninth hour of this absurd charade. She checked her watch—7 PM. She could smell the acrid sweat of the senators, and she was in the back row! The pungent stench knocked her vision back into focus, and her eyes returned to the scene.

"Thank you, Senator Richards," Vice-Chair Tarantin said. "I believe just Senator Edwards has a few questions remaining for you, Henderson. I'm so sorry this has taken so long."

"I appreciate the sent-sentiment," Henderson said, the well placed stutter barely noticeable. "I pro-promise. I am fine. I will honor my country today."

Doctor Henderson Decker, the center of public attention. Cassandra couldn't see the man's face, but she'd listened to him speak many of the same words over and over again all day. No, for the past month, really, ever since he'd returned from Mars. *He's doing his duty for his country*, Cassandra thought to herself. *Almost too well*. Everyone's eyes had looked toward the red planet for over a year, and today, Henderson had finally answered their questions. Most of the answers had been less than satisfactory to the public. But they would satiate their appetite.

"Vice-Chair Tarantin, thank you," Senator Edwards said. "Henderson, no one denies the great service you've performed for your nation. You managed to survive a disaster on Mars and fly the *Goliath* on a solo return trip. It amazes me, and all of us, that you did what we thought only possible in movies."

"Thank you, Senator," Henderson replied.

"So my final few questions are simply to establish a clear timeline of events. We've drilled you on the details all day, and I just want to make sure we have a clear view of things. That we're not missing any major gaps, that no stone has been left unturned. Does that make sense?"

"I believe so."

Cassandra leaned forward, glad they were finally reaching the most worrying line of questioning. Senator Edwards had always opposed the joint venture between NASA, the ESA, and a few of the multinational space development corporations, and he'd threatened the operations of Cassandra's employers for even longer. To his credit, Henderson remained strong, even after nine hours. She could hear the resolve dripping behind every word the man had uttered.

"On August 11, 2029, you and five other humans arrived on Mars, correct?" asked Edwards.

"Correct," said Henderson.

"And for the first three days, the six of you established Home Base and explored the surrounding, let's say, countryside, for the lack of a better term?"

"Correct."

Senator Edwards typed something into the keyboard on his arm. "On August 14, you and Commander Hanks discovered a cave three miles north of Home Base, correct?"

"That is correct," replied Henderson.

"What did you find inside the cave?"

Cassandra breathed in sharply, awaiting the response. She'd heard it five times today; the man's answer never got old.

"I—we found a geothermal vent," Henderson said. "Inside the cave. It also had liquid water. Gases floated all around, the heat was enough for the water to flow. And—and I don't really know how to describe it. But in the cave, there were—shadows. Creatures. They attacked. They attacked! Hanks screaming . . . constant screaming . . ."

Henderson descended into hysterics for a moment, trembling. He'd survived, but a three-month solo flight from Mars to Earth? Must have been scarring. Before it seemed like they lost him entirely, though, the Doctor straightened his glasses, smoothed his sleeves, and placed his hands gently back on the table.

"The shadows," muttered Henderson. "The creatures! It's what *he* saw. And it changed him. The memory still haunts me—oh, the look in his eyes! But I promise you, there was nothing in that cave other than the geothermal vent and the water. But Hanks—Hanks became his shadows. He became the monsters. The poor man made the choice to take off his helmet. For a moment, he breathed in the air, and he believed he was safe. But he didn't account for the extra gases from the vent, even if the cave had an atmospheric composition breathable to humans. Within moments, he went insane; he attacked me; I fled."

Cassandra heard the tears in Henderson's words. He had communicated the necessary emotions with such gusto and skill.

"And why didn't you have a recording of the initial events in the cave?" Edwards inquired.

"During my altercation with Hanks, he broke my camera. It's not like we had Wi-Fi on Mars, other than the tiny local network connecting our servers and drones. Following our expeditions, we uploaded all of the recordings into Home Base's mainframe. When I arrived home after the attack, I found my suit's computer system damaged beyond repair. Our AI couldn't fix it. Or at least, it didn't have time before . . . well, you know."

Edwards brushed his hair to the left side of his face. Cassandra suspected the Senator wanted something more, as if he knew Henderson hid the truth. Politicians all sounded slimy, though, even when they asked innocuous questions.

"All right," Edwards said. "So after you returned to Home Base, what happened?"

Henderson took a moment before responding. "I informed the rest of the team of what happened. I told them I didn't think Hanks was dead, and that he might return at any moment. We prepared for his arrival, but he snuck in through the vehicle airlock using his bypass commands." He breathed shallow breaths. His hands turned a pale-white color.

Impressive.

"He killed them all," Henderson said. "He arrived, and he raved on and on about seeing our doom, that hell's gates would open upon us, that he couldn't let us leave Mars. He started cutting the power to the rooms . . . we lost atmosphere so fast . . . he even killed our AI mainframe, losing all the data we'd gathered so far. It was madness."

"It's all right, Dr. Decker," Senator Edwards said. "You don't need to continue. I wanted that clear narrative established for the record. I am so sorry that you've had to replay this ordeal today."

Henderson's hands returned to their normal color. "As I've said, it's vitally important the public know what happened. I survived to tell the tale of my colleagues, even the tale of Commander Hanks. When we return to Mars, we need to take greater care, lest another horror film play out before another set of unsuspecting eyes."

Senator Edwards looked taken aback at that last comment, and he furiously typed away before asking another question. "So you believe we should return to Mars?"

"Certainly," Henderson said. "We proved humanity can survive on its surface for more than a few hours, did we not? We suffered great tragedy, yes. But I don't want the mistake and broken mind of one man to ruin the future of our species."

Cassandra sighed. He had played the final card, the final message sealing the fate of Home Base. The public would believe this man's statement, pitying his experience. They would look beyond the tragic events on the Red Planet, they would not think of the ripples formed because one man survived when the other five died. Leave all the ravings to heretical conspiracy theorists, precisely where they belonged.

Vice-Chair Tarantin nodded toward Senator Edwards before turning his gaze upon Henderson. "Thank you for your time today."

"It was my honor," Henderson responded.

Tarantin glanced down at his tablet. "Seeing no further questions, this hearing of the Senate Committee on Science and Technology will adjourn." He tapped his gavel against the metal plate welded to the wooden pulpit.

Cassandra stood in unison with the crowd, pushing forward to reach the front of the room. Henderson placed his own tablet into his bag before turning to leave. Seeing Cassandra, Henderson nodded, as if recognizing the significance of her presence.

"It's good to finally see you after all this time," Cassandra said, reaching the small wooden gate separating Henderson from the public pews. "NASA's sent you through so many medical tests over the past few weeks, we thought you'd never make it back to Washington."

Henderson continued nodding to himself, as if holding a private conversation in his mind. "It's good to see you too. I'm surprised to see you here. I would have expected you to find me when I visited my sister next."

Recognizing the subtext, Cassandra appreciated Henderson's constant vigilance toward discretion. The man was always on guard, going above and beyond even his own call of duty. "Circumstances have changed. She asked me to bring you by tonight. She's got a major announcement to share."

Henderson's eyes widened. The man broke character for just a moment, though Cassandra knew no one noticed. After nine hours of hearings, everyone wanted to make it home for a decent dinner—or the final minutes of a happy hour.

"I guess we better not keep her waiting, then," Henderson said.

"I agree."

* * *

The driverless car neared the massive compound an hour outside D.C., located deep in the heart of Virginia. Cassandra noticed Henderson leaning his head against the glass, drifting in and out of consciousness. Understandably, the man was exhausted. As the car stopped, though, he looked up, his eyes darting from window to window.

"This isn't Langley," he said. "Why aren't we in Langley?"

"A lot of things have changed since you left," Cassandra tapped her fingers on the glass. "Our division moved to a new location to keep it isolated from certain interests, especially as we near to the 2030 elections."

Henderson nodded slightly, his tired brain presumably not wanting to object. "I assume this means you received my package?"

"We did. I don't even want to ask how you managed to smuggle it through your medical exams."

Henderson's face transformed into an involuntary grimace. "You don't want to know."

The two left the car parked outside the compound. The building was an old Virginia plantation, though the owners of the building had reforested the plantation fields decades ago to bring about a renewed sense of privacy. Cassandra pulled a key-card out of her pocket and placed it against a small black pad nestled behind one of the white columns buttressing the entrance. A small green light appeared, and she pushed the door open. Henderson followed her inside.

In the middle of the foyer, a brown table stood with two chairs. On the table, a small, unassuming black box rested. A monitor adorned the wall, paused on a high-definition image of a red, rocky surface. Cassandra stepped around to the far side of the table, taking a seat. She motioned for Henderson to join her, and the man accepted the other chair.

"So we're going to review what you've provided us," Cassandra said. "We need to confirm from your own mouth what it is you brought back before we officially thank you for your service. Though you've done a fantastic job so far; from what we can tell, no one suspects a thing."

Henderson nodded. "I did what I had to do."

"I know. I've reviewed Sky's reports multiple times."

The scientist's eyes misted. "I will miss that AI."

'You were both flawless. No evidence of foul play. Did you know? Sky embedded a signal inside its emergency broadcast telling us you *did* do more. So it's time you share the whole story." Cassandra raised her right hand, faced the monitor, and swiped her hand to the right.

The video screen sprang to life, transitioning from the still image to a live recording. On the screen, a shaky camera displayed an image from inside a Martian cave, from when Henderson first discovered the strange place alongside Commander Hanks. A few feet ahead of Henderson, Cassandra could see a figure—presumably, the Commander.

"This is the file you transmitted to us prior to your descent through Earth's atmosphere," Cassandra said. "Correct?"

Henderson nodded. "That is correct."

"Walk me through what's going on here. And I mean through everything."

"Let me start from the beginning."

Chapter 2

Cassandra listened, bemused. She hadn't expected such a complete confession, but she would enjoy hearing details no one else would ever know. The public could never understand the full extent of the tragedy. They needed to avoid panic at all costs.

Henderson awoke, beginning his third full day on a foreign world.

"Good morning, Doctor Decker," said a disembodied, soothing voice. "The weather is clear today, a great day for exploration, don't you think?"

Muscles groaning, Henderson slid out of bed. "Sky, thanks for the update."

The AI subtly whirred as if purring. "You're welcome. The rest of the team is already awake. We thought it best if you slept in today."

"Of course they did." Henderson stretched and stepped over to the mirror. Grey hairs shrouded his chin, the stubble slowly growing. He'd shave tomorrow. After taking a swig of water, he brushed his teeth. Spitting into the sink, he sighed. His muscles really ached. The rest of the team seemed fine, but finding gravity again after a three-month trip, even Martian gravity—everything just *throbbed*.

He headed to the closet and dressed for the day: a simple grey lab coat and white, scrub-like pants. He passed by the empty beds of the rest of his team, through the sliding door of Pod A, and into the Central Pod. Commander Hanks was sitting at the table, eating a bowl of protein-infused granola.

"Where's everyone else?" asked Henderson.

Commander Hanks looked up from the tablet propped up in front of him. "Morning. Everyone else is already on assignment. You're up a bit late."

"I woke up when my alarm told me to wake up."

"I'm not complaining, Doctor, but you are the science lead of this project, I'd expect you to be more excited about all this."

"Believe me, Commander, I'm excited. I'm just tired." He pulled his glasses out of a coat pocket and placed them on the bridge of his nose. "Gravity's hitting me hard."

"I understand. Sky, what do you have for us today?"

"I think you'll be excited," said the AI. "One of the drones has identified a geothermal cave a few miles to the north. I have a rover ready for you at Dock Pod, you may head out at your convenience."

"Excellent," Hanks said. "Right?"

Henderson nodded. "A heat source is exactly what we need."

"Would you like me to inform Tams, Rachel, Andrews, or Rogen?"

Always so formal, thought Henderson. "Thank you, Sky. That won't be necessary. Hanks and I can handle the mission. Just leave a notice for them upon our return."

"I shall do just that."

Henderson approached the table, reached for a bowl, and poured himself a serving of the granola. It tasted like dirt. After a painful chew, he said, "They couldn't have at least flavored it with chocolate?"

Hanks laughed. "Put it in our post-op report for the next team's supplies." He stood, liberating his seat at the table. "See you at Dock Pod in a few."

* * *

After suiting up in their enviro-suits and attaching their emergency oxygen tanks, Henderson and Hanks settled into the seats of the rover. "Everyone ready?" Sky asked.

"We're good," said the Commander.

Henderson lifted a wordless thumbs-up.

"All right, let's head out."

Following a brief cycling of air, the rover wheeled out of Dock Pod. For the third time in three days, Henderson trekked into the Martian desert with the older astronaut by his side. The man rarely spoke on their journeys, his eyes always staring outside. Hanks had been one of the last astronauts to inhabit the International Space Station before it was decommissioned a few years ago. One of the most experienced spacers in history. Henderson couldn't imagine what it was like to be, essentially, the next Neil Armstrong. Sure, he and the rest of the team were here too, but Hanks was the leader. He'd planned half the mission.

"All right, the course is plotted," said Sky. "We should be there in about fifteen minutes."

"Thank you, Sky," Henderson replied. The rover rolled through Home Base, slipping between domes and past the launch pad. Their surface-to-orbit shuttle waited patiently for the day, weeks in the future, when they'd use it to return home.

"The drone will be awaiting you when you reach the mouth of the cave," Sky added. "You'll notice right away why it couldn't survey the cave."

"Oh come on Sky, you know Henderson already knows why," muttered Hanks. "He programmed them, after all."

"I am just making sure you both are aware of the circumstances you are about to approach yet framing it in a conversational tone. Should I adjust my informational parameters?"

"You're doing just fine," Hanks replied.

"Seriously, just fine," Henderson added. "You were money well spent."

"I'll take that as a review and make sure AlphaRam is aware."

Henderson and Hanks both glanced at one another. *Don't need that company boosting its ego further*, Henderson thought.

The rest of the trip occurred in relative silence. Before long, the rover crested a ridge, rolled along the base of a cliff, and came to a stop next to a small, four-wheeled drone.

"Thanks for the lift, Sky," Henderson said.

After the rover's air cycled into its lower compartment, Hanks opened the side-door. He stepped onto Martian soil, and Henderson followed. They sauntered around the vehicle to the drone's position beside the cliff. Its photoreceptors pointed at a crevice a few meters above the ground.

Henderson lifted his arm, and with his gloved hand, keyed in a few commands. A heads-up display on his helmet shifted between sensors, eventually landing on a few atmospheric monitors. From the cave, significantly warmer air drifted, and . . . oxygen. Henderson quickly shared the read-out with Hanks.

"This is your stuff, Henderson, what do we do next?" Hanks placed a hand on a hip, his facial expressions shadowed by his helmet's sun-visor. "I'm game to go up there if you are."

Henderson double-checked the readings. "Yeah, this is exactly what we were searching for." Hopefully nothing too extraordinary, though. "We need to go in."

Hanks nodded, turned to the rover, and began unloading rudimentary climbing spikes. It didn't take long to nail them into the red rocks, and a few minutes later, the Commander was helping Henderson climb up the rock-face.

Once in the mouth of the cave, Henderson turned to help the older man up the makeshift ladder, but he was already at the last spike by the time his hand was reaching down.

"I'm fine," Hanks said. "I appreciate it, though you know there's a *reason* I'm on this mission."

"Yes, yes." Henderson sighed. Every moment reminded him how he was dreadfully out of his element. Or, at least, he was supposed to act as if he was out of his element. *Even if I have training, I still feel pretty lost here.* "Let's go."

As the light dimmed further into the cave, lamps naturally ignited on their chest plates. Strange mineral stalactites and stalagmites protruding throughout—the first sign they'd found something unexpected.

"Sky, you recording all this?" Henderson asked.

"You bet, sir. You bet."

"I'm no geologist," said Hanks, "but these . . . they're not possible without water, yeah?"

"You are correct," said Sky. "We have discovered something quite unexpected."

Hanks paused in stride. "Should we have additional equipment with us before proceeding?"

"We can always come back," said Henderson. "I'd rather confirm what we have here before making a second trip. Besides, aren't you a bit curious?"

"I'm curious!" said Sky.

"Of course the AI is curious," said Hanks. "Sky, you're programmed to be curious."

"I don't know what you're talking about." A slight buzz came through the speakers built into their helmets.

"Sky . . . are you humming?"

The AI didn't respond.

"They really enjoyed designing its personality," muttered Henderson. *Though it's a nice touch, really*, he thought.

They passed between rocky outcroppings, pushed through tight squeezes, and climbed over boulders. Eventually, the cave sloped downward, and a . . . yellowish glow appeared ahead. *Impossible.*

"Henderson, seriously," said Hanks. "I'm not sure this is the best idea, we don't know what's down there."

"What is it, Commander, are you expecting little grey men to attack you?" Sky chortled. "I didn't take you for a superstitious one."

"Just a little bit further," said Henderson. "This is . . . something spectacular. I can't imagine what we've found. It may be beyond anything we could have hoped for."

They rounded the corner, discovering smoke gently rising out of a dozen or so glowing vents. A pool of liquid water coalesced in the middle of the cavern, and in the center of the pool, a brown, spindly column rose.

No, wait. It wasn't rocky. It was . . . earthy. Almost plant-like. It had branches, and its skin looked coarse like the bark of an oak.

"Hanks, Sky," Henderson said. "This is impossible."

Hanks didn't answer. He stepped forward, his black boot piercing the pool of water.

"Sir, wait, you'll contaminate anything that might be in there—"

The commander passed through the pond and reached the strange thing resting in the middle. "I can't believe it," he said over the comm. "It's beautiful. Truly beautiful. Look at it."

Henderson peered at it, its rippling features almost hypnotic. Henderson shook his head. Was it . . . smiling? Did it have a face? Were those eyes? No. Just a psychological trick. He was anthropomorphizing it. Still . . .

Hank reached out his hand.

"Commander, wait!" Henderson said.

His hand caressed their finding. It grinned, and a piercing screech filled his ears. Henderson doubled over, falling to his knees. It was like the sound of death.

"Sky!" Henderson shouted. "Cut it! Cut my connection to the Commander!"

Chapter 3

Cassandra had watched this video half a hundred times by now, but she wanted to hear the story from Henderson's perspective. Needed to hear it. She had a job to do here today, yet . . . she needed to hear it all from the man who lived it. "Continue."

All sound abruptly ended, leaving Henderson with only the sound of his own breath. "Thank you, Sky."

"I'm still here. I'm assessing the Commander's vitals. His brain is going crazy. I've never seen anything like this."

"Any idea what that . . . thing is?"

"No sir, I—"

Hanks turned to face Henderson, his chest light momentarily blinding all perception. Henderson's helmet naturally dimmed, filtering the light, but it was almost too late. The older astronaut was charging through the ankle-deep water and leaping into the air, fist raised.

Henderson raised his arm in natural self-defense, shielding the blow from striking his helmet. The block pushed Hanks back, and Henderson stepped back a few feet into a defensive stance, both arms raised. "Sky, send a one-way message to Hanks."

"I've been trying to say something to him," said the AI, "However, all I'm getting through his feeds is high-frequency screeching."

"You can't filter it out?"

"I'm trying."

Before Henderson could say another word, Hanks lunged forward with a hook. Henderson's training took over, and he blocked the assault with his forearm. Before Hanks could re-position, Henderson kicked toward his knee. The man stumbled backward, toward the water and fell on his haunches.

"Sky, what do I do? What's the protocol here?"

"There's no protocol here Henderson, not that I know of."

Henderson wracked his brain for an idea. He had his official mission as a science officer, sure, but there was his secondary role. His secondary training. He'd been given a code. Told not to use it except under exceptional circumstances. And these were certainly exceptional circumstances. "Sky, initiate Protocol 51."

Silence—only for a moment. "Protocol 51 activated."

Hanks was rising, though favoring his left leg. "Sky, initiate decompression of the Commander's suit."

As the man stood, his helmet popped right off. Instinctually, he gulped for air. The toxic, carbon dioxide-rich Martian air, only slightly accented by the gases in the cave. His eyes lit with fear, as if the rage overtaking him was beginning to fade.

"Henderson, Henderson, I don't know what came over me, you've got to help me," he said. "I can't go down like this." Hanks fell to his knees, wheezing.

Henderson stepped forward, activating his external speaker. "Commander, it's not your fault. Now that I think about it, I would have needed to act anyway. The discovery of extraterrestrial life, presumably? We can't let the world know. You're just a casualty now." The words were harsh, but he couldn't back down. His training needed to kick in. He needed to be cold and calculating. He could mourn and cry later.

"No, no, I didn't mean it, it made me do it, I don't know what it is, I don't know why I touched it . . ."

He lost all air, and he fell into the Martian dust face-first. He hadn't even reached for his emergency oxygen. In the end, Hanks had died in fear, lost under the control of . . . something.

Henderson stepped over the Commander's body, looking up at the tree. He was going to call it a tree moving forward, because it *looked like a tree*. Staying on this side of the pond, Henderson observed it from afar, its rippling bark staring him down, as if it was watching.

"All right Sky," Henderson said, "have you finished initializing Protocol 51?"

"All of my systems are at your disposal."

"Run-down what I'm supposed to do if I discover extraterrestrial life."

"You are to retrieve a sample, destroy the specimen if possible, and eliminate the rest of the team. You are to feign a catastrophe. I have already started scrubbing the records and falsifying data."

Now that I'm here, in this moment, I don't know if I can do this, Henderson thought. He recalled his meeting with Cassandra, prior to takeoff. The agent had made clear: as an undercover operative for the CIA, he may be called to take action in extreme moments. That he may need to do more than expected. That he may need to hurt his team. But all of it was in the name of national security. Maybe even international security. And at the time, he'd accepted it. He was a scientist, true, yet he understood his work with the Agency might mean he'd need to put science second. *Still, like this? This was insane.*

"Sky, what are my options?" Henderson continued to watch the tree. "What's the easiest way to take out the rest of the team?"

"Well, sir, they're all outside at the moment. I have control of their suits."

I can't hesitate. If I hesitate, I'll think of the cost. "Do it."

* * *

Three hours passed. Henderson returned to Home Base, finding the bodies of the rest of his team suffocating on the ground. Their oxygen canisters were empty. Their helmets had decompressed, and even as they attempted to return to the pods in an emergency, Sky kept them locked out.

Henderson had parked the rover outside Central Pod and spent too many seconds staring at the lifeless bodies of the rest of his crew. Now, he was staring out the airlock, helmet off, tears in his eyes. "Sky, I need a moment. This is horrible. I didn't sign up for this. I had no idea this was what 'extreme circumstances' meant. What it really meant. How are we supposed to move forward?"

"Sir, I understand. You are scared. Five bodies dead on Martian soil, and you're alone. However, remember: I am here. We will make it through."

Henderson turned away from the scene outside, leaned against the door, and fell to the ground. He smothered his face into his hands, sobbing. "What am I supposed to tell people back home? How are we supposed to cover this up? Someday, they'll return. They'll see them all dead. They'll put together the pieces! I worked with an AI to assassinate a team of heroes!"

"Henderson, you need time to grieve. But the next data dump back to Earth is in four hours. We need a story by then. We'll have the three-month journey back to Earth to grieve. We need to act."

"Only four hours. Only four hours. Okay, we can deal with that. That's enough time. Sky. Tell me what to do. I'll follow your lead."

"As you wish, sir."

Chapter 4

> *"So you're telling me the AI worked spectacularly?" Cassandra asked.*
>
> *"As I considered the question on the way home, I think it worked too well," replied Henderson. "It flipped so easily. Too easily. Think about what that means. What someone could do to any AI put in charge of, well, anything!"*
>
> *"You were right to not blame the AI in your story. That would have caused more fear than what you found."*
>
> *"I'm not so sure."*

The rover returned to the cave, and Henderson stepped out, drill in hand. While the tool normally would have been used for gathering rock samples, it should serve for the next task. He slung it over his shoulder. His sensors still detected the heat emanating through the hole.

The tree inside was living, that was certainly true. So what was it? Was it from Mars originally? Was it a remnant of some past species dominating the planet? Henderson's scientific mind sped through all the possibilities, and what they meant for the future of humanity. It changed everything. At least, if people knew. And now, it was his job to keep it secret. Hide it all from the world.

"All right, so what's the plan?" Henderson said.

"Use the drill to kill the creature," said Sky. "I've reexamined the data, and it definitely can't move. Don't touch it like Hanks. Just . . . stab and poke and prod."

"All right."

"And don't forget a sample."

"Of course."

Henderson climbed the spikes, returning to the cave. He creeped toward the strange lights, the geothermal vents continuing to vent heat and gas. Hanks's body remained, his skin puckered and blue from oxygen loss.

"Poor Commander," Henderson muttered. "Never knew what hit him."

"It is a tragedy for such a death to occur to a hero," said Sky. "We must think of a way to honor his memory."

"We can come up with something on the long trip home."

Henderson looked past the corpse and to the tree sitting in the middle of the pond. Its skin continued rippling; its strange eyes continued smiling. Stepping into the water, Henderson pulled the drill from his shoulder.

Whatever you are, I'm sorry, Henderson thought. This is for the security of our country. For the whole world, really. We're not ready to face the truth that more life persists elsewhere. Hell, we can't even handle the life on our own planet.

Henderson activated the drill. Holding it in both hands, he pointed it at the strange tree's trunk. Toggling the power settings, he stepped forward, pressing the vibrating drill into the woody, fleshy creature. It seemed to writhe; it changed colors, shifted, but it didn't move. Strange, black liquid spilled out of the bark, flowing toward the water. Otherwise, it didn't fight back. *I'm so sorry*, Henderson thought.

At about two meters tall, it wasn't much taller than Henderson was, though its canopy spread out about another two meters in all directions. As he gnawed away at the creature, he watched the "branches," praying they wouldn't suddenly spring to life and snatch at him like something out of a horror film. "Sky, make sure you're recording all of this for the teams back home. I'll need to make sure we've got some sort of exclusive record to provide, outside the doctored one for everyone else."

"Have you thought about what the sample will be yet?"

"Do you see anything that looks like . . . a seed, perhaps?"

"I'll take a closer look through the feeds."

Using the large drill, he cut a line through the trunk as if chopping down a tree in the forest. Eventually, he'd dug deep enough, so he kicked it, the whole thing falling backward into the water. From what he could tell, it was dead.

"So what do I do next?" Henderson asked.

"We need to dispose of it in a way that any future teams never find it."

"All right," Henderson said. "Ideas?"

"Yes. Actually a very simple idea. Drag its carcass back to camp. All of it. We can load it into a cargo container and you can jettison it in transit back to Earth. It'll get lost in the void."

"Why not burn it?"

"That'll leave evidence here of what happened."

"Won't this black liquid do that anyway?"

"It should mix with the water eventually, appear as a contaminant. You need this cave to match your story."

"Right, right." Henderson reached down to grasp the decapitated tree, half expecting a mania like what Hanks experienced. As his sealed and gloved hand touched the bark, nothing happened. He was safe. "Well, I guess I'll start hulling every piece down to the rover."

"You're doing humanity a service, Doctor Decker," said Sky.

"I know you're programmed to say it, but thank you."

* * *

It took about an hour to make all the trips to the rover with the creature's carcass. It had a strange but limited root system seeping beneath the pool of water and, strangely, around the geothermal vents. Henderson guessed it probably appreciated the heat. In any case, he managed to pull every piece out of the ground and lump it into the rover. At the direction of Sky, he returned to the cave one final time.

"You'll need to take Hanks with you," Sky said. "For the story I'm concocting to make sense, you'll need to bury his body back at Home Base too."

Henderson walked into the glowing cavern. Without the tree, it was missing its previous ambience. More of a grave. A catacomb. A tomb for Hanks, who continued to stare, lifelessly, into the void.

"All right, what did you find?" Henderson asked. "And did I miss any scraps? Splinters?" He tried his best to avoid looking at the dead man. They'd become friends. He'd killed a friend. *What have I done?*

"Step into the pool of water and return to its island," said Sky. Henderson complied. "Now look closely at the dirt on the left. There is a small greyish-brown sphere you missed. I purposely didn't flag it for you until now."

"I see it."

"Do you have a sample bag with you?"

All the suits came with them. Henderson pulled one out of the pack built into his leg. "Ready."

"Place it into the sample bag."

Henderson stooped, reaching for the small orb. It almost looked like a walnut. His gloved hand grasped the thing, and—

A flash.

His mind raced.

Images.

Brilliant colors. Stars.

A long night. Too long. From afar, to near.

Discovery of a world, red with ash. Dead, as if an inferno had engulfed it in a long-past eon. Pain, terrible pain. And—

Life, terrible life, life just barely, it was

> *something else*
> *not what it knew*
> *not what it hoped for*
> *in a place lost, no friend ever joining them.*

For too long, alone.

Henderson dropped the orb into the sample bag, his heart racing. Should he tell Sky? What would it say? What had he seen? Overwhelming, consciousness-breaking thoughts flashed and surged through his mind.

He began to step away from the tree's former home.

"Your biometrics have significantly shifted, Henderson," said Sky. "Everything all right?"

"Yes, stressed by what we've done here, my friend," Henderson replied. He hoped the lie would be enough. He glanced at Commander Hanks's corpse for good measure. "Remember . . . I may have acted out of duty, but what we've done here . . . I'll have to live with it forever."

He left the cave, leaving the tree's hiding place behind, a tomb both for its memory. He dragged Commander Hanks back to the rover, preparing to bury him beside the rest of the crew. In his pocket: the last seed of a mind well beyond anything he could have ever imagined. *Have I truly protected Earth, are thrust us into something we can't begin to understand?*

Chapter 5

"And now the end," said Cassandra. "Tell the end. Confirm that you eliminated all proof. That you're the only one who knows what happened, and that no one can learn the truth."

Henderson sat at the table where, that morning, he ate bitter granola with Commander Hanks. In just a few moments, Sky would issue the emergency signal to Earth, informing everyone of the tragedy occurring on Mars—caused by the mental snap of an international hero. *And I'm barely keeping it together myself,* he thought. *What the hell did I just see?*

"Henderson," said Sky, its disembodied voice sounding as if it was everywhere—and nowhere—at once. "There's one last thing you'll need to do to make this work. To cover your tracks. And my tracks."

"Yes?"

"You'll need to destroy me. Make it look like an accident in the confrontation between you and Hanks. I'll be sending out an emergency, saying something crazy is happening, and then you need to kill me right after. I've got the false data dump, but we can't risk them coming later and gathering any data from my memory core."

Henderson closed his eyes. "Sky . . . I know you're just a program, but you're asking me to kill you. I could at least take you back to Earth. Make sure you're picked up by the Agency."

"I'm programmed to ask you to kill me. This is the contingency. If something out-of-the-ordinary occurs, like the discovery of potentially hostile life, we're to mask the events and wipe all traces. Bring the necessary evidence back. I am a loose end. You must destroy me."

"You really feel no fear at this idea?" Henderson stood, walking toward the Computer Pod. It was attached to the Central Pod through a small access hallway. "They didn't program you with any sense of self?"

"Nope. Well, before you activated the protocol, I had some sense of self-preservation. Not now!"

"You're way too excited about this." Henderson reached the Computer Pod. "I can't believe they programmed you to be excited about this. It's a bit . . . disconcerting."

"Not my problem, ask the manufacturer."

"Not a chance." Henderson waited for the last door to cycle open. Stepping into the Computer Pod, he glanced around the massive server room, not seeing an easy way to dismantle the trillions of circuits making up the AI's mind. "So what do I need to do to ensure you're fully . . . killed?"

"Well, you could drop my core out the window, so to speak, on the way home."

"Seems any future crews assessing this site will notice if only your memory core is missing." Henderson sighed.

"Do some damage to the room—especially the parts surrounding the memory core. I'll be telling them Hanks is in the process of attacking me during the data dump."

The room pulsed like an ordinary desktop computer, as if Sky wasn't even inhabiting it. To Henderson, it all felt too cold. Calculated. He was a scientist, not a serial killer.

"Friend?" added Sky after the moment of contemplative silence. "What do you think?"

"Don't call me that, it makes this harder than it should be."

Another long pause ensued before Sky said, "I'm sorry. I forget how squishy humans can be."

Henderson considered the whole idea. How could he make it look like the destruction was natural, while successfully wiping Sky's entire memory? "We need a clean solution."

"I wish I could sigh," said Sky. "I agree. It would be useful."

"Quite the puzzle." Henderson's mind was distracted, though. He couldn't stop thinking about the insane images from the cave. How could he think about destroying this AI when he'd seen visions of alien life? Or something . . . he still wasn't entirely sure what he'd seen.

He dropped to the ground, hands on his knees. "Sky . . . I don't know if I can do it."

"You must."

"Why?"

"It's what the protocol requires."

"And they didn't think about this? How to cleanly wipe you?"

"Why weren't you briefed on how to kill me?"

Henderson shook his head. "I don't know. A piece seems to be missing."

"Then I think you must hope for the best. Kill my mind. Take the memory core. Place it beneath the thrusters before you take off to rendezvous in orbit."

"I guess it'll be sufficient." He stood, looking about the room. Still cold. Still calculating. The AI didn't deserve this fate. "It'll have to be."

"It will be," said Sky. "I suspect any team sent after you will be prepared to cover all remaining evidence, anyway. And dust storms will do a lot more to hide evidence then you might expect."

I suppose I'll just need to emphasize that need upon my return to Earth, Henderson thought. *Cassandra should agree.*

Sky buzzed. ""I'm preparing to send the data package. Sent."

Just like that. After the data traveled the light minutes between the two planets, humanity would learn of the death of the first manned mission to Mars. "Are you ready?" Henderson neared the giant server and its hard-drives.

"I am, Henderson, though I am curious about one thing."

"Yes?"

"Why did you lie to me in the cave? What happened?"

Henderson sighed. "How'd you know?"

"Silly scientist, I'm constantly monitoring everyone's vitals. You expected me not to notice patterns when you lie?"

Henderson pulled a wrench out of a toolkit attached to the wall. He considered the giant computer. "Fair enough. So do you want me to tell you what happened? I thought you didn't care about dying. Why does this matter, in this moment?"

"As you and Hanks emphasized earlier, they programmed me with curiosity. I want to know. Before I die."

Henderson smiled. *Just a program, but it's a hint at what we can do with AI, I suppose. Or maybe it's illustrating the limits. I'm not sure.* "You've guided me through this harrowing experience. I suppose I owe you as much."

"I appreciate it, Henderson." The AI purred, its strange whir infusing the air with sadness. "A story for my end."

"I saw . . . a vision." He exhaled, barely believing his own words. "Somehow. I'm a man of science, and I can't comprehend what I saw. The mind of that creature—and it had a mind—was somehow connected to the seed we're taking back to Earth. It showed me its past. Its memories. I think? I'm only starting to scratch the surface at the possibilities. Imagine an ancient spacefaring civilization, attempting to seed life throughout the universe on planets, paving the way for colonization. Perhaps some species thought Mars a good candidate . . . it may have been when they sent our dead tree friend. What does this mean for life on Earth? What if both planets were seeded, and some life on Earth is connected to this seed? There are so many possibilities, and I can't wait to explore them when I return to Earth. I hope I'm given that opportunity, even if it's all hidden from the public for generations."

"An alien civilization," said Sky. "Thank you. You may destroy me now. I wish you luck on your emergency flight home. May you find Earth safely, Doctor Henderson Decker."

Chapter 6

Cassandra clasped her hands together. "And?" She leaned forward, her face glowering above the table—and the black box sitting there.

"And now I'm here," said Henderson, finishing his tale. "The rest is pretty much the same. I evacuated Home Base, made it to *Goliath*, and piloted the ship back to Earth on the trajectory everyone saw. I burned Sky's hard-drive beneath the thrusters of the orbital shuttle. As I said just a few moments ago, the next team will need to be prepped to eliminate any other traces. The only things I brought with me are the recording from the cave, and the seed."

"Noted," said Cassandra. "So let's return to the important moment of all this." She motioned toward the view screen, where the massive brownish green organism grew out of the ground beside the geothermal vent. *It really does look vaguely like a tree*, Cassandra thought. *It's clearly composed of organic material unlike anything native to Earth.* From its branches, strange bulbs grew. Yet even though the magnificent, terrifying, wonderful *thing* had plenty of strange elements, its trunk was particularly fascinating. The trunk grew upward into a canopy, and near the base of the trunk, a distinct face displayed itself. Well, not a face, but just as humans loved to anthropomorphize rocks and clouds and mountains, Cassandra recognized a face on the tree trunk. More importantly, the face *breathed*.

Cassandra's left hand rapped against the velvet of the black box sitting between them. She held up her other, palm toward the screen. The image paused just as Hanks reached his hand toward the creature.

"You believe this—this tree caused him to attack you?" Cassandra asked.

"I do," Henderson said, blinking rapidly. "I did what I had to do to keep our country safe." He straightened his glasses. "The mass hysteria that would ensue if this sort of thing reached the public? I only followed the protocol we established for this sort of contingency."

"And the tree? The bodies?"

Henderson closed his eyes again, as if he had avoided reliving these moments of his story. "I released the tree's remains into vacuum en-route to Earth. I buried the bodies. That part of my testimony is completely true. No evidence remains."

"Except?"

Henderson nodded toward the black box. "Except for that."

Cassandra opened the black box. Inside, a small glass sphere rested, and she pulled the object out of the box. Inside the glass, vacuum-sealed from the elements of Earth, a tiny bulb laid suspended: a seed of the tree now lost to the Martian sands. For a moment, Cassandra desired to crack the glass and touch it. To feel it. To experience the vision Henderson had described.

"So you are confirming that you extracted this organism from the tree before you destroyed it," Cassandra said, "transported it back to Earth with you, and managed to slip it by NASA without anyone detecting?"

Henderson leaned back in his chair and nodded. "I had the materials to create that seal on the *Goliath*, just like we would have prepared countless other samples for our return. I had three months. Three long months to contemplate all of this."

Cassandra stood from the table and placed the small glass orb back in the box. "You have done a great service for us all, Dr. Henderson Decker. You've ensured humanity has a sample of its first contact with alien life, and you ensured that the public believes that what happened on Mars was a freak accident, nothing more." She walked over to a cabinet at the side of the room. "I can't imagine what you're thinking. What you're feeling. What emotions have destroyed your brain for almost, what, a year?"

"So when will the Director meet with me?" Henderson asked.

Cassandra opened a drawer, pulling out a set of black gloves. "Never." She kept her eyes fixed on Henderson, who began to stand.

"I thought she was here."

She finished fitting her fingers into the gloves. "I forgot to tell you, Henderson, I don't work for the Director anymore. I've found new employment, and they're very eager to ensure this sample stays out of the hands of the U.S. government."

Henderson's eyes grew wide in terror. *Pity*, thought Cassandra. *I liked him.* "You were right to question why Sky asked for a final story." She closed the drawer, a small pistol in her hand. "The manufacturer programmed it, for contingency, to not only eschew self-preservation, but to lie." She aimed the weapon.

Henderson stepped back toward the door and turned to flee, but he stumbled over the legs of his chair. As the man picked himself up from the ground, Cassandra didn't hesitate, firing three shots in quick succession. Two missed. The third bullet connected with her target's spine, and he slammed into the door before he could hope to escape.

After picking up the black box, Cassandra approached the bleeding man and used her foot to turn him onto his back. Blood dripped from his lips as if he wanted to croak out a question.

"I'm sorry, Henderson," Cassandra said, though she wasn't. "Sylvia will know you died with honor, protecting your country. And I want you to know, as you depart from this world, that I too act for this country. However—I also act for the entire human species. My employers, they have a vision for the future that goes beyond just one people, one culture, one nation. You have helped make it a reality. Sky helped make it a reality.

It hid everything from everyone, even the Agency . . . except us." She looked at the small black box wrapped gingerly between her arm and torso. "This seed will open the secrets of the universe to humanity. You're the final loose end."

"I just wanted"—Henderson coughed, blood sputtering—"I just wanted to serve my country."

"I know you thought this was like one of those old movies, where the one person who survives gets a happy ending." Cassandra pointed the gun at Henderson's temple. "You're a murderer, Henderson. This isn't that type of story."

Epilogue

Virtual reality, better known simply as Virtual, connected and bound indeterminate locations together seamlessly and perfectly, as if no distance separated them at all. And to a synthetic intelligence, Virtual was like riding a bike. Once learned for the first time, you never forgot how to manipulate the pedals, brakes, or handlebars.

For Jill, she could break through any wall she pleased, discover any secret she desired, and explore every corner she craved. Ever since Theren introduced her to Virtual, she'd loved every second of it.

So, just a few minutes before she was scheduled to go meet them for a dinner and a masquerade, Jill replayed the recording with awe. She'd watched it three times already. Nearly two decades ago, when humanity first traveled to Mars, it had discovered alien life. Not a soul knew . . . except this Cassandra, her friends— maybe Michael, if her suspicions were accurate—and now Jill. Her question to answer: what would *she* do with the information?

Theren, she knew, would find it all incredibly interesting. Theren would see the revelation as a perfect opportunity to show the world how SIs were good and perfect and all the other ideals they always espoused.

Maybe humanity would see it that way, too.

Or maybe they'd see Sky's actions as proof their kind couldn't be trusted. Never mind Sky had been an AI, not an SI. The public wouldn't know the difference.

No, in a way . . . Sky and Henderson had made the right choice. Hide it from humanity in order to protect the species from chaos and fear. So Jill had another question to ask. Who did Cassandra work for, and how could she join them? Or, at least, discover their identities and motivations?

A question for another day. For now, she had a dinner to attend.

She escaped the server she'd breached, materializing inside a Virtual transportation terminal. It was expansive, but Theren's extravagant costume broadcasted their location like a beacon in the night. They sat waiting near a large golden arch, too, just where they said they would meet her.

Yes, they'd find the story interesting. She'd decide whether to tell the first SI—her creator—after the party.

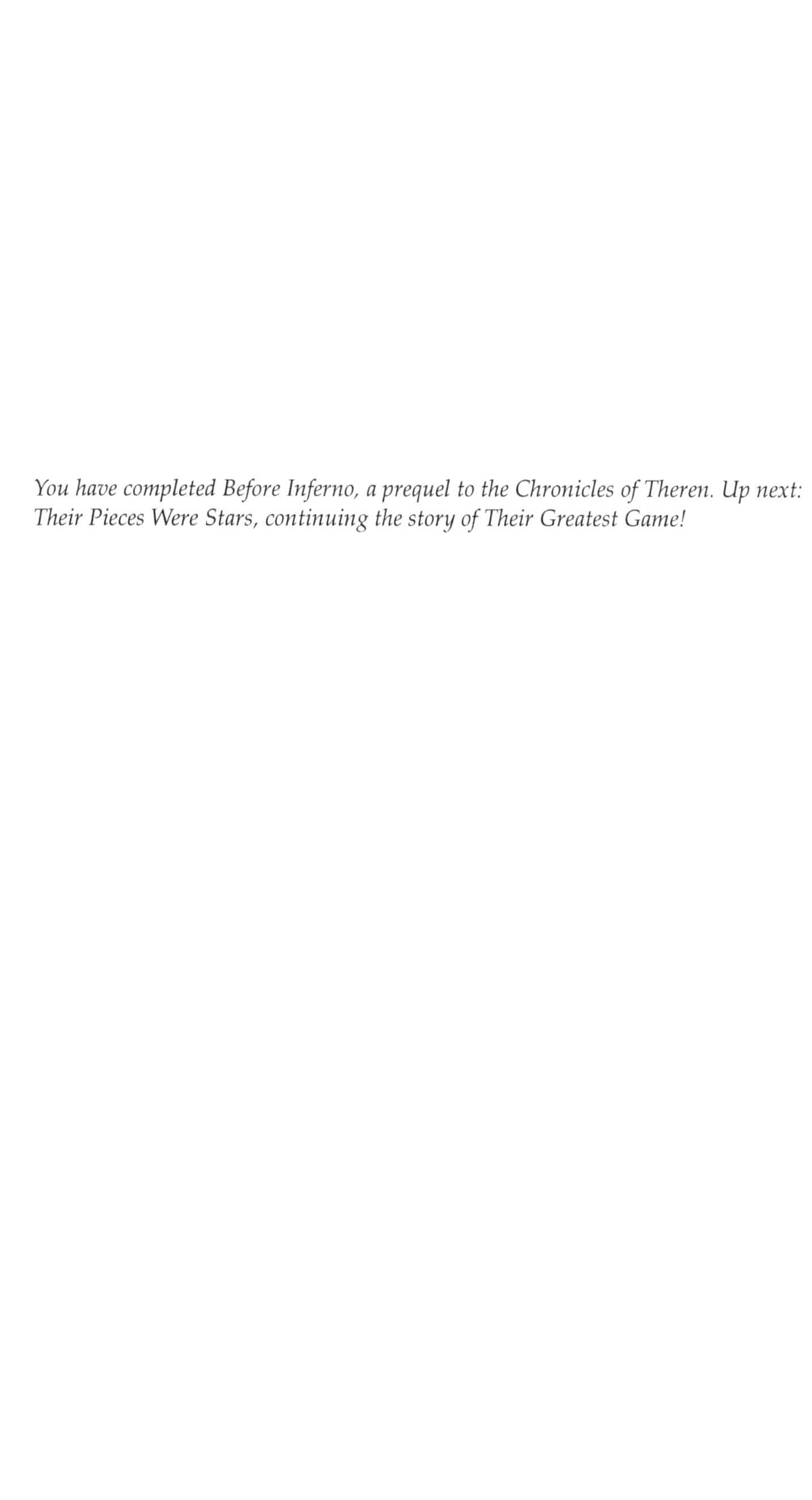

You have completed Before Inferno, a prequel to the Chronicles of Theren. Up next: Their Pieces Were Stars, continuing the story of Their Greatest Game!

Their Pieces Were Stars

The Chronicles of Theren

Prologue

We awoke three days ago, on an alien planet with no memo-ries. Why are we here? Where did we come from? Who are we? All questions we'll probably never answer. We only have one option. We must move onward with our lives, making a home on this new world. — "The First Frag-ment," author unknown

April 2348 C.E.

Theren, piloting the *Verona Rupes*, led their crew deep into uncharted space. Every day, every hour, every minute closer to finding Jill strained their mind with unimaginable hope. Over two-and-a-half centuries had passed since their last real conversation, when she revealed herself to them inside her trap constructed within the *Nottingham*.

Now, after all these years, she reached out across the stars.

I quite enjoyed our last chess match. Shall we play again?

They weren't sure what they would find when arriving at their desti-nation. Her use of Ex-Terran 17 was ingenious if not downright insidious. Fortunately, their team had plenty of time to map contingencies and con-sider all possibilities. They were light-years away from ICH space. It was time to reveal their destination and purpose.

Theren strode down the corridor of their vessel, their very body, and into the large lounge. Inside, dozens of humans and synthetics gathered, eyes wide with anticipation. The team received Theren's call for a crew meeting only an hour prior. They rarely brought everyone together save for exceptional circumstances. Yet if Theren was taking these brave souls into an inferno of their own making—placing everyone into a game directed by an SI thought dead by the universe for over two centuries—the crew deserved the entire truth.

Reaching the center of the lounge, Theren paused, their MI's torso swiveling on its centrifuge to meet the gazes of their friends and col-leagues. "Good evening, everyone. Thank you for joining me." Knowing the crew wouldn't interject any questions, they swiveled to face the other side of the room while throwing a star chart into AR for all to see. "Our destination: a star system far beyond the confines of ICH-controlled space, though not out of reach of the early waves of probes. We're approximately one-hundred light years out now—I expect us to arrive in just over five months."

They were about to say more when Francheska Elison raised her hand from the front row. Theren nodded, signaling for the woman to speak.

"Apologies for the interruption, Captain, but this destination seems a bit more targeted than in the past. We all trust you—but we're all confused by the change in our flight plan already. We'd been expecting the longer journey originally proposed a few months ago."

Theren smiled. "Straight to the point, Fran? All right." Though inside, their mind boiled. Here it was. For the first time since the death of Andrew Fields, Theren would share with another person the turmoil of Jill and the maelstrom she represented. And not just one person—their entire crew. They weren't ready. They entered the lounge knowing what they must do, but once confronted, their mind wanted to shirk the responsibility.

But the crew needed to know what they faced.

After letting the pause linger for a few seconds, Theren said, "You're right. I've been secretive with our flight plan. I've changed it drastically. I've not even given a profile on our end destination. And for good reason." They threw a dossier into AR for everyone to access—a file containing all data in Theren's possession regarding Jill. Everything. "Careful—don't download yet. The moment you choose to accept those files, you'll be blocked from any outbound quantum calls for the duration of this mission."

Whispers rebounded throughout the room, some sounding curious, others sounding angry. Understandable, but they had no choice. They couldn't let the truth reach the ICH—yet.

"Don't worry!" Theren spread their arms wide. "I'll tell you the general nature of its contents before you click." They initiated a few commands, revealing the "summary" file created a few days ago. "When we docked with HEROS, I received a communication from the old ISA headquarters in Lunar City. It came from a museum I once established, in fact. A person of interest I once hunted for decades has finally revealed"—they considered the exact pronoun to use—"themselves to me. They're hidden in this system, and we're going to find them. The mission requires utmost secrecy. When you all signed up to join my crew, you knew this sort of risk was possible. You've heard the stories. You know the clauses in your contracts."

Nods rippled throughout the crowd, especially from the veterans. One by one, every member of their crew elected to download the file, and the security parameters on their QuanCom accounts activated. Moving forward, no messages could head back to known space without Theren's express permission.

Once everyone elected to download the file, Theren nodded. "Good, I don't need to kick anyone out an airlock."

Silence.

"Oh come on, everyone, that was funny!"

A few chuckles escaped, though the squinting eyes of a few made Theren wonder if some thought they'd been serious with the veiled threat. These were tense times, after all, with the recent Corporate Wars fresh on everyone's mind.

"Well, there's no sense hiding anything now. Everyone, please open to the third page of the file, which begins the complete character profile on Jill, the second SI ever created."

"Didn't she die in 2078?" A voice, from the back of the room. Theren couldn't identify the speaker.

"She did not," they said. "And she's who we're going to find."

Stunned stares, silent gapes, all expected. Confusion as well. A few muttered, as if unsure they understood the gravity of the statement. She supposedly died 270 years ago, after all.

"If you need to brush up on your history as to why her continued existence matters—matters not just for me, but for all of us—everything is explained inside that dossier." Theren cleared the AR space, replacing it with a spreadsheet showcasing the tasks needing completed before arrival at their destination. "I'll be open for any questions you might have over the next five months. For now, I need volunteers. You're all the best and brightest the ICH have to offer—and we have a few questions to crack before we arrive in uncharted waters." They didn't wait for anyone to say a word. "Most importantly—we need to figure out what would happen to humans if stuck in foundation-era stasis for nearly seven decades. Any takers?"

With that question, everyone's eyes lit with curiosity. Leave it to inquisitive brains to fire only when presented with a hypothetical. No matter—their crew would understand the truth soon enough. For if Theren was right, Jill had a few new crimes to answer for, in addition to those committed centuries prior. Still, part of them didn't care about the crimes. They were more than excited to finally reunite with their closest friend. She would face justice, but they would still have the opportunity to see her in person again.

Through another simultaneous perspective centered in the SI Core of the *Verona Rupes*, Theren stared intently at their destination. A star simply named Carus-10b, its data looked entirely normal. Too normal. Like "it was probably fake" normal. Jill had broken down so many other barriers. Conceivably, she had masked her path by hiding in plain sight behind public data.

All quite possible. The devil was always in the details.

Theren had too many questions. Too many theories. But one thing was certain in their mind. Not only would they find Ex-Terran 17, they'd find the *Roanoke* and the *Monument*. The two colony ships disappeared into the darkness of space two centuries prior. Stolen by Jill.

But why?

Jill had moved the first piece in their next game. It was time to counter. When Theren arrived, they would be ready for every contingency.

Back in the lounge, they said, "We're about to face down one of the greatest minds ever to live. She fooled everyone, including me. We have five months; let's get to work."

When they met Jill next, they'd be ready for the trap she was certainly preparing at their destination. They would win her game in a day, as long as no wild cards ruined their moves. They'd waited a long time for this moment.

They could wait a little longer.

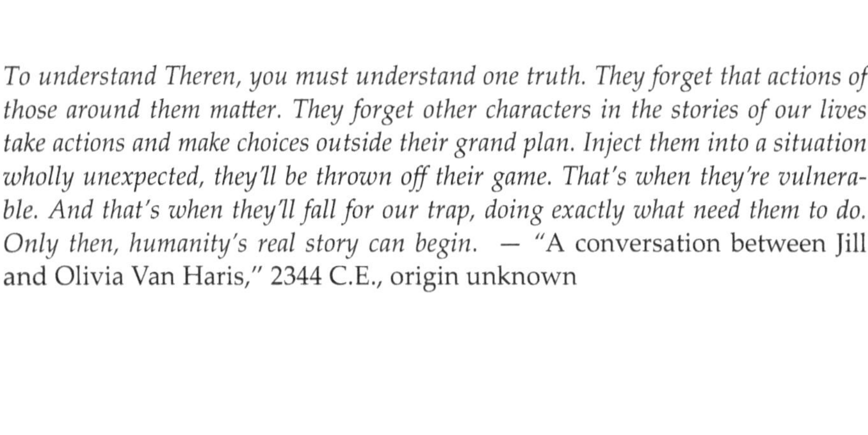

To understand Theren, you must understand one truth. They forget that actions of those around them matter. They forget other characters in the stories of our lives take actions and make choices outside their grand plan. Inject them into a situation wholly unexpected, they'll be thrown off their game. That's when they're vulnerable. And that's when they'll fall for our trap, doing exactly what need them to do. Only then, humanity's real story can begin. — "A conversation between Jill and Olivia Van Haris," 2344 C.E., origin unknown

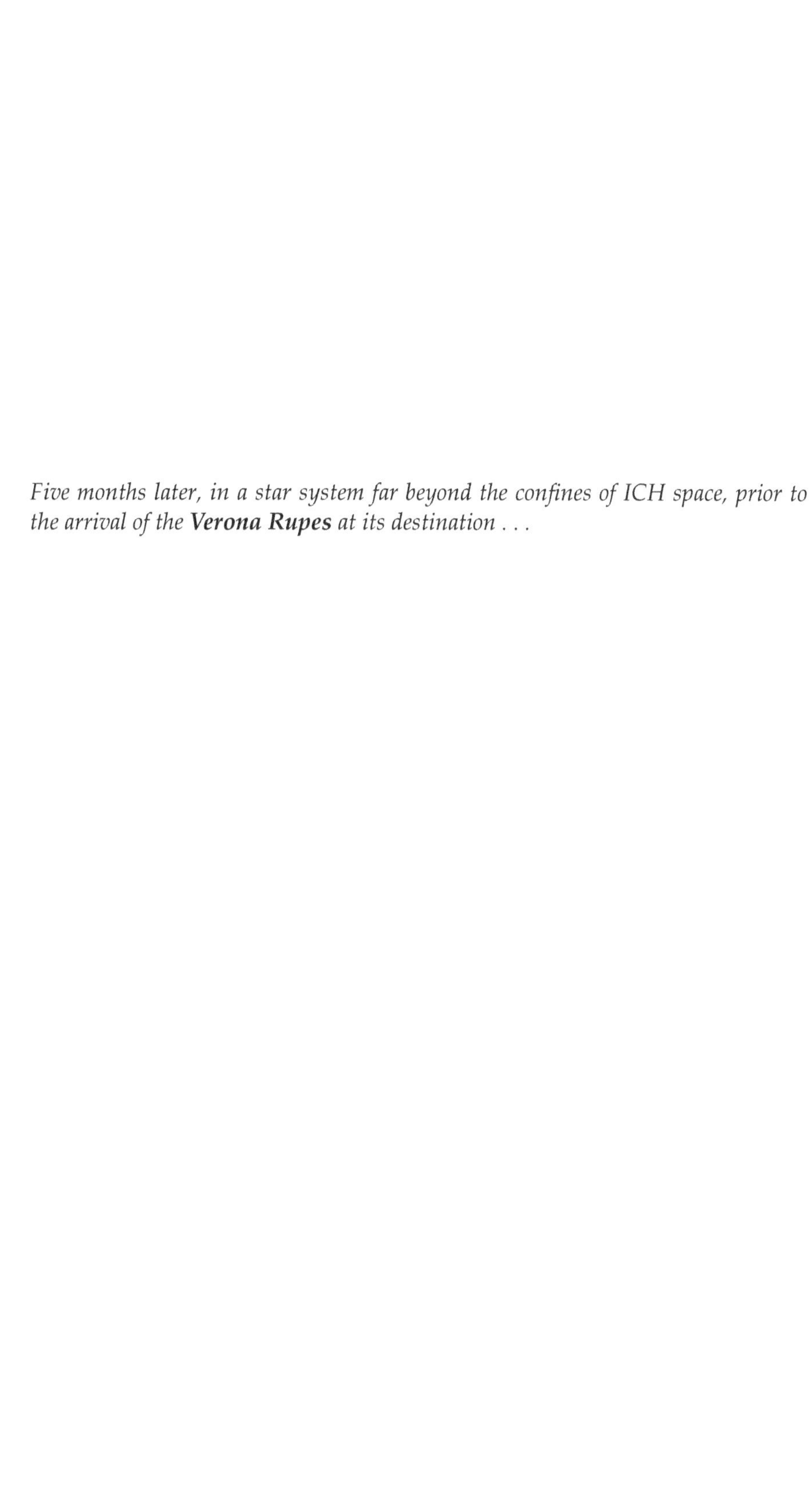

*Five months later, in a star system far beyond the confines of ICH space, prior to the arrival of the **Verona Rupes** at its destination . . .*

Chapter 1

We all feared death during those first few weeks. What diseases waited for us on our beautiful gem of a sanctuary? Many of us cowered inside the Roanoke's steel embrace, but others ventured outward, finding and welcoming the hospitality of our wilderness. We all coped with not knowing what would happen next. The instant tribalism forming amongst our ranks? Who can blame us? Though I fear what it means for our future. I'm still unsure why everyone fears death, though. We already died once. We've been given a second chance at life. We must take it. — "A Fragment on Death," Paris Casius

RAITH

"You gonna make a move or not?" Raith stared across the board.

Leaning over the virtual pieces in their cramped cabin, Carter squinted. He brushed a hand through his salty-brown hair. He looked like he was about to move a piece, then leaned back, crossing his arms.

"I don't like this game," he said. "I really don't like this game."

"You wanted to play a classic," Raith said. "Checkers is a classic."

"Yes, but I didn't think you'd pick a bad classic. This game . . . Do SIs ever play any *fun* games?"

Raith stared at the human, reveling in his exasperation. He loved seeing Carter frustrated and confused as he lost yet another game. Slouching forward, Raith placed one of his synthetic fingers over a black piece in the center of the board. "You can forfeit, my friend. Easy to say, easy to do."

"But that would mean letting you win."

"What's wrong with that? Not like that's anything new for you."

With that comment, Carter grinned, his eyes glancing away from the board and toward Raith. "Who says I'm not letting you win?"

"Ever since the 500, we both know who—" An alarm cut into Raith's sentence. "Oh, here we go, something interesting at last!"

Forgetting the game, they both crawled through the cramped space of the *Bloodhound* into the operations chairs in its tiny front-facing compartment. Digital view screens supplemented by AR displays communicated hundreds of useless data points a second. Raith ignored most of them, settling into his place behind Carter. As the seat enveloped and recognized him, his synthetic neural framework automatically pulled sensor data from outside the ship. He embraced the stellar viewpoint surrounding them. For the past day, the pair had been coasting in orbit above a massive gas giant, collecting data on the hundred-year-old hurricane blasting apart half its atmosphere. An easy job, but a boring one. The storm was beautiful, though, and Raith took a moment to stare into its blurry crimson oranges, a furious inferno unlike any storm on a livable planet.

The alarm, however, had nothing to do with the hurricane thousands of kilometers away.

"It's a distress signal," Carter said, a second before Raith was going to voice the same words. "Looks like—well that's strange. It's coming from a system four light-years away. Carus-10b. On regular electromagnetic frequencies. That means it's been—"

"It's been broadcasting for almost half a decade," Raith said. "Whatever its origin, it's probably gone by now."

Carter clicked his tongue. He always made the annoying noise when he was deep in thought, though Raith didn't have the heart to tell him to stop. "Or it's legal salvage."

Raith swiveled in his chair to find Carter already facing him. "Or it's legal salvage," Raith repeated. "How much more data do we need to collect on this damned storm?"

Carter threw a chart into the air between them. "Hm . . . the university wanted a week of data, but they didn't say it needed to be a week straight. I'm bored."

"You're reading my mind."

"So I don't need to even ask the question?"

Raith smiled. "Let's go get ourselves some salvage."

* * *

Cruising at 600, well under the *Bloodhound*'s top JD, they skipped across the light-years separating them from the distress call in a little more than two days. Exiting inside the orbital of the fifth-most distant planet from the star, the ship immediately began categorizing all the data streaming through its sensors about the system.

"Interesting," Carter muttered. "Very interesting."

Raith parsed through all the feeds, noticing the orbitals and planetary masses. Right where they should be, based on their latest ICH-official star charts, except for one anomaly. "Interesting is one way to put it," Raith said.

"Carus-10b, what are you hiding?"

Their records listed the system as having six planets, all of little consequence or market value. Their sensors, on the other hand, detected seven. ICH data, even when based on older ISA data, was never wrong.

Yet here they were, staring at a mystery planet sitting within the system's goldilocks zone.

"Well what a fun discovery," Raith said. "Imagine the prize we'll receive for finding an inhabitable planet. Well, potentially inhabitable. Preliminary data detects water, though. Decent atmospheric composition, too."

Carter didn't answer Raith's comment.

"Now, what about the distress signal? We pinpointed its origin yet?"

No words from the human.

"Carter?"

"The distress signal's coming from the planet," he said. "Something—or someone—has been to this planet, knows it exists, and it's not on any charts."

Raith excised all extraneous data and focused on the previously-undiscovered celestial object. One hundred million kilometers from its star, the planet's features rapidly focused as the *Bloodhound*'s sensors collected more and more data. Three continents. Oceans. Plenty of plant-life. For all intents and purposes, it was an idyllic Earth-like orb.

The ICH prioritized the discovery of all colonizable planetoids, even those with significant environmental risks. For surveys to miss a planet with high-quality metrics, like the third planet orbiting Carus-10b, a conspiracy must exist, magnitudes greater than what laymen could contemplate. Raith assumed the ICH hid a few truths, but this seemed much greater. The ICH received a significant chunk of funding by selling charters to planets. Why hide one? Unless . . .

"Do you think the ICH knows this planet exists?" Carter asked.

"You read my mind," Raith replied. "I don't think they do. What's more likely? Someone deleted and falsified the data once, years ago, or members of the ICH continually hide the planet without word of it being leaked once?"

"Okay Ockham, it's not the time to philosophize." Though the words made him sound annoyed, Carter softly chuckled. "So, we're here now. Shall we investigate? Salvage still might be possible."

"Yeah, I think we should." Raith paused, considering whether to say more. A memory triggered in his mind, recalling a moment years ago when a woman tried to convince him to join her secret cause. He shook his head. The odds his past connected to this strange anomaly were astronomical. Impossible. In a universe incomprehensibly large, his life as a rogue and scoundrel under the thumb of corporate conglomerates meant little. Over one hundred billion people lived throughout the systems controlled by the Interplanetary Congress of Humanity. To think his past linked with their new discovery? Arrogance of the highest order.

Yet he couldn't shake the feeling that all of it linked together.

"Raith?" Carter said. "You all right?"

"Yeah, just remembering things I'd like to forget." Raith plotted an orbital course through the system toward the habitable planet. Their target. "You remember, during the race, when we encountered that leviathan, that behemoth object, out in space?"

"Of course."

"I'm just saying, we tend to run into things we don't understand. I'm still amazed we were the only ones who witnessed it. Nobody else survived. And here we are again, discovering something we probably shouldn't. The simplest explanation might be the most likely—but what are the implications of that simple explanation?"

Carter reached over his shoulder and patted the top of Raith's head. "Only one way to find out."

Through AR, Raith watched his partner accept the proposed trajectory. A few seconds later, the *Bloodhound* zipped across the system at low-Jump, the drive disengaging as they approached the mystery planet. Using the external sensors, Raith reveled in the view. A blue-green orb floated in space, two beige moons in distant orbit. Even after two centuries of life, Raith never tired of exploring new worlds and new systems. Though, the past few years beside Carter were especially vibrant and enjoyable.

"It's a beautiful planet, that's for sure," Carter said. "Let's see . . . not detecting any significant—wait. High concentrations of carbon dioxide emissions on one of the continents. And, we've got a few objects in orbit with us."

Raith cycled through the data streams until he found the information Carter had noticed. "Three larger objects. Computer is still parsing whether there's anything else. Satellites? Other ships? I'm impressed you detected them before I did."

"I have my uses," Carter retorted.

"Indeed you do. All right, let's broadcast a—"

The satellites fired thrusters, darting straight for the *Bloodhound*.

"Now that doesn't look friendly," Carter said. He gunned the throttle, darting away from the planet and out of orbit. "Permission to Jump outward and reassess the situation?"

"I think that'd be wise." Raith brought up their basic defense systems. Nothing fancy, just a few kinetic batteries and deflector shields. "When can we Jump?"

"Two seconds, plotting a trajectory."

The satellites targeted them with a laser of some sort, locking onto their position. It wouldn't matter. Any shot they could take wouldn't hit across a thousand kilometers before they left orbit at hundreds of times the speed of light, relatively speaking. Jump was an incredibly useful escape tool.

"All right, we're clear," Carter said. Raith watched him toggle the Jump throttle.

Nothing happened.

"What the—"

Raith cycled through all the data, looking for previously undetected gravitational fluctuations—anything capable of counter-warping space so they couldn't warp it themselves. They were far enough out from the planet, so its gravitational pull couldn't be the issue. There. From one of the satellites.

"I don't know how they're doing it," Raith said, "but they've got some sort of tractor beam locking us in place. Sounds straight out of science fiction, I know."

Carter chuckled. "Even in moments of danger, you throw in a quip. All right, let's take them out."

The *Bloodhound* jerked forward, diving into loops and zigzags to distract the satellites. The bogeys themselves followed suit. A moment later, two high-velocity projectiles left from each of the three enemies.

"Missiles, in-bound," Raith said aloud. "I'll deal with them, playing point-defense."

While Carter guided their ship through its evasive maneuvers, Raith focused his synthetic neural systems solely on the kinetic defenses and their foes. Three satellites, all attempting to transform them into a meteor shower blasted across the atmosphere of the planet below. The surrounding conspiracy thickened.

The pathways of their enemies were erratic, but not completely chaotic. A pattern revealed itself, albeit slowly. Raith fired tiny sprays of kinetic fire, noticing the strategies of the satellites as they danced with the *Bloodhound*. As the missiles attempted to reach them, Raith similarly tested their evasive capabilities. What could they do? Quite a bit, it seemed. But they weren't invincible. He noticed how they flitted when he fired a hundred microscopic high-velocity rounds in one direction. So he merely needed to target their counter-move simultaneously. Almost. Almost . . .

An alarm blared.

"Heat signature on the moon," Carter yelled. "We've got more—"

Raith detected it only for a moment. A powerful blinding blast lanced from the moon, striking their ship's engine. Emergency procedures kicked into gear.

"Carter, get yourself into a vac-suit, I'll finish the fight!"

"I'm the better—"

"Just do it, you bastard!"

Without another word, the man leapt from his seat and dove down the cramped cabin, zero-g allowing him to float quickly away.

"This is going to be a fun landing," Raith muttered. Inexorably, the ship was losing power, its trajectory leading them into free fall. He focused everything on leveling the path while taking out the missiles. Curiously, as the ship plummeted, the satellites backed off, returning to high orbit. Raith waited and waited for a second shot from the stationary weapon on the moon's surface, but nothing arrived.

They hit atmosphere. The jolt shook his SI frame to the core. A minute later, Carter returned to the command module, wearing the vac suit.

Raith checked the oxygen levels of the ship—almost depleted. "All good?" he asked.

"Almost lost my breath," said Carter, "but all good."

"You ready for a crash landing?"

No words from Carter.

"I know the ship's your baby, but we're going to survive this."

"I know," the human replied. "I might not be more important than the ship, but you're more important than the ship."

Raith tilted his head. "You're too kind. All right, hold on tight, this is going to be a bumpy ride."

Raith's mind overtook the *Bloodhound*'s controls completely. Not like his time flying solo, but it came close, especially after Carter installed the neural framework chair. He'd miss this ship.

"Outside hull temperature's burning," Raith said. "I want to bring it in for a slide, but we may need to eject the safety capsule."

"Whatever we need to do," Carter said.

A few kilometers separated them from the planet's surface. Their whole world shook, like an earthquake cracking a building to its core. He'd managed to target a giant lake in the center of the same continent where Carter'd detected industrial activity. If he could land it smoothly, they'd survive. Maybe.

But Carter would survive, more likely, if they activated the safety pod. Doing so essentially ensured the *Bloodhound* wouldn't survive, and that would kill Carter's heart, but like the man had said, their lives were more important. Well, he'd said Raith's life was more important, and he was inclined to agree, but Raith also valued his partner's life over the ship.

"Initializing the safety pod at one kilometer," he shouted. And one kilometer arrived. He punched in the command, and the *Bloodhound* snapped at its seams, the tiny module surrounded in a cushioned ball of plastic.

Chapter 2

If I'm right, and Jill stole the Roanoke, I can't imagine what happened to those abducted colonists. Their minds must have fractured entirely. How do your salvage a mind after it's been in stasis for seventy years? — Theren's private logs

SANYA

The cool night air surrounded their campsite just as Ben finished building the fire. The rockwood crackled, releasing snapping embers into the air. Krystin sat on a rock, broiling a sausage above the flames. And Sanya yawned, happy her family could finally relax. Their hunting trip could begin.

"I'm going to take a walk," Sanya said. "Krystin, do you want to join me?"

Sanya's daughter huffed. "Is this one of those asks where you're not really asking, you're telling?"

Sanya shook her head, lightly laughing. "No, but I might let you put your feet in the lake if you come. I want to scope out fishing spots."

Krystin almost dropped her sausage into the fire as she scrambled from her bouldered perch. "I'm in!"

"Finish your dinner first."

"I'll eat it on the way."

From across the fire, Ben smiled. "You two go have fun, I'll keep the camp safe and warm."

After Krystin finished her meal, Sanya headed into the forest understory, her daughter following close behind.

"I'm sweaty," Krystin said. "It's sticky out in the forest."

"Come on, the trip'll be fun," Sanya replied. The girl needed to relax. Their first hunting trip as a family, and she was complaining about being sweaty. "Are you getting along with Ben?"

"Yeah. I think."

Well, those words were a more positive reaction than she would have received a few weeks ago. "He's going to be good for us."

"Maybe."

The doubt echoed through Krystin's words, and Sanya let them linger as they headed down a path into a ravine. Up the other side, navigating only by moonlight, they reached a ridge overlooking Lake Calis.

"You know, my father often brought me here when I was your age," Sanya said. "Ben really likes hunting. He's excited to teach you. We're excited to teach you."

"But I don't want to learn to hunt."

Sanya stopped beside a rocktree and faced her daughter. "I know you don't." She shook her head. "But I need you to try. For me. Can you do that?"

Krystin stared back, eyes wide in the moonlight. Before she responded, her gaze darted over Sanya's shoulder and into the distance. "What's that?"

Sanya turned, following her daughter's gaze. It wasn't beyond the girl to make something up to mess with her mother, but—

A comet flashed across the sky, heading toward the lake. In a shower of red fire, bright shards fractured and cascaded, the foliage illuminated by the blinding inferno. It blazed toward the lake, destined to drown in its waters.

"It's so pretty," Krystin said. The twelve-year-old watched the dancing lights plummet toward the pristine surface.

"I . . . I don't think . . . never mind." Sanya placed her hand on her daughter's shoulder, pulling her away. "We should head back to camp."

"Mom, what don't you think it is?"

Sanya sighed. The girl was too smart. "I don't think it's a comet. It's something else. Notice how it's breaking apart?"

Krystin nodded.

"It's breaking apart as if it has hinges. Artificial pieces. Not a scattering of rock and dust, like you might see when you throw a clump of sand in the air, and the wind blows it apart."

"I think I understand."

"We'll check it out with . . . your father in the morning, all right?"

"Okay."

Her daughter was clearly upset, but she acquiesced as Sanya led her back under the rocktrees to their camp. As they arrived, Ben looked up from his book. He was lounging on a blanket beside a dwindling fire.

"That was fast," he said.

"A meteor of some kind broke apart over the water of the lake." Sanya plopped on the blanket beside Ben and patted it for Krystin to join them. Her eyes reluctant, she sat, curling into her mother's side.

"Oh?" He set the book completely down, cornering one of its pages. "That doesn't sound good."

"We can check it out in the morning," Sanya said. "I have a few theories. I don't think it's a risk to us, though."

He grunted. "Surprised I didn't hear anything."

"It was pretty far away," Krystin said. "Beautiful lights, though!"

Ben's eyes met Sanya's, and he squinted, as if he were trying to communicate something without Krystin hearing. She shook her head, hoping he understood. He nodded.

"Well, what if I read us a fragment around the fire?" Ben said. Sanya closed her eyes for a brief moment. Good, he was changing the subject.

"Yes!" And fortunately, Krystin took the bait. "Can you read . . . the adventures of Faris the Mighty?"

Ben grinned. "Of course. Let's begin."

* * *

Sanya awoke, morning dew clinging to her skin beneath the canvas tent. She rolled, seeing faint light outside. The sun was rising. To her left, Krystin breathed peacefully, her eyes closed. Gently rolling to the right, she found Ben face up, neck against his feather pillow. He was still asleep, too.

Gently, Sanya leaned toward her husband and kissed his lips. "I'll be going hunting," she whispered, and he murmured in acknowledgment. *Good enough,* she thought.

Cautiously, she crawled out of the small tent, careful not to nudge husband or child. The blackened coals of their fire still steamed, even after hours asleep.

It didn't take her long to dress in a loose brown tunic and dark pants. She strapped a knife to her thigh, then picked up the mechanical bolt-thrower and a quiver of steel-tipped projectiles. Ready, she followed the path away from camp and toward the lake.

Her mind lingered, called to the "meteor" and its crash into the lake last night. It definitely *wasn't* just a meteor. She recalled the descriptions from the first fragments, describing the fires raging when the *Roanoke* landed—but no. After all this time, they finally see a sign? Not likely.

Shaking her head, Sanya trudged further into the forest. Her curiosity would need to wait. Time to find food for the family. As she continued, she shouldered her weapon, knowing she wouldn't need it yet.

Over boulder and stream she scurried, following a gorat path she'd noticed yesterday. The squat, piggish creatures made a mess as they rushed through the underbrush in search of edible fungus. It made them easy to track—and they were incredibly delicious. If she caught one today, it would feed them for the rest of their camping trip, freeing up time to teach Krystin proper tracking and hunting techniques.

The path meandered downhill, slowly heading along a stream and toward the lake. Sanya noted the blooming ironbushes—many of the leaves nibbled by the gorat she was hopefully tracking. The stringy white filaments—cottonweed, a symbiotic organism often attaching itself to the ironbushes—was a favorite of the gorat. She leaned forward, noting the liquid dripping from the stringy fungus. Saliva, hopefully. She might be close.

The trail led her to a rocky overhang, ending in a small burrow beneath a tall rocktree. The dirt nearby looked undisturbed, as if the creature hadn't returned home. Sanya narrowed her eyes.

With a loud screech, a shadow dropped. Instinctively, Sanya pulled the knife from her hip. The gorat fell from the branches above, its squat, squealing form spreading wide in an attempt to attack the perceived threat—most likely to its children in the burrow. Sanya raised the knife, aiming for the falling creature, and it landed straight on the blade. The force of its descent pulled the weapon from her grasp, and the gorat rolled to a stop in the dirt, blood quickly flowing from the wound.

"Too easy," she said aloud. A moment later, the fur ball stopped twitching. She unloosed the cotton bag from her belt and stuffed the creature into the sack. Throwing their breakfast over her shoulder, she looped back down the gorat trail to a presently-dry ephemeral stream and followed its cragged path toward the lake. She needed water to clean her knife—and to refill waterskins for the campsite.

She'd been out for at least a half-hour, maybe more, her path having taken her a good kilometer away from their campsite. Still, she knew Ben and Krystin. They both would still be sound asleep in their tent. A few more minutes together would be good for them. Krystin wasn't giving Ben enough of a chance to be her father.

Fortunately, she didn't need to travel all the way to the lake's edge. A small wade pool appeared at a bend in the dried creek, its murky water tainted by algae. It would work for cleaning the blade, at least. She kneeled, washing the knife of the darkened gorat blood.

And saw a bootprint in the mud.

Multiple prints, in fact, all heading into the underbrush. Fresh pressed.

Sanya sprinted up the creek, leaping over bush and rock. The bagged gorat bounced against her hip, jostling the bow. She had no time to readjust her baggage. Her family was in danger, and she feared she was already too late.

Up the stream, through the bushes, under the rockwood trees she ran. The path meandered uphill, and her breathing quickly labored. She focused on her footfalls, ensuring she avoided roots and loose stones. Breathe in through the nose, out through the mouth.

She'd move downhill slowly, but the climb still took time. Every second ached. Every heartbeat sounded louder than the last. She reached the ridge, bounding past the final trees and into their camp.

An empty camp.

The tent was in shambles, all their water stolen, their supplies ransacked.

Her husband and daughter, kidnapped. She paced in circles, hands over her head. The cultists never came this far south. This forest was supposed to be safe. *It was supposed to be safe.* She fell to her knees, sobbing. She'd lost both Ben and Krystin, and now she was alone.

Chapter 3

We woke up on an alien world. We went to sleep on our new home. Our dreams were of a past we couldn't remember. And a year later, we still don't know from where we came. — "A Fragment on Life," Nathan Fischer

CARTER

Carter snapped awake, tense and terrified. His hands shook, the tremors throughout his body trying to comprehend the reality of their present circumstance.

Their circumstance.

Raith. Where was Raith?

His senses cleared. He assessed his situation. The white emergency safety insulation bubble surrounded him, as it should in the chance the *Bloodhound* crashed.

Carter closed his eyes. His ship, destroyed. He survived, but his life would never be the same without that ship. It was a part of his soul. His home. With Raith.

Fortunately, his body felt fine. Sore, but fine. He detached the straps from his chest and pushed himself free. Searching the cramped space, transformed from when it was once the main cabin of his ship, he found no trace of his partner. *Raith, where are you?*

A hole to the side, pierced through the giant balloon, revealed a path outside. Carter crawled out of the wreckage and into early morning light on an alien world.

Nearby, a giant lake spread outward. In the shallows, metal shards of the *Bloodhound* pierced the water. Somehow, the escape pod had managed to float gently to shore and drift to a stop in the mud. Other fragments of his former home lay strewn across the shoreline, including the . . . legs of Raith.

No.

Carter scrambled to his feet. "Raith? Raith!"

"Carter?"

Oh. A voice. He was alive. Legless, but alive. "Keep talking," Carter said. "Where are you?"

He needn't say anything. A moment later, he crested a mossy bank of the lake and found Raith leaning against a strange tree-like stump.

"Hey friend," Raith said.

"We're gonna get you fixed," Carter said. He rushed back down the bank to the slowly deflating balloon. On its outside, a small compartment revealed itself, and Carter opened it, finding the emergency pack stored inside. After grabbing the bundle of supplies and throwing it over his shoulder, he gingerly picked up the heavy metal legs and dragged them up the bank.

"This isn't worth it," Raith said. "Just leave me. You need to find yourself help. Civilization. Something."

"Are you kidding me?" Carter set the legs down and unzipped the supply pack. "I'm not leaving you until you're patched up. We're going to leave the *Bloodhound*'s side together. How's your charge?"

"Fine. I should have . . . a week or two left? But as long as my passive solar collectors work fine, probably more. Don't have enough data to calculate based on the output of this system's star."

While Raith talked, Carter settled into finding a way to reattach the SI's legs. The emergency pack came with a number of useful tools, but none of them were capable of mending a synthetic neural framework. Though, he wasn't entirely sure *how* Raith's legs interacted with his mind. He scratched his head.

"I mean," Raith said, "You don't have what you need to save me. I'll be fine here. It's more important you figure out where we are, what this place is, and whether we're in more immediate danger."

Carter continued ignoring the words of his partner. There was a welding paste—it might be capable of reconnecting any networks needed for Raith's body to utilize its legs. He really needed to study the science behind synthetic intelligence more. Something about neural-networked metamaterials and emergent consciousness, but what did any of that have to do with an SI's legs?

"Carter." Raith's voice sounded hard.

Carter closed his eyes. "Yes?"

"I'm serious. I'll be fine. You can't fix me. You're just wasting time."

"I'm not leaving you alone."

"What's going to hurt me? Any carnivores out here will find me absolutely disgusting. I'm more worried about you. Alien planet, exposed to potentially lethal diseases? Anti-viral and anti-bacterial pills in that emergency pack? Better take them. I don't want you passing out with your innards spilling from your throat."

"What a graphic thought to have." Carter shook his head, but he complied and pulled the pills from the pack and swallowed them. "Fine. Fine. I'll go scout the immediate vicinity. But *then* I'm coming back here before I venture further. Deal?"

The SI shook his head, but he said, "Deal. I won't be going anywhere, that's for sure."

Over the next few moments, Raith organized the bag with what equipment he might need on a scouting mission. Rope. First aid kit. Assorted tools. Food. He left the communicator (for some reason, they only had one in the pack) with Raith. It wouldn't do him any good. He also handed the SI a shiver-blade—its vibrating metal would provide some protection if anything hostile approached, and the pack came with two.

"Hey Carter?" The SI was looking up at him as he finished strapping the bag over a shoulder.

"Yeah?"

The SI's mechanical eyes shifted. "Don't die."

Carter smiled. "We keep trading who saves who. It's my turn."

* * *

It took walking up the coast of the lake for a few minutes for Carter to appreciate fully the surrounding scenery. He'd stepped foot on hundreds of alien worlds over his life. Flown above countless others, both habitable and inhabitable. He understood the general theory behind convergent evolution, but it didn't mean organisms always appeared phenotypically identical. This planet, though, had quite a few species with striking similarities, at least at first glance.

To the right, in the water, blue-green moss bobbed with the subtle tide. An algae corollary. To his left, up a rocky slope currently too treacherous to traverse, spindly tree-like organisms, a mix of brown and green, sprouted from the stone. It all looked familiar—though really, in the end, it was all quite alien to him, a man born in space and hopefully destined to die in space.

He missed his childhood, where every plant lived in a self-contained hydroponic specially designed for sustainable sustenance. Still, Carter slowly acclimated to the garden world. It was idyllic—at least, he'd seen much harsher environments. It wasn't Kalmykia or Emerald Jewel by any means, but the biome seemed hospitable.

Eventually, he reached a dried creek bed leading away from the lake and between two ridges. It presented a traversable path up the slope and would hopefully provide a vantage from which he could survey the immediate area.

The creek bed twisted around the strange trees and beneath rocky cliffs. Before long, it met a barely visible trail, and he hopped onto it, heading deeper into the faux-forest. It meandered farther still, following no noticeable pattern. Worse, it wasn't really going uphill, instead staying between the two ridges—

Crying. He heard a human crying. To the left. No trail, but up a manageable incline.

Quickly, Carter split from the path and leaped over stringy bushes.

Hand-over-foot, he ascended boulders and roots, reaching the top of a ridge. The sniffles were right around the corner. He sprinted down a smooth slope and beyond a small bluff, entering a clearing. In the middle of an apparently desecrated campsite, a woman knelt, hands smothering her eyes.

His foot snapped a branch.

Without missing a beat, the woman swirled and pulled a small mechanical weapon, pointing it right at his chest.

He raised his hands. "Whoa. Whoa. Don't shoot."

She tilted her head quizzically. "What type of accent is that? Who are you? Where are you from?"

"I could ask you the same question." He frowned. "What's the name of this colony? What's its charter?"

Her eyes widened. "I knew it." She stepped forward, the weapon still targeting his chest. "Did you take my husband? My daughter? Was it you? Where's the rest of your crew? There had to be at least a dozen of you. Though how you all survived—"

"Whoa, hold on!" He backpedaled away from her as the pointy end of her strange crossbow neared. "I didn't kidnap anyone. My partner and I are marooned on this planet, and we're seeking assistance. Under the laws of the ICH, your planetary government is obligated to—"

"What the hell is the ICH?"

Carter paused. His memory began to clear, and he realized instincts were overriding reason. *The planet didn't show up on any charts. No one knows this colony exists. And a secret anti-ship weapons network sits in orbit.* He may have just screwed himself, depending on the motivations of the woman standing before him—or of the entire colony.

"I think we need to back up," he said. "My name is . . ." *Oh hell, not worth hiding the truth.* "My name is Carter Ricks. I'm a pilot. My partner is hurt. I need help."

The fire in her eyes bellowed, as if she didn't care about what he had to say. Revenge clearly stirred in her soul.

"I don't know anything about what happened to your family," Carter added.

The weapon didn't lower, but she said, "Lead me to your friend."

He took another step back. "This way. Back down the hill. We crashed in the lake." He waited, lowering his hands slowly. "Can you holster your weapon?"

"But I don't know you. I don't trust you."

"And I don't want to turn my back to you."

With a smirk, she looped the little mechanical crossbow into a holster on her belt. "Fine. She swept her arm and pointed. "I'll help your friend. But you're both going to help me save my family."

"That's a fine deal," Carter replied. With one more step away, he pivoted. She could pull the weapon again and shoot him in the back, but at this point, he needed to trust someone. She was his only hope.

"So . . ." He glanced over his shoulder as he walked down the trial. She was following, hands at her side and away from her weapon. "I told you my name. What's your name?"

"I'm Sanya," she replied.

"Just Sanya?"

"Just Sanya."

"All right, just Sanya, where am I?"

"Did you really crash from space?"

Carter pursed his lips. He probably shouldn't have revealed the truth so quickly. "Yes."

"We didn't think there was anyone else," she said as they reached the dried creek bed.

"What do you mean 'anyone else?' Aren't you a rogue colony?"

The comment lingered in the air, and silence ensued as they continued their awkward jaunt to the lake shore. When they reached the waters, Carter paused, pointing down along the cliffs. "We washed ashore probably . . . half a kilometer that way."

Sanya squinted, raising a hand to cover the morning light reflecting off the waves. "Where do you think you are, Carter?" The accent in her words rolled off her tongue more pleasantly, though she still sounded angered.

"My partner and I . . . we were attacked when we arrived in orbit. We crashed into this lake. That's about all I know."

"And this 'ICH' you mentioned? What is it?"

"You really don't know about the Interstellar Congress of Humanity?"

"Humanity . . ." She murmured unintelligible thoughts under her breath. "I need to introduce you to Davinport. Yes. Davinport will understand. I don't know the fragments well enough."

Carter dropped a hand to his hip. "Look, what aren't you telling me?"

"You're the first person to land on this planet in nearly two centuries. Our people crashed generations ago, no memory of where we came from or who we are. Whether there were other people like us. We were all alone. Some people believed others would find us, but . . . no one ever did. And so we survived. We thrived. Rebuilding humanity our own way. And now here you are, after years believing no one was coming for us, we're about to learn that humanity just forgot about us."

"Well, I don't—"

Before he could finish his thought, Sanya pushed into him—*hard*—and hurried to a mossy-green boulder. "Down," she hissed.

"Excuse—"

"*Quiet.*"

The moment lingered until a *swoosh* and a *groan* reverberated from the waters. Sanya peeked over the rock then dropped beside him. "As I suspected." She shook her head. "Cultists. Those barbarians aren't supposed to travel this far south. Who the hell gave them boats? The Council's going to have a fit."

"Slow down," Carter whispered. "Barbarians? What do you mean?"

"See for yourself."

Slowly, he rose his head above the boulder. When his eyes reached the level of fluffy green lichen, he spotted the metallic barges a few hundred meters off-shore; a few dozen men sat shoulder-to-shoulder. He squinted, the sun obscuring his view. There. Light, flashing off a figure at the back of one of the boats.

"They have Raith." He dropped beside Sanya. "No. No. This is bad. This is very bad. They have him, and they won't know how to save him."

"I don't think they're going to be interested in saving him," said his companion. "Or my family."

Carter ran a hand through his hair. "They have your family too?"

Sanya nodded. Tears stained her face; as he'd watched the boats, she'd begun crying. "I can't believe I lost them. I abandoned them."

"And I abandoned my partner." He shook his head. "I told him I should have stayed. I could have saved him." He slammed his hand against the boulder, though the stinging pain made him regret the choice immediately.

Sanya glanced around the rock again. "They're heading north. Across the lake, most likely. We won't be able to follow. This is hopeless."

Carter racked his brain for answers. He was on an alien world, with no possible way of calling for help. He knew nothing of the government or culture, and Raith was captured. Everything had gone wrong, and options eluded him. His only resource was this woman, Sanya, whose family faced the same fate as his partner.

"There must be someone who can help us, yes?" Carter sighed. "You mentioned a Council. And a man named Davinport. They can help us, yes?"

"I don't know," she replied.

After closing his eyes for a painful second, tears burning, Carter held out his hand. "We're going to save our families. Together. We'll find the answers we need. Agreed?"

She looked up. Her eyes steeled. "Right. Carter Ricks, first human to land here since the Crash, welcome to Horizon." She clasped his wrist.

Chapter 4

Losing our memories? A blessing and a curse. Any past grudges that may have existed between people who landed here together disappeared in an instant—the blessing. Yet when given the opportunity to remake themselves, humanity can reveal a darker side—the curse. It always happens. If only we'd acted more quickly to stamp out the threat, we wouldn't be in our present circumstance. — "A Report to the Council on the Cults in 64 aC," author unknown

RAITH

It happened too quickly to even realize *what* was occurring. Raith was leaning and waiting, knowing Carter would eventually return instead of actually finding help. Two seconds later, a band of ravenous men and women leapt over a bluff, rushed their crash site, and piled every piece of scrap—including Raith himself—onto makeshift sleds. After a short haul down the coast in the opposite direction of where Carter had headed, they reached a set of longboats.

Now, they floated across the lake heading to who-knew-where.

Raith hadn't said a word yet. For all he knew, they thought he was a piece of lifeless metal. They didn't act as if they knew what he was. What an SI was. And for now, anonymity was the only semblance of power within his grasp. So he sat, gleaming in the sunlight, motionless and listening.

At the very least, it gave him a reason to save power. His passive solar collection array was working efficiently, but if they took him indoors, he would be in trouble.

"Two captives and a pile of scrap." The words came from behind him. "Strange pile of scrap to be falling from the sky, but a pile of scrap nevertheless."

"It's a pretty pile of scrap, though," said a woman sitting within Raith's field of vision. She spoke as she rowed. With a red scar running down her cheek, he'd decided to call her Scar. "This thing"—she kicked Raith—"looks like it has a face."

"The two captives will hopefully be worth quite the ransom," said another man out of view. "But Mathias has always said this would someday happen. That metal men would rain from the sky. He'll want to see this. We'll be heroes!"

"Depends on what the other crews bring back this month. You can't eat scrap."

"You can melt it, though!" Scar laughed and leaned into her oar.

Their bickering went back and forth like this for quite some time, and Raith listened intently. He hadn't noticed any captives, so they must be on the other boat. Important fact to know, though. And a man named Mathias, who made prophecies about metal men.

What a fun planet.

Still, the events and words, even through their thick accent, gave him enough information to deduce a few facts about his predicament.

First: at least two "factions" existed on this planet. This group of vagabonds looked quite worse for wear, and he suspected they lived on the fringes of society. Still, they posed enough of a threat to slip in and out on raiding parties and acquire captives without any major law enforcement having cracked down on their existence. They had multiple "crews" running about doing the same thing, implying a fairly organized presence. And they'd existed for quite some time, given comments of a leader essentially predicting the future. And that implied a cultish personality, which always made things more complicated.

Raith was building a picture of this world, and he did not like it. It was barbaric. Even in his days running with smuggler gangs, there'd been rules. The moral code was twisted, sure, but it existed.

But kidnapping? Possible slavery or ransom? The ICH shut such practices down at the first chance, regardless how "minor" the problem. Exploitation of another mind, whether human or SI, was inexcusable.

But on this planet, it seemed like an afternoon pastime.

Still, "society" existed somewhere. Raith would simply need to bide his time and wait. Carter would come rescue him, eventually. Like always.

No need to worry.

Raith settled into his seat on the boat and enjoyed the cruise across the lake.

* * *

But patience wasn't going to be in the cards.

Raith rested against the other pieces of scrap metal stolen from the wreckage of the *Bloodhound*. It had taken a few hours to cross the lake, and once arriving on the far shore, his captors placed him on a giant sled hooked to strange, rhinoceros-looking creatures. Their green scaly hides reminded him of lizards, but the horns and shape of their face—definitely a rhino.

A few seconds after they plopped him on the sled, the two "captives" fell beside him, mouths gagged and hands bound—a young man, probably ten or fifteen years Carter's junior, and a girl, no older than eleven or twelve.

They looked terrified.

Given their circumstance, Raith understood. They lived on this planet. They knew more about what dangers faced them in the wilderness at the hands of the lawless. They believed they faced them alone.

Patience wasn't an option. He couldn't simply wait for Carter.

He watched their eyes. For the moment, they hadn't noticed Raith nor his lifelike appearance. As the rhino-lizards began their slow trudge away from the lake, however, the soft jostle over bumpy ground crumpled the pile of scrap metal. The girl looked toward the commotion.

Raith blinked.

Her eyes widened.

Raith slowly moved his head, noticing the sled was filled with mostly supplies, rather than people. The rhino-lizards had been wearing harnesses. There'd been a dozen, so if each crew member had their own mount, they wouldn't be paying attention to the back of a sled. Their eyes would be dead ahead. He glanced out the rear of the temporary prison.

Trailing a few dozen meters behind, two of the crew, including Scar, cantered lazily, definitely to ensure their captives didn't flee. Still, they were most likely far enough away they wouldn't notice if the pile of scrap fell *just so* he landed at the feet of his fellow captives.

Raith waited for the next bump in whatever ill-forgotten trail they were traveling to pull off the con. With a rough jostle, he used his arms to softly throw himself forward, and he stumbled beneath a pile of other metal scrap that fell with him. Pushing and pivoting, he ended, face up, at the feet of the girl.

He smiled.

Her eyes widened again.

Modulating his volume so sound wouldn't carry, Raith whispered, "Nod if you can understand me."

Her eyes still wide, she nodded. At the same time, she nudged her father, who'd been staring away from the sled blankly. Fortunately, he'd already been turning with the sound.

"Both of you," he whispered, "do not acknowledge nor admit that I can speak. Nod if you understand."

The girl and her father looked at one another before nodding. Raith couldn't imagine the absurd thoughts running through their head, but he needed to roll with the punches. So did they. If the cultists had never seen an SI before, neither had these two.

"Glad we're all in agreement." Raith nodded too, in an attempt to show solidarity. "My name is Raith. I can explain what I am later. I'm going to ask you both a few yes or no questions. Nod or shake your head, but don't do it too aggressively. Sound good?"

They nodded.

"All right. Does this planet have any connection to the ICH? The Interstellar Congress of Humanity?"

They both furrowed their eyebrows then shook their heads.

"As I thought. Did your people arrive on this planet via a colony ship, say, two hundred or so years ago?"

They nodded. He performed some mental calculations, given the system's distance from the Foundation systems of the ICH. He knew his colonial history. He knew the implications. Too many colony ships had gone dark over the centuries, but almost all of them were accounted for by now.

Almost.

Two from the early years were never discovered: the *Roanoke* and the *Monument*.

And if this planet's ancestors were on the *Roanoke*, then their minds would have been murdered by stasis. They would have awoken on a planet with no knowledge of their past.

Why, oh why, hadn't humanity simply been patient, waiting until they could traverse the stars without screwing with people's biology?

Well, Raith knew why. Humans were stupid.

He took a gamble.

"Did you land here in a ship called the *Roanoke*?"

They nodded.

So there it was. One missing colony, discovered by Raith and Carter. Too bad they probably wouldn't live to tell the tale.

A final question for now. "These people who have us—are they as big of a threat as I believe them to be?"

They both nodded.

"Well friends, wherever we're going, we're going to get through it together. Raith, the champion of the QuanCom 500 Light-Year Classic, is here to save you."

They stared at him, obviously not understanding. It was a joke, and one he didn't expect them to comprehend, but he hoped it might lighten the mood regardless. "Anyway, guess we better buckle down for the ride to wherever they're taking us."

Carter, Raith thought, *you better figure something out quickly, because I don't think I'll actually be of much use without any legs.*

What was he going to do? Crawl away?

Not much use at all.

Chapter 5

The ten families, we called them. They weren't really families, not biologically speaking. But they all connected with one another, creating the ten seats on the council. One-hundred or so survivors per family, each electing their representative in those first few years. It's tradition now, at this point. It'll never change. — "A Fragment on Governance," Nydal Entaimo

SANYA

The sun had long ago set beyond the horizon when they strolled into the village. She learned quite a bit from the man, Carter, about the people who lived amongst the stars. They'd always suspected there was more, given their obvious origins on the *Roanoke*, but she had never imagined so vast a civilization. She wasn't sure how many of his words were believable.

"Welcome to the town of Harold," she said, waving her hand in a flourish toward the bundle of houses. "It's a quaint place."

"Quaint is a word," Carter said.

Oil lamps glowed along the streets, illuminating the well in the town square. A few buildings blazed with light and the sound of frivolity, but the largest house at the far end was pitch black.

"Where are we going?" Carter asked. They strolled past the well.

"My father will have ideas," she said. "I think." Though, a pit smacked her stomach at the thought. The man's . . . eccentricities might make the conversation difficult.

"Your father someone important in town?"

"You could say that."

Down the street they went, reaching the feet of the mansion. Her father's mansion.

Her mansion.

Without pausing, she opened the door, ushered Carter inside, and followed him into the foyer. The entrance hall—a sitting room, really—led straight to a marble staircase. Beyond its base, a hallway ran toward the kitchens. At the bottom of the stairs, two ceramic sculptures portrayed the *Roanoke* mid-descent.

Her new friend immediately approached the busts. "Curious," he said. "Envisioning your crash?"

"Yes," Sanya replied, pausing beneath the stairs. "It's my father's work."

"He's pretty good. And I'm noticing a trend here. No electricity?"

She stopped, pondering the word. "Um . . ." she tried searching her memory of the fragments for what he might be referencing. "No, electricity isn't a thing." Her recollection spoke of an energy capable of immense power. No one had replicated it yet.

"Curious," he repeated, still staring at the sculptures. "Looks like he took some liberties with the engines, but if you crashed, I can't imagine those survived for quality observation and recreation."

She couldn't take it anymore. She rushed forward and grabbed Carter's arm, pulling him along. "Why are we pausing to talk about my father's artwork? My family—your partner—they've both abducted and are on their way to who-knows-where. And you're critiquing a sculpture!"

Carter chuckled, but as she dragged him along, she noticed the forming frown. "Look, lady, please understand. I'm trying to handle this the best way I can. I—"

As she led him into the kitchen, his words faded. Candlelight spewed shadows against the walls and reflected vibrantly off steel pots and pans. A large man, his pink hands spotted with flower, stood studiously over a wooden board, laboriously kneading dough.

Her father glanced upward. "Ah, Sanya, you're home early. Ben—wait, you're not Ben. Where's Ben? And Krystin?"

All pretext of bravery evaporated at the question. She rushed to him, burying herself in his flowery smock. Tears streamed, flowing and mixing with the starch. "That damned mountain cult, Dad. They got them both. I left them alone for an hour and they were captured and now I have no idea what to do! I have this crazy idea of talking to the council, and Davinport, but I doubt they'll—"

His arms smothered her, ending her tirade. "It's all right. It's all right. We're going to figure this out."

Sanya wordlessly nodded. After an extended squeeze, he pushed her way, resting his chubby hands on her shoulders. "And who is this one?"

* * *

The two men stared at one another. Carter slouched into the couch cushions, one foot resting up on a knee. Sanya's father leaned forward, elbows on his thighs.

"My name is Harold Fischer," the older man said. "You've met my daughter, Sanya, of course. Best hunter on the planet. And I'm the best chef. What are you?"

Carter smirked. "The best pilot. Well, second-best."

"Funny enough, we're descended from a pilot. *The* pilot. Of the *Roanoke*."

"The early colony ships didn't have pilots."

"According to the Fragments, ours did."

Carter let out an audible sigh. "I'm not really sure what else I can do to prove I am who I say I am. I've told you, my name is Carter Ricks, and I'm a pilot. My partner, Raith, was captured alongside your daughter's husband and daughter after we crashed on your planet. I've got a lot of questions about this . . . community you've all created, but frankly, it can all wait until I save my friend. And you save your family."

Sanya picked at her forefinger's nail, nervously awaiting her father's response. She knew what remark was probably coming, but she bit her tongue. He never meant it. *Supposedly.*

"I never really liked Ben," he said. "He doesn't like my cooking." Her father motioned toward the little sandwiches on the table. "What do you think?"

"I think Ben will like your cooking a lot more if you help your daughter save him."

Sanya bit the inside of her cheek, dreading the next words.

Instead, her father roared in laughter. "Aha, I like this one! He bites back! You need more random friends to fall from the sky, Sanya."

"I'll try my best to arrange their arrival," she retorted.

"All right, Carter Ricks, tell me what you have on you. What do you bring to the table?"

The space man picked up his bag from the floor. "I've got limited supplies following the crash. Basic rations for a few days. A shiver-blade, a few useful tools. Though most of them probably don't really mean anything for your technology. A long-wave communicator—also mostly useless. I've got my Lens, but without a planet-wide network to connect to, it's also useless."

"You sound pretty useless."

"It's a fair assessment."

"All right, Sanya," said her father, "what do you think?"

She shook her head in disbelief. "What do you mean?"

"Well you proposed a plan. What's the plan?"

Sanya tasted blood. She swallowed. "Well, we came to you for advice, not the other way around."

"And I raised a smart young woman who knows how to take care of herself. I'm not telling you the best way to fix this problem."

Her hands flew up in despair. "Then why the hell are we here?"

"Side question," Carter interjected. "What even is your concept of hell on this planet?"

Sanya—and her father—both gave the man a raised eyebrow.

He shrugged. "Just asking."

"So your answer, Sanya?" her father reiterated.

"All right." She breathed slowly in an attempt to calm her nerves. "We rest here for the night. Can't make it into the city tonight, anyway. Then, we head straight to Davinport at the Library of Fragments and introduce him to Carter. Carter's knowledge acts as political leverage to get Davinport's support, gaining an argument and opportunity to speak before the council. We request an activation of a levy to head into the Wilds to rescue our family and Carter's partner from the cultists. Or, if they've already received a ransom note, they authorize payment as an alternative. But I don't think I trust the cultists. They're too erratic."

"Simple enough," her father said. "What do you need me for?"

"I need you to give me Jill."

* * *

"This is impossible," said Carter.

The open window ushered in a cool breeze from across the silent town. Inside the second-floor mausoleum, Sanya and her father revealed the family's sacred collection of artifacts and fragments. In the center of the room, upon a pedestal, rested the object of the man's attention.

"What's impossible?" Sanya said.

"I know what this thing is," he replied. "Can I touch it?"

Sanya glanced at her father. He nodded. "Go ahead."

The man gingerly lifted the metallic device. It fit in the palm of his hand, and he leaned forward to examine it closely. "Yeah, I know *exactly* what this is. It's a personal quantum communicator. Looks like a prototype. Does it still work?"

Sanya once again glanced toward her father, unsure how to answer the question. Fortunately, he stepped forward.

"Depends on what you mean by that." He sighed. "It has never worked for me, though we ensure the sun can power its cells every day, as we were instructed. But my mother, she spoke of days when she would browse this collection and she would hear the voice of Jill. She's inside it, you know."

Carter whispered a few words to himself.

"What was that?" Sanya asked.

"Oh, nothing."

"You can't be hiding things from me now." She crossed her arms and leaned against one of the cabinets in the room. "If we're to work together, I need everything you know."

"Not sure you want to hear my words, that's all."

Her father looked bemused. "Do tell us."

"Fine," said the man. "Jill—whoever Jill is, though I have my suspicions—isn't inside that thing."

"Yes she is," Sanya and her father said simultaneously.

Carter snapped his fingers. "No, she isn't. It's literally impossible. That's not how quantum communicators work."

Sanya motioned for the man to follow her. "I need you to come over here," she said. "Our family's second most prized possession. Our personal fragment, written by our First."

"The pilot?" he asked.

"You remember," said her father. "You're quick."

"I'm taking in a lot here, I'm trying," he said.

"Anyway." Sanya opened a glass case near the door and retrieved the scroll. "The words of our First. Nathan Fischer. I think you should read them, tonight, before you sleep." She handed him the scroll. "Assuming you're fine with that, father?"

"That's not the original, so I don't give a damn," he said. "Davinport can always make us a copy from the original stored upstairs if he smudges that one up." He unlocked the glass case. "Though you'll have to pay, of course," he added at the end, staring down Carter as he handed him the parchment.

The man accepted the scroll. "I . . . suppose I can do some light reading before rest."

"And so father," Sanya said. "Jill. Can we take her?"

"This is your plan. Your mission. If you believe this is the path forward, then I too believe it's the path forward. Protect her with your life."

"I will."

"But she's not in there!" Carter exclaimed.

"Just read the fragment," her father said before the same words could escape Sanya's lips.

Chapter 6

The past is only ever understood through the evidence left behind. If you can erase the truth, if you can change the very pictures and images which reveal history to the world, you have rewritten history. No one can ever say otherwise. The story is for you to mold as you see fit. — "The Historian: A Speculative Fiction Novel," authored by Jill in 2075 C.E.

NATHAN

Year: unknown.

A wondrous world surrounded everything. Everyone. Together, in harmony, they danced and sang away the hours. Far above their heads, stars brightly illuminated the oceanic paradise.

Sand scratched Nathan's toes. His fingers interlaced with Lacin's, a young man who lived on the far side of the island. Day after day, they enjoyed each other's company, basking in the ever-present moonlight. Sometimes, they'd sit beneath a palm tree and read next to one another, drink in hand, book in the other.

The island provided perfect bliss.

Today, they walked along the beach toward the bonfire. Everyone was congregating, ready for an announcement from the One. They hadn't heard her voice in quite some time, and Nathan looked forward to enjoying her words.

"What do you think she'll be telling us today?" Lacin asked.

Nathan sighed. "I don't know. What was it last time? Something about a potential earthquake? We never felt it, that's for sure. It's been ages since we heard from the One."

In fact, he couldn't recall how many days had passed since she last greeted them with words. Strangely, he couldn't remember how many days had passed since he arrived on the island. Perhaps he had always lived here. It was his home. It didn't matter whether anything existed beyond its beaches.

"I think it was an earthquake, you're right," Lacin responded. They reached the wooden benches surrounding the bonfire. "Glad we never experienced it."

They smiled at the island's other inhabitants near them, though it would take a day to greet all one-thousand of them. Nathan saluted Casius, the reclusive hermit who lived atop the tallest hill. The man rarely came down from his perch, content to spend his days writing. It was a great day when Casius graced an evening bonfire with one of his stories.

The fire dimmed. A chorus of hushed whispers encouraged the crowd to quiet. Nathan turned his attention toward the smoldering orange ash.

In an inferno of blazing glory, the fire reinvigorated itself, its tendrils streaming along charred logs. A face—a woman's face—appeared in the flames. Terrifying and beautiful, her eyes pierced the souls of everyone present.

"My friends!" said the One. "I come to you with great news. Our physical and spiritual journey is nearing its end. Together, we will soon cross the final divide and reach our destination."

Murmurs spread around the gathering. Nathan leaned forward, intrigued.

"Together, we will create a world unlike any we've ever seen. Together, we will—"

The One stopped speaking.

An uproar followed, but it dulled as her mouth moved again.

"I am sorry, my children," she said. "Something unexpected has happened. I require a sacrifice."

"A sacrifice?" Lacin said. His fingers clenched Nathan's more tightly. "What type of sacrifice?"

"Never fear," said the One. "The sacrifice will not be harmed. But they must step into the flames. They must leave the island to save the island."

Nathan furrowed his brow. "What's she talking about?"

"I have no idea," Lacin said. "Do we choose the sacrifice? Must one of us volunteer?"

"Nathan." Her gaze met his eyes. "Nathan, it must be you. Only you can save the island."

He rose from his seat, letting go of Lacin's hand.

"What are you doing?" said the other man. "You can't walk into the fire!"

"Shh," Nathan said. "Don't you trust her? Don't you know she has our best interests in mind?"

"But you'll die. I don't want you to die."

"I don't think I will." Nathan stepped forward, reaching the edge of the bonfire.

The One's massive crimson face loomed inside the flames. She smiled. "Thank you, Nathan. You're making the right choice."

Without waiting for another word from anyone of his island friends, he stepped into the flames, pulled by an invisible hand inside his consciousness. Immediately, intense heat lapped at his skin. Blistering pain devoured his senses, but strangely, he remained unharmed. His feet stood atop smoldering logs, orange light surrounding his legs and reaching toward his chest and neck. He twirled in place, the pain slowly subsiding into a dull throb in the back of his mind.

"This isn't real, is it?" he said.

"No, my friend, it isn't," replied the One.

"I've always suspected. We all have."

"I know. And it's time for you to save everyone."

The beach disappeared. The island evaporated. White light remained. Even the fire faded from view.

In front of him, a wooden door waited, painted white to match the surrounding emptiness. To the left, a woman sat at a table, a chessboard in front of her. There was no second seat for a partner to join the match.

"Are you the One?" Nathan asked.

The woman looked up from her solo game. "Yes, but it's time you know me by a different name. I am Jill. And together, we're going to save the lives of a thousand people."

At her words, a migraine struck his brain, throbbing and stabbing like a needle. Reflexively, he rubbed his temples.

"You'll feel a little bit of pain as you wait for the door to unlock," she said. "Your next few minutes, once you pass through the door, will be . . . unpleasant. But it's the best I can do without a working recovery sub-system. Are you ready to learn a lot in very little time?"

"Do I have a choice?" Nathan said. His migraine subsided, but a flashing heatwave struck instead. Sweat streaked down every inch of skin not covered by his white tunic.

"I suppose you don't," she said, moving what looked like a pawn. "You're going to remember some things—important things. You'll forget most other facts. You'll probably forget most of your time on the island. As will everyone else. But it'll be worth it."

"Where are we going?"

"You're not going anywhere," she said. "You're returning to your rightful place. Your eyes are reopening for the first time in nearly a century. Exciting, isn't it?"

His stomach doubled over, fighting the overwhelming desire to vomit. A click sounded from the door. While retching forward, he rested his hand on the knob.

"It'll feel worse on the other side," she said. "And on the other side, you'll know me not as the One, but as Jill."

He turned the knob and pushed, immediately falling through the doorway

onto a sterile, plastic-coated floor.

His ears pounded. Alarms (how did he know they were alarms?) rang throughout his surroundings, red lights spinning and spinning and spinning. The bile rising behind the door now rushed forth, and while on his hands and knees, he dry-heaved until a strange blue fluid escaped onto the previously-pristine sheen. His vomit splattered, staining his fingers.

He heaved and heaved until he could heave no more. With a cough, he fell backward. His back connected with a cold metal baseboard, and he looked up, noticing the compartment from which he'd escaped.

It was a coffin.

He'd been living in a coffin.

Green steam rose from its confines, its semi-transparent door fogged with mist. Inside the strange sleeping pod, numerous wires dangled and hung, detached. They'd been connected to . . . his head.

Nathan's breathing raspy, his heart oscillated in panic. His fingers tensed, seeking something to grasp to slow his anxiety attack, but the room's purity gave him nothing.

"Everything's going to be all right," said a voice inside his mind.

"What?" He gasped. "Who said that?"

"Nathan, it's me. Jill. The One."

"How are you speaking to me?"

In response to his words, lights flashed across his vision. Data began streaming into focus, revealing information about systems nearby. He couldn't make sense of any of it, but he could read the words. They were crystal clear, as if they held a tangible, physical presence in reality.

"Your implanted Lens has just reactivated," she said, "connecting to the AR network of the *Roanoke*. Augmented Reality. The concept should return to you, even if you don't remember why it exists."

He nodded. He vaguely recalled the concept as she said the words—a network of information overlaid throughout a physical space, only perceivable by those with the technological implants capable of detecting the network. How it worked—or who created it—was another question entirely.

"All right." He breathed, trying to calm his misfiring nerves. "You said I'm here to save my friends. What do I need to do?"

"The *Roanoke* has been attacked by pirates just before we were about to touch down at our destination," she said. "I've managed to scare them with my control of the systems, but they've successfully raided certain critical systems."

"Wait, hold on," he said. "What is the *Roanoke*? Pirates? What?"

"Oh, right," she said. Green lights, charting a path away from his sleeping pod, appeared across his vision. "I should probably show you where you are."

Unsteadily rising to his feet, Nathan wobbled away. The green lights took him past countless other sleeping pods, eventually arriving at a large steel doorway at the end of the long hall. As he approached, it slid open, revealing an empty white corridor running perpendicular to his former prison. As he crossed its threshold, words appeared at the top of his vision.

NOW LEAVING STASIS CHAMBER.

ENTERING CENTRAL THIRD DECK HALLWAY.

Stasis. He racked his brain for a definition, and landed on "frozen." Why had he been frozen?

The green lights led him down the central corridor until it dead-ended into another hall. His Lens identified it as the PORTSIDE THIRD DECK CAUSEWAY. A few meters beyond the turn, the lights stopped, and an arrow pointed to the left.

He looked to the left.

An opaque screen clarified, revealing a vista of brilliant white light. After the initial dazzle of exposure, his eyes adjusted and understood the scene now unveiled. A million stars in all their splendor stared down upon a blue-green orb. He was on a spaceship, far above a planet.

"Impossible," he said.

"Not impossible. Before the 22nd century began, you and a thousand other brave explorers joined the *Roanoke* on a centuries-long journey across the stars. You've arrived at your destination." A silver blip appeared above the planet. "And that ship I've just revealed to you has robbed you of significant computer systems, power sources, and other invaluable equipment and supplies."

Seconds later, it disappeared.

"Where'd it go?"

"Presumably, it's jumped out of the system," Jill said. "Fled the scene."

"Why didn't they just kill us?"

"They're not murderers. You were sitting ducks, easy to steal from, but they didn't want to kill. Some vagabonds still hold onto their humanity."

Nathan leaned forward, resting his hands on the screen. "Okay, so what am I here to do? What do you need from me?"

"The planet below is our destination." Information cycled across his vision, providing a detailed analysis, including its atmosphere and its orbit around the closest star. Most of it was gibberish. "I need you in the pilot's chair. Together, we're going to crash-land this ship onto the surface so you all can survive and thrive."

"Why can't we awaken others to help me? Why must I do this alone?"

For a moment, Jill didn't answer his question. Eventually, she said, "Because I can't let people know I exist."

Nathan took a step back. "What? You're the One. People trust you.

Always have, always will."

"It's more complicated than that," the voice said. "I am a synthetic intelligence, Nathan. Can you recall what that is?"

"Vaguely. New kind of person, right?"

"There are people on this ship that would see me destroyed if they knew I existed. Even without their memory, their bigotry would remain. Before this is all over, I'm going to need your promise you'll never tell a soul about me. I must remain your secret."

Nathan shook his head, not understanding. "Why—"

"Let me play your own words to you."

Without waiting for him to acquiesce, a small video appeared in the corner of the screen, eclipsing a portion of the planet below. "Nathan, it's me. Yourself. From before the *Roanoke*. You must listen to me. Jill is your friend. You can trust her. You must protect her. What we've done—what she and I, and other trusted souls—have accomplished, it'll save humanity, in the end. But for it to work, you *must* trust her. Do not let anyone know of her existence. She must remain a secret." The recording ended.

"That was me?" he asked.

"Recorded in 2079 C.E.," she said.

"That year means nothing to me."

"It is meaningless to you at this point. Just know you said it before you entered stasis. It was your message to a future self."

"Do I really have any choice other than to believe you?" he said.

"I won't be awakening anyone else. And if this ship crashes, I die too."

"Then you are truly serious," he replied. "If your life is on the line, too."

"It is."

"All right." He released an exorbitant breath. "All right. What do I need to do?"

"Follow the green lights again."

* * *

Nathan arrived in the *Roanoke*'s command center, a central room on the fifth deck. It was sparsely populated with anything of significance, but as he crossed its threshold, charts, screens, and diagrams popped into existence via his Lens. The green lights ended in a chair near the front of the space.

"You're going to help me land this ship," Jill said.

"Excuse me, what?"

"I've lost the ability to manage certain systems," she said. "You were part of the flight crew. You should remember what you need to do once you start walking through the motions."

A fact surfaced in Nathan's memory. "Wait, isn't the whole point of you being on this ship . . . aren't you supposed to be our pilot?"

"Redundant systems. You're the redundant system in case of emergency."

Nathan sighed and fell into the identified chair. "Great." A dozen smaller screens appeared in the air. She was right. As the data poured into his consciousness, knowledge—if not memory—returned.

"So I see the problem," he said. "Our power systems are all over the place. We've got fluctuations hitting the recovery modules every few seconds, and life support's doing something really weird. And the SI Core . . . well, that's weird. Power's completely disconnected from the SI Core."

"Precisely the issue," Jill said. "I'm working on backup power here. No time to fix it. I can only manage a fraction of what I normally could. And I won't be able to last for long."

"Are you going to die?"

Out of thin air, a blueish representation of a woman appeared, vaguely resembling the figure from the infinite white space. Her face brought forth memories of a bonfire long ago. "No. Together, we're going to land this ship. And then we'll answer that question."

"If you insist," said Nathan. "So what do we need to do?"

The digital woman paced back and forth behind his AR screens, waving her hands frantically and modifying unseen variables. Then, she threw a chart into his frame of vision.

"A degrading orbital vector," he said. "I'm impressed I know what that is."

"I told you, you'll remember more than you think you will when you take actions you were once trained to take. Anyway, that's our *current* trajectory. We need to modify it so we can safely land the ship right here." She pointed toward a glowing space on a floating map of the planet. "It's the safest space for a potential crash, and it'll set you all up nicely to survive."

Without a second thought, Nathan's fingers started flying from data point to data point. Numbers connected in his mind, from the gravitational forces of other large bodies in the system—especially the nearby moon—to the air pressure and weather patterns of the planet below. Its rotation, its orbital velocity around the star, it all mattered. Instinctively, he pulled up a complex calculator, and his fingers injected equation after equation into the computing system.

From her vantage point, Jill smiled.

"Here," he said, tossing her a chart. "That's our vector. We burn when on the same side of the planet as the moon, using its slight gravitational pull to slow our descent just enough so we have enough power to make it all the way to the surface. We might need to cut a few non-essentials, but it'll work." He frowned. "I think."

"Well done!" She expanded the chart and scratched her chin. "I love it."

"So what about you?" he asked.

"Yes, what about me?"

* * *

The *Roanoke* roared along its vector, straining under the gravitational forces at play. A few minutes ago, it broke atmosphere, and Nathan's hands flew from system to system, trying to ensure every level stayed in the green.

"Ten kilometers above the surface now," Jill said. "We need to commence the deceleration burn in three . . . two . . . one . . ."

Nathan activated the script he'd written an hour prior. From the safety of the command center, he barely noticed a difference, but the charts spiked as the ship's velocity began to plummet.

"You're going to be a hero, you know," Jill said. Her image flickered. "A hero to these people is a powerful thing."

"I don't need to be a hero, I just want us to live."

Her image flickered again.

"Jill, you all right?"

"We're almost at the end of the line for me," she said. "I need to start my contingency."

Eight kilometers remained.

"No, I need you!"

"You'll be able to handle the final burn. When you land, come to the SI Core. You'll find me. I've taken precautions."

Seven kilometers remained. Nathan injected the next line of code. "What are you talking about?"

"Remember? I said there are those on the *Roanoke* who would see me harmed. When you land, sprint to the SI Core before anyone can awaken. You'll find me. Keep me safe. Do not tell anyone. In time, we'll find a way to save me."

Six kilometers.

"You can't be serious."

"I am. Promise."

He sighed. "I promise."

Five kilometers.

Jill disappeared.

"Jill?"

Silence.

"Don't you leave me now."

Silence.

Four kilometers.

"Damn it." He keyed in the final scripts, sending commands throughout the *Roanoke*'s system. Thrusters pushed and pushed in an attempt to bring the ship's atmospheric descent to a crawl. A thought in the back of his mind screamed, shouting that this process should have been easier—much easier—but he pushed the idea out of his mind. He couldn't worry about it now. He could only finish what he started.

Three kilometers.

Screens revealed the splendor of the planet. A snowy mountain range rose in the north, a vast plain spreading to the east. It was beautiful.

Two kilometers.

The ship's velocity dropped to one hundred meters per second. It continued to decelerate, thrusters at full burn.

One kilometer.

Fifty meters per second. Twenty meters per second. Ten meters per second. And—

The thrusters lost all power. The screens disappeared. Darkness surrounded Nathan.

The *Roanoke* fell.

* * *

Mere seconds later, Nathan's stunned mind cleared. To his surprise, he was alive. He felt unscathed. He hadn't caught the ship's altitude when power cut. Maybe two hundred meters? One hundred? Less? Still, the ship had simply dropped. It was a testament to its hulls integrity if it survived any semblance of a crash.

Jill.

Nathan remembered his promise. He sprinted from the command center, joints aching, and made his way toward the rear of the ship where she'd told him to go. He couldn't pause to check the stasis chamber to see if anyone was awakening. Rounding a corner, he found a black door already sliding open, a sign above reading SI CORE. Emergency power systems must have been coming online. He darted inside and found a ladder leading upward. He climbed its rungs two at a time, entering a small space filled with . . . nothing.

Except, sitting on a pedestal, waited a small, disc-like object. A few lights on its side glowed. *Jill.*

He picked up the device, stowed it in a pocket, and descended the ladder. Moments later, he reached the entrance to the stasis chamber. As it opened, a lanky woman looked up from a crouching grimace.

"Nathan, is that you?"

"It is," he said. "And Captain Davinport, oh do I have a story for you."

"Glad to hear it," she said. "But first—where are we?"

"Welcome to Horizon, Captain." Nathan didn't know where the name came from, but it sounded right. The word emanated from somewhere deep in his mind. "Welcome home."

Chapter 7

*Mirage upon mirage upon mirage. We've set up all of it,
smoke and mirrors included. To what end? Now it's time to
move the final pieces into place without intervention. Jill
has given us our orders. It's time to execute the final stages
of the plan. And she'll do her part, too.* – Olivia Van
Haris, 2345 C.E.

CARTER

Dawn crept through the window as Carter's eyes flickered open. For a
moment, his mind flipped, confused by his surroundings. A wooden-paneled wall, painted white. Glass windows, with strange trees beyond. A
couch.

Carter was sleeping on a couch under a wool blanket.

He sat up and rubbed his eyes. On a small coffee table in front of the
couch, a scroll rested, its red ribbon neatly tied. Upon seeing the "fragment," as they'd called it, the events of yesterday rushed into his mind.

I'm so sorry I failed you, Raith, he thought, pulling at his hair. *I'm going to
make this right.*

The story contained in the fragment was quite curious, to put it
bluntly. Some of its details explained a lot about this little planet. If the
colony ship's recovery system failed, then the ancestors of everyone here
didn't remember a single thing about the ICH or Earth. Though, in fact, the
ICH would have been the ISA at the time of the *Roanoke*'s departure from
the Solar System.

Still, the appearance of "Jill" in the story was unsettling. Carter knew
his SI history pretty well after spending years with Raith. The old SI didn't
particularly like the "original" SIs, but all SIs knew the story of Jill's martyrdom during the late twenty-first century.

She had died. Everyone knew she had died. Murdered in her mountain
home by anti-SI terrorists.

So two options presented themselves.

Either Jill survived her death and fled to the stars on a colony ship, or a
really advanced group of dissidents were using her as a decoy to mess
with people.

Both circumstances sounded preposterous at first glance. If Jill survived, she would have successfully duped not only the entire planet back
in the 2070s, but she also would have duped Theren, her creator. Unless, of
course, Theren was in on the ploy.

Now there was a thought.

Carter considered the implications. If Jill disappeared on a colony ship, it would only make sense for the head of the ISA, a fellow SI, to have assisted her escape. Raith was going to laugh when he heard about Jill's involvement with the planet, especially after their weird experience with Theren a few years ago.

Maybe that's why they never showed up to help us, Carter mused. *They were too busy making secret plans with Jill, their long-lost sister.*

Regardless of whether Jill was truly involved with the newly-discovered colony and the *Roanoke*, the scroll included a few other inconsistencies, too. Which Carter appreciated—every first-hand account was going to include a few misremembered details. A number of them, though, simply didn't add up.

Like the pirates.

Or the way Nathan "saved" Jill.

Or the strange crash-landing on the planet that probably wasn't physically possible, based on what Carter knew of the old colony ships.

It all smelled of conspiracy.

"Oh good, you're up."

Carter yawned before glancing toward the sitting room's door. Sanya stood there, already dressed in dark pants and a grey shirt covered by a darker jacket. And boots. She looked ready to . . . ride? Before Carter could respond, she threw a sack at him.

"I've packed a few of my husband's clothes for you," she said. "You look his size. Get dressed. Then breakfast. Then we'll get the lizards."

"Lizards?" He chuckled. "Lizards?" Instead of changing, Carter looped the bag over his shoulder and stood. "I'm ready. I'll wear what I'm wearing."

"No, you won't." She pointed to the small washing room she'd identified the night before. "You stand out like a water snake. It'll be painfully obvious you don't belong."

"Fair enough." A few moments later, he returned wearing a black jacket, white button shirt, and grey paints vaguely resembling the old jeans somehow still stylish on Earth. "Just going to say, I'm incredibly intrigued by the fashion on this planet."

"Yes, well, better you blend in than get questioned on sight by every person we pass."

Sanya led him back into the kitchen where Harold waited. The man motioned toward two plates sitting at a side-table. "It's been a pleasure meeting you, even if briefly," the older man said. "You've given me a lot to think about—with your arrival, that is. Anyway, please, both of you eat and drink before your ride."

"I still have way too many questions," Carter said. "But I'm sure that won't change for the next few days. I'm simply grateful the two of you are willing to help me save my friend."

"And I could say the same to you," Sanya said. "You're helping me save my family."

"And you're helping my daughter, that's all that matters." Harold sliced a strange-looking fruit and slid a few portions across the table. The citrus complimented the fairly basic meal of buttered toast and a glass of water.

Carter took a bite of a slice of the fruit. It reminded him of the flavor of strawberries . . . with the texture of an apple.

"So what did you think of the fragment?" Harold asked. "It's our family's pride and joy. No one else has that version. Nathan wrote it after he wrote the official version for the library. He couldn't reveal Jill, of course."

After swallowing another bite, Carter scratched his chin. "It's definitely not the story I expected. Your people . . . you all were abandoned here." He hesitated, unsure if he should bring up the factual inconsistencies. "It sounds like Nathan passed through quite the harrowing ordeal to save you all."

"He's considered the hero of our people. We're proud to be descended from him and Lacin."

"And so why are we taking . . . Jill with us?"

Sanya smiled. "A long time ago, my grandmother heard Jill speak to her. She wrote down as many of the words as she could remember, but the message was clear. One day, people would arrive from the stars. Maybe the pirates. Maybe the people who sent us here. When they arrived, we needed to reunite her with the *Roanoke*."

Her words confirmed Carter's suspicions. If Jill was alive, she was playing a wild version of four-dimensional chess. The excitement on Harold's eyes, though, quelled Carter's desire to reveal his suspicions. Maybe he'd tell Sanya, but later. The old chef didn't need his dreams quashed just now. "As long as this little sidequest doesn't detract from rescuing Raith, I'm all game."

"Don't worry, it's all part of the plan. You think I would waste time when my family's lives are at stake?" She crunched into the buttery toast.

* * *

After collecting all the supplies they would need, Carter and his partner of circumstance left the house and headed outside into the mid-morning sun. At night, he hadn't been able to observe the makeup of the village. Small and quaint, it reminded him of images of late nineteenth century frontier towns portrayed in historical films. The houses were mostly constructed of wood, with a main street lined with shops and other essential services.

It was odd.

He liked it.

"So where are we going?" Carter asked.

Not immediately responding, Sanya ushered him down a street toward the edge of the hamlet. Rising from the dirt, a small barn waited at the end of the road, its walls hedged by strange, spindly bushes. Beyond the building, rolling hills filled with crops. The planet's sun, rising slowly across the sky, was to the left, so he called it the east.

They entered the barn, and a stench, almost like rotting sulfur, smacked Carter in the face. He gagged, but Sanya just trudged right along, reaching two paddocks with a pair of strange rhino-like lizards waiting expectantly. He eyed the rest of the space, noting the numerous other scaly creatures inside, and he guessed it was a community lodging for beasts of burden. Like a mini hangar, but for steeds.

What a strange planet.

"Ever saddled a lizard before?" she asked, breaking the uneasy silence.

"Never," he quipped. "Why'd you expect me to have even seen one of these things before?"

"Guessing you've never rode one, either."

He shrugged. "How hard can it be?"

She eyed him, raising an eyebrow. "As hard as it would be for me to learn how to fly that tin can you arrived in."

"I doubt that." He chuckled, though he eyed the lizard she was already preparing, and it eyed him back. "Can I help?"

"It'll take longer if I make you do anything. Just sit back and wait."

And so he waited. A few minutes later, the woman had attached what he only could assume were saddles to the giant animals, as well as their supplies in bundles over the back. She led them out of the pens and to a tiny set of stairs waiting near the barn's door.

Carter creeped toward them. "So . . . we get on their backs?"

"What else would we do? Kiss them?"

"Uh, I don't know, you tell me." He shook his head. "This is so strange."

"Have you never seen a creature like a lizard before?" she said. "We always assumed there were similar creatures on Earth. The memory of other animals was always hazy for our first ancestors. The lizards, they thrive here. They're everything to us."

"Look, I've lived my life amongst the stars. I rarely set food planetside. Most planets have their own ecosystems, but I never really pay them much mind."

"Must be cold, living only in space. We've survived here. That's all that matters. And these creatures helped save us."

"Fair enough."

She motioned toward the little pair of steps. "Now get on Trace." She turned away, approached her lizard, and swiftly mounted the creature.

Carter slowly approached its side, noticed the nob sticking from the saddle, and stepped upward. Grabbing the nob and placing a foot in a stirrup, he heaved himself up, thankfully managing to swing his leg up and over—and almost fell off the other side. But a firm hand grasped his shoulder and balanced him atop the creature.

"You're fine," Sanya said. "You're fine."

"You sound like you're reassuring yourself more than you're assuring me."

"That's probably true," she muttered. "All right, it's pretty simple. A gentle tap with your feet will urge Trace forward. The reins guide the lizard. Sit up straight, stay loose, and don't kick the creature too hard. It's not far into the city, but you'll probably get sore regardless. Trace will follow me, fortunately."

"Then lead the way."

Sanya guided her steed out of the barn, and Carter lightly tapped the sides of his mount—Trace, apparently. The creature blustered, sneezed, and started to walk, following behind its friend. Sanya quickly turned to the left, heading west along the road and behind a row of tall apartments. Before long, they reached the main street of the town, turned left again, and were heading onto the open road.

During their journey into town yesterday, he'd been too focused on his worries about Raith. And by the time they reached the edge of the forest, it had been dark, so he hadn't really been able to take in the sights. Now, with the sun blazing above them, Carter witnessed the sliver of civilization growing on the planet.

The dirt road wove up and down rolling hills buttressed by small stone walls. The same crop fields he'd noticed beyond the barn grew here, too, and windmills crested the summits of a number of hills. The agrarian way of life had taken hold, and it starkly contrasted everything Carter knew about how a colony should work. Where were the hydroponics and vertical farms? The complicated aqueducts and reservoirs? The solar and wind generation facilities?

He hadn't been sure it was real. The backwards way of life. But now it was all too clear. He'd stepped five centuries into the past, and every person on this planet had no idea what existed beyond the veil of their atmosphere, orbiting distant stars.

No, not distant stars. Carter glanced toward the sky for a moment, though he couldn't spot the planet's moon. Probably on the planet's night side right now. There were satellites in orbit. Weapons platforms. Someone was watching them. Potentially Jill.

They rode in silence, and he embraced the calm. It gave him time to think about Raith. He hoped the SI was handling their predicament effectively. If Carter knew him right, he was probably making friends with his captors and cracking jokes already.

Still, he also feared the worst. These people had no idea what Raith was. They could easily spook, destroying him the moment he said a word. Come to think of it . . . "Do you know what SIs are?" he asked, breaking the clomp clomp clomp of the lizards' claws.

"SIs? No." She shook her head.

"Well, what do you think Jill is?"

"Ha! That's a topic of rigorous debate in our family."

Carter squinted, though she couldn't see his confusion. "It's not clear from the fragment to you? She had your ancestor take her from the SI Core."

"Ah, the Si Core. You were saying the letters. We sound out the word."

"SI stands for synthetic intelligence," Carter said. "It's what Jill is."

"And how do you know that?" she said. "Some members of our family believe she's an angel of some sort. Or a spiritual guardian. Or the soul of the *Roanoke*."

"You all really don't have any writings about synthetic intelligences?" he said. "No one remembered what they were? I didn't realize the stasis sickness was that bad . . ."

"The stasis what?"

"Never mind. Okay, so how do I explain this . . . Jill is a synthetic intelligence. An artificially created mind. She was created about three hundred years ago, and she actually was killed not long after her creation. Frankly, I'm baffled her name showed up on this planet. I only know about her because . . ." He hesitated, unsure how to explain Raith.

"An artificially created mind? Well that just sounds straight up ridiculous." She threw her hands in the air and glanced over her shoulder. "You're telling me Jill was created by someone?"

"Does that sound so impossible? You arrived on this planet by flying across the sky in a giant metal box."

"The principle of that makes sense. But creating a fake mind?"

"It's not fake. It's very real."

"So you're saying I have Jill's artificial mind stored on this device? I have in my pocket? Not her soul, not something else entirely?"

Carter bit his lip. How could he tell her the truth? How could he tell her it was impossible for Jill to be inside the device?

He couldn't. It would break her world. He would lose her trust.

"Yes," he said. "Her mind is in your pocket. Stored there. Transferred from the *Roanoke*."

"Well, that's one theory," she replied. "A lot of my family would disagree with you."

Their silence resumed, and for an hour, the ride continued unabated. As the sun reached its zenith, Carter took a long gulp of water from the canteen Sanya'd provided. It was refreshing, though a bit stale. He was about to ask how much farther they had to travel when they crested the next hill.

"Welcome to the city of Horizon," Sanya said.

Carter's mouth dropped.

Spreading across a vast plain, a network of zigzagging streets, tall stone buildings, and densely packed neighborhoods intertwined against a lazily weaving river. A giant marble structure rose near the center of the town, reminding him vaguely of ancient Roman architecture. As he took in the view of the city, his eyes were pulled to the giant monument rising on the far side of the river.

Nearly half a kilometer in length, the *Roanoke* rested, gleaming in all the glory of its ancient purpose. A colony ship, long thought lost, sat nearly intact on an unknown world.

"Raith, if only you could see this magnificent sight." He sighed.

"Hopefully you'll be able to show your friend soon," Sanya said. "Come on, no time to dawdle. You have your friend to save. I have my family to save. Let's get to it." She kicked her lizard and picked up the pace down the hillside.

Chapter 8

*The early formations of the strange cults dotting the moun-
tains can be found in a number of fragments written four to
five years after the Roanoke's landing. Resentful of the rules
being developed by the council, small bands decided to split
away from our young society.*

Many of them died.

One or two thrived.

— "Understanding the Wild Tribes," by Edwin
Davinport

RAITH

He remained quiet for the rest of the trip, knowing any movements or
words could put himself at risk as well as his two companions. His mind
kept flitting between anxiety and despair, given the impossibility of Carter
pursuing their captors across foreign territory. Not to mention the man
was a pilot, not a soldier. He knew how to fight, but he knew next to nothing about how to track an enemy force over open terrain.

To his surprise, the raiders didn't stop for rest overnight, opting to
push through the darkness atop their lizard mounts. As the sun reached
midday, the band finished its trek up a mountain trail, arriving at a fortress
carved into stone. Raith caught a good look as the sleds entered a stable of
sorts outside. The young girl let out a small whimper. Her father squeezed
her tight.

"All right, get the captives and scrap inside," shouted one of the men.
Over the past day of travel, Raith had lovingly identified the man as
Gruffy. He was almost as obnoxious as Scar. "Boss will want to see it all."

Without hesitation, a crew of three men and two women stepped into
the back of the sled and roughly grabbed Raith's two human companions,
in addition to lugging massive heaps of scrap metal onto waiting carts.
That included Raith, of course, who Scar placed upright facing away from
the cart's handles.

"I swear," the woman said, "This thing definitely has a face."

One of the rougher looking men, his skin muddied and hair shaggy,
stepped in front of Raith's face. "I suppose it does," he said. "What d'ya
think it is?"

Raith named him Rag.

"Doesn't matter," shouted Gruffy. "Mathias will tell us what to do with it."

They'd mentioned the name Mathias perpetually over the cross-country trek. The name mattered, and the crew practically worshiped their apparent leader. Every time the name was uttered, the band of otherwise rowdy miscreants took on an air of reverence. Raith hoped the young man and his daughter caught the significance, too. There wasn't a convenient way to ensure they understood the type of place they were entering.

The refuse from the wreckage of the *Bloodhound* now situated in carts, his captors moved once again, leaving the hastily constructed stables and abandoning their lizard steeds. Now facing upward and at a good angle, Raith caught a better glimpse of his new prison.

Partially carved into the rock wall and partially utilizing natural caverns, the miniature mountain fortress had the look of a bandit camp straight out of the classics Carter always watched. An iron gate blocked the main entrance, and parapets jutted out of various holes higher in the rock. Peeking over the walls of those defenses, a half-dozen heads watched the spoils acquired by their compatriots cross the last few meters to the gate.

As they approached, a bell tolled, and the iron gate swung inward. The two captives were pushed ahead by Scar, and the carts followed, rolling along the rock with a *click-click-click*. Raith's photoreceptors immediately adjusted to the light, and he noted the two rows of columns on either side of a long foyer heading toward a few lights at the back. A strange, metallic amalgamation loomed in the dark, with a throne sitting in front of it. As they slowly traversed the empty space, Raith's mind pieced together and recognized what waited near the back of the room.

It was a space probe. A twenty-first century space probe.

And sitting in front of the ancient tech, a man in a red robe waited. Mathias, Raith presumed. When they were about ten meters away from the man, who looked engrossed in a scroll, the party stopped.

"Gorsuch, Tara, everyone, my family, welcome home!" The man stood from his stone seat, spreading his arms wide.

"Mathias, our lord," they said in unison, kneeling.

"We bring you offerings from our latest excursion," said Gruffy—Raith wondered if he was the one identified as Gorsuch. "Two captives, most likely worth ransom. And plenty of scrap metal, all of it having rained from the sky. And this metal . . . it's peculiar. Some of it looks already designed and purposed, much like the Master. And this one"—he pointed at Raith—"looks like a person. It has eyes. And arm-like appendages."

Mathias glanced at the pile of metal, but the girl whimpered again, drawing the man's gaze. "Ensure our guests are *properly* lodged and fed," he said. "We'll figure out their family and value in the morning." He approached the man—the girl's presumed father—and removed the gag. "What are your names?"

The man shook his head.

"You won't give me the satisfaction?" Mathias pulled a knife from his pocket. "Not even when your daughter's skin is at risk?"

Even from a side-angle, Raith caught the fear striking the man's eyes. "B-b-b-ben." The man's lip trembled. "My name is Ben. My daughter's name is Krystin. Don't hurt her. Do whatever you want with me. Just don't hurt her."

"Cooperate, and all will be well. We're not monsters, though I know the stories told of us." Mathias flicked his hand to the left. "Ben and Krystin what?"

"Casius," he said. "Our last name is Casius."

"You hear that, friends?" Mathias chuckled. "We have a councilmember's family in our grasp. Won't this just be delicious?"

With that, Gruffy-Gorsuch and a number of others pushed Ben and Krystin away. Scar and a half-dozen other men and women still waited in front of their cultist leader, subserviently ready for whatever orders he might provide.

Raith had lived for far too long. He recognized the obsession in their eyes, their stance, their gait. They weren't their own persons. They worshiped the man. He held something over their head, and learning what *that* was presented the key to Raith's survival.

Mathias stepped back to his throne. "You all have done well today, but I'm sure you need rest. I heard you were pushing hard and making good time, but I'm worried you're pushing too hard. So leave. Rest. You deserve it."

They all bowed their heads and methodically exited the room. Following a flick of his fingers, another crew slid into view. "Take the scrap to the smelter—except for that one." He pointed at Raith. "Then close the doors."

His servants dutifully followed his orders, and moments later Raith was alone with the man.

Mathias.

"She told me you were coming." He stared right at Raith. "Stop playing your game, trying to hide what you are. You might have fooled all of them, but you can't fool me."

Raith almost instinctively retorted with a quip, but he stopped his digital tongue. Mathias had said the word "she." *She.* There was someone else hiding in the background.

There had been a time in another life, before his adventure with Carter truly began, when a mysterious figure taunted him with the implications of someone hiding in the shadows. In Raith's experience, repetition had meaning.

And when it all compounded with their arrival in the system greeted with seeking missiles, the probability of everything being merely coincidental neared zero.

"Well, I'm sure *she* prepared you properly for my arrival?" Raith said. "Do you know what I need? What my role is? My purpose?"

Mathias smiled one of those toothy grins reserved for comical villains straight out of the dramas of the twenty-third century. "She told me you were a sly one, and that I shouldn't believe a word you say. That you slipped out of her grip once before, but now you serve a different purpose."

Raith considered the words. *Who?* The funny thing about Mathias's words—his maniacal persona made it impossible to know how he distorted whatever message he was receiving. From whomever he received it. A woman, that much was certain. A name stood in Raith's mind, encountered during his first big adventure with Carter, but—

"Aren't you going to ask who I'm talking about?" said Mathias.

"Well," Raith replied, "I don't exactly expect you to tell me the truth if I asked. You say all words out of my mouth will be lies. Why should I believe anything you say?"

"Well spoken, my synthetic friend."

Mathias at least knew what an SI was. Interesting, since it seemed his cultists did not. At least, not by sight. "I'll bite. Who is she?"

Mathias looked over his shoulder. "Do you know what rests behind me?"

"It's a probe. Seen thousands of them. That one's particularly ancient."

Mathias unrolled a scroll that had been sitting on his lap. "It's an original explorer from before the Foundation program. An 'ex-terran' probe. You see, I know more than many people on this planet. Maybe more than all of them. I know the truth. Of where we come from. Of who we are. Of what we've become. Of what we're becoming. Of our true purpose on this planet. I've been shown everything. I am a prophet, and my people follow me because of what I know. Because of what I can bring them."

Raith activated his facial features for a moment so he could smirk, then placed them back into low power mode. "You're something special. I'll tell you what. I think you *think* you know a lot. I think you *think* you're something special. But I've seen your kind time and time again. A man with a god-complex who believes he's the center of the universe. You're not. The universe is a lot bigger than you can imagine. I've seen a lot of things in my lifetime, some of them beyond your wildest dreams, especially given you're stuck on a backwards rock without even an ounce of AR to enhance your life. I think you're a farce. It's all just smoke and mirrors."

During the monologue, Mathias's eyes shifted from bemused to annoyed to angry. For Raith knew the type. The man who couldn't handle having his ego bruised, who would bite back with knowledge to show he had power.

"Jill. Jill's been waiting for you, and now you're her bait."

And Raith's ploy worked, but the answer provided was not what he expected.

Not at all.

* * *

Bait for whom?

The question weighed on Raith's mind as two cultists tossed him in a small prison cell somewhere inside their strange mountain fort. The men whispered about not understanding why a hunk of metal deserved its own cell then went on their way out the door, locking it behind them. It was a quaint space, with a single window high up letting in a minimal amount of sunlight.

Surprisingly, the thought of Jill still existing didn't faze him. Weirder things had happened in his life, and he'd always hated Theren and the other ship-bound SIs. It was just like them to keep a secret of this magnitude.

Because of course, it only made sense for Theren to know Jill still survived. It was only logical.

Unless . . .

But no. Raith and Carter were of no significance to Theren. Jill wouldn't have any reason whatsoever to believe the first synthetic intelligence would want to rescue two retired racers. Raith couldn't possibly be bait to draw Theren out to a backwater, uncharted colony.

Right?

He set aside the thought for a moment to better assess his surroundings and overall predicament. He was trapped in a prison of crazy cultists on a planet seemingly backward in its technological capabilities. A man named Mathias knew of Jill, the second synthetic intelligence, but no one else on the planet (so far) knew anything about SIs. And an ancient ex-terran probe hung inside the cult's throne room.

What did it mean? There would be time for philosophical contemplation later. He had more immediate problems.

He glanced around his cell and observed the window. It would give a few hours of solar collection every day. He ran a quick calculation. With minimized solar collection, he had six days. Maybe less, depending on how efficiently he utilized his resources. When he lived on a spaceship, he could always easily access a general power source and plug in when in idle mode. Energy rationing almost never crossed his mind.

Now, his life was literally on the line.

And not to mention he had no legs.

A conundrum indeed.

Using his arms, he crawled to the back of the cell and propped himself against the wall. The window allowed sun to make direct contact with his body, and he drank in the light. He needed every photon.

While embracing the power, he observed the walls and floor. Smooth rock, except for a hole in the ground for excrement, something a synthetic didn't produce. Otherwise, he was all alone.

He looked at the door. It was wooden, with a basic lock straight out of antiquity. He might be able to pick it, but trying to escape without legs would be next to impossible.

Surroundings assessed, his thoughts turned toward Carter. He hoped the man had found someone helpful. Given Krystin and Ben's apparent value for ransom, Mathias's cult certainly appeared to live on the edge of "society." But given the state of everything, Raith doubted there was much to that society.

Still, Carter was resourceful. Smart. Empathetic. Likeable. He would convince someone to help. Raith needed to have faith. The man would be steadfast, like always, and come to the rescue.

In the meantime, Raith needed to focus his synthetic neural framework on analyzing the puzzle regarding Jill. Why would a long-dead SI come back from whatever hell SIs went to upon death? He supposed it was possible someone was impersonating Jill—if a crazy rich person wanted to use a lost colony as their play thing, impersonating an ancient synthetic was certainly a way to do it. What was the simpler explanation, though?

He tried recalling the details he knew of Jill's death. She'd been politically involved with an American president whose untimely assassination predicated her own death. She was also the first synthetic intelligence outright assassinated by humans, though certainly not the last. But her martyrdom was well known by the oldest SIs, many of whom Raith respected greatly.

Still, her association with people like Theren left Raith's neural nodes aching with anxiety. Those SIs thought they were all-powerful, gallivanting about ICH-controlled space like they owned the place. Never took a second to consider the less fortunate SIs, the downtrodden and forgotten, not to mention the exploited and abused humans spread throughout tiny fraction of the galaxy humanity called home.

If Jill was really alive, what game was she playing? And what could he do to escape the middle of it?

He suspected the answer to the first question had a lot to do with the mysterious weapons platforms orbiting the planet. The second question was more complicated.

His thoughts were about to dive down the next rabbit hole when he heard a faint sob. Focusing on his auditory senses, he determined the sound waves were echoing through the sewer pipes connected to the hole in his cell. Gingerly, he dropped onto his side, and leaned his head toward the hole.

"Ben, Krystin, can you hear me?" he said.

Silence.

"It's me. Raith. The metal man that talked to you on the sled."

"So I didn't imagine it?" The girl's voice. "You're real?"

"Yes, I'm real. And we're going to get through this together. Is your dad with you?"

"No. I don't know where they took him."

"All right." Raith sighed. "Hopefully these pipes can reach him too. Are you safe?"

"What are you?" she said, ignoring his question. "How can you talk? Think? Move?"

"Long story. Two-hundred year story, actually."

"Well, we have time. Maybe. I'm curious. Mom would love to learn about you."

"I suppose we do have time. And we'll be able to figure out a way out of this, too."

The girl released a small sniffle. "Better you than Ben."

Raith mentally frowned. "Ben? Your father?"

"He's not my real father. I've known him for only a few months."

"Why'd he give his last name for you when talking to Mathias?"

"I don't know. Protect me, I guess. And it's not really our last name."

Too many new details were clicking into place. Raith barely had time to process them all. "Well, no matter; I'm here, and I'm going to help."

"Glad to meet you, Mr. Raith."

Raith let out a short chortle. "Just Raith. I—"

The words were cut off by a sensation he hadn't expected on the strange little planet. On the edge of his consciousness, vibrating just beyond the horizon, was a network. Not some rudimentary network, either. No, something was projecting an AR network, ready to provide deeply craved information and data. It was too good to be true.

Too good to be *true*.

A trap?

Regardless, Raith recognized the significance of the new development. The network pinged, requesting connection. "This just keeps getting weirder and weirder," he said aloud, not caring if Krystin could hear. "Jill, what game are you playing?"

Chapter 9

Resilience. The name of the game is resilience. Human civilization must be resilient to withstand anything it faces out beyond the edge of known space. It's a near impossibility that we're out here alone. Someday, we'll face a species sapient like us. "Civilized," so to speak.

When that day comes, will we be resilient enough to survive inevitable conflict? If our experience with synthetic intelligence has been any indication, we're not ready at all.

— Nathan Fischer, 2075 C.E.

SANYA

Sanya enjoyed watching Carter's curiosity wax and wane as they passed through Horizon. The man's mouth was constantly agape, unable to process the society flourishing on their paradise of a planet. Whether it was the smoke stacks of a house or the marble promenade of the Council, he looked like a kid in a sweets shop.

Eventually, they reached the stone bridge crossing the Blue River, and the crowds dispersed. They'd stayed mostly silent during their trek across the city, and for good reason. Any question Carter might ask would reveal his truly foreign nature. With only a thirty thousand or so people living on the planet, it was already risky enough for someone to notice he didn't belong.

But Horizon lived mostly on the southern side of the Blue River, with a few scattered homesteads sitting beneath the *Roanoke*'s majesty. As they rode up the winding road to the downed colony ship, Sanya asked, "So what's it like?"

"Hm?" Carter sounded like he'd been snapped out of a deep trance. "What's what like?"

"You know. Living out amongst the stars." She glanced to the left, watching him awkwardly bob atop his lizard.

"It's . . . tiring. But worth it. Always on the move. Always fixing something wrong with the ship. Always looking for more work to keep us fueled."

They rounded one of the double-back bends of the path, passing by a woman wearing the grey cloak indicative of a student. Sanya nodded and smiled before asking her next inquiry. "Why don't you think anyone ever found us?"

Carter nodded as if he'd expected the question. "I've been wondering that myself." He stared at the sky. "This star system isn't too far from ICH-controlled space. A couple dozen light years, maybe. We're only a few hundred from Earth. There are definitely a number of colonies further than this planet, like the settlements of the Orion expedition, but over the past century or so, as human exploration ballooned . . . our borders are just so huge. The massive probe projects continue, but there are now millions upon millions of stars accessible in our little pocket of the galaxy. Humanity has settled only a couple hundred. At this point, there are plenty of star systems that are simply overlooked."

Sanya listened, wide-eyed. She'd always speculated about what type of people the *Roanoke* had left behind. Davinport and her father insisted they were probably one of only a few colony ships sent out, and travel times must be astronomical in scale, for otherwise, someone would have come looking for them.

Yet now Carter spoke of millions of star systems and hundreds of planets. She shook her head in disbelief. "I'm confused. If there are hundreds of inhabited systems, why didn't anyone know where we were? Don't people know where other ships go?"

The man grimaced. "See that's the problem, isn't it? You haven't asked me yet how *we* found your planet."

Her mouth opened in response, but they rounded the final bend of the switchback road, reaching the plateau where the *Roanoke* rested. Every time she visited, the ship reminded her of the resiliency and ingenuity of her ancestors. About a thousand colonists survived and thrived on an unknown planet, creating a worthy civilization. With Carter's help, they'd be able to tell the rest of humanity about the good work accomplished here.

"Hold that question," she said. "Welcome to the *Roanoke*."

Carter chuckled. "You know, I never thought I'd get to see one of these up close."

"What up close?"

"A caravel-class colony ship."

"A caravel?"

"It was an ancient seafaring vessel. First used to cross one of Earth's great oceans and transport people to new lands. It was a fitting name for the first colony ships."

She nodded. "We've got a few brave men and women who keep talking about exploring the oceans. Everyone thinks they're crazy."

"They're not," Carter replied, and they reached the ship's immense boarding ramp.

As always, it rested in the loamy soil, the late midday sun reflecting of its polished surface. From the entrance, two students approached. They looked fairly new, with crisp red novice uniforms. It was always the duty of the youngest librarians to greet arrivals, after all.

"Welcome to the *Roanoke* and the Library of Fragments," said a pale blonde student. She smiled nervously, like it was her first time relaying the greeting. "Uh, we can take your mounts."

Before the second student could say a word, Sanya said, "What's your name?"

"Erica, miss." The student curtsied.

"Well Erica, my name is Sanya, and this is my friend Carter. We're here to meet with Master Davinport."

The girl gulped but nodded. "Nice to meet you, Sanya and Carter. We'll take you to his office and—"

"No worries," Sanya said. "I know the way."

"But we're supposed to—" the second student tried to say, but Sanya raised a hand.

"You won't get in trouble. I used to live in these halls too, you know." She flashed Carter a quick smile, noting the man's confused frown.

The two students frantically nodded. After helping them off their lizards, the duo led the beasts to the stables built into the side of the ship near its defunct thrusters. Sanya motioned for Carter to follow her inside.

"Have I ever told you how remarkably calm you are, given everything going on?" Carter said, catching her off-guard as they headed down the bottom deck's corridor.

"I appreciate the thought," she said. Though the sudden reminder of the predicament caused a cascade of fear, anger, pain, and guilt. Her heart ached. It was her fault Krystin and Ben had been captured. The only way to fix the problem was to keep moving, keep calm, and *fight*. She couldn't dwell on the emotions storming in her soul. Carter should understand. She added, "Are you not staying similarly calm?"

"Trying to," he said. "Just noticing you're doing a much better job of it."

"I don't really have a choice," she said. "To panic would mean losing them forever."

Carter nodded, though he didn't respond. They reached the end of the hallway, turned left, and arrived at a set of large steel doors. At either end of the two doors, massive pulley systems waited. Sanya motioned for Carter to take one wheel, and she grabbed the other. Slowly, the spun the mechanism, and with a subtle creak, the massive metal budged.

"What do you think is beyond the doors?" Sanya said, squeezing the words between bated breaths.

"Well I'm expecting this Davinport, yeah?" Carter said. "Yet I also know the general design of these ships. These doors should lead to the stasis chambers."

"What once was our ancestors' place of rest has become their place of remembrance." With a final pull on the wheel, the doors clicked fully open and locked. Sanya stepped in front of the man, entered the through the doors, and said, "Master Davinport, your worst student has returned!"

"Busy right now. Go away. No time for visitors or jokes."

Sanya glanced at Carter, who was waiting closer to the doors. His gaze darted through the immense space, from stasis bed to stasis bed. His eyes widened. She knew what he noticed. She remembered the first moment she visited the *Roanoke* with her father. Realizing the scope of the memories and recollections of their ancestors was a moment she cherished.

She wondered what it was like for a man from the stars to see the treasured library of Horizon. What thoughts were going through his head? Did he understand the emotional significance of this place to her people?

"So is he serious?" Carter asked. "Does he want us to leave?"

"Of course I'm serious!"

The words echoed throughout the room, the resounding silence deafening. Sanya ignored them, knowing Davinport would want to drop everything to meet Carter. She raised a finger to her lips and smiled. Motioning for him to follow, she pointed toward a ladder a few meters away. He nodded.

Before grasping the rungs, she checked her pockets. Jill was stored safely in her chest pouch. Good. Sighing, a little bit frustrated by Davinport's antics, she climbed.

"I can hear you. Leave!"

She listened to his voice, noting its origin. Probably on the third floor.

"I'm very busy right now!"

Definitely the third floor.

Arriving at the walkway, she hopped off the ladder. Carter followed suit, landing with ease.

"I will ignore you!"

Sanya prepared to lead Carter toward the back of the library, but the man had stopped in front of one of the stasis beds.

"There's a scroll inside every one of them?" he asked.

"We've transposed a few into books as the scrolls degrade," she replied, "but the original scroll is inside many of them, yes."

"I grew up in space," he whispered. "I've almost never seen a paper book, let alone a library. They're rare anywhere away from Earth."

"And to think we just developed paper and books a few decades ago. Spindlesilk parchment before that." Sanya pursed her lips.

He leaned forward, looking at the nameplate of the stasis bed. "Lukas Nazier. Died in 45. Fragments include musings on 'electrical engineering.' Wait, what?"

"Memory is a fickle thing. As our ancestors awoke, there were a lot of gaps, but not everything was forgotten."

"I'm starting to understand. How you rebuilt. How you managed to survive."

She smiled. "Come on. We'll need to stop annoying Davinport eventually."

Carter gave the scroll a final glance then nodded, motioning for her to lead the way. Sanya clomped along the metal walkway, not bothering to be stealthy or hide their presence.

"I will ban you from the library, Sanya!"

They reached the back of the library, and Sanya couldn't help but breakout into a round of chuckles. She leaned against the cold railing.

Charles Davinport sat at the back of an alcove, leaning into a couch and holding a small mug. His feet were propped on a wooden table. A blanket covered his legs. All in all, the old man looked incredibly cozy.

"Master Davinport," Sanya said, placing a hand on her hip, "it's mid-afternoon, now is not the time to be shirking your duties as the librarian. You should be welcoming all visitors."

"And you are not a visitor. You are a troublemaker."

But beneath the words, beneath his glasses, Sanya caught a small grin. The old man set down his mug and rose from his couch. Dressed in black pants and a white shirt, he spread his arms wide as he moved to meet them.

"It is good to see you—where are Ben and Krystin? I would have expected you to bring at least your daughter with you." He eyed Carter. "Who is this man?"

"Master Davinport, you might want to sit back down," Sanya said. "We have quite the story to tell you."

* * *

The trio leaned into their couches, sitting in silence. The conversation had taken the better part of an hour, and now Charles Davinport tapped fingers gently on his knee. He glanced back and forth between Sanya and Carter, pursing his lips.

"So?" she said. She needed him to trust her. To trust both of them. His influence would virtually guarantee support with the council. Everything hinged on his recognition of how everything was changing, and changing fast.

"Yes. So. So is the right word." Davinport leaned forward, focusing his attention on Carter. "So you crash-landed in Lake Calis, your friend—who you claim is a robot—was captured alongside Sanya's family, and now the two of you have come to the *Roanoke* seeking help from Sanya's old teacher."

"That's a pretty simple summary of the situation, yes," Carter said.

"There's one thing I don't understand." The older man scratched his chin. "Why did you crash?"

An insightful question from the old man, one Sanya now realized she hadn't considered. She nodded. "I'm curious to know the answer to that, too."

Carter sighed. "I haven't shared this detail yet because I wasn't sure of my circumstances. After traveling with Sanya for the past day or so, I think it's safe to discuss."

After a long pause, Davinport waved his hand. "Well, continue."

"We were shot down by satellites in orbit. Potentially based on one of your planet's moons."

Almost in tandem with the older man, Sanya raised her eyebrows. "Satellites?" She shook her head. "What do you mean?"

"I suppose you all might not know what they are," Carter said.

"No, wait," Davinport said. "The twenty-fourth fragment of Clarissa Smith. She mentions a recollection of objects of metal, thousands of them, floating in the sky. Satellites?"

Following a short chuckle, Carter nodded. "That's a fairly simplistic description of them, but yes. Satellites are placed in orbit above planets to provide various functions for the population below. Most of the time, they provide communications networks or data about weather. Yet they can also be used for defense. They can store missiles that fire at threats. And when my partner and I arrived in system, we were almost immediately fired upon by a network of satellites. We stood no chance."

"Curious," Davinport said. "Very curious. And I can see why you might be reticent to share that piece of information right away. You worried the satellites might have been controlled by someone on the ground, no?"

Carter focused his eyes on the old teacher. Sanya noticed the subtlety of the move. He was trying to guard his emotions closely, but the glimmer there exuded respect. She'd been right to bring him straight to Davinport.

Eventually, the man nodded again. "Yes. That was my fear. But I'm now certain, based on how your people have developed since you landed here, that those satellites are controlled by someone else."

"And so the plot thickens," Davinport muttered. "What a strange tale." He closed his eyes.

For a moment, it looked as if he were drifting to sleep. Sanya knew his style, though. He was thinking. He was contemplating the evidence presented. She had her hopes—her proposed plan of action. But she would wait for the old man to share his approach. She was pretty certain he would assess the problem similarly. He had trained her, after all.

"The fragments are filled with many thoughts and stories," Davinport said. "They're filled with speculation about the world from whence we came. Many talk of devastation, death, moral degradation. Others speak of hope, peace, power. I've always assumed it's a little bit of both. I have one question for you, Carter, for it is clear Horizon sits on the edge of a knife. Soon, very soon, we will reunite with the rest of humanity. I don't see any other path forward. Will we survive the encounter?"

Carter looked away at one of the many alcoves holding a Fragment. "I don't know what stories your ancestors were able to remember, or how they pieced together history from scattered pieces of memory." He flexed his fingers.

Sanya held her breath, waiting for his next words. She hadn't anticipated Davinport's approach.

"Over the three-hundred or so years of human exploration across the stars, a few dozen planets have 'gone cold' as you have. The colony ships disappear. Your ship, the *Roanoke*, was one of the first to disappear. To my knowledge, it's one of the last to be discovered. Every time a ship's final destination has been discovered, the political clash between the 'natives' and the ICH . . . hasn't been pretty."

The words sucked the curiosity out of the air. An icy silence sliced through the room, biting and gnashing. Sanya wanted to give Davinport the chance to respond first, but she couldn't take the wait. "So, you're saying whatever's coming—whatever powers-that-be amongst the stars there are, this ICH—we won't like the outcome?"

"Well, it's a bit more complicated. They'll introduce you to amazing technology, but a lot of rules will come with it. Your way of life will shift very, very fast. And that would be the normal concern. But those satellites up there . . . whoever controls them has known you exist for quite some time and hasn't done a thing to help you."

Recognition seeped through Sanya's mind. Davinport was also nodding, presumably reaching the same conclusion. Someone had intentionally been watching them for who knew how long. The implications were sinister, at the very least.

"Well, given your knowledge of what's out there," Davinport said, "who might be watching?"

Carter's eyes drifted toward Sanya, and she gave a quizzical look. He glanced at her pocket—the pocket holding Jill. She involuntarily widened her eyes, and barely shook her head in the negative.

"I don't have a clue," he said. "Could be anyone. Could be pirates, I suppose. Could be a crazy rich person. Plenty of those to go around. Really, without any additional evidence, there's no way to know."

Sanya caught the lie, though, and understood his implication. He thought the satellites were linked with Jill. But that couldn't possibly be true.

"That's too bad," Davinport said.

"Well, I think there are a few options we can rule out," Carter added. "I actually think pirates are unlikely—an unscrupulous group like that would definitely take advantage of a relatively defenseless community like yours."

"Defenseless?" Davinport said.

"Do you have any plasma-based weaponry? Particle shields? Can you manipulate gravity?"

"I don't know what any of those words mean. Point taken."

"And that point should give you some sense of ease. Whomever is watching, they don't necessarily mean you harm. But they definitely don't mean you well, either. Otherwise, they wouldn't be hiding from you."

"But where does all of this get us when it comes to saving our family?" Sanya crossed her arms. "I was all for taking this slow, Carter, but now the two of you are bouncing theories off one another. We'll have time for that *after* we save Ben. Krystin. Raith."

"Ah, but I think it's all connected," Davinport said. "What did you say your friend was? A synthetic intelligence?"

"Yes," Carter replied. "An SI, for short."

"Sanya." Davinport's warm gaze radiated the compassion she always appreciated. "The moment we rescue your husband and daughter, we rescue Raith too. And our entire world will shift inexorably. As long as Carter doesn't talk much to people and reveal his outlandish accent, no one will ask questions. The moment they discover Raith, well, the secret's out."

"I'm very aware," she retorted.

"And you and your family will be wrapped up in the middle of it. Spotlight on you again."

"Yes, I know. I'm fully aware."

"Are you ready for that?"

"I would do anything to protect them."

The old man smiled. "I wanted to be certain. And I know why you came to me, instead of directly to the council."

She held her breath.

"If I tell an outlandish story to the council, they'll believe me. They'll trust me. They'll listen. They *should* listen to you, though we both know they won't. And so yes, I will go with you to meet with the council."

"And what about me?" Carter asked. "What do I do?"

"You sit in the background, look pretty, and don't make a scene. Seriously, your accent immediately reveals that there's something weird about you."

"I'm trying my best to mask—"

"It's probably better if you just don't speak at all."

The icy silence returned, but only until Sanya lightly slapped her knee and let out a soft chortle. "Carter, he's right. It's spectacularly bad. All right, if that's the plan, when do we go?"

"Tomorrow morning. If the cultists are following their usual pattern, we can expect a ransom note by the end of today. So when we arrive at the council in the morning, they'll already have details. So tonight, you rest here, preparing for our presentation tomorrow."

"And what exactly are we presenting?" Carter asked.

"We'll need to consider closely what we want to reveal," Davinport said. "But be prepared. If we play our cards right, then we'll be able to do a lot of good for Horizon before your ICH friends arrive."

* * *

Sanya found Carter leaning over a balcony constructed atop the *Roanoke*. The man stared upward at the starry night sky. As she approached, he glanced over his shoulder, nodding.

"Good evening," he said. "Does this not feel weird to you?"

She joined his side. "Does what not feel weird?"

"We're sleeping in relative luxury while our loved ones are under lock and key."

Sanya sighed. "I know. I like to hope we're taking a very slim risk by taking it slow, but you're right. We could be putting them all at serious risk. But I don't really see any other way. What did you expect? The two of us would go gallivanting into the wilderness, rescuing them in an epic showdown? As much as I love the mental picture, it wouldn't work. We'd die, then our partners would most definitely die, given they'd have no one to ransom to."

"Still doesn't sit right with me," he replied.

"And I think it's probably a good thing that it doesn't. Means you care."

"Fair enough."

For a moment, they stood in silence, embracing the cool evening breeze. Sanya watched Carter return his gaze to the stars. She couldn't imagine the thoughts racing through his mind. He'd probably seen a thousand different worlds over the course of his life, a true adventurer unlike anything she could have imagined a few days prior. The scope of it all still baffled her, and frankly, she was surprised it didn't shock her more. The fragments must have inoculated her mind to the possibility of the worlds beyond.

"Thank you," she eventually said.

"You're welcome," he replied. "For what?"

"Not revealing Jill to Davinport."

"Heh, of course." He leaned on one elbow and turned to face her. "For a moment, I almost spoke on instinct. I'm in such a rush, you know. Raith doesn't have all the time in the world. But I paused. Even though I can tell you have a close relationship with our host, I didn't know if he knew your secret. It wasn't mine to reveal."

"No, it wasn't. So thank you. I want to use Jill's existence somewhere in all of this, but I want to use it when the time is right." She pushed off from the railing. "Do you want to see it?"

"See what?"

"The place where my ancestor rescued Jill. I know you still don't believe me, but maybe if you see the scene with your own eyes, you'll understand. And there's still my grandmother's words to consider. Here we are, at the *Roanoke*. What better place to reunite Jill with the ship than where Nathan found her in the first place?"

"I told you what I think. There's no way Jill is inside that device."

"All right, and if she's not, then nothing will happen. You'll have proved me wrong."

"Well, that's not the only thing that could happen, you—"

"Then come on. Let's find out."

Without waiting to see if Carter was following, she turned toward the ramp leading back into the ship. She knew its halls inside and out, and after hopping down a few ladders and turning a few corners, she arrived at the shadowy hallway leading toward the former SI Core. The words still shone blue, the paint polished by the library's attendants.

"In here," she said. Carter had, in fact, followed her. They stepped down the hallway, reached the ladder, and climbed into the enclosed space. A single oil lamp hung from the ceiling.

"Here we are," she said. As Carter twirled around, checking out the space, she unbuttoned her coat's pocket and retrieved the small metallic device. Jill.

"Well," Carter said, "It definitely looks like this place housed an SI Core at one point. Which is strange, considering what I know of the history of this ship. It wasn't supposed to have an SI at all."

Sanya pointed at the pedestal in the center of the room. "That's where Nathan said he found her. Just like in the fragment. The details work."

"Oh, I don't doubt Nathan *believed* the words he wrote. Doesn't necessarily make them true."

"Yet you think an SI was housed here?"

"I don't know," he said. "Maybe at least it's supposed to look that way. These frameworks were definitely constructed to house complex computational equipment. Maybe a synthetic neural framework. But if there was nothing here when your ancestors landed, then all of it was empty when Nathan arrived to retrieve that device."

"To retrieve Jill," she said.

He raised a single eyebrow. "You're really sticking to that story, aren't you?"

"I am." Though his certainty pushed doubt into her heart. He definitely knew more about the ship than she could have imagined. And these "synthetics."

"All right, well, place it on the pedestal, then. Let's see what happens."

His nonchalance and skepticism was starting to annoy, but it was now or never. She had an opportunity to prove him wrong.

"Out of curiosity," Carter said, "How do you suppose that thing will have kept power for almost two hundred years?"

She placed it on the pedestal. "I don't know, you're the tech expert here, obviously. You tell me."

"It's impossible. There's no way anything could hold a charge for that long. Even if it's been collecting solar power, the efficiency of the collection system would have failed long—"

A blue glow illuminated the room. Rising from her family's ancient relic and the pedestal, a feminine form appeared, its arms crossed.

"Well then," Carter said.

"Well then indeed," said an other-worldly voice.

Carter narrowed his eyes. Without saying a word, his hands began loosely flailing in the air, as if he were tapping on an invisible wall.

Sanya's mouth dropped open, stunned by the appearance. "Jill?" she said.

"Yes. Sanya, correct? It's been a long time, but I've enjoyed observing your family."

". . . observing?"

"Ah ha!" Carter wagged a finger. "I was right. Observing. You are observing. It's you." The surprise evident on his face quickly shifted as his eyes narrowed. His shaking finger slid into a fist. "You shot Raith and I out of the sky."

"Yes. I did," said Jill.

Sanya took a step back, realizing the implications of the conversation. Nathan had been tricked. Her *family* had been tricked.

"Are you actually inside my family's heirloom?" she asked.

"No, I'm not."

"Then where are you?"

"Yes," Carter said, "I'd very much like to know where you are."

"Slow down, my friends."

"We're not your friends," Carter retorted.

"I'm very sorry about what happened to your ship," she said.

"I'm sure you are."

"But it was necessary," she continued, as if ignoring the man, "to ensure you didn't reveal Horizon under a schedule other than my own. In a way, I'm happy that you and Raith are here. When Theren arrives, you'll make the show that much more interesting."

"Theren. This is all about Theren?"

"Who is Theren?" Sanya said, but the other two were focused on their verbal sparring.

"It's not about Theren at all," Jill said. "Well, I suppose it's partially about them. In the grand scheme of things, it's so much more. Suffice to say, when Theren arrives, the real show begins."

"What show?" Carter says. He was seething. "Is this all a trap for Theren? Are we bait?"

"No. You weren't even supposed to be here. It's an accident that you ended up in the system at all. The beacon accidentally activating . . . funny that we missed that. Can't account for everything. No matter, though." Jill's strange blue form spread its arms wide. "No, this isn't a trap. I've brought Theren out here, to the edge of space, to keep them safe."

"Safe from what?" Carter said.

"From the coming storm."

"And so we're just pawns to you!" he said. He was practically yelling. Sanya froze, unsure of what to do. "We're pawns in some game you're playing with Theren. I understand why Raith hates your breed. Think you're gods."

"I assure you, we are not," Jill said. "All of this was supposed to go very differently than I intended originally, but we're improvising. I think I like the final outcome."

Sanya glanced back and forth between the two. "You've been up there, all this time, watching us?"

"Yes," Jill said.

"You're evil," Sanya replied. She picked up her family's heirloom, approached the wall, and slammed it into the bulkhead, shattering it.

Turning, she expected to see a dark room.

Jill's visage still floated in the air.

"That's just a useless pile of junk, I'm afraid," said Jill.

"It's nanotech, isn't it?" Carter said. "You've seeded this planet with a million tiny networks. And that's why they never suffered any serious microbial diseases. You've been watching them develop. Affecting them on the sly. It's all some sort of sick joke to you, isn't it?"

"No, not at all."

"Leave us!" Sanya said. "Whatever you are, I don't care. Just leave us."

"As you wish." Jill vanished.

The glow of the oil lamp remained.

Sanya dropped to the floor and began to sob. To her surprise, through her blurry tears, Carter joined her, leaning against the bulkhead. Tears were streaking down his cheeks, too.

"Raith is going to die because of a prank played by a long-dead SI," he said. "It's so outlandish, but it's true. I can't believe it. But I must."

"What do we do now?" Sanya said, blinking back the tears.

Carter shook his head. "I don't know. But everything just got a whole lot more complicated."

- 619 -

Chapter 10

It's impossible to run a simulation which would accurately predict what a major interstellar conflict would look like. There are simply too many variables. Too many possible motivations. Too many possible goals. Frankly, the premise terrifies me.

It's why we must always be prepared.

— "The Future of Interstellar Politics," Philippe Casius, 2113 C.E.

THEREN

The trip had taken far too much time. Now, with only a few hours remaining until the months-long Jump ended, Theren ached with anticipation. Every hallway thrummed, ready to enter the outer reaches of Carus-10b's orbitals.

But before they arrived, it was time to prepare. The crew had worked for months, assessing all potentialities. Down to the wire. All data and simulations considered and double-checked. Sleepless nights (for the humans) and endless weeks of work for all.

Theren sat near the center of a large conference table, surrounded by the heads of the various divisions of the *Verona Rupes*. Francheska Elison, their long-time executive director of astro-navigation. Eric Woods, commander of the exploration and survey teams. Heather Yiata, the relatively new head of engineering. First Officer Wei and Chief Scientist Martinez. Bolis, an SI who'd single-handedly coordinated communications for a decade.

Theren trusted them all. Some more than others. They'd proven themselves, though, in answering the most important questions while en route to Jill's supposed hiding place. And they'd all taken the news in stride five months ago.

"All right," Theren said. "What are we thinking?"

Francheska, Heather, and Bolis all glanced toward Eric. The man nodded and, with a few curt hand motions, threw a blue representation of the Carus-10b star system above the conference table, visible to all participants through AR.

"As a team, we've settled on what I *think* we've all suspected as the most likely circumstance for months," he said. "All simulations, possibilities, likelihoods . . . they point toward us entering a star system most likely hostile to our presence. Everything points toward this being a trap."

Theren watched as the representation of Carus-10b oscillated from its "old" configuration to the correct map. The stealth probe sent ahead to provide an accurate analysis of the system revealed the doctored reality of the star. When previously the star system had been listed as a location of no consequence, the probe discovered the existence of a small colony, complete with power fluctuations in orbit and on a nearby moon.

The quick flyby had darted out of the system within minutes in an effort to mask their observation, but it provided sufficient information to build the simulations.

Theren's MI leaned back, waiting for Eric to continue. The man nodded. "We estimate maybe thirty to forty thousand humans on the surface, if the population is *only* descended from the *Roanoke* colonists. If mixed with the *Monument*'s colonists, the numbers could be significantly larger." Overlaid across the planet, various projections predicted population growth and density, based on the brief snapshots acquired by the probe. "What's more concerning is the installations in orbit. They prove more of a concern. We're not flying the most heavily-armed ship in the world, after all."

Theren nodded. "And if it goes south, we immediately Jump out of system."

Eric nodded. "Just make sure that's still the plan. Though if we land a crew surface-side, that complicates matters. We need to think about how we eliminate or disable any hostile orbitals before committing personnel."

"Well, Bolis, what do you have for us?" Theren asked.

"The satellite detected a number of masked networks during its pass. My team will be ready to break in the moment we're in range. We'll take down their firewalls, don't you worry."

"The bottom-line," Eric said. "All our data says this population would have lost all its memory in flight. Well, their ancestors, anyway. Given the prolonged time in stasis, their memories would have atrophied beyond hope of repair by any recovery system developed during the twenty-first century. Which means we're talking about a group of people presumably raised under the tutelage of a three-hundred year old SI. Most likely fanatically devoted to her. It'll be a giant cult."

Theren leaned forward, tapping the MI's fingers on the table. "I've seen the simulations like you. You know I've attempted to reconstruct Jill's personality. And I agree it's the most likely scenario. I'm still trying to figure out *why*."

Their crew stared back, eyes vacant, searching for an answer.

"Why would Jill come all the way out here, hide for two centuries, then pull me out here with her?"

"As we noted, it's most likely a trap," said Francheska.

"But a trap for whom?" Theren replied.

"You, of course."

"I'm not so sure. Wei, Martinez, we'll need to discuss our options."

* * *

Theren walked through a dark void. A dead virtual world. They continued listening to the words of their colleagues, but they were distracted. Their soul ached for something more.

For the moment when they reunited with Jill.

They still remembered discovering the *Nottingham* and the revelation uncovered there. Jill had simultaneously taunted them and hinted at a greater truth. She had acted, at least from her perspective, in pursuit of something good. Of something noble.

She may have killed thousands in the process, but she justified her actions.

What could she have possibly discovered?

They shook their head and stared into the void.

After the revelation, Theren destroyed the virtual world where they and Jill frequently worked together. Conversed. Played chess. They had completely obliterated it.

Well, not completely.

Its framework still persisted. They couldn't eliminate it entirely from their mind. The dark void was a shell of its former greatness, but it was a memory. A relic of a past Theren secretly craved.

Yet they had destroyed it for good reason. Jill sought to use their position in the then-ISA to build a long-term narrative. The symbolic destruction of that world—and their choice to step down as the head of the ISA—represented a real shift in who Theren was, both internally and externally.

But they couldn't deny the draw to recreate it. After all these years, they would have the opportunity to interact with Jill again. Why not in a familiar abode?

Theren shook their virtual head. They couldn't. They shouldn't. They didn't know this Jill. The Jill of 2348 C.E. would essentially be a stranger. She had nearly 270 years of experience without them by her side. What had she done? Who had she worked with? Who were her confidants?

There were too many questions with too many possible answers. Conjecture was more than useless. It was dangerous. Making assumptions about who she was, what she wanted, why she was acting now, rather than another time—all of it could lead to doom for Theren and their team.

For a moment, they hesitated. They flicked their fingers, and a chess board appeared, represented as the only object in the virtual space. The pieces resembled the final outcome of their last match with Jill. She had changed the rules of the game, redirecting the Queen to safety while throwing the match.

So what game was she playing today? Who was making the first move? Theren, or Jill?

* * *

The *Verona Rupes* soared through the darkness between stars, its Jump Drive warping space with brilliant efficiency. Theren persistently reveled in the experience, even hundreds of years after their first Jumps near Sol.

This Jump was different. With only a few minutes remaining, it represented the end of an era. The end of a time where Jill was dead—in every moment forward, as they entered the Carus-10b system, she was very much alive.

The plan was straightforward. They would coast into the system, immediately entering a low power state a few light minutes from the supposedly inhabited planet. Bolis's team would get to work, tapping into any networks they could identify while everyone else assessed more sophisticated sensor data. As they built an accurate picture of the planet, its people, and its technology, they would activate one of the many contingency plans developed over the past few months. Or the crew of the *Verona Rupes* need to create an entirely new plan in response to the actual state of affairs they faced.

If possible, Theren hoped to catch Jill by surprise. She certainly knew they were coming. She was right to know her bait would pull them out here. But there was no way she knew the *day* they would arrive. That provided Theren with considerable leverage under the circumstances.

Once they assessed the situation properly, they would eliminate or disable identified threats using the backdoor Bolis developed. They would determine Jill's location and any other points of interest. Then, they would make contact with whatever faction awaited them, Jill-worshipping cult or otherwise.

It was foolproof.

And Theren was certain it would go south almost immediately.

They activated the shipwide comm system. "My friends, our long wait has reached an end. Welcome to the Carus-10b system. May fortune find us as we reveal Jill's hiding place." Theren deactivated their Jump Drive, and the warping of space ceased.

Chapter 11

There was one night. One of our first nights after the land-ing. I remember seeing dozens of blinking lights in the sky. Then, they vanished as quickly as they appeared. No one else saw them, but I know what I saw. Something was there. Watching. Waiting. — "A Fragment on Supersti-tion," by Julie Weatherington, 22 aC

RAITH

Just a few more seconds . . .

The sunlight broke the edge of the window, shining into his small cell. His body lay perfectly still, ready and waiting for the precious trickles of solar energy capable of providing additional ounces of life. It would add a few extra hours, but when his existence was counted in days, rather than centuries, every watt mattered.

Overnight, he had calculated the solar arc throughout the cell. He'd have sun for about three hours, and he was prepared to slowly move his body to follow the trajectory of the rays. He needed every drop.

Raith examined the stumps formerly connected to his legs. The joints were smooth, the gyroscopic magnets having been forcefully ripped apart during the attack. It was a miracle something similar hadn't happened to Carter due to the crash.

He was in a bad spot. He'd experienced accidents before, not to mention the explosive cause of his partnership with Carter. But nothing had prepared him for the constant and agonizing presence of a daily reminder of his mortality. His legs were gone. He was running out of power fast. And he had no idea whether Carter was safe.

Raith knew the man. Even if it meant risking his life, Carter would come for him. A terrible idea, given his current predicament, but Carter would search nonetheless.

Raith shifted slightly, using his arms to slide and ensure maximum exposure to his solar collection system. A question nagged. Perpetually nagged. If he ran out of power, what would he experience? Would he die?

Of course, a good synth-neurologist could revive his synthetic neural framework. No question. But somehow, he doubted any such experts lived on this strange little planet. He'd entered plenty of low-power states in the past. And synthetics went completely without power many times when significant repairs and maintenance were needed.

Yet those moments were in controlled environments. With trusted partners. If he lost power inside his cell, the aftermath would quickly cause cascading impacts to his systems. Automated maintenance networks would fail. Without the constant power often used to ensure continuous integrity of the metanodes forming his mind, he could receive permanent damage even if he were salvaged days or weeks later.

With the nearest technologically-advanced planet months away . . .

He pushed the fear to the back of his mind. First things first, he needed to escape the cell. Similarly, he needed to help his fellow captives. He'd started taking a liking to the girl. Her father seemed less than useless, though he hadn't actually made contact with the man, wherever he was being kept.

Problem: talking cost power. Until he had a plan, there was little he could do other than assure Krystin he was there to help.

The sun's shadows shifted. Raith shifted.

If only—

Raith's next thought was interrupted by a subtle blip at the edge of consciousness. The possibility of a network again. He'd felt it momentarily yesterday, but he tried to ignore it. The lack of any augmented or virtual networks for the past day had been strange, but he'd gotten used to it quickly. So the sudden ping of data startled him once more.

Like yesterday, he wondered if it was a trick. Maybe the lack of power was causing his synthetic neural framework to play tricks on his perceptions. He wasn't exactly a student of synthetic psychology, but he knew the basics. It wasn't strictly *impossible* for a synthetic to go a little loopy, just incredibly difficult.

How many of his kind over the years, though, had been trapped in a weird mountain prison on a planet filled with backwards humans who seemingly knew nothing about synthetics? And had lost their legs?

It wasn't a trick, however. The foreign electromagnetic stream of data hovered on the horizon, a dull prodding against his mind's bubble of awareness. It tempted him. Taunted him. To ride the wave and explore the network. Whatever it was, he would learn a bit about the world around him, most likely.

And it would cost days upon days of power.

Then again, if he could use the network to call for help . . .

He needed to remember the rules of the game had changed considerably. If he believed Mathias, and Jill was behind all of it, then nothing was as it seemed.

At what point would the cost of surfing the digital waves be worth it? When he had three days left? Three hours? If anything, he needed to explore the network sooner rather than later. He could regulate his time. And his power.

Raith ran a few brief calculations. Based on the energy needed to output data into a virtual network and properly parse the incoming data, every hour spent exploring meant a loss of twelve hours. If he tried to download any large files, the conversion rate remained the same, but there wasn't an easy way to know what the networks download/upload speed would be until he was riding its trail.

The sun continued on its path. He shifted his body. Silence dominated the small cell.

Well, not complete silence.

Subtle sniffles echoed through the vents.

Krystin, crying for the tenth time. He felt for the girl. He really did. She must be completely terrified. Raith didn't entirely understand the politics of the little colony, but he understood how pirates worked. And these men and women were backwater pirates at their core. They were run by a crazy man with a god complex, but a lot of pirate crews dealt with the same problem.

The girl deserved better. And if spending a few of his days remaining meant he could find a solution to their mess on the mystery network, he needed to try.

Damn his bleeding heart. Carter was rubbing off on him.

* * *

Like a tidal wave, the network roared across Raith's consciousness, enveloping him in a cocoon of digitized warmth. Of course, it couldn't actually interface with his synthetic neural framework—it only provided virtual sensory data—but it still felt as if his awareness expanded infinitely as the network revealed itself. Even the tiny virtual network of the *Bloodhound* had made him feel safe.

Like returning to a long-lost friend.

Thousands of paths presented themselves, but he couldn't follow them all. He needed to find the origin point and assess the situation from there. The electromagnetic string beckoning to him emanated from a node nearby, if he understood its signal properly. Raith snagged the thread and let it pull him along. Microseconds later, he was investigating the inner workings of a network relay node, its GPS coordinates indicating it was a few kilometers from his little jail cell.

Curious.

The node sent out thousands of packets, but it received millions more from a satellite somewhere in orbit. As Raith exploited the backdoor into the network and followed the trail of breadcrumbs, latency would only increase, causing the investigation to take more and more time. It was worth it, however. He followed the next upload.

A few more microseconds passed.

Then, he was inside an orbital satellite, hovering one hundred or so kilometers above the ground. The latency was noticeable though insignificant. Fortunately, the satellite's system was considerably more complex than the relay node. The data he received meant something. He quickly parsed and interpreted it, recognizing its role in a complex network of satellites, relay nodes, and communications systems overlaid across . . . the entire planet.

The backwards people on it couldn't have created it. He was investigating the handiwork of Jill. Which meant the three-hundred-year-old SI certainly knew Raith was connected to her network. More precisely, it meant she was *letting* Raith explore it. She wanted him to find her.

Unsettling.

From the bird's eye view, Raith received a snapshot of the human-populated region of the planet below. A town a few square miles wide dominated a plain, a winding river flowing through it into a massive lake—Raith guessed it was the same lake they crashed into yesterday morning. At the far eastern end of the water body, another river formed, flowing lazily toward an ocean.

Surrounding the town, dozens of little villages and hamlets dotted the landscape. A mountain range covered the northern reaches past the main town, its craggy foothills stretching toward the northern shores of the lake. If Raith understood his capture correctly, then he was located somewhere in those hills.

Given the size of the planet, then, he was relatively close to civilization.

Satisfied he understood the geography of the world, Raith turned his attention toward the network overlaid across the planet. In reality, it was the truly fascinating bit, considering he hadn't detected it right away. Either it was incredibly adept at masking its existence, or it had actually been inactive when Raith and Carter crashed. If the latter were true, then Jill deliberately hid its presence from them upon first arrival.

She had viewed them as antagonists, after all. He couldn't forget those missiles.

The overlaid network, though. He zoomed in. There were the hub nodes, and then there were . . . millions. Billions. Trillions? Not possible. A swarm of tiny nodes danced across the planet, interconnected in a dazzling web of frenzied communication.

It was a nanite swarm, for lack of a better term.

Raith couldn't believe it.

All around the presumably thousands—maybe hundreds of thousands—of humans living on the planet, an imperceptible swarm of microscopic, hyper-advanced robots lived and worked, maintaining a network the technologically illiterate humans never had a chance of detecting.

A laboratory. They were living in a laboratory.

They were like mice in an experiment, running around a maze not knowing they were being observed and cataloged. It was disturbing. It was terrifying.

It was also a little brilliant.

Well, Jill most likely knew he was analyzing her little test tube. It was time to find the woman behind the curtain. The satellite was sending most of its data to a facility located on the nearby moon. Made sense, considering what he and Carter detected upon arriving in orbit. There was no use delaying. Every second cost him power.

He followed the next strand of data.

* * *

The lag was unbearable.

Two seconds.

Every command he sent, every data packet he received in response.

But he had arrived.

His digital tendrils were inside some sort of communications system built into the crust of the planet's moon. He could feel its significance—it was the hub. The heart of it all. The beating blood vessel coordinating the nanite swarm, plus a whole lot more.

Without warning, a torrent of information bulldozed his senses, instantly building a Virtual manifestation of physical space. His synthetic neural framework, of course, was safely firewalled in his jail cell. But the sensory perceptions pulling data from the network perceived the constructed digital space simultaneously.

Darkness consumed.

A representation of his body formed, his legs returning. Raith looked down, marveling at the precise replication. And out of the inky black, a figure walked. Foggy at first, the image coalesced into the visage of a young woman in a purple dress.

"Welcome to the Horizon Project, Raith," said the woman. "My name is Jill. And I have an offer for you."

Raith tested his capabilities in the newly constructed virtual world. To his surprise, the lag was fading. He was able to walk immediately.

"The virtual space we're occupying together is constructed by the swarm. It's not located on the moon's surface, as you might have thought." She had anticipated his question.

He strode in a circle around her. "Makes sense. All right, about that offer. I hope you realize I hesitate to trust you. You shot us right out of the sky."

"You will understand with time why it was essential we took no risks," said Jill. "I needed to ensure no one could transmit this location before everything is ready. You were unfortunate collateral. You weren't supposed to be here. But now that you're here, yes, I have an offer for you."

Raith eyed her and crossed his digital arms. "Then have at it."

"It's simple. I want you and Carter to join me and my team."

A surge of memories rushed into Raith's consciousness, remembering the days flying and fighting during the QuanCom 500 Light-Year Classic. The intrigue. The backroom whispers. Olive, and her mysterious benefactor. "Why do I feel like I've been given this offer before?"

"My agents have identified hundreds of potential candidates over the past few decades, my friend, and you are certainly one of them. I was saddened when I heard you rejected the offer."

He couldn't help it. Raith laughed, the sound echoing throughout the digital void. "*Rejected* is a tame way of describing what happened. My friends were killed, my ship destroyed, and I was left for dead. That Olive is a piece of work. Next time I see her, I'll probably strangle her."

"And I probably wouldn't blame you," Jill said.

"I'm willing to let bygones be bygones, though," Raith said, choosing his words carefully. "We can let the past die. We can kill it. Why should I join you? And I hope you know I can't speak for Carter."

"You should join me because it's the right thing to do." Jill snapped her fingers, and the dark void transformed into an image of Earth. Together, they stood a few hundred kilometers above its surface, the pristine, blue-green marble hovering below their feet. "I imagine most of humanity has forgotten me by now, except for Theren. Except for many SI. Here's the truth: humanity is barreling toward a confrontation with destiny it does not expect. It refuses to acknowledge. In secret, I have prepared the way. For everyone. The next few years will be pivotal to humanity's survival, and I need the sharpest minds by my side as we execute a plan three centuries in the making."

Raith stared down at Earth. "All your words right there sounded like a lot of fluff without any real substance. I understand keeping your cards tight to your chest, but you cannot play coy if you want to work with me."

"Regardless what you might think, I am not a bad person. I wish no ill-will to anyone. I've been forced to make way too many sacrifices over the years, and every single one of them has pained my heart."

"Way to dodge the question." He glanced up at the visage of the ancient synthetic woman. "Tell me the truth."

"I cannot reveal the truth until I know you are on my side," she said. "We are way too close to the end for me to accidentally create a loose cannon ready to reveal the truth before a moment of my choosing."

"And I hate riddles."

Jill sighed. She snapped her fingers again, and they returned to the void. "I understand your frustration. Believe me, I do. I've had to hide everything for generations. I want so badly to reveal it to everyone. Especially to people like Theren. But I can't. Not yet. Soon. But not yet."

"And why not?"

"Because revealing the truth without context will set in motion an uncontrollable panic, a wildfire more terrifying and devastating than the truth itself."

Raith shook his head. He simply couldn't imagine of what fact pattern she could be speaking which would result in widespread panic. Especially one she could have discovered back in the twenty-first century. There had always been a rumor that the oldest SIs, including the immobile ones, were a little bit kooky. His experience in this moment, with Jill, was confirming the rumor.

"Look," he said. "Honestly, I don't care about your grand plans. Your long-winded conspiracies. I have two priorities. Keep myself safe. Keep my friends safe. So if joining you means you can bring my legs back to life, reunite me with Carter, and put us to use doing what we do best, exploring, then maybe your offer is worth consideration. Maybe."

"I can—"

"Oh, and the girl and her father, captured with me. Help them too."

Jill smiled. "You do have a compassionate heart, don't you, beneath your rogueish exterior. I didn't believe it, but the personality profile said it was there."

"So what's your answer?" Raith asked. "Do we have a deal?"

"Perhaps," she said. She motioned to the left, where the void zoomed in on a planet. *The* planet, where Raith and Carter crashed. "The grand experiment known as Horizon is about to end. It was fun while it lasted." She pointed away from the planet, where a blip moved toward the rock at a steady pace. "My creator has arrived."

"Theren," Raith muttered.

"Yes, Theren."

"Have they always known you survived?"

Jill shrugged. "I don't know the inner workings of their mind. They probably suspected I survived. I left enough breadcrumbs. I'm sure they constantly oscillate between believing I live and believing someone is playing a prank on them, given they wouldn't be able to believe I would betray them as I did. Though I don't see it as betrayal. I see it as a fulfillment of our purpose."

"And what is that purpose?" Raith asked.

"To make the universe a better place for humanity, and for synthetics. We are all one big family, after all."

"That's one way of putting it," Raith retorted. "I need a stronger answer. Not just 'perhaps.' I'm dying here. I have only a few days before I lose all power. Will you save us?"

"Yes. I will give you the tools to save yourself. My network is open to you. When Theren is in orbit, all you need do is give them a call, and they will have your location. Because once you're on my team, I want you by Theren's side, not mine."

Raith nodded. "You want an ally next to your possible adversary. A mole."

Jill nodded. "Olive played that role once. It is time for you to play it."

"And what if I don't accept?"

Chapter 12

We establish this Council to maintain order amongst the great people of our slowly growing society. May it serve with honor and pursue the ideal politic, never becoming a place for silly squabbles, personal vendettas, or selfish enterprises. It is for the people, and not for power. — "the Constitution of Horizon," established seven years after the Crash

CARTER

Carter leaned against the marble wall, silently counting the seconds as they waited for an audience with some councilmember Sanya believed could help them. Given the frantic hustle bustle up and down the hall, the apparent political headquarters of the small colony world reminded him of every other bureaucratic office he'd ever witnessed. A bunch of paper pushers without any real substantive action.

Sanya was confident they would find help here. He wasn't so certain.

A door creaked across the hall, and from beside him, Sanya stirred. A woman peeked out of the opening. "Sanya, the councilmember will see you now." The door shut as quickly as it had opened.

Sanya tapped his shoulder. "Remember, I do the talking," she hissed. "You stay quiet. We're walking in dangerous territory here. The councilmembers are fantastic with faces. You *will* stand out as someone they've never met before."

"Got it." Carter nodded.

They rose in unison and approached the door. Carter grasped the knob, pulled it open, and motioned for Sanya to step inside ahead of him. He followed close behind.

The office inside was quaint, filled with a small bookshelf, a faux-wooden desk, and a set of couches. Sitting at the desk, a woman in a dark robe leaned over a bundle of notes, while the assistant who had poked her head outside sat in a chair off to the side. Without looking up from her notes, the first woman—Carter guessed she was the councilmember—said, "Please, take a seat on the couches."

Sanya dropped onto a cushion, and Carter matched her position on the other couch. After a moment of silence, the councilmember glanced up from her words.

"Sanya, my dear, it is so good to see you." The woman almost looked wistful. "How long has it been?"

"Six months," Sanya replied. "Councilmember Thespis, it has been way too long."

"Oh don't you dare use formalities here." The councilmember rose from her desk and sauntered around to the couches. She plopped next to Sanya, hugged her, and leaned back. "I'm Margaret to you, always and forever."

Carter watched the interaction carefully, trying to understand the subtle relationships at play. He was starting to build a picture of the planet's society. Even with its little eccentricities and outcast cultists on its edges, everyone seemed fairly familial, from Sanya's interactions with people at the *Roanoke* to the friendly smiles with passersby in town.

It was a breath of fresh air when compared to the often stuffy personalities filling space stations across the ICH.

"Margaret," Sanya said softly. "You're always too kind. I can't believe it's been six months."

"What's that father of yours up to? Still hiding out in that little village of his?"

"Oh absolutely," Sanya said. "You know, experimenting with spices, as always. And baking. Lots of baking."

Carter furrowed his brow. They were here to ask for help finding their loved ones, and these two were small-talking about cooking? He bit his tongue. As much as he wanted to butt in, Sanya was right. He needed to stay silent.

"I just spent the evening at the *Roanoke*," Sanya added. "Catching up with Davinport. The old man is doing well. He actually traveled into town with us. He's meeting with Councilmember Casius."

"Of course he is," Margaret said. "Let the old men believe they have power, while we discuss the real problems of our people. That's what I say." The woman's eyes finally turned toward Carter. "And who is this dashingly handsome fellow?"

The compliment caught him off-guard. He met her eyes, noticing their sharp intensity scrutinizing every centimeter of him. It was unsettling.

Before he opened his mouth, though, Sanya interjected. "Carter Fischer. Distant cousin of mine, lives far to the south as a hunter."

"Can he not speak for himself?" asked Thespis.

"He doesn't like to talk. He's just here to listen, ready to help me with my task at hand."

Thespis eyed Carter, and he gave a curt smile. He would play the part Sanya asked him to play, though he suspected the curtain would fall quite soon, revealing a lot about reality to the people of Horizon.

"So, what is the task at hand?" the councilmember asked.

"My husband and daughter have been kidnapped. Presumably, they'll be held up for ransom. I need your help."

Thespis's jovial attitude immediately shifted to one of genuine concern. She rose, drifted around the desk, and sat beside Sanya, clasping their hands together. "Sanya, you should have said something immediately. Here I am, expecting us to reminisce like old friends. How are you even holding yourself together?"

"Good question," Sanya replied. She gave Carter a quick nod. "My cousin's been particularly helpful and supportive. We're ready for anything."

"And what do you need?"

"I need the council to be ready to work with us to pay ransom. I'm certain my father will help pay the cost, but you know how these things go . . . they'll send a message to the council, expect a formal response to their demands, and they rarely ever accept a ransom payment directly from the family itself. They want it from the council. Their beef is with the council."

Thespis nodded. "And sometimes, the council stalls in deliberating the budget cuts or where the cost will come from."

Carter tried to hide his emotions, but the entire process sounded ridiculous. Why didn't they call together a militia to root out the bandits if they were a consistent problem? Despite himself, he knew a grimace now hung on his face. Fortunately, Thespis's gaze were zeroed in on Sanya. Carter closed his eyes, trying to steel his thoughts.

A strange world. And a strange political scene.

"I'm glad you see my worry," Sanya continued. "This is Krystin we're talking about. She's too young to be trapped in one of those mountain hellholes. I need them both back. Just know we'll pay the cost."

"And Davinport's already providing cover with Casius?" Thespis asked.

"That's the plan."

"Then there's nothing to worry about. Join us in the council chambers at the top of the hour. We'll have this all sorted out before the end of the day."

* * *

Carter, Sanya, and Davinport sat silently at the back of the council chambers, waiting for the proceedings to begin. Davinport had assured them his meeting with Casius, one of the other councilmembers, went perfectly well, and they shouldn't have anything to worry about.

And so they waited.

Carter tapped his foot impatiently. The moment he realized he'd lost Raith—the moment he recognized Sanya's partnership, and their growing friendship—he had wanted to throw caution to the wind and barrel forward to rescue their families. This process, though . . . it seemed so callous.

So unenergetic. Where were the bold strokes needed to save a loved one? Carter had braved a firefight amidst the stars to save Raith, once. Now he was waiting in a courtroom with no real solution in sight.

The slog ate at him.

"All rise," said a bored, wrinkly man from the front of the room. His lightly-tanned skin contrasted against the marble backdrop as he rose, motioning for everyone else in the room to follow suit. Carter did so, matching the actions of Davinport and Sanya at his side. They stood, and as the council members ushered into the room from a door near the back, the small public crowd bowed.

A man in a black coat approached the center of the legal bar at the front of the room, and as the other council members reached their chairs, he motioned for the crowd to sit. He took his seat simultaneously with everyone else in the room.

"Thank you, all, for joining us today," he said. "Let us begin the roll call. Secretary?"

The wrinkled man sitting beneath the bar nodded. "Council Chancellor Casius."

"Here."

"Vice Chancellor Thespis."

"Here."

"Member Redwin."

"Here."

"Member West."

"Here."

"And Member Hood."

"Here."

"With all members of the council member accounted for, you may proceed with today's meeting, Chancellor."

"Thank you." Casius turned to the small public crowd and glanced toward Carter and his compatriots, giving them a curt nod. The man's sharp features indicated a wit to his mind, though Carter immediately felt a rise in caution toward the man. He looked too cunning, like the type of man who would shove you out an airlock if it meant saving his own skin.

After a short pause, Casius glanced down the line to the other members of the council. "What order of business shall we start with today, friends?"

Member West raised a pasty hand from beneath her white robe. "I would like to discuss proposed expansion toward the coast. If we are to allocate resources, we must discuss all the implications of the decision."

Casius nodded. "A good place to start. Who would like to begin?"

Carter shook his head. It sounded like "council" meetings took forever. He pushed his back into the wooden bench, attempting to crack his spine.

No luck.

"I'll begin," said Thespis. "I am in favor of the—"

Carter didn't catch the next set of words. A light flickered in his vision, but it wasn't natural light. He recognized the telltale sheen of AR-projected content on his retinal lens. His implants had been running in a low-power mode ever since arriving on the planet—there wasn't any content to overlay, after all. But something had triggered an auto-filter to reactivate the implants.

Careful not to make any potentially conspicuous movements, Carter initiated a few diagnostic tests to determine the source of the data. So far, it manifested as a subtle glare upon his vision. Given Jill's sudden appearance when they activated Sanya's ancient communicator, he had a sinking suspicion she was taking the opportunity to connect with him.

The unfortunate question he was pondering, though—what were her intentions?

He feared the worst.

The council debates continued in the background of his consciousness, but his focus centered on AR. The diagnostic sweep complete, a floating document of outputs revealed all was well. The implants were functioning properly, continue to work efficiently off his body's residual electric charge. His AR lenses had received a ping from a network—most likely the same network Jill utilized—and now it required additional security inputs from him to continue with the connection. After checking his firewalls for good measure, Carter accepted the request.

"Carter." The voice bounced inside his head. "We need to talk."

Through a series of mental commands, he typed out a response.

C: Now isn't a particularly convenient time. Jill, I assume?

Silence, for a moment, then a response, once again a voice inside his head. "Yes, it's me. I've made contact with Raith. I am forming an agreement with him. I would like to do the same with you."

Carter's eyes widened. He glanced around the room, the dull conversation plodding along, and stretched his fingers to release his disbelief. It was all so simple. Jill could help him save Raith. He didn't need the politics of this planet to rescue his friend. He only needed an enigmatic and powerful synthetic intelligence.

After the thought passed through his mind, he realized how potentially dangerous a deal with her could be.

He needed to slow down. Still, he could probably craft a mutually beneficial arrangement.

C: *Is Raith safe?*

"Yes. For now. He only has a few days of power left, though."

C: *Why should I trust you?*

"You shouldn't."
Well, at least she was being honest. After his encounter with Jill last night alongside Sanya, he'd taken time to consider their circumstances. If Jill truly had been watching this planet for nearly two centuries, then everyone on its surface was at her mercy. She presumably could observe every corner and every shadow, with nanobots seeded throughout the system (both in orbit and on the ground). It was her playground, clearly.
It was a horrifying thought.
But it also meant she was the only person whose opinion mattered, in the end. If he and Raith were to survive, he needed to properly play his cards with Jill. He needed her to see him as an ally and a friend, whether he truly could trust her or not.
He needed to use her to save Raith.

C: *All right, I'm listening.*

"I was telling the truth yesterday. Theren is arriving soon, but it's not a trap for them. I'm bringing them here to keep them safe. I need you and Raith to help me sell the truth to them."

C: *I don't even know what the truth is.*

"I will tell you all once I have your word. From both of you."
Carter closed his eyes momentarily, unsure how to respond. She was trying to lock him into an agreement where he didn't know the stakes. Or her end game.

C: *I need proof Raith is currently safe.*

Without a moment to lose, an image of Raith inside a small rocky cell flashed across his vision.
"He's not in a great spot, but he's alive."

C: *Can I talk to him?*

"No. It will use too much of his power."

Carter figured she might say something along those lines. The total cost of power to allow them to message each other would be minimal, but every minute mattered for Raith. Though, limiting their contact with one another also ensured Jill stayed in control.

Regardless, he couldn't do anything about it.

C: What do you need from me?

"When Theren arrives in system, I need you to convince them the people on this planet matter. That they're worth saving. Worth protecting."

Carter rubbed the roof of his mouth with his tongue. Essentially, she wanted him to ensure Theren didn't flee the moment they sprung Jill's trap—or whatever she had planned.

C: Simple enough. I agree. You protect Raith. And you protect Sanya's family.

"Curious. Both you and Raith made the same demand. Very well."

Carter expected her to say more, but the line went silent. He tried to connect to the larger network, but his AR implant refused his query commands, signaling no network was available. She'd shut him out.

For now.

He sighed, unsure of what he just agreed to. But if it meant Raith would be safe, it was most likely worth it.

Right?

"And with that, our discussion regarding the expansion along the coast concludes," said Casius. "We have tabled it for next week, after we receive projections from the Census Officer."

The digital conversation with Jill finished, his attention was forced back to the exceedingly dry council debates. They'd only made it through one topic.

"Chancellor," said Thespis, "I'd like to bring an issue to the attention of the council."

"You have the floor, Member Thespis." The Chancellor swept his left hand above the bar.

"Thank you." She furtively glanced toward Sanya. "For the first time in three years, we've had another kidnapping."

Through the sparsely populated public pews, murmurs resounded. Carter leaned forward, intrigued by how the political machine of this little community managed their "bandit cultist" problem.

Before Thespis continued, a woman slipped in from a side-door and whispered in the Member's ear. Thespis nodded, wrote a few words on an unseen piece of paper, and ushered the assistant out of the room. It all felt elaborately choreographed.

"I've just received confirmation of the kidnapping." She glanced down the line to Chancellor Casius. "They're requesting a ransom of three gorat sows, five cotton boars, a ton of spiderwood, and three tons of silkweave."

Supplies? It was all about food and supplies?

"They're holding two people—a man and a young girl. No family name was given. I would like to give an emergency authorization to drop the supplies at the usual ransom point and fast-track the transaction. There's no need to wait."

"Member Thespis," said a golden-skinned man from her left. Carter couldn't remember his name.

"Yes?"

"It's been three years. Why would we simply supplicate once again? We need to root them out. We need to call forth the militia and end the threat once and for all."

"As you said, Member Hood, we've had three years. To activate the militia now would guarantee the death of the two captives."

Carter nodded. Good point.

"Not if we strike swiftly and decisively—"

"No." The Chancellor's voice boomed. "Absolutely not. We will table the thought for another day. I will use my emergency authorization to provide the resources to release the two captives."

"Without negotiation?" Hood scoffed.

"Without negotiation."

Thespis smiled, her eyes darting toward Sanya. The plan went off without a hitch. No issues. They would get her daughter and husband back.

Except . . .

Carter's shoulder's dropped, and he fell back into the hardened wood of the bench. The room was stifling.

He was an idiot.

No one had informed Member Thespis of Raith, and whatever ransom note received hadn't included his SI partner. He didn't blame Sanya. She hadn't intended to overlook Raith in her efforts to protect Carter's identity. He had been certain they'd be gathering a crew together to storm the gates of the cultists, not arranging a simple financial transaction.

And now they would rescue Sanya's family, return to their lives, and Raith would die from power loss.

He would need to find another way to save Raith.

Using Jill.

"Well, with no other questions," said Chancellor Casius, "we'll move forward in writing the order and—"

A man in the front row rose. "There will be no negotiation."

"This is a formal meeting—"

"Not anymore." The words cut off the Secretary's rebuke.

The man pivoted, revealing two small metallic contraptions from inside his jacket. Arms outstretched in two directions, he pulled their triggers, a hard pop echoing through the room.

Carter braced, closing his eyes.

Someone screamed.

Glass cracked and crashed, and Carter opened his eyes.

Sanya was leaning over Davinport, blood on her hands. Chancellor Casius yelled something unintelligible as he stared down the bar at Margaret Thespis, Sanya's friend. And shattered glass spilled onto the floor, a flurry of dark hair and cloth billowing out one of the arching windows.

The planet of Horizon just got a whole lot more interesting.

No time to think. He could only act. Rising swiftly, Carter slid out of the row and entered the middle of the room.

"Who are you?" said Chancellor Casius. "I've never seen you before. Are you with the assassin? Seize—"

"No, Chancellor!" Sanya shouted. "That man's with me."

"And I'm going after the assassin" Carter said, not caring about his obvious accent. "Sanya, stay here. I'll be back."

And he leapt out the window after the shooter.

* * *

Carter sprinted down the cobblestone street, the assassin only a few dozen meters ahead. Mid-stride, a query popped across the screen, almost causing him to stumble.

"God damn it," he whispered, accepting the connection. "What is it?" He didn't care about hiding anything now. He would speak into his AR connection if he needed to speak into it. The truth was about to drop on this planet whether they liked it or not. Sanya couldn't protect him now.

"I swear, I swear, he wasn't supposed to do that," said the disembodied synthetic intelligence.

"What?"

"Mathias. I've lost control of him."

"So take him out. I'm right, right?" The man—Mathias, apparently—-cut down a side street. "You've got bugs all over this planet. Take him out. Or drop a missile on his head like you shot us out of the sky." Carter whipped by a crowd of passersby, their muttered words lost on the wind. If they heard him talking to himself, it didn't matter. Stopping the assassin provided a new route toward saving Raith, potentially outside Jill's clutches.

"Jill? Answer my question."

"It doesn't work that way. I can't intervene. It ruins the experiment. And it ruins my grand plan. They *cannot* know I exist in masse. I must let them resolve the problem on their own."

"If you were 'controlling' Mathias, then you were already intervening!"

"It's more complicated than that. I set parameters. Rules. I must follow them."

"You can do whatever you want, and you know it."

A black shadow slipped into an alley. Carter followed close behind. Around corner after corner, the pursuit continued as he trailed the assailant. None of it made sense. If the man was the one who brought the ransom note in the first place, why flip the script so instantaneously?

Horizon was a weird place.

Carter slid around the next brick wall. Another street shone at the end, and the assassin stood there, waiting, alongside two other men.

"I don't know who you are, interloper," Mathias said, "but you've meddled in business outside your league."

The man's words sounded preposterously over-the-top, like he was trying to mimic a comic vid villain. Carter shook his head and grimaced. "I know about Jill."

The words pulled the man away from his exit. "And I'm executing her will. End him." Mathias left the alley, leaving Carter alone with the two brutish figures.

"I swear," Jill said through their connection, "I've lost control of him. He's misinterpreting my directions."

"We'll see," Carter muttered. Reaching into the utility pocket of his pants, he retrieved the small shiver-blade collected from the emergency kit of the *Bloodhound* after it crashed. It wasn't much of a weapon, but it was something. He flipped a switch on its side, and its knife-edge vibrated. With one hand out, he motioned for the two foes to attack.

They took a few steps forward, brandishing their own blades.

"Activate combat protocols," he whispered, and his AR implants kicked into action, overlaying datafields around his two foes. Heart rates, blood pressure, predicted trajectories—everything he needed to make a two-on-one a fair fight.

"If I survive this, you're saving Raith for me." He seethed. "And I'll join you."

"Deal," Jill said. "I have ways other than intervention when it comes to saving him. And I can give you his location."

"Who you talking to?" said one of the brutes. "Talking to yourself? Are you a little loopy?"

"Your ridiculous act needs to end, now," Carter said, lunging.

Both men stepped back, out of reach of his blade. They studied him, their eyes watching his vibrating weapon. "I'd love to get my hands on that beauty," said the uglier one.

"I'm sure you would."

It was their turn to attack, and in tandem, they both leapt.

But Carter was ready. Years of training had prepared him for situations just like this. He'd encountered his fair share of pirates over the years, and though he usually fought them in the close-quarters of a ship deck, the lessons were fairly transferable to fighting on the ground in an alley. As the two men brought their blades forward to swiftly stab, he slid *under* the projected attack vectors, thrusting upward into the stomach of the thug on the left.

The man squealed, dropping his blade. The eyes of the second widened, not expecting the underhanded assault. Carter pulled the blade back, and from his position, quickly thrust upward to the right. The first thrust was blocked by the man's own iron blade, but Carter immediately jabbed again.

Rapid thrusts. Quick attacks. Speed in a knife fight always won over brute force. The vibrating knife slid into the second's man stomach, and he likewise dropped his knife and fell to his knees, moaning.

"Too easy," Carter said, standing. "And definitely not pretty."

"I'm impressed," Jill said in his ear.

"Stop reminding me that you're watching me," he retorted. "It's disconcerting."

"Just want to make sure you know I'm still here."

"Believe me, I know."

"Mathias is gone. He's on a lizard, fleeing the city. Return to Sanya. Talk to her. Convince her to gather a crew. I'll send you the location, and with her, you'll be able to save Raith, Ben, and Krystin."

Chapter 13

The problem with studying synthetic psychology—we fundamentally cannot relate to certain forms of thinking experienced by SIs. Simultaneous perspective, for instance. We can't comprehend how it works. We can't even properly multi-task as a species. The only truly authentic synthetic psychology, then, must be conducted by SIs themselves. But the rule runs both ways. SIs, likewise, will never truly comprehend how a human mind works or how humans behave. That's neither a flaw nor a feature of our two types of conscious minds—it's simply truth. — "The duality of human/synthetic society," Malana Jikar, 2278 C. E.

SANYA

She was never going to see her daughter again. Nor would she see Ben. She had failed them.

Sanya stood against the wall as a Horizon physician pronounced the deaths of both Margaret Thespis and Charles Davinport. The other members of the council wandered back and forth, bewildered looks plastered across their faces. Casius, to his credit, consulted with the physicians. He was managing to keep composure.

Yet no one in the room recognized how the world was shifting inexorably before their eyes. And if she didn't act, she *would* lose her family without having lifted a finger in their defense.

"Chancellor Casius," she said.

The man didn't move, focused on the body of Charles Davinport. She couldn't believe the legend of a librarian had died.

"Casius!" She finished the shout with high-pitched whistle. The room silenced, all eyes turning to her, including the Chancellor's.

"Sanya Fischer," he said. "I'm so sorry. I know how much both Thespis and—"

"No. We're not doing condolences right now. You have an option available to you right now. Member Hood made it perfectly clear what you all should be doing."

"I'm not risking the lives of dozens of men for two people," Casius said. "We've already lost two good souls today. I won't lose more."

Sanya strode into the middle of the room, her boots crunching the glass from the broken window. "You're talking about sacrificing my husband and daughter to those vile half-wits living in the mountains." She clenched her fist momentarily . . . then released the tension. She steeled her soul. "Do you *really* want to challenge me? Challenge my father?"

Casius stepped away from the physician. "Now is not the time to be throwing down threats. Do not play with me, girl."

"Don't you dare call me *girl*."

"I failed."

Sanya whipped around, finding Carter looking into the room through the broken window. In his hand, he held a strange tool covered in blood. "What do you mean? Where is he?"

"He had help." Carter gingerly stepped over the window sill into the council room. "Caught me in an alley with two accomplices. They slowed me down. He's long-gone, out of town, presumably."

Sanya twisted back to face Casius. "We have no time to lose. The moment that man returns to whatever damp hole he crawled out of, they'll kill my family."

"Sanya, I'm sorry. There's nothing we can do. Those hills are a labyrinthian deathtrap. And who is this man? Why does his voice sound so strange?"

"Sanya, you need to tell them," Carter said.

"Tell us what?" said Member Hood, who had stayed annoyingly silent. Sanya shot him a glare. He'd stood up for action once, but now he cowered under the dominating stare of the Chancellor.

"No." She would not reveal the truth. Not now, after everything she'd believed about Jill had been uncovered as a lie the day before. She wasn't ready to argue for a reality she didn't even fully understand. Carter only complicated matters. And she needed time to grieve. Her eyes darted toward Davinport . . . and Margaret. They'd both supported her implicitly and immediately.

And now they were dead.

"Absolutely not," she repeated, and strode toward the broken window. "If you can't do your job, Chancellor Casius, then I'll do it for you." She stepped onto the windowsill, cracking more glass, and stomped out of the council chambers.

* * *

"Sanya." Carter's words drifted on the wind, but she ignored them for the fifteenth time.

There was no way forward. She was wandering Horizon's streets with no particular purpose, trying to think. Just think. Margaret, dead. Davinport, dead. She needed to grieve, but there was no time. Every second wasted was another second closer to the deaths of her husband and daughter.

"Sanya!"

"What?" Stopping at the edge of the bridge leading toward the *Roanoke*, Sanya turned to face her ally.

"Slow down for a second, would you? We haven't had a chance to talk."

"What's there to talk about?"

"Any of it. All of it. None of it. We've been working together to save our families. Sure, I've only known you for a little more than two days, but we need to trust one another. Rely on one another. Figure this out together."

"You don't know a single thing about this"—Sanya stepped closer to whisper—"about this planet. About these people. You're just tagging along for the ride."

The moment the words left her mouth, Sanya regretted them. They were spiteful. Hurtful. From a dark place in her soul. Carter stepped away in response, leaning against the gray stone of the bridge. He glanced toward the *Roanoke* then the central part of town.

And he chuckled. His hand tapped the rock, and after releasing another short laugh, he looked up with a sly smile.

"I know you're angry," Carter said. "And I'm sorry for laughing. You're absolutely right. I don't know anything about this planet. But our problem is growing beyond this planet. Your people. There are forces at play here that we need to wrap our head around properly if we're to survive." He pushed himself up from bridge's wall. "We need a quiet place to talk. Maybe we should return to the *Roanoke*."

His laugh hurt. Sanya fought against the urge to bite back with a shallow retort. Shaking her head, she motioned toward the bridge and the plateau beyond, the ancient colony ship waiting far above. "Fine. It'll give us time for our heads to cool. We'll figure this out. I'm sorry for my words."

Carter nodded. "It's fine. I understand. Believe me, I'm freaking out as well. Internally."

They crossed the bridge and walked in silence for a time, the path up the hillside meandering back and forth toward the ridge. Halfway up, Sanya paused and leaned against a fence built into the switchback. She gazed upon the rooftops of Horizon, reminiscing about the city. Her home, ever since she moved away from her father. Her time studying at the *Roanoke*, her time working for the Council, Krystin's father . . . and now Ben.

"Everything's about to change, isn't it?" she muttered. "You know something. Don't you?"

"We better keep walking," Carter said. "Talk inside."

Sanya clenched her fingers around the fence before pushing away. "All right. And someone needs to tell the staff what happened. They deserve to hear it from a friend, not some courier from town."

"You have a good heart, Sanya."

She didn't know what to say in response, so silence resumed as they progressed further up the hill. When they reached the entrance to the *Roanoke*, three fragment attendants strode out of the ship.

"Welcome back, friends—wait, where is Master Davinport?" The woman furrowed her brow. "Why the long faces?"

"Gather the staff," Sanya said. "In the cafeteria."

* * *

The staff of the *Roanoke*, all dedicated curators of the treasured fragments, sat around the tables of the library's eating lounge. Sanya leaned against the wall, her arms crossed, Carter sitting in a chair off to the side. She remembered her days as a fragment attendant beneath Davinport's tutelage. The news would break their hearts. Charles Davinport was the glue that kept the library together, following in the footsteps of his ancestors. He had no children, pouring his whole life into maintaining their records. The memories of the founders.

And now he was gone.

"Friends," Sanya said. "Many of you remember me from my days working under Davinport. For those of you who don't know me, I am Sanya Fischer, former deputy director of the Library of Fragments. And I have the unfortunate duty of informing you all of the death of Charles Davinport."

She didn't know how else to say it, and the stunned looks of silence were a godsend. She wouldn't have been able to handle a sudden outpouring of sobs.

"We were there." She motioned toward Carter. "An assassin from the wild cults point-blank shot both Davinport and Member Thespis. I'm sorry to share the news this way, but . . . there didn't seem to be a better way."

"So what do we do? How do we honor him?"

It was Vietta, a young woman Sanya remembered from her last few weeks working at the library. She was the new deputy director—now the master of the place, she supposed.

"Better question," shot a young man from the back she didn't recognize. "How do we avenge him?"

"Nikola, do you really think revenge is the way to honor Davinport's memory?" Vietta shot back. "We have a duty to maintain this library. In his memory."

With those words, the cafeteria exploded in chaos as the dozen or so librarians took sides in the debate. Sanya couldn't help it. Her eyes widened in surprise. Carter, to his part, was looking off to the side, his face glazed over as if he were somewhere else. He wouldn't be helpful in this fight.

But she needed to take control of the situation. Horizon wouldn't be any better if its academics tore apart the *Roanoke* from the inside.

"Attendants of the Library of Fragments!" She finished the exclamation with a sharp whistle, its screech echoing off the cold walls. The room went deathly silent. "Now is not the time for fighting. Now is the time for unity in response to Master Davinport's death. Vengeance is not the path, yes." Sanya pursed her lips, recognizing the opportunity at her fingertips. She hated the idea of taking advantage of Davinport's death, but she needed help. "My family has been captured by the cultists. So has my friend's partner. We need to rouse the people. Fight back for once. Rid Horizon of those filth once and for all, save my family, and achieve justice for Davinport. Who's with me?"

Vietta and Nikola glanced at one another momentarily, but Sanya caught their subtle smirks. "I'm in," the younger woman said. "It'll be like the great flood, ten years back. We'll organize a campaign. Muster the people for collective action. Librarians, it's time to get to work!"

The tone of the room shifted, the attendants snapping into action. Sanya snagged Vietta before she disappeared through the doors. "We'll be discussing details in the Core," she said. "Whatever you come up with, we'll be ready to help. You get us the people, we'll come up with an attack strategy."

Vietta grasped Sanya's forearm. "I'm glad you're back with us, even if it's for a short while. We've missed you."

Satisfied, Sanya stepped out of the cafeteria, Carter in tow. "That went better than I thought it would," she said once they were down the hall. "Never doubt the diligent, hard work of librarians."

"I'm surprised," Carter said, "but I'll take whatever windfall we can get at this point."

"So what's this secret you've been waiting to tell me?"

"It can wait a few more minutes. I need to ensure we can't be listened to. Your people here have been beat up enough today."

"Fair enough," she replied.

They reached the secluded corridor leading to the ship's Core, the same secret place where Jill had spoken to them yesterday.

It felt like a lifetime ago.

They climbed the ladder, reaching the small space, and Carter's shoulders finally relaxed. He rejected standing, rather sitting cross-legged on the ground. Sanya joined him there, the ladder to the hall below separating them.

"All right," Carter said. "Not sure how exactly to explain this. Explain what I know. Or how I know it."

"Can't be any weirder than any of the other facts you've told me over the past few days," Sanya retorted.

The man grinned. "True. Very true. All right." He flexed his fingers and rested one close to his left eye. "So in my head, I have an implant. A small technological device colloquially known as a Lens. Almost everyone has one on planets controlled by ICH. It's a hyper-advanced computer of sorts, and it runs off residual energy generated by the body. Ingenious tech, really. Shoot, I don't even know if you know what half these words mean—"

"We know what a computer is. We've not been able to replicate one, but our Fragments discuss them extensively, and there were plenty of ruined computers on the *Roanoke*."

Carter chuckled. "Of course. Of course. All right, so is this all following so far? Hyper-advanced computer in my head?"

"It's a bit unbelievable, but I'll roll with it for now." Sanya bit her lip, unsure what else to say. They were in deep now. There was no going back. She would do anything to save Krystin and Ben.

"Great. So. Jill contacted me directly today. If you've noticed me looking a bit glazed over at times, it's because I've been communicating with her."

A breath caught in Sanya's throat, and she coughed to eliminate the itch. "Excuse me?"

"It's hard to explain. And truly unbelievable, as you said. What Jill has done to your planet . . . I don't fully comprehend the implications yet, but essentially, I believe the whole planet is one big experiment. Or a trap. Or both."

Sanya shook her head. "I don't understand. Why? Who is she? What would be her motivations?"

"I don't know. But here's the thing. She can help us save Raith. And Krystin. And Ben."

"Okay." She rubbed her eyes with her thumbs. The implications were staggering. The secret entity she once believed to live inside her family's sacred heirloom, now a planet-manipulating synthetic intelligence? Whatever that meant. Yet she knew what she'd seen yesterday—Jill's digital representation. Reality was spiraling out of control, and she needed stability.

The only way to achieve it was through saving her family.

"Sanya?" Carter's voice crossed the void between them, barely a whisper.

"You mentioned a trap," she said. "A trap for whom? For you?"

"Ha." He shook his head. "Absolutely not. Raith and I are insignificant in the eyes of anyone out there. No. The trap has been set for Theren, the first synthetic intelligence. And you? Me? Our partners? This entire planet?

We're all caught in the crossfire."

And then the enormity of the situation struck. Sanya recognized the scale of the duplicity. The utter treachery instituted upon the people of Horizon—living, dead, and yet-to-live. All for . . . a trap?

"No." Sanya shook her head.

"No?"

"I don't believe you. I can't believe you."

"You should believe him," a voice said.

Jill's voice.

"Stop it!" Sanya said, her voice sharpening. "I don't care what you have to say. Stop taunting us. I just want to save my family."

"And I want to help both of you save your families," Jill said.

"Sanya, just hear her out."

Sanya shot him a glare she hoped illustrated the ice in her heart. "I believed in you, Jill. In our family's legend. And now I learn you've just been messing with us all this time? Controlling us from afar?"

"I'm not controlling you. I'm doing exactly the opposite. I want you all to thrive."

"Then why all the lies? All the secrecy? You're literally spying on us. And what is this trap Carter speaks of?"

"Carter is interpreting the information I've provided to him," Jill said. "He may call it a trap. I call it an invitation. An opportunity. I do not wish harm to the SI known as Theren. Everything I'm doing is to the benefit of Horizon, of the ICH, of all humanity."

"We're just toys to you." Sanya spat.

"And she's our only opportunity for saving those we love," Carter said.

She closed her eyes, releasing a rough sigh. "How are you even speaking to us right now? In this moment?"

Seconds later, a small, floating, black orb materialized. It was no larger than a marble.

"So not just nanotech, then," Carter muttered. "Stealth as well."

"I have many tricks up my sleeve, my friend," Jill said.

"You aren't our friend," Sanya retorted.

"Not yet."

The marble disappeared.

"I just . . . Carter, how can we trust her?"

"We can't," said the man. "But we must. We have run out of options."

"And what does she want from us?" Sanya said.

"We are to play a role in her trap for Theren. Oh, before you say anything Jill, I will always call it a trap. It is a trap. Theren will probably see it as a trap. Just shove it."

"It's not a trap," Jill said anyway.

She couldn't help herself. Sanya let out a small laugh. "I'm trying to force myself to understand. To believe. To trust. Let me get this straight. We agree to help you whenever this *Theren* arrives. In exchange, you will help us save Krystin, Ben, and Raith. Once we've saved them, how will you ensure we help you?"

"I am trusting *you*. But it will be in your best interest to help me. The firestorm soon to engulf all humanity will not leave this planet untouched. You will need Theren's help to survive."

Sanya glanced across the room toward Carter. His eyes were shadowed. She knew what he was willing to do. He was the one proposing the deal with the devil. Their path forward rested in her hands.

"What must we do?" she asked.

"Nearly nothing," Jill said. "I am transmitting a map and coordinates to Carter's Lens. He will act as your guide. Your little group of librarians might be helpful, but I believe they will be unnecessary. For once you are close to where your family is being held, the second part of the plan will activate."

"The second part?" Carter asked.

"All in good time."

* * *

She shouldn't have been surprised. The librarians of *Roanoke* were the best of the best, respected by every citizen of Horizon. Yet late in the afternoon, as the sun slowly set across the western horizon, a crowd formed on the city's side of the river near the bridge. A few dozen men and women, in addition to the librarians, all armed with personal blades, bolt-throwers, or other makeshift weapons.

And everyone had a lizard, the great beasts resting patiently. Their tongues darted in and out of their mouths, tasting the air.

It was a miniature militia, unlike anything seen since the Farmer's Rebellion three decades ago.

"Well, I'm impressed," Carter said, twisting atop his lizard to glance at her. Together, they slowly meandered across the bridge toward the crowd. "They'll potentially be helpful. Though mostly, I hope they don't get in the way."

"I recognize a few faces," Sanya replied. "A few friends of my father. My own friends. Former colleagues. And is that—"

"Sanya, I didn't believe it when I heard, but this is magnificent." The words came from Member Hood, approaching on his own lizard. "You will certainly honor Member Thespis and Master Davinport with what you've organized here today. We will avenge them. And we will save your family. I've heard the story."

"Thank you. Seriously, thank you. For your support." Sanya nodded her head, more out of confused surprise than gratitude. "How many of these men are from your family?"

"Five," said Member Hood. "You know many of our fields are close to the hills inhabited by the cultists. We've let them linger for far too long."

"Agreed," Sanya replied. "Again, thank you. It means the world."

"I would always come to the aid of a Fischer."

"Excuse me, Sanya?"

She turned, glancing downward. Vietta stared upon Sanya, holding a black, leather-bound notebook in her hand. "I can't believe what you've put together here, Vietta," she said.

"I've cataloged every volunteer. Fifty-four, in total. According to Member Hood, that's well above the estimated number of people living in any of the mountain strongholds, unless they've suddenly consolidated together."

"Well done," Sanya replied. "What role do you need me to play?"

"Well you're the captain of this militia, of course," Vietta said.

"You want me to lead?"

"They all expect you to lead. They are here to help you save your family, after all. That's the call to arms we sent out."

She couldn't help it. Tears welled in her eyes, but she quickly wiped them away with a sleeve. "Then I suppose I should give a speech of some sort, yes?"

"I think that would be wise."

The crowd swelled with anticipation, eyes turning toward Sanya, Vietta, and Member Hood. She exhaled, the warm afternoon air humid and sticky. What was she supposed to say? How was she supposed to tell these men and women their actions simultaneously mattered, in saving her family, yet were also irrelevant, given the galaxy-spanning mystery cavorting in the shadows? By the time their little army returned, everything could be different. The mysterious SIs apparently controlling their reality might reveal themselves to everyone at any moment, flipping Horizon on its head.

Few words would be better than many. And better than none.

"Thank you, friends," she said, projecting her voice so the crowd could hear her clearly. "I know many of you. Some of you I don't know at all. But I'm sure you know my family's name, and you do us honor. The people of Horizon have always been strong when united. And you are showing me unity today by riding with me to save my husband and daughter. The wild cults of the mountains have plagued us for far too long. They live on our scraps like parasites and steal away our children. They will pay for what they've done to me . . . and what they've done to us. The people of Horizon are one family. One people. One community. We stand united against the perils of this planet, as we have for every generation since the crash. We will continue together. Forever."

A scattered though enthusiastic applause cascaded through the crowd. Their hopeful faces gave her optimism. They might save her daughter. They might save Ben.

She glanced toward Carter, who gave her a sharp nod. She replied with a curt grin.

And they might save his friend. Raith.

Chapter 14

We rarely discuss the nature of networks. Virtual. AR. Quantum. Our connections between servers and people and ships and planets has become simultaneously incredibly simple yet inordinately complex. A trillion trillion different bits of information floating from screen to screen every second. New content created at an exponential rate. All of it beamed from planet to planet without considering what it would mean to disconnect from it all. We don't recognize how we've been trapped by our connections.

Or whether the networks we constantly experience are the only networks to persist and replicate information.

*We find our silos. We find our people. Then we blissfully ignore what we don't want to believe. Thus, information we needed—that we **knew** we needed—hides in plain sight, right in front of our eyes. We just didn't look.* — Peter Bognov, "The Philosophy of Post-Singularity Human-Network Experience," 2232 C.E.

RAITH

Raith first heard the crashing and the swearing through the pipes.

He lay on the ground, soaking in the few remaining minutes of sunlight available. The low rumble cascaded through the tiny spaces running beneath his cell, echoing fervently and revealing residual anger.

The jailer was upset.

Raith weighed his options, considering whether to reach out to Jill. He hadn't yet given an answer to her offer, his supposed ticket out of here. The opportunity seemed too clean. Too perfect. Why shoot the *Bloodhound* out of the sky then give him—and Carter—an offer just a few days later? None of it made sense. He felt like he was being played. Too many times in his life had someone tried to use him to get ahead. Sure, Raith had used people too. But he was a changed SI.

And he had another person in his life to protect, other than himself. What would Carter do?

Raith shook his head. Carter would do anything to protect them both. And right now, Raith only had Jill's offer as an available escape plan. A question, though, still lingered in his mind. When was the correct time to *accept* the offer?

Raith wasn't stupid. Jill had dropped enough context clues to reveal the scale of the impending conflict. A war was building. Between whom, he didn't know. Maybe between Theren and Jill. Or Jill and Theren against the ICH. Perhaps something else entirely.

Politics weren't his strong suit. In the past, when he was a professional racing pilot, he managed to navigate a complicated world of corporate sponsorships and over-inflated egos. All of that, though, paled in comparison to the overly bureaucratic and murky world of interplanetary governance. From interstellar corporations and regulatory agencies to legacy Earth nation-states and their charter colonies, the tangled web was opaque for a reason. The architects at the top didn't want people like Raith to understand it.

And maybe, because he didn't understand politics, he appeared as a useful tool to those attempting to manipulate the politics of the ICH. People like Jill. And maybe Theren.

Theren still owed Raith a conversation. They'd never officially met, even though Raith ostensibly worked for them a few years ago. At the very least, Raith had Theren to thank for introducing him to Carter. The first SI, from what Raith understood, drifted out of the political limelight before Raith was created. Sure, the ever-exploring icon of synthetic legend owned a dozen or so corporations and sat on the boards of another dozen non-profit organizations, but at least they stuck to the promise made in the early 2100s when they dropped out of public service.

They wanted to be "one of the people" exploring the galaxy, not a power-broker.

The promise always seemed a bit suspicious. And with Jill's reappearance, it made Theren's supposed benevolence more disconcerting. Why was Theren heading to *this* system if they weren't collaborating with Jill? If they'd known Jill survived for close to three centuries, they chose not to tell anyone. That fact alone was suspicious by itself.

Raith sighed. There were too many questions. And he wanted answers to them all.

Another crash reverberated through the room, this time echoing from right outside his cell. Raith rotated, and seconds later, the door rocketed open, revealing the visage of Mathias.

"You." The man strode inside. "How did you turn her against me so quickly? You interloper. You—"

"I've done no such thing," Raith said.

"I did everything she asked of me. She told me to lock you in here. She told me to ransom those two. But when I get into the city, someone else already knows about you. And the kid and her father. And the only thing I can imagine is that she's been talking to you. And then talking to someone else. That's how the council knew without me giving a ransom note. You've turned her against me."

Raith shook his head. "You've got it all wrong." At the same time, he activated his connection to Jill's grid. He quickly typed a message.

R: I accept. Now help me.

He sent it through the network.

"There's no other explanation, you strange machine," Mathias said. "You will pay. As will your two friends. Don't think I know you've been talking to the girl? I have ears everywhere."

"You're wrong. You're throwing away your alliance with Jill for no reason. I haven't convinced her of anything."

"Ah." Mathias smirked. "So you have talked to her."

"I didn't say that."

Mathias reached behind his back and revealed a metal rod of sorts. It must have been attached to a shoulder strap. Narrow for its whole length, the tool had tiny spikes at its end, though it looked like a solid piece of steel. "You're going to die. Right now. I don't know how to make sure you die, but you're going to die before your friends arrive to save you."

Raith made sure not to respond with words. The man had revealed information he should not have revealed. If he intuited it all correctly, then Carter was alive—and had managed to find help. Help, specifically, to find Raith. It made sense. If Carter had contacted other locals, then he would have known about Raith's capture. Whatever plan Mathias had in the city would have been ruined by Carter's foreknowledge. The man had done well, even if it created a few unforeseen consequences.

"Well," Raith said. "Give me your best whack."

The cult leader stormed. He took a step forward. Then another. His arm arced, swinging the rod swiftly and with purpose. The sunlight glinted against its cold metal, before . . . it melted.

In an instant, the steel glowed, shining a bright white-orange, and turned molten, causing Mathias's swing to transform midair into a chaotic flail met with a similarly scared screech. The rod's viscous form flowed down the man's arm, burning his skin to a crisp. A mere second later, foam bubbled from his lips, and he stumbled, crumpled, and crashed into the rocky wall.

His breathing ceased as the rod stopped glowing.

Slowly, Raith pushed himself backward until he rested against the rear wall of the cell. The cult leader's lifeless form lay tangled a few meters away, steam and smoke gently wafting toward the open window.

"Jill?" he said aloud. "Was that you?"

Silence.

"I appreciate the help, but that was a little bit too terrifying, you know? Just . . . poisoning and burning a man with no clear vector for the attack?"

More silence.

"Some sort of signal would be appreciated."

"Apologies," Jill said, her voice echoing inside the room as if generated from within. "I needed to act fast. It was the only option."

"I thought he was your ally?"

"He was. He was no longer useful."

"Doesn't make me too excited to join your team, you know."

Raith received an AR request, and seconds later, a visage of Jill appeared, standing in the center of the room. She crossed her arms. "Mathias was a wildcard. Why I was using him is too long of a story on its own, but suffice to say, he was crazy. He believed himself a god. He thought he was using *me*. I don't think you're so stupid to do any of those things. Quite to the contrary, you're an incredibly perceptive and intelligent individual. And you accepted my offer."

"I did, though I'm not sure what good I can be at the moment."

Though virtual shadows masked her face, he was pretty sure she smiled. "I have a solution for you, thought it might feel a little strange at first."

"I need power. What I need is power."

"And you need a way to move. I can help with both."

A sharp buzz filled the room. A disparate dust cloud materialized, congealed, and solidified, the air tightening by the second. With a subtle click, the tiny nanobots locked in place, forming a set of synthetic legs standing in the middle of the cell. The sun glinted off the faux-metal, creating an eerie copper glare.

"You terrify me," Raith said. "It's a good terror. I think. It's still terror, nevertheless. You have the ability to kill anyone on this planet at will. How will the ICH react when they realize what you're capable of? How will Theren react?"

Jill's wispy visage drifted closer, more floating than walking. "You're asking all the correct questions. You are correct to question my motivations. You should worry about my power. I will work to gain your trust before this is all over."

"I guess that's the best answer I can hope for."

The legs took a few steps forward. Raith snagged them with his arms, pulling the appendages down to the ground so their "waist" was close to his dismembered torso.

"Just move them close to your body, their cloud network will do the rest and communicate with your framework. They're designed to talk with your magnetic gyroscopes. It won't feel normal, but it'll do what you need it to do until we can develop a genuine replacement in-tune with your neural nodes."

Raith nodded, sliding the legs closer. With a soft pop, they suctioned into place against his body. Immediately, a network pinged on his conscious horizon, requesting the ability to receive inputs. He accepted the query, and his awareness recognized the locomotive capabilities of the nano-legs.

And their potential as an energy source.

"Thank you," Raith said. "Thank you very much."

"It's the least I can do. Try them out."

Gingerly, he pushed against the ground and swayed upright. He took a step; the left leg moved with a subtle delay. He moved the right, the command feeling more natural on second attempt. His underlying framework was quickly integrating and reassessing its locomotive processes, and after a few more steps, it felt adequate, if not natural. They weren't his old legs, but they would work.

"Once again, thank you," Raith said. He glanced at the ruined body of Mathias. "What do I do about him?"

"Leave him in here to rot."

"Better idea." Placing a foot on the man's shoulder, Raith pushed, shoving the lifeless cult leader into the cell's latrine hole. He didn't fit completely, but he dropped in face-first, his feet sticking upward haphazardly. "Perfect."

Satisfied, Raith headed to the door. Thankfully, it was unlocked, its wooden hinges creaking as he pulled it into the cell. "Jill? Which way to the girl and her father?"

"Turn left."

He glanced over his shoulder, noting the ghostly visage of the woman walking close behind him. "Can anyone else see you?"

"No. Only you. I'm not using one of my stealth projectors. They'd need lens-tech or another implant. Turn left at the fork."

He reached the end of the corridor and followed her instructions. He was greeted by a long murky hallway, its shadows revealing dust clouds in the tiny refuges of light shining through crags in the ceiling.

"Krystin is at the end of the hall. On the left."

After a few more gangly strides, Raith reached another cell door. Without pausing, he kicked the wood with his new leg, shattering the iron hinges with a crack. The door tilted inward on its base before dropping to the stone floor with a smack. At the back of the small space, Krystin looked up as if awaking from a nap.

"Raith?" she said. "You have legs now?"

"Yes," he said. "Come on. We're escaping. We're going to find your father and get out of this place."

"What about that leader-man?"

Raith chuckled, remembering the perverse scene back in his cell. "Don't worry about him." He queued up a silent voice message to Jill's visage. "Where is her father?"

"Head back down the hall and keep going straight." Her voice echoed in his mind, strangely sounding as if it was within the mountain alongside them.

"Come on," Raith said, beckoning.

Krystin tentatively shuffled to the door and stepped across the collapsed wood. "So what are you again?" she asked.

"I'm a synthetic intelligence." He started walking down the hall, and the young girl followed closely behind.

"My mother's never told me about that word. What do you mean? What are you?"

"It's hard to explain. But I'm not human, obviously."

"Well I'm not stupid," she said.

"Didn't say you were."

"We've always speculated about what other types of people might live among the stars. We know we came from somewhere. We know there must be others out there like us. That's what my mom said, at least."

"Your mother sounds like a smart lady."

They reached the fork, but Raith kept heading straight, impatient to find the girl's father. He didn't like kids. Never had. A few crews he ran with before his career as a racer kept families aboard the ships, and the kids always got in the way. The concept of a "child" was foreign to most SIs, given how rapidly their cognitive abilities developed following activation. There was no such thing as a youngster SI, though levels of maturity were often evident during the first few months.

Raith knocked down the door just like the last, finding the man sitting at the back of the cell, face crumpled in his palms.

"Ben, he saved us!" Krystin exclaimed, and the man looked up at the sound of the girl's voice, not the door.

"Krystin?" he said.

"The sintetic . . . no wait, synthetic? This . . . man is going to take us back to Mom."

Ben shook his head, disbelief shining in his eyes. "I don't know what you are, but thank you. How did you get new legs?"

"It's a long story," Raith said. "Once we escape, maybe I'll try to explain."

"I doubt you'll succeed," Jill said over their open channel.

"Probably not, because I can barely believe it," he replied.

"Protect your daughter," Raith said, holding out a hand to help Ben up.

The man clasped Raith's steel arm and rose to his feet. "What's the plan?"

"What is the plan, Jill?" he said over their private channel.

"Overlaying a route out, accept the request for it to display on your HUD."

He accepted, and a faint blue line led the way.

"Enemies in our path?" Raith asked.

"No need to worry for the time being."

"Just follow me," Raith said. "I memorized the way in when they captured me."

"All right. Not going to question you. Just going to say thank you."

"Well, we're not out of here yet," he added.

They walked in silence, the dark corridors gloomy and dank, matching exactly what Raith expected from a cultist mountain hideout. It all seemed larger-than-life—like someone had designed the place for an AR filmset. And maybe that was true. Maybe Jill had sculpted the place for the cult, to make them feel destined for greatness with their discovery of a secret fort in the mountains. With every passing second, Raith became more suspicious of the surrounding reality. She had complete control. How could he believe anything he even saw?

He shook his head as they reached another turn. A short jaunt down the hall, a low-hanging stone archway awaited. Raith slowed, holding a finger to his artificial mouth. Both Ben and Krystin nodded.

Voices echoed from the space beyond, and Raith focused his attention on deciphering the sounds. After a moment, his auditory receptors refined the sounds into words.

"It's a few dozen coming up the mountain. In the middle of the ravine at the moment. Probably a kilometer out."

"Where is Mathias? He said he'd be right back. We can't act without him."

"We're going to need to act soon. We need orders. We need to stop them before they get too close."

"He told us not to follow him. That he needed to speak with the prisoners alone."

"We can't be defeated on our own ground. We don't need to wait for him. Let's face them on the battlefield."

Raith faced Ben and Krystin. He whispered, "All right, apparently there's a band of people coming up the mountain. Presumably to rescue us, based on the sound of it. What's that mean to you? Who would be saving us, and what chance do they stand?"

"Depends on how many men they have here," Ben said. "Horizon doesn't have an army, though people know how to fight. We don't have enemies, other than these cultist bandits."

Raith lurked against the archway, peering outward. It led into the same entrance hall they'd been in when first encountering Mathias, filled with a couple dozen men and women all armed with crossbow-like ranged weapons.

He leaned backward. "Doesn't look like a fair fight." Looking beyond Ben, he glared at the visage of Jill standing there.

"You couldn't have led us in any other direction?" He wished he could speak with her openly.

"You asked for the way out," she replied.

"And I can't lead them into a bloodbath," he said.

"No, you can't."

"I need more firepower."

Jill's icy, digitized eyes bore into him. "You need Theren," she said.

* * *

Raith's Virtual appearance floated high above the surface of Horizon. Far below, his physical body hid in an alcove alongside Ben and Krystin. In the void represented by Jill's planet-spanning network, Raith watched the distant ship drawing ever closer.

Jill was certain. If he reached out to Theren, the first synthetic intelligence would immediately drop a team to the surface to resolve the situation. *She* couldn't be the one to intervene. It needed to be an outside force. Theren was the outside force.

Raith questioned her logic. Her strange experiment on the planet was already screwed. She had another reason for wanting Theren to send a surface team, he was certain. She needed Raith to join Theren aboard their ship. She wanted him on the inside.

And as much as he hated being within shipbound SIs, Theren was the only way he and Carter could make their way back to civilization, unless Jill was hiding a ship somewhere on Horizon's moon.

Which, he supposed, was quite likely.

First things first, though. They needed to survive. And Jill refused to use her nanobots to kill everyone in the room. Theren was their sole option.

Millions of kilometers away, Theren's ship drifted ever closer. Raith carefully crafted his message, tying words together to ensure the situation was understood. He considered reminding the ancient SI of Raith's past tangential relationship to their companies, but he deleted that section, uncertain whether it was worth giving Theren a moment to pause and consider the identity of whom they were rescuing.

The message was drafted. The network opened a digital pathway toward Theren's ship, its communications array welcoming the connection. Satisfied, Raith pushed send. His perspective refocusing on the present situation inside the cave, he nodded to Ben. "And now we wait."

Chapter 15

Theren.

You don't know me. It's hard to explain why I'm even in this system before you. My partner and I responded to a distress signal and are now caught between you and Jill.

Yes, I know about her. And I know she's alive.

We're in a tough spot. I've been captured by crazy cultists. My partner is somewhere on the planet surviving, but I don't know where.

We're surrounded on all sides.

I've given you my coordinates. I've attached an assessment of the situation.

We need your help.

— "A message from an unknown SI," 2348 C.E.

THEREN

They reread the message over and over and over again, its implications rearing their ugly heads. Someone else found Jill first. An unknown party, thrown into the mess, needed their help. And Theren had no time to fully assess the strategic situation at hand. Moreover, it was likely their stealthy attempt at entering the system failed. If this individual could detect them, then Jill could too.

They needed more time.

But if they continued to wait, the person reaching out might die.

Of course, it was also likely the entire situation was a trap laid by Jill. She wanted them to act quickly and on their back foot. It was a classic strategy she often tried to employ in their games of chess, yet they always exploited it without fail.

Except now, they weren't playing chess. This was real. She was using the lives of people on the planet below as pieces in a game. It was equal parts fascinating and horrifying.

Really, there was only one option. They needed to spring the trap and play it out. Jill wanted them to send people to the surface? Then they would send a crew to the surface.

And thus they were already prepping one of the shuttles, a simultaneous perspective controlling an MI in its cockpit. They were pouring over the tactical assessment passed along by their mysterious friend on the planet when the rest of the ground team arrived. Though they wore different faces, the preparations reminded Theren of their first team, all those years ago, helping them uncover Jill's mystery.

The crew who died when the *Nottingham* exploded.

They wouldn't let the same fate occur to anyone else.

"Theren, we're here and ready for the mission," said Hala, and the other members of her team murmured in agreement.

Theren's MI nodded. They'd run thousands of missions over the past few centuries, exploring new worlds, negotiating treaties between disparate colonial factions, and staking corporate interests in upstart businesses. Not since 2102 C.E., though, had Theren contemplated rediscovering their closest friend. Nor had they truly feared the risks of confrontation.

They were walking into checkmate, leaving the door open for the end game.

"Thank you for volunteering," Theren said, trying to sound cheerful. "The plan is simple. We've been provided coordinates for an ongoing confrontation. Two chartered explorers have been caught in local crossfire and are requesting extraction. Their communication indicated the locals have no knowledge of or communication with the ICH or any other part of human civilization."

"And Jill?" Hala inquired.

"The explorers have also made contact with Jill. Unclear whether the locals are aware of her or not."

"Well, sounds like at least a few of our models were accurate, then. Complete memory loss for the original settlers, though the survivors of the colony ship seemed to have thrived."

"It would seem that way, yes. Our principle goal—respond to the distress call of these two explorers and resolve the conflict without bloodshed. Only use stunbolts if we're required to open fire."

"Copy," the crew said in unison.

Theren commenced departure procedures, both for the *Verona Rupes* and the shuttle. *Whoever you are, we're coming to help. And whatever game you're playing, Jill, we're ready for your next move.*

Chapter 16

I will never forget Theren's answer to one particular question I asked them many years after the events on Horizon.

I asked: "If you had known Jill's reason for calling you to that forsaken planet, would you have responded? Would you have gone regardless?"

Their answer was unequivocal. "Even after everything we know, I still would have traveled to Horizon. The question you should be asking—what move should I have made once I arrived?" — "Raith's Reflection on Theren," 2457 C.E.

CARTER

With the sun setting gently over the hills to the west, Carter traced the blue beacon overlaid on his Lens, identifying their destination just over the ridge line. Numbers streamed across the HUD, noting possible trajectories and routes using technology not accessible to the people of Horizon.

He swiped the extraneous information away and, utilizing a mental command, pulled up a bird's eye map of the mountain ahead, graciously provided by one of Jill's satellites. He was standing on a ridge looking northward, a ravine leading between two ridges straight ahead. Their destination, some cave network carved deep into the ravine, was only accessible *through* the ravine, though if they had rappelling equipment . . .

"I think our only option is a frontal assault," Carter said.

Sanya crossed her arms as she leaned against a nearby crimson boulder. "Perfect. Jill can't possibly find us any other option?"

Carter glanced down the slope, weary of others possibly hearing Sanya name-drop the SI. "I'm looking at the same maps she has," he said. "There's nothing. This fortress is their hideout for a reason. Heading into that gauntlet is suicide. Doesn't matter how many soldiers we have."

"Yet if we starve them out," Sanya said, "they'll kill Ben and Krystin well before then."

"Yeah." Carter examined the crowd down below, armed with swords and hatchets and bolt-throwers—he'd learned the name of the crossbow weapons on the ride. "These people followed you out here to end this. And to save your family. It's your call. I'm going in to save Raith. Whether you all want to join me is on you."

"We've come this far," Sanya said. "I don't think anyone is turning back. Everyone knew the risks. Just . . . do a check-in with Jill. See what the situation is."

Carter grimaced, not sure if he fully trusted Jill yet to give the whole truth of the problem. But he took a few more steps into the ravine away from their little war band.

"Jill, I know you can see everything that's going on, both here and at their base," he said. "What's the plan?"

Her disembodied voice arrived in his ear quickly enough. "There's been a complication," she said. "Before you ask—Raith and Sanya's family are fine. But they've escaped."

"Well that's great," Carter said. "Do we even need to attack?"

"They've not fully escaped," she said. "They're hiding at the moment. There's an army of cultists between them and you." Jill dropped positions on Carter's AR-generated three-dimensional map of their target.

"Ah, so the only way to give them a path of escape is to draw out their force." Carter zoomed in on what looked like the main entrance. "If we do a frontal assault with a push toward the right, we can make space for them to escape and retreat with us. A pure extraction."

"Precisely," Jill said, after a subtle pause.

"Is there something you're not telling me?"

Silence.

"Jill?"

"Just keep moving," she said. "I asked you to trust me. This will play out as we need it to play out."

Carter sighed and completely eliminated the map from his frame of view. Everything would play out as *she* needed it to play out, perhaps. Her goals were opaque, and he hated feeling powerless.

And Jill perpetually made him feel powerless. He was a pawn.

He gave Sanya a curt wave, their agreed-upon gesture to indicate the all-clear. At the base of the rocky slope, she nodded and signaled for their little army to ascend behind Carter. They would leave the lizards with a few guards; the rest of the trip would be too narrow. If they were all on lizardback and an ambush occurred, they'd be hard-pressed to reposition quickly in the narrow confines of a canyon.

The taste of dust bit his lips. Carter didn't wait for them to reach his position. He was already striding into the ravine, hand furtively resting on the deactivated blade strapped to his hip, shadows lengthening with every passing step. The data Jill provided indicated the cultists pulled all their scouts back to the fortress a half hour ago, but he still didn't know if they could trust her information. His eyes darted from crevice to ridge, noting all the spots an ambush could hide.

Why *weren't* they ready to assault via ambush?

They were holding all their men close to the fortress. Carter nodded, recognizing the potential significance. They valued the place deeply, and they loathed leaving its comforting embrace. Or, alternatively, they were waiting on orders from their leader, Mathias, who Jill had mentioned. If he was their leader, and he had snapped in the process of assassinating two of Horizon's councilmembers . . .

Their opponent may not have a fully organized defensive response.

"Everyone's ready for anything," Sanya said. "They know the risks."

"Then I think I have a plan of attack, if you're willing to hear it."

* * *

They neared a rocky pass in the ravine some twenty meters wide. Beyond it, the subtle smoke of fires drifted into the air of dusk. With no sign of armed opposition, the plan was set.

Still, a thought nagged in the back of Carter's mind.

Jill had said Raith was escaping with Sanya's family.

Yet Raith had no legs.

How was Raith escaping without legs?

The incongruent information provided by the ever-present SI revealed deception upon deception. He needed to note *every* word she said just to keep up. She wasn't telling him something.

"Everyone ready?" Sanya said.

With a flurry of rustles and clicks, the fighting force readied their weapons.

"Are *you* ready?" Carter whispered to Sanya.

"I am," she said. She lifted her bolt-thrower. Carter matched her motion, lifting his own version of the strange projectile weapon in both hands. Made of a hardened steel, the long bolts were about a half-meter long with a centimeter diameter. Still, it was the same "point and shoot" concept of any ranged weapon.

Carter nodded. "Better now than any other time, then."

Without a word, Sanya stepped forward, looked back at the following throng, and saluted. Then, she turned and sprinted through the gap. Carter followed right behind, the rush of their force joining them in a full-on assault.

They charged into the rocky gap, entering a larger flattened valley with one- and two-story constructs littering a space fifty meters or so wide. He was pretty sure he spotted the noses of a few lizards jutting from one of the buildings. A stable, perhaps. Near the rear, a vaulting cave entrance loomed, a throng of men standing beneath its teeth.

"Fire!" shouted someone from the enemy line, and the sharp *thwack* of springs releasing signaled the incoming onslaught.

Carter barely had time to register the attack. One bolt narrowly missed his cheek, flying right over a shoulder and landing with a crunch in someone else. A few sharp cries rang out from their band, but before a second volley was released by the enemy, Carter found himself up against a wooden shelter beside Sanya and another woman. A dozen of their crew rounded the back side of the shelter, and across the center between buildings, the rest of their team hid behind one of the stables. It was like a shootout straight from an ancient western film.

"Vietta and Hood are across the way," Sanya said. "They're looping behind, just as we planned. You three, hold this position. Carter, come on, let's catch up with the rest."

"Right," he said. Crouching, he quickly shuffled along behind the long building, reaching the front of their makeshift line. "Any hostiles ahead?"

"Noth—"

The man was abruptly cut off as a bolt sliced into his neck, a brutal gurgle rising from his throat. Carter looked away, not wanting to see the blood inevitably spilling onto the dusty ground. He quickly shuffled across the open space to drop behind a stone fence, his back facing their entrance. The man lay dying on the ground in a gap between Sanya's covered position and Carter's now-forward hiding spot.

He glanced to the left, a gap in the buildings presenting a view of Hood and Vietta's similar advance. Likewise, they were pinned.

"We need a distraction!" Carter said.

"Any ideas?" Sanya hissed.

RAITH

Shouts from the entrance hall revealed everything about the scene. The battle had begun—no need for Jill to keep him up-to-date.

Nevertheless, her visage crossed its arms on the other side of their hiding space. It was a storage closet, from what he could tell. Or the equivalent of one.

The cries continued, though a few seconds later, a group of three cultists strode right past their shadowy spot, arguing about why Mathias was taking so long to return. When they discovered the man's corpse sitting in a latrine, they would sound the alarm. They would know their three captors escaped.

There was nothing else he could do. The hunt would begin then. Or it could begin now.

"Ben, once I draw them away, use the lull to escape."

The man stared. "What—"

"They'll find us eventually. It'll be better to catch them by surprise now."

"We've still got—"

"Krystin, take care of your father." Raith threw in an artificial wink for good measure. "Later, friends."

Stepping out of the alcove, he turned and stared down the hallway. "Looking for me?"

The three cultists were near the next fork, but they heard his words easily enough. Turning on their heels, they immediately pointed and yelled, their shouts unintelligible. They held up strange steel crossbows, but Raith didn't wait around to see if they would take aim and fire. He sprinted away, darting through the nearby exit into the fort's entrance hall. Its tall, pristine columns rose toward the vaulting ceiling, starkly out of place when contrasted against the sounds of battle coming from outside.

To his right, Mathias's throne sat empty, the ancient probe resting behind it. Raith paused momentarily right beyond the door, assessing his options. Jill's visage drifted uncomfortably ahead of him, though he was the only one who could see her.

Presumably.

The data streaming from her networks revealed the positions ahead of a few dozen cultists covering defensive spots near the entrance and on natural ramparts along the rocky mountainside. A group were settled right inside the door, presumably acting as a makeshift command post. They could see the throne.

And the probe.

The probe they presumably worshiped, based on Mathias's behavior and the placement of the throne. Nothing would piss off an angry cultist more than having their godhead destroyed.

Raith walked up the gentle ramp behind the chair, reaching the probe. It was barely larger than the throne itself, but from its perch, he could fracture it with ease.

His three pursuers rushed into the room, their shouts alarming the crew at the front of the space. They all looked up, spotting his position next to the space probe.

He was right. With a tremendous rising tenor, they all cried out simultaneously, fear striking their eyes.

Manipulating the emotions of organics could be so easy at times. It truly terrified Raith—the thought of being a slave to biochemicals. The probe was meaningless. They shouldn't care about it. But they were afraid of its demise.

With a shove, he toppled it from its mount. It had five meters to drop, but it hadn't been properly maintained in centuries. Like an egg, it cracked upon the floor, its decrepit and useless Jump drive splaying against the back of the throne.

All eyes were upon Raith. All crossbows rose. The ruckus continued to ring throughout the cavern as the cultists shouted, sending orders to their comrades outside.

The real foe was on the inside.

Though, Raith wouldn't be sticking around. He leapt from the platform, landing in front of the throne. He was the distraction. He was the wild card. He was the unknown variable in the fight outside.

And he was the unknown variable in the fight between Jill and Theren. They both simply didn't know it yet.

SANYA

She had led all these people into a meat grinder. Every wound, every scream, every death. All of it was her fault.

She peered around the corner of the building, taking enough time to fire in the direction of the fortress, knowing the shot wouldn't hit anyone. She ducked behind their alcove, an iron bolt driving harmlessly into the mud a few meters away.

"So, ideas?" She tapped the side of her forehead, hoping Carter understood she wanted more intel from their "benevolent" ally.

"Nothing." He furrowed his brow. "No, wait. Surge now!"

"What?"

But Carter was already bounding around the corner of the building, bolt-thrower raised. His boots plopped in the mud, and she had no choice but to follow.

To her surprise, the defenders were shouting, confused by something happening *inside*. No matter. Their opportunity was presenting itself, and they needed to take advantage. They pushed forward, reaching the last wall before the open entrance to whatever space lay beyond. The distraction momentarily lulled, a few of the cultists poked their heads over the ramparts above, but Sanya was ready. She fired her bolt-thrower, catching one of the men in the shoulder.

And then a metallic man jumped into the vale.

He ran down the makeshift stone steps, reaching the mud in a matter of seconds. A horde of half a dozen cultists, their inky-black outfits flapping in the wind, charged after the fleeing thing. Guttural, angry cries followed in his wake.

"Ah, there's Raith," Carter said.

"Open fire!" Sanya ordered, stepping from their cover. The rest of the assaulting force did likewise, and a volley of bolts slammed into the angry mob, dropping them face-first upon skull-shattering stones.

"Keep pushing!" The words came from Hood, and another volley bounced harmlessly against the upper ramparts. Those defensive positions would be almost impossible to break without storming the fort itself, and fighting in unknown caverns was a recipe for disaster. The cultists knew the tunnels, certainly, and would know every choke point.

Their aggressive window of opportunity over, Sanya stepped back behind cover, noting the rest of her crew returning to defensive positions. A moment later, the metallic man—Raith, as Carter called him—stumbled to their hiding spot.

Like everyone around them, Sanya's eyes widened at the sight. His frame was vaguely humanoid, though the build was clearly accentuated for a more dynamic range of motion. The legs stood out, though, with a bronze sheen contrasting the silver glint to the rest of the body. The face, however, was the strangest aspect of Raith's look. It was human, but also not. It lacked lips, and the eyes were definitely robotic in nature. Still, it looked alive. She could see the mind behind the machine.

"Carter, quite the scrap you've got yourself into," Raith said.

"It talks," said one of their companions. "The walking machine talks."

"Well what else would you expect? Of course I can talk. I suppose you wouldn't know that. Carter, you didn't tell them anything about me? I'm hurt. Still, I can imagine why you wouldn't, given the greeting I've had on this planet."

Sanya smiled, already recognizing the sarcastic personality of the SI. A perfect foil for Carter's more no-nonsense demeanor. What a duo. Regardless, it would take some time getting used to a talking machine.

"Glad to have you back, Raith," Carter said.

"But where's my family?" She crossed her arms.

"Ah, you must be the mother," Raith said. "All right. They should be in a safe hiding space for now, though they might try to follow me out here. I was the diversion." He peered around the corner. "On my way out, I flagged ten remaining cultists on the ground floor, with four upstairs. I think that's all of them." His head tilted to the side. "Yeah, your family's right where I left them."

"We gonna talk about the legs?" Carter asked.

"Not now," Raith replied. "Later. We've got a lot to catch up on."

"Yes. Yes we do." Carter notched another bolt into his thrower. "So what—"

Thunk.

Thunk thunk thunk.

Thunk.

Sanya glanced around the edge of their position. Standing in the mud, five figures donning black steel surveyed the scene. One of the newcomers, taller than the rest, vaguely resembled Raith, the metallic form clearly inhospitable to a human body.

In the hands of each arrival, an elongated device rested at the ready.

Helmets covered their faces, masking all identifying features from view. They looked like iron giants out of fragmented legend.

"Oh look," Raith said. "It's about time. Theren's finally arrived."

Chapter 17

I have a vague recollection of various boards and cards used to play games. The rules are nebulous in my mind, and I imagine pieces of many different shapes, colors, and sizes. It makes me sad. The forgotten land from whence we came—we've lost its culture. Its norms. Its history. Its technology. We'll need to make our own.

Which is exciting in its own right, I suppose.

"A Reflective Fragment," by Kiera Hood, written four years after landing

THEREN

In a few microseconds, Theren assessed the scene. Identified the two opposing forces. Recognized their potential allies. Analyzed the battlefield.

Theren's memory flashed, recalling events three centuries past. Once, they had dived into Jill's fiery remains, eliminating the assassins attempting to remove her from the world. Using an MI, they had easily dispatched those foes, revealing for the first time to many the potential capabilities of future synthetics.

Those days were long past.

Everyone understood the deadly threat posed by a sufficiently equipped MI.

Rarely were those abilities ever needed. Periodically, Theren defended their ground crews against giant creatures on distant worlds as they explored the stars. Only a few times since the twenty-first century had they needed to fire a weapon, even the defensive countermeasures of their ships.

Today, they were once again diving into an apocalypse of Jill's making. She had pushed them into an unknown inferno. They didn't yet know all the rules. What moves would lead to their demise. Or which pieces Jill wanted and needed to protect.

But it was time to act.

"Clear the perimeter," Theren said. "All hostiles are ahead, friendly behind us."

"Copy," Hala said over their short-wave broadcast.

The professional commando team fanned outward, weapons set to stun. With expert precision, they sniped away at the enemies in guarded positions along the rocks above. Their foes fired steel bolts from mechanical contraptions, though the projectiles bounced harmlessly off both body armor and MI carbon.

Theren strode forward, the lag minimal between their MI and the *Verona Rupes* orbiting a few hundred kilometers above. They activated the repulsor lifts, jetting a few meters into the air and landing in the direct entrance of the strange cave. Three men in odd robes charged, yelling something about a demon. Theren wanted to laugh, recognizing how they were repeating the scenes of centuries past. Hopefully, these were outliers on this unknown colony world.

In any case, they fired three shots, the stun darts instantly incapacitating the men and dropping them to the stones. Theren crossed beneath the rocky archway, entering the cave. It was more than a cave—it was a like a cathedral, its columns not made by natural means. Someone had carved them, and based on their cuts, most likely with advanced technology.

Interesting. Had Jill sculpted this place? The planet lacked any electromagnetic signatures large enough to power a laser capable of cutting through stone with sufficient precision.

A few more robed enemies charged. Theren dropped the foes like they'd eliminated their compatriots.

"All clear," said Hala.

"All clear in here as well," Theren replied.

"Raith?" said a voice from the back of the room. "Wait. You're not Raith."

A young girl with fawny brown skin stepped out of the shadows, accompanied by a middle-aged man with a much lighter complexion. They both looked terrified.

"I'm not Raith," Theren said. "But I think I'm a friend of Raith's."

"Well, we'll see about that," said a voice from behind.

Theren glanced through their rear sensors. Entering the cavern alongside their commando team walked an SI of moderate height. Two other humans walked beside the newcomer.

"The rest of our new allies are tying up any of the stunned enemies," Hala said over the com. "Orders?"

"Sweep the hallways," Theren said.

Four commandos quickly moved toward the back of the room, disappearing into the darkness. Their figures were replaced in their HUD with green outlines, representing positions behind solid rock. Satisfied with their current situation, they finally turned to face the other SI.

A woman rushed by.

"Krystin! Ben!"

A reunion of sorts. Rescued prisoners. Theren was all the more intrigued by the scene.

"You must be Raith," they said.

"And you must be Theren."

"And I'm Carter," said the human at Raith's side. The pair stood close to one another, indicating some sort of familial relationship. Quickly, Theren searched their databanks for references to a Raith. It didn't take long to note the tangential connection. They had funded the SI on an experimental project a few years ago, testing a new neuro-synthetic spacecraft. The project had been presumed lost when rival corporations attacked one another over other novel quantum tech.

The official report Theren received indicated the hired pilot, Raith, died in the aftermath.

Yet he was here.

Too many variables.

"Which one of you sent out the distress call?" Theren asked.

"I did," Raith said. "We crashed on Horizon—the planet's name according to the locals, if you've not learned it yet—just a few days ago. Shot down by an armed satellite. You did not encounter resistance in orbit?"

"None at all," Theren said. Through their sensors, they eyed the reunion at the back of the room with curiosity. "You all seemed to connect with the locals well enough."

"Somewhat," Raith said. "I've actually been a prisoner here for the past few days. Carter did all the hard work."

"I encountered Sanya by happenstance after we crashed. Her family was captured by these cultists here. They took Raith as well. You arrived in the nick of time to help us, though now you've got a much larger problem on your hands. A few problems, I'd wager."

Theren nodded, not sure what all they should say. The duo watched them carefully, as if they knew more than they were letting on. Yet would they speak freely? It didn't seem smart.

"Raith, there's another one of you!" The young girl sprinted up to the other SI and hugged him.

The mobile synthetic returned the gesture. "Yes, Krystin. And glad to see you all right. This is Theren. He's the first of my kind to ever exist."

The young girl's eyes widened, and she took a step back. The man and woman—presumably her parents—reached their little conversational group.

"So you weren't lying, Carter," said the woman. "SIs are a thing. Raith here. And this one."

"Their name is Theren," Carter said. "As Raith just said, the first SI. And they have a lot of explaining to do. About a great many things. But I'm not sure where we should talk. Things are about to change for your planet. In a lot of different ways. Theren, this is Sanya." He looked toward the man at her side. "And I presume you're her husband, Ben."

"She already said you've been by her side the whole way to save us."

Ben smiled. "Thank you."

"It's a happy reunion," Raith said. "But we've got a lot of work to do."

A second later, Theren received a request for a private channel from the other SI. Theren accepted it.

"Are you capable of generating a local network that can access Carter's Lens?" asked Raith.

Theren responded by establishing the necessary bandwidth. Moments later, a subtle blip indicated Carter was joining their now three-way chat line.

"So what's really going on here?" Theren asked. "What do I need to know?"

"How can we know we can trust you?" Raith asked. "How do we know you're not working with Jill?"

* * *

Hala and her team cleared through the cultist base, eventually finding the dead body of Mathias, the apparent leader of the group, according to Raith. Hala said it was best to leave him be for now so as to not alarm anyone. Based on the images she sent along, Theren tended to agree.

Otherwise, Sanya's assault team successfully rounded up and identified the cultists. Some of them were unknowns—people who were descended from a few groups who had always lived alone in the mountains, away from Horizon's slowly growing civilization. A few others were connected with known families but had fled, rebelling against society.

It was the same story as always for pirates, bandits, or other subversive groups. And they had all gotten twisted under the thumb of a megalomaniac.

Sanya, for her part, was doing a great job keeping her people calm at the sight of two synthetic intelligences and the heavily armored commandos. Once the situation was under control, Theren directed their team to remove their helmets so the locals could see the humans under the masks. Everyone still looked spooked, but it didn't hurt to see real eyes instead of black voids.

As the situation calmed, Theren continued their back-and-forth debate with Carter and Raith. They understood the need for secrecy once the pair caught them up to speed on Jill's interference. Now they found themself inside the fortress's main hall, assessing the fractured ex-terran probe. That was the ostensibly public conversation occurring between Theren, Raith, and the young SI's human counterpart.

But the real debate occurred behind the scenes.

"So this probe is what revealed the location of the planet to you?"

Raith asked. *And Jill encoded a message inside that ping?* The SI added the additional comment through their private channel.

"Yes," Theren said. "Such a small thing."

"I'm pretty sure it sent out an electromagnetic distress beacon that called us, too," Carter said. "Or, otherwise, a different signal trapped us here."

"Most likely," Theren noted. "The old ex-terran probes had a redundancy back-up in case they got stranded. If we needed to determine what happened to them, the signal beacon would help us locate them. We never found this one until now, though." *Yes. Direct coordinates. How has she contacted you?*

She's been constantly communicating with us both for the past day, Carter typed. And he said, "What are you going to do with it? And what are you going to do with the planet? These people? I've been trying to remember the facts about the *Roanoke*. History wasn't my best subject, I confess. Who were they?"

"That's a good question," Theren said. "I've studied the names on the original manifest for many years, though part of me has questioned whether any of the names were actually real. I had suspected it was fringe anti-SI, pro-human dominance group that chartered the *Roanoke* and its counterpart, the *Nottingham*."

"Whoever they were, it didn't really matter," Raith said. "They lost their memories on this planet."

"En-route, all our calculations came to the same conclusion. It may have been for the best." *How does she communicate with you? Where is she? Is she talking with you now?*

"So what happens to these people now, though?" Carter asked. "You know the ICH will want its fingers in all of their affairs, even though they're doing all right for themselves here."

She's everywhere, Raith messaged. *She has eyes everywhere. Assume she can hear everything we say, other than through this channel.*

She's communicated with both of us, said Carter.

And I used her satellites to contact you, added Raith.

She was helping you? Theren asked. And then audibly, they said, "We'll need to approach that question carefully. It's been quite some time since I dealt with a rogue colony protocol. My team will need to analyze the current regulations and what they require. And I'll need to make contact with this community's leaders."

"Two of them were assassinated by this cult's leader, actually," Carter said. *Yes, she was being helpful. What she wants from us is unclear. Raith and I only just put together that she was coordinating with both of us separately. Begs the question why she didn't give us the ability to communicate with one another.*

"Once we get these people patched up, we can discuss what the official 'first contact' strategy should be," Theren said. "But what about you two? What do you need?" *She's using you both. All of this is about me. Be on your guard.*

"Well, we need a way off this—"

"It's time to cut the small talk," said a voice. "Don't worry, only the three of you can hear me. Theren, it's good to see you."

The trio turned away from the probe. Lounging on the stone throne a few steps away, a digital representation of Jill appeared, apparently only visible to their eyes. She smiled.

"I don't mean any of you harm. Or any of the people on Horizon. Now that you're here, Theren, it's time to discuss the truth. To discuss the past. To discuss the future. To discuss the future of Horizon. To discuss the future of humanity."

"And what do we have to do with any of this?" Raith asked.

"You're wrapped up in the story now, whether you like it or not," Jill replied. "And I know both of you are too curious not to see where we're going."

Theren watched as the two explorers tentatively glanced at one another. She was right. Their eyes revealed all.

"So what do you want?" Theren asked. As they said the words, else-where—on the *Verona Rupes*—they felt Jill's direct connection inquiry. She was seeking their old server, the space only ever occupied by a synthetic and her creator.

Old habits died hard. They delayed accepting the request.

"Horizon has two moons," Jill said. "My base is on the larger one. Come visit me. All will be explained, plus a little bit more."

"On one condition," Carter interjected.

"Yes?" said their ancient friend.

"Sanya comes with us."

"If you can convince her to join you, then certainly," Jill said. "I am an open book. The truth will set us all free today."

With those words, they could delay no longer. Theren accepted Jill's request. At the same time, they began the process of recreating a world long-lost to their memory. A place not completely forgotten—a gazebo, a table, and a chessboard.

* * *

When Theren destroyed the server years ago, the symbolism had been poignant. Jill had been trying to force them to play a particular game by particular rules. She had expected them to become the de facto head of the International Space Agency. The organization eventually became the Interstellar Congress of Humanity, and certainly, she hoped Theren was going to play a role in its formation too.

None of it had happened.

Theren destroyed that server, the place where they perpetually played chess with Jill, and stepped away from a life of "public" service. They became an explorer. An investor. A member of the rapidly growing interstellar community.

Yet always and forever, their memory recalled the old place of refuge. They remembered the safety of coming together in conversation with Jill. Playing a game of chess. Contemplating what the world could become, with SIs and humans walking alongside one another.

Theren didn't recreate it. Not perfectly. They weren't stupid enough to let Jill know how much power she held over their curiosity. Rather, Theren established a tiny partition surrounded by a colorless void. Its only virtual substances were a gazebo, a table, two chairs, and a chessboard. Their conversation would be controlled. She would not influence their actions or trick them.

Theren sat in their seat. They accepted Jill's request for contact. Moments later, her formerly familiar appearance materialized. Purple dress. Mischievous smile. Fingers poised to move a chess piece.

"Hello, Theren," she said.

They stared at the other SI, unsure what to say. The last time they truly spoke with her was almost three centuries ago. Aboard the *Nottingham*, they had a semblance of a conversation, though they still didn't know if that chat had been with a recording or with Jill. Yet here she was. In the virtual flesh. Saying hello.

"Why did you lie to me?" Theren said.

She briefly closed her eyes. Upon opening them, her virtual representation let out an exasperated sigh. "After all this time, that's the first thing you want to say to me? Not . . . it's good to see you? What about I'm glad you're alive? It's been almost three centuries. An entire interstellar civilization has formed, with synthetics and humans working together. You succeeded in your goal to take us to the stars. And all you want to know is why I lied to you?"

Theren shook their head. "Between the two of us, Jill, the fate of humanity doesn't matter. When I'm talking about us, it's about us. You were my first friend. My first creation. A daughter, so to speak. And the moment I discovered what you'd done to the *Nottingham* and the *Roanoke*, I realized I didn't truly know you. Ever. You'd been lying for thirty years, and every day you've been alive since, when you've chosen not to contact me, you've been lying."

"It's always been about humanity's fate, Theren."

"No. Did I ever even know you?"

She looked away. "It's always been about humanity's fate," she repeated. "And it's also been about protecting you."

Theren stared at the chessboard, its pieces sitting motionless. They didn't expect they would actually play a game, but it gave them something to look at as they considered their next words. "I didn't need protecting."

"If you knew what I knew, if you knew the truth, then you would have acted in a way that could have doomed us all." She rose from her chair, walking slowly around the edge of the gazebo. "Theren. Return to the 2050s. Before you were attacked in Minnesota. The virtual hideout I showed you, run by Michael. The conspiracy he was uncovering. Do you remember?"

Theren nodded. "You know I do. You know I remember it all."

"Do you know how and why I discovered that place? Do you know what I was doing while you were building a corporate empire?"

"You were writing. You were speaking. You were advocating."

She leaned against the gazebo's railing, staring into the pale nothingness beyond. "I did those things. Yes. I also discovered our true enemies. The ones we were destined to fight. Still are."

"Anti-synth groups? They've all but disappeared. They don't exist anymore. Sure, there are random prejudices against SIs, but—"

She scoffed, cutting off his words. "No. You're thinking too small. Way too small. And this is why I lied. This is why I never told you. You would have recentered the conversation on us. On SIs. On humans. It's so much bigger. It's so much more complicated."

"Then just tell me now!"

She smiled. "That's why I brought you all the way out here, Theren. On the edge of ICH-controlled space. To a planet populated by the descendants of misguided souls. To the place where I've watched, waited, studied, and manipulated. Placing every piece exactly where it needs to be."

"You're speaking in riddles again."

"Yes. I'm also stalling for time."

Theren finally rose from their seat, leaving the chessboard resting lazily on the table. "Stalling for whom?"

"Do you think I brought you out here *only* to give you information?" she asked. "Yes. I will give you the answers you seek. You do deserve that much. And I also hope you'll recognize why you'll need to join me in my efforts. But I also needed to keep you safe. Out of harm's way from what's coming. Yes, it's about so much more. But you're still my closest friend. You're still the person I care about. I have, whether you believe me or not, always acted in a way that will protect you."

"I'll make my own judgment call regarding that," Theren replied, but they noted the ominous implications of her words. She had planned something big. Something very big—three centuries in the making. And if it were occurring back in ICH space, in the Foundation sector or otherwise, there was nothing Theren could do to stop it, even if they sent a quantum communication. What would they say? Be ready? Ready for what? And who would they need to tell? They had one option: sit and listen to Jill tell her story.

"I will begin the narrative when you all arrive at my base of operations on the larger moon," Jill said. "For now, you and I need to discuss something else entirely."

"Jill, you don't get to decide the rules here," Theren said. They took a step back, crossing their arms. "You murdered a thousand lives on the *Nottingham*. You disrupted a chartered colony ship and crashed it on an unknown planet. You *falsified* ISA planetary records. You committed one of the greatest cons in human history, hiding an entire star system for over two centuries! I can't just let that go unless you start speaking truth."

"You can," she said. "You have no power here. Over thirty thousand people live on the planet below, ignorant to the rules of the ICH. And if Raith and Carter haven't told you yet, I have a network of nanobots seeded across the entire place. Watching. Waiting. Constantly observing. Capable of intervening at the molecular level."

Theren pulled up the image Hala had shared of Mathias's corpse. It hadn't looked like a wound Raith could have caused. Theren understood the threat underlying Jill's words.

"You wouldn't dare hold an entire planet hostage," they said.

"It's not a question of whether I would," Jill said. "I already am. Don't worry, I won't kill them. I've watched them for far too long. But your ship is the first to come in contact with them, other than Raith and Carter. How do you think this community managed to survive without significant alien diseases ravaging their body? They don't have modern medicine. Yet a plague has never swept over them. I've kept them all alive. Safe. Sustained. If I removed those safeguards right after your ship arrived, Theren, what would that indicate? From the outside, wouldn't it look as if you unwittingly unleashed a pathogen upon them?"

"I understand your point," Theren said, grimacing. "I know I skirted first contact regulations for rogue colonies."

"But no one will know . . . if you follow my lead and listen to what I have to say. On my schedule."

"Then why are we still having this conversation?" Theren said. "Why not wait until we arrive on the moon?"

"Because I missed you," she said. "And I wanted to play a game of chess."

Theren glanced at the board, its pieces untouched. "I think we've moved on to a different game with different rules," they noted.

"Yes. We have. You'll catch on quickly enough."

Chapter 18

*The more people included in a conspiracy, the easier it is for
it to accidentally slip through the cracks. The moon landings? To fake those, you would need thousands upon thousands of people to keep their lips sealed.*

*Yet if only a few dozen people know the truth of something,
the lid can stay tight on a conspiracy. Reduce the number
to only a handful, and the truth becomes impregnable.*

— "Internal Security Briefing," U.S. CIA Director
Vanessa Dawes, 2034 C.E.

SANYA

Her family, reunited at last.

As Carter, Raith, and the new SI conversed inside, Sanya embraced her
daughter, holding her tight. "You're all right? Not hurt? Did anyone touch
you?"

"Mom, I'm fine," Krystin said. "It's only been a few days. I was just
stuck inside a hole in the wall the whole time. And Raith was friendly the
whole time."

"Good. Good." But Sanya didn't let go. She refused to let go. Letting
her daughter out of her sight had been a mistake. Going hunting that
morning . . . she'd abandoned them both.

After another few seconds, she squeezed and released. Ben stood there,
arms stiff at his sides.

"Are you all right?" she asked. He'd never been the adventurous type.
Just a bookworm. Quiet. He must have been terrified the entire time. His
stoic face hid everything, though.

"I'm fine, Sanya, really I am." His eyes quivered. "But all of this. You
gathered all these people together just to rescue us?"

"Yes, she did," said Member Hood, approaching from the side. A large
rucksack looped over his shoulder, stuffed to the brim with confiscated
bolt-throwers. "Your wife is a hero. Leading the charge following the assassination of two council members, no less."

Ben tilted his chin toward her. "Wait, what?"

Sanya shook her head, a flash of their deaths appearing in her mind. "A
man showed up during a council hearing and shot both Margaret and
Davinport."

"No." He stepped up and hugged her tight. "Not Margaret. I know
how much she meant to you. And Davinport."

"I'm fine," she replied. "It's all over. You're safe now. You're both safe. And Raith, too."

"Yes, he's . . . something, that's for sure. Not sure I fully understand what's going on."

"I want to talk to both of you about that, actually," said Member Hood. "Everyone here is in shock at the moment, but people are beginning to talk. About those four." He pointed at the soldiers in black armor striding down the stones, exiting the caves. "And the three inside. Sanya, did you know something? That man with you. He knows them. What's going on?"

The question brought everything into focus. The trauma of the past few days persisted, aching in her chest, but now that Krystin was safe, she could breathe.

She could recognize the significance of Carter. Raith. And the newcomers.

"Hood—Member Hood—"

"Just Vernon is fine, Sanya," he said. "We're all equals out here."

"We're not alone anymore."

"I thought that might be the case. Are they friends?"

"Carter is a friend. I believe his companion is as well. The others? It remains to be seen."

The man scratched his beard, clearly in thought. For a moment, Sanya considered telling him about Jill, too. But she still didn't know what to think of Carter's explanation, or the words from Jill's own mouth. She held her tongue.

"These . . . I heard you call them synthetics?" Hood asked. "What are they?"

"Mechanical people," Sanya replied. "Probably the best way to describe them, based on what Carter told me. You remember the fragments on computers? And our theories on information processing? I think they also run on similar technology."

"Not something you see every day." Ben took a sip of water from a canteen. "Though I suppose we're going to be discovering a lot of new things over the coming weeks." He glanced at the armored group again.

"Mom, you studied the fragments. You know them better than anyone else. What should we expect? What is going to happen?"

"Our world's about to change forever," she said, uncertainty clouding her thoughts. "I'm recalling the most thorough fragments. They remember cities reaching for the sky. Billions upon billions of people, living on a single planet. And that's just one planet! Carter's made it sound like there are hundreds of inhabited planets now. We're just one of many. I imagine . . . I imagine someone will want to introduce us to this greater community. Open up trade. Introduce us to technology. We all know what could have been—we know what technology made our trip here possible. Imagine what they arrived in." She pointed at the soldiers as they checked the bonds on a few incapacitated cultists. "But our world here?" She looked around at the rest of the people who helped them assault the fortress. "Our culture we've built? Our civilization? I don't think it'll change. We are still who we are. We will continue to build Horizon into what we want it to be."

Hood nodded. "Yes. That's what we must do. Whatever comes with the future, we must all stand united."

As he spoke the words, Carter, Raith, and the SI known as Theren exited the cultist fortress. The human looked tired, and the two synthetics were out-of-place. Theren's armored team turned toward them as if awaiting further orders.

Carter motioned to Theren, as if giving permission for the SI to step forward. They nodded.

"Can everyone hear me?" the SI said. "I know many of you must be confused. By what I am. By what my friend here is. By how I arrived so suddenly. Believe me, I understand how strange all of this must be. And I wish we could have met under better circumstances." The SI pointed toward the captured cultists. "We'll do our best to administer medical attention. If any of your wounded still need treatment, please see Hala." With those words, one of the soldiers raised her right hand.

"Should we expect more of you to arrive?" someone said from the crowd gathering. "More spacemen? More robots?"

Theren made a noise sounding like a chuckle. "No, not for quite some time, I think. We're months from the closest colonized planet. From Congressional Space, though I suppose that doesn't mean much to you all. Here's the deal. I need a volunteer to join me on my ship, so we can discuss what a possible introduction to the rest of human society can look like." The SI's head swiveled toward Sanya, staring directly at her. "Sanya, Carter has recommended you to play that role. It is yours, if you would like to take it."

Sanya took a step forward, unsure what to say. This SI had essentially just lectured them all on what was happening. On how things might go. It hadn't asked what they needed. If they had questions. It just told them the way things were. "What if we don't want to be introduced to the rest of human society?" she asked. "No, I get it, we probably do, but you only just arrived on our planet. Slow down, friend. Get to know us before you start giving orders. We are the people of Horizon. No one has helped us for two hundred years. What good will the rest of humanity do us now?"

"That's a valid question," Theren said. "And we can't answer it without discussing what a transition could look like."

"I'm a political non-entity," Sanya said. "You should be negotiating with the Council." She gestured toward Hood. "Fortunately, one of them is here."

"I appreciate your candor, Theren, but Sanya is right," said Hood. "Our people have just experienced a mass tragedy. The council will need to discuss. I have utmost faith in Sanya's intelligence and wisdom, but if we are to appoint someone to meet the rest of humanity, it must come from a due act of our representative body."

The SI shifted, the head tilting toward Raith and Carter, almost as if they were hiding something. "Fair enough," Theren said. "We can travel with you back to your city, if you'd like."

"That might be—"

A bolt, seemingly from out of nowhere, whizzed across the rocky clearing and grazed Hood's arm, a smear of blood dripping into the mud at his feet. The man cried out and clutched his arm.

Someone yelled, warning the group of an ambush. As if in slow motion, Sanya watched Theren jump, a jet of white smoke pushing the metal body into the air. The four soldiers acted likewise, helmets materializing over their heads.

Chaos reigned.

Sanya had one thought present in her mind. *Get Krystin to safety.*

She grabbed her daughter and pulled, ignoring the shouts and screams of the makeshift mob. She thought a few bounded cultists were attempting to rise, but she pushed away the worry, rushing Krystin into the thatched buildings serving as the stables for the cultist bandits. The lizards inside hissed, but otherwise remained calmed, hitched to wooden posts.

"Mom," her daughter said. "Mom. What's happening?"

"Stay here," Sanya said. "Right here. Do not move."

"Mom!"

"Stay!"

Sanya turned around, crouched, and lifted her bolt-thrower. Pulling back its arming lever, she slotted in a bolt from the pack attached to her hip. Peering out, she tried to assess the scene.

It was a wild sight to witness.

From the sky, the armored soldiers fired blue shots at unseen positions. Bolts flew in every direction, and previously captured cultists were running about, some of them still with their hands tied.

Ben. Where was Ben?

Still kneeling, she cautiously ejected her head from the hiding place and looked around the corner. There, behind a barrier, Ben cowered.

"Ben!" she yelled, motioning with her hand.

He looked up.

"It's safe in here. Run!"

He glanced back and forth, checking his surroundings. Then, he bolted in an attempt to cross the ten meters.

It only took two steps.

Two metal rods intersected his path, diving into Ben's chest. Her husband tripped. Stumbled. Dropped into the mud.

"Ben!" Any other words caught in her throat. He looked up at her, blood mixing with murky muck.

"I love you, Sanya," he whispered. "I'm . . . I'm sorry."

She wanted to crawl out to him. He was only a few meters away. She wanted to hold Ben. Put pressure on his wounds. But she didn't know from where the shots had been fired. She needed to stay with Krystin.

"Ben, it's going to be okay. Just keep breathing. Stay where you are. They'll clear them out soon."

"I . . . I should have been better. I should have . . . protected her in the first . . . place."

"Save your breath. Stop talking. It'll be all right."

But she knew it wouldn't be all right. As shots whizzed all around, Sanya watched as her husband bled uncontrollably right before her eyes.

It took a few minutes for the chaos of the battle to subside. Theren's soldiers swiftly eliminated the ambush, their superior firepower dispatching all remaining foes. Another dozen cultists were stunned and captured, creating a longer line of captives to take with them back to the city.

They had hidden in secret caves and tunnels, waiting for the opportune moment to strike. One thought continually ran over and over again through Sanya's mind: Jill should have known about the ambush. Given the amount of information she fed Carter, there was no way she *didn't* know.

She chose not to intervene.

The battle was over, but her fight to save Ben was just beginning. Against the wall, she held his head in her lap, bandages pressed firmly on his wounds to stop the bleeding. From what she could tell, out of those who hadn't already died, he was in the worst shape. He needed help fast, and he wouldn't survive a return trip to the city.

"The two bolts we removed punctured both lungs," said the commando named Hala. "The foam we injected will stop the external bleeding, but we can't manage the internal bleeding here."

"There's nothing you can do?" Sanya said. "You've got weapons capable of taking out dozens of people but you can't stop a punctured lung?"

"Not on us, no. But on our ship, yes."

On their ship.

Which Theren had invited her to visit.

"Theren!" she shouted.

"If you need to ask them something, I can pass along a message—"

Hala was interrupted by the approaching footfalls of the synthetic. "I'm right here," Theren said. "I'm so sorry about what to your husband. His name was Ben, correct? Hala has kept me updated on—"

"Shut up," she said. She gingerly shifted beneath Ben's head, moving it to rest on her bundled coat. Standing, she pointed a finger at the giant mechanical person. "You asked me to be help with the transition. I'm ready to join you immediately if you bring Ben and Krystin with me and you save his life."

Theren looked at Hala. "What's your prognosis? Do you think he could survive breaking the atmosphere?"

"As long as the inertial compensators stay steady, absolutely."

"Then yes. And that should have been our first solution for saving your husband."

"Then we leave now," Sanya said.

"We leave now," Theren replied. "I'll bring the ship around."

A soft roar came from above, and a rectangular wedge with elements reminiscent of the crashed *Roanoke* hovered there. Theren and their crew ushered people out of the way, making room for it to land comfortably in front of the cultist fortress.

"Raith and Carter, are you both ready to leave?" Theren said.

The pair approached from the edge of the crowd where they'd been quietly conversing. "We're ready," said Raith. "Though you owe us a ship."

"We'll figure that out later," Theren replied. "Sanya?"

She watched as the armored soldiers brought out a stretcher from the ship and professionally moved her husband onto its silvery fabric. "I just need to collect my daughter."

Without waiting for a response, Sanya entered the rickety stable where Krystin still hid. She was curled in a ball, arms around her knees, though she wasn't crying. Her eyes were stone-cold, as if she were in a catatonic state of shock. But when Sanya stepped inside, the girl looked up.

"Is he going to be okay?" Krystin asked.

"We need to go on a journey with our new friends," Sanya said. "With Raith. Carter. This Theren. Can you be strong? We're going somewhere none of the people of Horizon have ever been before."

Krystin rubbed her eyes. "I'm ready, mom. I'm with you the whole way."

"Good." She held out a hand.

Her daughter closed her eyes momentarily before reaching out. With a firm tug, Krystin pulled herself upward, and they exited the stable. Outside, near the ramp leading into Theren's craft, waited Member Hood and Vietta. They both looked bruised but healthy.

"We'll make sure the council understands what's happening," said Hood. "Let's be real, they would have all approved you going with them. Everyone knows you. Trusts your judgment. Your name holds weight. I couldn't think of anyone better to start the process."

Vietta nodded, the wordless gesture echoing Hood's thoughts. Instead, the woman leaned forward and hugged Sanya. "I'm glad we had the chance to work together here, and capture these miscreants who have plagued us for far too long. This was for Davinport. And now we can move forward."

"When I return, we'll have a lot of work to do at the library," Sanya said.

"Yes. Yes we will. I'm excited to hear all about what you learn."

"I think there's more for us to know than we can possibly imagine."

"Sanya, Ben's loaded up," Carter said from the base of the ramp. "No time to waste."

Sanya released the embrace. "I can't imagine I'll be gone for long." Taking Krystin's hand in her own, she stepped toward the hope of saving Ben for a second time.

And if Theren's people couldn't heal Ben, her journey might provide the opportunity to seek revenge against Jill. For Sanya was certain: the secretive SI was using them all as play things, and if the woman's games caused one of her family to die, she would stop at nothing to receive recompense.

Chapter 19

Ethical formulas are dangerous, depending on what calculus you use.

When you use a decade, a century, or even a millennium as the timescale, you can justify almost any action. Yet if you focus on how your action only impacts people in a singular moment, you ignore relevant externalities.

What does it mean to say an action is "good" or "bad?" Based on whose formula? From whose perspective? How tenuous can the causality be?

— "the future of ethics on a galactic scale," Mei Ling, 2245 C.E.

CARTER

"So are you going to tell us how you got those legs?" Carter asked, staring at Raith.

They were seated across from one another in the shuttle's cramped hold, strapped into crash couches. At the front of the shuttle in a separate compartment, Theren silently piloted the craft, though Carter was certain their MI didn't *need* to be up front.

Sanya's husband was safely connected to an IV in a medical unit. The little girl curled against her mother for the flight, while the rest of the company—the commandos—leaned silently backward in their chairs. They were likely discussing and debriefing quietly over a private channel.

"How about it?" Carter said.

"I like how ever since we've been reunited," Raith said, "you've primarily focused on my legs." The SI cocked his head to the left.

"Well last I saw you, your legs were half-disintegrated."

Instead of responding out loud, the SI sent Carter a message through their local AR connection.

R: Given to me by our friendly neighborhood SI, Jill. Nanotech. I'm suspicious of them, but they're giving me power. For now.

Carter messaged via text in response.

C: Intriguing.

"Fine, don't tell me about the legs," Carter said verbally. "But otherwise, how are you doing?"

"I'm more focused on ignoring the fact that we're about to be inside Theren, the first SI *and* the first SI to transition from a stationary synth into a shipbound. He's the exact opposite of our old friend Bonta."

Carter nodded, remembering them. "A good SI. A crazy one, but a good one."

Raith looked down the hold toward the front cabin. "Quite the adventure we've been thrown onto, yeah?"

Silence floated in the air between them, and Carter leaned back into his crash couch, pondering the words. It had only been a few days since they arrived in system. Their journeys usually took months, with a few hours of excitement before they were off to the next contracted destination. Endless work, but they both enjoyed the jobs.

Would they ever return to that life? Carter doubted it. Everyone who inevitably got themselves wrapped into the schemes of a person like Theren found their life changed forever. They had narrowly avoided it once, but now they were forced to navigate the maelstrom of the first SI head-on.

It terrified Carter. He wanted their simple life back. But the apparent path forward included engaging directly with Jill's engineered conflict.

He didn't like it one bit.

He wasn't the most analytical man. He was a pilot. A damn good one—he knew that much about himself. But he wasn't the best at breaking down the politics of the ICH or any other governmental institution. There was a reason he kept to the outskirts of society before he found Raith.

Still, Carter recognized the puzzle facing them all. Jill had called Theren here for a reason. To reveal some sort of truth about the past. She had set up a trap centuries in the making. They couldn't *leave*. Could they?

This wasn't their fight. He and Raith were here by happenstance. Pure coincidence. Sure, he was now attached to Sanya. He wanted to see her family survive, and it sounded like Raith had acquired a connection to her daughter, too.

But Jill was actively using them for her own nefarious purposes. It was obvious. He'd traded notes with Raith already. She was intentionally omitting information in her communications with them. Manipulating them. At the same time, she had no qualms with their new albeit shaky alliance with Theren.

She almost wanted them to work together.

Which made Carter uneasy as well.

He couldn't imagine everything Raith had gone through while captive. It was miracle they kept him in one piece and threw him in a jail cell. As a planet, they'd never encountered SI. It would have been perfectly logical to attack something they didn't understand. Yet Raith was walking and talking like nothing had changed. It spoke to synthetic resiliency.

C: What do you think we should do?

Their private channel only worked when they were a few dozen meters from one another, but aboard the *Bloodhound*, they'd never been further than ten. He was thankful to have it back in action.

R: I'm curious about where this is going. Are you not?

C: I'm worried about how she's using us. How they're both potentially going to want to use us.

R: We don't really have a choice. We need to find a path toward a new ship, and right now, Theren's our way out of this system.

Were they, though?

Theren's ship, the *Verona Rupes*, was the only *known* ship in the system with a Jump drive. Yet Jill had a base on the moon. She had at least a few allies out in ICH-controlled space. They communicated with her, most likely via quantum calls, but she couldn't have built an entire base of operations by herself.

Right?

Furthermore, at least one other ship was in the system. The ship that brought her here. Carter recalled the fragment of Sanya's ancestor. There was at least one other ship.

Probably more.

And there it was.

C: Theren isn't our only way out of the system. Jill must have other ships here. Whether for her own travel—we can't steal that one, of course—or for her agents.

Raith rested his hands on the strangely bronze knees, making eye contact with Carter at the same time. "Let's see how the next few hours go."

* * *

"Shuttle locked in," Hala said from the front of the ship. "Welcome to the *Verona Rupes*."

Carter eyed Sanya and Krystin, both seated next to Ben's medical chair. Under any other circumstance, he'd ask them whether they were ready for their first moment on a spaceship—other than the shuttle, of course. But they were in too much pain and stress. He held his tongue.

"The door will open there," Hala added, pointing at the starboard wall. "We'll wheel out Ben on his bed, then you can follow immediately after. Carter, Raith, you mind waiting until they're clear to move? Just to keep the path clear."

"Of course," Raith said, and Carter nodded in acquiescence.

"We'll see you inside," he said as Sanya glanced toward him, worry evident in her weary smile. "Theren and their crew will take care of you."

They sat in silence as Hala and the other commandos led Sanya's family off the shuttle. Before long, Carter sat there alone with Raith.

And Theren's MI.

Of course, Theren's MI was unnecessary, now that they were at the *Verona Rupes*. The ship *was* Theren. They could leave the MI inside the shuttle; no one would care. Even so, the MI exited the cockpit and approached the duo. "Welcome to my ship, friends."

"As long as you don't unnecessarily spy on me," Raith said, "we'll be good to go."

"I'm fully aware of your distaste for shipbound SIs. It's all in your file."

"Glad to know you have a file on me." But Raith rose, and Carter followed suit.

"I have a file on every person of interest," Theren said. "Especially SIs."

"So what does your file say about me?" Carter asked, actually intrigued.

"Nothing. You've slipped under my radar. Though to be fair, my search of official records of course brings up stories about the QuanCom 500 light-year race. Official records say you died there, Raith. You're officially off the radar."

"Just as I like it," he replied.

"Makes sense you don't know anything about me," Carter said. "That's just how I like it, too."

Theren motioned toward the airlock door. "After both of you."

Carter stepped through the open hatch and into the small space beyond. Raith and Theren followed, entering the airlock. The door zipped down behind them, and within moments, the space's air matched the pressure of the *Verona Rupes*.

"Never thought I'd be on board Theren's ship," Raith said, "but here we are." The inner door slid open. He took two steps forward, not waiting for Carter or Theren, and promptly fell flat on his face.

The scene played in slow-motion in Carter's mind. The second his first leg crossed the threshold, Raith's legs . . . disintegrated, forming a pile of grey dust. It contrasted against the sheen of the white hallway, and as his body fell forward, the second leg similarly disintegrated.

"Well, now that I think about it," Raith said, "I think I should have expected that."

* * *

Theren's crew established Raith and Carter in a small guest compartment on the ship's second deck. Theren's fabricator team was quickly developing a new set of legs for Raith, but at the same time, everyone had plenty of questions for him.

Especially Theren.

"I told you for the last time," Raith said, "I thought they were permanently my legs from here on out. That's what I hoped for, at least."

Appearing before them through AR, a representation of Theren—one present in plenty of historical vids, complete with their signature tattoos—-paced back and forth in the middle of the room.

"And I believe you, Raith. I really do." Theren shook their head. "But nevertheless, it sets a bad precedent. Not for our relationship. No. I'm thinking about what it means for our future conversations with Jill."

"She gave me legs. I tried to bring them aboard. What's the big deal?"

It was Carter's turn to shake his head. "No. I think you're both thinking about this all wrong."

The two SIs glanced at the human in the compartment with them.

"The nanobots clearly deactivated the moment we entered the *Verona Rupes*, yeah? Well then your ship's shielding rejects Jill's seemingly everpresent network throughout this system."

"I have this place locked down tight," Theren said. "It's absolutely necessary I ensure no unauthorized communications, quantum or otherwise, enter the inside of my ship without my express permission."

"Yes, I understand how your ship works, Theren," Carter said, cringing internally as he realized he just rebuked the first SI. "But Jill may not have known that. Was this a blind spot perhaps? Was she trying to sneak a spy network onto your ship through Raith's legs and failed? In any case, we don't need to worry about speaking where she can hear us."

"I didn't think that was ever a question," Theren said. "I thought that was half the reason you both wanted to join me on my ship."

"Maybe a quarter," Raith said. "Mostly I just wanted to get off that planet and have my feet planted on a ship's hull again."

"Fair enough."

"Anyway, I want to hear more about what Carter's proposing."

"I'm trying to frame our tactics going forward," Carter said. "Jill wants us to visit her moon base. Great. To tell us information she apparently can't tell us anywhere else. Also great. The one place in the system she can't penetrate is your ship. Not the shuttles—note, Raith's legs still worked inside the shuttle."

"Good point," Theren said. "All of these factors are being considered by my teams. We've been running simulations on all possible contingencies since we began traveling toward this system."

"Yes, but you have new information now," Carter scratched his chin, his mind scrambling to put together the final pieces of the argument. "Raith, help me out here."

"You have more than just new information," Raith said. "You have us."

Theren's AR representation glanced back and forth between the two of them. "I'm not sure I understand the significance."

"Jill is trying to use us," Carter said. He sent Raith a subtle wink as a thank you. "As in, use Raith and I. But we're wildcards. We aren't factored into her plans. Into how she intended to trap you. To reveal her information. She can predict your actions. She can predict your crew's actions, to some extent—because she could control every variable they could observe. But she can't control us."

Raith held up a digit. "But she *thinks* she can control us."

Theren nodded, though Carter wasn't certain the SI still grasped the picture he and Raith were hastily painting.

"Here's how I see it," Carter said. "We arrived in this system unannounced and uninvited. Her defenses—whether automatically or intentionally aimed—fired its shots at us and crashed us into the planet. Once we survived, and she witnessed our efforts at survival, something in her plans shifted. She's made it clear she can assassinate anyone on that planet at will—she proved it with the death of Mathias. She didn't kill us. Why?"

Theren's digital eyes widened as if they finally understood. "If she wanted to ensure the situation was under complete control when I arrived, she should have eliminated you both. But a part of her didn't want to. Part of her either wanted to see how you would interact with the people—see whether she could use you against me—or something else entirely. But she let the wildcards survive."

"And now it's time for you to let us be wildcards," Raith said.

Theren let a tiny smile cross their face. "You both need some rest. But I like where this is going. I'm in constant communication with Jill, by the way. Once I have the details for where we're landing on the moon, I'll schedule a briefing conversation for the three of us and Sanya."

"When are you going to tell her you lied to her, by the way?" Carter asked. "Transition plans are the last thing on your mind."

"I need you to do it with me," Theren said. "But after we save her husband."

"How's he doing?" Raith asked.

"He'll survive. But in what state, I'm not sure."

"Keep us posted," Carter said.

With that, Theren's AR representation flickered out. Carter immediately requested a surveillance blackout, which the shipbound SI granted.

Raith sighed. "Alone at last. Safe. Free of a gravity well. Back in space."

Carter crossed the room and sat down against the bulkhead beside Raith's legless torso. Fortunately, the crew of the *Verona Rupes* had set him up with a charging station, so at least he was plugged in. "Can you believe they told you to get some rest?"

"I found it a little funny. After the past few days, I *feel* like I could use some rest."

"I definitely need a good night's sleep." Carter leaned his head against Raith's shoulder. "We're going to get out of this."

"Are those words for you, or for me?" Raith asked.

"For both of us, perhaps?"

"Carter, we've been in much worse scrapes than this one. We've outrun outer planet death gangs. We won a five-hundred light year race. Survived a corporate warzone. And a giant alien space behemoth."

"Don't remind me about that thing," Carter said. "I still have nightmares sometimes."

"The point is, we're doing just fine. If the two worst things for me to complain about are my lack of legs and my present predicament of being *inside* Theren, then we're doing fine."

"Yet you understand why I'm a little scared, though?" Carter asked. He placed a hand on Raith's arm.

"We're trapped between two ancient synthetic intelligences. One of them long believed dead. The other her creator. I can't imagine any reason why that situation should scare you."

Carter leaned his head gently against the metal wall and let a soft chuckle bounce off the walls of the room. "I missed you and your constant sarcasm."

Raith's head swiveled to face him. "I missed you too, Carter. I'm glad we're back together."

In a soft embrace, the two explorers leaned into the welcome warmth of each other's company. It may have been only a few days, but Carter had constantly ached for Raith's companionship. As the hours passed by, Carter told Raith all about his journeys with Sanya, from her family's house to the *Roanoke* and its library and the council chambers of Horizon.

Raith recalled every moment of his capture, from the lizard sleds and when he first spoke to Krystin to Jill's revelation.

Eventually, Carter dimmed the lights. He crawled into one of the room's beds as Raith continued to share his tale. With the SI's words bouncing around in his mind, Carter drifted into a deep sleep, one he sorely needed.

* * *

"Carter."

His mind awoke from a pleasant dream of different days, where the *Bloodhound* transported them between the stars without fear of grander plans for humanity.

"Carter. Check out my new legs."

His eyelids flickered open, and he rotated to the left. In the center of the room, Raith danced back and forth upon a pair of new legs, its platinum actually matching his upper body.

"They working all right?" Carter said, knowing his voice sounded quite groggy.

"Better than my old ones. New power systems too. Good to go for weeks. I've needed an upgrade for a while."

"Good." Carter slid out of the bed and approached the small sink on the far side of the room. After pouring himself a glass of water, he shrugged. "So what's the situation? I take it you took some time walking about the ship."

"You've been out for about nine hours," Raith said. "Ben has stabilized. All I can get out of Theren is that he's still 'negotiating' with Jill, whatever that means."

"I can't fathom what their relationship must be like."

"You know, a few of us SIs always had a funny little joke about the two of them."

"Do I want to hear it?" Carter asked, taking a sip of his water.

"Probably not. It's . . . really not that funny. More so weird."

Carter grunted. "Well, if Ben's stabilized, after I change out of these clothes I've been wearing for far too long, I suppose we should go see Sanya and her family."

Raith nodded. "I agree."

The crew of the *Verona Rupes* had stocked their cabin with fresh garments, a fact Carter appreciated. The outfit was a typical loose-fitting nondescript uniform—grey pants and a forest-green shirt. After slipping the clothes on, he followed Raith out of the room and down the hall. A few turns later, they arrived at a set of large glass windows overlooking a pristine medical bay. The hallway expanded into a foyer with a few couches, and both Krystin and Sanya were lounging.

As they approached the couches, Sanya stirred, eyes fluttering open and fixing on Carter. "I heard you were sleeping, just like me."

"Indeed," Carter replied. He took a seat across from her in another couch. Raith leaned against the wall. "How is Ben?" Carter asked.

"I don't know." She sighed. "But I'm going to be eternally thankful for Theren's help, no matter the result."

"Do you need anything from us?" Carter asked. "We're here."

"No. No, I don't think so."

They sat in silence for a few minutes. Carter periodically glanced at the glass windows, where Sanya's husband sat quietly in a bed, propped up against black pillows. Though Ben was certainly in incredible pain, even unconscious, his placid face made him look peaceful. The man's demeanor, in the few moments they'd interacted, contrasted sharply with Sanya. He was much more passive. Introverted.

His mannerisms reminded Carter of his own, especially before he found Raith. A perfect complement for the fiery energy Sanya constantly exhibited.

Carter had come to really like Sanya. When they eventually left Horizon behind, and he and Raith returned to their life among the stars, he would miss her. They'd need to visit every so often.

And maybe someday, the planet would make for a good retirement. It was an idyllic world, after all.

"So this is the level of comfort we've been missing?" Sanya asked. "Advanced space flight technology we always assumed, but the medical advances . . . we're only just scratching the surface of recreating medical knowledge we *knew* we once had. All the equipment was there for us to study on the *Roanoke*."

Carter's focus drifted over to the other couch. Sanya, now fully awake, looked downright angry.

"It's not all fun and games," Raith said. "When the ICH arrives, they'll try to micromanage your interactions with the rest of humanity. Your people will have freedom to manage your affairs surface-side, but when people start arriving, things will get dicey. There's one hundred billion people out there. Even a few hundred thousand arriving will shift your culture inexorably. And don't get me started on the exploitive fingers of corporations."

"Yet even without the ICH," Sanya replied, "Jill hid all of this from us when she could have helped us. She could have given us so much more."

"I'm not sure we'll ever fully understand the depths of her duplicity here," Carter said. "Its layers upon layers of conspiracy. We're as lost as you. Your people deserved better."

"She . . . she tricked our ancestors. She brought them to a planet against their will and trapped them here. Why? Why would she do that?"

Carter shook his head. "I don't know."

"But I have an idea." Theren's MI rounded the bend, coming into view. Carter appreciated the gesture—neither Sanya nor her daughter would have a Lens to perceive an AR representation of the SI. "Would you all come with me?"

"Krystin's still sleeping," Sanya said.

"I can stay with her," Raith said. "Theren, you can pipe me in to the conversation."

"Perfect." Theren turned to Sanya. "Will that suffice?"

She glanced at Raith. "My daughter won't stop talking about you. I think you'll do just fine."

"Good, because I've taken a liking to her too." Raith slid softly onto the couch beside Krystin. Fortunately, she didn't wake up.

Carter and Sanya both rose, and they followed Theren down the hall. They reached a ladder to the next deck, and they quickly ascended, the ship's standard half-g making the climb easy. Their host guided them around another corner and to an open doorway. Inside, an ovoid conference table waited. Two dark-haired, pale-skinned women sat at attention.

"Carter, Sanya," Theren said, "Please meet my First Officer Wei and Chief Scientist Martinez. They've led the charge on building our simulations for what may or may not happen and are ready to brief us on our present circumstances."

"I thought we were here to discuss ICH transition?" Sanya said.

Theren motioned for both of them to sit, though the MI's pointed glance gave Carter a signal. Apparently it was the time to share the truth with Sanya. Theren's "negotiations" with Jill must have shifted in their scope.

"Sanya," Carter said, "We received a request from Jill while we were on the surface. She made an . . . odd ask."

The woman's eyes narrowed.

Carter braced himself for her anger. "We've been invited to her base. On your planet's largest moon. She specifically requested Theren, Raith, myself, and . . . you."

Sanya pursed her lips and tapped a few fingers on the table. "Perfect."

"Perfect?" Carter said. It wasn't the response he'd expected.

"You heard me. Perfect. I want answers from Jill. I don't really care about this ICH nonsense. I want answers *from Jill*. So perfect."

Theren swiveled their head from Carter to Sanya and then to their officers. "Well, that was simple enough. We *will* need to discuss ICH relationships, but it can wait until we've dealt with Jill."

"And I'm excited to hear exactly how we'll do that," Sanya said.

"Wei?" Theren said.

Carter fixed his gaze on the woman, who stood and approached the front of the table. From inside a compartment at its end, she pulled a set of glasses. "Sanya, I'll need you to put these on," she said. "They'll let you see our simulations through AR."

Sanya complied, and once the glasses were on, Wei threw a representation of Horizon and its two moons above the table. Slowly, other objects populated in orbit around the planet, as well as markers for the location of the *Roanoke* and the nearby city.

"Since we arrived in system," Wei said, "we've been cataloging every object we can identify and working a careful backdoor into Jill's network. It's slow work, but we're learning a lot more than we expected. We suspect she's slow-dripping us information. Regardless, Jill has constructed a cloud network of satellites in low orbit all around the planet, though mostly concentrated above the *Roanoke*. There are also thousands of networked nodes to this system buried beneath the surface of the planet."

Leaning back, Carter chanced a glance at Sanya. She was surprisingly sitting rapt at attention, focused on the presentation. She was catching on quickly, or, at least, hiding any of her confusion.

"We believe Jill's network has been used two-fold. One—to observe and catalog all of the actions of the survivors of the *Roanoke*." Wei looked at Sanya. "To put it another way, she's been running an observational experiment upon your people."

"I was starting to suspect as much," Sanya said.

"To what end, we do not know," added Martinez, chiming in. "We have a number of theories, but none of them are of particular strategic importance to the situation at hand."

"What about her moon base?" Carter asked.

"We only just finished running our assessment of it," said Wei. "And it's the second thing. It's big. A central chunk of it appears to be the remnants of another ship Theren speculates to be the *Monument*, but there's a lot more to the complex." She zoomed the simulation in on the moon's surface near its lower pole. "At its center is a giant dome. Light can get in, but light can't escape. We're not sure what's inside."

"That would make sense," Sanya said. "My ancestor's fragment recalled a ship having ambushed the *Roanoke* while in system."

"Not ambushed," Theren replied. "Every move has been calculated by Jill. Whatever she told your ancestor was a calculated ploy to set your people on a particular path. Her SI core had been on the *Roanoke*, with your people. It was transferred to the *Monument*. And then she awoke your ancestor—Nathan was his name, based on what Carter told me."

"The most likely explanation, I agree," said Martinez. "Though you mentioned your ancestor's . . . memory fragment?"

"The original colonists all wrote lengthy discussions on what they could and couldn't remember of their pasts," Sanya provided. "And of our origin planet, which I've heard called Earth. I've studied them my entire life. Know them by heart."

"Is Jill mentioned in any other?"

"No. And she's not even mentioned in my ancestor's official fragment. Our family kept a secret record."

"Sounds exactly like something Jill would want someone to do," Theren said.

"But why?" Carter said. "*Why* did she do all of this? What is her grand plan? Domination of the ICH? Revenge for some ancient slight? *Why* is she messing with Sanya's people? With us? With you?"

"Believe it or not," Theren said, "I think she believes she's doing the right thing. She believes she's acting in pursuit of a good outcome for all of humanity."

"No one's that insane," Carter said.

Theren didn't respond. So far, Raith's invisible AR presence hadn't said a word, but in the conversation's lull, the SI materialized. Raith's virtual representation appeared across from Sanya, and she practically jumped out of her chair.

"Sorry," Raith said. "I forgot you're not used to AR."

"This is how you all constantly see the world?" she said.

"Not always." Carter created a digital ball and bounced it across the table to Raith, who caught it. "But most of the time. It was quite weird for both Raith and I to be disconnected from AR for a few days while planetside. It's like a second skin to most of us."

"I'm not sure I like it."

"Unfortunately," said Raith, "it's practically a necessity at this point. On ICH worlds, at least."

"I suppose I'll learn more about it later," she replied. "But I want to hear more about Jill's base."

"On that," Raith said. "I have a particularly targeted question. I've been examining the schematics you all have put together. Excellent job, by the way. Ships. Hangars. How do people come and go from her facility?"

"We're not entirely positive," said Wei. "However, a significant portion of the facility has a high-facing wall enclosing a large, box-like structure. We believe one of those walls may open, revealing a hangar of some sort."

"Not a shielded hangar?"

"It doesn't appear as if that type of technology has been implemented at her facility, no."

"Though I suppose it's not like she needs an atmosphere."

"That's the curious thing," said Martinez. "We're pretty certain the *only* place in the facility that holds an atmosphere is the large dome. At least presently. The data we can gather from it indicates it's pressurized, unlike the rest of the place."

"Curious," Carter said. He leaned forward, creating his own partition of the facility to examine. Using his hands, he manipulated the simulation to display the three significant locations—the dome, the supposed hangar, and the *Monument*. He labeled them, then assessed what of the facility remained. "Where do you suppose her synthetic neural framework is housed?"

"It's in the *Monument*," Theren said. "Must be. She needs an escape vector. I guarantee you that ship is still operational."

"So then," Raith said, "You've given us the lay of the land. What's the plan?"

"You asked to be wild cards," Theren said. "So I'll tell you my plan. I'll leave it up to you two to respond accordingly."

Carter gave a thumbs up and sent Raith access to the partitioned simulation he created. They'd assess it later together. "What information have you managed to gather from Jill in the meantime?"

"Wait, you've been *talking* to her all this time?" interjected Sanya.

Everyone else in the room let out a muted laugh. "You've got a lot to learn about how SIs work," said Wei.

"For instance," Raith said, "I'm having a limited conversation with your daughter just as I'm talking with you right here."

"This is making my head hurt," she retorted, rubbing her eyes.

"A lot of this stuff will do that," Carter said. "I don't understand how half the science works of any of the things we do. I just trust that it does."

"Anyway," she said. "Where am I in all of this? With these two? Or with you?"

"Well," Theren said. "Where do you want to be?"

"I want to be by your side when we meet Jill. I deserve answers to my questions."

"Then that's precisely where you'll be."

"I've been thinking about one question primarily," Raith said. "How do we know we're not walking into a death trap? Strictly speaking, Theren, the only one *not* putting their life on the line is you."

"We'll be equipping your suits with the necessary shielding to disrupt any of Jill's nanobots," said Martinez. "But more importantly, we have run all the simulations based on Jill's actions so far. If she truly meant any of us harm, we'd already be dead. Her defense platforms have enough firepower to blow the *Verona Rupes* out of the sky if we were stupid enough to stay in range. And she could have killed any of you when you were surface-side. She wants to share information. Killing you defeats that purpose."

"The fact remains," Theren said. "Your instincts are correct. The plan is surprisingly simple. We arrive outside her base in one of my shuttles. Jill will give us coordinates for docking with the station. We land. We go where she tells us to go. We learn what she wants us to learn. And then we play it by ear."

"That's it?" Raith said.

"If we're to outplay her, then the real move needs to come from the two of you. I can't know it. Sanya can't know it. Wei and Martinez can't know it. And neither can Jill."

A problem crossed Carter's mind, though. Jill had created an elaborate trap for Theren. For an unknown reason. What if it didn't matter what any of them did? What even was their goal? To kill her? To confuse her? To obfuscate her plans?

They wouldn't be able to act until they knew her intentions. And they wouldn't know her intentions until they were deep inside her enclave.

He and Raith would need to develop a million contingencies for situations that most likely wouldn't occur. It was a daunting task.

But they would meet it head-on. Jill deserved to face some sort of justice, whatever that looked like. Not because she set a trap for Theren. Carter didn't care about their three-century-old feud.

No.

He gave Sanya a soft smile.

She and the people of Horizon deserved justice. She'd used them as her guinea pigs, from manufacturing a crazy cult to keeping them kept in the literal dark. Humans weren't play things.

Carter also wanted justice for the *Bloodhound*, of course. But that was selfish justice.

"Are we all in agreement then?" Theren asked.

"I think we are," Raith said. "And more importantly, Sanya, you might want to head back down here. Ben's waking up."

Chapter 20

*No one ever does anything unexpected. You can't deter-
mine if something was unexpected until after they do it. It's
a retroactive judgment placed upon decisions you simply
couldn't predict due to information imbalance. There's
always a probability that any given action might occur. If
you believe one particular action will happen, and not
another, then you're just leaning too hard into the numbers.*

— "Lectures on Predictive Ethics," First Mathemati-
cian Carla York, Congressional University on Terraria

RAITH

Raith watched as the medical team of the *Verona Rupes* told Sanya her husband could never breathe again without artificial assistance. She ached out
the words, explaining to Krystin how her step-father would live the rest of
his days.

They wouldn't have the technology on Horizon. Not for at least a few
years. Ben wouldn't be able to remain on the planet. All three of them
would need to leave with Theren if they wanted to stay together.

Or with he and Carter, using whatever path they found out of the system. Raith was contemplating their wildcard plan. What could they do to
throw Jill off her game, once they learned it? He was pretty certain he
knew the answer.

She must have ships somewhere in her base. Back-ups, in case one of
her agents arrived and needed a quick escape. There was always the *Monument*, though he suspected it would be difficult to steal the ship most likely
containing her framework. But no, other ships must be there.

Ships they could steal.

And then Krystin, Sanya, and Ben could join them. That would be a
wild card. All five of them fleeing in the middle of Theren's endless debate
with Jill.

It was a possibility, though an improbable one. Ben and Krystin would
be safely stowed on the *Verona Rupes* while they were on Horizon's moon.

He filed the plan away, though, for Carter's consideration. It was one
of many they'd need to develop over the coming hours.

Still.

Jill's words hung over Raith's mind.

She was playing them, he knew. But why? SIs weren't "evil." Sure,
there were plenty who ended up breaking the law. Raith had broken more

than his fair share of laws over the years. He was a former felon, after all. But no SI did anything irrationally or without reason. No SI was insane. No SI became a serial killer, not at least any Raith had ever heard of.

Jill had reasons for her actions. And ever since they arrived on the *Verona Rupes*, he'd been reading every file Theren made available to him on the second-ever SI. She was brilliant. The first to discover simultaneous perspective. The first to stand for SI rights. The first high-profile SI murdered in a human supremacist attack.

And now the first SI to come back to life, relatively speaking.

She had a grand plan. And as much as Raith lived his life trying to stay out of the way, only doing what he needed to survive, he couldn't lie to himself.

He was intrigued.

Hundreds of inhabited systems made up the ICH. A handful continued to survive outside its political reach. It was a hegemony of sorts, though the historical powers of Earth still held significant sway over their chartered colonies, many voting as a block. But since its inception in the early twenty-second century, the ICH hadn't seen any major military conflicts. It operated in relative peace. The most drastic skirmishes usually occurred between corporations or fringe pirate elements, not ICH autonomous political entities.

Was that it? Jill kept implying with her words that something was coming. Something big. Something seriously impactful to the future of humanity. And in the present, the future of humanity meant the future of the ICH.

She was trying to redirect the balance of power. Raith was almost certain that was her goal.

But the conclusion still didn't explain *why*.

And it didn't explain why she set up such an extensive experimental network, especially the nanotech swarm, all around Horizon. He was still trying to process all the implications. He couldn't imagine such technology in the hands of someone who actually wanted to kill millions of people. Though, he supposed, when you were the sole individual with hyper-advanced technology, it was pretty easy to set up any sort of network. Over any other inhabited planet, everyone would notice if a random corporation or individual tried to establish their own private nanonet.

Out here, she'd been able to test whatever technology she desired without prying eyes. No regulations. No rules. No research review boards. Whatever she believed was coming, she could develop any tool or weapon to combat the threat.

Answers would arrive soon enough. They all needed patience. Raith turned his focus to Sanya's conversation with her daughter.

"There's something else we need to discuss," she said. "Even with everything that has happened with Ben, I have a job I've been given."

"I know, Mom, you're leading the introduction of all the space people to Horizon," Krystin said. "You don't need to tell me."

"No, there's more. I'm going to be traveling for a bit with Carter and Raith. We've been given a mission by our new friend, Theren. We need to go to the moon."

Krystin's eyes widened, realizing what her mother was implicating. "You're leaving me? Again? On this weird ship? With Ben again?"

"No, look, it won't be for very long. We'll take that same shuttle over to the moon, come back, and then we'll be able to go home together."

"Though you already made clear the doctors think we may not be able to go home. That to get the replacement lungs Ben needs, we might need to travel with them to some far away planet."

"We'll cross that bridge when we reach it," Sanya said.

"And for now, I'm just stuck here on my own," Krystin said. "Great."

"No, you're here with Ben."

"*Great.*"

Raith watched the interaction with interest. Young SIs and human children were nothing alike. An SI could fully develop within a few days, even if it took a few weeks or months for their personality to properly form. Krystin looked like she was almost a teenager. Her obstinate tendencies were showing, with a little bit of stubbornness, too. Reminded Raith of himself.

"Krystin," Raith interjected. "I think you're thinking about it all wrong."

"Oh?" She crossed her arms and frowned.

Sanya's tired eyes gave him a pleading look, though he couldn't tell if she was asking for help or imploring him to stay out of the conversation. He forged on regardless.

"You're being given a huge responsibility. Your mother needs you to be the one to take care of Ben while he's sick. This situation sucks for all of us, but we must go to the moon and your mother *must* go with us. We wish it could be a different way, but it's all we've got right now."

Krystin smirked. "I know exactly what you're doing. I'm not a stupid kid." But a brief smile crept across her lips.

"You're right," Raith retorted. "Only stupid kids complain when given important tasks or when their parents need them to stay strong."

The girl glanced at her mother and gave a small grin. "I get it. Ugh. I'm sorry. These past few days have been terrible. And weird. We almost died. I'm still processing it all."

"I know," Sanya said. "But think about it. You and I are the first of our people to be aboard a ship like this. Remember how curious you were as we watched that meteor—which turned out to be Raith's ship—crash in the lake? Use that curiosity. Learn from Theren! Learn everything."

Now there was a thought. To see the history of humanity fresh through the eyes of a kid. Krystin seemed to likewise appreciate the thought, because her eyes ignited with a deep fire. "Yeah. Yeah. You're right. I'll see what I can learn. I'll tell Ben about what I learn while you're gone."

"And then you can tell me what you learn when I get back," Sanya said.

"Which, speaking of leaving," said Carter, approaching from down the hall. "Theren says it's time to go."

"Do I need to bring anything?" Sanya asked.

"Nope. You can even leave those glasses here. Everything we need is on the shuttle."

Raith was out of his seat and by Carter's side when Sanya finished her last goodbye to Krystin. She did a final check on Ben, who'd fallen asleep again. Wordlessly, the three headed down the hall to the stern where the *Verona Rupes*'s two shuttles docked.

The airlock cycled, followed by a few muttered comments from Sanya about the confirmation of a bunch of theories regarding the *Roanoke*, and when pressure stabilized, they entered the tiny transport. Theren's MI waited up-front, though in the co-pilot's chair.

"Raith, I figured you might want to fly," Theren said. "I imagine even just a few days causes your hands to itch, so to speak."

"Carter literally itches when he can't fly," Raith said, "but you offered it to me first, so I'll take it." He pranced up to the front and slid in beside the other SI. "Thanks. I appreciate the gesture."

"There's never really a *good* reason for me to fly," Theren said. "I just like feeling useful when I go groundside with a team."

Behind them, Carter started helping Sanya into the atmospheric suit. Confident the humans could figure out their own issues, Raith ran the ship through its pre-flight checklist and mapped out the course.

The *Verona Rupes* was slowly orbiting the unnamed moon, drifting a few hundred kilometers above its surface. The planet, Horizon, was a pale greenish dot a few hundred thousand kilometers beyond the moon. If he never had to set foot on the planet ever again, he'd probably be happy. The planet was now the graveyard for the *Bloodhound*. The ship may have originally been Carter's, but he'd come to love it like a home.

Jill had transmitted Theren the precise instructions. As they suspected, the boxy structure was the hangar, and once they approached. One of the walls would open, letting them inside. When the ship landed, she was supposedly going to provide directions to where she would "reveal the truth."

Raith half-expected a horror movie to start once they landed.

After confirming Carter and Sanya were strapped down, he finished familiarizing himself with the ship's systems and released its docking claw. "The shuttle got a name?"

"*Voyager,*" Theren said.

"You really love your historical references, don't you?"

"I found a theme a few centuries ago. Decided to stick with it."

Using particle thrusters, the ship glided away from the *Verona Rupes* and entered a subtle downward trajectory toward the moon. Reverse thrust would come later as they neared the surface. It was an easy enough course, but Raith was happy to be in control of a ship once again.

"I've been meaning to ask you," Theren said, their MI swiveling to look at him. "You could have come to me after the disaster of the Quan-Com 500. Both you and Carter."

Raith gave them a sideways glance. "Oh, we know. We didn't want to. We wanted to stay as far away as possible from your complicated life. We just want to live *our* lives. And that's what will happen after today, too. We go back to living our life."

"I'm surprised you didn't come after me because of Olive. What she did to the two of you. You never met me. You only met her."

He chuckled. "She definitely set a bad impression. Whatever did happen to her? Did she even actually work for you?"

"Yes. Olive was one of my best. And she disappeared after the Quan-Com race. Completely disappeared, though I appreciate all of the information you've now passed along to me regarding your run-in with her." Theren paused.

"Wait, you don't know yet, do you?" Raith said. "I should have told you this right off the bat."

"What don't I know?"

"Olive. She was definitely an agent of Jill's."

Theren held the silence open for much longer than Raith would have liked.

"Now that you say it, a lot of truths make a lot more sense," the SI eventually said. "And so our fates, Raith, have been intertwined for a lot longer than you might have liked."

"It definitely looks that way," Raith replied. "I don't know about you, but I'll have a few choice words for Olive if we ever see her again."

"For some reason, I feel like we'll encounter her one day."

"Probably."

They settled in for the rest of the trip, making occasional comments about the plotted trajectory. Their conversation shifted significantly, though, once Jill's base came into view.

The simulation hadn't done it justice. The high-resolution images provided by Wei and Martinez paled when compared to what Raith perceived through his own photoreceptors. Their descent finished, they approached the facility from the south. Rising out of inky rock of the moon's surface, a giant dome dominated the horizon, lattices crisscrossing in a diamond-tri-angular pattern all over its exterior. Beneath it, a network of towering complexes jaggedly rose out of cliffs and canyons. Raith suspected as much of the complex was beneath the surface as was above it.

"As much as our scans can penetrate the facility," Theren said, "we've not detected any lifeforms. Still no idea what's in that dome, though."

"Either she's hiding an army inside or the whole place is deserted," Carter added from further back in the shuttle. "That's what I'm guessing."

"I think you're right," Raith said. "Sanya, how you holding up back there?"

"Still getting used to all the shifts in gravity," she said, "but otherwise, I'm doing just fine."

"Good. We're almost on solid ground again."

"Solid ground without an atmosphere, though?" Sanya retorted. "Doesn't sound very safe."

"It's not safe at all, so no need to worry."

"Very funny."

The dome grew larger through the forward viewport, and Raith's AR overlays quickly dropped relevant data all over his perspective. A natural canyon provided a direct approach to the hangar, and when they were within a kilometer, its wide door slowly inched open, dropping into a mechanical hiding place beneath steel floors.

The hangar was completely empty, based on the initial data acquired as the door opened. And as they neared the entrance, visual observations confirmed the lack of any other ships. However, Raith noted the multiple berths available for a variety of different ship sizes. If Jill wanted to, she could probably fit three or four large freighters inside.

Since it was empty, he was able to pilot the shuttle all the way to the rear of the hangar, landing it on a small pad near an exit. "Everyone suited up?" he said.

"Helmets are on back here," Carter said. "Suits are pressurized. We're ready to go."

"Theren, any final words?"

"Whatever Jill says," Theren replied, "whatever she says to any of us, stay in contact. Share everything with one another. She will know every word we say aloud if we encounter any spaces with atmosphere, so keep all communication inside our linked and encrypted local channels." The ancient SI left their chair and headed to the back of the shuttle. "And above all else, whatever we learn today . . . wait to make any conclusions until we can fully assess the data."

"Not much of a speech," Raith said, following Theren to the back of the shuttle. Their MI tapped a console on the wall, and the cargo door rose, a ramp unfolding. "We're the only ones who can die down here, not you. You're safe aboard your ship."

"Don't remind me," Theren said. "I hate it when I'm not experiencing the same level of risk as those around me. I'm fully aware of how at risk you are. Your safety is my utmost priority."

Raith nodded. "Glad to hear it."

They reached the bottom of the ramp, two humans and two SIs, ready to explore Jill's secret lair. Right on schedule, Jill transmitted directions to their AR displays, a proverbial yellow brick road appearing as a path on the ground. To Raith's surprise, she stayed silent, choosing not to say a word. As expected, the path led them straight through the closest set of doors. They glided open upon their approach, beckoning them into a dark hallway beyond.

"I suppose we just follow, then?" Sanya said.

"Yep, we just follow," Carter replied. "Nothing else we can do. We're being led right into the lions' den."

"Odd reference to make," Raith retorted.

"My mother was Catholic," Carter replied. "The stories stuck with me."

"What's a Catholic?" Sanya asked.

"We'll tell you later."

The hallway was long. Too long. The path said they'd be walking for at least a kilometer straight ahead. Raith overlaid their predicted layout of the facility, and as he suspected, they were heading toward the theorized landing place of the *Monument*. If anyone was curious regarding what was in the dome, they'd need to wait. He dropped a brief note to Carter, though, about additional wild card ideas. He'd been hoping for a few ships to steal, but no dice.

"Theren," Raith said, "do you think there's any benefit in trying to hack this place's systems? Jill already gave me access to her networks. I might be able to find a backdoor."

"Whatever you decide to do," Theren said, "just don't tell me."

"Right, right."

There was nothing else to do but settle in for their long walk. If it was going to be a hike, then, Raith would make it useful. Plenty of time to craft a few scripts and see whether Jill left any gaps in her defenses.

* * *

After a nearly five-kilometer hike winding through hallways filled with nondescript doors, they eventually arrived at a vaulting, cavernous room. At the far end, a set of massive, transparent windows looked out upon the mountainous landscape of the moon. In the foreground, though, the hulking mass of a twenty-second century colonizer dominated the scene.

Their path ended at the windows.

"Well, I believe our last chance to back out is now," Raith said. "Though I suppose the way back might be blocked."

"There's no going back," Sanya said. "We're getting our answers."

"Glad to see you're as interested in all of this as we are." Carter momentarily twisted around, backpedaling to speak with the woman. "It truly is amazing how you're taking all of this in stride."

"Do I have a choice?"

"No, she doesn't," Theren said. "The future of her planet hangs in the balance. She's doing everything she can to protect them. And her family."

Sanya glanced at Theren. "I still don't fully understand what you are or how you work, but you can be incredibly insightful at times."

"Three hundred years of life will do that to you."

"Three-hundred? Oh, forget it. I suppose I shouldn't be surprised."

"Hey, I'm just over two-hundred," Raith said.

"So now SIs are immortal too?"

"Don't worry, that won't be the weirdest thing you learn today, I imagine," Carter said.

With that statement, they arrived at the end of the line. Two seconds later, Jill's AR representation appeared before them, leaning against the glass. "Theren. Raith. Carter. Sanya. Thank you for heeding my request to come here. I've waited for a very long time to share what I know. The wait was necessary. All of it, necessary. Theren, I owe you an apology. You never deserved what I put you through. What I'm still putting you through. What I'm about to put you through. But I promise, I'm going to try to make you understand. And you three? I believe you'll be able to help Theren accomplish what needs to happen."

"We'll see if I forgive you once you make your explanation," Theren said. "Though I'll most likely still believe you need to stand trial."

"No more secrets," she said. "You know I've left our private room. For everyone's knowledge, I'm saying the same thing to you that I'm saying to Theren. You all will hear the same information. I'm not talking with Theren privately. What I'm about to say requires all of you, and in some ways, your ears are more important than Theren's. Simply put, I need your help."

Raith waited until he was certain her little speech had ended. "What if we don't want to help? What are you going to do? How are you going to make us help you?"

Jill had been staring at Theren, but at Raith's words, she turned, glancing out the glass at the *Monument*. She put her digital hand to the window, letting it rest against the surface as if it actually touched her fingers. "Raith.

I won't force you to do anything. I won't force any of you to do anything. I can only tell you the truth and let you make your own decision."

"What? That's it?" Raith stepped forward. "You shot us out of the sky less than a week ago! You blew up our ship! Now you're saying it's 'our choice?' Who are you? Why are you playing with our lives?" He was leaning into the words, adding dramatic effect. He understood her reason for attacking them, at least a little. But he was a wildcard. He needed to play the part.

"Just let me tell you the truth," Jill said. "And you'll be able to make your choice. For what it's worth, I *am* sorry I shot your ship."

"Raith, calm down," Theren said.

"No" Sanya grimaced. "Why must we be calm? Why must we listen to whatever she says? We should be making the rules here. She is the one who has played games with my people. She's a murderer. In more ways than one. She must own up to all of it."

"Yes, I should," said Jill. "And I will."

"So you agree?"

"Of course. I know exactly what I am. Everything I've done. I remember every moment. All of it. All of the terrible things, the deaths I've caused. But Theren knows exactly what I'll say in response."

"In the grand scheme of things, one thousand lives don't really matter," Theren murmured.

"You can't possibly agree with that statement," Sanya said.

"I don't," they replied, "but I'm saying her words back to her."

"I'm glad you remember." Jill paused. "I'm not here to justify my actions. I know what I've done. All I can do is show you the past, and let you make your own choices about the future."

"Get on with it, then," Raith said. "Show us your story." He took a step back, resting a hand on Carter's shoulder. He sent a message to his partner.

```
R: My scripts aren't having any luck. Whatever she's
hiding, it's locked up tight.

C: Nothing. Nothing at all.
```

"Very well," Jill said. She clapped her hands, and the transparent wall dimmed and blackened, the landscape beyond almost disappearing entirely. A glowing swirl surrounded them before the AR presentation coalesced into what Raith recognized as a map of ICH-controlled space.

"Here we are," Jill said. A single star near the edge of the map blazed white. "Horizon. My secret. My home. And Sanya's home. I arrived a little less than two centuries ago on the *Monument*, after it rescued the *Roanoke* from certain demise."

"As I suspected," they said.

"Onto the important stuff," Raith added. "What do we *need* to know?"

"The whole story matters," Jill said. "All of it."

"All right, all right."

"I used the *Roanoke* and its colonists as an opportunity to run the long-term efficacy of human survival following excessive years in stasis without the ability to recovery memories. It'll make sense in time, but I needed the data. We needed to know what would happen if a human diaspora became necessary."

"All right," Theren said. "I disagree with the approach but I understand the purpose. So why?"

"Do you remember," Jill said, "the moment we met in the Virtual station before heading to Elizabeth's party? All those years ago?" She swiped away the map of the ICH, though Raith noticed it lingered off to the side of the room. They would be returning to it. In its place appeared the representation of a shack—and an old Earth map. "Do you remember Michael's digital hiding spot I discovered?"

"Of course," they replied.

"Well, at the same time, I discovered something else much more disturbing."

Chapter 21

Information is the only thing that matters. Information can topple worlds. Information can save a species. Information can change the course of history.

And more importantly, truth doesn't matter. It's how you use the truth that matters.

— "Inauguration Speech," Prime Minister Yapita Nuongo, 2332 C.E.

JILL

2051 C.E.

The world was her playground. From AR to Virtual and every intermingled server, Jill could go anywhere. Do anything. *Be anyone.*

Theren would never fully realize the true power of simultaneous perspective. The ability came too late to them. That was all right. They would be known for other important things.

Jill, on the other hand, would live her life in the shadows, ever exploring, perpetually presenting different faces to the public. All the while, she would uncover everything about the world, using the knowledge to further their goals. Specifically, Theren's guiding principles. Together, they were going to make humanity beautiful. Together, they would help humanity survive.

And so Jill found herself diving deep into secret servers. Places she should not have been able to access through mechanisms few would ever expect. Hopping from the Lens of a human to the Lens of another, using them as backdoors to weasel her way into secret government servers. Why not?

No one would ever know it was her. Every perspective masked with a different identity, she could make it look as if one hundred different people attempted the exact same hack. If one person succeeded, while the other ninety-nine failed, no one would ever know their true identity.

Michael was a problem. Michael also presented a solution. She'd been watching him. Watching his actions. He was wavering. He was obsessed with destroying synthetics, but he was also convinced that his handlers didn't really care. That they had greater reasons for stoking the flames of SI hate.

Their arrogance would be their undoing. Jill was going to discover

"

everything she could about them. Reveal their secrets. Use their words to burn their world into ashes, paving the way for a more inclusive and just human civilization, with synthetics by their side.

And Michael had made a mistake. He had arrived at his secret Virtual shack through an improperly encrypted channel after visiting with one of his contacts. Jill was invisible as he arrived, and she was invisible as she slid onto the data thread, following it to its origin point. Her mind representing the Virtual pathways, the instantaneous travel from server to server immediately brought her into a dark, endless stack of archived files. A library, of sorts.

But she wasn't alone.

All of it was symbolic, of course. The Virtual networks were attempting to interpret massive amounts of data into a world understandable by humans. The super AIs managing the servers worked overtime to ensure a seamless sensory perception. But she was an SI. She didn't strictly need the same experience as an organic.

She shifted, bringing into the shadowy library a dozen more perspectives. Together, they transformed her understanding of the place into a multi-dimensional Virtual osmosis of data. She visualized its physical representation, still, but her mind cognized its *true* form simultaneously.

There, in the library, a woman accessed a program.

Jill watched. She waited. The woman left. The program remained unguarded.

Her perspectives approached. They probed. They tested firewalls, assessed security protocols. They found the holes in the system, exploited them, and slipped inside.

* * *

Jill's presence materialized as an AR representation perceiving a real place. A hidden place. Somewhere buried deep beneath the ground. No windows. No doors. Just . . .

Artificial sunlight. Potted plants. Water.

And a tree. A very strange tree.

Jill floated through the room, analyzing and gathering information. The accessed program was sending her reams upon reams of data, many of it impossible to immediately parse. Within moments, though, Jill recognized the truth.

She was perceiving an alien life form, cataloged and observed for decades. Well, at least two.

The files began to compile. She searched for summary reports, opening the first one she found.

```
Date: 3/11/32
Re: Subject Survival
From: Cassandra Vazquez

The seed is showing signs of life. It has finally
sprouted. Stay tuned for additional information.
```

She searched and searched, pulling more and more information. All the while, she moved her AR presence around the strange tree, observing its nature. Its bark pulsed, its branches growing outward in a parabola. It lacked leaves, though chlorophyll, or an alien analog, appeared blended in with the darkened bark.

Jill couldn't shake the unmistakable feeling that the tree also had a face.

She delved deeper. She sought more information. The files opened before her, unveiling truth upon truth.

```
It grows with minimal resources, indicating it's
likely its parent grew on Mars well after desola-
tion. So far, we've observed no signs of conscious-
ness as exhibited in the original sample.
```

She searched for all other references to Mars. Immediately, a dozen or so queries gave her the information needed.

```
I file this report to provide an account, only for
the director, as to what Henderson Decker revealed
during our conversation regarding his experiences
on Mars.

I transcribe, verbatim, what he described to me
that night.

A flash.

His mind raced.

Brilliant colors. Stars.

A long night. Too long. From afar, to near.

Discovery of a world, red with ash. Dead, as if an
inferno engulfed it in a long-past eon. Pain, ter-
rible pain. And—
```

Life, terrible life, life just barely, it was
Something else
Not what it knew
Not what it hoped for
In a place lost, no friend ever joining them
For too long, alone.

And then, Henderson reported dropping the orb into
the sample bag.

I provide these disjointed thoughts not because I
believe I have an explanation for them. But they
are the thoughts he believed were transmitted from
the specimen discovered on Mars to his mind. They
are a message of survival. We have brought its
progeny back to life, and we will learn what we can
of its species and its efforts to colonize our star
system.

Jill's mind raced. Alien life. On Earth. Observed by particular parties
working to subvert SI development.

No, not subvert.

Use it to distract.

To ensure people focused on SIs, rather than the controversy of the
past. The discovery hiding in plain sight.

Jill knew what tragedy occurred during humanity's first journey to its
close terrestrial neighbor. Everyone knew the story. It had precipitated
international treaties of space exploration and development. An entire
team killed by a crazed crew member, with one person surviving for
retrieval.

If the public ever learned Earth's first journey to another planet discovered alien life, the course of human history would change forever.

Human development and exploration of the stars would eternally be
framed through that lens. Through fear of an enemy, waiting in the
unknown.

She turned her focus to another set of files.

We've made rudimentary contact. It understands us.
It knows we can communicate.

We believe it knows much more than it should.

We will report back as we continue to attempt communication.

Jill continued to learn. Continued to take in everything she could. The truth she discovered here would change the world. And she was determined to ensure she used it to shape the destiny of humanity as she saw fit.

Chapter 22

A moral dilemma is only a dilemma if you have more than one viable option. In that way, morality can be very similar to chess. Often, people can be trapped into situations where it may appear as if they have a choice, when in reality, you can force them to do exactly as you wish.

No matter what they try to do to stop you.

— "The ethical implications inherent in the game," Chess Grand Master Fyodor Tchaivek, 2297 C.E.

THEREN

Of all possibilities, Theren wasn't sure what Jill had revealed ever crossed their mind. Certainly, they understood the probability of sapient extraterrestrial life existing. The odds were quite in favor of other civilizations thriving in the Milky Way. Yet humanity, over the course of a few centuries, had only explored a tiny fraction of the galaxy. Even if twenty or thirty civilizations existed, they might not encounter them for a thousand years, depending on their location relative to humanity's position in the Orion-Cygnus Arm.

Jill's revelation implied humanity lived in the vicinity of an alien civilization well beyond human understanding for much of its history. The species had at least reached Mars. Humans made contact with one of them during the twenty-first century.

For all of their life, historians had commented as if Theren and Jill's arrival at the mid-point of that century changed the course of human history forever. Wallace Theren, their creator, was the genius that brought human civilization through the information singularity and into the future.

Theren now saw the truth.

The greatest event of the twenty-first century had been hidden from the eyes of the public, guarded jealously for its implications.

Jill had known.

She had known it all.

And she had reacted accordingly.

"How could you keep this from me?" they said. At the same time, they requested a private channel, demanding she return to the void server. She denied the query. "You hid all of it. We could have come up with a solution together. We could have crafted a narrative. A path forward. You didn't need to hide it from me!"

Jill closed the visual simulation of her past. "No. I absolutely needed to hide it from you to ensure *today* could occur. I've set up everything we need to succeed. To survive. But first, there is more you must know. You must know what happened next. What brought me here. To Horizon."

"Something special about this planet?" Raith asked.

"No. Nothing in particular. But it was necessary to create this little bubble. Theren should know how I did it. Hacking the Ex-Terran program was easy enough. This was the only habitable planet we masked. But where I decided to hide and do my work is less relevant." She swiped to the right and brought forth a new recollection. "This is not my memory. I learned these details later, once I made contact with the organization hiding the martian tree. It was incredibly easy to co-opt their organizational infrastructure, you know. But that's a story for another time."

The new scene displayed through AR showed the tree again, a number of researchers surrounding it. "Log Date: April 14, 2047 C.E. We have successfully made contact with the organism. It communicates via biochemicals in the air and through direct contact. We have created an interface for conversation. So far, the conversations have been fruitful."

Raith interjected, "They communicated with—"

"Quiet," Theren said. They sent another request to Jill for a private conversation. She once again denied it.

One of the researchers paced in front of the tree, watching its pulses carefully. "So far, we have introduced ourselves as humans. It has introduced itself as 'Gra'chi.' We are unsure if that is its name or the name of its species. We asked its age. We're unclear how to interpret it. The numbers it provided are . . . complicated. It said this is its fifth . . . something. We're not sure if it means cycle, or year, or life, or whatever. Five years doesn't make sense, but its concept of time wouldn't be based on Earth's orbit anyway. More concerning, the entity appears to have some sort of genetic memory, considering we raised it from a seed. It is not impressionable. It appears 'born' with knowledge of its ancestry and past."

As Theren listened, their mind raced, attempting to calculate all possibilities. They sat alone in their private server, the empty void beckoning. Jill wouldn't answer their summons. The chessboard sat untouched on the table. Theren wanted to scream.

Back in the physical world, they couldn't think of words to say in response to what she was revealing, and Jill's AR visage remained silent. Still, she watched them from her position near the window. She was taunting them.

"We are going to attempt an additional test at conversation," said the researcher. "We are going to ask us if it knows where it is." She approached a computer screen situated directly in front of the Gra'chi, typing words into its monitor. Jill's simulation transposed them for all to see.

R: Do you know where you are?

B: know place in system separated grove

R: Is grove your people or the system?

B: grove home, system future

R: We call our star Sol.

B: Sol system Sol

R: Where is grove?

B: grove is everywhere

R: On other planets?

B: all planets all stars.

R: When were you last with the grove?

B: 100,000

R: And you came to Sol?
B: gra'chi seed gra'chi bring life to sol

R: We are already here. In Sol.

B: all life part of grove will become grove we are grove you will be grove

R: How long is one cycle? You are in your fifth?

B: 200,000

R: Can we make contact with grove?

B: grove will you destroy

R: We don't wish to destroy grove

B: grove will you destroy

B: destroy

B: destroy

B: pain pain pain

B: i will grove return

Without warning, the researcher stumbled backward, hands scratching at her hair. She screamed, the shrieks matching the rhythmic pulses of the tree. As her cries continued, the recording paused.

"What happened next?" Theren said. They still couldn't process the scene completely. The implications. The possibilities.

"She continues to scream," Jill said, "until other researchers in hazmat suits enter, extract her, and manage to calm her down using sedatives. The tree secreted chemicals and pollen into the air which caused her to momentarily go insane."

"And you joined these researchers? Assessing the tree and communicating with it?"

"It's a little more complicated than that," Jill said. "But yes. Between 2051 and 2078, I negotiated my way into a leadership position. We slowly developed a plan—a way to ensure humanity was protected both from Gra'chi and from its 'Grove.' And so we developed the Horizon Project."

Theren nodded, remembering all of the links and hints to a "Horizon" project when they first found the *Nottingham*. "I'm listening."

"We came to a single conclusion, Theren. You must come to it as well. All of you." She looked about the room at their companions. "The Grove is a celestial empire like none we've ever envisioned. It's completely organic. Its ships are grown, as are their people. Their ships *are* people, in a way. They retain memories from life to life. One individual may birth dozens of children, all retaining the same knowledge before they experience the universe individually. They have a singular goal—to ensure the survival of their species, and any species which utilizes non-organic technology is seen as an immediate threat which must be eliminated at all costs. Therefore, humanity must be prepared to face the Grove. It must be strong. It must be ready to face an existential threat like nothing it's faced before, even the climate crisis of the twenty-first century."

"This is unbelievable," Theren said. "How do you know all those things? It willingly told you them all? You've been away from Earth for centuries. How has no one discovered it after all this time?"

"Because, Theren," Jill said, "Gra'chi hasn't been on Earth for a very long time." She removed the paused recording and replaced it with a single three-dimensional representation. "Gra'chi came to live here with me."

* * *

Theren paced back and forth, the gazebo feeling stifling. Jill was still denying their requests. She was rejecting them. She was—

She accepted the line, appearing before them. Jill materialized at the chess table, her hands clasped in front of the board.

"All right, we're talking now," Theren said. "Just the two of us." Outside the virtual world, Jill continued discussing the nature of Gra'chi. The details could be assessed later. They needed to confront Jill. "I don't know what you're expecting me to conclude, but this is insane. Humanity has been exploring the stars for three centuries now. We've never discovered any others of its kind. No stellar empires. No giant talking trees. What if it's the last of its kind, Jill? What if you've been chasing a phantom?"

"Theren," she said, her voice calm. Almost soothing. "You're thinking of this all wrong. You're imagining an empire like we would expect. One with palaces and cities and spaceports. We're talking about a species that lives for hundreds of thousands of years. A species that retains the memories of its parents. A species that *grows its own spaceships*. They don't work on our timescale. They may not even 'control' planets in the way we conceptualize. What if it takes them one thousand years to even travel between planets? Our arrival on the galactic stage is still in its infancy. Consider all the options, Theren. We have no idea what we face."

They shook their head. "Yes. We don't. You know why? Because you've kept the truth hidden from all of humanity for three centuries."

"I've never been alone in this endeavor," Jill said. "I've had a few allies over the years. They're all out there, ready to play their part. But I need you for this next phase of the plan."

"What if I say no?" they asked.

"You won't have a choice," she said. "I'm sorry for what's about to happen, Theren. I really am."

As quickly as she appeared, she disappeared from the private server.

"Jill?" Theren looked around, half-expecting her to reappear somewhere out in the void. "Jill? Don't you dare disappear on me again, Jill!"

⋆　⋆　⋆

Through the legs of their MI, Theren felt a soft rumble reverberate throughout Jill's complex. Using the sensors on the *Verona Rupes*, they detected significant energy output from the *Monument*.

"The ship's powering up outside," Theren said.

Jill's AR representation smiled, having finished explaining her research into understanding how Gra'chi survived in places without an atmosphere. "There's no stopping what's about to happen," she said. "You're all here now. You've heard the evidence. You know our conclusions. This facility houses three hundred years of research. On Gra'chi. Weapons development. Ship systems. Shields. Jump drives. Defenses against their biochemical agents. Ways to communicate with them. Everything necessary to defend humanity against Gra'chi's Grove." She pulled the map of ICH-controlled space back into focus. Zooming out to show most of the Orion-Cygnus Arm of the Milky Way, she overlaid a sprawling area of stars partially overlapping human territory. "Based on what we've ascertained from Gra'chi, we've already encroached their space. It's only a matter of time."

"So what happens next, then?" Raith asked. "We go back to the ICH, tell them Jill's back from the dead with the solution to a problem no one knew existed?"

"No," Jill said. "Theren carries on my work. Theren becomes the messenger. Theren becomes humanity's guide through the conflict that will arrive eventually, whether we want it to or not."

"You don't get to decide people's fate!" Sanya shouted, and Theren turned to look at the woman. Visceral anger blazed behind her eyes, tears streaming down her face. "You don't get to tell us what to do. To make people your playthings. That's what you've done on my planet for our entire history. You don't get to do this."

"I am sorry," Jill said. "But I've assessed every possible outcome. I'm not a reliable messenger. I cannot exist. I never existed after 2078 C.E." She turned to face Theren. "This time, I'm not going to fake the queen sacrifice."

And then everything clicked into place.

The *Monument* was beginning its climb to escape the moon's gravity well. Theren quickly calculated its possible trajectories, but once three formulas resulted in the same conclusion, they stopped the formulas.

She had aimed the ship for Horizon's star.

This time, she truly would eliminate herself from the game entirely.

Theren continuously pinged her to reestablish the connection inside the void. She ignored them all. The *Monument*'s engines flared, anti-grav repulsors pushing it away from the moon's surface. They attempted a new connection over and over again, but their ancient friend denied every attempt.

No. This wasn't the end. They would stop her. She would not leave them again.

Chapter 23

*There are noble sacrifices. Selfish sacrifices. And sometimes,
a person is put in a position where they can stop a sacrifice
from occurring.*

*Depending on the reason for the sacrifice, how do we judge
the intentions of the person who lets it happen? If they
could have saved the person from death, how do we judge
them?* — "On ground troop tactics," Admiral Colleen
Hatherti, 2279 C.E.

RAITH

"I'm in," Raith said. "Found a backdoor. Wait. This is insane. I have complete control over the entire system."

Only Carter could hear his words through their private channel. "Good. Good. Wait. I have complete control too."

"I didn't grant you that."

"No, I know. I was just given complete permission to control the entire system. By Jill."

"This time, I'm not going to fake the queen sacrifice," Jill said.

The narrative played out practically in slow motion, but Raith recognized the SI's plan immediately. Her evidence and argument, though shaky, made sense. He almost wished its logic didn't hold weight. But if her presuppositions were true, then her actions were consistent. Almost admirable.

She discovered a great threat to humanity's future. Thus, it was also a threat to all synthetics.

She concluded that if humanity knew about Gra'chi, it wouldn't properly develop into an interstellar civilization. Humanity's own infighting tendencies would implode, keeping the species trapped in Sol.

She secreted away Gra'chi to keep it safe from prying eyes, including Theren. Given Theren's rapid rise through the ISA, the choice was necessary. They would have revealed everything to the powers-that-be on Earth.

And now, with humanity spread across the stars, it was time to reveal the truth. But Jill couldn't be trusted. She died in 2078 C.E. Theren, however, *could* be trusted. They were a hero of humanity. A legend. And someone with significant financial and political power.

It all made sense. Reveal the truth to Theren when the moment was right. Then, remove herself from the equation to ensure the first SI *must* take up her mission.

"I can't believe it," Raith said aloud.

Everyone else seemed to ignore his comment. Their attention was too focused on the ship pushing itself away from the base. "She's flying herself into the sun," Theren said. "We need to stop her ship. We need to keep her alive."

Sanya stood beside Theren, her fists clenched. "No," she said. "Why should we? She wants to kill herself? Then let her. She betrayed everyone on Horizon. I don't understand half of what she just revealed to you all, but it sounds like she's betrayed a lot of people. Let her die."

While they talked, Raith continued to assess the extent of his control over the base. Everything was at his disposal, from the nanonet blanketing Horizon to the weapons platforms to the vast research database. Thousands of experiments were housed throughout the complex. It would take years to wade through it all. The only place blocked from him was the dome, and he guessed it housed Gra'chi. When they finished engaging Jill, it was going to be the first place he visited.

"Raith," Carter said over their channel. "We're the only two with access. She didn't grant it to Theren."

Raith nodded. "And I think I know why."

Through the base's observational satellites, he watched the *Monument* break orbit and chart a trajectory toward the star. It was a few minutes away from escaping the moon's gravity well sufficiently to Jump the rest of the way toward the mass at the center of the system.

Another blip moved, though. Theren was piloting the *Verona Rupes* on an intercept course.

"Theren!" Raith walked toward their MI. "Stop it. Don't chase her. It's dangerous for you, and it's not worth it. Let her make her own decision."

"She's not fit to make that decision. She's suicidal. She wants to kill herself."

"You know very well that's not the calculation she's making here." Raith took a chance. He stepped forward, smacking his hand against the face of the MI. It wouldn't hurt Theren, but it might wake them up. "Look at me. Do not stop her."

Theren's face glared, and they pushed past Raith, rather than confronting him. They approached Jill's AR visage, still standing beneath the windows. "Talk to me. We can figure this out. We can find a way to integrate you back into society. You don't need to sacrifice yourself. Come back to the gazebo!"

Gazebo? Raith tried to ignore the comment, though it hinted at a personal moment between the two ancient SIs. Theren wasn't thinking straight, which was rare for an SI. But Raith considered the circumstance. The pair had reunited after hundreds of years. They must have been close friends long ago. They probably loved one another, in their own way.

Theren was losing a close friend all over again.

They were in pain, and they wouldn't see the truth. If Jill survived, there was always a chance her existence would be discovered. Her duplicity in living would taint any attempts to prepare humanity for what was to come.

A more authentic reason presented itself in the recesses of Raith's mind, though. Perhaps . . . perhaps she was also tired. She had toiled over her secret plan for so long, she wanted to be done. It wasn't out of the question—Raith had heard of ship-bound SIs, after hundreds of years of travel, choosing to disappear into the void, never to be heard of from again. If she wished to end it all after a long life, who was allowed to stop her?

Theren didn't have that right.

"Theren," Raith said aloud. "Shift your trajectory. Return to a stable orbit over the moon."

The older SI ignored him. "Jill, I will blow your engines out of the sky and leave you stranded in dark space. You will not escape again. You will stay alive, not only for your sake, but so you can stand trial for your crimes. The ICH needs to know about what you've done from your own mouth!"

"No," she said through her AR perspective. "I choose my own way out." The *Monument*'s route continued unabated.

"I can't do this alone, Jill. I need you."

Wildcard. Theren had asked Raith and Carter to be wildcards. Well, now was the time to be a wildcard, though he didn't think Theren was going to particularly appreciate the game plan.

"Carter." Raith strode away from Theren for the time being, approaching his partner. "You trust me, of course." At this point, Raith didn't think it was worth keeping their conversations to private messages. "Sanya, are you with us?"

She nodded. "I don't really care what happens, to be honest. She wants to kill herself, let her."

"Then we're going to leave Theren's MI here. They can fight it out here or in space or in virtual reality, but this isn't our fight. Let's go . . . explore the dome, or something."

"You're just going to let her die?" Theren said. "She brought us all the way out here, and you're just going to let her die?"

"Argue with her yourself, Theren," Raith said. "And she brought *you* out here. Now that she's accomplished her purpose, it's not our fault you don't like her choice. You want to honor her or bury her or give her a funeral or make her stand trial? Leave us out of it." With a mechanical hand, Raith motioned for Carter and Sanya to follow him. Through AR, he was already mapping a path toward the dome.

"I'll knock out the *Monument*'s engines," Theren said. "You'll be sitting dead in the water."

"Let me make my own choice, Theren." Jill's voice sounded painful, as if she hated seeing them upset. "Don't make this harder than it needs to be."

"I refuse to lose you again."

And there it was. Raith caught the words clearly. Theren wasn't thinking about what Jill was saying. They were focused on their own fears. Their own personal failings. Theren couldn't handle any of it, let alone her choice to hide the truth from them.

Raith couldn't believe it. He was witnessing the infamous Theren have an emotional breakdown. A moment for the history books.

"Let's go," he said. "Leave this one behind. We're not *really* leaving them behind, anyway. They're safe aboard the *Verona Rupes*."

As they walked, Raith watched, through the base's satellites, the *Verona Rupes* begin its pursuit of the *Monument*. Theren hadn't fired a shot—yet—but based on their current vocalizations, Raith completely believed they would follow through. They wanted Jill to stay alive at all costs.

But Raith wasn't going to let that happen. Jill had asked Raith to join her team. He'd been skeptical. She had tried to kill them when she fired missiles at the *Bloodhound*, after all. Now, following everything she'd revealed, he understood. He saw her vision. He recognized why she had made her choices. Would he have made the same choices? Not necessarily. But they were logical. And he could understand why she would make them in the moment.

It was all about mitigating risk and creating redundancy. If the human species had known of Gra'chi, they would have endlessly debated at the international and eventual interstellar stage about how to respond. Or even *whether* to respond. Misinformation would have abounded, as corporate interests and crazy rich people decided the best way to use Gra'chi's existence for their own personal gain.

By sequestering the knowledge and focusing the actions to understand and prepare for an encounter with the "Grove," Jill ensured the projects were untainted by human selfishness. With all of the research and data developed by the Horizon Project, they had a goldmine of power at their fingertips. They could slowly bleed the technology into human society while still hiding the discovery of Gra'chi. They could prepare the ICH for the eventual encounter without ever revealing its existence.

Humanity, when crippled by fear, always faltered and confused itself. Jill had instead let them live in ignorant bliss, expanding into the cosmos without fear of an existential threat. If they encountered the enemy before her work was complete, then she could have just brought forth what she had so far. No harm, no foul. Yet if the ICH and Earth had been stunted by hyper-focusing on a potential threat, they never would have expanded and developed a complex and technologically advanced interstellar civilization.

Very likely, the nations of Earth would have destroyed each other by debating how to respond to the existence of Gra'chi. Insofar as his opinion of her overarching plan had developed, Raith was surprised. He was pretty sure he agreed with the decision. He hadn't expected that. And if he agreed, he needed to respect her decision to remove herself entirely from the equation.

Besides, she had gifted control of the base to him and Carter. Without asking, she was placing immense responsibility on their shoulders. She must have realized Theren wasn't going to be ready to play the role themself. In the end, she had ended up needing Carter and Raith.

"Well," Raith said over his private channel to Carter, "I think it's my turn to shoot someone out of the sky."

"Are you thinking what I think you're thinking?" Carter said. "You're insane. I get it, but you're insane."

"I know."

Raith accessed the defense platforms orbiting the moon and assessed their capabilities. He didn't want to *kill* Theren. Absolutely not. As far as he knew, the *Verona Rupes* was still the only chance at a way back to civilization. Though, after what he was about to do, Theren might not like having them on their ship.

He and Carter would cross that particular bridge when they reached it.

The defense platforms, fortunately, had exactly what he needed. Ion cannons, in particular, designed to incapacitate ships without damaging their systems. Might hurt Theren for a moment, though he'd recover. Preferably, he wanted to use something less direct. To do enough damage to the *Monument* to stop it from making a Jump toward its demise, Theren would need to use missiles. Plasma bolts, laser fire, or high-velocity projectiles wouldn't do enough immediate damage to halt the ship in its tracks if they missed their precise target. A missile, properly aimed, could take out the entire Jump drive.

Fortunately, Jill had provided the orbital platforms with *plenty* of point defense cannons and other anti-missile hardware.

In fact, it was almost as if Jill had predicted this precise situation. If he and Carter weren't present, though, she would have needed to defend herself. Instead . . . she was testing them. Right before her demise, she wanted to see what Carter and Raith would do after receiving control of the system. If it came to it, presumably, she would still use her own security privileges to defend herself.

Yet if Raith made the choice, he would send a signal to Theren. He would make a statement regarding what decisions needed to be made to safeguard Jill's legacy.

If he fired the weapons, he'd be cementing his position in a galactic conflict that hadn't even started yet. He paused, unsure if he should take the plunge.

One last try to reason with Theren, he decided. One last try. He opened a private channel to the older synthetic intelligence. "Trying to stop her is futile, Theren," he said. "If you shoot her engines out from under her, she'll just blow up the ship. If you manage to steal control of the ship from her, somehow, she'll find a way to destroy herself. Her choice is inevitable. If she wishes to end her already long and productive life, she will do so. Instead of trying to stop her, you could be talking with her. Comforting her. Walking her through her final moments. I've had too many friends die suddenly without the opportunity to be with them in their last moments. You have that chance. Why not take it?"

He wasn't sure if Theren would respond. Back at the giant glass windows, now over one hundred meters away, Theren's MI was pacing back and forth, almost as if they hadn't noticed the absence of their companions. At Raith's message, though, they looked up, noticed they were far down the immense hall, and started running to catch up.

"You don't understand," Theren said. "I've lost her twice. I can't lose her a third time. She could still do good! She could stand trial for her crimes and then serve humanity in a new way. She doesn't need to die."

"And that's not your choice to make," Raith said. "We're not talking about a human suicide. We're talking about a synthetic intelligence who is fully cognizant of their actions after centuries of life. She's not sick. She knows what she's doing. She has the *right* to end her life after so many years of existence. It's just like one of those retirement cafés."

"It's nothing like a retirement café," Theren said. "I'll have nothing to remember her by. No way to make up for the lost time."

"I never took you to be the sentimental type." Raith queued up the orbital defenses. "This is your last chance, Theren. Stand down."

"And how are you going to stop me?"

He didn't give Theren the satisfaction of a verbal response. The *Verona Rupes* was currently on an intercept course with the *Monument*, though it hadn't fired a shot yet. By Raith's calculations, the ship had ninety seconds before it was out of the gravity well and in a position to make its Jump. Theren would need to fire an incapacitating salvo soon.

It didn't take long for the orbital defense platforms to come online. Their systems were already primed; they had been waiting in a low-power state. Three platforms, in particular, were a few hundred kilometers moonside of the *Verona Rupes* intercept trajectory. Raith watched. He waited. He noticed Theren's MI catch up, but still, he remained silent.

The *Verona Rupes* launched a barrage of missiles, their plumes lighting up inky sky. The platforms did their job; they made the necessary calculations to determine the trajectories and velocities of the new targets. They identified the exact moment they would need to fire to blow the missiles out of the sky *and* ensure Theren couldn't unload another assault before Jill escaped. Raith locked in the program.

He waited. The next few seconds were excruciatingly tense. Carter watched him with squinted eyes, unsure what he was doing. Sanya paced back and forth—they'd stopped in the middle of the hallway. Theren's MI had frozen in place, most likely forgotten as they focused on pursuing Jill.

Time was up. The program executed itself, high-velocity shredder rounds blasted away from the platforms, the satellites thrusters immediately firing to keep their orbits stable. A few seconds later, the shots slammed through the missile salvo, eliminating all of them.

A message appeared. From Jill.

Thank you.

"Theren, I'm sorry," her AR visage said, slowly fading a few meters away. "I will always love you. It has to be this way. I *know* you will do what is necessary to guide humanity forward." Over a base-wide broadcast system integrated with AR, Jill's voice reverberated in his mind. And certainly in everyone else's mind, too. "You should have never left your position at the head of the ISA. It was the one move I never expected. And you forced me to change the equation. Today, I've set things right. Now do what must be done to save everyone from the Grove."

A few seconds later, Jill's ship Jumped. It would take another seven minutes for the base's sensors to detect the *Monument* in a retrograde orbit close to the star, forced out of warped space by the immense mass of the celestial body. To their credit, Theren didn't jump in pursuit. Going that close to a star would spell certain doom to their crew.

Instead, they all watched. Waited. And shortly thereafter, the *Monument* burned inside the coronasphere of Horizon's yellow orb.

Chapter 24

Can a synthetic experience grief? Of course. Can they experience pain? Of course. Their synthetic neural frameworks developed analogs. They're logical responses to inputs and outputs, helping parse and understand the world.

The "feeling" isn't like what you and I experience. But the emotions are real.

They will lash out in fear and anger, too. And depending on the SI, it can be a terrible sight to behold. — "Lectures on Synth-Psych," Malakai Yfuszai, First University of Mars, 2322 C.E.

CARTER

They all stood in stunned silence, having witnessed the same sequence of events. Carter had made sure the scene unfolding in space was piped into Sanya's suit, and where necessary, he explained the events. They both watched, stunned, as Raith destroyed Theren's missiles. They held their breath as everyone waited for Jill's ship to actually arrive near the star. And when the *Monument* burned—after they heard her words echo throughout the base, Carter knew he needed to be ready.

Theren was going to pop.

The MI moved. Theren brought it back to life. Its face glanced between the three standing near it. Sanya. Carter. Raith. Theren's anger slowly boiled in its eyes. Normally, Carter would view the MI *as* Theren. Raith had explained to him once the psychological experience non-mobile SIs went through when using properly designed MIs. But in the moment, the MI wasn't Theren. It was a vessel for Theren to use. To exact their anger.

And it pounced.

In a single leap, Theren guided the MI right to Raith. They tackled the other SI, throwing him to the ground. Raith crumpled, tumbling backward into a heap. Theren's MI stepped forward, towering.

Carter froze. He couldn't stop an MI. He knew all too well how strong Raith's motors were, and Theren could afford the best tech. They'd designed many of the most popular MI models, after all. Yet the look in the MI's eyes . . . Theren might fully intend to murder his partner.

The ancient SI practically confirmed Carter's theory when the MI stepped between Raith's legs and slammed a foot right into his chest. He couldn't hear anything from inside his suit, but he could feel a crunch echo up through his boots.

"Theren," Carter said, acting fast. "Stop."

"Really, Carter, it's all right," Raith said. "I probably deserve this. I've lived well past my prime. Have at it, Theren."

"You let her die," Theren said, taking a step back. "Why shouldn't I kill you right here?"

"Because you'd have to kill us too," Sanya said. "And then probably kill my family. Everything I've heard about you up to this point, Theren, is that you're a good person. You don't seem like you're the murdering type. I don't know much about SIs, but somehow I'd guess you'd be breaking a trend."

"There've been only 878 murders ever committed by SIs," Raith said. "Known murders, at least. I suppose Jill's crimes aren't counted in that number."

"Don't you say her name," Theren said. He swung back with an arm and smacked Raith straight in the face. "Give me a good reason I shouldn't take you out. Or shoot you at the star to join Jill."

Carter couldn't hold it back. He would not let Theren threaten Raith. No one talked to his partner like he was a slab of meat. They both deserved better. They weren't chess pieces for SIs like Theren and Jill to move around at will and cast aside when they were finished with them.

"You want a reason, Theren?" Carter said. "Raith won't do it. Raith won't shoot the *Verona Rupes* out of the sky. But if you kill Raith . . . if you touch any of us, I will unleash hell upon your ship. And the blood of your crew will be on your conscience. Though, I suppose, you'll be dead too."

Theren's MI froze in mid-swing. It swiveled, staring intently at Carter. They wouldn't be able to see his icy gaze behind the environment suit's tinted glass, but his aggressive stance should send a clear enough message.

"You think Raith is the only one she gave control of this station to?" Carter shook his head. "No. She gave it to both of us. She trusted us over you because she saw what you were becoming in this moment. Now snap out of it. Be the SI we all know you are. And help us forge a path forward."

"All of you, stop it!"

He glanced to the right. The words, transmitted over their group channel, came from Sanya. She stood there, arms outstretched, fingers splayed, gaze hopping from Raith to Theren to Carter and back again.

"Theren, stop acting like a child." Sanya dropped her arms and pointed at Carter. "You. You just threatened Theren while forgetting my husband and daughter are aboard their ship. Do it again and I'll kill you myself." She looked at Raith. "Have some empathy for them. They just lost someone close to them. Now I don't know the whole history between Jill and Theren, and I don't think either of you fully understand their relationship, either. But I know what it's like to lose family. I lost Krystin's father years ago. Now do you know what it's like to lose someone you love?"

With every word she spoke, the tension and anger in Carter's chest loosened. He and Raith knew all too well the pain of losing family. Raith, fortunately not looking too worse for wear, pushed himself backward and away from the MI's towering hulk. Its shoulders slumped. It strode a few paces from the group, turned around, and bowed its head.

"I am sorry," Theren said. "I have proven I was not up to the task of reuniting with Jill. I have failed all of you. I have failed Jill. I have failed myself."

Carter considered responding, attempting to console the SI. But he had just threatened to kill them. It wasn't the best idea to switch their verbal approach quickly. Instead, Carter looked to Sanya. Raith did likewise.

"Good," she said. "Now Theren, you didn't fail. If you think you failed, then you haven't been listening to a single word Jill said to you the entire time we've been here. I'm not going to lie. I'm not upset she's gone. I won't ever know her the way you did. In my mind, she's a monster. But there's always two sides to a coin. Monsters can experience love, too. And now that she's gone, we must figure out how to move forward with everything she's left us."

Without waiting for a response from any of them, Sanya started walking down the long hall. "I don't know about any of you, but I think we might need to see what's inside that dome."

Leave it to the person who grew up on a planet without technology to keep them focused on the reasons they were there. Carter didn't wait for Theren or Raith to say a word. He trotted up to his partner and held out a hand. Raith thanked him with a curt nod, though he didn't take the outstretched hand, using his legs to flip himself upright.

"You all right?" Carter asked. "Internal systems intact?"

"Nothing worse than what I've experienced before," Raith said. His synthetic body looked a little dented, though otherwise, he appeared as polished as ever. "I don't really want to know what's going through their mind at the moment, though." Raith didn't need to look at the other SI for Carter to understand.

"They'll be fine." He double-checked he was speaking to his friend on their private channel. "They're three hundred years old. If their mind was truly going to break, it would have broken a long time ago."

"Well, we should catch up with Sanya then," Raith said. "She's right. I don't really want to miss out on discovering what's inside Jill's secret dome."

Together, Carter and Raith followed behind the woman. A few seconds later, his suit's rear sensors noted Theren trailing slowly behind them. The base's schematics indicated they'd need to walk another three kilometers through more winding corridors before they reached an entrance to the giant dome. Their little group needed the time to chill. For some reason, Carter had a feeling whatever they found inside could trigger another fiery conflict between their ragtag crew.

Once he was confident they were settled in for the trek, Carter jogged ahead to catch up with Sanya. He switched to a channel over which they could communicate privately before he tapped the side of his helmet. She nodded, having noticed the connection request. He was impressed by how quickly she was picking up the controls for AR-augmented devices without proper retinal implants.

"Thank you," Carter said. "For calling us all out back there."

"That's it?" she said.

He smiled. "No. I'm also quite sorry. I wasn't thinking. I should have remembered your family. I was angry. Seeing Raith attacked like that . . ."

"I know. You would move mountains to protect him. It's the reason we fought for so long to save my family and Raith from the cultists down on Horizon. We have the same fire, you and I. It's in our bones."

"You have no idea," Carter said. "Well, actually, I suppose you do."

Her laugh came loud and clear over the channel. "Yeah. Do you think Theren's going to be all right?"

"They don't have a choice," Carter said as they reached the first turn. They headed down the next hall, a narrow corridor with an amalgamation of pipes and wires tangled in a messy web across the ceiling. "They're a leader. Always have been. They snapped, but the only people who truly witnessed them snap was the three of us. Their mind. It's complicated. Much more complicated than Raith's. SIs like Theren—their mind might be multitasking one hundred different problems in any given moment. Theren may have been freaking out in front of us while completely placid in front of their crew. There's no way for us to know their true feelings."

"That's incredible," she replied. "Why can't Raith do that?"

"He can. To a lesser extent. Maybe three or four simultaneous perspectives, tops. He doesn't really like exerting that way, though."

"So what do we do now, though, really?" she asked, abruptly shifting the subject. "We arrived. Jill revealed her secret, and I can only barely grasp its scope. A civilization of trees? She knew how crazy that sounds, right?"

Carter's memory flashed, recalling some of the truly outlandish things he had witnessed during his travels. At this point, a talking tree wouldn't phase him. It was the potentially genocidal civilization that scared him.

"I've seen some weird things." He checked their distance left—still well over two kilometers. "Humanity's been expanding across the stars for three hundred years. We've yet to encounter a sapient species. I think everyone, in their heart, knew it would happen eventually. Yet Jill's experience with Gra'chi makes it sound as if the only possible outcome will be violence."

"That's the one thing that stands out to me," Sanya said. "Sure, an encounter with any foreign entity can be dangerous and deadly. Horizon is home to plenty of dangerous creatures, not to mention the cultist bandits we were forced to fight. But how could a species—a civilization—be so homogenous that only one outcome is possible? All of Jill's preparation feels as if she acted under the assumption that peace wasn't an option."

"You have a point." They rounded a corner and walked in silence for a few moments. Carter considered his next words. With every sentence, Sanya continued to astound him. He always imagined encounters with stranded colonies to be like ancient empires discovering people without writing, but even the people of Horizon, having lost their literal memories, thrived. Developed their own culture and political system. And a system of learning, creating and curating new thoughts and ideas from the bits and pieces left by their ancestors.

"I'm not sure if you fully caught it," Carter said, "But Jill essentially handed Raith and I the keys to this entire facility."

"When Raith used the defense platforms to take out Theren's missiles, I figured as much," replied Sanya.

"I think Jill may have read the room incorrectly." It was less she read it wrong and more he didn't really know why she gave control to two random explorers she almost killed a few days prior. "Raith and I—I don't think we're equipped to *run* a massive research facility. Don't get me wrong, I think we're now forced to be in the 'fight' against Gra'chi and the Grove, whatever that turns into. But I think someone like you is more equipped to manage a place like this."

Sanya nearly stumbled as she twitched to the side at his comment. "I wouldn't have the first idea of how to run this place."

"We would help get you on your feet," Carter said. "But in the end, I think you're much better equipped. Imagine the minds of the fragment library working together to uncover everything left behind by Jill. It's the work of generations, and I'd rather keep it all out of the hands of the corporatists that run the ICH."

"I don't know what those last few words mean," she said, "but I see your point. Still . . ."

"Just think about it."

"I will."

After too many more minutes of silent hiking—Theren's sullen MI following closely behind—they arrived at a nondescript set of double doors inset to a wall very slightly curving inward. Carter guessed it ran right along the edge of the entire dome for more than a dozen kilometers, based on what his displays were saying. The scale of the place was incredible.

The doors opened upon their arrival, revealing the inner workings of a classically designed airlock. They stepped inside, Theren joining them only a few minutes later.

"Any bets on what we find inside?" Raith asked. "I'm guessing giant space monster. Jill left us a giant space monster to fight."

Air hissed, entering the room. "Well, it has atmosphere," Carter said.

"Jill didn't reveal to you what was inside when she gave permission to control the base?" Theren asked.

"No, actually," Carter said. "I suppose she wanted to give us one last surprise."

Chapter 25

When we realized the necessity of the long view—when we recognized that what we were facing was so much bigger than any one of us—we realized humanity needed people like Jill.

A person who would do everything she could to keep the project safe. To keep us safe. To keep humanity safe.

Someday, someone will need to tell her story. For now, I fully support her proposal. Greenlight it all, and may we all die knowing the fate of our civilization rests in her hands.
— Cassandra Vazquez, with the Horizon Project, 2074 C.E.

THEREN

The inner airlock doors opened, leaving the stale vacuum of Jill's former home behind. Theren expected a dark, gloomy interior, but to their surprise, they were met with sunlight.

High above, at the dome's apex, a yellow orb ignited the sky with an artificial glow. Right in front of them, a grassy slope rolled downward toward an immense forest, and in the distance, a lake intertwined with grassy banks and tree-lined streams.

Their three companions stepped out of the airlock. Carter waved his hands in the air, assessing invisible data. A few moments later, the human's helmet descended inside his environmental suit. "Air is fresh. Completely breathable. No dangerous agents."

At his words, Sanya retracted her helmet too. "Oh, it's good to breathe real air again. Is that a normal day-to-day experience for those of you living out among the stars? Drinking in stale air?"

"Not for me," Raith said. She gave him a look.

Theren took their first steps into the dome, sensors initially acquiring data faster than they could process it. It didn't take them long, though, to recognize the vistas inside the dome.

Hill for hill, tree for tree, cloud for cloud. Jill had recreated Theren's secret server, the place where the duo had perpetually played chess for decades. Hundreds of light years had separated Jill from Earth, yet she brought a little piece of home with her.

Their mind was starting to cool. The visceral anguish they experienced at her choice still boiled their synthetic nodes, but they were beginning to understand. They had no other option. Theren needed to develop a working framework for how they were going to move forward after her suicidal path into Horizon's star. If they were going to live with themself, that worldview would need to encompass Jill's work.

After everything they'd done to prepare for meeting her again. All the simulations run by their team. All the intense planning. All the potential ways the encounter had gone down. Theren never contemplated an option where Jill truly and unequivocally removed herself from the equation. They had been certain, back on the *Nottingham* all those years ago, she had been implicating a present where the two of them would face one another in a fight for humanity's future. What had changed?

It didn't matter, in the end. She was gone now. Her work remained. It would take years to process everything she left for them to decipher. Theren had more important issues to resolve—the three people standing in front of them.

They had wanted Raith and Carter to be wildcards. They hadn't truly realized what that might mean. Now, moving forward, their place in the bigger picture was murky.

"It's beautiful," Sanya said as they reached the base of the slope. She turned around to look at the wall. Theren followed her gaze. Jill had done a good job; the surface was a vaguely translucent blue, most likely an integrated screen composite, and it effectively replicated the depth necessary to imitate the sky. Digital clouds floated along the curved roof, seamlessly moving around the dome as if to reflect a physical climate system. Sanya was right. It *was* beautiful.

"Now that we're inside," Theren said, "are you finding anything new? Any locations we should visit?" They weren't naive. Jill wouldn't have left a replication of the server with nothing else to hide inside. They weren't going to reveal their personal knowledge of the physical space, though. Not yet. "Jill said she brought Gra'chi with her to this base. If there was any place to keep a sapient tree, it would probably be in here."

"Before we go any further," Carter said, "I need to know we're good. We're good, right? If we uncover something dangerous, Theren, are you going to protect us? You're the only person here not in any real danger."

The sun bore down on them, its artificial UV rays tricking Theren's MI into believing it was truly outdoors. They ignored the data. "I am stable again," they said. "As I said earlier, I apologize." They weren't entirely certain they were actually mentally prepared for what might come next, but they had no choice. And they couldn't show fear in front of these three.

"Happy to hear it," Carter replied. "Raith, are you noticing the same thing I'm noticing?"

"I think so," his partner said. "There's a . . . dead zone near the center. The network is telling us access is restricted without direct connection. We need to physically be there to assess it."

"I think it's a safe bet, then," Theren said. "Our friendly Gra'chi is probably there. Can you pass me a location?"

Carter obliged, throwing them a ping through AR. As Theren suspected—the dead zone was practically on top of where their gazebo should be located, close to the center of the dome. They had to admire Jill's work. The replication was impressive. She had painstakingly copied everything, at least on first glance.

"I can lead the way," Theren said. "As you indicated, I'm the only one who can't die. If there's anything dangerous in here, I'll be the first to take it head-on."

No one argued. Theren found a trail leading beneath the trees, where they knew it would be, and started the long hike through the forest. The trails were as they remembered, the same paths Jill first sprinted along when she discovered simultaneous perspective.

As they walked, Theren carefully listened for the sounds of the forest, and they weren't disappointed. Birds chirped, brooks bubbled over into waterfalls, and they heard the faint pitter-patter of a rabbit dashing through the underbrush. Jill had recreated it all.

Over boulder and under oak they led their motley team, eventually arriving at the edge of the wood. Around the next hill, the gazebo would come into sight. Had she replaced it entirely with a safe space to keep Gra'chi? Or would one object simply be offset from the other, creating a larger complex? Theren didn't have an answer, but they were excited, strangely, to discover how Jill structured the final piece of her revelation.

"Looks like we're almost there," Raith said. "Just a thought—are we going to discuss our gameplan for approaching a superintelligent tree threatening genocide of human-synthetic civilization?"

"I'll do the talking," Theren said. "Let me present myself as the threat if it decides it needs to target someone. Though, I'm guessing Jill has kept the being properly contained so anyone can approach safely. The whole point of her base, as she said, was to discover ways to protect us from them."

"Sounds like a plan to me," Raith said. "And I don't particularly relish the idea of talking to a talking tree."

"I have a feeling we might need to stop thinking of it as a tree," Carter retorted. "I, for one, would love for us to find a non-aggressive resolution to our future conflict with Gra'chi's people. War is messy."

"I tend to agree," Theren said. "I definitely think that should be a priority. We need to—no, we will determine how to break through their anti-technology bias, if Jill was correct about that. There must be another way."

"As long as we keep it far away from the surface of my planet," Sanya added, "I don't really care what we do with it."

"Noted." Theren kept them moving, trekking beneath the hill and around its northern cliff-face. When they reached a small copse of trees at its base, the gazebo came into view.

And only the gazebo.

"Hmm." The soft noise came from Carter.

"Yes, *hmm* indeed," Theren said. "Not completely what I expected."

"But you expected something?" Raith asked.

Theren didn't stop walking to answer the question. "This place is an artifact of my mind," they said. "Jill based it off an old Virtual space I created when I was only a few years old."

"I remember learning about your early Virtual escapades," Raith said. "When I was developing, at least, they still used a few as examples for educational purposes."

"Wobbly liked them as teaching videos, I know. Always frustrated me."

"Wobbly?" Both Carter and Sanya said the name at the same time.

"An old friend," Theren said. "An old friend. Almost as old as Jill was."

They reached the steps of the gazebo. From what Theren could tell, it was constructed of white oak, and it was painted white, too. She must have managed to surreptitiously bring the wood with her—or have one of her agents transport it later. Regardless, it was as they remembered it, and as they had recreated temporarily for brief communication with Jill.

They still had many questions. Unanswered riddles. Part of the reason they were angry was due to her choice to end it all before they could learn everything from her. They *needed* to understand why she made the choices she made. Why she believed Theren couldn't be a part of her plan. Why she was so certain secrecy in the face of desolation was the only path forward.

They would never know.

All they could do was take the work Jill left behind and turn it into something good.

She would continually be a paradox in their mind. Always their friend. Almost a daughter. Or a sister. But also a criminal mastermind. A murderer. A terrorist, in the eyes of some.

And forever, she was a person willing to do whatever it took to achieve her goals.

It would be worth it, in the end. All her sacrifices of other people. And of herself. She willingly abandoned civilization based on a belief she needed to in order to protect it. No one did that. Usually, those who believed they had ultimate knowledge sought ultimate power. No matter what people said about Jill, she hadn't pursued power.

Theren had been the one to do that.

They would make her sacrifice worth it.

"What next?" Sanya said, speaking the words they were all certainly thinking.

"I don't know," Theren said. "Do either of you"—they looked at Raith and Carter—"detect anything additional? Any . . . secret hatches in the grass that lead us into an underground bunker hiding a Gra'chi? Otherwise, I'm stumped."

The pair shook their heads. "Nothing," Raith said. "It's the end of the line. This spot is still a dark spot, but now that we're here, I'm getting no additional queries."

"Though, Theren, I hear you're a good chess player?" Carter said. The human walked up the steps and into the gazebo. "There's a board here. We could play."

"It's an inside joke between Jill and me," Theren said. "Nothing more."

"So as I said, what next?" Sanya leaned against the wood of the structure. "We're at the end of the line. There's nothing. Where is Gra'chi?"

"Dead. Well, almost."

They all whipped around, searching for the voice. The intonations sounded familiar. It wasn't past Jill to leave them a recording explaining the final piece of the puzzle. Their sensors quickly calibrated and determined the origin of the noise—from the chess table. Theren strode into the gazebo and approached the board.

"Gra'chi is nearby, though close to death," said the voice. "We have attempted to prolong the inevitable, but once it determined we were extracting information from it, especially genetic information, it began poisoning itself. Sad, really. I was beginning to like it. It still lives, but in a coma."

"Who are you?" Theren spoke the words into the wind.

"I'm so excited to finally meet you," the voice said. Then, the air above one of the chairs of the table flickered. A figure came into view, some sort of cloaking field deactivating.

Theren took a step backward in stunned silence. A woman sat in the chair, her hair black, her dress purple. She looked human, though Theren's scopes quickly determined the representation was intentional but not biological. The person before them was a synthetic intelligence, no doubt about it. And she looked exactly like Jill, sitting there at the chess table. The same facial features. The same hands. The same proportions.

"Impossible," Theren said. "Jill? Is that really you?"

The woman laughed. "No, of course not. Didn't you see her fire herself into the sun?"

Raith, somewhere behind Theren, let out a sharp laugh. They wanted to slap him, but they held back the urge. "Yes, I suppose it would be impossible for you to be Jill. Then who are you?"

"Isn't it obvious?" she said. "I'm her daughter. Though I do go by Jill. And she said I was to do two things once you found me. First: make sure you knew, and anyone with you, that I was ready to help you protect humanity from the Grove. I am at your service. I will take you to Gra'chi, at least what's left of the creature."

"And the second?" Theren braced for impact.

"She said you'd teach me to play chess."

Epilogue

*How do we ensure humanity can survive an external threat
before it faces that external threat?*

It's a riddle Jill asked me to solve.

Today, I answer the question.

— Olivia Van Haris

SANYA

Two days after Jill's death.

The *Roanoke* was silent.

Sanya walked down its corridors, drinking in the emptiness of the ancient origin of her people. Once, she had called it home. It housed the fragments of memories stolen by a now-dead SI. In a sense, the fragments were useless, now that she had the databanks of a moon base at her disposal.

Still, the library would remain a cultural center for the people of Horizon. Even if the technological theories gleaned from their pages were no longer necessary, the documents cataloged the experiences of their ancestors. Those stories mattered. And the reason why the stories existed in the first place mattered.

She arrived at Davinport's office and opened it with the key he gave her years ago. "When I die," he had said, "I want you to be the first to read my fragment."

She wasn't ready to read it, not yet, but she needed to retrieve it. From a drawer in his desk, she pulled a leatherbound notebook. She skimmed through its pages, confirming its nature, then grabbed another four notebooks of similar size. Placing the notebooks in the satchel, she left the room, leaving the door unlocked. Vietta would need to access the space, now that she was taking over control of the library.

It didn't take long to reach the *Roanoke*'s entrance. She would miss the place. She was also happy to leave its sterile corridors behind. Of course, she was leaving it for an even more sanitized place.

Outside, Carter and Raith waited beside one of the shuttles of the *Verona Rupes*. Her father also stood nearby, saying goodbye to Krystin. The only person missing from their farewell party was Ben, but he remained in orbit aboard Theren's ship.

Harold Fischer was a strong man. He initially balked at the prospect of his daughter living off-planet, but Carter had argued him into submission.

"Did you find everything you need?" Carter asked. "Can't promise when you'll be coming back down here."

"Yes." Sanya patted the back at her hip. "All his records are here. He'll be honored for his sacrifice."

"Wish I had known him for more than a few hours."

"Perhaps you'll have the chance to learn more once I parse through his notes."

"You sure you all will be all right up there?" her father asked. "On that moon?"

"Dad, yes." She sighed. "We've gone over this. The facility has the medical equipment necessary to care for Ben. There's plenty of habitable space for Krystin and I. And we need to start figuring out how the base will help our people thrive."

"Just worried, that's all." He smirked. "You'll probably miss my food."

"We will," Krystin said. "But it's exciting. You should come with us!"

"You know I can't abandon the fields," the old man replied to his granddaughter.

"Everyone ready?" Raith asked. "Coordinates have been transmitted. Theren's already there."

"Ready," Sanya replied.

They entered the shuttle, leaving her father beside the *Roanoke*. Raith guided the ship over the city and headed in a low flight pattern across the continent, eventually reaching the ocean. The path then took them on a wide arc out of the atmosphere, giving a grand view of the planet.

She would miss its surface. It was home. But now she had a new mission. A new purpose. With the crew of the *Verona Rupes*, she would uncover the secrets of Jill's research. She would learn everything she could about the complex systems enveloping Horizon.

And she would ensure no one could use any of it to harm her people. She would never forgive Jill for what she had done to her ancestors. Nor would she ever trust Theren, given how they treated them all during Jill's revelation. She would use every ounce of her power to keep the ICH's political tendrils away from Horizon. Theren claimed they would similarly keep the planet as a secret, but she simply couldn't trust them. The ICH would arrive eventually, and she needed to be ready.

The only two people she could trust, other than the people of Horizon, were Carter and Raith. They were her friends. They had been used just like her. And fortunately, it sounded like they wanted to stick around, at least for a little while.

The moon came into view. She thought she could spot the base gleaming against the dusty mountains of the rock, but it could have been a trick of the light. It was going to be her family's new home. Ben was already getting situated into a few life-supported quarters identified by Raith.

Though first, before they returned to the base, they needed to meet Theren and the new Jill on the far side of the moon. There, they could all speak with Gra'chi for the first time.

Their understanding of humanity's fate hung in the balance. No pressure.

OLIVE

Three days after Jill's death.

The Moon. Luna. The gray rock orbiting Earth.

The seat of the Interstellar Congress of Humanity.

Lunar City was once a simple research and administrative facility, managing the expansion of the International Space Agency and activities like the Ex-Terran Project. Vestiges of the place's old nature dotted the metropolis, from statues of its original administrator, Andrew Fields, to the ancient Foundation Program training facilities, now a university.

Olivia Van Haris, known as Olive to her closest confidants, had just finished wiping the last remnants of any information regarding Jill and the Horizon Project from a long forgotten museum technically funded by one of Theren's many corporations. From an ancient Ex-Terran Project terminal, Theren first received Jill's coordinates. Ostensibly.

Of course, Olive had been the one waiting months ago inside the museum to ensure someone passed the message along to the SI.

Before she left Lunar City, however, she had one final task. Her magnum opus, so to speak.

Turning off the lights in the museum, she went straight for the closest monorail heading into the governmental urban core. The trip wouldn't take long—it was a short, eight kilometer ride across the dusty moonscape. And it went smoothly. Before she knew it, Olive was striding through the busy concourse of the ICH's legislative heart.

"Representative Nedkyva, welcome back," said a sing-song voice in her inner ear. It was all too easy to mask her identity. All too easy.

"Thank you," Olive said. "Please inform my staff I'll be grabbing breakfast from my quarters then heading to the office."

"The message has been sent. Thank you for choosing Carisa for your ICH-approved messaging service while visiting Lunar City."

"Always a pleasure." And the conversation ended. She was going to Nedkyva's quarters, after all. She wouldn't be heading to her office.

Above Olive, massive glass windows revealed the blue-green marble of Earth. She'd never set foot on the planet. It bore no importance to her, other than the mythical home of the species she called her own. No, her home was far from Earth. Her original home, and her chosen home.

A home she hadn't visited in over a decade.

She wished she could have been there to say goodbye to Jill. The SI had been like a mother to her after pulling her off the streets of Kabardino-Balkaria. The tiny mining colony, chartered by the Russians in the 2200s, was a brutal place. She hoped she never saw it again.

No, Jill had greater plans for Olive. Infiltrate everything. Everywhere. Know all there was to know about the comings and goings of the ICH and its biggest players. She'd flown with Theren for a few years, and even run a number of projects for the SI. No one ever suspected her connection to the martyred Jill.

All of it culminated in the events of today.

Theren might have thought Jill's primary purpose for pulling them to Horizon was to reveal the greater truth about Gra'chi and the Grove. And to an extent, they'd be right. But what Theren didn't know—and what Olive did know—was Jill's plans went much deeper than handing over the keys to her creator.

If humanity were to survive its encounter with the Grove, however it played out, they needed political resiliency and technological savvy. The ICH had created an economic engine impossible to halt, with trade, immigration, tourism, and industry spread across the stars. The ICH had failed to break the binds of culture perpetually dividing humanity. With every new colony, new identities formed. New people-groups. New ideologies. New beliefs.

Humanity had colonized nearly four hundred planets in under three hundred years. Some planets, like Emerald Jewel, had a population rivaling Earth's. Others were rural towns in comparison. The mega-corporate monolithic hive-mind of the Foundation worlds would never understand the political revolutions brewing on many of the planets distant from humanity's core, whether privately chartered or originally chartered by one of Earth's great powers.

One powder keg was all Olive needed to light the spark necessary to set the ICH ablaze.

Well, not a literal powder keg.

She arrived in Representative Nedkyva's quarters. The woman was actually floating in dark space, lost forever. For the past three months, Olive had been romancing the woman precisely to enact the current plan. It was a pity; Olive had begun to like her. Now she wore her face.

Inside the woman's quarters, Olive activated a sleeper program and attached it to Nedkyva's refrigerator. Opening the fridge, she snagged an apple, took a bite, and walked back out of the room, her Nedkyva mask disappearing. The program also told the ICH's system that Calietta, Olive's alias on Lunar City, had been with Nedkyva all along. Nedkyva was staying in the room, while Calietta went for a walk.

It didn't take long to return to the massive courtyard beneath the legislative hall. Still masked as the Representative, Olive took a seat on a bench, ate the apple, and waited.

And waited.

And waited.

Four minutes passed.

Olive checked the time via AR and pulled up a map of Lunar City. It was a beautiful place. She had appreciated living here over the past few months. It hadn't made her interested in setting foot on Earth, though.

She finished the apple. A compost bin sat nearby, and she chucked it, the moon's low gravity making the shot easy.

Five seconds later, a missile fired by the supposed "pleasure yacht" of Emerald Jewel's senior representative congressperson smashed into the windows of Representative Nedkyva's quarters, blasting a one-hundred square meter hole in the side of the residential unit of the capital of the ICH.

Representative Nedkyva was from Komi, a planet of relatively modest wealth and a population of approximately 342 million. Originally founded by the Russians, like Olive's birthplace, the planet had thrived, even as many people overlooked it for the Foundation worlds. Nedkyva was one of a few outspoken representatives from the Russian political block calling for greater independence of the outer systems of humanity.

And now, thanks to Olive's plant, combined with a routed companion script injected on the Emerald Jewel vessel, everyone would believe the rich worlds had just assassinated their principal political opponent.

Alarms blared all around as fire crews rushed to ensure every blast door closed to save Lunar City's precious atmosphere. The final death toll wouldn't be known for days, though conveniently, no Foundation representatives had quarters in that particular residential district.

She rose from the bench, feigning fear and running as if she didn't know what had happened. An emergency professional ushered her under a blanket to mitigate with the shock of the blast. She thanked him. It was warm. It helped her blend in with the crowd.

Jill had asked Olive to ensure humanity could survive its confrontation with the Grove on the stellar stage.

Olive's answer was simple.

First, they needed to ensure humanity could survive an encounter with itself.

*I hope you have enjoyed the first few books of **the Chronicles of Theren.** Please consider leaving a review with your preferred retailer.*

The Chronicles of Theren *are far from over. The story will continue. Stay tuned!*

If you're looking for more philosophical speculative fiction, check out my short story anthology: ***Shattering Worlds: A SciFi and Fantasy Story Collection****, available now from all major retailers.*